# A MAGE'S APPRENTICE

# A Mage's Apprentice Series

Winds of Courage

Storms of Allegiance

Tempests of Truth

*And set in the same world:*

## A Mage's Influence Series

Seeds of Glory and Ruin

Vines of Promise and Deceit

Thorns of Hope and Betrayal

Forests of Grandeur and Malice

# A MAGE'S APPRENTICE

## COMPLETE SERIES

MELANIE CELLIER

LUMINANT PUBLICATIONS

HIDDEN CITY
NOMAD LANDS
Kingdom of CALISTA
VIRIDIAN RIVER
CELADON RIVER
CALINARA
LAKE ATERRA
CADENCE'S HOUSE
HUNTING LODGE
CELADON RIVER
NOMAD LANDS
Kingdom of TARTORA
TARONA
VIRIDIAN RIVER
N
W
E
S

CALINARA
LAKE ATERRA
ELDRIDA
CALTOR
TARONA
Kingdom of TARTORA
OSTARIA
TARIN
CELADON RIVER
VIRIDIAN RIVER

# WINDS OF COURAGE

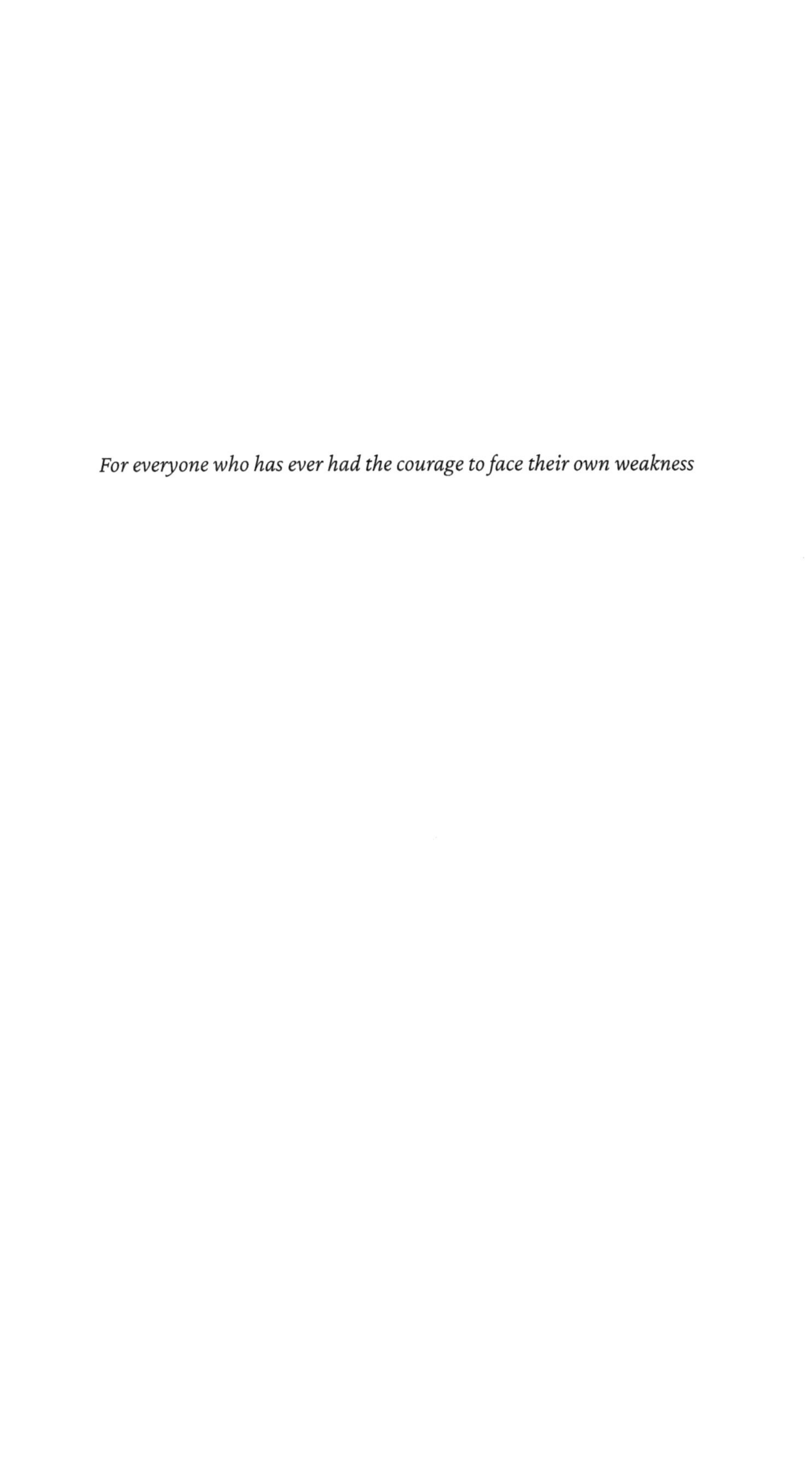

*For everyone who has ever had the courage to face their own weakness*

CHAPTER

# ONE

Rocky ran past, his lean, black legs flying as he joyfully circled the meadow. He would have made a fine sheepdog, but Father had been too fond of him, even as a puppy. When he took him into the house as a pet, he had claimed it was for my benefit. I had spent years begging for a dog who could live inside with us instead of outside as a working animal. But, given the way he doted on the tiny ball of fur, he didn't fool either Mother or me.

And Rocky responded to my father's love with a brightness that made us all smile. His unswerving loyalty would rouse affection in the coldest heart. Rocky might belong to Father first and foremost, but I always let him come for a run when I came out to inspect the fields.

A high yip made me freeze, my eyes skimming the fields as I looked for Rocky's moving body. He had disappeared.

Picking up my skirts, I ran for the spot I had last seen him. My heart contracted when I called his name and heard nothing in reply. The fields were bare and ready for planting, so there was no chance his lean body was hidden within the tall green stalks that usually covered the brown dirt. Where could he have gone?

I was moving so fast, I almost pitched headlong into a large crack in the ground that cut off the far corner of the field. The unexpected drop was hard to see from a distance, and Rocky had been running much faster than me.

I ignored the problem of the ditch's appearance—the earth in this area did shift occasionally, and it always meant days of work to restore the field. All I cared about in this moment was the missing animal.

I dropped to my knees in the rough dirt and peered over the unstable edge. Rocky gave a pitiful whine at sight of me, mustering the energy to thump his tail slightly against the ground beneath him. The effort made my heart twist. Even when injured and in danger, Rocky responded to the presence of one of his family.

"Good boy," I murmured, even as my mind raced.

He had survived the fall, which was my first worry, but it wasn't like him to just lie there. He would have risen if he was able to do so.

If I jumped in after him, would I be able to hoist him out and then scramble out myself? The trench was deep, but I might be able to manage it.

I leaned further over, trying to get a better look at Rocky's state. My eyes fell on one of his back legs which was bent at an unnatural angle.

As soon as I saw it, the blood rushed from my head, a roaring sound filling my ears. I fell back, gasping for breath and trying to suppress the light-headedness that was threatening to send me into unconsciousness. Forcing myself not to think of Rocky's injuries, I knelt in the dirt, my head hanging low as I debated whether I needed to lie down. The worst thing I could do right now was faint. Rocky was relying on me.

As the seconds passed, the feeling slowly faded, replaced by tears that welled in my eyes, stopping just short of falling. There was no way I could go into that trench to rescue Rocky. I was useless to him, just as I always was in this sort of crisis.

After several more ragged breaths, I risked standing. When my head and stomach remained settled, I called down to Rocky, keeping my eyes carefully averted as I did.

"I'm sorry, boy." I hoped my voice conveyed some reassurance. "I'm going to have to go for help. You just lie still until I get back."

His tail thumped again, and it took everything I had to turn and leave him. As I ran, making for the farmhouse by the most direct route, I could barely suppress more tears. Why was I so useless? Surely eighteen years should have been enough to overcome such a foolish weakness. Why did I never get any better? Just the thought—let alone the sight—of illness, injury, or the inner workings of the body was enough to set me off and make me more useless than a newborn baby.

I sped through dark brown fields which lay ready for spring planting, moving faster than was probably wise. But the thought of Rocky lying alone in the ditch drove me on.

By the time I arrived in the clear space between the front of the farmhouse and the barn, I was ready to collapse. But a distant bark reached me from across the fields, sending a shot of energy coursing through my limbs.

"Father!" I called between my gasps. "Come quick!"

He appeared from inside the barn, his steps quick and his brow drawn. "Delphine! What's wrong?"

I didn't usually make a fuss, so just the sound of my anxious tone had him worried. When he saw my expression, the lines of his face deepened.

"What is it, lass?" he barked. "What's happened?"

"It's Rocky." My breath had finally calmed enough for normal speech. "The earth shifted in the northeast field. There's a trench there now, and Rocky fell into it. I think he's injured, and..." I hesitated. "I couldn't get him out on my own," I finally finished in a defeated voice.

Father sent me a sharp look, glancing toward the farmhouse although there was no sign of my mother anywhere nearby. I knew better than to even allude to my weakness in her presence. Father had been with me the first time I encountered an injured animal as a child, and he had sworn me to utter secrecy, even from Mother.

I had instantly grasped the shame I brought to the family by being so weak, so I had been careful ever since, although it hurt to keep a secret from my mother. But I didn't want to see her wounded by my impediment—not when she had already grieved so much at only being granted one child.

Even back then, I had known that I carried the future of our farm on my shoulders. And how many times had Father said that farms required strength of both body and mind?

"He's too far down," I added. "We need rope."

I finally noticed the coil of rope slung over my father's shoulder, and affection rushed through me. Despite my unexpected arrival, and his anxiety, my father had kept a level head, grabbing a potentially useful tool on his way out. If Father expected strength from me, he expected even more from himself, exemplifying the kind of person who kept a farm thriving and prosperous.

"Let's go then," he said gruffly, clearly trying to hide his emotion over his beloved pet being alone and in danger.

I nodded, trying to hide my exhaustion as I hurried to his side. He set out across the fields, and I followed close behind. But within a short distance, I realized he was holding back his pace for my sake, aware of the fatigue weighing down my limbs.

"You go on ahead," I said. "I don't like the idea of Rocky lying there alone. Just don't try anything on your own. I don't think I could pull both of you out of there, even with a rope."

He paused, looking back at me with uncertainty.

"Go! Go!" I flapped my hands at him, and he nodded once before increasing his pace.

I followed as fast as I could push myself, the distance between us widening. Despite my warning, I doubted Father would wait for my arrival to begin the rescue process. I would likely find him in the trench with Rocky when I arrived.

Sure enough, when I finally reached the spot, there was no sign of my father. Peering carefully over the edge, I saw him easing the rope around Rocky's middle, murmuring reassurances as he did so.

I kept my eyes averted from Rocky's back legs, focusing on my father instead.

"Really, Father?" I put my hands on my hips. "Do my words mean nothing to you?"

He laughed gruffly. "I'll be fine, lass. You know that." He grinned up at me. "You get more like your mother every day. But worrying won't run a farm."

I rolled my eyes at his oft-repeated pronouncement.

"Neither will getting stuck in a ditch," I muttered but without heat. My father was stronger than I was in more ways than one, and there wasn't a ditch that could keep him contained. I was only quibbling out of the wish to be useful in some way.

It didn't take him long to finish securing Rocky. Despite the dog's injuries, he submitted to my father's actions without complaint, making my heart squeeze again.

Looping the loose end of the rope over his shoulder several times, my father prepared to climb back out. I leaned over, reaching down an arm, but he waved me away.

Frowning at the wall of dirt in front of him, he remained still for several moments. Curious, I leaned back over, trying to see what was happening.

At first I could see nothing, but then slight movement drew my eye. Pushing slowly from the rough dirt like a thick worm, the tip of a root appeared. There must have been trees in this area once, before it was cleared for planting, leaving behind this long-buried trace of their presence.

Another root appeared, pushing out of the dirt higher up the trench wall. It was followed by a third and a fourth before my father's shoulders slumped in fatigue, his face relaxing.

"That should be enough," he said.

I examined their placement. "You'll use them to climb out?"

He answered with his actions, placing his foot on the first of the roots and reaching up to grasp the highest one with his hand. With the help of the perfectly placed foot and hand holds, he was back up at ground level within seconds.

Frustration churned in my gut at this reminder of yet another way I was weaker than my father. His plants power might be considered barely middle strength, but it was endlessly helpful on a farm. Whereas I was entirely useless, unable to use any power at all.

Father didn't speak any criticism, though. Instead he handed me the rope.

"You pull from back here, and I'll pull from beside the trench so I'm on hand to help him over the edge."

He knelt in the dirt, gesturing for me to back up. As usual, he was silently protecting me from triggering my squeamishness, finding ways not to draw attention to it, although we were alone out here.

Blinking back tears again, I stumbled several steps backward. Father looked my way, checking I was in position as his hands tightened around the length of rope.

I planted my feet and leaned slightly back, bracing myself as I began the first pull.

"Stop!" The shout rang across the fields, making me start so violently I nearly dropped the rope.

Swinging around, I stared at the person hurrying in our direction. Who could it be? I could see at a glance it wasn't my mother, but there was no one else on the farm. When I was young, Father had a farm hand to help him, but our land was small enough that we had been making do with just Mother, Father, and me since I turned fourteen. We did occasionally have visitors from Tarin, the closest town, but they came via the road, not across the fields.

The figure was moving at speed, quickly becoming clearer. It was a woman—not old, but not young either. At a guess she might have had fifteen years on me. She appeared to be entirely alone, but she showed neither discomfort nor concern at approaching two strangers.

Her steps finally slowed as she reached me. Caution replaced my surprise as I took in the simple but expensive material of her clothes. Even their cut spoke of wealth, the design giving her an air of elegance even as she stooped to kneel in a dirt field. Lone travelers—especially women—were unusual, and even more unusual was a lone affluent traveler. I could only think of one group in society who would behave in such a manner.

Mages.

Churning anxiety, previously held at bay by the urgency of the situation, flooded through me. What was a Guild mage doing in Tarin, let alone on our farm?

I threw a frantic glance at my father. His hard expression showed he'd come to the same conclusion. I tried to think of what I could do to mitigate the situation, unsure if I should be shielding Father from the mage or the woman from my father.

But it was hard to process past the question being shouted silently inside my mind. Had she come for me?

Surely she hadn't come for me.

The woman seemed to confirm my conclusion when she didn't glance in my direction. Instead she was focused on Rocky inside the trench, my father's frozen, furious look doing nothing to put her off.

"If you pull that animal up, you'll cause him great pain and likely considerable further damage."

My father's hands relaxed around the rope, new concern showing in his eyes as he glanced at the trench. But when he looked back at the woman, his face hardened again.

"And how would you know anything about the matter?"

"I sensed his distress from all the way over on the road. His injuries must be significant."

My father frowned, so I forced myself to find my voice. "You have a healing affinity, then?"

It would have been remarkable good fortune if a healing mage happened to be passing by just as Rocky was injured. Mages of any affinity never passed our remote farm, let alone the specific one we needed.

Father shot her a look, and I knew him well enough to read the struggle behind it. The last thing he wanted to do was accept help from a mage, but if this woman could really heal Rocky, how could he refuse her services?

But the woman gave a regretful grimace. "I'm afraid I don't. But my influencer did." When neither of us spoke in response to this astonishing disclosure, she continued. "I'm an elements mage."

"You're elements cross healing, and yet you sensed Rocky from the road?" I gaped at her. "You must be very strong!"

Only those with a healing affinity had a connection with animals. Not even the strongest elements mage would be able to sense a dog's distress. And while it was true that someone with a cross influence had traces of their influencer's affinity clinging to their power, for that hint to be enough for such a thing…I shook my head. It was hard to fathom that sort of strength.

The woman smiled slightly, turning her attention toward Rocky in an obvious dismissal of the subject. Her lack of response shook loose the rock in my stomach. If she'd come for me, surely she would have taken the opportunity to boast of her strength. From what I had heard about Guild mages, that was their usual style.

"So you can't tell how injured he is?" I leaned forward to peer down at Rocky, concern at his unusually subdued demeanor overriding my worry about my own reaction.

"Not in any detail." The woman sat back on her heels with a sigh. "Even a healer would need physical contact with him to make a full assessment." She shot a quick glance at me. "But don't be too concerned. I heard him bark from the road, so he has some spark left."

I nodded briefly in response to her sympathetic smile before turning my attention to my father. His silence was uncharacteristic, but I could see he was still wrestling with his internal conundrum. Hoping to take the weight of interacting with a mage off his shoulders, I turned back to the woman.

"We need to get him out. You said not to pull him up, but we can't just leave him in there."

The woman turned to look at me, her eyes focused on me in a way they hadn't been previously.

"My name is Amara, by the way," she said.

I hesitated, unsure if I should attempt a curtsy despite my personal distaste for mages. If she could save Rocky, I was willing to put aside my pride. But a curtsy seemed out of place in the middle of a muddy field, so after an awkward pause, I settled on bowing my head respectfully.

It was less difficult to do than I had expected. Despite her background, something in Amara's gaze and bearing commanded instinctive respect. And I couldn't even hate her for the effect since her eyes held not only strength but also a warm spark that softened the overall effect.

Something about her made me think she would be a dangerous woman to cross—but that if you found yourself in need, she would help without thought of return. I shook my head to dislodge the fanciful idea. Our family knew well how alluring mages could be, but they didn't help unless there was something in it for them.

Amara gave me a pointed look, and I cleared my throat. "I'm Delphine."

She waited as if expecting more, but I said nothing. After a moment, she turned back to the trench.

"My influencer was unusual in that he specialized in both humans and animals," she said, referring to the mage she had apprenticed under. "I've seen many injured creatures, and from observing Rocky, I suspect he has injured both of his back legs."

"Both?" I squeaked, horrified.

I had seen one but since I'd looked away immediately, I hadn't registered the injury to the other. It would be impossible to hoist him out of the trench without jarring his legs repeatedly. If we damaged them enough, they might end up injured beyond the capacity of the single animal healer in Tarin. And if Halmir couldn't save the legs, Rocky would have no chance. A dog could survive with only one back leg, but not without both—not a dog like Rocky, anyway.

"I acknowledge it would be more helpful if I had a healing affinity," Amara said with unabated calm. "But my elements ability is not without its use here.

I'll bring him up, protecting his legs in a cushion of air. I can make sure they aren't jostled or moved."

She looked at my father. "Tarin must be the closest town. Is there an animal healer there?"

"Aye." My father nodded, breaking his silence. "Just the one, but he has enough strength for a simple break, and he should be able to set a more complex one on the path to healing." Obviously his concern for Rocky had won out over his hatred of Guild mages.

Amara smiled in satisfaction. "Excellent. I suspect they're clean breaks, so he should do well. As long as we can avoid causing further damage. Unless…" Her voice lingered on the word.

"Unless?" I asked, my anxiety for Rocky making the word come out sharper than I'd intended.

"Unless you think you've learned enough to heal him where he lies?" She turned to me. "That would be the best solution, and if the breaks are simple enough it shouldn't take much skill. As long as you have the strength, it could be accomplished, I suspect."

"What?" I stared at her, the earlier anxiety rushing back through me in a wave strong enough to make my knees waver. I drew in a deep breath, forcing my legs to lock and my back to straighten.

"I'm not a healer." I faced the woman, excess energy coursing through me. I had to grip my hands into fists to stop them shaking.

She raised her eyebrows, looking me slowly up and down. "I heard that the daughter of this house was born with a powerful healing seed. And you look as if you must be seventeen already. Are you not her?"

I looked away, unable to meet her eyes. So she had come here on purpose to see me, after all? If so, was she just pretending not to know that I hadn't had the seed of my power activated at seventeen according to the usual custom?

"Delphine is our only daughter," my father said. The pride in his voice made my eyes sting.

"I'm a simple farmer like my parents." I let my eyes roam over our barn and surrounding fields before returning to the mage. "Whatever you've heard, I'm no healer."

Amara continued to assess me, her gaze cool and curious.

"Interesting. You say you're no healer, and yet you don't claim an elements or plants affinity instead. So does that mean you do have a healing seed, but you resent your affinity? You wouldn't be the first. Since the foolish in the capital view the elements affinity as the strongest, some children wish for an elements seed. But healing is usually well-regarded also. Don't you find joy in knowing you can ensure the health and safety of your family and loved ones? Most people value that."

I met her eyes, my chin lifting. "I don't need to be a healer to keep my family safe. My parents are hardworking, and ours is a prosperous farm. I intend to make it even more so. I will earn the gold necessary to hire any healer our family might need."

The woman glanced at Rocky, not needing words to make her point.

I hated how quickly this mage had seen through to my hidden weakness. My healing seed was a horrible mistake since I would clearly never be a healer. I couldn't even help Rocky with my own two hands without almost losing consciousness. My parents used their plants power to aid our farm, but since I had been saddled with a healing seed, I could never follow in their footsteps in that way.

My fists tightened, and I carefully avoided looking at my father. He must be furious at the turn of the conversation, although he was clearly holding in his thoughts out of concern for Rocky.

"If you're trying to suggest that I should be activated so that I can provide healing in the case of future accidents," I said, "then you must know less of the world than I thought. My seed has been assessed as strong enough to qualify as a mage, and everyone knows mages don't live on remote farms. They go away to the Guild for their apprenticeships, and if they ever return from the capital, it's only to run healing clinics in cities and town centers or to pass through briefly at planting time or harvest. A healing mage will never be on hand in our fields. But I will be here. As I said, I'm no healer."

The woman's face shifted slightly, but I didn't know her well enough to read the emotion.

"It sounds as if it's the strength of your seed you resent, rather than your affinity," she said calmly. "It's a rare thing for a strong seed to be born to two weak parents—most families count it a great blessing."

My father muttered something under his breath that I hoped Amara hadn't caught.

"That is their business." I glared at her. "I will keep my eyes on my own business, and I request you to do the same."

I expected Amara to take offense at my words, but she didn't respond at all beyond a slight tightening around her eyes. After a silent moment, she turned back to the trench.

A whimper from within its depths dispelled my nervous energy and sent me to my knees so I could peer over the edge to check on Rocky. A gasp escaped when I felt a cross breeze on my face and saw Rocky rising slowly into the air. I turned my head to stare at Amara. She was already bringing him up?

Her attention was focused on the moving animal, but otherwise she gave no indication of being in the middle of a difficult task.

I wasn't sure what I had expected. Mages were merely people with a stronger seed than the seeds of normal folk. They didn't use their power in a different way, they just had the ability to do more. And when the adults I knew used their power in their daily lives, I never felt it. I wasn't sure why I had expected Amara to be any different. Had I thought the strength of her power would make it palpable?

A momentary curiosity brushed against my thoughts. If my seed was activated, and I could access my own power, would that give me the ability to feel others using their power?

I shook my head at my foolishness. Sensing power itself was the province of those with a power affinity—a seed so rare that no one I knew had ever met someone who possessed it. I had no time for fairy stories—my attention was needed in the daily toil of reality.

I leaned away from the trench as Rocky floated high enough to appear above its edge. Now that he was so close, I realized the breeze from earlier had only been the outer stirrings of a much more concentrated movement of air. A tight circle of wind moved impossibly fast, its speed and density creating a platform that lifted Rocky upward.

I shook my head in wonder. I had never seen a feat that required so much strength. I snuck an admiring glance at the woman next to me. Despite her lack of boasting, she must be strong indeed.

Amara followed Rocky's progress with her eyes, still using neither words nor gestures to direct the unnatural mass of air. My parents never needed outer movement to use their power, but then they had only the weak seeds of regular folk. Despite knowing mages were no different at base—merely stronger—I had always imagined them grandiloquently waving their arms in the air.

"Hold out your arms," Amara directed my father, and he obeyed without question.

The air carrying Rocky gently deposited him into my father's waiting arms. Rocky whimpered again, reaching up as if he intended to lick my father's face, but one stern word was enough to make him meekly settle back down.

"I have a small cart." Amara pointed toward the road. "It's not large, but I can take Rocky and one of you into town in it."

Father hesitated, his body rigid but his eyes glued to Rocky. I winced and hurried to his side.

"I'll go," I said softly, resting a hand on his arm. "I'll take Rocky."

He looked from me to Amara, and I could once again see him wrestling with himself. He wanted to stay with his beloved animal, but sitting beside a mage for all that way would strain him beyond bearing.

"Please let me go," I repeated, desperate to be of use in some small way. "I want to be the one to take him."

I saw the moment he capitulated, giving a single nod of his head before striding toward the cart. I hurried behind him, the two of us reaching it several steps before Amara.

"Watch yourself," Father muttered, shooting Amara a suspicious look. "She'll probably have all sorts of tales about a life of luxury at the Guild, but—"

"Do you have so little faith in me?" I hissed. "I'm not enough of a fool to be taken in by such things. I'm not like my uncle. I won't abandon you and Mother so easily."

Father's face softened as he nestled Rocky among the bags and parcels secured in the back of the cart.

"You're a good lass, Delphine, and you always have been. I trust you." His eyes narrowed again. "I just don't trust her."

Amara arrived, and he fell silent, jerking his head in a movement that could possibly be interpreted as a respectful nod.

"Don't worry about a thing," Amara said kindly, as if Father had protested about imposing on her. "I was already on my way to Tarin, and I won't rest until I see poor Rocky healed. You may be assured I'll take excellent care of both him and your daughter."

Father hesitated, as if that was exactly what he most feared, but I made a shooing motion from behind Amara, and he relented enough to make a small bow.

My eyes lingered on his retreating form as he headed back across the fields toward our farmhouse. When I finally turned back around, Amara was watching me, open curiosity in her gaze.

Uncomfortable, I moved forward to greet the horse harnessed to the cart. The mare had barely moved at all during the rescue process, merely positioning herself where she could graze on the grass that grew on the fringes of the road.

"She's a good girl," Amara said as I ran a hand down her neck.

The horse shook her head slightly in response, making her mane toss. I couldn't help but smile at how much the effect reminded me of Serena, one of the stronger apprentices in town—a girl as well aware of her own worth as this horse was.

With a final pat for the lovely mare, I pulled myself up onto the wooden bench at the front of the cart that served as a seat. As soon as I was settled, I wondered if I should have checked with Amara before climbing up. Perhaps she wanted me in the back with Rocky.

I hated the idea of bowing and scraping to someone just because they were a mage, but it wasn't her status pushing me to show respect for Amara. She had gone out of her way to help us when she was under no obligation to do so, and so far she had asked for nothing in return.

I cleared my throat as Amara climbed up beside me.

"Thank you for helping us."

She smiled across at me. "Of course. I couldn't just ride past an animal in pain. If it makes you feel more comfortable, you can think of it as something I'm doing for Rocky."

I nodded, feeling inside my pocket for the small pouch my father had slipped to me. Its leather was worn and soft beneath my fingers, its weight reassuring. It had the necessary gold to pay for the healing, so at least we weren't imposing on the mage for more than a ride.

But even as I was grateful for the coins, I wished we didn't have to part with our funds so unnecessarily. If only I wasn't so useless, I could have healed Rocky myself. A mage might have to leave home, but I could have activated my power at a lower level if only I wasn't crippled by my weakness.

What sort of useless person was born with both a healing seed and unconquerable squeamishness? It was a wasteful combination, and I understood my father's instinct for secrecy. Why would I want to advertise my shame?

"Don't worry," Amara added, perhaps seeing the discomfort on my face and misunderstanding the cause. "If the healing takes too long, I'll see you have a safe place to stay for the night."

I tried to smile although the expression felt false. Was she flaunting her wealth and philanthropy? Or did she think I would be eager to spend time around her?

Nothing could be less true. While I knew my heart was safe, my parents would worry the whole time I was gone. A lone mage wasn't the Guild, but it was a close enough connection to make them uncomfortable. My uncle had left and never returned, so I could understand their anxiety. I could only hope the healer would work quickly, leaving enough time for Rocky and me to make it home before darkness fell.

CHAPTER

# TWO

Our farm wasn't too far out of town, but the road felt interminable when every bump and swerve made the passenger in the back whine in pain. Rocky's obvious efforts to suppress his response only made it worse. Several times I had to restrain myself from urging Amara to go faster.

"You know this area better than me," she said after a particularly loud whimper from Rocky. "Is Tarin much further?"

"No, we should arrive soon. And it's not an especially large town. It won't take us long to reach Halmir."

"Halmir is the animal healer, I presume. In which case, I'm guessing he's located on the outskirts of the town. Is he on this side or the other?"

"He's on this side," I replied, impressed with her knowledge.

She gave me a look that held a suspicious hint of amusement. "For all the differences between towns, some things are always the same. Most townsfolk don't want a parade of injured animals being led into the house next door. Even in smaller villages, the animal healers live on the edges."

"That makes sense." I hesitated, frowning over her words. "You said *healers*, plural. Do some small villages have more than one?"

She shrugged. "It completely depends on the region and town." She hesitated, casting a speculative glance in my direction. "Are you younger than you look? How old are you, Delphine?"

I gave her a wary look, but she merely watched me in silence, waiting. After a moment, I sighed and answered.

"I'll be eighteen in the summer."

"Interesting." She turned her gaze back to the road ahead, so I couldn't see her expression.

After the tension roused by her question, her silence got under my skin.

"That's it?" I blurted, even as I scolded myself for not remaining quiet. "You're not going to lecture me about how I need to be activated?"

"It sounds like you've had enough lectures already." She cast me a quick glance, a slight smile curving her mouth. "Besides, I've been told to mind my own business."

I looked away, warmth creeping into my cheeks. It had been rude of me, given she was not only my senior but a stranger who had gone out of her way to help my family.

"I apologize," I said stiffly, and she chuckled.

"No, no, you mustn't backtrack now! I might think you're weak and an easy target."

The warmth in my face flared hotter. "You're mocking me."

She surveyed me for a moment before inclining her head. "It's ungracious of me, is it not? Now I'm the one who owes an apology."

I looked swiftly back at her, but there was only sincerity on her face. After an awkward moment, I cleared my throat.

"No, indeed," I said. "There's no need."

"Have you always lived with your parents on their farm?" she asked, her voice surprisingly gentle. "I think, perhaps, that you haven't spent much time around other youngsters."

I couldn't prevent a momentary grimace, but I banished it swiftly, loyalty to my parents flaring. When I was younger, I had longed to spend time with the other children in Tarin and had often complained to my mother. But despite my complaints, I had known she would never even raise the issue with my father.

Usually a loving, supportive figure in my life, any talk of leaving the farm would turn him silent and moody, sometimes for days at a time. When my mother finally explained why, I had become as careful about the topic as she was.

My father had always been prone to the occasional unexplained angry outburst, but it was only after the town healer tested my seed that the days of silent withdrawal started. And after my mother's explanation, it all made sense.

My father had an older brother who I had never met, and as boys they had been very close. My uncle had also been assessed as having an unexpectedly strong seed—although not as strong as mine. He had fallen just short of qualifying for a Guild apprenticeship.

Even so, the family had been elated, sure he was the key to turning around their fortunes. Even after my grandparents' sudden death, the two brothers had worked hard to keep the farm profitable, running it alone while they were barely more than children, and saving every coin they could. Every scrap of their savings had been pooled and used to send my uncle to the capital where he intended to seek training from the mages. Even if he couldn't be apprenticed to one of them, in Tarona he could find someone of a similar strength to his own to activate him. And with gold, he could purchase additional training from actual mages.

The brothers had been convinced my uncle's ability would ensure their future prosperity. And my father had been willing to work back-breakingly hard to keep the farm afloat alone for the two years of his brother's apprenticeship.

But my uncle had never returned.

Given he was alone, my father couldn't leave the farm himself, but eventually he had scraped together yet more coin and used it to seek information on his brother, who he feared must have died. He discovered his brother had abandoned Tarin, their family farm, and my father himself and had used their shared savings to establish a life for himself in the capital.

Instead of learning from the mages of the Guild and returning, my uncle had instead been seduced by the Guild's position and power—and by his own resentment at not being strong enough to join their ranks. Rather than accepting the reality of his lesser place, he had used the family savings to buy himself the lifestyle he thought he deserved.

My father was the strongest man I knew, and he hadn't been broken by the betrayal. He had found my mother and built himself a life. But working the farm alone had meant always working hard, without breaks. My father had once dreamed of a farm bustling with family, but that dream had been twice stolen from him—first by his brother and then by my parents' inability to have more children.

So I could understand how shattering my seed assessment had been for him. I was not only strong like his brother, but even stronger—actual mage material. And that meant that, just like my uncle, I would leave our farm and go to the Guild.

My father knew from bitter experience that if I left, I would be lost to him forever. Once again, he and my mother would be alone on their farm, and even the small family he had built would evaporate.

But I wasn't like my uncle, and I refused to go. There was no point in my being activated anyway. Not given my secret.

I wasn't sure who my birth had been a joke against, but it must have been against someone. The squeamish heir to a remote farm had no business with a powerful healing seed. I refused to be activated and not only make my life a misery but lose my family as well.

And here was a stranger criticizing the choices my parents had been forced into.

"I had no need to go into Tarin to school," I said coldly. "My mother taught me everything I needed to learn. And we always came into town for the festivals and celebrations. I don't need anyone's pity."

"No, I'm sure you don't—especially if the rumors are true." Amara spoke with an unexpected note of bright cheerfulness. "I assume you do, indeed, have a powerful seed? And it's a personal choice of some kind that you haven't been activated yet?"

Reluctantly, I nodded. Amara had already admitted to having heard of me. But she had been heading toward Tarin when she passed our farm, not away from it. So how was that possible? Halmir was always pestering me to go to the Guild and take up a mage apprenticeship. Had he sent word to the Guild of my existence? Surely they didn't care enough to send someone to fetch me?

I stiffened at the idea, giving Amara a sideways look. I had resolved back in the field that she wasn't after me, but the more I saw of her, the more I realized I couldn't trust my judgment on such matters. Amara was nothing like the mental image I had built of a mage.

"You do know you have mage level strength, don't you?" Amara asked into the silence, sounding concerned. "The local healer explained it to you, and all about seeds and activation? Sometimes parents have their own reasons for keeping things from their children."

My hands balled into fists as I leaped to my mother's defense.

"Of course my mother explained it all! And my parents had me assessed as a young child, just like all the other children in and around Tarin. The mage running the healing clinic at the time was clear about the results."

Amara nodded.

It was always the healers who tested children to determine the strength and affinity of their seed. A healing ability allowed someone to connect with living bodies in a way other affinities couldn't. All it took was physical contact.

Of course, any parents with a healing seed could take a guess at the affinity of their own children's seeds, as well as any other children they touched, but it was still common practice to have a formal assessment by the local healer. A certain level of strength and experience was needed to accurately gauge a seed's level, and no one wanted to raise false hope.

"So you knew of both your healing affinity and your unusual strength from childhood," Amara said. "You weren't kept in the dark, as I feared."

I sighed at her unpleasant assumption, restraining myself from launching to my parents' defense yet again. Instead I was swamped with memories. The shocking moment of my testing at the forefront, followed by the subsequent confusion. Everyone had heaped attention and praise on me after my testing—as if I had done something to earn my strong seed. But my father had gone silent, and without my mother's explanation, I had assumed his anger was directed toward me, although I couldn't work out what I had done wrong.

The inhabitants of Tarin had all assumed I would leave as soon as I turned seventeen, traveling to the distant Mage's Guild to start an apprenticeship that would make me a mage. No one had doubted I would be excited to leave my family and my whole life behind.

"It's not fair," I said, my frustration leaking into the words.

Amara laughed, a low, velvety sound. "No, who gets a strong seed isn't fair at all. But usually it's others making the complaint, not someone in your position."

I folded my arms across my chest. "I didn't ask to be born this way, and I don't want it."

Even without turning to look at Amara, my peripheral vision caught the crease between her eyes as she examined my face.

"I meant it earlier when I said most people hope and dream of a situation like yours," she said softly. "It's not a common thing to have a child whose seed far surpasses their parents. Most people follow the normal pattern of heredity in their ability as in everything else."

"It happens," I said quickly. "The current Master of the Elements was born to blacksmiths."

Amara nodded. "Of course. I wasn't denying the phenomenon, just saying that most people view it favorably. And most people see value in having a range of affinities within one family as well. Affinities often skip generations, and everyone has all three of the main affinities in their heritage somewhere, so it's fairly common."

I sighed, trying not to think how much easier everything would be if I had been born with a normal, weak plants seed, like both my parents. If that had been the case—as I had expected when I arrived for my testing—then I would already be activated by now and would have begun my apprenticeship under my father.

I pushed away the appealing image. It did no good to dwell on it. I didn't have a plants seed, I had a healing one. Even if I bound my strength by choosing a weak activator, I couldn't risk unleashing my healing ability. If I was constantly drawn to connect with the bodies of those around me, I would be fainting or vomiting more often than I was well.

"I don't mean to pry," Amara said, a statement I found less than believable given her number of questions so far, "but I just want to be completely sure both you and I understand the situation."

She paused briefly, and when I didn't protest—already resigned to allowing the conversation to go its course—she continued.

"You are aware that your seed will lie dormant and unusable until it is activated by someone else's power? It doesn't matter how old you get, you'll never come into your power on your own."

"Of course," I said, impatient. "Seeds might become ripe for activation sometime around your seventeenth birthday, but they don't change after that without activation. Believe me, I could hardly be unaware given how many times Halmir and the local healer have badgered me since my seed ripened four months before my last birthday."

"Four months?" Amara gave me a speculative look. "If you were ready for activation that early, you really must be strong."

"You can't tell?" I asked, the petulant note in my voice embarrassing me.

She smiled. "No, my healing cross-influence doesn't extend to anything that subtle. I'm as much in the dark on such matters as you are. But your local healer must have run those sorts of tests hundreds of times. He or she would know what they're doing."

I shrugged. "I don't know why they bothered checking. It didn't matter when I was ready—as I kept telling them. Four months before my birthday, or four months after, I had no intention of abandoning my home and family to go to the Mage's Guild."

My tone colored my final two words with more emotion than I had intended to reveal, so I fell silent. Amara's eyes were on the road again, but her face had a false stillness that told me she was purposely hiding her thoughts.

"Don't you care about sacrificing your potential?" she asked eventually. "Your seed gives you the possibility of great strength, but it's only a possibility. You'll also be limited by the strength of your activator. With a seed as strong as yours, only a mage influencer will allow you to realize your full potential. From what you're saying, you must have been told that a hundred times. And yet you truly don't care?"

I sighed, disliking hearing the familiar lecture on the lips of a stranger—and a mage at that. "If I could give my seed away, I would do so happily. I have no interest in becoming a mage." My voice dropped to an irritated mutter. "And you're right that I've heard it a hundred times. Even the mayor herself lectures me every time she sees me. I really don't need to hear it again from you."

"Apologies," Amara said lightly. "I have a particular reason for wanting to fully understand your situation."

A particular reason? I gave her a suspicious sideways glance. Was she really sent by the Guild then? I reviewed everything I'd said, a hint of uneasiness appearing. I hadn't spoken flatteringly of mages or the Guild. Was I risking harm to my family by speaking so openly?

"I have to ask, though," Amara added after a moment of heavy silence. "The mayor?"

I sighed. "It's been a long time since Tarin sent anyone to the Mage's Guild for an apprenticeship. They seem to think it will boost our town's status to ship me away."

*Not that it did Tarin any good when my uncle sought out the Guild*, I added silently.

"Perhaps they're thinking of your return rather than your departure," Amara said gently. "Smaller towns can find it difficult to secure a senior healer to run their healing clinic, so having one of their own as a qualified mage is an appealing prospect."

"Who's to say I'd ever return?" I said shortly.

"You fear the Guild would keep you prisoner?"

Was that amusement in her tone? I shifted uncomfortably, remembering my earlier concerns.

After a moment, Amara gave a light chuckle. "While there are those in the Guild who would be astonished to hear me utter any defense of it, I can assure you they're not in the habit of taking their students prisoner. Healers, especially, are encouraged to return to their home regions once they've received their qualifications. There's always a shortage of healers in the more remote parts of Tartora."

I shot her a surprised look. Her words made it sound like she was no supporter of the Guild. But that was impossible. As a mage, she was bound to the Guild. It wasn't an optional connection.

"So you know that in your case, realizing your potential means going to the Mage's Guild in search of a mage influencer," Amara said thoughtfully. "But you're refusing to do so."

She frowned, although she looked more intrigued than unhappy. "For some reason, you don't want to be a mage."

Silence fell in the wake of her statement.

I couldn't deny any part of what she'd said. But neither did I want to explain my reasons.

"I've never encountered anyone like you before," she said when I didn't speak. "I've never even heard of a similar situation."

Again she waited, as if expecting me to say something, and again I stayed silent.

In truth, I didn't have an aversion to being a mage, but to the Guild itself and the lifestyle of the capital. But the two were inextricably linked.

Mage wasn't an official rank but rather a general honorific for anyone who had completed an apprenticeship with a member of the Guild. Since Guild members only activated young people of similar or equal strength to themselves, completing such an apprenticeship was sufficient to earn you the title. And completing such an apprenticeship also made you a member of the Guild—bound to both its privileges and its control.

Once again, I surreptitiously examined Amara. Despite my initial aversion, I was already starting to warm to her. She was nothing like I'd imagined a Guild mage to be. And she clearly had strength that would distinguish her, even among other mages. It was even possible she was a master, although she didn't act like a member of our kingdom's top elite.

Every mage began as an apprentice and after two years graduated to become a proficient. The majority of mages remained proficients for their whole lives, the cachet of their magehood enough to carry them through life. But those with sufficient power and control to pass the mastery exams were permitted to take the title of master, beyond which rank there was only affinity head.

Since the affinity heads generally held their position for many years, few masters ever reached such heights. Given the political nature of the role, I wasn't sure all masters even desired such a promotion.

The three affinity heads not only ruled the Mage's Guild, under the collective title of the Triumvirate, but they also joined with the king to govern the kingdom. The king was prohibited from passing laws without their input, with the Royal Mage standing between them as liaison. It was a system designed to allow the people a voice within the kingdom's governance—a fallacy that had always made me angry.

What ancient authorities had thought the strongest of all mages were representative of the people? It was clearly a system designed by those who had never known anything but power. To them it must have seemed logical that a society dominated by various guilds should be represented by the guild at the top of that hierarchy.

When I had raged about it in my lessons as a child, my mother had always tried to defend the thinking. But while I could acknowledge her words, I could never truly embrace them. Mages might be essential to the smooth running of the kingdom—ensuring everything from our health and our defense to our weather—but they didn't understand the life of the common Tartoran citizen. It would benefit no one for the crown and Guild to be at odds, but it didn't necessarily follow that their unity always benefited the common people either.

I finally spoke into the silence, curiosity getting the better of me. "Are you a proficient or a master?"

Amara laughed, and it occurred to me that perhaps it was a rude question—like asking a farmer if they owned their own fields or only rented them. But she smiled at me easily enough.

"I passed my mastery exam many years ago."

As I had suspected, she was a master. Given her actions back on the farm, it was no great surprise.

I twisted to look back at Rocky who thumped his tail enthusiastically in response to my attention, although the movement made him whimper. Awareness of his presence and his pain pressed against my back, and I struggled to refocus on Amara.

"We were fortunate you happened to be passing by at that moment," I said, my concern for the dog making my words genuine.

Amara hesitated. "Good fortune, indeed," she said eventually, and I frowned.

"What is it?" I asked.

She laughed again. "You're not slow, despite this foolishness over your seed."

"It's not foolishness," I said, bristling.

"Oh?" Her eyebrows arched, her face settling into a thoughtful expression. "You're very confident in your opinions on this topic. Can I assume, then, that your parents support you in this matter?"

I hesitated. My father backed me wholeheartedly, but my mother had always disagreed, arguing that I had a responsibility to use the gifts I'd been given. It was why she had never suggested activating me herself, even though she didn't know about my squeamishness.

Amara clearly picked up on my hesitation, her perception stronger than I would have liked.

"I'll admit I half expected to arrive and find you already activated," she said. "While I've never met someone who resented their strong seed, my old master once encountered a family who didn't want their child to leave home. In that case, one of the parents activated the boy the moment he was ready, thus locking him to their own level for life. It was a sad waste, but there's no way to undo an activation."

"You mean you *were* looking for me!" I exclaimed, latching onto the important part of her speech. "The Guild sent you after me?"

When I shifted in my seat, inching away from her, she launched into speech.

"Halmir did send word of your existence and unique reluctance to the Guild, and it happened to reach my ears. But given all the recent upheaval and unrest, the Guild is too busy to track down unwilling potential members. I came entirely on my own initiative." Her mouth twisted into a self-deprecating smile. "It was curiosity that drove me mostly, if I'm honest."

I relaxed slightly, although I couldn't entirely regain my former ease. How far did Amara's curiosity go, and what was she willing to do to satisfy it?

Amara smiled at me, either not noticing or choosing to ignore my discomfort.

"I must admit, having met you, my curiosity has only increased."

I stared straight ahead, my jaw clenched.

"Relax, child." Amara chuckled. "I don't intend to pry into your life, and I certainly don't intend to report anything back to the Guild."

Her words surprised me enough to make me look at her. As soon as our eyes met, her smile widened.

"I hope you'll let me satisfy my curiosity on another matter, though. I'm curious to know the thoughts of such an unusual thinker on cross influencing."

"Cross influencing?" I stared at her, trying to keep up with the abrupt change of topic. How had she known I held unpopular opinions on that matter as well?

"Well?" she asked, readjusting the reins and looking entirely at ease. "Don't tell me you have no thoughts on the topic because I won't believe you."

Reluctantly I grinned. She really was perceptive.

"I think everyone is too obsessed with strength," I said.

Amara laughed. "They are a little, aren't they." She gave me a conspiratorial smile. "It's always nice to meet someone who thinks differently."

I shook my head, amazed. Could Amara really be a Guild master? Given the way she talked, I wouldn't have believed it if I hadn't seen her power for myself.

Your affinity allowed you to connect with those aspects of the world around you that aligned with your seed, and having an influencer who was of the same affinity consolidated and strengthened those connections. So traditional thinking held that you should be activated by someone with the same affinity wherever possible. But my argument had always been that while doing so increased your power, it also limited it.

Did Amara—a master mage from the Guild—agree with me?

She had admitted to being cross-influenced herself. Her seed was elements, making her an elements mage, but she had chosen to be activated by someone with a healing affinity. Why?

Had the healing mage in question merely been the strongest available option? Or was it just a sign of Amara's own strength? Was she so powerful she didn't need to worry about further shoring up her strength? Or was there some other reason behind her decision?

"Why did you choose to be cross-influenced?" I asked.

I knew why I had always had an interest in the other affinities and the possibilities of cross-influencing, but Amara was different from me. She didn't have a reason to desperately hope another affinity could overpower her own.

How often had I wished that being activated by one of my parents—who could connect with the crops of our farm as well as the earth itself—was enough to cancel out my healing ability.

"I know it's not the popular choice," Amara replied, "but I see cross-influence as a positive thing. It's incredible, the way we're never entirely free of our activator. Just that one small moment of activation leaves our power forever tangled with traces of theirs—that's why their strength and affinity influence us so strongly. By allowing your power to be colored with traces of a different affinity, you expand the reaches of your power and open up the possibility for all sorts of different abilities. I've spent considerable time researching how it was used in the past, and I firmly believe that the popularity of cross-influencing will eventually rise again."

I grinned slowly. "You sound like you're on a one-woman mission to spread word of its benefits."

Seeing the light in her eyes was almost enough to make me reconsider the idea that cross-influencing might be the answer to my problems after all.

Amara smiled back. "I do feel strongly on the matter. Although I admit cross-influencing can cause minor complications in the training process."

I nodded slowly. Training was one of the reasons for the lack of popularity of cross-influencing. The law stated that anyone who activated another person was required to take on their apprenticeship. It ensured everyone received training in the use of their power and that the training came from someone with a similar level of strength. But the requirement could become awkward when the teacher and student didn't share the same affinity.

"I believe the answer is for mages to form small training groups," Amara said, clearly warming to a favorite topic. "That way an influencer is still responsible for their apprentices' training, but the apprentices can also benefit from training sessions given by a mage of their same primary affinity."

"Is that how they do it at the Guild?" I asked, curious in spite of myself.

Contempt flashed across her face. "Of course not. The Guild is hidebound and rigid. And almost all apprentices choose an influencer of their own affinity anyway."

"Oh." I wasn't sure what else to say, but my interest in the woman sitting next to me had just risen dramatically.

I had thought she would be horrified if she realized the extent of my feelings about the Guild. But it was almost as if she shared my aversion to the institution.

But how could that be true of a master mage? Who exactly was Amara, and what was she doing traveling alone through this out-of-the-way part of the kingdom? She couldn't possibly have come all this way just for me.

"You must be wondering why I brought up cross-influencing." Amara's voice startled me out of my thoughts.

I remained silent, not willing to admit to my extreme curiosity and completely at a loss as to what might come next.

"I wanted to be sure I understood your situation before I extended my offer," she continued. "Especially since it's not one I've ever made before." She took a breath. "Delphine, you obviously have a reason for not wanting to be a mage, but I get the impression some of your dislike of the idea is directed at the Guild itself. Given that, I wonder if you would consider an apprenticeship offer from me?"

"An apprenticeship?" I asked blankly. "With you?"

She laughed. "I can't offer you one with anyone else."

"I..." I tried to think of a polite way to turn her down. Was this why she had offered to transport Rocky into town? If I told her I wasn't interested, would she abandon us both by the side of the road?

"I can consult with your local healer, if you like," she offered. "But I'm confident my strength is great enough that I wouldn't limit you in any way. I don't have a healing affinity myself, of course, but you've already heard my opinion on that matter."

"I'm not interested in a Guild apprenticeship," I said stiffly, concerned about her reaction but also irritated that she would suggest I be activated after I'd already expressed my opinion on the matter so clearly.

"I understand you don't want to go to the Guild," she said. "That's largely why I made the offer. I am a Guild member, of course, but are you aware there's more than one kind of Guild apprenticeship?"

"I...what?" I stared at her.

"Officially, every graduate of a Guild apprenticeship is a member of the Guild—whether they want to be or not. It's the Guild's way of controlling those of us with strength." She sounded resentful, but she brushed off the emotion to continue. "And, therefore, every apprenticeship completed under a qualified mage is a Guild apprenticeship. There's no rule that says the apprentice ever needs to step a single foot inside the Guild itself. They don't run classes, remember. And some of us Guild mages choose to occupy ourselves outside of the capital."

"You mean you don't normally live at the Guild?" I asked, latching onto the least confusing part of her speech.

She grimaced. "I spend as little time as possible there. I'm what's called a traveling master."

"A traveling master?" I stared at her. I had never heard of such a person.

She sighed. "There's all too few of us, unfortunately, so I'm not surprised you haven't heard the term. But some of us care about the kingdom beyond the capital and major cities, and we believe our power should be of use to all." She smiled. "Don't worry, I pay my way easily enough and can afford to take on an apprentice. Tarona might hold much of the kingdom's wealth, but there is still gold to be found elsewhere. The rest of the kingdom is far from destitute, and my abilities are often in demand."

"You're saying that if I apprenticed to you, I wouldn't need to go to the Guild or the capital?" I asked, so shocked it was hard to think. "You want me to travel with you? For two whole years?"

Amara nodded. "You have a gift, Delphine, and I don't believe gifts should be wasted."

Her words sounded so much like my mother's that it was hard to dismiss them.

"I don't have a healing affinity like yours," she continued, "and I don't even have a plants affinity, like you wish you had. But an elements affinity can be very useful—for farmers as much as anyone else."

"You want to activate me?" I repeated. "Yourself?"

"I believe I've already mentioned that I'm not qualified to offer on behalf of anyone else," she said with a chuckle.

"I'm sorry," I said, unsure how polite I needed to be given the unexpected turn of the conversation. "But I'm not interested in leaving my fam—"

"My offer has come as a surprise, of course," she said, calmly cutting me off. "Take some time to consider it."

"I don't need ti—" I tried to say, but she cut me off again.

"Take some time to consider it."

I opened my mouth only to close it. I would look foolish if I kept insisting. I could just as easily wait before refusing her offer for a second time.

I could even admit there was a certain intrigue to the idea. She wasn't insisting I travel to Tarona—most likely never to return—like everyone else did. But she still wanted me to activate my healing seed which made the idea untenable. I just hoped I could get away with not telling her why.

"I'll talk to your parents, of course," Amara added, and my heart sank.

Maybe I should make more of an effort to convince her immediately, after all. My mother would love the idea, while my father would almost certainly resent both it and Amara herself. The last thing I wanted was to introduce tension into our home.

But I couldn't find the right words to convince her—not without revealing the weakness my father had sworn me to secrecy over. So instead I just kept sneaking glances at the mage beside me. The master mage.

A traveling master, apparently.

I might not want to accept her offer, but that didn't mean I wasn't intrigued by Amara herself. The more she spoke, the more mysterious she grew.

She said she'd never taken an apprentice before, so why did she suddenly want to start now? Why, exactly, did this woman want to activate me of all people? And how far was she going to go in her attempts to convince me?

# CHAPTER

# THREE

"Is that the animal healer's house?" Amara pointed ahead at a comfortably sized home that stood out among the smaller dwellings on the fringe of the town.

Her words jerked me back to the pressing matter at hand, and I nodded confirmation. When I turned to look at Rocky, he couldn't even muster the energy to acknowledge me, sending my concern spiking.

As soon as Amara pulled her horse to a stop, I leaped down, running forward to pound on the house's front door.

"Halmir!" I shouted. "Hurry!"

The door was yanked open in seconds, but the older animal healer wasn't on the other side.

"Delphine!" The girl in the doorway sounded surprised and pleased to see me. She peered over my shoulder. "What's wrong? Has something happened to one of the cows again? Do you need Father back on the farm?"

I shook my head. "It's Rocky. He fell into a hole and has badly hurt his legs. We brought him here."

"Rocky?" The girl's ready sympathy flared, her face falling.

Miranda always found an excuse to tag along when her father was called out to our farm, and no one who had met the friendly dog failed to fall for him.

"You cannot be the healer," Amara said from behind me, her light tone taking any sting from her words.

Miranda gasped when she saw the limp form in Amara's arms. Stepping back to clear the doorway, she let the woman and dog inside. I peered back toward the cart, checking the horse's reins were secured to the hitching post before I followed them inside.

Miranda had darted ahead, calling loudly for her father, and Amara was already halfway through the house in the girl's wake. I hurried to catch up with her and direct her the rest of the way. I had visited often enough to know how to find the treatment room at the back of the house with its attached fenced yard.

By the time we reached the room, Halmir had appeared, joining us at the large table in the center of the space. Amara briefly outlined the accident that had befallen Rocky, while I tried not to focus on either her words or the room itself. Being here always made me uncomfortable. The air was heavy with past treatments and the weight of future expectation. Halmir had long hoped that I might assist his daughter in the future running of his clinic.

My heart rate picked up slightly—a natural response to the pressure, no doubt. I ignored a heady, breathless feeling that didn't quite fit. That hint of hopeful excitement had nothing to do with Amara's proposal. It was only relief that Rocky was finally receiving the help he needed.

Since Amara's assistance had prevented further injury, Halmir should be able to restore Rocky to his previous strength. The animal healer's seed hadn't been strong enough to qualify as a mage, but he had been close. I had often heard him tell the story of nearly being chosen for a Guild apprenticeship. We were fortunate to have him in Tarin.

As soon as Amara gently deposited Rocky on the table, Halmir leaned over him. I tried to look away, knowing the danger and telling myself I wasn't interested in the process anyway. But I couldn't keep my eyes from sliding across the room to latch onto Halmir's hands as they gently cupped the dog's heaving sides.

My fascination warred with the churning in my stomach and lost.

"I'm going for a walk," I announced abruptly.

Halmir was too absorbed in his task to acknowledge me, although none of the rest of us could see any outward sign of the connection he had forged with Rocky. Amara gave me a sharp look, however, and I turned away from the mix of censure and speculation in her gaze.

Miranda, who had been standing close beside her father, bounded to my side with a sunny smile. "I'll come with you."

I shrugged and hurried from the room. I didn't mind if I had company or not, I just wanted to get away from the stifling atmosphere of the healing room.

Outside, I headed up the street toward the center of town, not really seeing the houses on either side of me as they grew larger and more prosperous looking. Night had started to fall, but the lingering hints of daylight were bolstered by the moon, which was already hanging in the sky, nearly full. I had no issue seeing the road in front of me.

"It's always distressing when someone you love is in pain." Miranda placed a gentle hand on my arm, her face full of sympathy. "But you don't need to worry. It sounded like a straightforward healing, and my father has never failed at one of those." She hesitated before continuing. "And I'm sure he won't charge too much. You came to us, after all, so it's not as if he had to spend a long time traveling out to the farm. And he likes Rocky, you know." Her voice brightened by the end of her speech, as if she'd succeeded in convincing herself.

I smiled back weakly, wishing my discomfort stemmed from something as simple as payment. What was wrong with me that I couldn't even spend a few minutes in Halmir's healing room? And yet neither could I overcome the fascination that made me want to try.

Miranda linked her arm through mine and smiled brightly up at me. The younger girl had always followed me around ever since we were little. Having her appear every time my family visited town had annoyed me when we were younger—back when I'd wanted friends my own age. But my perspective had changed after my testing. Everyone in town was interested in me after that, but only because of my seed. Miranda was the only one who had liked me from the beginning. I even began to imagine that if I'd had my longed-for younger sister, she might have been something like Miranda.

"If you wait just a little longer," she said, "then we can get activated together. I know Father would be delighted to take you on." She squeezed my arm. "Wouldn't it be the best fun to be apprentices together!"

I managed a pained smile. It wasn't the first time Miranda had made the suggestion, and my refusals never seemed to make an impression on her. The longer I remained unactivated, the more convinced she became that we would be trained together.

Despite my irritation, part of me couldn't help amusement over her definition of *a little longer*. She wasn't even sixteen yet, despite already being taller than me, and her seed wasn't mage strength, which meant she would likely have to wait for her seventeenth birthday for activation. All the adults in Tarin seemed to think every month I delayed was a wasteful crime, but apparently well over a year was nothing to my friend.

"Miranda," I said wearily, but she cut me off, her tone as cheerful as ever. I suspected she knew what I was going to say and didn't want reality intruding on her happy fantasy.

"Oh, look!" She pointed toward two figures ahead of us.

I squinted through the half-light, trying to identify them. I didn't know everyone in Tarin—we didn't spend enough time in the town for that—but I knew the more prominent adults as well as all the other young people around Miranda's and my ages.

I didn't recognize the people loitering down the side road, though. They were tall, their bearing confident and shoulders broad. These weren't the youths I was used to seeing in town.

I frowned back at Miranda. What was she doing spending time with men who must be nearly ten years her senior? Other than her inexplicable devotion to me, she had never been one to chase after the older children or want to hurry into adulthood.

A young woman appeared from the other direction. She joined the men, a friendly greeting on her lips as she looked at the taller and more confident of them. I relaxed slightly at sight of her. Serena was a year older than me— already nearly finished with her plants apprenticeship—so she wasn't a particular friend of Miranda's, but at least she was familiar.

"Friends of yours?" I asked, trying to sound more relaxed than I felt. It seemed darker now than it had before, although I hadn't noticed the last of the daylight slipping away.

"Oh yes!" Miranda smiled happily. "Shall I introduce you?" At my look of uncertainty, her nose wrinkled. "I know they're a bit old, but you shouldn't mind that. They're only passing through Tarin, and they have the funniest ideas. They've completely broken the monotony around here, so all the young people hang around them. See."

She pointed toward the small group where the arrival of yet another person seemed to confirm her words. The new arrival was another familiar face, a gangly youth a little younger than me who liked to complain loudly about his father, Tarin's blacksmith. I usually avoided him, so it took me a moment to recall his name—Stefan.

I frowned, although I understood the situation now. Many of the youths in Tarin found life in a small town monotonous. They couldn't understand why I didn't leap at the chance to run off to the capital. Naturally they weren't close friends of mine, but I still understood their perspective somewhat. Even I would have found remote town life constricting if it hadn't been for the wide-open fields of our farm and the unswerving love of my parents.

The newcomers, however, were another story.

"What kind of grown men spend their time roaming the kingdom with a bunch of youths? Are they trying to make themselves feel important or something?"

Miranda's face fell, and I immediately felt bad for repaying her friendliness with harsh judgment.

"I'm not saying I want to go following them off to the new land they're always talking about," she said hurriedly. "I just find them amusing." Her lips twisted. "There isn't much else of interest happening around here."

I forced a smile. If the men were recruiters for Calista, then their presence made more sense, although I was surprised they'd made it as far as Tarin.

"Sorry, don't mind me," I said. "I'm just in a crotchety mood because of worrying about Rocky."

Her expression lightened, and she gripped my arm in sympathy. "Of course! I'm the one who was thoughtless. You'll be wanting to get back to him." But even as she said it, her eyes glanced wistfully toward the group of four down the side street.

"Yes, I should be getting back." I removed her hand from my arm, giving it a squeeze. "But you don't need to come with me. Like you said, it's a simple healing and your father will have everything well in hand. Just because I need to return doesn't mean you have to."

She glanced at the small group again before giving me an uncertain look. "You really don't mind walking back on your own?"

I laughed. "Of course I don't. I'm not exactly a stranger in Tarin. I won't lose my way."

She brightened further. "No, of course not. I'm being silly again. I'll be off, then."

She sped away from me, throwing a smile and a farewell wave over her shoulder. I watched her go with a smile of my own. No matter how many times I had tried to shake Miranda loose when we were children, I'd never been able to do it. She always managed to win me over.

Shaking my head at my own foolishness, I turned back toward Halmir's house. But something made me pause, glancing back. I had told Miranda to go, but I was suddenly having second thoughts about leaving her behind.

Tartora's northern neighbor of Calista had been nothing but dangerous, poisoned land for generations, its surviving population scattered into Tartora and the nomad lands. Now that the land itself had been restored, it was understandable that its new rulers were recruiting subjects from among the descendants of the refugees. From what I'd heard, you didn't even have to have Calistan blood to be accepted in the newly reformed kingdom. A willingness to do the work of rebuilding was all that was needed, although a strong seed was appreciated. But surely the Calistan recruiters weren't encouraging underage children to leave their homes?

I tried to reassure myself with Miranda's own words. She had said she wasn't interested in Calista, that she just found the men's tales amusing. And the gatherings themselves must have been safe enough. If they were raucous or dangerous, the town mayor would have put a stop to them before now.

But still I hesitated.

Without forming any real plan, I faced back toward the men and their cluster of attendant youths. The group was on the move now, and I found myself trailing them, staying just far enough back not to attract attention. If Miranda saw me, she would find it odd, but none of them looked in my direction.

As they moved toward the end of the street, I began to berate myself. What exactly was I doing? Halmir would be finished by now, and Amara must be wondering what had happened to me. Why was I following this group? I wasn't even close enough to hear their conversation, although they were talking animatedly. What did I think was going to happen?

I couldn't answer the question, and my progress slowed. Just as I was about to turn back, a sharper tone ahead caught my attention. The voice had lifted enough to reach my ears, although the exact words still weren't clear. I frowned, peering into the shadows that enveloped this section of the street. The houses here were closer together, less of the moonlight making it between their hulking shapes.

The anger seemed to be coming from the blacksmith's son, and dismay filled me when I saw he was facing Miranda, clearly berating her for something. She shrank back, and I increased my pace again.

Before I could make any progress, however, several things happened at once. Stefan and Serena took off toward the edge of town at a half-run. The two men followed, each of them gripping one of Miranda's arms as they hustled her along with them. Before I could even shout a protest, a shadow detached from the darkness of one of the houses between me and the running group, forming into the shape of a man.

His height and the breadth of his shoulders immediately called to mind the fleeing strangers. Apparently there were three strange men in Tarin, not two. And this one carried an exposed sword in his right hand.

Were the others dragging Miranda somewhere more secluded so that he could dispose of her?

My concern transformed into full panic, and I threw myself at the man's back with a guttural scream. My fear lent me strength, and I leaped high enough to get my arms around his neck, wrapping my legs around his middle as my weight cut off his airway.

He gave a strangled grunt and thrashed violently, nearly dislodging me. I clung on tighter as he dropped the sword, his hands coming up to claw at mine. I held on as tightly as I could, but I couldn't resist his strength as he pried my grip apart. As soon as my hands were loosened, he gripped the top of my arms, flinging me over his shoulder and onto the ground in front of him.

I landed hard on my back, the breath pushed from my lungs as I stared up at a terrifying face.

The darkness clung to him, his inky hair and the black leather of his clothes blending with the night behind him. Only the light skin of his face and hands stood out, an unnatural contrast of light against his shadowy form.

The expression on his face was as black as the deepest shadows, however, his features twisted with anger. He stooped to retrieve his blade, and I cowered away, my hands coming up in an instinctive gesture of defense.

Instead of attacking, however, he merely stepped over me, disdain in his eyes as his attention returned to the empty street where the others had previously been. He clearly intended to follow after them, so I rolled to the side, my hands flashing out and catching at his ankles.

He stumbled, only just catching himself before he joined me on the ground. Cursing, he spun to glare at me again.

"I won't let you hurt my friend," I said breathlessly, pushing myself up to my knees.

"Grey isn't your friend," he said in a deep, rough voice.

I stilled, surprise making me pause in my attempt to grab at his legs.

"Who?"

He also stilled, throwing me a look of equal surprise.

"I don't know who you are," I said, recovering my determination and my voice, "but I won't let you hurt Miranda."

"Miranda?" He glanced from the empty street to me, letting out a low groan.

"I won't let you hurt her," I repeated, lunging forward in an attempt to grab him around the knees and trip him up.

He stepped easily out of reach, and I barely kept my balance, scrambling inelegantly back to my feet. Racing around him, I blocked his passage down the street. He let out another mumbled curse, shouldering his way roughly past me.

I darted around to cut him off again, this time grabbing both his arms to hold him in place.

"What do you want with her?" I asked, breathless.

"Want with her?" He sounded incredulous. "What could I want with a girl too foolish for her own good?" It was obvious he wasn't just talking about Miranda. "If you're really her friend, you shouldn't have gotten in my way."

"I..." My words stuttered to a stop as I registered his piercing blue gaze which seemed to cut all the way through me, judging everything he saw.

Hadn't his eyes been black before? It must have been a trick of the shadows because there was no denying the brightness of the blue now. And how had I mistaken his age? Despite the breadth of his shoulders, he wasn't as old as the other men had been. At a guess I would put him within reach of my own age, perhaps a year or two older, although he carried himself with a confidence and assurance far beyond mine.

With the full force of his attention on my face, I could barely breathe. How could someone so attractive be so menacing? He must turn heads wherever he went, but I couldn't decide what stood out more—the handsome lines of his face and bright color of his eyes or the thrill of warning and fear that coursed through me as a result of his attention. Every nerve in my body was telling me to run from this man.

Gritting my teeth, I held my ground. It didn't matter what he looked like or how well he could wield his sword. Miranda was what mattered, and I wasn't going to turn tail and flee.

"What are you talking about?" I asked, proud of how steady my voice sounded.

He ripped his arms from my grasp. Moving too fast for me to block, he flipped our places, grabbing both my wrists in a crushing grip.

I gasped and tried to pull away, but he held me in place, leaning forward until he took up all the air around me, making it hard to find my breath.

"If your so-called friend is never seen again, you can blame yourself." His low words were sharp and cutting.

"What?" I gasped. "What do you mean never seen again? What are you going to do to her?"

Impatience twisted his features. "Me? What am *I* going to do to her?" He flung me away from him, looking down the empty street before whirling back to glare at me. "If you're really so clueless, you should never have gotten involved. Thanks to you, I've just wasted weeks of effort. And who knows when I'll get this chance again."

I faltered back a step, feeling my certainty draining away. None of his words made sense.

"What are you talking about?" A creeping dread filled me. "Are you...are you not with those men?"

He shot me a contemptuous look, his face answering my question as the situation crystallized in my mind. I had thought I was protecting Miranda, but I had actually been barring a potential rescuer. Heat rushed through me, and my legs trembled.

"You said she might never be seen again. What did you mean by that? Who are those men? Where have they taken Miranda?"

His eyes were lidded now, the storm of emotion gone from his face, although the tense lines of his body told me he was eager to be on the move.

"That is something I would very much like to know," he said. "But they're experts at covering their tracks. Now that we've lost them, I won't find them again. Not unless I can work out which town they'll be appearing in next."

"Next town?" I asked, still dazed.

He half turned to go. "Your friend won't be with them then, though. She'll be long gone."

CHAPTER

# FOUR

"Wait!" I lunged forward and gripped his closest arm with both hands, holding on firmly when he tried to shake me loose. "What do you mean? Where will she be? Are you saying they'll kill her? If those men have just kidnapped Miranda, we have to go after them before they get too far away."

"Did they just kidnap her?" His words made me freeze. "Is that what you saw? Are you sure?"

"I—" My rushed assurance faltered as I replayed the scene in my mind. Was that what I'd seen? Now that I considered the matter closely, I wasn't entirely certain.

It had been Stefan who had yelled at her, not either of the men. My instincts had been shouting about danger, but it was possible the strangers had been supporting her after the confrontation rather than dragging her away.

But if that was true, why were we talking about never seeing her again? Nothing about the situation made sense.

"If you're completely certain she didn't go with them willingly, we can turn the town out to join the search." The stranger's eyes were locked on me, and I could feel the tension of his muscles beneath my hands, as if he was ready to launch into action at a word from me. "There might be some slim hope of finding them if we have everyone helping. But if we do find them, and she denies being taken by force..."

I hesitated—only a matter of seconds—but when my hands fell away from his arm, the tension drained out of him, replaced with the earlier frustration.

"When you say go with them..." I asked, still trying to make sense of the situation.

"Willingly or unwillingly, your friend is gone," the stranger said shortly. "And she won't be back. I knew they were making their move tonight, which is why I haven't let them out of my sight for hours."

He gave me an accusing look, but I was too horrified to take any notice.

"You can't mean you think she's run off with those people? Miranda would never abandon her father like that! If that's what you meant, then of course I'm sure she didn't go willingly."

He shook his head. "Unless you're willing to swear you saw her forcibly dragged away, it won't be enough. This isn't the first town they've visited."

"Not the first town? Who are they?"

"That is what I've been trying to find out for a long time. And thanks to you I have to start all over again." He began to stride away from me, but I raced after him.

"Wait," I said again, and he paused, although I could easily read his desire to be gone. "What am I supposed to tell Miranda's father?"

He shrugged. "Tell him what you like. That's not my problem."

His callous attitude made me stiffen and glare at him. "How can I possibly explain where Miranda's gone when I don't understand myself?"

For a moment I thought he was going to stride off without an answer, but with a sigh he remained in place.

"I think you'll find he's not as surprised as you seem to think he'll be."

"What?" I stared at him.

"Not even the most advanced concealment skills could have protected Grey for so long if he was openly taking people by force. There's a reason he targets youths—there's always a few who are willing to abandon everything in search of adventure and riches."

"Not Miranda," I said with certainty. "She's not like that."

"Did I say they all left with him willingly? I wouldn't be following him if I believed that."

"Then how come—"

"Grey is persuasive, and he targets his victims with care. If you have some proof I'm not aware of, by all means, please come forward with it."

His superior look made me want to smack him, but I kept my distance. My body was still shaking with leftover tremors from our earlier proximity.

"Today was my chance, but I lost it," he said. "Thanks to you."

"I was trying to help." My voice sounded weak even in my own ears. I cleared my throat. "Maybe it's not too late. Maybe together we can find—"

"Don't even think about it." The stranger's eyes narrowed, his face transforming instantly as the earlier menace returned. "I don't want help from anyone, let alone you."

I shrank back before I could stop myself, but I forced out words anyway. "I won't just abandon Miranda. Of course I have to try to help."

"You would be a hindrance, not a help. If you really want to help your friend, then stay out of my way next time. If I never see you again, it will be too soon."

He strode away without a backward glance, and this time I didn't try to stop him. I still didn't properly understand what had just happened, but anger had consumed my earlier instinctive fear.

How could I possibly have known he was trying to stop this Grey and rescue Miranda? I hadn't meant to get in his way, and yet he dismissed me without knowing a single thing about me. How did he know I couldn't help? Who was he to reject assistance so confidently?

I forced my trembling legs back toward the main street. I had to tell Halmir what had happened. Perhaps he would be able to rouse the town, even if the stranger wasn't willing to do it.

My legs didn't cooperate, moving more slowly than I asked them to. I kept replaying what had happened in my mind, but my encounter with the dark stranger already seemed more dream than reality. Would anyone even believe my account? What if he had been nothing more than a madman, and I would find Miranda already back home, having bid her friends goodnight while I fought with a stranger in the street?

That hopeful thought made me pick up my pace, but I couldn't truly believe in it. The stranger might have seemed dreamlike, but he had never seemed mad.

As I approached the edge of town, I massaged my left wrist which ached after his tight hold. What power did he have to give him such confidence?

Fiery defiance rose inside me. He had dismissed me as weak and worthless, but if he'd known about my seed—if I'd been activated—he wouldn't have dared grab me like that. He wouldn't have dared to even let his skin brush against mine.

Healers needed skin to skin contact to send their power into someone else's body, but once they had that contact, there was nothing stopping them using their power to still a heart as easily as start one. Elements mages might have the flashiest power, but the most feared assassins had a healing affinity.

I swiped angrily at the tears that had appeared on my cheeks. If I had access to my power, I wouldn't have killed anyone, of course, but I could have taken down the stranger and stopped Grey—or whatever his name was—from taking Miranda. I could have helped my friend.

But only if I was activated. I had been convinced for so long that I could never activate my power. I had been so set and sure on my course. But then Amara turned up out of nowhere with a path I had never considered and suddenly everything around me seemed less sure. What if it was possible to find a way around my squeamishness after all? What if I could fully access my power without ever going to the Guild?

Halmir's house loomed in front of me, and I pushed the door open without pausing to knock. Light and sounds from the back of the house led me to the treatment room.

I didn't have time to absorb who was present before a furry blur launched himself at me, tongue out.

I cried out in protest, telling Rocky to stop even as I dropped to my knees and wrapped my arms around him. It was the sort of confusing mixed signal Father would never have allowed—even toward an animal who was a pet rather than a working dog—but I was too relieved to see him healthy to care.

"He's been pacing ever since I got him down." Halmir's amused voice came from over near the table. "I think he was wondering where you were."

I dredged up a small smile as I considered how best to broach the more important topic of Miranda. I came up blank, realizing there was no easy way to say it.

"Does Miranda know someone named Grey?" I blurted out, standing and finding Halmir with my eyes.

He immediately stiffened. "Don't tell me she's gone off with him again! And at this hour!" He sounded annoyed rather than worried, and I relaxed slightly.

"She's gone off with him before?" I asked. "And she came back?"

"Came back?" This time there was a trace of concern in Halmir's tone. "I only meant she spends more time hanging around him than I'd like. All the local youths are enamored of his stories about faraway wealth and luxury." He snorted. "A waste of time and energy, but I can't keep her trapped at home all day every day."

I could hear his fondness beneath the words. Halmir had always been a doting father, perhaps because his wife had passed away while Miranda was young.

"She went off with Grey and another man," I said reluctantly. "Along with the blacksmith's son and Serena."

Halmir sighed. "I never liked her hanging around with the older youths, but she's become good friends with that Serena in the last year. She even stays out late some nights, which she never did before." He hesitated. "The ladies of the town tell me it's normal for a daughter to start to rebel around this age."

"Miranda? Rebelling?" I frowned at him. "She's never seemed the rebellious type."

I tried to remember if she'd made any particular mention of Serena on my more recent visits to town, but I couldn't recall her doing so. But then, she might have avoided the topic on purpose. Serena was no fan of mine. Before my assessment, hers had been the strongest seed in our generation, and she wasn't one to appreciate competition. Miranda knew we didn't get on.

Halmir looked away, rubbing at his jaw. "Miranda's seed is similar to mine. She wouldn't have been accepted into the Guild ten years ago, but times are changing. Tarona and the Guild are different now. If she travels to the capital, she might be able to secure an apprenticeship with the help of one of those new power mages."

Amara made a politely skeptical noise that alerted me to her presence. I kept my focus on Halmir, though.

"She doesn't want to go," I guessed.

He sighed. "She kept saying she didn't want to leave me. And then suddenly she was barely speaking to me and instead spending her time with those newcomers and all the others who hang around them. I tried telling her that her behavior just proves she doesn't want to be stuck here with me forever, but that wasn't received well."

Amara chuckled quietly. "I can imagine. It's a difficult age. But she doesn't have to make an immediate decision. You said she's only fifteen, didn't you?"

Halmir nodded while I tried to order my thoughts. The stranger had seemed certain Grey was hurrying Miranda out of the town, but it was possible they'd merely been moving somewhere else within the town limits. If I made a big fuss now, and Halmir tore the town apart searching for Miranda, I might just deepen the current wedge between them.

"They met on a side street," I said slowly. "And then they all disappeared off in the other direction to me. I was just worried that..."

Halmir sighed. "I apologize, Delphine. Miranda shouldn't have abandoned you like that."

"Oh no, no." I waved my hand to dismiss his words. "I told her not to worry about me. I know my way back well enough."

I smiled, but even as I did, my heart sank further. It was true I'd told her to go to her friends. If she really had been kidnapped, I could have prevented it by insisting she return with me.

"The thing is," I said, "I met a stranger—a different stranger, I mean. He seemed to believe they were all on their way out of town."

Halmir's lips thinned, pressing together. "If she's gone jaunting out of town, then she's taken things too far this time. And so I'll tell her next time I see her."

I cleared my throat. "This other stranger seemed concerned they weren't going to return. That they were gone for good." I looked at Halmir hopefully. "That's nonsense, surely?"

To my surprise, Halmir gave me a smile, moving over to pat me reassuringly on the shoulder.

"It's kind of you to worry about Miranda, Delphine. You've always been kind to her, and I appreciate it. Don't be too concerned. This is only a phase, and I'm sure it will pass soon."

I hesitated, but I couldn't think of anything to say. The stranger's words of challenge kept echoing in my mind, making me question my memory more and more. I could no longer be sure I'd seen Miranda hustled away at all.

"I may only be a new acquaintance," Amara said with a smile, "but I already have the impression that Delphine is too responsible by nature to have experienced that particular phase. You needn't worry." She directed the last words to me. "Halmir is right that it's a perfectly normal phase many young people go through. Your friend will return to her usual self soon, I'm sure."

Halmir returned her smile, nodding his agreement, and I fell silent.

"We should leave Halmir to his evening," Amara added. "It's past time for us to be moving to the inn." She thanked him, sweeping me from the room before I could protest.

"The inn?" I tried to gather my scattered thoughts. "I don't need to go to the inn. Now that Rocky's been healed, he and I will head straight back to the farm."

I stepped outside, the excited dog on my heels. Breathing in the cool evening air, I tried to reassure myself with Halmir's words. Miranda would be back at any moment.

"Don't be ridiculous," Amara said briskly, capturing my full attention. "It doesn't matter if you're going to be my apprentice or not. I was the one to bring you into town, and I can't allow a child to go wandering off into the night alone."

I rolled my eyes. "I'm hardly a child."

She gave me an impatient look. "You've already told me you're only seventeen, so don't claim you're of age now."

She sounded so sincere that I subsided, accepting the inevitable. It was ridiculous, of course, to treat me as if I were a child. The official age of majority might be nineteen—since activation happened at seventeen, and official apprenticeships lasted two years—but no one considered seventeen- and eighteen-year-olds to be children. They might not have legal status, but everyone was treated as an adult once their seed was activated.

At least, that was the case among normal folk. Perhaps it was different in the capital, among the upper class members of the court and Guild? Not for the first time, I felt a swell of sympathy for the poor children born into those families.

An image flashed through my mind of the young man I had tackled in the street. I was willing to bet my whole farm that no one treated him like a child. Did his arrogant assurance come from a powerful seed? If I could wield my own power, would it give me confidence like his?

My steps slowed as I realized what I was considering.

Amara slowed as well, matching my pace and regarding me with patient curiosity. She wasn't going to ask me anything, instead waiting for me to speak.

I drew a deep breath. "What exactly would being your apprentice involve?"

# FIVE

Amara's brows rose almost to her hairline. "This is an abrupt change," she said lightly. "What exactly happened with your friend?"

I ignored the question, my dislodged thoughts now moving at fever pace. I couldn't shake the lingering feeling of weakness or the clamoring thoughts that told me I had to make sure I was never helpless again. I had thought the best way to be strong was to avoid my power setting off my squeamishness. But when confronted with a true threat, it was my lack of power that had made me weak.

If I had been activated, I could have protected myself and helped Miranda. And there hadn't been any injuries or illness involved, so I wouldn't even have fainted while doing it.

If my power was activated, I didn't have to do anything with it that I didn't want to do. At least, I wouldn't have to once my apprenticeship was complete. I could return to my farm and continue with my life as normal, but I would have a powerful weapon ready at my disposal. Surely I could endure for just two years?

My stomach tried to rebel at the thought of what might be involved in my apprenticeship, but I clamped down on the feelings, suppressing them with all the force of my will. The next time I encountered that arrogant man, I wouldn't be the useless villager he clearly thought me.

I drew a steadying breath. *If* I ever encountered him again. The odds were against it. The stranger had given the impression he was following Grey all over the kingdom—and that he intended to continue doing so. He wouldn't be staying in Tarin now that Grey was supposedly gone.

I shot a glance at the woman beside me. Amara had claimed to always be on the move herself. Had she encountered Grey before? Would she perhaps encounter him again?

If I accompanied her, would I have the chance to get to the bottom of whatever was going on? An image of the dark stranger rose in front of my eyes. He'd told me to stay away from the whole situation, but how was it any more his business than mine?

Did he think he was at the center of everything, just because he wasn't some weak villager from a remote corner of the kingdom?

I had seen firsthand how differently you were treated when you had a powerful seed, and I resented it on Miranda's behalf. I doubted youths from the capital had started disappearing. If Miranda had been snatched, it was because she came from a remote part of the kingdom and didn't have important relatives or a strong ability. Was Grey just getting away with his villainy because no one cared?

*No one except that stranger,* an unwelcome voice said, and I pushed it away. Whatever that man's motivations, I hadn't seen any traces of compassion in his manner. He didn't care about Miranda or any of the other people he claimed had been taken. If I had to guess, perhaps he had some rivalry with Grey.

As my anger rose, my determination rose with it. Everyone had been telling me for years that my strong seed came with a responsibility to make use of that power. I had been doing my best to ignore them, but this was a situation I couldn't ignore.

I drew a deep breath and turned to Amara. She was watching me in silence, giving me the space to sort through my thoughts. Her consideration made it easier to speak my new resolution.

"I've changed my mind. I want you to activate me. I'll be your apprentice for the next two years if you'll take me with you on your travels."

She stopped, cocking her head and assessing me with her eyes. "I thought it was going to take longer to persuade you."

I brushed off the flare of resentment at her certainty of eventual success. After all, she'd been proven right.

Something else made me hesitate, though.

"You said it won't be a traditional healing apprenticeship, right? Since you aren't a healer. You'll just teach me to control my power?"

Amara resumed her progress toward the inn, and I hurried to keep up.

"There certainly won't be anything traditional about the apprenticeship. But, of course, I'll take the responsibility of being your influencer seriously. I'll arrange training from healers whenever I'm able."

I drew a slow breath, not meeting her eyes. If we were traveling constantly, how deep could the healing training go? Surely not very. I would be fine.

"When will you activate me?"

She chuckled. "Why the hurry?"

I just shrugged, unwilling to explain my reasoning to her.

"Don't you think we should discuss the situation with your parents? You're under age, after all."

Uneasiness stirred inside me at the thought of telling my father about my decision. Mother would be delighted, and I hoped Father would accept this solution since it would keep me away from the Guild. But his dislike of mages went far deeper than mine.

"The law is clear on the matter of activation," I said, hoping she hadn't noticed my hesitation. "I might not officially be of age for well over a year, but everyone has the right to choose their influencer for themselves. My parents have no legal say in the matter."

Her brows knit, her eyes searching my face. "No legal say, perhaps, but I had the impression you're close with them. Don't you want to talk to them about it?"

I shrugged again. Whatever my parents' reactions, I had no intention of telling them the true reason for my change of mind. Telling them about Grey or the stranger who was following him would only make them worry for no purpose.

"I would still feel more comfortable if we spoke to them first," Amara said as we arrived at the inn door. "We can ride back to your farm first thing in the morning."

I hesitated again before nodding agreement. The churning emotions in my middle were giving the situation a false urgency. Tomorrow would do just as well as today.

Rocky barked, attracting the attention of the innkeeper who shooed him back outside.

"You can't bring animals inside!"

"But he's just been healed." I glared at the man. "He needs to rest."

"He can rest in the stable easily enough." The man's expression left no room for argument. "If you feel the need to be with him, you're welcome to sleep there yourself."

"Very well, I will." I stalked off in the direction of the stable doors, Rocky frisking around me in an excited manner that undermined my words about rest and recuperation.

Inside the stables, I found an empty stall with a layer of fresh hay that would make a comfortable enough bed. I had just plopped down into it when Amara appeared.

"You won't convince me to go inside," I said before she could speak.

She smiled slightly, dropping a pack into the corner of the stall. "Did I try to do so?"

I gaped at her. "You're going to sleep out here, too?"

"A master has no business sleeping in a proper bed if her apprentice is in a haystack. This is my promise to you. If you become my apprentice, I can't guarantee two years of ease—in fact, I can almost certainly guarantee the opposite—but I can guarantee that whatever you go through, I'll be there by your side."

"I—"

Her promise, solemnly delivered, made me feel like my decision had been hastily made—but also that my instincts had served me well. Amara was the sort of master I could not only follow but also respect.

"Thank you," I said at last.

She smiled and lowered herself into the hay with a sigh. "My own horse and cart have been attended to by the inn's staff. In the future, we'll often have to do it ourselves. Do you have experience with a vehicle like mine? I can only assume you're familiar enough with horses."

I filled her in on my years spent caring for the various farm animals as well as driving our own simple cart. She listened and asked respectful questions, the conversation only finishing when I yawned widely, setting her to yawning as well.

"Enough for now," she said. "We'll talk to your parents in the morning, and if they're in agreement, I'll activate you."

*And we'll stop off to see Halmir on our way out of town,* I thought as I drifted into sleep. Surely Miranda would be back home by then.

<hr>

Unfortunately, our morning's visit to Halmir proved my hope unfounded. Miranda had not returned, and the animal healer had lost his relaxed attitude from the evening before.

"To tell you the truth," he told us, "it seems you may have been right. Word in the market is that Grey fellow left town last night, taking some of our youths with him."

"Let me guess," I said, my heart sinking. "The youths are Stefan and Serena."

He grimaced. "That's right. And my Miranda apparently. But she's not the type to run off." He didn't sound entirely convinced of his own words, though, and I remembered the way he had talked about his daughter the night before.

"You mustn't doubt her," I said quickly. "I don't think she's really changed, not underneath. Nothing she said to me gave the impression she was about to run off."

"Then what am I meant to believe?" he asked. "That she was kidnapped?"

The fear in his eyes was enough to explain why he preferred to think his daughter had left willingly.

"The other parents don't seem surprised," he said in a heavy voice. "It sounds like their children have been more open about their dissatisfaction and desire to leave Tarin."

"I don't—" I stopped, not sure what to say. If only I was confident I'd seen her abducted, I would be able to speak up freely. But I couldn't be sure of what I'd seen. "Is anyone looking for them?"

"They've been traced out of town, heading north, of course, but we don't know the exact route," Halmir said heavily. "And no one in Tarin has a strong enough ability to track them. We would need someone from the capital for that."

I bit my lip. I could keep insisting that I didn't think Miranda left willingly, but what would it achieve? I had no evidence to convince the town with —I didn't even have a strong eyewitness account—and Halmir was right that he had no hope of finding them on his own.

But it wasn't true that we had no one with a strong ability in Tarin right now. I glanced at Amara, and she caught my look, raising her eyebrows before turning to Halmir.

"North, *of course*? What makes you so confident they're heading north?"

"Because Calista is north. I never paid much attention to those fellows— I'm too busy for nonsense—but according to Miranda and the others, they were always going on about the glories of a new land. From the way some of the youths talked, that man had them convinced it's some sort of paradise up there."

Amara frowned. "Those men were Calistan?"

"Who else could they be?" Halmir asked dismissively. There aren't any other new kingdoms sprung from the rocks. And everyone knows the Calistan crown is scouring Tartora and the nomad lands for recruits to repopulate their new kingdom."

Amara continued to frown, obviously bothered by his words although they made sense to me. After a moment of silence, Amara spoke.

"I was intending to continue on my journey imminently," she said to Halmir. "I'm not an expert tracker, by any means, and I'll be heading northwest to Ostaria initially. But after that I'll be turning north more directly, and I'd be more than happy to keep an eye out for any sign of the runaways."

"Yes," I cried, leaping in. "Of course we'll look for Miranda! Don't worry, Halmir. One way or another, we'll find her."

"We?" He looked back and forth between us. "Are you leaving, Delphine?"

"Delphine has agreed to become my apprentice," Amara said calmly.

Halmir whistled. "I was starting to think I would never see Delphine activated."

I glowered at him, but my emotions softened when he grasped my left hand in both of his.

"Thank you, Delphine. You've always been kind to my Miranda, and she's always admired you. If anyone can convince her to come home, it's you."

"I—" Once again I swallowed my words. I didn't think it was a matter of convincing Miranda, but that didn't change my intentions. I would rescue her and bring her home safely.

"Of course," I said. "Try not to worry."

The weight of responsibility sat heavily as we extracted ourselves, and it kept me silent all the way home in the cart, Rocky behind us among the bags. When we pulled up in front of the familiar farmhouse, Amara didn't immediately get down.

"Are you having second thoughts?" she asked.

"What?" I started and turned to her, trying to shake loose my lingering concerns. "No, no, not at all. Sorry."

She smiled. "That's good." She paused, examining me with a creased brow. "Is it your friend, then?"

I bit my lip, wondering how open I should be with Amara. She'd said she was willing to help look for Miranda.

"Yes, I'm worried about her," I said.

"Is that why you've accepted my offer?" she asked slowly. "Because you want to look for your friend?"

I considered, wanting to give her an honest answer. It seemed the least I could do if we were going to bind ourselves to each other for the next two years.

"No," I said slowly. "At least, it's not the whole reason. But I do want to be able to help people like her. I don't know why I have this seed, but my mother is right—I don't want to waste it."

She nodded, looking pleased rather than upset with my mixed answer.

I climbed down slowly, more nervous than I'd expected now that it was actually time to face my father. My earlier thought that he would see this apprenticeship as a satisfactory work-around now seemed less and less likely. Would he think I was betraying him, just like his brother had done?

My breath quickened, as both my parents emerged from the house. Rocky had alerted them to our arrival with a series of excited yips. He had already leaped down from the cart and was racing around the yard, sniffing every-thing as if he suspected it had changed in his short absence.

As soon as my father appeared, Rocky raced to him, pressing against his legs and happily receiving pats and words of praise.

"You're back," my mother looked torn—clearly relieved at my return but also uncomfortable at the presence of a mage on our farm. "I'm pleased to meet you, ma'am," she finally added with a respectful nod of her head.

"The pleasure is all mine, I assure you." Amara gave a friendly smile and held out her hand.

My mother looked from the hand to Amara's face, clearly taken by surprise by her humble attitude. As Mother took Amara's hand to shake it, her manner warmed noticeably.

"We're so grateful for your assistance with Rocky. And for bringing our daughter back safely. I understand Rocky might have been in real danger without your intervention."

Amara smiled and demurred, probably thinking that my father had reported positively on her assistance. I knew it was far more likely he had been enraged at being forced to accept the help of a mage.

"I'm sorry for any worry we caused you by not making it back last night," Amara said. "I generally try to avoid traveling after dark, so we stayed at the inn. Your daughter was very devoted to Rocky's care. I was impressed."

My mother glowed with pride, and I moved forward to give her a hug. She had always been supportive of me, the only tension between us my refusal to take an apprenticeship with Halmir.

Praise of me had been the only thing needed for Mother to warm to Amara, despite her mage status. She beamed at the other woman, one of her arms wrapped around my shoulders.

"Thank you for taking our Delphine under your wing."

"Actually, about that..." Amara glanced at me as if she wasn't sure if I wanted to tell them myself or have her do it.

A sharp twist in my gut made me want to delay, but there was nothing to be gained by doing so.

"I've agreed to be Amara's apprentice," I blurted out.

"What?" my mother cried, her voice halfway between shock and delight.

Usually my parents agreed on everything, and my mother had never shown anything but understanding and compassion for my father's occa-sional outbursts and silent withdrawals. But on the matter of my activa-tion, she had always stood firm in opposition to the two of us. Father might support my not being activated, but Mother had always held out hope.

But it was my father who drew my attention, his silence louder than my mother's exclamation. Every line of his body was stiff and taut, his face frozen in a mask of disapproval.

I slipped out of my mother's grip and hurried over to him, my words falling over themselves.

"Amara is a traveling master. She doesn't live at the Guild, or even spend time in the capital at all. She travels around to small towns like Tarin. As her apprentice, I'll travel with her. Apparently I don't ever need to go to the Guild at all. I can graduate without them."

My father's stance relaxed slightly, although his expression remained displeased. I pressed on, slowing down as I chose my words more carefully.

"Amara's an elements mage, as you know. So she won't be teaching me healing. But we both believe there's value in cross-influencing, and she'll still be able to teach me the necessary control."

I glanced briefly at Amara to find her watching me with a hint of confusion on her face. I fell silent, my face flushing. Did Amara think I was insulting her teaching before she'd even begun? I couldn't backtrack my comments though since they were intended to convey a message to my father that neither Amara nor my mother would understand.

My father finally moved, swinging his head to look me in the eyes.

"You want to leave us?"

I swallowed. "Just for the two years of my apprenticeship. I'll have a chance to see the latest farming techniques from across the kingdom, and then I'll return to help put them into practice here. I can't do anything about not having a plants seed, but at least I should be able to use my power to help us a little. It would be better than being completely powerless."

"Would it?" he asked gruffly, not breaking his gaze.

I took a step closer, lowering my voice to plead with him.

"Please, Father. I don't want to always be weak and powerless and vulnerable."

A shadow crossed his face, and he shot a look at Amara, clearly wondering what had happened during my absence. He wasn't entirely wrong, but I didn't want him to blame Amara.

"It's not her," I whispered, even more quietly. "But I want to be able to protect myself. I want to be able to protect all of us."

I could hear the fierce note in my voice, despite the quiet volume, and apparently my father could too. The skin around his eyes tightened, but he slowly nodded.

I couldn't be sure if he actually agreed or if he had simply accepted that there was nothing he could do to reverse the momentum that had already begun.

"You'll really be all right?" he murmured, and I knew what he was referring to.

"I'll find a way to be all right," I said. "I have to. I'll overcome *all* my weaknesses, and then I'll return."

He nodded again and turned to Amara.

"It seems the mages are to steal away my daughter, after all."

"Father!" I hissed, but I couldn't help a slow smile spreading across my face.

His agreement might be reluctant and halfhearted, but it was still agreement. He didn't intend to disown me for aligning myself with a mage.

"I'm grateful to you for loaning Delphine to me," Amara said, cautious but polite. She clearly knew there was something going on here she didn't understand, but she didn't press for answers. "I waited to activate her until we'd talked to you, but I can do it now if you're both in agreement."

"It seems like a dream!" Mother turned to me with a smile. "Have you truly agreed to this, Delphie?"

I grimaced. "Is it so hard to believe?" But even as I said the words, I realized it was. I had always been so set against activation, with my father as my staunch supporter. "You know that means I'll be leaving for two whole years, right?" I added, wondering how she could be so happy about the prospect.

My mother's arms wrapped around me in a tight hug. "I'll miss you every day, of course I will. But loving your children means wanting them to have a full life and to fulfill every bit of their potential—even if that means they have to spread their wings and leave for a time. Your father and I have each other. We'll survive just fine."

My brow creased as I considered the practicalities. "Will you, though? You'll need help for the farm."

"Then we'll get it," she said firmly. "We've done so in the past. It's not as if we have to pay for your apprenticeship." She looked to Amara for confirmation, and the mage nodded.

"That's correct. I will fund my apprentice for the entirety of her training, including food and board. In return, I will receive any earnings from our combined efforts in those two years."

"That's fair." My mother looked at my father, as if daring him to protest. He remained silent.

"It won't be a life of luxury," Amara warned, looking a little concerned. "The life of a traveling master isn't as glamorous as life at the Guild. We'll be sleeping by the road rather than in a castle. But if Delphine assists me with any particularly high-paying tasks, I will likely give her a bonus."

She had meant her words as a caution, but she couldn't have said anything more perfect. I wanted to throw my arms around her, but I restrained myself, only allowing a slight upturn of my lips.

My father responded as I'd hoped he would, unbending even further, and even nodding acknowledgment of Amara's words.

A terrified sort of elation swept through me. This was really happening. I was going to become a mage after all.

"Do we need to have some sort of ceremony or something?" I asked, not wanting to delay in case I lost my nerve.

"Ceremony?" My father stared at me blankly while my mother chuckled.

"To activate me," I said, flushing. I'd never seen an activation before since I didn't have any older siblings to go through it ahead of me.

"I've seen families and mages who like to make an event out of it," Amara said diplomatically, "but it's not at all necessary. The consequences and responsibilities that come from activating someone are significant, but the act itself is easily done."

"Will you do it right now, then?" I asked, gritting my teeth. I'd never bothered to ask my parents what it felt like, but surely it had to hurt to have a hidden seed inside you cracked open.

"If you're sure?" Amara met my eyes squarely, and I held her gaze.

"I'm ready."

She turned to my parents. "Do you have any objection or any reason for us to wait on the activation? I don't need to be on my way immediately, so there's no great hurry."

I thought of my father's moods and of the unknown fate of my friend and frowned. It would be better for us to be on the road immediately. Now that I'd made my decision, any delay chafed.

"No, no, there's no reason to wait," my mother said, clearly afraid I might change my mind if we didn't take the opportunity immediately.

Amara smiled slightly, as if guessing the reason for her sense of urgency. "Very well, then. I'll activate Delphine now."

# CHAPTER

# SIX

I waited, expecting her to raise a hand or speak or do something discernible. She neither moved nor spoke.

"Well?" I asked impatiently. "Do I need to do something?"

Amara's smile grew. "It's done."

"What?" I stared at her. "What do you mean? You're saying I've already been activated?" I patted down both arms as if expecting to find something different about my body.

"Take a moment," she said. "Don't think about your own body, focus outward."

I hesitated, confused by her words, but I could sense an earnestness behind them. Although I still couldn't feel a difference, I knew with certainty she was speaking the truth about my activation.

I froze, wondering where the certainty had come from. She had so far proved herself to be a trustworthy person, but it hadn't been that. The certainty was rooted somewhere inside me, a sense that didn't brook any doubt or opposition. Amara had spoken the words, and her body had radiated truthfulness.

Her body? Where had that thought come from? The more I considered it, however, the more certain I felt. It had been her body itself that had told me the truth of her words.

I turned slowly to look at my parents. As soon as I focused on them, I felt an acute awareness of their presence. I could almost hear the blood flowing through their veins and the breath pumping in their lungs.

A sense of unclouded happiness flowed over me a moment before Rocky bounded around the corner of the house and dashed toward us. I expected him to make for my father's side, but instead he bounded straight to me, panting and wagging his tail. When he reached me, he stopped, leaning against my leg.

His happy contentedness pressed against me as heavily as his physical form. It was like the pain I had sensed from him in the cart the day before, but magnified many times over. Had the earlier sense been a result of my seed? I had always assumed everyone sensed such things, but now that I considered the matter more closely, I hadn't always felt it so clearly. My awareness of Rocky had grown as my seed reached maturity, even before it was activated.

And now that my power had awoken, even that stronger sense of recent months seemed like a whispered echo. It was nothing compared to how aware I was of everyone around me now.

I couldn't possibly doubt any longer. I had clearly been activated.

Amara held her hand out to me, and I stared at it. Was this another part of the process? Was I supposed to bow over it or kiss it or something to pledge my loyalty to her as my influencer and my master for the next two years of my apprenticeship?

She chuckled. "Just take it."

Hesitantly, I reached out and lightly clasped her fingers.

Gasping, I jumped back, breaking the contact. My heart raced and sweat broke out along my hairline as I stared at her.

"I...That was...I..."

"Unlike with my own elements affinity, healers need physical contact to make full use of their power. The fact you're sensing anything without physical contact is a sign of your strength." Her tone remained calm and positive, but her smile had faltered at my reaction.

I gulped in several breaths, slowly nodding as I commanded my body to calm itself. To my surprise, it obeyed, my roiling stomach settling. I blinked, too startled to speak. That had never happened before.

"Be careful," Amara said in a low, urgent voice. "In these initial weeks while you're learning control, you can protect others by avoiding physical contact, but you can't close off your connection with your own body."

"I...How did you know?" My opinion of her rose even further.

"Don't be too impressed." She sounded rueful. "I'm actually demonstrating my inexperience. I've never been involved with training a healer before. I should have warned you to be careful before I activated you."

"Is Delphine in danger?" my mother asked, fear in her voice.

Amara hesitated, her lips twisting. "Again, it's my error for not fully informing you of the dangers. I don't want to deceive you in any way, so I will acknowledge there is a small amount of risk. Some risk exists for all newly activated mages, due to the strength of their power. It's one of the reasons we have such strict rules around apprenticeships and learning control. But that risk is amplified for healers—even those with a weaker seed can make a fatal error."

"Fatal?" my father asked gruffly.

"Only in the rarest of cases," Amara said quickly. "And I can assure you that despite my initial misstep, I'll keep a close eye on Delphine going forward. I won't let anything happen to her."

My parents exchanged a long look before my mother nodded. But it wasn't as if they could do anything at this point. Amara had activated me now, and the law was clear on that point. Whether we liked it or not, she was my master for the next two years.

During the entire exchange between Amara and my parents I had remained frozen in place, terrified of doing something dangerous unintentionally. My fear must have shown because Amara turned to me.

"Don't you worry either, Delphine," she said in a soft, calming voice. "The fact you're older than the average apprentice will help you here. You have more experience and natural control, and that will aid you in bringing your ability into line."

"I don't understand what I did." The words came out in a tight, unfamiliar tone.

"Please relax," Amara said, smiling this time. "You won't accidentally use your ability by moving your body or speaking."

I nodded but couldn't bring myself to make any more substantial motion.

Amara hesitated, looking toward my parents. My mother seemed to pick up on her message first, taking my father's arm.

"There is plenty to be done on the farm still, so we'll be about our work. But you should make yourself at home inside." She gestured toward the open door of the farmhouse. "I'll make some tea and see if I can dig out some left-over cake. This is a moment to be celebrated."

My father stiffened at her words, obviously not at the point of celebrating my apprenticeship to a mage. But at least he didn't say anything aloud.

Amara thanked them both and guided me across the yard and inside the house. Seating me in an armchair, she pulled over a second chair so she could sit right by me.

"Now that your seed has been activated, you have full access to your power. You don't need to summon it or use any words or actions to access it. The power is part of you now, the same way your limbs or your eyes are part of you. If you want to pick up a cup, or kick a ball, you can do so with a single thought. Your mind instructs, and your body obeys. It's the same with your power. Our aim in our training will be to make your use of power as controlled and instinctive as the use of your limbs."

An amused chuckle preceded my mother's arrival with a plate full of slices of lemon cake.

"I wish you luck, Master Amara," she said. "Our Delphine didn't master walking until she was nearly two. She was determined not to fall, so she preferred not to take a step at all rather than practice walking and fall over constantly."

"Makes sense to me," I muttered.

Amara hid her smile behind her hand. "We can move slowly at the beginning, but it will be necessary to practice with your ability."

"But how can I risk *falling* if I'm operating inside someone else's body?" I asked, fear washing over me.

"It's good to have an appropriate level of caution," Amara said. "There are other aspects of your power we can focus on for now. When we find a healer with enough experience and strength, you'll be able to work alongside them and observe without putting anyone's life at risk."

I drew a shaky breath, liking the sound of working on other aspects of my power. I had no desire to start messing around with anyone's insides.

"The important thing for now," Amara said as my mother disappeared back to the kitchen, still chuckling, "is not to put your own body at risk. You've just gained a connection with all breathing creatures, and it's like you've just gained an extra arm. Except this limb is clumsy and poorly connected to your brain, so if you have a fleeting thought about hitting someone in the face, it just might reach out and try to do it."

I considered what had happened earlier. I had commanded my churning stomach to settle, and it had obeyed, as if my will had gained new control over my body. It turned out that was exactly what had happened.

"Is that how those other apprentices died?" I asked in a shaky voice. "They thought about their heart stopping or something similar, and their power obeyed their thoughts?"

"That's right, but you really don't need to be too concerned. We haven't had a death like that in Tartora in over a generation. Just exercise caution for now, and you'll gain the control you need in no time. The first thing we'll work on is awareness of your ability and when you're using it. Once you're clear on that, you won't accidentally make use of your power."

My mother returned with cups of tea, and I forced myself to focus on the cup in my hands and the warm liquid moving down my throat, refusing to let my thoughts wander. She kept up a stream of conversation with Amara which helped, telling her about my preferences and quirks in the embarrassing way only mothers do.

I held onto the discomfort, using it to distract myself as I let her sweep me away to pack my bags. Amara said she had plenty of room in the back of the cart, so I ended up packing two large bags, even slipping in several favorite books, and my larger writing kit. My mother would want regular updates on our travels, and I looked forward to being able to tell her about the parts of the kingdom she had never had a chance to visit.

When we finally came back downstairs, I had calmed, no longer hyper-focused on every thought and action. Amara had joined my father in our absence, the two of them inspecting the small collection of horses in our stables.

"Delphine will soon surpass me in this area," Amara said as they walked back inside together. "I can only sense a problem in the vaguest way, and I can't fix it. She'll soon be able to pinpoint exactly where the problem is and fix anything that isn't too complex. Eventually, given her strength, she'll be able to heal almost anything at all."

I grimaced, sudden discomfort assailing me. I'd been so focused on my fight with the stranger, and then on getting permission from my father, that I'd never stopped to wonder if I was being dishonest by not revealing my squeamishness to Amara. She thought she had taken on an apprentice who had the potential to be one of the kingdom's strongest healers. Would she still have taken me on if she knew the truth?

Before I could get too twisted up in the thought, my mother appeared, bearing a tray of delicacies. Apparently lemon cake hadn't been sufficiently celebratory.

My father rubbed his hands together at the sight of his favorite smoked sausage. He seemed to have softened toward Amara significantly during their time in the stables—perhaps as a result of her willingness to get her hands dirty on a small and inconsequential farm. He must have seen the same thing I had—Amara wasn't like the Guild mages of the capital, the ones he hated.

Making an appreciative noise, he raided the platter. But just as he popped a round of sausage in his mouth, Rocky raced through the open door with a particularly loud bark. The dog must have smelled the sausages, which were also a favorite of his.

My father jerked in surprise, twisting to peer at the animal. I just rolled my eyes, reaching toward the tray myself. Father would no doubt soon be feeding Rocky sausage, although he always told me off for hand-feeding the dog.

But my father didn't bend down, and a sharp cry from my mother made me startle. She leaped to my father's side, taking my gaze with her. Horror filled me as I took in his appearance. Fear twisted his face and his body spasmed, although he wasn't making a sound.

"He's choking!" Amara said sharply.

She whacked him on the back, but although his whole body shook, he still didn't make a sound, his hands pressed against his throat.

Amara spun to me. "Delphine! Quick! You can save him!"

"What?" I gasped, fear making me shake. But even as my mind stuttered, my legs were already carrying me toward him.

He dropped to his knees, and I knelt beside him. But my hands gripped together, squeezing tightly as I remembered the sickening rush when I made contact with Amara. Even now, I couldn't quite bring myself to touch him.

"Quickly," Amara instructed. "I'm sorry, Delphine, but there's no time for caution now. If you want your father to live, you're going to need to do the best you can."

"But what if I..." My words trailed off as my father reached out himself and gripped my bare arm.

Immediately I was overwhelmed with a jumbled awareness of every part of his body. I could sense every vein and all the blood pulsing through them. His heart still pumped, but his lungs were no longer contracting. His other organs jumbled together in my mind, although I couldn't name them all. I didn't have the knowledge to bring order to the parts I could sense. Instead they all pressed on me at once, clamoring for attention.

My stomach responded immediately, my senses swimming and my gut churning. Any second I was going to be sick.

Instinctively, my mind cried out for everything to stop, trying to find enough space to think clearly. I didn't speak aloud, but instantly I felt a change. I could still sense all the parts of him just as clearly, my mind just as overwhelmed, but the sense of pulsing movement had disappeared.

My father's body went limp, his hand slipping off my arm. Instantly the connection between us was severed.

I dived forward, my own body's reaction forgotten as I reached for his arm myself this time. Both of my hands clung onto him as a distant, wordless scream tore from my own throat.

*No, no, no, no!* my mind silently recited, desperately willing his systems to return to normal, and his blood to start flowing again.

The returning rush of movement in his veins hit my senses with relief this time instead of overwhelm, but the momentary relief from intense fear unlocked the tight clamp on my stomach and I retched, my stomach starting to spasm.

"Delphine!" Amara's commanding voice cut through the chaos in my body and senses, her hand landing heavily on my shoulders and her fingers digging in to the point of pain. "Settle your stomach now. Focus! Your father's life depends on it."

Desperately, I pushed aside my confusion and fear and commanded my stomach to settle, just as I had earlier. The spasming muscles immediately subsided, the burning in my throat receding as my stomach's contents resettled into place. I coughed, trying to suck in air, but I couldn't afford to waste any more time on my own body.

"Can you sense something out of place?" Amara asked urgently in my ear. "Something in his body that doesn't belong there?"

As soon as she said it, I could feel it. How had I not noticed it earlier? His body was rebelling against the foreign substance, trying desperately to expel it, although he couldn't suck in the air needed to cough.

"I can feel it," I said, not sure how else to explain it. It wasn't actually the sense of touch, any more than it was sight. But the inside of his body was as clear to my mind as if I could see his throat with my eyes or touch his heart with my hand.

"Contract the muscles of his throat just below the sausage," she instructed. "Follow its progress up until you push it all the way out."

Trembling from head to toe, I tried to focus on his throat. I didn't know how to identify his muscles from the other internal parts of him, but I hadn't needed to know the details to soothe my own stomach.

"Squeeze," I whispered, speaking aloud in an attempt to focus my thoughts as I silently instructed his throat to contract.

His muscles tightened, and the foreign substance moved, inching upward. Elated, I focused even harder, contracting his throat all the way up until the substance popped free. Every part of his body sagged in relief as he sucked in a huge gulp of air.

I collapsed, our contact breaking again and the mess of confusion in my mind fading. My father was coughing, but weakly, both hands at his throat. As he pulled them slowly away, I paled. His skin was red and swollen and would clearly soon be mottled with bruising.

"Your neck! I—" I burst into tears without completing the sentence.

He tried to speak, but his voice was too rough and hoarse to be understood. Reaching out instead, he pulled me into a hug. My mother wrapped her arms around both of us, her tears falling on my ear.

"He's alive, Delphie," she wept, "that's all that matters. The bruising will heal."

I looked to Amara for confirmation, and she met my gaze steadily, her face serious.

"You're the healer here," she said. "You tell us."

My eyes widened. I was trying my best to ignore the jumbled sensations coming from my parents' bodies due to their embrace. The last thing I wanted was to purposely dive back into my connection with my father's insides.

"Don't try to heal him," Amara instructed. "You're not advanced enough for that. Just have a look."

I drew a deep breath and reluctantly focused my attention. I was so terrified of accidentally sending my power an unintentional command that I was barely letting myself think at all.

To my surprise, his throat already felt familiar, though. My mind latched back onto the part I had earlier manipulated, and I could feel the bruising. Nothing seemed permanently crushed, however. As far as I could tell, there was no damage that wouldn't heal on its own.

With a sigh of relief, I extracted myself from my parents' arms. The peace that descended once we were out of contact felt more comforting than the contact had.

The thought made my heart squeeze painfully. Would I never be able to comfortably embrace anyone again?

"Don't worry," Amara said at my side, once again seeming to read my mind. "You'll get used to it, and then you won't even notice—unless you want to."

I gave her a tremulous smile, wanting to believe her words were true although it felt unlikely.

I cleared my throat and focused back on my father. "Your throat should get better. Although it might hurt for a while."

"Thank you, Delphine," my mother said, tears in her eyes as she reached for me, only to stop and let her hand drop. "You were activated just in time."

Delayed shock hit me, my whole body trembling uncontrollably. My father had just died, if only momentarily. If I hadn't asked Amara to activate me today, he probably would have stayed dead. Delaying my activation for so long suddenly seemed foolhardy in the extreme. What had I been thinking?

Memory of my earlier sickening awareness of his internal organs swept over me, reminding me exactly why I had never desired this life. Saving my father had brought home the value of learning more healing, but every part of me rebelled at the idea of spending more time connected to the bodies of others. How many hundreds of hours of practice would it take to achieve the necessary mastery?

I sank down to sit on the floor, putting my head in my hands. The will might be there but my body and mind were traitors, working against me. What if I couldn't do it?

# SEVEN

I tried to convince my father to travel into Tarin to go to the healing clinic, but he refused, unwilling to spend money on something that would heal naturally, especially when the injury didn't stop him working.

"What if I'm wrong, though?" I asked Amara after my father grew tired of listening to my worries and stalked away toward the stables. "I have no idea what I'm doing." My volume dipped. "I nearly killed him! I stopped his heart beating."

Even Amara looked a little shaken by the revelation, but after a moment, she fixed me with a determined look.

"But you got it started again. You don't understand yet, but that speaks to your strength. You have more awareness and control than a weaker seed would have at this point. You need to trust yourself. If your sense was that he'll heal fine, then I believe it's true. My healer friends tell me that anatomical education and knowledge help, but a lot of it is still instinctual.

"And the stronger someone's seed, the more they instinctively understand how bodies work. It's why many of the strongest healers end up focusing on research instead of running healing clinics. If they can make breakthroughs in understanding and healing techniques, then weaker healers can put that increased knowledge into practice. In the long run, that means more people can be helped. Much of your medical training will be about learning prevention, early intervention, and healing techniques that use less power. For someone as strong as you, there will always be the option of brute forcing your way through a single complex working."

I let her words wash over me, focusing on the impromptu lesson to quiet my racing thoughts and frantic heartbeat. For a moment I even imagined myself as a researcher before I abruptly remembered that my future was already set. I wouldn't spend it at a healing clinic in the capital, but right here on my family farm outside Tarin.

At least Amara had succeeded in calming me down. And preparing the evening meal with my mother calmed me further. The familiar action brought a much-needed sense of normality to my final evening at home.

I slept in my bed, and Amara slept in our guest room—a more comfortable night for both of us than the previous one in the stables. I suspected I would be wise to savor every night spent on a soft mattress from here on. The next two years looked likely to bring all sorts of different sleeping environments.

I was reluctant to leave while my father was still injured, but both my parents were insistent that we start on our way the next morning.

Now that the decision was irrevocably made, my father seemed eager to have us both gone. And while my mother was grieved over the farewell, she was no less encouraging of our departure. From the surreptitious looks she kept directing at my father, I could guess why.

Who knew how bad his mood would be in the wake of my activation and departure? And it would surely only grow worse the longer he had to restrain himself due to the presence of a mage in his house. At this rate he might withdraw into himself for days.

Amara hadn't pressed for our departure, but she didn't fight it either. She even waited patiently while I bid a lengthy and tear-filled farewell to my parents. My mother risked a single, brief hug, pulling back quickly at my intake of breath when we made contact. My father, by contrast, was restrained, speaking very little. But tears sprang to my eyes when he gruffly told me to take Rocky with me.

"I couldn't separate him from you!" I told him. "Rocky would be miserable without you."

Rocky himself tried to make a lie of my words by pressing himself against my leg. Two days ago, I would have sworn the animal would never choose to be separated from my father, but since my activation, he had been following me like a shadow.

I knelt down and buried my face in his neck, ignoring the discomfort that came with the contact. Commanding him to stay, I whispered that he needed to watch over Father. I was afraid of his reaction and how it might hurt my father, but he seemed to take my words to heart. Thumping his tail against the ground, he licked me once before trotting over to stand at alert at my father's feet.

With a teary smile, I rose and climbed into the cart. After a final round of waves, we started down the road that led away from the farmhouse.

"Are you all right?" Amara asked after several minutes of silence. "With the physical contact, I mean."

I tried to surreptitiously wipe away my tears. "I tried to build a wall, like you said."

"A wall?" She stared at me curiously. "I said that?"

"Didn't you?" I frowned, trying to remember. Now that she was questioning me, I couldn't actually remember her speaking those exact words. "I guess not. Isn't that what you meant, though? That I need to separate my consciousness from my new awareness?"

"Did it work?" She looked at me sideways, her eyes alight with curiosity.

"It helped a bit." I sighed. "Not as much as I'd hoped."

"What I actually meant is that you'd grow accustomed to it," she said. "So that over time, you wouldn't notice it consciously anymore. Like with the sky. If we're outside, it's always there in our vision—blue or gray, cloudy or clear—and if we have a reason to think about the weather, we'll take note of it. But most of the time we have no active awareness of it."

"Oh." I felt like an idiot.

"I'll be interested to hear how it goes, though," she said. "If you partially succeeded in building your wall today, then practice should make it stronger."

My eyes flew to her face. "You want me to keep working on it?"

"Of course! This sort of thing is exactly why we need to vary how we handle activation and training in Tartora. Just like there's much to be learned from cross-influencing, there is always insight to be gained from fresh perspectives and approaches. We lose that when we gather everyone at the Guild and train them in the same way. I want to encourage you to think differently, Delphine, not force you to be like every other healer apprentice."

Her words eased a lingering tightness in my chest. I had only agreed to apprentice with Amara because she seemed different, but after the fiasco of my activation, I had forgotten that fact in the wave of fear.

I managed to produce a smile, although it was a little shaky.

"Thank you. I'll continue practicing it, then."

"Excellent. And make sure you keep me apprised of your progress. I want you to explore your own path, but as your influencer, I'm also responsible for you. I may not be a healer, but I am an experienced mage, and it's my role to keep you safe and ensure you learn the necessary control."

"Yes." I shivered, remembering the moment my father's heart had stopped beating at my command.

"Like right now," Amara said.

"Now?" I asked, startled.

She nodded. "I don't intend to introduce formal lessons to our daily schedule—we won't be sitting down at a desk and studying each day. I believe there is far more to be learned from experience. But some reading will be required, as well as some direct lessons from me. Travel days like today provide an excellent opportunity for such activities."

I murmured agreement, pleased to hear I wouldn't be confined to lessons like a child again. Was that what mages did to their apprentices at the Guild? I was doubly glad I'd refused to go there if so.

"As I told you yesterday, our first focus needs to be on helping you acquire the necessary level of control to prevent any damage to your own body. That's something we can practice while traveling."

She looked sideways at me. "I don't need to tell you how much clearer your senses are now. You can experience that for yourself. I'm relying on what I've been told by healer friends, but I understand you're now able to sense all those parts of your body that operated subconsciously before. I'm glad it doesn't seem to be overwhelming to you like physical touch is."

"What?" I frowned, trying to understand her words. "What can I sense?" I looked down at my body. I didn't feel any different.

The horse pulling the cart—a calm mare named Acorn whose presence radiated contentment—faltered, as if in response to a tightening of the reins. I looked up to find Amara staring at me.

"You don't sense your own body?" Her sharp tone scared me.

"Should I?" Panic rose up, making my voice shake. Was something wrong with my power? Or worse—with my body?

Acorn resumed her steady pace, a calm mask descending over Amara's features as well.

"Please don't be alarmed," she said. "Remember that I have no experience training a healer, let alone one as strong as you. I'm sure there is some obvious explanation I've overlooked."

A crease appeared between her brows. "Have you noticed it at any point? I'm talking about things like the beat of your heart. Is your strength allowing you to instinctually push it into the background, like we were talking about earlier?"

She gave me another sharp look. "You had a strong reaction when I first talked about using your power on yourself. Had you already done that?"

I bit my lip as I tried to remember the exact order of the various distressing events of the previous afternoon.

"Yes, I—" I hesitated, cutting myself off and then rushing to continue with different words. "It was after the activation when you had me touch your hand. I touched you for the first time and felt your...insides." I gulped. "I instinctively calmed myself after that. And then again when I needed to heal my father."

I knew I wasn't being entirely accurate in my description of what I'd done —hiding behind the word calming—but I wasn't ready to admit the full truth to anyone, let alone a master mage.

"It sounds like your awareness of your own body only awoke after making contact with someone else and feeling theirs," Amara said thoughtfully. "That seems reasonable enough. Your power was still in the process of awakening. But now you say you're not sensing anything at all?"

I shook my head, gathering the courage to speak. "Not in a constant way. But I could try to see what happens when I focus on it if you like?"

She considered. "It was certainly an unusually traumatic activation. So perhaps small deviations are to be expected. If you could make the attempt, I would be interested in what you find."

I nodded, my attention too focused to allow for words. Amara had warned me against tampering with my own body in these early weeks. I had done it in order to heal my father, but that had been an extreme situation. I should avoid doing it again if I could. I just needed to sense my body without interfering with it.

But would I cope even with that much? I had barely made it through every instance of physical contact since my activation. Could I focus on my insides without setting off my most hated reflexes?

Slowly, reluctantly, I tried to think about the blood pulsing through my veins and the rise and fall of my lungs. A queasy feeling in my stomach accompanied the thoughts, but it was a familiar feeling, not born out of my ability. I could sense nothing else.

"I..." My lips twisted, worry filling me again. "I'm sorry, I can't feel anything unusual."

"Hmmm..." Amara seemed to have left behind any trace of concern, consumed by professional curiosity instead. "Your reaction to contact with others is intense, and your first interaction with your own body was bound up in that reaction. Why don't you try touching me?"

"On purpose?" I asked, wide-eyed. "And actually focus on your body without a wall? But you said I should avoid that for now—that it could be dangerous."

"I trust you," she said calmly. "You won't attempt to change anything inside me, I'm sure."

My head started vigorously shaking of its own accord. "But what if I make a mistake?"

"I trust you," she repeated, something implacable in her tone.

She was my influencer and my master for two years of training. Refusing to cooperate with her lessons wasn't an option. I could see myself dragged before the Triumvirate at that rate.

I stretched out a hand toward her arm, but just before it made contact, it froze, trembling slightly. Amara spoke again, her voice warmer, the words wrapping around me and soothing my anxieties.

"As soon as you make contact, you'll be able to sense every part of my body. Do your best to ignore that. Those sensations are just a jumping point to allow you to feel yourself. Focus inward."

I drew a deep breath, but Amara spoke quickly before I could make contact.

"But don't change anything about yourself, remember. All we want today is awareness."

I nodded, and before I could change my mind, thrust my hand the rest of the way forward to wrap around her wrist.

Instantly I was overwhelmed with awareness of Amara's internal systems. I threw up a wall as I had done earlier, although I couldn't explain how I was doing it. It was like my mind's eye could see the red bricks stacking on top of each other one by one.

I wasn't fast enough, though, and the wall had cracks and holes, limiting its effectiveness. My stomach churned, and I had to use all my willpower not to use my power to calm it.

Instead I tried to expand my awareness of myself beyond my belly, searching for veins and heart and lungs. My head swam, saliva filling my mouth.

"Stop, stop!" I managed to gasp, and Amara pulled back on the reins.

Acorn slowed to a halt, and I almost fell out of the cart, I managed to make it to the side of the road before the contents of my stomach came up. My belly retracted and spasmed as it expelled my breakfast, only calming once it was fully emptied.

Amara leaped down to join me, one hand rubbing circles on my back while the other handed me a water skin. I took it gratefully. Rinsing my mouth, I spat out a mouthful before taking a large drink.

"I'm sorry," I said when I could speak again. "It seems like some of that celebration food must have disagreed with me."

Amara's circling hand froze before resuming its previous pace.

"You poor thing," she said. "I know I told you not to use your power on yourself for now, but if you need to settle your stomach, that should be safe enough." She hesitated as if she wanted to say more but didn't speak.

"Thank you," I said, feeling a flush mounting up my cheeks. It was only the first morning of my training, and I'd already disgraced myself.

Amara's kindness as she helped me into the cart only further exacerbated my guilt and embarrassment. I should tell her the full truth of what had just happened. But no matter how many times I decided to speak up, I couldn't bring my mouth to actually form the words. What sort of healer felt sick at the mere mention of a wound, let alone at the sight of actual blood? Knowing what was coming, I should have refrained from eating the food my mother had prepared.

In the aftershock of my run-in with the stranger, my anger and the sour taste of my fear had overcome my normal caution. But now it was hard to recall the intensity of those emotions. What had I been thinking allowing Amara to activate me? I could clearly never be a healer.

"It's all right," Amara said softly as she directed Acorn to resume walking. "You'll soon get the knack of how to heal yourself—and others too."

I pressed a hand to my head, wishing a healing ability included the power to erase unpleasant memories.

"How did you go, though?" Amara asked after a brief moment of silence. "Did you sense anything before we had to stop?"

"I could sense you clearly," I said slowly. "I tried putting up a wall to block it out, but it was only partially successful. It was enough to calm my mind somewhat, though, so I did try to focus on myself like you said."

"And?" she prompted when I faltered.

"I got nothing, beyond a sudden awareness I was about to be sick."

"Nothing?"

I shrugged, not sure what to say.

"Let me think about it some more," she said. "In the meantime, we'll try something different. The positive side to this situation is that you don't seem to be an imminent danger to yourself. So we can work on building up your control in general. I'm confident we'll work out what's going on eventually, and when we do, you'll find it a lot easier to handle if you've already learned some general control."

I nodded, trying not to show my uneasiness. What was she going to ask me to do?

"I had the impression yesterday that you can sense people and animals around you without needing physical contact," she continued, and I released a shaky breath.

This part of my power didn't scare me. This was the part I liked.

I sat up straighter. "Yes, I can. I realized I could sense it before as well, but it was so faint in comparison that I didn't think anything of it. It's not like when I make contact—it's not all blood and internal organs. I would describe it more as a general sense of their presence. With people, if I'm close like we are right now, I can sense the most basic body functions, like your breathing, but with animals, it's more a general sense of their current state—whether they're in pain or afraid or happy. I can tell that Acorn is mildly pleased to be plodding along in such pleasant weather."

Amara chuckled. "Suddenly you're all words. Clearly I just need to find the right topic."

I flushed and slumped back on the hard wooden seat.

"Don't stop," she said with a smile. "That wasn't a criticism. It helps me if you talk. I want to understand what's going on in your mind. It will help me be a better teacher."

"All right, I'll try," I said, feeling awkward and wishing I didn't have anything to hide.

"Those external senses you're talking about are because of your strength," she explained. "Healers below mage level generally have little to no ability to sense anything without physical contact. Even someone as strong as Halmir would only have the vaguest external awareness."

"Really?" I frowned at her. "But you were able to sense Rocky from as far away as the road, and you don't even have a healing affinity. I know you have a healing influence, but I thought that only gave you echoes of your cross affinity, not advanced abilities."

"No, you're right," she said. "While I have an unusual sense of connection with both humans and animals for an elements mage, I can't actually heal at all. The only conclusion I can come to is that the awareness you're feeling—which I also have to a lesser extent—isn't actually an advanced ability. Rather it is a basic ability that is accessed only by those with greater sensitivity."

"You mean that it's the overall strength of your power that allows you to share that part of the healing ability?" I asked.

"Exactly." She sounded pleased. "And it makes it a good place for you to start. It's not only an external ability, but one that shouldn't require great skill, control, or effort from you. You won't even need to be nervous since it's non-invasive."

I sat up straight, my eyes fixed eagerly on her face. Did I really get to start with such a pleasant part of my ability?

"What do you want me to do?" I asked.

"I'm curious to see your range," she said. "Try to relax and reach out with your mind. Tell me what animals you can sense around us."

"Reach out with my mind?" I tried not to sound nervous. I didn't want to fail at my first proper lesson.

"Why don't you close your eyes this first time?" she suggested. "It isn't necessary, but it might help to remove distractions until you're used to it.

Essentially it's the same as looking into the distance or listening for sounds from far away. You're just reaching with a new sense you didn't have before. It should be just as instinctive. You just need to learn how to recognize it."

I drew a deep breath and closed my eyes, trying not to scrunch them tightly. To my surprise, the moment I concentrated on reaching outward and feeling for life around me, my sense expanded. Amara had been telling the truth when she said this new sense was as embedded in my mind as my sight or hearing.

"There are birds overhead," I said.

"How many? And what type of birds? How far away are they?"

I scrunched up my face, trying to concentrate. "There are two in the skies above us, both birds of prey, looking for their next meal in the fields below. And there's a group of more than ten birds in that clump of trees on our left."

"More than ten? You can't be specific?"

I grimaced, my eyes still clamped shut. "They're moving, darting around and among each other, so it's hard to tell. But they're all the same type."

"Can you tell which type?"

The more I tried to focus on the small, quick-moving animals, the more confused I got. I let out a long breath and relaxed. Amara kept talking about instinct—maybe I was trying too hard.

As soon as I stopped concentrating so intensely on the birds, the answer came to me.

"They're sparrows."

"How do you know?"

"I...I'm not sure. I can just tell."

Was that the wrong answer? Was there something specific about the birds that I should have been able to identify?

"Good." Amara's response made me relax, and I reminded myself that this wasn't an audition. I already had the position as Amara's apprentice, and she couldn't legally get rid of me. I didn't have to know everything from the beginning. The whole point of my training was for me to learn.

"What about on the ground?" she asked. "Is there anything living at ground level among the trees?"

I didn't reply as I directed my awareness below the birds.

"I can sense five squirrels, a large family of rabbits, and..." I frowned. "Too many mice to count."

"I feel sorry for the closest farm," she said with a chuckle, and I winced in sympathy.

"Hopefully they have good cats—or even better, someone with a healing affinity."

Amara nodded. "There's no affinity that isn't helpful on a farm. The earth and growing things, the weather, and animals are all central to farm life." She carefully kept her eyes on the road ahead. "I know you would have preferred a weaker, plants seed, but I feel like there's more to your reluctance to be activated. I don't suppose you want to tell me the other reason?"

"Other...other reason?" I stammered, unable to hide my shock.

"If you're still not ready to tell me, it can wait." She still didn't look at me, her voice calm and even.

"I don't..." I cleared my throat. "That is, I'm not sure what you mean."

She chuckled softly. "Really? Don't concern yourself then." I began to relax, only for her to add, "We can talk about it another time."

I tried to think of a response but couldn't come up with one.

"How far away do you think those trees are?" she said as if the previous conversation hadn't happened.

I looked to my left automatically, but I'd never been good at estimating distances.

"I have no idea, sorry."

"I would guess two miles," she said thoughtfully.

"That far?" I peered at the trees, acknowledging that they appeared smaller and further away than I'd remembered. I was surprised I'd even noticed them at all.

"That's an impressive range already," she said. "Especially for creatures as small as a mouse. But I'm curious if you can go further. Try reaching ahead of us along the road. This stretch of road is straight, so we can see a long way, but can you sense beyond your line of sight? There's a small hamlet ahead. Can you feel the people there?"

I squinted at the empty road ahead of us. My family's rare trips away from our farm had always been in the other direction, toward Tarin. I'd never come this far on this road, so I had no idea how much further the hamlet was. I was as curious as Amara about my ability, though.

I shut my eyes and concentrated, reaching along the road. At first there was nothing, just a vast blankness as if I was trying to stare into a pitch-black room. But just as I was about to give up, I felt something brushing the edges of my awareness. Straining, I latched onto the rhythmic feeling of breathing. People.

"There are people," I said breathlessly. "But they're far away."

"How many?" Amara asked.

I counted, moving slowly so as not to miss anyone.

"Nine," I said at last. "Three children and six adults."

I opened my eyes and looked up at her. "I almost gave up before I reached them. How far is the hamlet?"

"While your eyes were closed, we passed a road marker indicating ten miles." For the first time during the morning, Amara's voice held a slight tension beneath her usual calm.

"Ten miles?" I asked, awed. "Is that far?"

For a moment, Amara hesitated before slowly nodding. "Very far. To be honest, I wouldn't have suggested the exercise if I'd realized we were still so far out. I don't know any healers who can reach that far."

"But..." I gaped at her. How could that be true? Amara was a Guild mage and a master. Surely she knew all the kingdom's master mages, even the healers.

Slowly she began to chuckle. "For the first time I'm questioning my own rashness. I can only imagine what Hayes would have to say about my stealing you."

"Hayes?" I asked, completely confused.

She laughed again. "Sorry, I was talking to myself mostly. Hayes is an old friend and—more importantly—a healer. He would berate me for locking you into a traveling apprenticeship with an elements mage when I didn't know the full extent of your strength. The situation in Tartora is starting to change at last, and our strength is growing again after many years of gradual decline. But strong mages are still in short supply."

"You don't need to worry about that," I said, "since there was no way I was going to the Guild and apprenticing under this Hayes, or anyone else. You didn't steal me away from a healing mage."

She grinned at me. "Do you promise to tell him as much?"

"Of course." I smiled back. "You're my master now. I'll always have your back."

"I'm starting to wonder why I didn't take an apprentice earlier," she said. "It's nice not to be alone."

I looked back at the road as my cheeks grew rosy. It was hard to grasp what she was saying about my strength—surely I couldn't be anything so very special—but it felt nice to have my presence appreciated. Despite my fears, the more I learned about Amara, the more certain I became that I wasn't going to regret my rash decision to become her apprentice.

"It's too late for recriminations anyway," Amara said cheerfully. "For now, we should continue the lesson. I want you to alternate between reaching for the hamlet and monitoring the animal life around us. The more you practice, the easier it should become to use this ability. And I want to know when the hamlet stops being a stretch to reach. Let me know when you can feel the people comfortably."

I nodded and immediately swept the area, sensing a number of small ground animals as well as a few new birds in the sky. It was surprisingly relaxing reaching out of myself and focusing on the world around me. The animals were all intent on their normal business, unbothered about things like affinities and seeds and apprenticeships.

As I reached down the road again, a jarring note disrupted my peace. I leaned forward, my eyes closing as I tried to focus.

"What is it?" Amara asked sharply.

"Pain," I gasped out, shuddering. "So much pain. I think something is dying."

CHAPTER

# EIGHT

"Dying?" Amara's voice anchored me in the cart, reminding me that the pain I was sensing wasn't my own. "You said something, not someone? It's not a person?"

I shook my head, trying to push past the overwhelming strength of the pain to identify the animal behind it. I failed, once again submerged in the animal's distress. The intensity of the sensation even overwhelmed my usual nausea.

Before I realized my own intention, I had scrambled to my feet. Without waiting for Acorn to stop, I flung myself down from the cart. Staggering, I only just managed to keep my feet under me, setting off at a sprint down the road.

"Delphine!" Amara shouted after me, but I could barely hear her through the intensity of my focus.

My breath was soon coming hard and fast as my legs protested the unusual level of exertion. I didn't slow, though, veering off the road as I reached a spot level with the animal.

A few trees lined the road, wild grass growing beneath them. A flash of sickening red caught my attention at the base of one of the trunks. Something had brushed against the bark and left a streak of blood. My stomach turned over, but the spike of panicked energy suppressed the reaction, as if my body was already too overloaded to process its usual reaction.

Following more drops of red, I ran to the last of the trees. Slumped in the grass against the trunk was a small bundle of red and orange. Dropping to my knees, I reached out both hands and pressed them to the rough, sticky fur.

Relief filled me at the sense of movement and life inside the fox. It was still alive, although its heartbeat was weak and getting weaker by the moment. I had no way to tell what predator had attacked it, but its gashes were deep, and it was losing far too much blood. Without the intervention of an animal healer, it had only minutes left to live.

Familiar fear filled me. But this time it wasn't at my weakness but at my lack of experience and knowledge. I was the only possible healer in range, but I had no idea how to heal such deep gouges.

A hand landed on my shoulder, and a soft voice spoke.

"This is the way of things in the animal world," Amara said sympathetically. "You're not responsible for this."

I shook my head stubbornly. "I don't care how natural it is, I can't just leave her to die without even trying."

Amara paused. "If you're sure you want to, you can try. I don't see how it could do any harm, as long as you accept that you might not be successful."

I scrubbed at the tears on my cheeks and nodded. "But what do I do? I have no idea how to…"

"You didn't know how to expel that food from your father's throat, either." Amara's voice steadied my erratic emotions. "Until you get further training, you'll have to rely on instinct. And brute force," she added. "You have the advantage of strength which most people don't."

The fox now lay frighteningly still beneath my gentle grip, so I focused on the connection between us, urgency driving me forward. My power was still an unfamiliar part of me, but I directed it to the torn and damaged parts of the fox. Commanding it to restore the animal's body, I tried not to think too closely about what that meant, instead allowing my mind to float along the veins, muscles, tendons, and bones in the damaged areas.

Although I knew nothing about fox anatomy, my ability knew which parts felt healthy and which broken. Sweat broke out across my forehead as I willed the damaged, wrong-feeling parts to fix themselves.

I felt it as it happened—the skin closing back over, the muscles knitting back together, and the veins reforming, using the fire of my power as their fuel.

Fire? I frowned at the instinctive description. Was I burning her?

I nearly pulled my hands away but stopped myself just in time. I couldn't feel any burn damage. It wasn't that sort of heat. My power just felt like fire and wind, sweeping through the fox's insides.

At last, I could find no remaining spots of wrongness or damage inside her. I slumped backward onto the ground, my head sinking into my now bloodied hands.

My whole body shook with aftereffects from both the exertion and the emotions. The peace radiating from the fox in place of the earlier pain was calming, but I could still feel myself hovering on the edge of shock.

Amara gave a soft sigh. "That's a lot less noisy."

I looked up, her voice grounding me and helping fight back the confusion and dizziness.

"You could feel her pain as well?"

Amara nodded. "But only as an echo compared to what you must have felt. I couldn't feel it at all until I got closer."

"But is she really healthy now?" I asked, struggling to believe I'd really managed the healing without making any mistakes. "She was so close to death."

Amara's lips twisted apologetically. "I have no idea, sorry. But if there's anything wrong, she doesn't seem to be feeling it. When we reach the next town, we can have their animal healer check her over."

"We can bring her with us?" My hands tightened around the warm body still resting in my lap. "Really?"

Amara looked down at me and the fox and chuckled. "Was there an option where we left her behind? You both look pretty attached at this point."

I flushed, not wanting to admit that I hadn't expected a master mage to make any special accommodations for an apprentice. I had once again misjudged Amara, and it was time I stopped doing that. She was obviously nothing like the mages at the Guild who lived self-centered, indulgent lives.

Unaware of my thoughts, she took one of my arms and helped haul me to my feet, my own arms full of the fox.

"I think we'd better get both of you cleaned up," she said ruefully. "Unless we want to scare the townsfolk."

I looked down at myself, and my eyes widened. I'd been too distracted earlier to worry about how much blood was being smeared across my clothes. And the poor fox looked even worse, her fur matted with sticky red.

But now that the crisis was passed, sight of the bright red made me sway, the blood rushing from my head and a roaring filling my ears. I tore my eyes away and gulped, trying to clear my mind of all thoughts.

"There's a stream not too far down the road," Amara continued, unaware of my sudden reaction. "We can make early camp there for the night and get you both cleaned up and this lady fed and settled. I know I'm always ravenous after a healing. If we stop there, we'll be able to reach Ostaria comfortably before nightfall tomorrow."

I gulped, my stomach heaving dangerously. I'd just successfully completed a proper healing. I couldn't disgrace myself now by vomiting.

But when I reached with my power, intending to just settle my stomach, nothing happened. Like earlier, I couldn't sense my own body at all.

I frowned and glanced at Amara. Should I say anything?

But she'd already climbed back up into the cart and was beckoning me to follow. The surprise of my failure had distracted me just enough to settle the immediate danger, so I hurried over to join her. As long as I kept my eyes on the horizon, and my mind blank, I should make it to the stream.

We reached it without issue. A tributary of the western Celadon River, it wasn't wide, but it flowed briskly. Within minutes, all the red had washed away, making me grateful for the water, however icy.

The fox proved more recalcitrant, but I ruthlessly dunked and scrubbed her. And even the cold soaking didn't entirely shake her out of her shock. I suspected if she'd been in a normal frame of mind, I never would have succeeded with the bath at all.

With the last traces of her injuries gone, I was able to breathe easily again. As long as I kept my mind from wandering back to the scene beneath the trees, I shouldn't have any more trouble.

"Don't worry," Amara told me when she caught me sending worried glances toward the resting animal as we prepared the evening meal. "It's normal enough to be sleepy after suffering such significant injuries and then a major healing as well. I saw it often in the animals my old master healed. Some would require a full day to come back to a normal state of awareness."

I looked at the fox again. "Did we do the right thing in bringing her? Maybe she has a den of kits somewhere."

"I don't think she would have left them if so," Amara said. "Not at this point of the year. But you should be able to tell."

I looked from the mage to the animal. "I should?"

"Connect with her and ask yourself whether she's recently given birth. You should be able to sense the answer. According to my old master, the traces left on the body are very obvious." She shrugged, clearly apologetic not to be able to give me more direct help.

Crossing slowly over to where the fox rested by the fire, I knelt down cautiously, not wanting to alarm her. She merely flicked her tail, however, waving it once in a gesture of communication I didn't recognize. I glanced back at Amara who was watching us.

"I think she's quite a young fox," she said. "And she seems to have taken to you." She sounded amused.

"I would hope so after my effort on her behalf," I muttered, but my heart wasn't in the complaint. I couldn't help smiling at the sight of her, curled by the fire, plump and healthy.

Now that she was clean, I could see she was an elegant vixen with a fiery orange coat, mottled black on her tail and legs, and contrasted by the white that ran from the underside of her chin all the way down her belly.

She would have looked like a small dog, if not for the indefinable air of a wild animal that hung about her, even while she accepted our ministrations.

Reaching out a gentle hand, I settled it on her thick coat. She raised her head to look at me but merely lowered it again after a moment's gaze.

As expected, just the sensation of her insides was enough to send my own roiling. Without the shock and urgency of our earlier interaction, there was nothing to suppress my normal squeamishness. I tried to push past it, glad we hadn't yet eaten our meal.

I focused my mind on the question of whether the fox bore signs in her body of a recent litter. But as the seconds stretched, my mind grew fuzzy. Gasping, I pulled my hand free but stayed in my crouched position, letting my head hang low as I struggled to push back the lightheadedness. Hopefully Amara hadn't noticed anything.

I finally pushed back to my feet, moving slowly. Joining Amara, I took over the job of spooning out the simple stew she had prepared.

"I think you're right," I said once we both had a bowl full. "I can't explain why, but I feel certain she's only newly grown into adulthood and hasn't had any kits yet."

"Well done." Amara gave me a smile I didn't deserve, making me shrink inside.

At least my stomach had calmed enough for me to enjoy the warm dinner. As my belly filled, my enthusiasm slowly returned.

"We should give her a name." I scraped clean the last of my stew.

"She looks like part of the fire sitting there," Amara said. "Is a fire name too obvious for a fox?"

I laughed. "No, why should it be? I don't even know any other foxes with names. What about...Ember?"

"I like it." Amara looked at the fox. "What do you think, girl?"

She opened one eye and looked between us before closing it again. We both laughed.

"I'm taking that as a yes," I said. "Ember it is." I hesitated. "But do you think she'll leave once the shock of the healing wears off?"

Amara frowned. "It's hard to say. She is a wild animal. But it's possible she'll feel bonded to you now. The power in your healing ability already calls to animals—you saw it with Rocky and even with Acorn."

"Acorn?" I directed an astonished look toward the tethered mare just inside the circle of our firelight. "I haven't noticed her directing any particular affection my way."

Amara laughed. "She's normally extremely cantankerous and greatly dislikes everyone but me. I've never seen her so docile in my life. I don't think

I could have taken on an elements or plants apprentice. She would have ended up biting them."

"Acorn?" I asked again, still unable to believe it.

"I swear it's true," Amara said through a laugh. "The fact you can't believe me just shows how much of a transformation she undergoes in your presence."

I was still marveling at Amara's claims as I harnessed the horse to the cart the next morning. She gave me no trouble, pressing her head against my side in what appeared to be affection.

"Is it my power making her do this?" I asked Amara as she put our tightly rolled bedrolls into the back of the cart.

"Well, that and the sugar cubes in your pocket." She grinned and went back for our packs.

Acorn let out a whuffing breath as if in agreement with Amara. Shaking my head, I retrieved two cubes and held them out in my flat palm, grinning as she eagerly gobbled them up.

Ember strolled over and leaned against my leg. I picked her up, cradling her in my arms. Her furry warmth already felt familiar, and a pang shot through me at the idea that she might disappear by the end of the day.

Climbing carefully into the cart, I settled her in my lap, reminding myself that she was a wild animal, and I couldn't hold onto her if she didn't want to stay.

The day passed quickly, the weather beautiful and the road smooth. It was a well-maintained thoroughfare since the western half of Tartora was blanketed in farmlands and most of the produce was transported north or south via one of the rivers. Tarin was in the southwestern part of the king-dom, so we sent most of our crops further west to the Celadon, which formed Tartora's western border. I had often heard townsfolk talk of making this journey northwest to Ostaria on the Celadon River, but I had never made the trip myself.

"What's it like?" I asked, unable to suppress my curiosity.

"Your parents never took you to Ostaria?" Amara asked. "I know Tarin is much closer to your farm, but Ostaria is considerably bigger and hosts a lot more travelers."

I sighed. "I would have liked to, but we couldn't leave the farm. There's never been anyone we could trust it to in our stead, and neither Father nor Mother wanted to leave the other to manage the farm alone. Not when it would have been a multi-day trip. They never even took me south to see the ocean, since that's just beyond reach of a day trip."

It was all true, if not the full truth. I was certain Mother would have found a way to get us to both the beach and Ostaria if it hadn't been for Father. Any mention of a trip provoked one of his bouts of silent moodiness. Just the idea of traveling reminded him of what had happened last time someone left the farm, as well as the fact that he had expected to be managing it alongside his brother. If I had grown up alongside my uncle—and hopefully an aunt and cousins as well—how different my life would have been.

If Amara picked up on the undercurrent in my tone, she didn't comment on it.

"I'm sorry you won't get a chance to see the ocean anytime soon, given we're heading generally northward, but I hope you like Ostaria. I've always had a fondness for it, and in particular for one of its inns. It has an especially excellent washroom." She sighed with remembered pleasure.

"Washroom? Is that significant?" I asked, confused. The only inn I'd ever visited was the small one in Tarin, and even then only a couple of times. I didn't think I'd ever made use of their washroom.

Amara nodded fervently. "It all comes down to how many bathtubs they have and who manages them. If they only have one tub, you have to hurry in and out because there's always someone waiting, and if the attendant isn't skilled enough, they might only be able to keep the water warm. Bath attendants always have an elements affinity, but they vary in both strength and skill." She hummed to herself in remembered pleasure. "The attendant at the inn in Ostaria can keep the bath at the perfect temperature for each patron, no matter how long you stay in. I once soaked for over an hour, and the water never cooled."

I blinked, unsure how to ask my question without sounding rude. "But you're an elements master. Why do you need the attendant to keep your bath warm?"

She laughed. "Of course, I *could* do it myself, but the whole point of soaking in a tub is relaxation. I don't *want* to do it myself."

"Oh." I considered the point. "I suppose that makes sense."

Since we didn't have anyone with an elements affinity in our household, baths were something to be hurried through, everyone rushing to take their turn before the lukewarm water cooled. I had never been one for long soaks.

I sighed. "Every farm should have someone with each of the affinities. It would be a big help."

Amara raised an eyebrow, looking down at me with a hint of amusement in her expression. "This is a change of sentiment."

I flushed. "I never thought a healing affinity was bad for a farm. I just think a plants affinity is more helpful. My parents won't always be around to keep the crops growing healthily."

I bit my tongue, wishing I had the courage to confess my other reason for wanting a different affinity, but a rider approached from behind, moving fast to overtake us, and the moment passed. More and more traffic appeared as we neared Ostaria, and we ended up traveling behind a closed carriage, carrying passengers who must have been more wealthy than either of us.

I glanced several times at Amara, wondering if she might know them—perhaps they were even mages—but she showed no special interest in the carriage. If I hadn't seen her power for myself, I would doubt her claims of mastery. She seemed in every way like a normal traveler.

Ostaria was big enough to qualify as a small city, having a wall all the way around and guards at the gate. The guards showed little interest in us, although they kept us waiting for some time while they spoke to the occupants of the carriage and bowed them through the gates. When it came to our turn, they merely waved us through.

Amara caught me frowning after the carriage and laughed.

"Avoiding that sort of thing is part of the reason I travel with just this cart," she said. "Believe me, it gets old very fast."

"Do you think you might know whoever is in there?" I asked.

"I hope not," she said lightly, not elaborating.

I was too interested in our surroundings to push her harder. The cobblestone streets were broad and clean, bustling with people in the late afternoon sun. All types of vehicles could be seen, along with plenty of foot traffic.

The stone houses themselves were neat and well kept, many suggesting occupants of comfortable circumstances. I could immediately see why Amara had thought Ostaria of greater interest than Tarin. The city was much larger, more prosperous, and busier than the town I'd grown up near. Even the colors seemed brighter and more vivid, flowers growing everywhere in window boxes or small, well tended plots, and the shops boasting awnings in varied shades.

When I finally finished staring around open-mouthed, I realized Amara had been watching me with the amusement back in her eyes.

"I thought you would like it," she said, and I grinned back at her unabashedly.

"It's the most interesting place I've ever seen."

"Just wait until we reach the inn." She urged Acorn to pick up her pace, despite the congestion of the street.

"Until we reach the baths, you mean?" I asked, making her chuckle.

"When you live your life traveling, you learn to appreciate what familiar comforts you can find."

Her words made my insides contract. How long would it be before I enjoyed the familiar comforts of home again?

But I couldn't take my decision back now. If I wanted to run my family farm one day, I first needed to complete my apprenticeship, which meant I was better off focusing on what was before me now rather than getting lost in homesickness.

"Here we are," Amara called triumphantly, turning Acorn into the court-yard of a large inn.

A groom appeared within seconds, running to Acorn's head. He looked concerned, the worry only disappearing slowly when Acorn accepted his presence calmly. When he sent Amara a questioning look, she burst out laughing.

"See, I told you Acorn acts differently with you around, Delphine. Even the grooms here remember what she's normally like."

She stepped down, helping me to alight without disrupting Ember who was looking around with great uncertainty. By the time we were both safely down and able to move toward the inn's doors, a stout man had appeared, his manner and dress declaring him the innkeeper.

Before he could do more than welcome Amara, however, a woman pushed forward to take his place. Clearly his wife, she was full of effusive welcome for Amara. The traveling master was obviously a well-known and liked guest.

When her eyes fell on me, however, her expression stiffened, her smile disappearing as her eyes fastened on Ember.

"Is that a *wild animal?*" she asked, her voice too loud. Her expression made it clear she would have liked to say something more disparaging but was held back by Amara's status.

"She is a patient," Amara said, unshaken by the woman's transformation.

"A patient?" The innkeeper and his wife exchanged a look. "Your patient, Master Amara?" he asked cautiously.

She smiled, although her expression seemed a little too calm, more like a mask than true emotion.

"Goodness, no. I haven't changed affinities since my last visit."

Both the innkeeper and his wife chuckled awkwardly at this impossible suggestion.

"The fox is the patient of my new apprentice, Delphine. Delphine has a healing affinity."

"Apprentice?" The innkeeper's wife stared at me, more astonished at this news than she had been by Ember's presence. "I've never known you to have an apprentice, Master Amara!"

"There is a first time for everything," Amara said lightly, although there was a hint of impatience behind her words, suggesting she was bored of the conversation and ready to be ushered inside.

I couldn't help marveling at the perfect blend of authority and civility in her manner. I had never seen this side of her before, and I suddenly found it impossible to think of her as a regular traveler. When needed, she knew how to carry the weight of her true status.

"You're most welcome, Apprentice Delphine," the innkeeper said.

"Most welcome," his wife affirmed, even bobbing a curtsy. "But I'm afraid you can't bring a wild animal into our inn. What will the other patrons think? The fox will do well enough in the stables, I'm sure."

Despite her general deference, the steel in her voice made it clear she didn't intend to budge on the issue. Amara must have come to the same assessment because after only the smallest of pauses, she nodded.

"Delphine, you take Ember over there." She pointed to the side of the inn where a separate building stood, also fully enclosed within the inn's outer wall.

As I glanced over, the groom from earlier led Acorn inside the second building, which had to be the stables.

Amara gave me a significant look. "I'll see you up in our room."

I frowned, having no idea what she was trying to silently communicate. After an awkward moment, I nodded and hurried away, looking over my shoulder in the hope of some final sign.

But Amara was already stepping through the inn's doors, accompanied by both the innkeeper and his wife. Whatever she wanted me to do, I was going to have to work it out on my own.

CHAPTER

# NINE

I walked along the front of the inn toward the stables, trying to look like I knew what I was doing. No one paid me any notice thanks to the arrival of a carriage full of new customers. When I reached the corner of the inn and rounded it, I found myself in front of the stables.

A groom came hurrying out, bumping past me with a barely muttered apology, his eyes focused on the team harnessed to the carriage. The glancing blow of his shoulder didn't hurt, but it spun me slightly, facing me toward the side of the inn. My eyes latched onto a plain wooden door.

A daring thought popped into my mind. Amara had said only two things. That I should come over here, and that she would see me in our room. But she must have known I wouldn't abandon Ember to be alone in the stables, especially while the fox was still in a state of shock. Had Amara intended me to smuggle Ember into the inn?

I put my hand over my mouth, stopping the giggle that was trying to bubble up. Was a master mage really encouraging me to sneak a wild animal into an inn over the protests of the innkeeper?

Once the idea had taken root, I couldn't shake it, however. I had taken on responsibility for Ember's healing, thus making me responsible for her until she regained full alertness. Amara might not be a healer herself, but her influencer had been, so she understood that. She also knew we wouldn't let Ember destroy the room or bother the other guests. Was this her way of avoiding an unnecessary fight with the innkeeper and his wife?

A flurry of activity approached, and I pressed myself back against the stone of the inn wall. A parade of grooms trooped past, leading the four-horse team from the carriage into the stables. None of them paid me any notice, so I shuffled along until I was next to the side door.

As soon as the last of them had disappeared, I darted a glance around the courtyard. It was empty now, the guests having entered the inn with the innkeeper. Spinning, I grasped the door handle and pulled, hoping I wasn't going to find it locked.

I released a breath as it swung open. The inn's servants must use the door for access to the courtyards and stables. Ducking inside, I pulled it closed behind me as quickly as I could without making any noise.

Peering around me, I waited for my eyes to adjust. No lanterns or candles had yet been lit in this section of the inn, making the air around me murky in the semi-darkness of dusk.

As soon as my vision improved, I hurried down the long, straight corridor that led into the depths of the inn. From the little I knew of inns, guest rooms wouldn't be in this section of the building. My best bet was to find some stairs and get up to the next level.

Wrapping my cloak around Ember, I slowed my pace at the sound of voices. The background hum suggested several people were talking at once, so I was likely hearing either customers in the main room or staff in the kitchens. Either way, I wanted to avoid them.

I was about to turn back and start trying doors when I reached a staircase so narrow I hadn't noticed it before. Gripping Ember more tightly, I dashed up the stairs.

My haste was nearly my undoing since my feet outpaced me, and I slipped half way up. My free hand flew out, barely managing to steady myself on the stone wall. I froze in position, my heart beating rapidly, and Ember stirring in my other arm.

She gave a soft yap that set me into motion again.

"Quiet!" I said, and she instantly subsided, bowing her head.

"Sorry," I pressed my free hand on her head, instantly contrite. "I just don't want anyone to find you, girl."

When no one appeared at the top or bottom of the stairs to challenge me, I started upward again, moving more cautiously this time. I reached the top without further incident.

The staircase opened onto a much wider corridor, this one carpeted. I stepped out, confident I'd found the domain of the guests. But once in the hallway, I stopped, unsure how to proceed. I couldn't knock on every door looking for Amara.

While I was still hesitating, unsure how to proceed, a door opened, and a familiar figure stepped out. Amara looked the other way first before turning in my direction and spotting me.

"Ah, Delphine, there you are," she said calmly.

I hurried over to her, relieved.

"Sorry to keep you waiting," I said breathlessly. "I wasn't sure—"

"Inside." She gestured toward the open door behind her.

I ducked around her and scurried inside, only breathing easily once she'd followed me and closed the door behind us.

"I hope I was right about what you meant me to do." I pushed my cloak aside, revealing Ember curled in my arm.

Amara smiled. "I can see you and I are going to deal well together."

"Won't we get in trouble?" I looked doubtfully around the lavish room.

The carpet underfoot was thicker than I had expected, and the curtains were heavy brocade. It must have been one of the inn's best rooms.

"Don't worry," she said. "I didn't want to make a fuss in front of other customers, but both the innkeeper and his wife have a soft spot for me."

"You helped them in the past, didn't you," I guessed.

She smiled slightly. "It was a minor matter, but they've been more than gracious ever since."

I considered the possibilities. "Did you keep the inn safe from a serious storm? Or maybe prevent it burning down?"

She turned a laugh into a cough. "The latter."

I shook my head. "No wonder they like you."

"I try not to take advantage of it, so we do need to keep Ember out of sight of other guests." She pointed at a large wooden box sitting by the fireplace, a rough woolen blanket at its bottom and a small dish of water at its side. "As you can see the innkeeper has already provided."

I gaped at it while she made no attempt to hide her amusement.

"The innkeeper doesn't have standards that are quite as strict as his wife's," she said. "And if we're fortunate, he'll have talked her around by tomorrow, so we won't need to be quite so surreptitious in the future."

Relieved, I deposited Ember in her new temporary home. She sniffed all around the box in a dainty fashion before settling herself on the blanket and closing her eyes.

"She seems to approve." I surveyed the room again, taking in the two heavy wooden beds, pushed up against opposite walls, and the matching dark wood of the furniture. "So do I. I've never stayed in such a fancy place."

Amara's eyes crinkled. "I should warn you that not all our nights will be spent in such pleasant surrounds."

"Of course not," I said absently, wandering over to the bed that had my pack on it. "We slept on the ground last night, after all."

"I applaud your adaptability," Amara said.

I turned, looking suspiciously for any sign I was being mocked, but she had already crossed to her own pack.

"Should we go downstairs to eat?" I asked, remembering the smells that had accompanied the chatter of voices from earlier.

"No." Amara shook her head firmly. "First the washroom."

I laughed. "I should have known."

"Come on," she said. "You're going to enjoy this."

She was soon proven correct. Given the hour, all three of the wooden tubs in the female washroom were available, and we happily claimed two. A quietly spoken assistant appeared as soon as we sank into the water, adjusting the water temperature at our request. I asked for mine as hot as I could bear, ready to enjoy every moment of the luxury.

In the end, only our rumbling bellies chased us out, and the attendant teased us about our wrinkled state as she handed over dry towels for our use. Amara laughed back, clearly recognizing the girl from previous visits. Her praise for the girl's skill with the bathwater turned the attendant's cheeks fiery red, and she bowed us both out of the room much more deeply than Amara's status required. She'd probably be boasting to her friends within hours over receiving such a compliment from a master mage.

Given the lateness of the hour, we headed straight for the dining room, gorging ourselves on a perfectly cooked meal. As I leaned back from my empty plate, I groaned.

"I can see why you like this place. You might have to roll me back up the stairs."

Amara grinned and hauled me to my feet. "Come on, lazybones. You can manage a single staircase."

Grumbling but smiling, I followed her back to our rooms, a napkin wrapped bundle weighing down my pocket. I had selected the rarest looking bits of meat to bring up for Ember, the best I could manage until she was well enough to hunt for herself again.

But when we entered the room, the box by the fire was empty.

"Ember?" I spun to examine the large room. "Where are you hiding?"

I knelt, peering under first one bed and then the other. When there was still no sign of her, I looked toward Amara in concern.

"You're sure she's not under there?" Amara's brow creased. "Maybe she was scared by some sounds from the corridor?"

I shook my head. "She's definitely not. And I can't see anywhere else in here for her to hide."

I hurried over to the window, realizing for the first time that it wasn't actually a window but a door leading onto a narrow balcony. And it was ajar.

"Oh no," I whispered, stepping outside and peering down toward the back of the inn and a small, well tended garden.

"She's gone?" Amara's voice was gentle. "She must have recovered then."

"She was probably hungry." Tears pricked at my eyes. "I shouldn't have left her for so long. I should have brought food up more quickly."

Amara's hand rested on my shoulder. "We always knew there was a chance she wouldn't stay."

I nodded, not trusting myself to speak. The emotions were surprisingly overwhelming. The fox was the first animal I had healed, and I couldn't help but feel I'd failed her. We hadn't even had her checked by the local animal healer.

"I'm going to go after her," I said, not meeting Amara's eyes.

"Delphine," she said softly, but I shook my head stubbornly.

"My healing hasn't been checked by an actual qualified healer yet. I can't just let her run off. With my ability, I should be able to sense her location if I can just get close enough to her."

Amara hesitated for a moment before nodding. "Very well, then. But don't stay out too late." She must have recognized that I wasn't going to give in easily.

Murmuring my thanks, I grabbed my cloak from where I had left it on the bed and hurried down the corridor to the main stairs. I forced myself to slow down enough not to trip as I had on the way into the inn, but within moments I was outside in the courtyard.

I didn't waste time circling the building. The garden was small enough that I had been able to examine the whole thing from the balcony. There hadn't been any sign of Ember.

Pulling up the hood of my cloak against the chill in the evening spring air, I hurried through the inn's gates and onto the streets of the city. The crowds had largely dispersed, most people heading home for the evening meal, I assumed. There was still enough traffic for me to feel safe, however, and I threw my full attention into the search for Ember.

As soon as I reached out with my ability, as Amara had shown me, I was overwhelmed with heartbeats and the pulsing sense of flowing blood. There were too many people in close proximity, and their presence overwhelmed everything else.

I groaned. I was going to have to search the old-fashioned way, after all.

Striding forward as quickly as possible, I began to patrol the streets closest to the inn, looking down alleyways and keeping my eye out for gardens of any size.

My eyes were soon tired from flicking this way and that, straining for any sign of red fur. Assuming the fox would avoid crowds, I moved further and further away from the well-traveled area around the inn and into the back-streets.

Only when I heard furtive voices did I realize the background noise of the streets had decreased significantly as the people thinned. I had been trying too hard to ignore the sense of so many bodies around me and hadn't noticed when they disappeared.

I could still feel people in the houses on either side, but it felt quiet enough that I might have some hope of identifying smaller animals as well. I sent out my awareness, searching for the now-familiar sensation of Ember's internal systems.

I had passed over five dogs and seven cats, and had just latched onto something that might be a fox, when a name caught my ears, shattering my concentration. Grey.

Looking up, the emptiness of the street struck me again but with different import this time. I was alone in the backstreets of an unfamiliar city.

My heart took off, racing at a frantic beat that was strong enough to break through to my new senses. Without thinking, I instructed my heart to calm down, and the beats instantly dropped so substantially that my head spun and I nearly collapsed. Gasping, I corrected myself, only breathing freely when the lightheadedness passed. As soon as my heart returned to its regular rhythm, I reinforced the wall protecting my body.

The second I did so, I noticed the voices again. They were coming from a nearby alley, the speakers just out of sight. I edged closer, trying not to make any noise with my steps. My heart had sped up again, but I determinedly ignored it, keeping my focus on the speakers.

When I reached the alleyway, I cautiously peered around the corner. Two men were facing each other, paying no particular attention to their surroundings. They were standing in front of a wooden door that gave access to the side of a large building. It appeared to be a shuttered warehouse that would have looked abandoned if not for the two men.

One of them shifted slightly, making me gasp and draw back. It was definitely Grey—the taller of the men I'd seen in Tarin. His image was imprinted on my mind given how many times I had gone over the memory of Miranda being dragged away.

Halmir had been convinced Grey and the others were heading north to Calista, but here they were in Ostaria. Was it just a stop on the way to the northern kingdom? Did that mean they were still gathering more recruits before returning home?

I squeezed my eyes shut, thinking of the door. Had Miranda, Serena, and the others been sent ahead to Calista already, or was it possible they were right here, behind that door?

I reached out with my power, suppressing a gasp when I sensed more people inside the warehouse. Part of me wanted to storm straight inside, but there were so many of them. And I didn't even have a way to confirm if Miranda was among them. For all I knew, they could all be Grey's henchmen.

I slowly inched to the side and peered around the corner again. This time I focused on their words instead of their appearance.

"We need to do better here than we did in Tarin," Grey said, his tone annoyed.

"We will," the other man assured him. "Ostaria is much bigger, so it will be easier to go unnoticed by the authorities. I've already found a few youths who are showing interest. I've told them you won't appear unless they can gather a crowd, so they've promised to spread the word."

I sucked in a breath. They were planning to abduct more youths here in Ostaria?

But even as I had the thought, I rubbed the back of my neck, uneasy. If I was honest, it didn't sound like they were talking about abducting people. If they were taking the time to charm and sway the Ostarian locals, maybe I really had been mistaken about Miranda.

I peered into the growing darkness. Whatever had happened that night in Tarin, I didn't intend to give up my search for my friend. Even if she'd made a rash decision in the heat of the moment, I didn't doubt she was regretting it by now. She wouldn't abandon her father like that—not when she was all he had.

Their voices dropped in volume, and I edged further around the corner, straining to hear. If Grey confirmed the youths were inside the building, I could take that information to the authorities of Ostaria. Even though it wasn't their own people in question—yet—they might be willing to act, for the sake of the neighboring town and their lost children.

I had nearly rounded the corner completely when a heavy hand landed on my shoulder, making me shriek. Twisting, I tried to peer up at the new arrival, but the hand tightened, holding me in place. I managed only the general impression of a tall, muscled man.

He moved his hold down to the top of my arm, taking the other one as well and hustling me into the alley, pushing me from behind. Both Grey and his companion had turned at the commotion and were watching me with wide eyes.

I struggled to break free, digging my heels into the ground when I couldn't shake myself loose. The man merely tightened his hold, lifting me completely off the ground.

I screamed, as much in frustration as fear, and tried to kick back at him.

My blows seemed to have no effect, however, and within moments I was deposited in front of Grey.

I made one last attempt to writhe free, but the hands holding me in place only tightened even further. Sighing, I gave up momentarily, instead meeting Grey's gaze defiantly.

"You have an eavesdropper," the man behind me said matter-of-factly. "What do you want done with her?"

"Let me go at once," I said immediately. "What can you be thinking? The streets belong to everyone."

"My words do not, however." Grey examined me with a calculated gaze. Behind it was something else, though, and my insides clenched in fear at the sight of the concern on his face.

I knew well that there was nothing intimidating about my appearance. If Grey was worried at the idea of my having overheard his conversation, then he must have said something sensitive before my arrival. What had he said, and how was I going to convince him that I hadn't heard it?

I cleared my throat. "I don't know who you are, or why you're lurking back here, but glancing down an alley hardly makes me a criminal. I'll be returning on my way now."

Despite my bold words, my captor made no move to release me.

Grey stepped forward. "Who are you?"

He stooped slightly to put his eyes on the level of mine, his mesmerizing green gaze pinning me in place as effectively as the hold of his henchman. This was a man used to commanding obedience. Somehow I knew that whatever he ordered, the two men with him would obey without question.

"Maybe she's heard about us," Grey's companion said, sounding smug. "She looks about the right age."

A flash of interest leaped in Grey's eyes as he assessed my face.

"A new recruit, you think? She certainly looks seventeen." He grinned at me. "Shall we take a look and see if you meet my requirements?"

Something in his gaze made me shrink back, but I couldn't go far given the human mountain holding me in place.

"You're going to test her?" Grey's companion sounded shocked.

Grey threw him a lazy smile. "Why not? There's no one here to go telling tales."

He looked back at me, something crackling in his gaze. Despite myself, I could feel the magnetism of this man. No wonder he managed to entrance youths in every town he visited.

His expression slowly transformed, however, his brows pulling together and his mouth turning down.

"What's her affinity?" his companion asked. "Does she have any strength?"

Grey's unhappy gaze tightened, burning with something disturbingly like curiosity.

"You can't tell?" His companion was clearly even more shocked by Grey's failure than by his decision to test me in the first place. "What do you mean you can't tell? That's impossible."

"And yet…" Grey smiled, the effect chilling as his eyes held mine. "You've suddenly become very intriguing, young lady. Let me get a hold of you."

He reached out a hand for one of my bare wrists, and I jerked backward so violently that I took my captor by surprise, sending us both staggering back several steps.

If Grey wanted physical contact, did that mean he was a healer like me?

*Healer or assassin,* whispered a terrible voice in the back of my mind, making me break into wild thrashing. Already off balance, my captor's hold loosened slightly, further galvanizing my efforts.

But Grey stepped closer, unfazed by my desperate resistance. His hand loomed toward me, his fingers assuming a terrifying aspect I had never attributed to a hand before.

Tears squeezed from the corner of my eyes, running down my cheeks. I didn't know what was going to happen when Grey touched me, but I didn't want to find out.

A streak of movement distracted us both just as he was about to make contact. I looked sideways in time to see an orange blur launch itself at Grey's arm, sinking sharp, pointed teeth into his wrist.

CHAPTER

# TEN

Grey shouted in pain, whipping his arm back and forth until the fox attached to it went flying through the air and hit the wall of the warehouse.

"Ember!" I screamed, struggling anew.

Grey turned back to me, an ugly look in his eyes. His good hand gripped the puncture marks on his other wrist, red drips welling between his fingers and slowly dripping to the ground.

"Bring her here," he said, but I was too distracted by my terror for Ember to feel fear on my own behalf.

She lay still at the base of the wall, although my power told me she was still breathing—for now. Without touching her, I couldn't tell the extent of the damage.

I struggled against my captor, trying to get free to go to Ember, but it was no more effective now than it had been earlier. The man pushed me toward Grey, and despite my resistance, I moved closer.

Before we reached him, however, a deep growl emerged from the depths of the alley. We all turned in time to see a fifth person appear from the darkness.

Moving too fast for my eye to easily track, he struck Grey's companion in the back of the head, sending him to the ground. I shouted a warning as Grey lunged toward the attacker, bare hand outstretched, but the assailant seemed aware of the danger.

He was already covered from head to toe, a scarf concealing all of his face except his eyes, and he remained a constant blur of motion, denying Grey the opportunity to pull at his clothing. Deftly avoiding his grasp, he approached me, a blade appearing from somewhere to spear toward me.

I screamed and cowered down, allowing the steel to flash past me and bury itself in my captor's shoulder. The man grunted, finally letting me go.

As soon as I was free, I ran toward Ember, nearly falling in my haste. I slid to a stop, stooping to press my hands against her fur. Every sense was heightened, my blood thrumming through my veins, and I had no time to think of being sick. Faster than I would have thought possible, I pushed my healing power into her, mending the broken ribs and making one damaged lung whole again.

A curse sounded behind me, and then the breathless voice of my rescuer spoke in my ear.

"Come on!"

A gloved hand grabbed my wrist, tugging me so hard I barely had time to scoop up Ember. Stumbling, I tried to get my feet under me as I let him pull me out of the alley.

Grey was only steps behind us, his hands outstretched as if he meant to grab at the exposed skin of my face.

I threw myself sideways as we rounded the corner onto the main street, just evading him. A wagon rumbled in our direction, and I heard Grey's soft curse as he stopped his pursuit, fading back into the alley.

My rescuer didn't slow, however, tugging me along the street and round turn after turn. Only when we reached a more populated area did he finally slow, stepping into the first alley we passed and shoving me against a wall.

I gulped down air, trying to catch my breath as I peered around him out onto the street.

"They didn't follow us?" My words died as I turned back to him and found piercing blue eyes boring into me.

Unforgettable eyes.

"It...it's you," I stammered.

The stranger from Tarin unwound the scarf from his face, revealing an expression of disgust. "That should be my line. Here I thought my luck had been startling when I stumbled on Grey again so quickly. I should have known better. My luck was never that good."

"I...You were there watching him?"

"I think he has his converts in that warehouse. Not for much longer, though—thanks to you. They'll all be off to some new hideout long before morning. And now Grey knows about me as well. I'd managed to stay out of sight before this."

He sounded furious, but I was too distracted by his earlier words.

"You mean Miranda *was* back there?" I turned toward the street, consumed by a futile desire for action. "I thought you said she'd be sent somewhere else by the time Grey surfaced in a new town?"

"That's his usual mode of operation. For some reason he's doing things differently this time." He didn't sound like he thought that was a good thing, but I was delighted at the idea Miranda might be here in Ostaria with me.

"We have to tell someone before they have a chance to move."

He raised an eyebrow. "Who exactly would we be telling?"

I faltered, my face slowly falling.

"They'll already be on the move anyway," he said. "Grey doesn't hesitate."

He fell silent, watching me. I gulped, unnerved by his scrutiny. Abruptly, he stepped forward, trapping me against the wall. His tall frame took up my whole vision, only the warmth of Ember forming a barrier between us.

My body quivered at his nearness, although I tried to keep it from showing in my expression.

His eyes roamed over my face. "Something about you fascinated him," he breathed. "I've never seen him react to someone like that. It's rare for him to use his power to test someone, but it's never failed when he did." His gaze tightened. "I've never heard of that particular test failing for anyone with enough strength to perform it."

"What—" I swallowed, trying to moisten my dry mouth. "What do you mean *test*? Like the healers do with children's seeds? I've guessed Grey is a healer, but healers need contact to test someone's seed."

He frowned. "Exactly how ignorant are you?"

Defiance rose up in me, but I forced it down. I needed answers more than I needed to assuage my pride.

"Assume very," I said shortly.

He sighed. "Master mages are permitted to probe the power level of another person. It requires great strength, which limits how many can do it, but the Triumvirate felt the need to limit its use even further. Officially, only those who've passed the mastery exam are permitted to test others."

"Why?"

His mouth twisted slightly. "It's considered a highly offensive thing to do. Supposedly, if you've reached mastery level, you've demonstrated sufficient control and sense to only use the test when absolutely necessary." His derisive tones suggested he doubted that assumption.

"Grey is a master mage?" I gasped.

He rolled his eyes. "Not officially. He certainly hasn't passed the mastery exam. I don't think he's even officially a mage. But I suspect he has the strength of a master."

"How is that possible?" I asked slowly, trying to make sense of it.

To be so strong, Grey must have had a powerful influencer. But everyone with that level of power was a member of the Mage's Guild, and completing an apprenticeship under one of them would make Grey a mage as well. Grey couldn't have master mage level power without having a master mage as influencer. Which meant he must be an official mage of the Guild.

My head hurt thinking around in circles.

"Not everyone completes their apprenticeship," my rescuer said, reading my confusion.

I frowned up at him, but I couldn't read the thoughts behind his guarded expression. Did he mean Grey had been activated by a master mage but had abandoned his apprenticeship and thus never qualified as a mage himself?

"I have no idea how you're in Ostaria at all," my rescuer suddenly burst out, "but what in the kingdoms were you doing in that alley? You not only got in my way *again,* you've now attracted Grey's attention in a dangerous way. You should get out of town immediately."

I bristled. There was no way I was running if Miranda might be here in Ostaria.

But it didn't seem like the right moment to say as much.

"I was looking for her." I held Ember out slightly, and he glanced down at her, his face softening slightly for a moment.

Despite myself, my attitude toward him softened an equal amount. I couldn't help but like others who liked animals. In fact, now that I thought about it, he hadn't emerged to challenge Grey until Ember needed protecting.

For some reason, the thought sent a giggle bubbling up out of me. This man had been unmoved by my struggles but had been helpless to resist coming to the defense of one small fox.

"Her name is Ember," I said, when he looked at me with a wary expression, as if he feared I might have fallen into hysterics.

Ember lifted her head, regarding him with a steady gaze before raising her tail in the air.

"She approves of you." I giggled again before clapping my free hand across my mouth. Maybe I really was in danger of hysterics after the unexpected events of the evening.

My rescuer looked at me again, and that slight softening still lingered. I gulped, my pulse speeding up as I became aware of our proximity, the two of us pressed against the wall of the dark alley.

But his expression hardened again, his eyes becoming diamonds, sharp enough to cut. I shrank back against the stone behind me, but I still couldn't forget his earlier look.

"My name is Delphine," I said softly.

He blinked once, my introduction apparently taking him by surprise. After a moment, he leaned back slightly, easing the atmosphere between us.

"I'm Nik," he said gruffly.

I smiled, surprisingly pleased to know his name.

"Thank you for rescuing me and Ember back there."

"Are you sure she's all right?" He glanced down at the fox.

I nodded. "She wasn't initially, of course, but I'm a healer. I healed her before I picked her up."

"A healer?" His eyebrows rose. "A healer strong enough to complete a healing that quickly and then speak of it so flippantly—despite still being an apprentice, which you must be from the look of you." His eyes narrowed, his gaze turning introspective as if he was talking more to himself than me. "Exactly what sort of power do you have, I wonder? I think I'd like to see what interested Grey so much."

"What does that mean?" I asked sharply.

He grinned at me, the expression half-amused, half-menacing. "Grey isn't the only one with the strength to probe a mage."

My mouth fell open. "You're a master mage?" My voice dripped with skepticism. "There's no way you're old enough to have sat the mastery tests."

"Passing the mastery tests is only an *official* requirement," he said with a hooded gaze I couldn't interpret. "Grey's words apply in this alley as much as the other. There's no one here to tell on us." He paused. "Unless you're planning to report all this?" There was definitely a mocking note to his final question.

"I—" I tried to think of something intelligent and cutting to say and failed.

What would the authorities of Ostaria make of this outlandish story? I couldn't even imagine trying to explain it all to them.

There was Amara, of course. I could tell her, but what could she do to bring this man to account?

"Exactly," he said with the same satisfied amusement.

I expected him to make some further boasting comment or even a further request, but he remained silent. A slight stiffening of his muscles told me he was doing something, but I felt nothing.

After a moment, he pulled back, clearly surprised.

"My power can't connect with yours at all. It's like there's...a wall there, or something."

"A wall?" I stared at him, my mind whirling.

I'd built a wall by mistake when I'd misunderstood Amara's words. She'd encouraged me to strengthen it at the time, so I hadn't thought there was any harm in it. But then, later, when I'd tried to connect with my own body, I'd failed. I hadn't understood why at the time, but could it be because of the wall I'd put in place?

The more I thought about it, the more sense it made. Earlier that night, I'd accidentally slowed my heart, but I'd been so distracted, I hadn't noticed the significance of being able to connect with my body again. If it had been my wall blocking my access earlier, I could only assume I had let it drop after time passed without any incidents, unwittingly allowing myself access again.

And yet, the first time I used that access, I had again responded on instinct and put the wall back in place, reinforcing it in the process. My fear at having access to my own body had taken practical expression. And that instinct had protected me from Grey's testing. But I'd shown I could take the wall down and put it up at will. If I could do it on instinct, surely I could do it on purpose.

"Just give me a second," I said.

Nik frowned but didn't interrupt as I slowed my breathing and brought my ability to the front of my awareness. Ember and Nik's heartbeats sounded loudly, their bodies pressing against me, but I pushed past them, turning my focus inward. Now that I knew what I was looking for, I could sense the wall.

Forcing myself to work against my instincts, I dismantled it brick by brick, willing myself to open up. Immediately I felt every system in my body thrumming and alive. Panting, I tried to push the awareness away before I lost the contents of my stomach all over Nik.

"Quickly," I gasped out. "Test me again."

This time I was so connected with my body that I felt the presence of an outside force. But it had no sooner made contact than it pulled away again.

Nik staggered back two steps, his eyes growing wide.

"You're strong!" he said as I slammed the wall back into place, sagging against the stone behind me with trembling legs.

He stepped forward again, grabbing my upper arms roughly, his eyes burning into mine.

"You're mage strong," he said. "More than that. You could be a master one day. How is that possible? Why aren't you at the Guild? *How are you not at the Guild?*"

"I…" My words stumbled over themselves at his intensity. "I…I've only just been activated. My influencer is a traveling master. Wh…Why?"

"This isn't good." Nik finally let me go, stepping back and allowing me to breathe again. "This is very bad. You've already intrigued Grey enough that he's going to be looking for you. And once he makes skin-to-skin contact, he'll be able to find a way past that wall of yours."

"And that would be bad?" I asked hesitantly.

"Of course it would be." He raked a hand through his dark hair. "As soon as he discovers your strength, he'll be determined to have you."

"Have me?" I squeaked, wishing I didn't sound so terrified.

"Grey focuses on seventeen- and eighteen-year-olds—those whose power is activated, or ready to be, but who are still young and susceptible. But he hasn't been fool enough to tackle the capital, let alone the Guild. Which means he hasn't been able to get his hands on youngsters anywhere near as powerful as you. Children with seeds like yours go to the capital sooner rather than later. You represent an unusual opportunity—one he won't want to let slip by."

"You're saying Grey will want to abduct me too?" My hold on Ember tightened enough to make her squirm, and I forced myself to relax my grip.

I glared up at Nik, although none of it was his fault. "He won't find me such an easy target."

A reluctant smile tugged at Nik's lips, making me lose my breath again. I hadn't seen him smile before. And this had only been a half-smile, so I could only imagine how devastating a full smile would be.

"Unfortunately you said you've just started your apprenticeship," he said. "Despite your power, you won't be a match for Grey."

"My master is, though," I said, confident my faith in Amara wasn't misplaced.

"Your master?" Nik raised an eyebrow, considering my words. "Yes, you'll have to let them know immediately. They can take you far away from here."

My mouth snapped closed, unease filling me. Amara didn't know Miranda, but she did have a responsibility—both moral and legal—to me as her apprentice. If I told her what had happened, would she act to protect me, whisking me straight out of Ostaria and leaving Miranda and the others in Grey's clutches?

Nik's eyes narrowed as he watched my face, as if he could read my thought process. He had told me to leave Ostaria—did that mean he would tell Amara himself if given the chance? I spoke at random, hoping to distract him.

"Why do you care? Don't tell me you're worried about me?"

He drew back even further, scoffing. "Worried about you? Hardly. You've been nothing but a menace since you first appeared. But running into you just might be the best luck Grey's had so far, and I'm against anything that helps Grey."

"Why do you care so much?" I asked, genuinely curious despite my initial intention of distracting him. "Do you know someone in that warehouse like I do?"

"Me?" He turned away slightly, laughing scornfully. "You think it would still be standing if that was the case?"

I shivered slightly at the threat in his tone, even though it wasn't directed at me. I couldn't help feeling a slight thrill at the idea of being loved by a man like this—someone willing to overcome any obstacle to help me.

"Why, then?" I asked, desperate to drive out the foolish thoughts. "You don't seem old enough to be an official."

"An official?" While his laugh held some actual amusement this time, it still had a dark edge. "Hardly. But that doesn't mean I'll let Grey tear this kingdom apart."

"Tear the kingdom apart?" I frowned at the dramatic overstatement.

When he stayed silent, I prompted him again. "What do you mean?"

He still didn't speak, however, and when he turned back to me, his calculating eyes told me he was thinking of something else.

"Shall I see you safely back to your accommodation?"

I was instantly on alert, remembering my earlier fear. There was no way Nik was worried about my safety. Was his offer a ploy to find Amara so he could convince her to take me out of Ostaria? Amara had both the means and the right to make me obey if she decided we were changing plans and moving on immediately.

"That's unnecessary," I said quickly. "I can find my own way."

"Can you?" His face told me he doubted it but wasn't going to push the matter.

"I suppose you'll go back to the warehouse now, just in case," I said. "If you find any clues, will you let me know? I have a friend there, remember."

"Do you intend to leave me your address?" he asked with a hint of amusement.

"I..." I bit my lip. "I'm sure we'll run into each other on the streets again at some point."

Nik stepped forward, leaning over Ember so his mouth was beside my ear. His lips brushed against the wisps of hair there, making my breathing stutter and stop.

"I sincerely hope not, Delphine the healer," he whispered, his words chasing out the thrill of his nearness.

Abruptly pulling back, he gave me a look laced with amusement, as if he knew the effect he had on me. Before I could think of anything to say, he strode out of the alley and was lost in the evening traffic of the main road.

I gaped after him, trying to pull myself together. Eventually I balled my hand into a fist and hit it against my leg.

"Why can I never think of the right thing to say to him?" I asked Ember.

The fox didn't reply.

# CHAPTER
# ELEVEN

By the time I reached the room at the inn, my nerves were shredded. I'd been as jumpy looking over my shoulder for Nik as I had been looking for Grey and his men. But no one on the streets had shown the least interest in me.

As soon as the door closed behind me, I slumped against it with a sigh of relief.

"You didn't find her?" Amara's sympathetic voice snapped me out of my distraction, reminding me I wasn't alone.

"Actually…" I pulled my cloak aside to reveal Ember.

Hoping to head off any further questions, I busied myself settling the fox in her crate and providing her with the package of food that was still in my pocket. But when my flurry of activity finally ended with me preparing to climb into bed, Amara spoke again.

"What happened? You looked shaken."

I stopped, my back to her, one hand on my blankets.

"I ran into Grey—that man who was in Tarin and might have taken my friend."

"Miranda was her name, wasn't it?" Amara sounded happy. "So she's here in Ostaria? That's wonderful news. You can clear the whole situation up, and we can see her back on her way to her father."

I turned around slowly. "I didn't see Miranda or either of the other two from Tarin, just Grey and a couple of his followers. I don't know for sure if Miranda is here."

"Did you ask this Grey?" She was watching my face a little too closely for comfort, so I tried to smile.

"I didn't get the chance to ask."

"That's too bad." Her eyes suggested she knew there was something I was holding back. "We can only hope we run into him again."

Her words reminded me of my own to Nik, as well as his response, and I almost leaped into bed, pulling the blankets up to half cover my face. There was at least one person on the streets of Ostaria who I wasn't likely to run into by chance. He would clearly be avoiding me like the plague in the future.

"Do you want to leave Ostaria? We could move on sooner than planned if you like," Amara said, showing she understood more than I'd shared.

It was kind of her to refrain from prying and to offer me a way out. But I couldn't accept the escape she offered.

I replied quickly and firmly. "No, indeed. I haven't even had Ember checked over yet. There's no reason to hurry off—especially if Miranda might be here. We told her father we'd keep an eye out for her."

"Very well." Amara climbed into her own bed but paused just before extinguishing the one remaining lantern. "But I hope you know you can come to me with anything that's bothering you."

"Thank you," I whispered into the darkness as the lantern light disappeared.

---

I slept fitfully, Grey chasing me through my nightmares, sometimes with Nik at his side, and sometimes with Nik standing against him.

Nik had said that if Grey managed to touch me, he would find a way around my wall. So every time I saw him, I added bricks to it, building it higher and thicker, locking myself away.

I woke in the morning, panting and more exhausted than when I'd gone to sleep. Amara had already disappeared, and I wasn't surprised to find her in one of the bathtubs. I was grateful for a soak after my long night and didn't comment that we'd already washed the night before.

The breakfast provided by the inn was as delicious as the evening meal had been, and we were both full and sparkling clean by the time we took to the streets of Ostaria. Amara didn't hesitate as she led me only a few streets over to a cheerful stone building with a large, enclosed yard.

"I thought you said animal healers are normally on the outskirts of towns," I said as I examined the clinic with interest.

"Ostaria is large enough to have many healers," she explained as she rapped loudly on the large wooden door. "Along with a small hospital staffed with healers from the capital, it has more than one animal healing clinic. There's one on both the northern and southern sides of the city to cater to farm animals. And this clinic mainly sees animals from within the city itself."

"For pets, then," I said, secretly impressed at the luxury of it. "Are you offended, girl?" I crooned at the animal in my arms. "You're not a pet, are you?"

Amara raised an eyebrow as Ember stirred sleepily before resettling.

"Do you think it's a bad sign that she's sleepier than yesterday?" I asked. "I can't feel anything wrong inside her."

"Don't forget that foxes are mostly nocturnal," Amara replied. "Yesterday she was dazed but awake—this is more like her normal state during the day."

"Oh, of course." I felt like a fool. I should have realized that for myself.

"Don't worry," Amara said. "That's why apprentice healers study so much, despite their instinctive understanding of healing. It helps to know about anatomy and behavior since your ability can only take you so far on its own."

I nodded, but the door opened, cutting off further conversation.

A smiling, older woman greeted us, ushering us inside with only the faintest flicker of surprise when she saw what type of animal we'd brought with us. She had on a plain gray gown in serviceable wool with a crisp white apron over the top, everything about her screaming competence. I didn't doubt that every nook of the clinic was sorted and organized.

"The healer is with another patient now," she said, ushering us to a waiting room and gesturing toward a row of seats against one wall.

She put one hand on Ember's fur, a look of vague surprise crossing her face. She didn't comment, however, beyond a reassurance that the healer would be with us soon.

"Is she not a healer?" I whispered to Amara when the woman disappeared out of the room, leaving us alone. "Why did she make contact with Ember, then?"

"She would have a healing seed, I'm sure. Every employee at a clinic and hospital does. But it's likely a weaker one—well below the level required to qualify as a mage, certainly. So she wouldn't be the one healing pets, but she likely does an initial screening of new arrivals."

"But the main healer here is a mage?"

"I am," a cheerful voice said as a tall man strode into the room, an amused smile on his face. "Would you like my exact qualifications?"

"Oh no...no." I stood up and gave him a half bow. "I didn't mean—"

"Don't tease my apprentice, Clay." Amara strode over to meet him, pressing one of her cheeks against his in greeting.

"Your apprentice?" Clay pulled back to stare at her in astonishment. "You can't mean it."

"Of course I mean it." She gave him a reproving look. "Would I joke about something like that?"

"I'm impressed!" He shook his head. "And here I was thinking you were getting too old to ever change your ways."

"Amara isn't old," I said defensively, pulling the man's attention back to me.

He inclined his head courteously. "I'm most grateful to hear you say so since I'm several years older again. I'm Clay."

"I'm Delphine. And this is Ember." I held her out, and he looked at her with curiosity.

"Do I dare ask how your apprentice comes to have a fox for a pet, Amara? Or what manner of ailment she suffers? I'm not exactly an expert on foxes, I'm afraid, but she looks like a fine specimen from what I can see."

"She isn't exactly a pet," Amara said. "And we're not exactly here for a healing."

"Not exactly, hey?" He grinned. "Sounds like a story that needs tea." He raised his voice and bellowed, "Tara!"

He'd barely finished the name when the lady from earlier reappeared with a tray in her hands holding a teapot and several cups.

"Excellent." Clay's smile grew even broader. "I remain convinced that you possess a yet-undiscovered affinity for always knowing what's needed and when."

She scoffed, although she couldn't quite hide her smile as she placed the tray on a small table between two of the chairs. "It's called age, wisdom, and experience—something none of you youngsters would know anything about."

"See?" I couldn't help smiling myself. "I told you Amara isn't old."

"Old? That young thing?" Tara winked at me before sailing back out of the room.

Clay chuckled. "Tara is a true gem. Runs this clinic like clockwork and keeps everything shipshape. It was a mess before I hired her."

"I can only imagine," Amara said dryly. "I'm glad I never visited in those days."

"Didn't you hear what she said?" Clay asked with a wicked twinkle. "You were probably a baby back then."

Amara laughed and moved toward the tea tray, while Clay turned to me, his eyes going to Ember.

"She's clearly not in any distress," he said.

"No," Amara agreed. "As I said, we didn't come for a healing. She was badly injured by a larger animal, but Delphine has already healed her. We just came for you to check the healing."

Clay's eyes flew up to my face. "Your apprentice is a healer?"

"She is," Amara said calmly. "Unfortunately it means I can't check the healing myself. That's where you come in."

Clay threw back his head and laughed. "Amara finally gets herself an apprentice, and she has a healing affinity. I don't know why I'm surprised. You'd never take someone with an elements seed, would you?"

"Naturally not." Amara's eyes twinkled at him over a steaming cup of tea.

"May I hold her?" Clay asked, holding out his hands toward Ember.

I handed her over, surprised at my reluctance. Would Ember protest? But she barely stirred, and I reminded myself Clay was a healing mage with the same connection with animals that I shared.

He was silent for only a moment before his smile returned.

"I can see no sign of injury, although she has the feel of one newly healed. Well done, child."

A smile spread over my face as my shoulders sagged in relief. I hadn't realized how tense I'd been waiting for his verdict.

"What was the nature of her injury?" he asked. "Amara said it was significant?"

Some of my relief faded, replaced by embarrassment. "I'm sorry, I don't know what was wrong. Only that she had several large gashes which had damaged half her body, including some organs. I...I'm not sure which ones," I admitted.

His eyebrows rose so high they almost disappeared into his hair. He looked across at Amara.

"You aren't teaching her anatomy? I know you have different ideas, but that's too much. You can't take on a healing apprentice and not provide basic education. She can learn it from a book if you don't know enough to give lessons."

Amara merely looked amused by his stern lecture. "Calm yourself. Of course she'll need to learn anatomy, although I shan't attempt any lectures on the subject myself. I'm not withholding education, we simply haven't had the chance to begin yet. I only activated her three days ago. In fact, I was hoping you might be willing to give her a guiding hand to get started for as long as we're in Ostaria?"

"Three days ago?" Clay handed Ember back to me, astonishment on his face as he examined me for a second time. "And you healed her yesterday? From injuries that severe? On your own?"

"Of course not," I said hesitantly. "Amara helped me."

"Amara...Amara helped you?" He stared at me before suddenly looking across at Amara and bursting into laughter. "I know you put great stock in cross influencing, old friend, but don't tell me you claim to be able to heal now?"

"No, of course not," Amara said with a sour note. "Delphine merely means that I provided her verbal guidance. Very general guidance."

Clay shook his head as his chuckles subsided. "Remarkable. Truly remarkable." He gave me a cautious look, loaded with curiosity. "I don't suppose you'd consider allowing me to..."

"Of course you can test me," I said quickly, eager to cooperate with Amara's friend and the first healing mage I'd ever met. "I don't mind."

I tried to dismantle my wall to allow him access, as I had done for Nik. It resisted, however, and I barely managed the necessary crack before I felt the brush of foreign power touching mine.

The opening I had created might have been small, but it set me shivering at the sudden rush of awareness. First Ember's body in my arms and then the more distant thrum of Clay and Amara washed over me, making my stomach rebel.

It only lasted seconds, however, before my wall sprang back into place. I took several calming breaths as Clay turned from me to Amara with a raised eyebrow.

"You found her on a farm somewhere? I'm no longer surprised you changed your ways and finally took an apprentice, but why wasn't she already at the Guild? I know some of the smaller towns have to make do with weak healers, but don't try and tell me any tester could have missed strength like that."

"I didn't want to go to the Guild," I said firmly, hoping he wasn't going to take offense.

He merely grinned—a response that seemed as natural to him as breathing.

"You're well matched, then." He glanced between us.

When his and Amara's eyes met, something unspoken was exchanged, a communication I couldn't even guess at. Whatever history they had went much deeper than the one I shared with my influencer.

"So do you intend to specialize in human healing or animal healing?" he asked, focusing back on me.

"I haven't even considered the question," I admitted. "Everything happened in a bit of a rush."

"I'm planning to take her to the hospital next," Amara said. "Since she's never been out of Tarin before, she's never seen one."

"Well, I'll be most happy to offer what instruction I can during your stay," Clay said. "I have to put my best foot forward if I'm going to win such a powerful future healer to the side of the animals." He winked at me, and I blushed at the implication that I was someone mages would want as an ally.

"Very proper," Amara said with a nod. "The healers at the hospital can do the same. But you should all remember that Delphine doesn't have to be locked into one or the other. She does have other options."

I couldn't think what she meant for a minute until I remembered her own master had specialized in both. Was that what she meant?

"Of course you would say that." Clay chuckled. "But in the interests of objectivity, I hope you're going to tell Delphine that there are advantages to specializing in one of the main branches—and choosing which one early. Especially since you'll have limited access to healing mage teachers."

He sent an inquiring look at Amara. "At least, I assume you're planning to continue with your traveling ways?"

"Of course," she said. "I believe the variety of experience will make up for anything Delphine misses in consistency. And I'm not going to pressure her into making a decision before she's ready."

"Fine, fine!" Clay held up his hands in laughing surrender, turning the conversation in other directions.

The two of them chatted for a while longer, catching up on the doings of friends and acquaintances I didn't know. I was happy to stay out of the conversation, drinking the cup of tea Amara offered and taking comfort in Ember's solid warmth.

Clay wanted me to pick a specialty, and Amara wanted me to visit clinics and hospitals and begin my training, but I still hadn't told anyone about my embarrassing reaction to blood. I hadn't even told Amara about my wall growing out of control. Now that I heard her talking to Clay and making plans for my training, it felt like a betrayal on my part. I hadn't been a good apprentice so far.

It was time for me to do better. I would confess the truth as soon as we left the animal clinic.

CHAPTER

# TWELVE

D espite my resolution to tell her about the wall as soon as we left, we'd barely made it back onto the street before she was pointing across at a larger, taller building made of imposing white marble.

"That's the hospital?" I gasped.

Amara chuckled. "Ostentatious, isn't it? But they have good reason. All the hospitals in Tartora are built that way since it makes them visible and memorable. People need to know where to go in an emergency, and many people who aren't familiar with Ostaria come here just for the hospital."

I nodded. I had known a couple of families from Tarin who had made the journey with a sick or injured family member who needed more complex care than the local healer could provide.

I stopped in front of the broad double doors, gazing up at the building. It was larger than I'd expected and must employ many healers of varying strength levels. Was that why Clay had been so sure there would be someone here with the time and willingness to train me?

I glanced back to the animal clinic, speaking hesitantly. "It's fortunate you have a friend like Master Clay here."

"Fortunate?" Amara followed my gaze before looking back at me. "It's true he has both skill and experience which is ideal. And he has strength, too, since Ostaria is large and lively enough to attract a few master mages. Being on the river with easy access to the capital helps in that regard. But while there aren't masters in all towns and villages, I still have friends everywhere I go. Don't get the wrong impression. I might travel alone, but I'm not lonely.

And I won't have any trouble finding you healing instructors across the kingdom."

"Sorry," I said quickly.

She shook her head, smiling at me. "You don't need to apologize. I'm as new to being an influencer as you are to being an apprentice. If you're lacking relevant information, it's because I failed to impart it to you. I'm the master here—it's my job to know what you need to know and when."

She inclined her head toward the imposing building. "On which note, your master is saying it's time to visit your first hospital."

I nodded, looking away and hoping my cheeks didn't look as pale as they felt. If she noticed, she didn't say anything, leading the way through the doors without hesitation.

I followed much more slowly, my dragging feet wanting to turn and run. I was already terrified, and I hadn't even made it inside. But when she ordered me inside as my training master, I couldn't refuse—especially not when I hadn't explained my reluctance yet.

A stark white hallway, free of any decoration, led into the depths of the building. Doors opened off both sides, many of them open. Rooms of varying sizes could be seen, the larger ones filled with rows of beds, while the smaller ones held a single bed each, along with a desk and chairs.

"Those are treatment rooms." Amara pointed through an open door at one of the smaller rooms. "The larger ones are for patients who need to stay for longer periods of time."

"Stay?" That explained the size of the building. I'd been wondering why it needed to be so large when it was surely staffed with strong healers, unlike the clinic back in Tarin. "I thought they had mage healers here. Can't they heal the patients within minutes?"

"They do have mages," Amara said. "But that doesn't mean anything and everything can be instantly healed. The most complex healings can take even powerful healers an hour or more, and there are never enough strong healers to go around. Many people have to be satisfied with partial healings, leaving it to time and their body's own effort to finish the job. Some of those patients are able to go home to recuperate, but some stay here under observation by healing assistants."

"Assistants?" I asked. "Are they regular people with weaker healing seeds like at the clinic back home?"

"Yes, that's right. There's a whole team of them working here."

"I see." So even in this impressive building, not everyone could be healed of everything. I frowned, gripped by a sudden concern. "If they don't have the strength to heal everyone..."

"Don't worry," Amara said with a knowing smile. "Those in greatest danger are treated first, regardless of their ability to pay. The crown funds all the kingdom's hospitals, as well as the clinics in smaller towns like Tarin. Strong healers are expected to serve for some time in one of them before they're permitted to open a private clinic to cater to wealthier clients."

I bit my lip. I'd vaguely known that the clinic at Tarin was funded by the crown, but I hadn't considered the issue more broadly. The picture she painted didn't align with the one I had grown up with—a picture of arrogant mages living lives of luxury and indulgence. I had thought Amara must be an exception, but what if that wasn't true?

I shifted uneasily, pushing the thought away. Just being here was uncomfortable enough without adding further unease.

"So everyone in here has a complicated issue that can't be easily healed?" I asked, glancing into a room that had over ten occupied beds.

Amara shook her head. "It isn't as simple as that."

"A lot of them are just old," said a cheeky voice from inside the room. "They've grown resistant to healing, as we all do eventually."

A girl appeared, looking too young for the crisp white apron she wore.

Amara greeted her with familiarity. "You've finally been activated, then?" She nodded at the girl's outfit.

The girl smiled proudly. "Last week."

Amara turned to me. "This is Hazel. She's been hanging around the hospital, getting underfoot, for as long as I've known her."

"It isn't fair our seeds aren't ready for activation until we're *seventeen*." She gave me a conspiratorial look as if she expected me to agree with her sentiment, and I managed to scrape together a slightly astonished smile. She must have taken it as agreement because she continued breezily on. "Thankfully there's plenty to be done around a hospital that only requires a pair of strong hands. I've been observing the healings and helping out in the wards for years. But it's much more interesting now I can use my ability. Don't you think so?"

She fixed me with a wide-eyed look, her pause stretching long enough to make it clear she actually expected an answer this time.

"Oh, well..." I couldn't quite think of anything more intelligent to say, given how terrified I was of this building.

Hazel laughed, a high, bright sound that made several of the patients smile.

"I can tell you're an apprentice, like me, because you have that dazed, slightly nauseous look most of them have when their masters first drag them along here."

I started, giving her a closer look. Was my nausea really showing on my face?

"I suppose you have an elements affinity like Amara?" she continued. "You'd be surprised how many elements mages go funny at the sight of blood. Most of the ordinary folk think it's foolish of mages to require their apprentices to have a basic knowledge of the other affinities, but I think it's sensible. Most of the elements and plants apprentices look like you when they first arrive—but most of them have gotten over their nerves by the time they leave. There's nothing as frightening as the unknown."

She beamed at me, showing no hint of judgment for my perceived weakness.

"Actually, Delphine is a healer like you," Amara sounded amused.

"A healer?" Hazel turned enormous eyes on me.

Despite the fact she was even younger than me and had barely started her apprenticeship, I still squirmed under her scrutiny. She'd already shown she saw too much.

"You don't look like a healer apprentice at all," she said frankly, making Amara laugh again.

"Do you think there's a particular appearance required to be a healer, Hazel?" Amara reached out and pinched a strand of the girl's hair. "You've always been a rascal, but that's a bit much, even for you."

"I don't mean her physical appearance." Hazel cocked her head to the side examining me. "It's her manner, her..." She waved her hand around vaguely, as if unable to find words to express her meaning. "You've known me for years, Master Amara. You've seen what I was like since I was small. Usually healer apprentices are like me—they've spent years itching to be inside the hospital, healing people. By the time they finally arrive, they're full of excitement, not dread."

I cleared my throat. The speed and cadence of Hazel's speech made her sound flighty, but she was startlingly perceptive.

"I think Delphine is probably in shock, poor thing." Amara patted me on the arm. "It's a big leap from life on a farm to the hospital in Ostaria."

"Did you come from a farm?" Hazel sounded genuinely interested. "I grew up here in Ostaria, so I can't imagine an isolated life like that. Did you like it?" She continued on without giving me time to answer. "I guess Ostaria must seem as large and impressive to you as I imagine Tarona must be." She sighed wistfully. "I've always wanted to go to the capital. I hear the main hospital there makes this one look tiny."

"Once you've completed your apprenticeship, you can apply to work there," Amara said, and Hazel brightened immediately.

"That's the plan." She looked at me. "So you've never been to Tarona either? I suppose you'll be going soon now you're a Guild apprentice." She sighed again. "I was so disappointed when I got tested. I only got as far into the hospital as the testing room, but even that was enough to know I never wanted to leave. So it was no surprise I had a healing seed. But I was so hopeful I might have surpassed my parents and been strong enough for a guild apprenticeship."

"You weren't far off," Amara said kindly. "Which means you'll always be welcomed in the hospitals of Tarona. You know better than me that there's more than enough work for everyone."

"That's true!" Hazel brightened quickly, giving me the impression she wasn't the sort of person to stay down for long. "But still, you're lucky, Delphine." She smiled at me without any trace of ill will.

I smiled back, afraid the expression looked pained. The familiar feeling of being an impostor swept over me. A proper healer should be drawn to healing, like Hazel. Wasn't that the work of the seed inside them?

So what had gone wrong with me?

"I'll get one of the masters," Hazel said, stepping further into the corridor. "They'll want to greet you, Master Amara—and meet the new healing apprentice, of course." She laughed. "I'll try to find one of the more amiable masters for you—one who won't give you a scolding for stealing a powerful healer away to your cross-influencing cause."

She had only taken a few steps away when I spoke, my voice sounding a little desperate. As much as I didn't want to speak up around Hazel, I wanted to expose my weakness to an unknown master healer even less.

"Everyone keeps telling me I'm so strong, but if that's the case, shouldn't I be able to get some sense of those people?" I gestured at the row of beds inside the closest room.

Hazel whirled back, a confused look on her face. Amara also stepped forward, a frown creasing her brow.

"What do you mean? You can't sense them?" Amara gripped my arm. "Not at all? But you could feel the people in that hamlet from ten miles away."

"Ten miles?" Hazel gaped at me. "You could get a healing sense of people ten miles away? But you can't feel the people in that ward?" Her eyes lit, clearly intrigued by the mystery. "That makes no sense."

My stomach swirled. I didn't want to be any stranger than I already was.

"Can you tell anything about them at all?" Amara asked. "Give it a try."

I reached out, as I had on the road, but there was nothing. Why hadn't I noticed how peaceful it was inside my head? It had been the same earlier at the animal healing clinic, but I'd been so focused on Clay's assessment of Ember's health that I hadn't noticed.

"I can't sense anything at all," I said, the beginnings of panic sounding in my voice. "Has my ability disappeared? Is that possible?"

"No, it's not possible," Amara said firmly. "Give me a minute to think."

I tried to recall the last time I'd used my ability or felt anything in relation to it. It had been at the animal clinic, but only for a brief moment when Clay wanted to test me, and I'd lowered my wall to allow him in.

"My wall!" I gasped.

I tried to turn my attention inward, but I was just as shut off from my own body as I was from the people and animals around me. I couldn't even feel Ember in my arms, and I had physical contact with her. No wonder I'd been coping with my squeamishness so well.

"Your wall?" Amara frowned. "What do you mean?"

"Sorry, I meant to tell you earlier, but I didn't get the chance. Last night I worked out why I couldn't sense my own body on the road. I'd completely walled it off."

"Walled it off?" Hazel moved closer, eyes alight with curiosity. "What does that mean? Is it something I could do?"

I ignored her, focusing on Amara. "At first the wall was just protecting my body. But it protected against more than just my own power. I had to lower it to be tested." I swallowed. "I think...I think I was working on it in my sleep last night. I had terrible dreams all night, and I remember trying to make my wall stronger. I thought it was just a dream, but my subconscious must have actually been doing it. It was harder to lower the barrier for Master Clay than it had been the evening before. And now my sense of other people is blocked off as well as my sense of myself. I've accidentally made it too strong."

"Fascinating," Amara breathed, the worry in her eyes replaced with interest. "Who knew such a thing was possible? I'll have to consult with Master Colton as soon as I get the chance."

"Master Colton?" I stared at her.

"He's the Master of Healing," Hazel said, almost bouncing in her excitement. "The head of the healing affinity."

I barely restrained from snapping back at her that I knew who he was. I wasn't totally ignorant. I was just highly uncomfortable at the idea of anyone having a conversation with him about *me*.

"Don't worry," Hazel said, once again seeming to pick up on my emotions. "All the stories say he's the least intimidating of the affinity heads."

But as terrifying as the idea of Master Colton was, I had more pressing concerns.

"How can I continue my apprenticeship if I can't access my power?" I asked, gripped by the new fear.

"I'm sure it's not that drastic," Amara said in what was clearly meant to be a soothing voice. "Why don't you try taking down the wall now? You said it was harder to do with Clay than it had been earlier, but not that it was impossible."

Her slight emphasis on *earlier* probably went unnoticed by Hazel, but I caught it with a sinking feeling. I'd spoken without thinking and all but told her I'd been tested the night before while I was out looking for Ember. While we were apart. She wasn't asking me questions now, but that didn't mean she wouldn't later.

"All right," I said, too distracted to quibble. "I'll try."

Focusing with difficulty, I tore at the wall, ripping a much bigger hole than I'd done for Clay.

Instantly I was slammed with sensation. My awareness of Ember—the only one I had physical contact with—was by far the strongest, but every person in the hospital was easily within my range. And almost all of them had something wrong with them, a taint in my awareness that pressed at me. Illnesses and injuries bombarded me from every side.

My eyes jerked to the closest patient, fastening on a bandage around his arm. It had to be an old dressing because red had seeped all the way through the white layers. My stomach lurched.

I tried to reach for my power to settle my nausea, but already roaring filled my ears. It blocked out the alarmed voices of Amara and Hazel as spots of black grew across my vision, filling my head with cotton wool. I forgot all about my power and instead put out my arms, reaching blindly for something solid.

My hand found nothing but empty air, and I collapsed, darkness closing around me completely.

CHAPTER

# THIRTEEN

I came back to consciousness slowly, keeping my eyes closed. The first thing I noticed was the blessed quiet. Nothing was assaulting my senses anymore. Slowly, I cracked open my eyelids, nervous about what I would find.

My surroundings were unfamiliar. I wasn't back at the inn.

Looking around the room, I saw white walls and a wooden desk. I groaned. I was still in the hospital. Given the quiet, that had to mean my wall was back in place.

"You're awake?" a familiar voice asked, and I finally noticed Amara sitting on a chair in a corner of the room.

"What happened?" I cleared my throat, trying to get rid of the croaky rasp that had sounded in my words.

"You collapsed." She pulled her chair forward, placing a cool hand against my forehead. "Although you were briefly unconscious, Hazel assured me you didn't need a more senior healer." Amara cocked her head to one side, watching me with a concerned gaze. "I hope my trust in her wasn't misplaced?"

"I..." I paused as I considered checking myself and remembered that would involve opening my wall. "I feel all right?" I finally said.

Amara sat back with a calculating look. "I know you've been keeping something from me. But the beginning of this apprenticeship was so sudden. I didn't want to press you until we had a chance to get to know each other better. I was hoping you would decide to confide in me yourself. But it's clear the issue is a bigger one than I realized. I think it's time you told me exactly what's going on."

I winced and pushed myself into a sitting position.

"I was going to tell you. I'd already realized I needed to, and I was actually going to say something on the walk to the hospital, only then it was so close." I shook my head at the silly reason for my failure to speak up.

"Well, now seems like a good opportunity," she said with a wry smile.

I took a fortifying breath, feeling as foolish as I had the first time I'd been overtaken by the symptoms as a young girl.

"I'm squeamish," I said in a rush. "I can't see blood or injuries without getting sick and faint. Even just talking about an illness or how our insides work makes me feel lightheaded. And no, it's not just all in my head," I said defensively, although Amara hadn't said anything. "They're physical symptoms, as you saw. If it's sudden, or if I try to ignore the symptoms, I end up fainting."

Amara stared at me. When the silence grew too long, I laughed awkwardly.

"Have you ever heard anything so ridiculous as a squeamish healer? Now you can see why I think my affinity is some sort of mistake. I'm not a healer. You heard what Hazel said. Healers are excited to heal. They want to be around illness and injury so they can fix it. I'd love to be able to fix it, of course, but that would require me not turning into a second patient within seconds of my arrival." I gestured around the treatment room. "I'm worse than useless."

"So that's why you constructed the wall," Amara said thoughtfully. "I was wondering why an idle comment had taken such root. It turns out it was fueled by desperate need."

I sighed. "I might as well not have any power at all."

"Nonsense," said a cheerful voice from the door.

We both turned to see the smiling face of Clay.

Part of me wanted to slide under the blankets to avoid the humiliation I'd brought on myself, but the other part of me was too interested in his words to run away.

"There's no need for you to look so pained, Apprentice." He came into the room, standing beside Amara's chair and looking down at me. "This is merely a minor inconvenience."

"Minor?" I shook my head. "If I access my power, I lose consciousness. That doesn't seem minor to me."

He looked sideways at Amara, putting on a stern expression that seemed out of place on his face.

"This is the problem with your much vaunted cross-influencing. If you'd been a healer yourself, you would have known how to help your apprentice through this. Even as an elements mage, if you'd been at the Guild, her symptoms would have been recognized."

I sat bolt upright, my hands clenching around the blankets. "You mean I'm not the first? This happens to other healing apprentices?"

Clay chuckled. "Of course! Did you think you were special?" He winked at me.

"It's not common or anything," Hazel said, popping into the room from where she'd clearly been listening in the corridor. "It hasn't happened to anyone apprenticing here at the hospital—at least not in the years since I was tested for my affinity. But I did once hear it mentioned by one of the master healers. He had a previous apprentice who had the problem."

"And what happened to them?" I focused in on her, not even caring that she had inserted herself into the conversation.

"The master didn't go into detail, but it sounded like a minor problem that was dealt with in the first months of the apprenticeship. Master Clay will probably know more." The smile she gave him was slightly strained.

"Yes," Clay said, sounding amused at the apprentice's discomfort. "Even I, a lowly animal healer, know enough to deal with something like this."

Hazel's eyes widened slightly at having her prejudice called out, although Clay was clearly unbothered by it. When I looked back and forth between them, Clay caught my confusion and grinned.

"I never had any hope of luring Hazel into specializing with animals. She had her heart set on the hospital from the beginning."

"Of course," Hazel said promptly. "Why would I want to focus on animals when there are *people* needing healing?"

"I thought all healers loved animals?" Amara sounded amused. "Because of your connection with them."

"Of course I love animals," Hazel said. "It's not that I want them to suffer. It's just that people are so much more—"

"Precisely," Clay said, neatly cutting her off. "Which is why I, for one, am grateful so many healers want to specialize in healing people. It allows me to focus on animals without guilt. Just like I'm sure you're grateful there are other healers wanting to specialize with animals."

Hazel nodded, looking suitably chastened.

"See, this is why you shouldn't push your rivalry so hard," Amara told Clay disapprovingly. "Young people always take this kind of thing too seriously. Both specializations should be working together. I'm sure you have things you can learn from each other."

Clay looked at me. "I hope you, at least, mean to offer me some sympathy!

Here I am, beset on every side, after rushing over here at the first word you were having difficulties."

"Oh! You came for me?" I gulped. "I'm so sorry for causing you so much inconvenience. I didn't mean—"

"Stop, stop!" He held up his hands to silence me. "I was only joking, Apprentice Delphine. Of course I came. I've already promised my old friend that I would help with her new healing apprentice, after all. And you shouldn't listen to either of these two. There's no real rift within the healing affinity—merely a friendly rivalry. We need something to keep us occupied in this small town."

He winked at me again, and I fiddled with the blankets. After a lifetime spent between my farm and Tarin, it was impossible to think of Ostaria as a small or boring town.

"Delphine has had a rough enough day without any further teasing," Amara said sternly. "I will even acknowledge my own deficiency in this matter. Please explain what is needed, or if you cannot, find me a healer who can."

"Ouch, Amara, you wound me." He was still smiling at her, though, so he didn't seem to have taken any real offense. I'd never met anyone who joked like he did, and I found myself wondering what it would be like to be his apprentice.

It didn't seem like a bad picture. Would specializing with animals be easier than healing people? I could imagine spending my life working with people like Clay, bringing peace and wellness to people's animal friends.

I tucked away the appealing image for later. For now, I couldn't even consider specializing in anything until I could actually use my power.

"Squeamishness is really something other healing apprentices have encountered?" I asked, struggling to accept the incredible news.

"Really, truly," Clay said in a voice that was somehow both serious and warmly reassuring. "It's a rare condition, but it's familiar in the Guild, at least among the healers. For some reason, it's more prevalent among those with a seed of mage strength than among the ordinary population."

"How interesting!" Hazel exclaimed. "I wonder why? Is it the strength of the seed that sets off some sort of opposite reaction?"

Clay threw her a smile. "Perhaps? It hasn't been properly researched since it's a condition that's easy for the apprentice to overcome themselves."

Wild, unbelievable, heady relief swept over me, followed by a hopefulness I hadn't felt since I was a small child. I wasn't irreparably broken. I could be fixed. I could learn to use my power. I could be useful, just like I'd always dreamed.

If only my father was here so I could tell him the good news.

As soon as the thought occurred to me, a horrible chill lanced down my spine. It would be news to my father...wouldn't it?

For a horrifying moment, I considered the possibility that my father had known all along that my squeamishness was a known condition for healer apprentices and could be cured once I came into my power. Had he deliberately lied to me to keep me crippled and chained to his side?

I quickly rejected the thought. My father had a plants affinity, as did my uncle, and their parents before them. He had never had much to do with healers of any strength, and Clay had said squeamishness was an uncommon affliction. There was no reason to think my father would ever have encountered it or heard of its cure before.

But he could have found out. There was no denying that reality. From Clay's comments, it was a well-enough known condition that surely either Halmir or one of the string of healers at Tarin's healing clinic would have heard of it. And if they hadn't, I was sure Halmir, at least, would have contacted the Guild to ask about it. He had been trying to convince me to agree to an apprenticeship for years.

My father might not have deliberately covered up the solution, but he had kept me from discovering it. He had used my affliction for his own purposes.

I slumped back against the bed, overwhelmed. Now that I had opened the gate to such thoughts, they came flooding into my mind. How long had there been an element of uncertainty lurking inside me, ruthlessly suppressed and ignored? It seemed obvious now that I should have questioned my father's perspectives, but I also understood why I hadn't. I had been terrified of overturning the only world I knew.

But the cracks had already begun to show before now, hairline fractures appearing soon after I met Amara—a image entirely unlike his portrayal of them. I still hadn't properly questioned his teachings, though—the habit of years too strong to break.

Until now. Once the thoughts had begun, they wouldn't stop, tumbling out one after another and building a picture I wished I didn't have to face.

My father had latched onto my squeamishness, blowing it out of proportion as a tool to keep me chained to the farm. As long as I believed I had no hope of ever using my power, I would have no temptation to run away to the Guild.

My stomach churned, a familiar feeling, although a new cause. Lying in this hospital bed, I was seeing my father through a whole different lens.

How much pain had I suffered—both physical and mental—due to the unfortunate combination of my squeamishness and my healing seed? And instead of bringing me relief, my father had encouraged that pain. He had allowed his own hurt and prejudice to poison my life. He had deliberately kept me weak in order to control me.

That wasn't love. It wasn't the role of a parent as my mother had explained it.

Tears dripped unheeded down my cheeks as I realized my mistake. If only I had told my mother the truth. Unlike my father, she would have left no stone unturned in seeking a solution.

Fresh pain gripped me as I realized my father had known that. He had known my ability was the one issue my mother would never bend on, and so he had driven a wedge between the two of us, telling me my affliction was a shame I needed to keep hidden, a burden that would cause her grief.

Because of my father, I had never been truly open with my mother.

My head swam, and I closed my eyes. Through all the years of frustration and anger over my joke of a seed, one constant had been certain. My parents loved me, and they would always be my safe home and my support. My insides clenched as that foundation cracked, the silent roar of it reverberating through me.

I had never once doubted that my goal was to qualify as a mage and return to my family to run our farm. But just the thought of facing my father made sweat break out on my palms. Had he ever loved me at all? I felt too betrayed and angry to think clearly, and all I wanted was for my mother to wrap her arms around me and tell me everything was going to be alright, as she had so often done when I was a child.

But even the thought of her had lost its soothing effect. Instead guilt gripped me. My mother had never done anything to earn my mistrust. I should have seen through my father's deception and told her the truth from the beginning.

A hand took mine, lightly squeezing. I opened my eyes to find Amara looking at me, a concerned crease between her eyes.

"I wish I'd known from the beginning, and I'm sorry I couldn't tell you were suffering in silence. But you heard Clay. We can fix this, and you will become a great healer."

I swallowed, consumed in equal parts by a desire to pull my hand out of hers and to throw my arms around her. I wanted to believe that she would look after me—that she would help me fix all my problems—but I had once believed my father knew all the answers as well.

"Of course you'll be a great healer!" Clay said. "Especially since you have Amara to guide you. Who knows what great contributions you'll make to the healing affinity. In fact, I'm already curious to hear more about this wall of yours. It explains how you were holding Ember so casually earlier."

"Is there something significant about that?" I looked from him to Amara who looked just as blank as me.

Clay laughed. "Between your holding her and the way you'd healed her, I thought you were the most advanced apprentice I'd ever encountered. I was almost ready to throw my support behind Amara and speak up at the Guild on the benefits of cross-influencing."

"What do you mean?" Amara asked. "Was there something strange about Delphine carrying Ember?"

"Wait," I gasped, feeling terrible for not noticing earlier. "Where is Ember?" I looked wildly around the room, but she failed to appear.

"Is that the fox?" Hazel asked. "She took off like a shot when you collapsed. I hadn't even noticed her under your cloak until then, or I might have made some effort to catch her."

"She's probably back in her box by the fire by now," Amara said. "There's no need to look so concerned, Delphine. She's a wild animal and knows how to look after herself. It isn't even her first time wandering around the streets."

I hesitated before sighing and nodding. I still didn't feel entirely comfortable about her disappearance, but there wasn't anything I could do about it right now. I was just glad I hadn't landed on top of her when I fainted.

"But why is it significant that Delphine was holding Ember?" Hazel asked Clay. "Don't you animal healer types always have animals hanging off you?"

"Delphine was only activated three days ago," he said.

"Three days?" Hazel gaped at me. "And you're carrying a pet around with you?"

"She's not a pet," I said automatically, but my focus was on Clay. "I still don't understand…"

"You look older than me," Hazel said, "so I assumed you'd been an apprentice longer. I wouldn't dare touch anyone—human or animal—without my master with me. There are always new apprentices at the hospital, and it usually takes months before they're confident enough about their control to risk it."

"Oh," I said foolishly, their surprise now making sense. "Yes, of course. I had some trouble like that myself before I made the wall."

"Wall?" Hazel asked. "What does that mean?"

"Delphine has blocked off her ability." Amara spoke for me, her attention on Clay. "It was a defensive measure at first, because of her nausea, and it's worked—but a little too effectively. It seems to be growing in strength and getting harder for her to dismantle."

Clay rubbed his chin. "I can't say I've heard of anyone doing that before. It sounds like it could be a useful tool for new healing apprentices, though. I assume you at least knew enough to warn her when you activated her? Those first few weeks are a dangerous time for new healers."

Amara nodded. "Of course. I think I inadvertently pushed her toward creating the wall. But what do you usually do to keep your apprentices safe instead?"

"Terrify us into being more cautious than we've ever been in our lives," Hazel said promptly. "I can't even think about my own body without having a panic attack."

Clay looked at her with a raised eyebrow. "You've never had a panic attack in your life, troublemaker. We'd all sleep more easily if you had a bone of caution in your body."

She laughed. "I don't know what you're talking about." She turned to me. "Actually, I recite multiplication. It was my hardest subject in school and brings back terrible memories. It never fails to distract me."

Clay nodded, looking back at Amara. "Distraction is the usual technique. Train their minds to be disciplined. Keeping your thoughts under tight control while healing is a useful skill, so the training achieves multiple purposes. Even experienced healers need to be cautious when they're oper-ating inside someone else's body."

He surveyed me with narrowed eyes. "If you could put that wall up and down at will, it would actually be an ideal solution for squeamish healers in those first weeks while they're still learning basic control. Those who suffer nausea like you usually have a hard time until they can be trusted to heal themselves."

"Can't their masters heal them for that first period?" Amara asked. "I know I can't do it for Delphine, but surely you..."

He shook his head. "We can help during an actual healing, and we do help new apprentices while they're training. But once their seed is activated, the new sensations are so intense that they're usually suffering almost constantly. Since the symptoms have a mental cause rather than a physical one, we can't just permanently fix them. They would need constant masking."

Amara frowned. "Are you sure it can't just be fixed? Healers can treat illnesses of the mind."

He sighed. "Only some of them. The best and strongest healers can treat problems in the brain, but some mental conditions aren't created by damage or imbalances."

"Sometimes people's brains are making them sad," Hazel continued for him, "and sometimes their life is what's making them sad. In the second case, all we can do is mask the symptoms for a short while to provide some relief. The patient has to use that space to find their own healing."

"Are you saying I'm doing this to myself?" I asked indignantly. "That it's all in my head? Do you think I'm faking the physical symptoms?"

"Of course not," Clay said. "Your symptoms are real. The brain controls everything, so just because something originates in the brain doesn't mean it stays there. I'm not saying your physical symptoms are fake, I'm saying there isn't a physical malady I can treat—and that includes inside your brain. This isn't strictly an illness at all. Something in your nature makes you more uncomfortable with the idea of injury than the standard person. Your body is merely responding to the discomfort in your brain."

"So what can she do about it?" Amara asked when I stayed silent, processing Clay's words.

"As I said, it's possible to temporarily suppress the physical symptoms," he said. "For us healers, we can choose to suppress our symptoms indefinitely. And the stronger the healer, the more successful we'll be at that task. Usually we don't recommend it as a permanent solution since it ignores the underlying issue. But in the particular case of being squeamish, a temporary solution is almost always enough to solve the problem. Because a healing apprentice has constant exposure to what triggers their squeamishness, they grow used to it over time. Plus they gain a sense of empowerment from being able to heal the ailments they encounter. Combined, those two elements are enough to overcome the original discomfort."

He looked at me. "I can't say how long it will take in any individual's case, but you'll be able to operate as a normal healer as soon as you gain enough control to safely suppress your own symptoms. Some level of the squeamishness may always remain, but it will drop to a manageable level well before your apprenticeship ends."

"Well, that's a relief," Amara said briskly. "I was afraid we had a more serious problem on our hands."

"Um, it sounds serious to me," I said, sliding down to lie on my back and stare up at the ceiling.

I knew Clay's words should spark the earlier wild elation, but it was hard to feel hopeful with the specter of my father's betrayal hanging over me. I had longed for a usable seed so I could ensure the safety and future of my family and our farm. What did it mean to gain that longed for power just as all desire for that safe family haven was ripped away from me?

Two years had seemed long just days ago, but now it felt far too short. I didn't want to face the decision about what I would do once it was over.

"This wall could cause problems," Clay said, pulling my mind away from the spiraling thoughts about my family. "But with most uses of power, practice is all that's needed. As long as the desired activity is within the capacity of someone's seed, then practice is the key."

Hazel groaned. "You sound like the masters here at the hospital. Practice, practice, practice."

Clay ruffled her hair. "Some things are universal. Ask the elements and plants apprentices and they'll tell you the same thing."

She stepped out of his reach, patting her hair back into place with an indignant look.

"I do sympathize," he said with what looked suspiciously more like amusement than empathy. "You make me glad my own youth is behind me."

Amara snorted. "We can all be equally thankful. You were the most obnoxious apprentice."

"Me?" He clapped a hand to his chest. "What are you talking about? I never let the need for endless practice get me down."

"Exactly," she muttered. "No one should be that cheerful all the time."

Hazel and my gazes met, and we both tried, unsuccessfully, to suppress laughter. Amara smiled at me.

"I'm glad to see you looking a bit more cheerful. Do you feel up to getting out of that bed now?"

Guiltily, I sprang up, pausing briefly as all the blood rushed out of my head at the sudden movement.

"Steady there." Clay lightly gripped my elbow. "I think the usual approach for cases of nausea will work well enough for you, despite the complication of the wall." He let go and turned to Amara. "She needs to learn control and how to discipline her thinking. So don't hold off on starting her training—but focus for now on the peripheral areas of the healing ability that don't involve actual healing."

She frowned. "You mean testing children's seeds?"

He nodded. "And truth testing as well. That will give Delphine the opportunity to take down her wall and practice using her ability in environments where everyone is healthy. And, of course, Ember should stay home on those excursions, and physical touch should be avoided as much as possible. Delphine seems to be a fairly extreme case, so just sensing people at all might cause some discomfort, but if they're healthy, then exposure should deal with that fairly quickly."

"Testing people," I said slowly. "That sounds doable."

"I have no doubt you'll take it in your stride." Amara stood. "And since you've recovered for now, I think the first thing I should do is get you out of this building. Clearly the hospital will have to come later."

I couldn't have agreed more, so we hustled outside, bidding our farewells to Clay on the street. He promised to check up on my progress regularly before watching us set off toward the inn.

"I'm sorry I can't take you out of Ostaria altogether," Amara said regretfully.

I stiffened. In all the excitement of the day's activities, I'd temporarily forgotten about Grey and Miranda, but thoughts of the Tarin girl came rushing back at Amara's words. We couldn't leave until I'd tracked her down.

"I don't want to move on," I said quickly, earning a curious look from my influencer.

"Having so many people in one place can't be helpful for your comfort," she said. "But if you're going to train in the side aspects of the healing affinity, you need to be in a larger center like this one. They do much more regular truth and seed testing here than they would somewhere smaller."

"Yes, of course. That makes sense." I nodded enthusiastically.

She narrowed her eyes at me. "Don't think you're off the hook. I know there's more you're not telling me."

I froze, falling behind a couple of steps, but she reached back and tugged me forward.

"Relax." She shook her head. "I think you've been through enough today. I'm not planning to force it out of you."

*Yet.* The unspoken extra word hung heavy in the air between us.

"I'm sorry," I said softly.

She smiled at me. "I've already told you that I expect it to take time between us. I meant that. I want you to learn to trust me as your master and as a person, and I realize that doesn't start with me forcing you to tell me all your secrets."

"I..." I paused, my mind struggling to take in her words and my thoughts pulled back to my father who had wanted my secrets to stay buried forever. I couldn't force myself to make sense of it all. Eventually I spoke again. "Thank you. I appreciate that." I couldn't think of anything else to say.

If Amara picked up on my heavy mood, she gave no sign of it, her smile turning smug. "I should have known I would be an excellent master. I don't know why I waited so long."

I gave her a startled look, and she winked at me. Gratitude washed over me as I realized she was purposely lightening the mood.

"Clay is a bad influence," I said, chuckling, and she laughed back.

"I always enjoy seeing him again."

I gave her a surreptitious look. Did Amara have a deeper interest in Clay than just as a colleague and old friend from her apprentice days?

She showed no self-consciousness, however, and I could hardly ask her after she'd shown such forbearance about my secrets.

"I do want to tell you everything," I said, my words surprising even me. Keeping my secrets had been a mistake in the past. "My mind is just in a bit of a muddle at the moment. Once I have it all straight myself, I'll definitely tell you."

Amara smiled. "Thank you."

She maintained her supportive demeanor that evening when I announced after the meal that I was going out for a walk. I expected her to protest about me going alone, but she seemed to think this was all part of the thinking process and raised no objections.

Ember—who had indeed been safely back in her box—perked up with the arrival of twilight, making it clear she wanted to join me. I scooped her up for the short journey out of the inn, but once we were loose on the streets, I set her down so she could stretch her legs.

She stuck close to my heels, easily losing herself in the night shadows that swirled around my cloak.

I had no particular destination in mind, but I'd been telling the truth when I said my mind was in a muddled state. I needed space and movement to have any hope of untangling it.

On top of the hurt, confusion, and hope, I couldn't shake lingering embarrassment. Amara had given no indication that she found me a deficient apprentice—in front of Clay, she had even taken the blame on herself as my master—but I wanted to be an apprentice who made her proud. She had taken a chance on me, and I hated letting her down so immediately.

Enclosed in the inn room with her, the feelings of inadequacy had grown, but out here in the cool air and the darkness, they began to unravel. Clay had seemed impressed by my strength and my healing of Ember, and Amara continued to be fascinated by the wall I had accidentally created. Even Hazel had been nonchalant about the nausea. I was the only one overthinking the issue.

But how could I not after the years I had spent believing it was an insurmountable problem? Years of anxiety fueled by my father. The father I had thought loved me.

I shook my head and increased my pace, letting the physical activity drive out the poisonous thoughts. Ember brushed against my leg, and her presence steadied me. Even after I'd dropped her earlier, she'd chosen to return to me. Animals didn't lie and manipulate for their own purposes. Their love was as straightforward as it appeared, and I accepted her devotion like a balm for my heart.

The faint stirrings of my initial excitement returned. Soon, I would be able to freely use my ability. I would be able to protect Ember—and other animals like her—from pain and illness.

"Don't get ahead of yourself," I muttered aloud. "For now, you need to keep that wall in place. Which means you're better off focusing on Grey than on healing."

Just the sound of his name sharpened my senses. He was somewhere near, and Miranda might be too. If I could find and rescue her, then Amara and I wouldn't need to be bound to Ostaria anymore.

But I knew almost nothing about the city. I had no idea where to even begin to look. The only thing I could even think to try was retracing my steps from the night before.

Nik had seemed certain Grey and his people would be long gone from the warehouse, but I couldn't help feeling a spike of anxiety as I approached the alley where they had trapped me. I pushed past it, though, entering cautiously.

Ember hung back, as if she also remembered the place, but it seemed as deserted as expected. The door that had been behind Grey and his companion stood unprotected.

I pressed my ear against it. After hearing nothing but silence, I worked up the courage to try opening it. It swung inward without any resistance, nearly sending me staggering. I stepped inside, flinching when the door swung closed, leaving me in near blackness.

I held my breath, but I could still hear nothing. I seemed to be truly alone in the large, empty space.

Shaking myself, I turned back to the door. I needed to find a way to wedge it open so I could get some light in here. Perhaps I could find some clue Grey had left behind.

Even as I thought it, I knew it was foolish. What helpful thing could he possibly have left behind? But I wanted to be doing something, and I couldn't think of anything else.

Before I could reach the door, however, the handle moved. I stiffened and threw myself against the closest wall, hoping to be out of the line of sight of whoever was coming in.

Had Grey or one of his men returned?

The door swung all the way open, and I tensed, ready to run if the new arrival spotted me. But I had barely absorbed the presence of the tall, dark figure before he was moving.

Spinning and leaping too fast for me to escape, he trapped me against the wall, the feel of cold steel against my throat keeping me still.

CHAPTER

# FOURTEEN

The door clanged shut, plunging us back into darkness. For an endless moment, we stood frozen in position, before I remembered I was no longer helpless.

My mind reached for my wall while my hands flew up to grasp my assailant's wrists. All I needed was skin-to-skin contact, and I would become a weapon far more deadly than the blade he wielded.

But my searching fingers found nothing other than the leather of gloves and several layers of material. My assailant's grip tightened just as a growl sounded from close to the ground.

We both froze before a flurry of movement provoked a muttered curse. My attacker stepped abruptly back, swinging his leg up. A muted thump was followed by a high whine.

"Ember!" I screamed, stumbling toward the sound of the whine.

"Ember?" repeated a deep voice.

A light flickered and flared, a lantern illuminating our portion of the empty warehouse. Nik, dressed in his usual black, was staring at me with a horrified expression.

"You! *Again!*" He sounded furious.

When I didn't respond, too frozen with a mix of shock and relief, his expression turned disgusted. "You're fortunate I didn't kill you."

"As are you!" I snapped back, my temper surging. "Healer, remember?"

He laughed derisively, extending one hand and arm. Between his sleeve and his glove, there wasn't so much as a flash of visible skin.

"Do you think I would go into battle against someone like Grey without armor?"

I bit my lip. So it hadn't been chance that my attempt at skin-to-skin contact had failed.

Another whine sent me rushing toward the bundle of orange fur on the ground, although with my wall down I could already tell she was all right. As I knelt beside her, I glared over my shoulder at Nik. "You kicked her!"

His eyes narrowed. "She bit me." He gestured to his boot which had a visible bite mark in the leather.

"Good girl," I muttered quietly, bending over her.

She was breathing shallowly, something making her uncomfortable, and guilt overtook me. She had behaved in an aggressive manner totally unlike her natural fox instincts, and she had done it to protect me. Again.

Placing a gentle hand against her fur, I forced myself to focus on her injuries. As soon as I made contact, nausea sprang to life in my stomach, the burst of energy that had been holding it back since I pierced my wall no longer sufficient.

My head swam, and I used my power to steady myself, easing my symptoms before reaching into Ember.

"You fractured one of her ribs!" I exclaimed accusingly, even as I strengthened the bone, smoothing it back into wholeness.

Nik shifted uncomfortably. Did he actually feel guilty? Was he capable of such an emotion?

He cleared his throat. "I didn't realize it was her. I thought something rabid was living in here."

I rolled my eyes but stayed silent. Despite my earlier tone, I couldn't exactly fault him for reacting defensively to an attack in the dark.

When I finished the healing, I sat back, relieved to break the contact. As soon as my wall snapped back into place, I sighed.

"Do animals develop a resistance to healing as well?" I tried to count how many times Ember had been healed now. "Ember really needs to stop throwing herself into harm's way for me, or I'm not going to be able to heal her so easily anymore."

"It must be nice to have someone so loyal," Nik muttered, so quietly I almost didn't catch the words.

I twisted to look at him, sadness filling me at the closed expression on his face. Did Nik have no one in his life to show him loyalty? Is that why he spent his time roaming the nighttime streets of town after town, passing through like a phantom?

The loneliness of such an existence made me shiver. Ember pressed herself against me, as if sensing my momentary melancholy. I ran a hand over her fur, murmuring my thanks before slowly climbing to my feet.

"I suppose I don't need to ask why you're here." Nik sounded sour.

"Yes, that should be obvious. I'm not sure why you're here, though. Weren't you going to investigate this place last night?"

Nik ignored my accusation. "What were you planning to do if my guess was wrong, and Grey was still here? This is the last place you should be."

"I guess I trusted you," I said with more confidence than I felt.

Why *had* I trusted his words so implicitly? I'd done the same thing earlier when he'd said Miranda would disappear before Grey resurfaced, and yet he'd been wrong on that occasion by his own admission. I knew nothing about this man, so why did I put so much stock in his words?

"Trust me?" Nik laughed darkly. "Don't be a fool."

"Are you not trustworthy, then?" I met his eyes steadily.

For a moment he was silent, staring back at me, an arrested look in his gaze. But with a quick shake of his head, he broke the moment.

"I have it on excellent authority that I can't be trusted at all."

I frowned, saying nothing as I watched him. Nik had been surprised I wasn't at the Guild, but why wasn't he? He was a mage and couldn't have long finished his apprenticeship. Had something happened to turn him against his influencer and send him off on his own?

"Maybe I am a fool, then, because I trust you," I said firmly.

His eyes flashed to mine, not able to hide his surprise.

"At least in regards to this," I added. "I believe you're set against Grey and his theft of Tartora's young people."

Nik relaxed slightly, but my next words made him stiffen again.

"Do you hate the new kingdom? Is that why you're so set against Grey?"

"Hate Calista?" he scoffed. "Save a kingdom and see what thanks you get. Of course I don't hate Calista."

I raised an eyebrow. "Are you trying to say you were the one to save the fallen kingdom? Because you don't look much like Queen Cadence."

He gave a bark of genuine laughter. "I'll take that as a compliment."

I rolled my eyes. "Everyone knows Calista's new queen was the one to restore the fallen kingdom from its cursed state, reintroducing the world to power mages and ushering in a new era of growth in power."

"I see the propaganda has reached even the remotest parts of Tartora," Nik said.

He had denied hating Calista, but his words only reinforced the impression he was prejudiced against Tartora's northern neighbor—once a wasteland but now restored and in the process of being rebuilt.

"Are you saying it wasn't Queen Cadence who saved Calista?" I asked.

He sighed. "Of course I'm not saying that. Everyone knows it was her." His words had a slight mocking lilt, echoing mine earlier. But he seemed to mean the words. "She just didn't do it alone."

I laughed. "Are you saying that when she ventured into the fallen kingdom, she chose *you* as one of her companions? That was more than a year ago, had you even graduated your apprenticeship then?"

His eyes slid away from mine, and I snorted. Of course he hadn't.

"If you love Calista so much," I added, "I don't know why you're so set against its emissary."

"Grey isn't Calistan," Nik ground out through his teeth.

I put my hands on my hips, pinning him with a skeptical glare. He whirled away from me, striding toward the closed door.

"I don't know why I'm wasting my time on this conversation," he muttered as he walked. "If you want to believe Calista is the problem, go right ahead."

I ran after him, grabbing his arm to hold him back.

"Wait! If you're so sure it's not Calista, explain it to me. Who else wants to steal away our best and brightest young people? Everyone knows the Calistans need people to repopulate their abandoned land. Tarin is way down south, but we still had a family who chose to head north last year."

I shook my head, remembering the buzz their departure had generated in the town.

"Everyone says the Tartoran crown is sympathetic to the new Calistan king and queen," I continued. "I've even heard people claim King Marius shows more care and affection for them than he does for his own children. Otherwise he wouldn't be turning a blind eye to Grey."

Nik ripped his arm from my grip, turning back to me. I drew away, unnerved by the fire in his eyes.

"The Tartoran crown isn't turning a blind eye to Grey! And they certainly wouldn't do so just because he was Calistan!"

"Are you sure?" I asked, gathering together my courage. "I've heard Princess Morgiana is doing a similar thing to Grey—traveling around and gathering young people to send to Calista. Clearly the Tartoran royalty are enamored with the new kingdom."

"You think," his voice dropped low, vibrating with danger, "that the princess is going around abducting children? And that the crown is allowing it to happen?"

"I..." I stumbled back even further. "No, I don't suppose the princess would be *abducting* people. I guess Grey has been a bit overenthusiastic."

Nik drew a deep breath. "Tartora has agreed to allow those with Calistan heritage to return to their homeland if they wish to do so. They're even allowing free immigration by those without Calistan heritage. But they have good reason for it. Tartora is gaining something in the exchange, even if no one bothered to explain it to the villagers of Tarin."

I straightened at the scorn in his voice. "But they explained it to you?"

He shrugged.

My eyes narrowed. "If you know so much, explain to me why the king hasn't stopped Grey, then."

"Because he doesn't know about him," Nik snapped.

"Why haven't you told him, then!"

He turned away from me. "You think the king of Tartora would listen to me? When I have enough evidence, I'll take it to the capital myself."

"Will you?" I asked, genuinely curious. "Are you sure you don't want to solve the problem single-handedly?" I hadn't received the impression he was someone interested in working as part of a team.

His shoulders stiffened slightly, and he didn't respond. I smiled with satisfaction. I'd read him correctly after all.

But a moment later I sighed. Whatever his motives, I had no hope of finding Miranda without Nik.

"You really believe the king is unaware of Grey?" I asked. "How is that possible when he's taking young people from all over?"

Nik turned back to me, the anger on his face replaced with sadness.

"You said Grey was stealing away our best and brightest young people, but it's not the best and brightest he's taking, is it?"

I stared at him, shaken by the question.

"If it was," he continued, "Grey would never have gotten away with it for so long. Instead, he targets the dissatisfied, the malcontents, the troublemakers. The ones who don't fit neatly into their communities and who the authorities could do without—the ones they sometimes privately wish would disappear."

"But that description doesn't fit Miranda at all!" I protested.

"No," he agreed. "Grey isn't as cautious in the villages because he thinks no one there matters. If he was more careful in the countryside, he might have even avoided leaving discontented rumors in his wake. But he caught the people's attention because his dismissal of them presses on an existing nerve. The countryside know they aren't valued equally, and now they think the crown doesn't even care if they all leave for Calista. We can be grateful, though. Grey's attitude shows his overconfidence, and that sort of confidence will eventually lead to a misstep. And that's when we're going to catch him."

"Are we just going to wait, then?" I asked.

He paused partway to the closed door. "We?"

I joined him, Ember at my heels. "Yes, obviously. I have to find Miranda, and even if I could somehow sneak her away, I can't just leave Grey free to continue abducting other people. I want to help gather enough evidence to convince the authorities."

"*We* aren't going to do anything," he growled. "I will be finding the necessary evidence and taking Grey down. The best thing you can do is stay out of my way."

I stalked around him, positioning myself between him and the door and giving him my best glare.

"You tested me yourself, so you know I'm a powerful healer. Are you really saying it wouldn't be helpful to have a healer with you?"

"That depends on the healer." He gave me a contemptuous look. "You can't even look after yourself, let alone anyone else. If I have to keep rescuing you, I won't get anywhere."

"You rescued me one time! The other times we were fighting each other. Think how much more effective we could be if we work together."

He shook his head and tried to brush past me, but I held my ground.

"Fine," I said, trying a different tack. "You might not want me helping you, but I'm not giving up on this. So you can either choose to work with me, or we can keep tripping over each other like we have been so far."

Nik stilled, his expression telling me my words had found their mark. I tried not to smile too broadly. While I did think I could be of help, I couldn't deny I would be gaining more than him in a partnership. Everything I knew about Grey so far had come from Nik, who had been tracking him far longer than me.

"Don't slow me down," he snapped, and I bit my lip, trying to suppress my excitement. From Nik that was the closest thing I was going to get to enthusiastic agreement.

He held up his lantern and scanned the interior of the warehouse. The light wasn't enough to fully illuminate every corner, but it looked convincingly empty. If it hadn't been for Nik's arrival, my visit here would have been useless.

Nik must have concluded the same thing because he strode the rest of the way to the door and pulled it open. But instead of striding outside, he knelt in the open doorway. The door attempted to swing closed, banging against his hunched back, but he ignored it.

Splaying the fingers of his right hand against the packed dirt beneath us, he closed his eyes.

Seconds ticked by in silence and even Ember stepped forward to sniff at the ground next to his hand as if searching for what was holding his interest. My curiosity grew too great to be contained.

"What are you doing?" I asked, the words abrupt and loud in the empty space.

"I told you not to get in my way," he said through gritted teeth, not opening his eyes.

"You're the one in my way," I muttered. "You do know you're in the doorway, right?"

His eyes sprang open, and he straightened in one fluid movement, suddenly looming over me.

"I don't need or want a partner. If you insist on coming along, at the very least stay *silent*."

I gulped and nodded, annoyed with my own compliance. But I wanted his cooperation, and I hadn't had the chance to prove myself yet. I should have stayed silent in the first place instead of provoking him.

"Can you explain now?" I asked in my best meek tone.

He eyed me suspiciously before sighing. "I'm tracking them. When I came back here last night, they were gone, of course. But they hadn't managed to clear out the entire building."

"So they did it during the day?" I looked around the empty space. "Why didn't you watch for them and follow them when they came back for it?"

"I did," Nik growled, hesitating before adding, "But I have to sleep sometime."

"You missed them?" I stared at him, wondering why I was so shocked. Of course he needed to eat and sleep, like anyone else. A smug feeling crept over me. "Are you sure you can do everything by yourself?"

His eyes narrowed. "Naturally I had a backup plan."

"Communing with the dirt?" I quipped, but he cocked his head and gave me an arrogant look that was quickly becoming familiar.

"I know all about your ability," he said, "but you haven't even asked my affinity, have you?"

"I—" I stopped, realizing it was true. I knew he was powerful—his ability to test me had proved that—but in the chaos of our previous interactions, I'd never even considered his affinity.

"You're a plants mage?" I guessed.

His half smile seemed to confirm it, although he didn't say anything.

I frowned down at the dirt beneath us, trying to remember anything about the plants affinity that might be relevant. Both of my parents had it, but they didn't have mage-level strength. My mother's education plan had included more detailed descriptions of each of the affinities, but I couldn't recall anything of relevance.

"I know you're powerful," I said slowly. "So I'm sure you could bring all sorts of wondrous plants springing to life in the middle of this building, but I'm not sure how that would help us right now."

"Do you think that's the only thing plants mages can do?" He sounded contemptuous, but I refused to shrink back this time. He spoke as if I was looking down on his affinity, but nothing could be further than the truth.

I straightened, facing him defiantly. "People with a plants affinity are the backbone of this kingdom! Those plants they grow feed every person in Tartora from the poorest child to the king himself. And, as well as filling our bellies, those plants also clean our air, brighten our days, feed the animals, and preserve the land itself. Ensuring the health and growth of the kingdom's plant life isn't a minor thing."

Nik stared at me, for once bereft of speech. After a moment, he recovered himself enough to raise one eyebrow.

"Don't tell me I've found a healer who doesn't think healing is the pinnacle of the affinities?"

I turned away, pushing past him to exit the warehouse.

"What, nothing to say in defense of healing?" He needled as he followed me, Ember slipping between us.

"The relevant point is finding Grey," I said firmly. "Which leads me back to my original question. What exactly were you doing back there?"

Nik looked as if he didn't want to answer, but after a moment he relented.

"I stayed awake all night and most of the day, but I had to sleep for a few hours in the late afternoon. Your arrival woke me."

"My arrival? But not Grey's people carrying out bags and parcels and who knows what?"

He shrugged. "They must have come while I was in the deepest part of my sleep. The important thing is that they came recently and in a quieter part of the day. They probably timed it for dusk when their activities would be partially obscured. That means I still have a chance of tracking them through the ground."

My mouth dropped open. "Is that possible? I've never heard of such a thing! I know those with a plants affinity also share a connection with the earth itself, not just the things that grow in it, but that's..."

"Obviously the average person with a plants affinity couldn't do so."

"What about the average plants mage?" I raised an eyebrow as I waited for his response.

"I never said I was average." He smirked at me, looking far too pleased with himself.

When I just narrowed my eyes, he sighed again.

"I don't care what's normally done, I only care about getting the results I need. I had to come up with a new strategy after I lost Grey in Tarin thanks to a certain someone..." He gave me a significant look before continuing. "Have you heard of elements mages who can track people through the air—a bit like a dog following a scent?" He looked down at Ember with a half-smile. "Or a fox."

I nodded. I vaguely remembered my mother mentioning it in a long-ago lesson. It had only interested me because of the relation to animals.

"But you're not an elements mage," I said, and he stiffened, the muscles across his arms and shoulders tightening as he clenched his fists. Unsure what I'd said wrong, I hurried on. "Can you do the same thing through the earth?"

"I'm not so much using the earth itself as the network of roots within it," he said after a loaded pause. "I got the idea from...someone I know. He used the root network to send messages, and I worked out how to combine that idea with the tracking ability of an elements mage."

"You mean you came up with that idea yourself in the last few days? So you're the only one who can do it? That's brilliant!" The compliment slipped out before I thought to filter it. His ego was already unnecessarily inflated without me further flattering him.

"It might only work because I'm plants cross elements," he said, his manner suggesting he was being drawn into speculation in spite of himself.

"You're cross influenced?" I asked, astonished. "And you have master-level power? That's really rare! You need to talk to my master. She would love to meet you. She's elements cross healing."

"She?" He stared down at me. "Your master is a woman? And she's elements cross healing?" He raised an eyebrow. "You're apprenticed to Master Amara?"

My mouth dropped open. "You know her? You know my master?"

Fear rushed through me as I remembered that I had been intending to keep them apart. I'd already been worried he might convince her to whisk me away—and that was before I found out they knew each other.

"Of course. I—" He started to speak before cutting off his words, a closed expression slamming over his face as if he realized he'd said too much. "Never mind. That doesn't matter. You said yourself that what matters is finding Grey. And the longer we stay here yapping, the older the trail gets."

"But..." I sighed and let it go. He was right about the trail and finding Grey. And what was I trying to achieve anyway? It's not like I wanted to push him into meeting Amara.

Nik eyed me suspiciously for a few moments, but when I stayed silent, he knelt once more, pressing his hand against the ground. When he stood again, he didn't speak, merely striding deeper into the alley in the opposite direction to the street.

I kept my curiosity inside, scrambling to follow him as he hurried toward the dead end. When we reached the wall, however, I realized it wasn't a dead end at all. The brick wall was broken by a simple door that gave access to whatever was on the other side.

Nik attempted to open it, but it remained stubbornly in place.

"It's locked," I said, disappointed. "Can we circle the building and find the spot from the other side?"

Nik gave me an amused look, purposely holding my eyes for several seconds before looking back toward the door. I followed his gaze and gasped.

The door no longer looked much like a door. The dead wood of its planks had somehow sprung back into life, the wood around the latch covered in so many green shoots that it resembled a plant more than part of a building. The lock itself had disappeared completely, the metal dropping free of the writhing wood.

"What? How?" I gaped at Nik.

"Plants mage, remember?" he murmured with a satisfied smile.

I nodded shakily, feeling every bit the ignorant apprentice. We'd been investigating together for mere minutes, but it was increasingly obvious why Nik had originally spurned my offer of help.

Pushing the door open, Nik ducked through. He didn't bother to hold it open behind him, and I barely caught it before it whacked me in the face. The small rudeness restored some of my shaken confidence. Seeing his power at work didn't change his annoying, arrogant personality.

Ember and I followed him through the door into a second alley. This one was much shorter than the previous one, however, opening almost immediately onto a broad street. The thoroughfare was well lit but almost deserted at this hour.

Nik stopped just before stepping out of the alley, kneeling again to feel the earth. When he stood, he turned right, and I followed without comment.

He led the way in the same manner through several turns. We were soon on back streets where the buildings crowded close together, in some cases looming over the street itself in a way that made me shiver. One or two of them looked old and decrepit enough that they might collapse on our heads.

Nik was unshaken, however, ignoring our surroundings, except to follow the trail only he could sense in the ground beneath us. And while I wouldn't have admitted it out loud, I took courage from his presence.

We eventually reached a building that might have been another warehouse, although it was smaller and more run-down than the previous one. It was in a much shabbier area of town, backing against the city wall.

Nik held out an arm to stop me. "This is where they went." He spoke quietly but with confidence.

I nodded, afraid to speak in case I attracted attention from someone inside. Scanning our surroundings, I noticed a pile of crates against the neighboring building. They appeared to be empty, most of them too splintered for use, and they would no doubt have been cleared away before now if they'd been left in a nicer area of the city. They would serve us well, though.

I pointed toward them, and Nik nodded. Before either of us could move, however, the door into the run-down warehouse began to open.

# FIFTEEN

Shock held me immobile, but Nik sprung into immediate movement. Grabbing me around the waist, he whisked me with him, pulling me behind the crates so quickly that I couldn't get my feet properly under me. I would have collapsed to the ground if he hadn't kept his arm around me, pressing me firmly to his side.

Ember seemed to understand Nik's intent because she didn't protest his hold this time, staying silent at our feet as Nik peered through the crates. Several people had appeared in the street and were milling in front of the door.

I willed them to move off, but they lingered. I couldn't see all of them clearly through the occasional gaps in the piled crates, but I thought I recognized the brute who had held me captive in my one encounter with Grey, as well as the other man who had been with him.

I twisted slightly within Nik's grasp, trying to get a clearer view. Was Grey himself with them? What about Miranda?

I couldn't see either of them, but my eyes fell on a different familiar face. I gasped at the sight of Serena in the streets of Ostaria, and Nik stiffened, his free hand clamping over my mouth.

I stilled, realizing my mistake. No one was rushing toward us, but several of them were looking in our direction. Their suspicious glances seemed too weighty for one stifled gasp. Had someone caught a glimpse of movement as they emerged onto the street?

"I'm telling you, I think someone's there," one of the men said, confirming my fears. "Can you see something behind those crates?"

Nik and I both froze, not even daring to breathe as we held our positions.

The man who had been beside Grey at our previous encounter peered toward us. From the way the others deferred to him, he appeared to be their leader, and I could see he was torn.

"Grey wants us back quickly, and we won't manage that if you're jumping at every shadow," he told the first speaker.

"It wasn't just a shadow!" the man protested. "And we should smash down those crates anyway. Anyone could be hiding there watching us."

"Still scared of that man from yesterday?" Serena asked in a scoffing voice. "The one in black?" She spoke tauntingly, as if she didn't take any threat seriously, but I caught the nerves in her gaze as she glanced at the crates.

"Who said anything about being scared?" the enormous one asked, weighing in for the first time. "I'm more worried about who's going to be expected to do the work. Are you going to be carting off crates, little girl?"

Serena turned her back in the characteristic, petulant gesture I remembered from Tarin. Thanks to her attitude I had never warmed to her—an attitude born of the relative strength of her seed compared to others in the town. Her sense of superiority had alienated her from more than just me, and that isolation had turned her into a perfect target for Grey.

I peered at her, noticing the slight shake in her hands, and the way she was trying to hide it. She might have brought her situation on herself, but I still felt stirrings of pity.

The large man was still eyeing the crates with distaste, but the leader seemed torn. He took a hesitant step in our direction, and I felt Nik's muscles tense. Was he preparing to draw his blade, or was he preparing to silently use his ability? Either way, I wanted to help, but I had no idea how.

Nik's hands dropped away from me, but before either of us could take any further action, movement exploded at our feet. Ember leaped into the middle of the pile of crates with a growl, and we could do nothing but duck down out of sight as the whole pile shuddered and shook.

High squeaks and hisses sounded from beneath the wood as several streaks of movement exploded from the bottom, racing past the group in front of the warehouse. They all jumped, obviously more unnerved than they'd been letting on.

After a moment of stunned silence, the leader gave a strained chuckle.

"I'll acknowledge it was more than shadows," he said to the concerned man. "But you must be jumpy if you're mistaking a nest of rats and a stalking cat for people. I imagine those crates provide a nice hunting ground for the local felines."

The whole group relaxed, apparently satisfied with the explanation and eager to return to their original task rather than clearing away abandoned rubbish. Within moments, they had all disappeared, heading toward the more populated part of the city.

"Should we follow them?" I asked once I'd regained my breath.

Nik shook his head. "They'll be on a supply mission, so there's nothing to be gained by that."

"Will they steal supplies?" I asked, wondering if that could be an avenue for gaining official attention.

Nik shook his head. "They won't do anything to draw negative attention to themselves. Not yet. You'll note they even took a couple of the youngsters to make the group less remarkable."

I sighed. "Sorry about making a noise. I recognized one of them from Tarin."

Nik looked down at me with an unreadable expression. "Your friend?"

"Sadly, no. It was another girl—one who appeared to leave willingly. But if Serena's here, that's a good sign that Miranda is too." I looked at the closed door of the warehouse, dropping my voice even lower. "Should we have a look inside?"

Nik hesitated, clearly wanting to say yes. But after a quick glance at me, he gave a decisive shake of his head.

"Didn't you see? One of them went back inside. Grey and whoever else is in there will be on alert now. They may even come out to investigate. We should go immediately. If they can't find any further evidence of our presence, they'll hopefully dismiss their concerns and remain here for now. We can come back tomorrow night."

I hesitated, examining his face. I had the distinct impression he would have considered going in anyway if I wasn't here. But he was right to be cautious. Apparently my presence was already doing him good—even if he didn't appreciate it.

I couldn't resist throwing him a cheeky grin as we hurried off in the opposite direction to that taken by Grey's people. "If you'd been on your own back there, they might have come investigating behind those crates and found you. Are you glad you have a partner now?"

Nik stalked forward, not even looking at me. "If I hadn't had to reveal my presence last time—thanks to you—they wouldn't have been on such high alert. And besides," he glanced down at Ember who trotted at my feet, "it wasn't you who saved us. I will concede that the fox, at least, is helpful."

I huffed, but his words distracted me.

"Do you think she went after those rats on purpose?" I asked. "Was she trying to distract those men and shield us?"

Nik frowned, his eyes lingering on her elegant form as she kept pace with us. "Foxes are intelligent, but I've never known one to act like she does. She seems devoted to you."

I bit my lip. "I've already had to do major healings on her several times. It's worrying me, actually. Her behavior is very unusual for a wild animal."

"Animals are always drawn to healers," he said. "Even before their power is activated, although the effect increases afterward. Healers' pets are always unusually devoted. It seems like your power has created a connection between the two of you. At the very least, it seems to have raised a strong protective instinct in her."

I reached down and scooped her up, holding her small body close in my arms.

"I just hope it doesn't get her killed."

"You're a healer, aren't you?" he said callously. "So don't let her die."

"It's not always that simple," I muttered, but I let the point drop since we'd reached familiar streets near the inn.

I stopped abruptly, making Ember look up.

"I know the way from here," I said to Nik.

He looked like he was going to protest, but after a moment he just shook his head and turned to stride away. I blinked after him in surprise before recovering enough to call after him.

"Farewell to you too."

He didn't even break stride.

"I'll see you tomorrow night," I added, and that made him falter.

After a moment he continued, however, not having turned back to me.

"Rude," I muttered as I watched him disappear into the night. "Even if it was you, Ember, and not me, we did still save him back there. If he can't manage a thank you, he could at least say goodbye."

Sighing, I hurried the rest of the way to the inn, not wanting to be scolded by Amara for staying out too late. Nik was no doubt hoping I wouldn't appear again, but I'd taken careful note of the route to the second warehouse and had every intention of returning.

---

I woke with my mind full of Nik and Grey and the brief glimpse I'd had of Serena. I had no interest in the day except to hope it passed quickly so night would fall again.

Amara, however, had other ideas. She dragged me out of bed with far too cheerful an expression.

"Don't worry," she said, misinterpreting my reluctance. "I meant what I said yesterday. I'm not going to drag you back to the hospital.

We're going to try something different today. No illness or injury involved."

Despite my earlier disinterest, my curiosity rose at her words. The idea of using my power without the specter of the nausea was more appealing than I'd anticipated.

We ate a hearty breakfast in the main room of the inn, and to my surprise, Amara had Ember join us. The fox sat calmly on a cushion by my chair, accepting the admiring glances and comments of passersby, and even accepting choice scraps from the hands of her admirers.

"See," Amara said with an amused look. "The innkeeper's wife came around eventually—once she saw Ember isn't going to cause any trouble. She's more softhearted than she looks."

I wouldn't have believed it possible if I hadn't seen the woman sneaking Ember morsels of breakfast from her own hand, but I was relieved not to have to hide the fox in my cloak anymore.

When we ventured out into the streets, Ember stayed behind, happily curled in her box by the fire. The innkeeper had even promised to send someone up to check on her while we were gone.

True to Amara's word, we bypassed both the hospital and Clay's animal healing clinic. As we passed the latter, Amara spoke.

"You'll need to start studying anatomy soon, like Clay said. Thankfully you can learn it from books well enough, so you won't need a regular tutor. But I'll try to ensure we make regular visits to places like Ostaria that have experienced healers available."

"Do I need to start today?" I asked reluctantly. Just the thought of the books' contents made my stomach churn.

She shook her head. "No, I haven't even purchased the books yet. Clay will help me with that while we're here, since Ostaria is large enough to have a dedicated bookstore. But I want to wait before handing them over to you. Once you have the necessary control to keep your physical responses suppressed, you can start the reading. Otherwise I'm guessing you'll have the same problems you had in the hospital."

She gave me a questioning look, and I nodded fervently, full of relief. Once again, Amara had proven she had my best interests at heart.

"So where are we going today?" I asked, looking around with curiosity.

We'd reached the center of the city, an area I hadn't visited yet since my nighttime wanderings had taken me to the fringes.

"In small towns like Tarin, parents take their children to the local healing clinic for testing," she said. "Most such towns have only one healer of any significant power, and he or she is responsible for testing seeds as well as healing. But Ostaria has many healers, and they want to limit the number of children traipsing in and out of the hospital just for testing. So healers are rostered to make regular visits to the schools and offer testing there."

"Schools?" I asked. "Is Ostaria big enough to have more than one?"

Amara nodded. "I know in villages like Tarin, many children are taught by their parents, as you were. It's a practical option when many families live out on farms. But in the cities and even the larger towns, all children attend school. They aren't actually tested in class, of course, since their parents want to be present. Instead they put aside a room for the healers to use on the specified day and parents can book a time."

"Let me guess," I said. "One of the schools has a testing day today?"

Amara grinned. "As luck would have it, yes. It's a fairly junior healer rostered on today, so I don't know him, but he was more than happy to have an apprentice visit."

I suspected it was Amara herself he was more interested in meeting, but I kept quiet. He was willing for us to be present and that was all that mattered.

# CHAPTER
# SIXTEEN

The school turned out to be a neat stone building, larger than the average house but smaller than the hospital. It had an enclosed yard full of children, most of whom were running in all directions.

As we approached, a woman stepped outside the building and rang a large bell. The children immediately stopped their play and raced over to form a ragged line, chattering loudly the whole time. The woman beamed at them, her motherly vibe making me smile. I would have enjoyed coming to a place like this every day.

A pang made my smile fall away. Every decision my father had made to keep me on the farm had taken on a new light now. Had he been afraid that if I spent more time in Tarin, I might find a solution to my problem?

We hung back as the children streamed inside, standing near a couple who pressed close together, looking anxious. When the end of the line passed them, they called to one of the children, and he broke off from the others to join them.

"Mother! Father! Is it nearly time?" He looked more excited than nervous, and the woman mustered a smile for him.

"As soon as the other children are settled, we'll go inside," she said. "I'm sure you'll get an excellent result."

They had to be the first family on the list for the day's testing. I turned to confirm it with Amara and noticed someone at the very end of the line of children. The boy was gazing wistfully at the small family grouping, looking reluctant to go inside and leave his friend.

When the child due for testing caught sight of him, he smiled broadly and waved for the other boy to go inside with the others.

"I'll come to class as soon as I've been tested," he called to his friend, thrusting his chest forward proudly. "And I'll tell you all about my awesome seed."

The other boy grinned and hurried toward the doors, but the father grabbed at his son's arm, frowning.

"Why are you talking to him?" he asked. "I thought we told you not to have anything to do with him. A good-for-nothing like that—without even parents to set him straight—will just drag you down. You'll see once you've been tested. You're worth far more than a street child like that."

I stiffened, my eyes flying back to the other boy, hoping he hadn't heard. He was just disappearing inside the building, but from the rigid set of his back, I suspected he'd caught every word.

My heart sank as I thought of how happy he'd been for his friend only a moment ago. Had the second boy already been tested and found to have a weak seed? Was that why the other father despised him so much? Surely it couldn't purely be because the lad was an orphan?

Amara sighed quietly, drawing my eye. She looked as sad as I felt.

"The crown ensures every Tartoran gets an education," she said softly, "but there's only so much they can do to combat prejudice."

Anger welled inside me. "Everyone talks about our seeds like they're a great leveling force, allowing those born to poverty and obscurity to rise as high as the Triumvirate itself. But our seeds are still just an accident of birth. It's no more that child's fault that he has a weak seed than that he has no parents."

Amara nodded. "Why do you think I choose to be a traveling master rather than living in luxury in the capital? Those of us with powerful seeds owe a debt of service to the rest of the kingdom. We were given more at birth, so we must give more back as well."

Tears sprung to my eyes, fueled by an unexpected rush of gratitude. My own father had kept me trapped, but Amara—a stranger to me—had chosen to seek me out and set me free. She was the opposite of the mages he had taught me about—spending her life helping those who lived far from the glamour of the capital.

I couldn't even blame my father's attitude on his poverty and disadvantage. My mother had lived the same life as him, but she had still chosen to love me selflessly—even if that meant letting me go. My uncle might have been the one to commit the first wrong, but my father had chosen to let those wounds fester until they stunted us both. That decision hadn't harmed my uncle, who knew nothing about it—it had harmed my father and ultimately me, someone he claimed to love.

I blinked furiously to fight back the tears. My anger with my father was still fresh, and it was hard to reconcile with the images of my childhood that kept resurfacing. I could feel my father, sturdy and solid beneath me, as he hoisted five-year-old me onto his shoulders. I could hear his voice telling me that everything I could see was mine, even the sky itself—that here, on this dependable land, I would always have a home.

I wanted to lash out at the father in front of me. To tell him that his love for his own child wasn't enough to justify his attitude toward the boy's friend. Did he want to poison his son with his own narrow-mindedness? Couldn't he see the damage he was doing?

The words remained inside, barely restrained. Regardless of this stranger's behavior, he wasn't the real target of my anger, and it wasn't my place to harangue him.

"Come on," Amara said softly, not mentioning the moisture in my eyes. "Whatever we think of those parents, that boy still deserves to be tested just like every other child. We can't let our feelings get in the way of the job we're here to do."

"Wait, *we're* here to do?" I asked, shock replacing the messier emotions swirling through me. "I thought we were just here to watch the local healer?"

"We're here for you to learn, and what better way is there than by doing?" Amara asked in a suspiciously prim tone.

I groaned, my earlier indignation entirely swallowed by my anxiety. "What if my wall gets in the way?"

"You'll find a way around it," Amara said calmly. "I'm sure of it."

I swallowed, trying not to look as terrified as I felt. I only hoped she was right.

"Oh, you're already here!" A young man rushed into the school yard, stopping beside us and bowing to Amara. "I'm running a bit late."

I hid a smile at his distracted air. He had the feel of someone who was late a lot.

"I'm Bjorn." He stuck out his hand toward me, before noticeably starting and pulling it back. "Oh, sorry! I nearly forgot you're a new apprentice. You won't want to touch anyone."

"I'm Delphine," I managed while Amara grinned openly at us.

"And you must be Master Amara, of course." Bjorn bowed to her again. "It's an honor to meet you. I've heard a lot about you."

"Not from Clay, I hope," she said with a laugh, and Bjorn laughed as well, ushering us ahead of him into the school.

As we stepped inside, I glanced back and saw the small family still lingering outside, their curious gazes fastened on the three of us. The interested look in their eyes made me wonder if Bjorn's greeting had been more calculated than it appeared. After his respectful, almost awed, reception of Amara, I doubted they would object to our presence at their child's testing. Whether they would be equally calm about a new apprentice doing the actual testing remained to be seen.

The room set aside for our use was small but painted in a bright, cheerful yellow and with a small vase of flowers on the large windowsill. Bjorn busied himself bringing in two more chairs so that six chairs stood in a rough circle.

"The testing itself is a simple matter, of course," he said. "But many parents are anxious and full of questions before and after. We leave plenty of time for each testing so that we don't have to hurry anyone along."

"A nice day off for you healers." Amara winked.

He laughed. "That entirely depends on how many disappointed parents we get. Last time I was here, one of the children had a different affinity from both of her parents and a lower strength than they'd expected as well. Her mother burst into tears as soon as I announced the results, and her father kept insisting I'd made a mistake and demanding I call for a more experienced healer to retest her."

I winced, although he seemed to find the memory more amusing than traumatic. If a parent responded to a fully qualified healer that way, what would they say to a mere apprentice?

Bjorn caught my expression. "Don't worry, Delphine. If anyone causes trouble with you, we'll just dazzle them with Master Amara's qualifications."

She grinned. "I may have an elements seed, but I'd like to see any parent tell me they need a more experienced mage in my place."

Bjorn chuckled. "I'd enjoy seeing them try. But thankfully the vast majority of parents are reasonable, and most children test according to expectations."

"Is it really so unusual to get a surprise?" I asked, remembering my own testing. The healer had been shocked by my seed, but I had always imagined it was a result of his inexperience.

"It's unusual for strength, at least," Bjorn said. "Affinities are harder to predict from parentage since everyone has all three in their family background somewhere. But even so, there's still a strong correlation between parents and children. And even for those who diverge, it's not usually a surprise to their families since they'll have seen hints of it already. Even the youngest healer children are usually good nurses, for instance, and they're always drawn to animals. And elements toddlers love to wander out into storms. It gives their poor parents heart attacks if they're not elements themselves." He chuckled. "My younger sister was like that. Most of us in my family are healers, but she's elements."

Amara smiled reminiscently. "I remember being fascinated by storms as a youngster. The bigger, the better."

I shivered. "That sounds horrible. I like to be curled up safely inside when it starts thundering."

Amara tilted her head, looking at me closely. "*Does* it sound so horrible? Take a moment to really think about it."

I frowned. My initial instinct was to insist that I knew myself, but it was clear Amara was giving a lesson of some sort, so I obeyed. To my surprise, I couldn't seem to remember what had sent me scurrying inside in the past. Just thinking about the crackle of electricity in the air was exhilarating. Why had I always hidden from storms in the past?

Bjorn looked from my arrested expression to Amara's amused one, and then back again, curiosity in his gaze.

"We've had a rather action-packed beginning to Delphine's apprenticeship," Amara told him. "She hasn't had a chance to think about what it means to have an elements influencer." She turned to me. "You still have a healing seed—nothing can change that. But you're not just a straight healer now. You're healing cross elements, and as you grow in your ability, you'll discover all sorts of ways in which the lingering effect of my power has influenced yours."

"Like a plants mage who can track someone through the ground," I whispered to myself.

"What?" Amara's brow creased, and I bit my lip. I hadn't meant to speak aloud.

Thankfully a knock at the door saved me from having to answer. As Bjorn stood up to usher in the boy and his parents, I mentally kicked myself. I needed to be more careful.

The parents responded to Bjorn's introductions with respect, showing Amara the same deference they'd witnessed Bjorn showing her in the yard.

"As you would no doubt be aware," Bjorn said, "we often have apprentices here in the testing rooms. But we're honored today to be joined by the apprentice of Master Amara, who is one of the youngest masters in generations."

I noticed he carefully avoided mentioning her affinity. She didn't correct the omission as she gracefully received a second round of even more deferential greetings from the two parents.

The boy in question looked a lot less interested in our identities, finding it hard to sit still on his assigned seat. As he bounced up and down, I smiled at him. From what I'd seen outside, he was confident in his results and eager to get back to his classroom so he could boast to his friends.

"I'm sure he has an elements affinity like me." The father clapped his son on the back, a proud look in his eye. "My father has one, too, as did his father before him. I'll be inheriting the family smithy soon, and of course I'll take my son on as my apprentice when he reaches age."

"Unless he's even stronger than you," the mother said with a hint of excitement. She turned to Bjorn. "I'm sure he doesn't have a plants seed like me—he's far too attracted to fire." She shuddered dramatically. "But he could be stronger than either of us, couldn't he?"

"It is certainly possible," Bjorn said diplomatically, although I could read on his face he didn't expect it.

"It would, of course, be an honor to send our son off to the Guild to become a mage," the father said with a glance at Amara. "But a son to inherit the forge after me is all I ask for. As long as he's strong enough to discern pure metals from tainted ones, to keep the furnace at the right temperature, and to keep himself safe from burns, I'll be happy."

I got the distinct impression he would prefer his son wasn't too strong. While a mage son would bring honor to the family, he would never run a smithy in Ostaria. Anger flashed through me as I once again saw my own father in this man.

I drew in a slow breath as I fought the feeling down. This man wasn't my father, and he had already stated he would send the boy to the Guild if he was strong enough. It was hardly a crime for him to want to train his son himself, or to want to pass on the family business.

If I could extend understanding to this man, was I being unfair in blaming my father for doing a similar thing? Was he really so unjustified in wanting to keep me around?

Not in wanting, I realized with a swell of sadness. I didn't blame my father for wanting me to stay, I blamed him for taking away my choice. And more than that, for doing it in a way that left me bound and weak. If he had succeeded, I might have lived my whole life without ever having access to a central part of me.

That would not be this boy's fate, regardless of his results today, and that was the essential difference. One way or another, he would have access to his full self, and today was the first step toward that future.

Determination filled me. Everyone thought I could do this testing, so I was going to believe in myself too. I glanced at Bjorn, ready and willing to start but unsure what was actually involved.

"Don't worry," Bjorn said to the boy in a cheerful voice. "It doesn't hurt at all. In fact, you won't feel a thing. You're lucky because you're going to be tested twice. Apprentice Delphine will test you and so will I."

Relief filled me. Despite my sudden confidence, I preferred knowing my findings would be backed up by someone more experienced. And from the expression on her face, the boy's mother felt a similar relief. I smiled at her, and she smiled tentatively back.

Bjorn turned to me with an encouraging nod. "You go first."

I glanced at Amara, still unsure how I should go about the testing.

She leaned close enough to speak quietly into my ear. "Take down your wall first. You're not in physical contact with anyone, and no one here is injured, so it shouldn't be too overwhelming. For the actual testing, you'll need to touch the boy, but when you do, try to focus on his seed and don't get caught up with his other systems."

I gulped, unsure how I was supposed to do that. But the boy was already holding out his arm obediently, so I couldn't delay any further.

Pushing past my natural reluctance, I tore down a section of my wall, bracing for the inundating wave of sensation. It wasn't as bad as I'd feared, however. Amara had been right.

Had I already started to become desensitized from exposure, as Clay had predicted? The six healthy bodies in the room felt less overwhelming than my parents' presence had back on the farm.

Slowly I reached out my hand and placed it lightly on the boy's forearm. Immediately my awareness of everyone else dimmed to almost nothing as my power surged into the boy's body, encompassing every part of him.

The rush of blood through his veins and the pumping of his heart and lungs pulsed through me. But when my stomach clenched in response, my head spinning, I sent part of my power breezing through my own body, blowing the sensations away.

My stomach settled and my mind cleared in the wake of my power. Relieved, I smiled and focused back on the boy. Carefully not thinking about his heart or lungs, I looked instead for something inside him that wasn't linked to a physical organ.

Now that I was free of other distractions, I sensed it almost immediately. Deep inside the boy, something coiled, its sleeping power calling to me. I instinctively recognized the feeling of heat and wind and crackling lightning.

"Elements," I said, surprising myself with my certainty. "He has an elements seed as you predicted."

Both parents and the boy himself smiled, as did Bjorn. His encouraging expression made me look down, noticing for the first time that his hand also rested lightly on the boy's outstretched arm. The healer clearly wasn't waiting for my assessment before doing his own testing, he was just keeping quiet to give me a chance to speak first.

A wave of relief washed over me. Bjorn and Amara must have discussed it ahead of time, and he knew how inexperienced I was. He was already in contact, ready to use his power to protect the boy if my control slipped.

Bolstered by the realization that I had back up, I considered the boy's seed again. It was surprisingly easy to sense his affinity, but how did I measure his strength? And how did I communicate something so unquantifiable to his parents? I tried to remember the wording the Tarin healer had used when testing me, but I couldn't recall the details. He'd been too excited, and I'd been too shocked to take note.

I had no choice but to betray my ignorance in front of the family. I looked across at Bjorn. "How do I tell how strong he is?"

Bjorn rubbed the back of his neck with his free hand. "That's a little difficult to explain. It basically comes down to experience and exposure to enough seeds. That's why apprentices do lots of testing in their two years. After a while you start to get a feel for it."

"That is most unhelpful," Amara said disapprovingly. "Surely you can tell her something."

Bjorn thought for a moment. "You felt the seed easily," he said eventually. "From there it's just a matter of how strongly you sense the affinity coming from it. Once you've felt a few different seeds, you'll be able to judge the difference."

"That's all very well," the father said abruptly. "But what about my son? Surely one of you can tell us his strength?"

"He's of middle strength as a non-mage," Bjorn said with a broad smile. "Likely similar to your own strength, I imagine—and certainly sufficient for the blacksmith tasks you mentioned. You need have no hesitation about activating him yourself when the time comes."

"Middle strength!" his mother exclaimed in delight, pulling him into a hug.

His father beamed, only slightly less enthusiastic at the news.

"I was a little worried he might be weak like me," the mother confessed quietly to Amara and me as the father clapped his boy on the shoulder. "But everything is perfect now."

I smiled back at her, pleased that my first attempt at testing had gone so smoothly. If only every family was as happy with the results their children received.

Unlike the long questioning session Bjorn had described, the family moved out of the room quickly, leaving us to discuss the matter without them. I felt I'd been of no help at all, but both Amara and Bjorn praised my efforts.

"How could you possibly tell the strength when you have nothing to compare it against?" Bjorn asked. "And you can't look at the strength of those already activated for comparison either. Unlike me, you might have the strength for it, but it would be a major breach of etiquette."

"Goodness, yes, don't do anything of the kind, Delphine," Amara commanded. "You'll face enough scrutiny given your unconventional apprenticeship without offending people into the bargain."

"Come now, surely that's an exaggeration," Bjorn protested. "I'll admit news that you've taken an apprentice has generated a fair bit of interest and excitement among the mages in Ostaria. But I haven't heard anyone say anything negative."

Amara smiled. "That's because mages willing to make a home outside the capital are already more broad-minded than their fellows who stay welded to the Guild. Why do you think I prefer to live my life out here?"

Bjorn snorted. "You might be right on that point. But does that mean you're planning to take Delphine to the Guild to undergo official scrutiny?"

I stiffened at the suggestion. Amara hadn't mentioned anything like that.

"Not imminently," she said. "But I imagine our travels will take us through the capital at some point. If Delphine is going to be accepted, then Master Colton will need to examine her, at least."

I gulped. "I really don't care that much about being accepted."

Bjorn and Amara both chuckled.

"Don't let Amara prejudice you," Bjorn said. "The Guild isn't such a terrible place. And it's become even more lively since the exchange with Calista." When I gave him a questioning look, he added, "We're training some of their young mages in preparation for founding a new Calistan Mages' Guild. So our Guild is bursting with young people right now."

"I've heard rumors about that," Amara said. "Maybe I really will find it a changed place."

"Excuse me?" A nervous voice from the open doorway made us all look up.

The next appointment wasn't for some time, but the family had obviously arrived early and noticed we were already alone.

Bjorn ushered them in, and we went through the same process as with the previous child. It was a girl being tested this time, and she looked utterly terrified.

Bjorn was gentle in his manner with her, explaining the process patiently before asking her to hold out her arm. When she finally did, I rested my fingers on it as lightly as possible before sending my power into her.

It was harder to find her seed than it had been with the boy. I had thought experience would make it easier, but apparently my one success had made me cocky. I did eventually manage to locate a sense deep inside her that reminded me of my farm back home—something warm and green and growing.

Bjorn had also connected with her, but this time he didn't wait for me to speak first. Focusing fully on the family, he spoke in a sympathetic tone as he explained that the girl had a very weak plants seed.

Both parents were clearly disappointed but remained subdued, neither of them demanding a retest. The father asked a few questions about what sort of prospects there might be for his daughter while the mother struggled to contain the silent tears streaming down her cheeks.

I focused on the girl, who hadn't lifted her head since her testing.

"Do you like plants?" I asked, using the same voice I used when meeting new farm animals for the first time.

She didn't lift her head but managed a slight nod.

"I'm not surprised," I said. "I'm a healer, and I've always loved animals."

She looked up at that, frowning. "But I thought they said you were strong. I'm weak."

Her head immediately dipped again, as if she was startled by her own voice.

"That's true," I said. "But weak or strong, we both have an affinity. Since yours is with plants, that means you have a connection with the ground and with growing things. I grew up on a farm, you know, and I always wished I had a plants affinity."

She looked up again at that, interest in her eyes.

"Even though I didn't have any plants power at all, I was still able to help my parents a lot," I continued. "There's plenty to be done on a farm, even if all you have are your own two hands. I'm sure you could find work on one, regardless of your strength."

"I'd love to live on a farm," she said wistfully. "There aren't enough living things in the city."

Her mother straightened at her daughter's words, the tears stopping as she gave her husband a defiant look.

"And why shouldn't she! My brother has a farm, and he's always complaining about needing extra hands. Now that we know the truth of her situation, there's no reason to hold out for something better."

The husband threw his wife a look, but on meeting the steely determination in her eyes, he sighed and nodded.

A broad smile immediately transformed the girl's face.

"Really?" she asked. "I can go to uncle's farm?"

Her mother laughed. "Not immediately, child. You've only just started school this year! But when you're older. Your uncle might even take on your apprenticeship himself. I'm sure there's something he could teach you, even if you only have a touch of power like me." She sighed. "If you'd been elements, I would have activated you myself, of course. There are plenty of roles in the city for those with an elements affinity, even if it's not a strong one."

The mother escorted her daughter out of the room, having now launched into a lecture on the need to focus in school, and the father trailed out behind them. I sat back in my chair with a sigh. That had nearly been a disaster.

"Well done, Delphine," Amara said.

I looked up and met her eyes, flushing at her approving look.

"I can see you have a natural knack for connecting with the children," Bjorn agreed. "Some healers don't, and no amount of practice helps. They're the ones who always hate being rostered on for this job."

The next family had a boy whose healing seed was even easier to identify than the first boy's had been. Bjorn declared him to be of high non-mage strength, leading to great excitement from his parents.

They spent nearly the whole allotted hour asking questions of Bjorn and trying to ascertain their son's potential future options. By the time they left, I was exhausted—although I hadn't had to answer any of their questions myself—and more than ready to break for lunch.

CHAPTER

# SEVENTEEN

"That one was so much easier," I said as we sat outside in the sun to eat our packed meal of bread and cheese. "I struggled with the girl."

"That's because she had a plants seed," Bjorn said around a large mouthful. "And she was also weak. That's the worst combination for you."

"Why does it matter what her affinity is?" I asked when my own mouth was empty.

"You're healing cross elements." Amara cut Bjorn off before he could speak again with a full mouth. "So you have a connection to both those affinities. But the power connected to plants is totally foreign to you. And since a weak seed is harder to sense in general, a plants seed is doubly so in your case."

"Are you cross-influenced?" I asked Bjorn.

He chuckled. "I'm a good Guild boy, not a rebel like Amara here. I only just had enough strength to qualify as a mage, so I was eager to make the most of it."

"So do you find it hard to identify elements and plants seeds, then?"

He shrugged. "It's harder than with a healing seed, but I've tested enough children now that I can identify anything easily enough. You'll be the same soon."

Excited chatter and laughs rang out as the doors of the school building opened and children flooded into the yard. We stayed in place against the building wall, watching them as they began to eat and play.

I smiled to see the delight they had in the spring sunshine and the company of their friends. Most of them would have been tested in their first year of schooling, but none of them were old enough for activation yet. What seeds hid inside them?

Without consciously meaning to do so, my words sparked my power. Before I realized I was reaching out, I had connected with one of the girls playing hopscotch close by.

Her elements seed sang to me, crackling with lightning. It was stronger and easier to sense than the blacksmith's boy's had been. Was that because of my increase in experience?

My power reached for the girl hopping just behind her. She had a healing seed buried inside, its power calling in kinship to my own. But despite the familiarity of her seed, it was definitely harder to sense than her companion's.

So it hadn't just been an increase in my experience, then. The difference was in the girls' strength. This was what Bjorn had described when he talked about needing comparison to recognize the level of strength.

I was reaching for the next closest child, eager to compare their seed as well, when I realized what I was doing. I gasped, attracting both Bjorn and Amara's attention.

"Is something wrong?" Amara asked.

"I thought healers needed physical contact," I said breathlessly. "So how did I just test those girls over there?" I pointed to them. "I didn't plan to do it, I was just thinking about their seeds, and the next thing I knew, I connected to them."

Bjorn's eyebrows shot up, and Amara turned to him, looking confused.

"Do you know what she's talking about? I also thought healers needed physical contact to test seeds."

He put his bread down. "Actually it's a little more complicated than that." He paused, looking at me. "You really tested them from over here?"

I nodded. "Was that wrong of me? It's not like testing another mage, is it?"

He laughed. "No, don't worry, no one's coming after you with pitchforks. Testing children's seeds is unexceptionable—as long as their parents have already brought them for testing. It might be a little rude to do it to a very young child who hasn't had their seed assessed yet, but those girls would have been tested years ago."

"Did you test them?" I asked. "Does the one on the left have a strong elements seed and the one on the right a weak healing seed?"

Bjorn squinted at them. "It wasn't me. I only joined the roster for this school at the start of the year, so I haven't tested anyone that old. And I rarely remember which seeds belong to which children, anyway."

"Can you check them now, then?" I asked. "I want to know if I got it right."

Bjorn shook his head, although a smile lingered around his mouth. "I can't tell from this distance."

"You can't?" I frowned across the school yard. "But it wasn't hard."

Amara burst into laughter. "Please remember you're my apprentice and anything you say or do will reflect on me. So don't go shaming your elders, please."

Bjorn grinned. "Since the only mages you've really interacted with have been Master Amara and Master Clay, I'll forgive you. But please remember that most of us don't have your strength."

I flushed, stammering out an apology. "I'm so sorry. I wasn't thinking."

"Please always think in the future," Amara said, but her eyes were still laughing.

"In answer to your question about physical contact," Bjorn said, "even the strongest healers need physical contact to actually change anything in someone's body. But as you know, a mage can sense certain things about people and animals from a distance. For the strongest mages, that includes testing children's seeds. But you likely haven't heard of it, Amara, because us healers are creatures of habit. Since we train to use our ability through physical touch, most of us prefer to use it wherever possible, even if it isn't strictly necessary."

I shuddered. I felt the exact opposite. I was most comfortable with those parts of my ability that I could use without physical touch. I had only tested those two girls so instinctively because I hadn't had to touch them to do it.

"Just because something is usually done a certain way is not a reason you have to do it that way, too," Amara told me firmly. "If you can test children without needing physical contact, by all means, do so."

"There's certainly no issue with it," Bjorn said. "Although you may want to experiment with both approaches to see if you notice any difference. It's possible that being in contact will give you more detail."

A loud cry followed by an even louder cheer pulled my attention to a tree on the far side of the yard. The blacksmith's son from earlier had climbed halfway up the trunk, trying to keep pace with his friend. I recognized the other boy as the one who had been labeled an orphan by the blacksmith. Apparently the son had defied his father's orders and was continuing to play with his friend.

"What about that boy?" I pointed at the second boy who had now reached the top branches of the tree. "I don't suppose you know about his seed?"

Bjorn peered in the direction of my pointing finger. "I don't recognize him. Why?"

I shrugged. "I just wondered." I didn't want to go into the conversation I'd overheard that morning, but I couldn't shake a lingering sadness for the boy, who likely had a weak seed.

"The boy we tested this morning was old for testing," Bjorn said. "He must have been late to start school. So his friend's parents probably brought him for testing last year."

I frowned. "But he doesn't have any parents."

Bjorn's face fell. "An orphan, is he? How tragic." He picked his bread back up and resumed eating. "Sometimes guardians aren't as diligent about bringing children in for testing. Eventually a teacher will notice and book him in themselves if necessary."

I stood up, unable to let it go so easily. If this boy lacked conscientious guardians, he was already at a disadvantage. Why should he wait to identify his seed?

I walked to the foot of the tree, trying to peer up through the leaves. I couldn't see much, so I called for the boys to come down. They both slid down so fast, I suspected they weren't supposed to be climbing in the first place.

When they finally stood in front of me, their guilty expressions confirmed it. But a moment later, the expression on the face of the blacksmith's son cleared as he recognized me.

"You're the healer!" He nudged his friend. "The one I told you about. She's a master!"

Both boys stared at me with awed faces, and I laughed. "Actually I'm an apprentice. My master is sitting over there." I pointed back to Amara. "Congratulations on your result," I added to the boy who'd spoken.

He swelled with pride, nudging his friend again, and I turned to the second boy.

"What about you?" I asked. "What's your affinity?"

He had been gazing at me curiously, but at my words he looked down at the ground and scuffed his toe in the dirt.

"He hasn't been tested," his friend said for him. "He never had an appointment."

"Would you like me to test you now?" I asked.

The boy's head sprang back up, his eyes wide. "Would you really? Right here?"

I smiled. "It's an easy thing to do. And it doesn't hurt or anything."

"I'm not worried about that," he said with a confidence that made me believe his words.

I reached out with my power, slipping easily through the cracks I had made earlier in my wall. As soon as I connected with him, I felt his seed. It pulsed in the middle of him, a warm and friendly presence.

I pulled back out, finished with my test, although the boy didn't know anything had happened.

I turned back toward the two I'd left behind. "Bjorn," I called, waving for him to join me. "Could you come over here?"

"Is there something wrong?" the boy asked, alarmed.

I shook my head. "Not at all. You have a healing seed, I'm sure of that much. And I think..." I let my words trail off. "I just want to confirm something before I say any more. I'm only an apprentice, so I'm new at this."

The two boys exchanged wide-eyed looks as Bjorn and Amara both crossed the yard.

"It turns out he hadn't been tested," I said to them both. "So I just had a look, and I think..." I turned to Bjorn. "Can you check for me? I'm sure he has a healing seed, but—"

Bjorn reached out a hand, and the boy obediently placed his own in it. Bjorn's eyebrows rose and he whistled. "Well, that's unexpected."

"What is it?" his friend asked. "Is there something wrong with him?"

"Far from it," Bjorn said. "Young man, you have a healing seed of medium non-mage strength." He glanced at the other boy. "It's stronger than your friend's here."

"Medium strength?" both boys echoed in unison.

"Wait until Father hears that," the blacksmith's son crowed. "He was so sure you had a weak seed like your parents, but you're stronger than me!" He didn't seem in the least upset about being surpassed by his friend. "I'm always telling him he's wrong about you." He turned to Bjorn. "Does that mean he'll work at the hospital, like you?"

Bjorn looked at the other boy. "Would you like to? You're strong enough that there's every chance you'd be accepted for an apprenticeship at the hospital. We take on people of a variety of strengths."

The boy slowly shook his head, looking dazed. "Actually, I've always wanted to work with animals."

"Finding an animal-focused apprenticeship should be equally feasible," Bjorn said. "You can talk to one of the animal healing clinics, or even one of the larger farms. There's no rush, since you're a long way off seventeen."

I frowned, looking at the boy. He might be a long way from activation, but what was his life like now? Did he need somewhere to call home?

"How do you feel about horses?" I asked.

The boy's eyes lit up. "I sometimes hold the reins for people who need to step into a shop. Some of them will give me a coin for the task, but I do it happily even if they don't."

"What are you thinking?" Amara asked, but I shook my head. I didn't want to speak up in front of the children when nothing was confirmed.

The afternoon flew past as I tested more children—this time trying it first without physical contact and then with. I could see why most mages preferred contact—it made everything sharper and more focused. But that was the exact reason I disliked it.

By the time we returned to the inn, I was exhausted. But when we entered the yard, I swerved toward the stables instead of the main building. I thought Amara would protest or question me, but she just followed silently.

Inside the dim aisle, I greeted those horses who had their heads over the half walls of their stalls. Stopping to rub each nose, I murmured praise, understanding the young student's interest in the animals. They were intelligent, affectionate, and useful. Seeing the horses here made me miss the faithful ones I had left behind on my parents' farm.

But conscious of Amara's silent presence, I limited my time with each horse, making my way toward the tack room halfway down the length of the stables. Sticking my head inside, I found an older man polishing a saddle.

He nodded his head but offered no other greeting and made no attempt to rise. I smiled at this sign that he didn't care about rank or station.

"I don't suppose you have need of any youngsters to fetch and carry for you?" I asked.

He stopped polishing and leaned back in his seat, looking at me speculatively. "Fetch and carry? I can't imagine you're interested in such a thing, miss."

I laughed. "No, not me. I mean a much younger child. Maybe seven or so?"

The man scratched his chin. "That depends."

"He has a healing seed of medium to high strength and a strong affection for horses." I hesitated. "And he's an orphan."

"Ah." The man sat forward again and resumed his polishing. "So that's the way of it."

My heart sank.

"Tell him to come see me, and I'll size him up."

"Really?" I stared at him, wondering if I'd somehow misunderstood.

He looked up and raised an eyebrow. "Send him round. I'll make up me mind once I see him."

"Thank you!" I wanted to say more, but I didn't think it would be welcome, so I beat a hasty retreat instead.

Amara was waiting for me with raised eyebrows.

"I know." I gave her a guilty look. "I'm interfering."

"Don't expect a reprimand from me for that." She chuckled. "You'll soon learn I have a terrible reputation as a busybody."

"I find that hard to believe. Everyone seems to love you."

"Not everyone." She grinned. "And, of course, most people don't use the term *busybody* for a master mage. But one or two may have told me I like to stick my nose where it doesn't belong."

I laughed. "Did those people live at the Guild?"

"Maybe." She put an arm around my shoulders and guided me toward the inn door. "Come on. Let's get something warm in your belly. You did a good job on your first proper day, apprentice of mine. A very good job."

CHAPTER

# EIGHTEEN

I would have liked to fall straight into bed after the evening meal, but I knew Nik would happily investigate Grey without me. And knowing him, he wouldn't tell me what he'd found either. If I missed my chance to meet him tonight, I might not be able to find him again at all.

At least Ember had the energy I lacked, dancing by the door in her eagerness to be gone. Amara smiled at sight of her and didn't question my departure, probably thinking I was taking the fox out to stretch her legs.

As I exited the inn, I couldn't shake my guilt at not telling Amara what I was doing. But hopefully Nik and I would find the evidence we needed that night, and then I could tell Amara everything and ask her to take me to the relevant authorities.

My worry over finding my way back to the abandoned warehouse proved groundless. I remembered the route more easily than I'd expected. And even Ember seemed to know where we were going, growing more and more restless the closer we got, as if she had no desire to return.

Eventually I scooped her up, afraid she might run off and be lost in the night. As soon as I felt her solid warmth against my chest, I realized I had picked her up for my sake as much as hers. I was nervous and her presence was reassuring, even if she was just one small fox.

When I neared the warehouse, I slowed, eventually sliding along the wall of the closest building, doing my best to keep to the shadows. There didn't appear to be anyone around to see me, however, and the door was firmly closed.

I reached out with my power, thinking to count how many people were inside and to check whether any of them were near the door.

I counted one in close proximity to the front of the warehouse and pushed further on, looking for the others. I found nothing, however. I frowned. Had something happened to affect my range? Why couldn't I sense them?

And where was Nik? Had he come earlier—during the day even? Was he trying to avoid me? Panic rose inside me, a fizzy feeling that made it hard to keep still.

How long should I wait for him? If Grey had gone out leaving only one guard behind, it was an unexpected opportunity. Did I need to take a look inside the warehouse on my own?

My arms tightened around Ember, and she squirmed in protest. I forced myself to take a deep breath, pushing the panic down. This wasn't the time to do anything rash.

While I was still reassuring myself, the door swung open so violently it smashed against the wall. I jumped, nearly colliding with the pile of crates. I managed to save myself before making contact, but a small squeak slipped out.

Footsteps sounded, and Nik appeared. The two of us stood for a moment, staring at each other before he sighed.

"I should have known it was you," he said.

"Was the person in the warehouse you?" I gasped, suddenly hit with a foolish fear. Had I misjudged the whole situation? Was it all a set up, and Nik was actually working with Grey?

Nik's eyes narrowed, and he held up a hand. "Stop."

"Stop what?" I eyed him warily.

"Stop whatever nonsense is going on in your head right now."

I flushed, hoping the meager moonlight wasn't bright enough to reveal my embarrassment.

"I don't know what you're talking about. Although I would like to know what you found in there. Where are Grey and his followers?"

"They're gone."

"All of them?" I frowned. "Well, shouldn't we—" I broke off abruptly. "Wait. What do you mean by *gone*? As in, gone out to one of Grey's meetings? Or gone to a new warehouse?"

"As in, gone from Ostaria. I already tracked them as far as the city wall, but I lost their trail there." He turned suddenly and slammed his fist into the wall of the warehouse. "I missed them again!" He punched the unforgiving stone a second time.

When he drew back his fist again, I dropped Ember and grabbed his elbow with both hands.

"You're going to injure yourself if you keep that up."

He shook me off violently, pulling away, but he didn't throw any more punches.

"If you already tracked them out of Ostaria," I said slowly, "what are you doing back here?"

He stilled, his back to me. "I came back to check for anything they might have left behind. I don't think they were originally planning to move on so quickly. They were still scouting the local youths. Grey hadn't even started winning over any followers yet."

"That's a good thing, at least," I said tentatively, trying to draw him out of his black mood. "We didn't rescue anyone, but at least there aren't any more victims."

Nik didn't move, so I stepped closer again, circling him so I could see his face.

"Do you think they left Ostaria so quickly because of us?" I asked.

"It's likely," he said in clipped tones. "But I don't like it. It doesn't fit Grey's pattern, and…" He trailed off, looking at me with an intense expression.

"You still think Grey's after me, and you don't understand why he's run off like this," I said slowly. "But coming after me is a serious risk, given my apprenticeship to a master mage. You must be mistaken about the risks he's willing to take."

"Perhaps." Nik didn't sound like he believed it.

My eyes focused on his right hand. He wasn't wearing his usual gloves, and his knuckles were bright with red.

My hands reached out of their own accord, taking his injured hand in both of mine. The sudden skin-to-skin contact was shockingly intimate in the moonlight. A gesture that had once meant little had gained new meaning since the activation of my power.

"You've hurt yourself," I said softly.

His muscles clenched, but he didn't pull away. When I looked up, he was watching my face intensely. My breath caught in my throat.

"I can heal this for you, if you like," I whispered.

He didn't move or speak, and I took his silence as permission. Cracking open my wall, I let my power slide into his hand, soothing and healing the broken, bruised parts.

It was a minor injury, and the healing only took seconds. But I didn't let go of his hand.

Reaching for my handkerchief, I wiped at the blood that now stained smooth, unblemished skin. But the silence was like a heavy weight, so I blurted out the first words that came into my mind.

"Did you really come back to look for evidence? Or did you come because you knew I would be waiting for you?"

He ripped his hand away, snatching the handkerchief from my grasp and rubbing it roughly over his stained skin. As soon as he was finished, he dropped it in the dirt at our feet.

Despite his sudden burst of activity, neither of us stepped back. Instead, he leaned in, closing the distance between us even further.

"Don't get the wrong idea, healer. I'm here for Grey, not you. The best thing you can do is run far, far away."

But his dismissive, intimidating manner didn't have its usual effect. I could still feel the lingering sensation of my power connecting us. Instead of shrinking away, I leaned in as well.

Keeping eye contact, I reached out and took back his hand, gripping it in both of mine as I had before.

"I could kill you right now, and there's nothing you could do to stop me," I whispered.

He held utterly still, his eyes boring into mine in the semi-darkness.

"I'm not useless, and even Grey knows that, apparently," I continued, still not flinching from his gaze. "Stop telling me to leave—I'm not going anywhere."

I swayed even closer, and I thought, for a moment, that I read capitulation in his eyes. He took a breath, but whatever he'd been about to say or do, I would never know.

A voice cracked across the night like a whip, making us spring apart.

"What exactly is going on here? What are you doing in this part of the city, Delphine?"

I stared at Amara, horrified. Had she followed me here?

It seemed the only possible explanation.

"Who exactly are..." Amara's terse words faded as she looked more closely at Nik. Both of her eyebrows slowly rose toward her hairline as she fell into silence.

After a loaded pause, she spoke again. "Nikolas. This is indeed a surprise."

"Amara." The slight bow of his head seemed more insolent than respectful, making my brows knit together. When he'd mentioned her previously, he'd used her title and seemed at least neutral toward her, if not actually respectful.

"You've certainly grown up." Amara's eyes flicked from him to me, but I couldn't read their expression.

"And you look exactly the same." He stood with his back straight and stance rigid.

My eyes flew between them, trying to make sense of the interaction. What history did they have, and what did Amara know about Nik?

"What exactly have you been doing on these night walks of yours, Delphine?" Amara asked, making me forget all about my own curiosity.

Remembering the position she'd found us in, I flushed and hurried into speech.

"We've been tracking Grey—looking for Miranda and for evidence we can use to have him arrested."

"Grey?" Amara's eyebrows shot up again. Whatever she'd been expecting me to say, that hadn't been it. "Say that again. Grey is here in Ostaria?"

"Not anymore," I said regretfully. "They must have left sometime during the day today which means we just missed Miranda. Nik was able to—" I cut off abruptly when I caught the slight shake of his head.

Did he not want me to mention his tracking ability in front of Amara?

"Were you healing him when I arrived?" Amara asked. "Is that why you were holding his hand?" She looked like she wasn't sure if that was better or worse than her first assumption. "Just how dangerous is this Grey person?"

"I..." I wasn't sure how to answer.

I had healed Nik, but not because of any danger from Grey. But somehow I didn't think it would help either of us to tell Amara that Nik had injured himself in a fit of fury. Unfortunately, that left me floundering, and Amara turned to Nik.

"I don't know who Grey really is yet," he said. "But I intend to find out. And I intend to stop him before he tears Tartora apart."

Amara's brows creased. "Tears the kingdom apart? You think he's a real danger, then?"

"I know he is." Nik met her gaze firmly, conviction on his face.

Amara's frown deepened. "And you thought it was a good idea to involve my newly activated apprentice in this mission of yours?"

"It wasn't exactly his idea," I rushed to say. "I'm the one who insisted on helping. Because of Miranda. I promised Halmir I'd rescue her."

Amara ignored me, keeping her focus on Nik.

"You may have chosen to throw your life away, Nikolas, but that doesn't mean you can treat the lives of others cheaply."

He stiffened, his face darkening. "I told her she should leave. In fact, I told her Grey—"

From where I stood off to the side, I shook my head vigorously, and he cut off whatever he'd been about to say. My shock at his compliance was so great I went still—just in time to avoid being caught by Amara who threw me a suspicious look.

Earlier in the evening, I'd resolved to tell her everything, but given her current anger, it didn't seem like a good time for Nik to mention his totally unfounded theory that Grey had some special interest in me. Especially since Grey's latest behavior didn't support the idea at all.

Amara drew herself up, her eyes turning icy. "I had intended for Delphine and me to make an extended stay in Ostaria. Leaving now will be inconvenient. But I clearly need to get my new apprentice away from your influence."

Nik took a swift step forward, his face furious. "You elements mages have always looked down on the rest of us, but—"

He broke off as Amara grew in front of our eyes. Tiny threads of lightning crackled up and down her arms as she transformed from my kindly mentor into a figure of terrifying power. I stumbled back a step, and even Nik stopped, his face tensing. He was also cross elements, so he had to be sensing the energy crackling over her as easily as I could.

"I don't think I'm superior because of my affinity," she said in a voice that was menacing despite its low volume. "I am superior because I'm a master mage while you are nothing but a reneger."

The word crackled across the space between them, hitting Nik like a physical blow, although I'd never heard of a reneger before.

Both his hands balled into fists, but he said nothing. When the silence grew too painful, I hurried to fill it.

"I like Ostaria, but I'm also happy to leave since Miranda's no longer here. Grey will have headed north toward Calista, so we should go north as well. We might be able to catch up to them."

Amara spun to face me, looking displeased. Nik flinched slightly in response, a subtle gesture I nearly missed.

"Why would he have gone north?" he asked in his most scoffing tone. "Haven't I already told you to forget about Calista?"

"Are you saying you tracked him south?" I asked disbelievingly.

"I'll be leaving by the south gate at dawn," he replied.

"If I could believe that, we wouldn't have to leave at all," Amara muttered.

Nik gave her a challenging look. "Are you calling me a liar?" His eyes flicked briefly to me at the end of his sentence, but I couldn't read the expression in them.

Amara also looked at me, taking in my confused face before turning back to Nik.

"Before today, the thought would never have occurred to me. But finding you here like this..." She trailed off, her eyes narrowing before she began a new sentence. "North does seem a more logical direction for Grey to go."

"Are you saying you believe this nonsense about Grey abducting

Tartorans on behalf of Calista? If so, by all means, assume he's fleeing north to his home." He sounded both disgusted and unsurprised.

Amara drew in a long breath, settling back to her usual self, although her face was still steely and her eyes sharp.

"If Grey is truly abducting people, then of course I don't think Calista is behind it."

I frowned, surprised by the strength of their conviction on the matter. Who else could Grey be working for?

"You can stay here or go south, whichever you prefer," Amara continued. "It's no business of ours. We will go north as soon as possible."

I bit my lip. If Nik had really tracked Grey south, then that's the direction we should be moving. But what if Grey had gone south temporarily just to throw off any observers? Regardless of his kingdom of origin, it still made most sense for him to be moving north. What was there south except the endless ocean?

Amara looked at my face and sighed. "If you really want to find Grey and your friend, this is for the best anyway. Nikolas can check south, and we'll look for Grey on the northern road. If we see any sign of him, we can report it immediately."

I wanted to protest. If the matter could be resolved just by reporting Grey, we would have done it already. But I could tell it wasn't the moment for objections. Amara had clearly made up her mind, and I was already in a shaky position given my secret nighttime activities.

"Do as you wish," Nik said tightly.

He looked from Amara to me, and I wondered if I was imagining a softening in his expression. The fingers of his left hand brushed across the knuckles of his right, touching the place where his injury had been.

"Thank you," he muttered, and I blinked twice, wondering if I'd misheard.

"You're...welcome," I finally managed to say, and he nodded once.

"Take care, healer."

Again I was too astonished to properly reply until he'd already wheeled around, the moment passing. He stalked away, not bothering to offer a farewell to Amara.

I watched him go, trying to understand what had just happened. It certainly didn't seem the right time to ask Amara for her impressions.

Ember gave a sharp bark, and Amara nodded.

"I agree. It's time we were home in the safety and comfort of the inn."

"I don't think that's what she was...I mean, yes, I agree," I corrected myself hurriedly.

Amara gave a tired laugh. "Oh relax, child, I don't intend to bite you— however displeased with you I currently am."

I nodded vigorously and fell in silently behind her as she led the way back toward the inn. Several times she looked back at me, sighing and opening her mouth as if to speak. But each time she decided against it, waiting to begin until we were both wrapped up in front of the fire with a cup of hot tea.

I expected a lecture, but instead she just looked at me.

"I suppose you have questions," she said. "I have some too."

"What's a reneger?" I asked, the query bursting out of me and taking us both by surprise.

"Of everything that happened, that's what you're most curious about?" She sounded amused, and I was glad to recover a more familiar atmosphere between us.

"I don't think I've ever heard the word before."

"It isn't needed often, I'm glad to say." She sighed heavily. "A reneger is someone who abandoned their apprenticeship, never completing their training. There are mechanisms in place for replacing a master in the case of injury, illness, or neglect of duties, but to abandon an apprenticeship completely..." She shook her head. "Reneging on your apprenticeship is utterly forbidden, and being a reneger means being an outcast from both the law and society."

I stared at her, a number of things about Nik making more sense in light of her words. A shiver ran over me at the thought of what it would be like to be so completely cast out.

"Is that why he's so determined to catch Grey?" I asked, mostly to myself. "Does he hope to win back a place in society by completing a great service to the kingdom?"

Amara shook her head. "I'm sure he knows better. A reneger can't come back just by accomplishing good deeds. The law has imposed the harshest of penalties for reneging in order to act as a deterrent. Otherwise young people would be abandoning unfavorable apprenticeships all the time. And that would be dangerous for everyone. Without proper training, a person's power becomes a threat to themselves and to others. And this is one case where the privilege of the strong is no assistance. The more powerful someone is, the greater the possibility of danger."

I remembered the power Nik had demonstrated and blanched. He must have been activated by a master mage—so how had he come to leave such a prestigious apprenticeship? Was the reason he hadn't reported Grey to the authorities that the authorities were after him too?

Amara sighed again. "I would like to think Nikolas was interested in redemption, but there's only one way to regain your previous status after becoming a reneger. You must return to your abandoned master and complete your apprenticeship." She looked at me. "Do you really think the man you met has the necessary humility for such an undertaking?"

I grimaced, not needing to answer what was clearly a rhetorical question.

"So why is he so determined to catch Grey if he'll remain an outcast afterward?" I asked.

Amara shrugged. "I have no idea. We were never close given he's fifteen years my junior."

"But you know him." I watched her face closely.

She kept her gaze on the dancing flames. "He wasn't studying at the Guild while I was there, of course. He was a young child in my student days. But even then, he was considered one of the kingdom's most promising future mages."

"Then why—" I began, but she cut me off.

"What I'm more interested in is you, Delphine. Since you're my responsibility."

I gulped, effectively distracted from my question.

"Why didn't you tell me what was going on?" she asked, and I winced at the disappointment in her tone. It hurt far more than any lecture could have.

"I was going to tell you. In fact, I was planning to tell you tonight." I paused, aware of how weak the excuse sounded. Especially since I'd used it before. With a deep breath, I hurried on. "The truth is that I thought you'd do exactly what you are doing and hurry us out of Ostaria if I told you. And I didn't want to leave while Miranda was still here."

I expected her to reprimand me, but instead she looked guilty which only had the effect of making me feel worse.

"I know you're just thinking of my safety," I added. "And I know it's your job to watch over me for as long as I'm your apprentice. But for me, rescuing my friend is worth taking some risks."

Amara sighed. "The sentiment does your heart credit—if not your good sense. I'm sorry that we can't think alike in this, but at the end of the day, I'm the master and you're the apprentice. It's up to me to make the decisions."

She rubbed the back of her neck, her lips compressing into a thin line. "If both Nikolas and Grey have left Ostaria, we could stay after all."

I made a small noise of protest, and she met my gaze.

"Despite what Nikolas said, you still think Grey's gone north?"

"I think it's a real possibility."

She shook her head. "Fine, then. We'll compromise. We'll head north which is away from Nikolas, at least. The last thing you need is to get tangled up with a reneger. And on the way we can look for signs of Grey." She gave me a stern look. "Not that I want you investigating him on your own."

I nodded enthusiastically. "I can agree to that. I swear I won't go out looking for him alone."

Amara's suspicious gaze went to Ember who was pacing the length of the room, clearly unsettled.

"Ember doesn't count," she said, and I laughed.

"Foxes and all other animals do not count," I agreed, and we finished the evening with shared laughter—the last thing I'd expected when she dragged me home.

# CHAPTER
# NINETEEN

In the end it took us several days to leave Ostaria. During that time, Amara appeared to have genuinely forgiven my deception. When I had agreed to my activation, I had known I was putting myself under her authority for two years, and she had confirmed her position in the hierarchy. But she had also been reasonable, consultative, and forgiving—treating me like a member of her team rather than a mindless inferior. And, as always, I couldn't help comparing her to my father.

I had been a child in his care, but I had also been a person, and he had denied me the right to have a voice in my own life. The comparison made me angry, but it also made me feel guilty. When I had deceived Amara, she had forgiven me—shown me kindness even. Was I going to take her gracious example and spurn it?

But no matter how many times I resolved to forgive my father and let the past go, I couldn't shake the bitterness of his betrayal. In the same way that the good memories of his love and care stopped me from seeing him as a monster, the enormity of his betrayal stopped me from embracing the future I had once imagined for myself.

All I could do was hope that time would help—or at least that it would reveal a different, better future.

We visited Clay several times. He was dismayed at our early departure and was clearly aware there was a reason behind it. He didn't push Amara to explain, however, instead clearing his schedule for us. At the bookstore, he chose anatomy books for my future studies, and at his clinic, he helped me practice basic control exercises.

Thankfully Amara was true to her word and the books were stored with our luggage, all our immediate focus remaining on the development of my control. As well as working with Clay, she took me along to a second testing day at a different school, and by the end of it I could identify the feel of a seed's strength without needing to refer to the official tester.

I even managed to find the orphan boy from the first school and conduct a hurried introduction with the stablemaster at the inn. The man's words were gruff, but the boy didn't seem in the least daunted, instead appearing delighted to be surrounded by horses. Neither of them noticed when I slipped away, and I took it as a hopeful sign.

Whenever we walked the streets of the city, coming and going from lessons or errands, I caught myself watching for Nik out of the corner of my eye. It was foolish, since he was long gone from Ostaria, but I couldn't shake the instinct.

In the end, I was grateful when we finally rode out on Amara's small cart. I would likely never see Nik again, and I needed to leave thoughts of him behind and focus on my studies instead. When I next encountered Grey, I wasn't going to be weak and helpless.

Ember perked up when we left the city walls and entered the countryside. Seeing the change in her made me nervous. I'd grown used to her warmth by my side, but I couldn't stop her from returning to her natural habitat if she wished to do so.

I slept restlessly the first night on the road, but when I woke in the morning, Ember was still curled at my side, her nose toward the dying fire.

"I think she's too attached to you to leave at this point," Amara said as we packed up camp and climbed back into the cart, the sleeping fox curled among the bags.

"Is it wrong of me to keep her?" I asked, plagued with guilt now that I'd gotten my wish.

"It would be if you tried to keep her by force. But if she chooses to stay, there's no reason for you to feel guilty."

I frowned at the horizon. Her words sounded good, but was it as simple as that?

I tried to put my worries into words. "I've healed her several times now— and most of those were injuries she received because of me. If I accidentally bound her to me with my power, is that really her free choice?"

Amara frowned sideways at me, clearly considering her answer.

"It does you credit that you're concerned about it. But remember the state she was in when we first found her. She would have died without your intervention."

"Are you saying she owes me her life?"

Amara shook her head. "Not that, exactly. I'm saying that her only options were death or a connection with you. Surely you don't think the former would be a better option?" She smiled down at me, and I reluctantly smiled back.

"No, I guess not."

Amara paused, looking at me again. "Maybe it's time for the speech."

"Speech?" I stared at her.

She grimaced. "Apparently I should have given it to you in our first lesson—yet another of the ways I'm deficient as the master of a healing apprentice, as Clay pointed out to me."

"I'd rather be your apprentice than anyone else's—even Master Clay," I said, earning a smile from Amara. "So what's this speech given to all healing apprentices?"

"I'll probably get the exact words wrong," she said ruefully, "but it boils down to the fact that the power inside you has the ability to both heal and destroy in equal measure."

"We're called healers," I said in a subdued tone, "but people with my affinity also make the best assassins."

Amara's lips pressed together. "Exactly. You wield the power of life and death more directly than the other affinities. Apparently that ability can go to some people's heads."

"You mean they become dangerous?" I asked.

She frowned. "It's more complex than that. Many healers spend their whole adulthood saving lives, and it's an admirable pursuit. But it's admirable because every life is unique and valuable. Saving lives doesn't give you a right to those lives—and it doesn't give you credit in some invisible ledger."

"Invisible ledger?" I blinked at her.

She laughed. "That bit was confusing to me, too. But I gather there have been cases the healing affinity doesn't like to talk about publicly. Cases where healers felt that the lives they had saved gave them the right to take other lives—as if they were exchangeable, a life for a life."

I sucked in a breath. "That's horrible! You don't need to worry about that. I'm definitely not about to go on a killing spree—no matter how many people I may one day save."

"I'm glad to hear it," Amara said in a tone that was a little too serious. "It would reflect badly on me as your influencer."

I snorted. "Yes, the one and only problem with that scenario."

She smiled, but after a moment, grew more somber. "In all seriousness, though, I think it applies in this case as well since the principle goes both ways. When you heal someone, it's a gift given in the moment. Just as you don't have any claim to the rest of that person's life—or anyone else's in exchange—you also aren't responsible for anything they may choose to do afterward. You didn't impose a burden on Ember, you gave a gift, and she chose her response. Don't take away the value of her choice by trying to take responsibility for it."

I considered her words in silence.

"Well," I said at last, "consider me suitably humbled."

Amara chuckled. "Oh no, you're much too young for that. I'm sure it will take at least another ten years before you can make such a claim. Maybe twenty."

I laughed back. "So I need to be roughly your age to achieve true humility?"

She winked. "Naturally. Whatever age I am at the time, of course. When you reach my current age, you'll find you still need another ten or so years."

"I can only be grateful I have such an example to aspire to," I said with enough gravity that we both laughed again.

"With that out of the way," she said when our mirth subsided, "I want you to spend our travel time focusing on identifying people and animals around us. It isn't something healers usually do because most aren't strong enough for it, but it will help you develop your control and hone your senses."

I happily agreed to such a reasonable request and spent the next weeks doing exactly as she'd asked. We traveled northeast along the road that ran beside the Celadon, sleeping in the open or in hay barns we found along the way.

Our progress was slow since we stopped in every hamlet or village even vaguely close to the road. None of them were large enough to have an inn, but most of them were familiar with Amara and had requests to make of her.

She used her elements power freely when asked to do so, accepting whatever gifts of food and provisions were offered in exchange. But I noticed that she spent more of her time training the villagers than performing acts beyond their ability. Although she was powerful herself, she seemed to have mastered many of the ways that someone with a weaker elements seed could maximize the use of what power they had.

"If I can help in the moment, of course I'm happy to do so," she told me when I finally asked her about it. We were packing up camp in the morning, and she continued working as she spoke. "There are plenty of things that can only be done by a stronger ability. But I can't be in every village on every day. My dream is to always leave a community more capable than when I arrived."

"It's an admirable dream." I thrust away the inevitable thoughts of a father who'd wanted to cripple rather than empower me. "But shouldn't the villagers be learning those skills from their activators? Isn't that the point of the apprentice system?"

"That's the theory behind it," she said. "And it works well in the bigger population centers. But in the more remote regions, there are many people who never travel at all—sometimes whole communities of people have never been further than the closest trading center. So their knowledge pool never grows. They miss new developments and often have a limited knowledge pool to begin with."

I climbed onto the cart, musing on her words. The picture she painted was a familiar one since my own family had never traveled beyond our small town. If there was something that could be accomplished by my parents' abilities that was unknown to the farmers of Tarin, how would they ever learn of it?

"That was the life I was choosing," I murmured. "I might have lived my whole life without traveling beyond Tarin."

"But you didn't." Amara settled beside me and signaled to Acorn to get moving.

The horse lumbered into a slow walk, and I spoke quietly, almost under my breath.

"Because you came. I didn't live that life because you came."

"No." She looked across at me. "Because you chose something different."

"But also because you came."

"But also because I came," she conceded, a distant look in her eyes. "And that's why I do it. That's why I'm a traveling master. Because sometimes, someone has to come."

She turned and looked at me, and something passed between us—something heavy that I didn't yet have the courage to name. Shaking my head slightly, I reminded myself that I still had almost two years of being an apprentice, and that Amara herself was still young. She wouldn't be retiring any time soon, so there was no reason to get maudlin and start thinking about passing of torches and other such foolishness.

The day was a sunny one, and it was no hardship to turn my mind to my training. The time passed quickly as I identified the various animals around us. Not being near any larger villages, we barely passed any other travelers, but we found a stream in the late afternoon and made camp beside it.

I prepared the fire pit, proudly coaxing a flame into life. Once it had taken hold of the branches, I sat back and smiled at the friendly warmth. I might not be able to control fire, as Amara could, but the impact of her influence left it feeling like a pleasant and welcome companion.

At first I had complained that it was pointless for me to learn how to start a fire when Amara could produce flames from her fingers. But she had rightly pointed out that I wouldn't always be with her. She seemed to think she would be remiss in her training if I didn't learn how to properly prepare, start, maintain, and douse a campfire—a different skill from managing the fire in the fireplace at home.

"Look at you, ready to set off on your own." Amara sank down beside me with a weary sigh.

I snorted. "Hardly that. But you were right—I'm glad to know how to manage a fire. Just like I'm glad to be immune to minor burns thanks to your cross influence." I looked ruefully down at the hand I had absentmindedly used to adjust a burning branch.

"Make sure you say that to Clay next time you see him," she said smugly.

I sighed, thoughts of Clay bringing a reminder of all the comforts of Ostaria. They seemed a long time ago now. "I wonder if I'll ever see him again."

"Of course you will!" Amara pulled out the ingredients for the evening meal. "I have a fondness for Ostaria, so we'll definitely be back. You still have nearly two years of your apprenticeship, remember."

I looked at her out the corner of my eye. Was it the city or the master healing mage she had a fondness for? As usual, her face gave me no clue as to whether any warmer feelings lay beneath her words.

I yawned widely, although I'd done little in the way of physical activity all day. When I yawned again, even more widely, both the ground beneath me and the air around me seemed to tremble slightly in time with my body.

But when I stilled, the rumbling continued.

I turned to Amara to find her staring upstream, her body and face frozen. The sound grew and intensified, cracking and rushing as if we were camped next to a raging river instead of a sleepy stream.

"Amara?" I said just as the trees along the stream were hit by a wave that appeared to be made more of dirt and logs than water.

"Amara!" I screamed as the debris-filled water rushed toward us.

I jumped to my feet, but the flood had already crossed most of the remaining distance. Within seconds, it would crash over us, Acorn, and even our cart.

I gasped, scooping up Ember from next to the fire and leaping the short distance to Acorn. Throwing my arms around her neck, I braced my legs wide. Shielding Ember between us, I waited as a second passed and then another. Nothing hit us.

Breathing raggedly, I turned around.

Amara still sat where I had left her, her brow furrowed and her hands in her lap. The water and debris had shifted, however.

Instead of bearing toward us in a wide wave, the flood had narrowed, its level rising to tower over me but its edges confined to the stream bed. My mouth fell open as I watched the unnatural phenomenon of a tower of dirty water raging past me.

I stretched out one arm, ready to dip my fingers into the passing water.

"Don't!" Amara snapped, making me snatch my arm back.

She finally moved, giving me an exasperated look. "Can't you see how much debris is in there? Do you want one of your fingers broken from a passing branch? I've had to channel a lot of force into that flow. It's moving quickly."

"You did this?" I asked, although the answer was obvious.

Amara didn't answer, her gaze growing distant. I slowly sank back into my previous position beside the fire, marveling at the power Amara had to be using to divert an entire flood.

Gradually the height of the towering river rushing past us lessened, indicating less water was being channeled along the bed of the stream.

Amara spoke again, sounding less strained. "It's reached the river and is dissipating. The Celadon is large enough here to absorb it, but I need to guide it some way downriver, just to make sure it doesn't cause unforeseen problems."

I held my breath, not wanting to disturb her in any way. Elements mages meddled with the natural environment, and they had to be as careful of unforeseen consequences as healers had to be of accidentally stopping someone's heart with a stray thought.

Eventually the color of the passing water began to clear, the height of the stream returning to only twice its usual flow. Amara gave a sigh and relaxed, her shoulders slumping.

I gulped, trying to find my voice. "Did we nearly just die?"

Amara rolled her shoulders, stretching herself slowly.

"Hardly. I'm an elements mage, remember. If I hadn't been distracted talking to you and preparing the meal, I would have sensed the water coming even sooner. As it was, we were never in any danger."

I pressed my hand to my racing heart. Apparently my body hadn't quite absorbed that message yet.

Slowly my calm returned, however, and I noticed that the animals were entirely unalarmed. Apparently I was the only one who had given in to terror.

"I think your healing cross influence has rubbed off on Acorn or something," I said. "She doesn't seem like an ordinary horse. Aren't horses supposed to have excellent senses? But she didn't even seem to notice the flood. She wasn't bothered by it at all."

"We've always gotten on well." Amara smiled at the horse affectionately. "But she's changed since your arrival. I've noticed animals are much less likely to panic in the presence of a healing mage. Did you even notice that your instinct was to run to the animals?"

I blinked. Wasn't that the natural thing to do?

"Let me guess." Amara grinned at me. "You're thinking that anyone would do the same? I can promise that's not the case. Our seeds affect us from birth —to the point where it's hard to even imagine seeing life through a different lens from the one given by our affinity."

"Oh." I considered her words. "But in this case, a little concern wouldn't have been out of place. We got lucky. If you weren't an elements mage, we could all be dead right now. Where did the flood even come from? It hasn't rained for two days."

"That is a very good question." Amara turned stern eyes upstream.

"What do we do now?" I asked. "Surely we can't just make camp as if nothing happened?"

"No." Amara sounded slightly dangerous, her words carrying some of the lingering power that had diverted a flood. "We need to find out exactly what is going on here."

CHAPTER

# TWENTY

It didn't take us long to douse the fledgling fire and repack our belongings. We had camped between the stream and a dirt track that branched off from the main road and disappeared uphill. It seemed the logical path to take, but we couldn't follow it for long. Beyond our campsite, it had been washed away by the flood, leaving only muddy ground littered with branches and rocks.

Amara stopped to survey the sodden earth ahead, her hand resting lightly on Acorn's mane. She had chosen to walk beside the horse's head rather than take her usual place in the cart, and I felt awkward holding the reins in her stead.

Glad for the excuse, I clambered down and joined her in front of the cart. "A plants mage would be helpful about now. There's no way Acorn can pull the cart through that. The wheels would get bogged almost immediately."

"Are you sure a plants mage is what's needed?" Amara asked in a light tone that seemed out of place in the situation.

I frowned at her. She had to be tired after her earlier feat—was she getting lightheaded? Should I suggest she sit down?

She met my concerned look with an amused smile, nodding toward the wheels of the cart. I looked down and gasped.

Instead of resting on the ground, as they usually did, all four wheels were floating about an inch above the dirt.

"What...is that?" I asked in a strangled voice.

Amara laughed. "Elements mage, remember?"

I had a sudden memory of Nik accusing Amara of being a typical elements mage who thought her affinity was the greatest of the three. It had seemed unfair at the time, but her grin told me even Amara couldn't escape traces of the infamous elements arrogance. I rolled my eyes.

Amara continued to smile. "Consider this another impromptu lesson. Your power is useless to connect with anything outside the bounds of your affinity, but that doesn't make you powerless. It just means you need to find a different way to achieve your ends. Here, it may have been logical to wish for a plants mage to harden the mud, but it's not the only possible solution. I've put a small cushion of air under each wheel which should allow them to skate across the top of the muck. The flood moved through quickly enough that the bog shouldn't be too deep. As long as Acorn can make it, we'll be fine." She looked at the mud ahead, and her expression turned rueful. "I hope you don't mind walking through that, though. We probably shouldn't add to the cart's weight unnecessarily."

"Never mind me! Amara, even the strongest mages have limits. Your power isn't endless, and you just stopped a flood. You're going to collapse if you try too much."

She laughed. "Thank you for your concern, but I'll be fine. I was a master long before you were even ready for activation. I know my own limits well enough."

I examined her, looking for any hidden signs of exhaustion, but she looked as relaxed and confident as ever.

"Well...if you're sure," I said hesitantly.

She shook her head. "Anyone would think you were the master and I the apprentice. Come on, let's get moving. It's only getting darker."

She patted Acorn on her flank, and she lurched into movement. The cart slid easily behind her, Ember perched on the seat, ears up and tail high, as if she were the driver.

I smothered a laugh, unable to properly process the surreal scene. After a moment I hurried forward myself, though, not wanting to be left behind.

The mud was sticky, making each step difficult, and I had to pay attention to the ground in the gathering gloom, trying to avoid obstacles that might trip me up and send me face first into the muck. My calves and thighs were soon burning, and by the time we saw lights ahead, my eyes ached from squinting in the near darkness.

"Aha!" Amara's voice floated back to my position at the rear of the cart.

I mustered the energy to increase my pace enough to join her by Acorn's head. As soon as I reached her, the questions died on my lips.

Before us was the obvious cause of the flood.

We had been moving slowly uphill, but here the land sloped more steeply upward, and at the top was the remnants of what had once been a dam. A poorly constructed one from the looks of it.

"The villagers are fortunate their houses are on the high ground above the dam," Amara said in a neutral voice. "Otherwise they would all have been swept away when it burst."

"But we weren't so fortunate!" I cried, not as capable of taking an objective view of the situation. "We only survived because of you. If it had been any other travelers instead of us …"

"Yes." Her tone hinted at emotion behind the calm after all. "And that's why we'll be having an urgent conversation with the villagers before the night is over."

I winced, my sympathy taking an abrupt swing toward the unknown villagers. Their bad night was about to get a lot worse.

It took us a while to pick our way up the final slope and around the edges of the dam and what remained of the lake behind it. But as soon as were past, the path appeared again. A soft thump told me Amara had released the air cushions on the wheels, and I gave her another surreptitious examination, trying to work out how close she was to the edge.

She still gave no sign of being any more tired than usual, however. There was no hint of hesitation in her stride as she marched into the middle of the village.

We were spotted immediately. The villagers were all outside already, standing huddled around lanterns, their faces full of fear, confusion, and anxiety.

"Who's in charge here?" Amara called in a loud voice, and the people exchanged panicked looks.

After a long moment, a young man stepped forward.

"Our village is too small to have a mayor or official leader. Whatever you have to say you can say to all of us."

Amara took her time, letting her eyes roam over the crowd.

"Then I assume you'll all be taking responsibility for what just happened? I've seen the dam you built, and I feel certain the proper construction permissions were skipped."

Murmurs swept the group at her words, and several people broke off the fringes of the small crowd to disappear into the nearby homes. The young man who had spoken earlier looked undaunted, however, and I couldn't help admiring his courage.

"You can see the size of our village for yourself," he said. "Construction permission from the crown requires consultation with a plants mage. Do we look like we could afford that?"

Amara's eyes roamed over the crowd again, this time moving further to examine their houses and the livestock fenced nearby.

"It's a small village, certainly, but you look prosperous enough." She tilted her head, her gaze piercing and attitude authoritative, and I saw the man flinch.

But he quickly rallied. "Only because we built the dam! Before it, we were struggling to survive. To afford the funds for proper construction, we first needed the wealth the dam brought. It was an impossible situation. What were we to do?"

Amara didn't soften. "Seek consultation with a plants mage post construction, of course."

"But that would be admitting what we did!" a woman called in protest. "And why should we do that when we're so out of the way here that no representatives of the crown ever pass through?"

"The king isn't uncaring toward his people," Amara said sternly. "He doesn't require mage consultation because he wishes to drain the coffers of his people. Mages need to be involved in such large-scale construction projects because a poorly built dam is a danger to more than just its creators. You were fortunate that it burst when there was an elements mage downstream, or you would have had deaths on your conscience as well as illegal construction."

"A mage?" The cry rang out from several lips. "You're a mage?"

Everyone moved back, the ring of empty space around us growing until the young man was the only one still facing us. He no longer looked confident now, his face equal parts guilty and fearful.

"We truly meant no harm," he said.

Amara sighed, her straight posture softening. "That, at least, I believe. I've already examined what remains of your dam, and for now there is no further danger."

"You did?" I whispered from just behind her. "But how can you tell? You're not—"

"A plants mage? No." She glanced back at me. "I have no special insight into the rock of the dam wall, but I can sense the water it's supposed to be holding back. It's telling me there are no further cracks that will let anything through. What remains in the lake will stay there for now. We can safely sleep for the night and look more closely in the morning."

"You intend to stay here for the night?" the young man asked cautiously, having overheard her words.

"Naturally." Amara raised an eyebrow, daring him to object. He didn't.

"Was there anyone downstream when it burst?" she asked after a moment of silence. "If you have anyone dangerously ill or injured, my apprentice is a healer. She's inexperienced but strong, and she'll do her best if the situation is urgent."

I gulped, fixing my eyes on his face as I waited for what I hoped was a negative response. It took him a moment to reply, however, looking between us in confusion.

"She's your apprentice? And she's a healer?"

"Yes, yes," Amara said, weariness showing for the first time. "She's cross influenced. That is hardly the most noteworthy thing happening here. Do you have need of her services?"

The man focused on me, sounding a little dazed. "Not immediately, no. I don't know of any urgent need."

"Good." Amara echoed my own sentiment completely. "In that case, we'll sleep."

I moved a step closer, being as surreptitious as I could. I didn't want to get my head snapped off for hovering, but when Amara stumbled slightly over a stone, I couldn't help bracing her under her elbow. Sure enough, it earned me a reproving look.

"I'm not about to collapse, Delphine. You don't need to look so worried."

"Sorry, Master Amara." I grinned, unrepentant. "I can't help it."

The young man bowed. "Master Amara? And Apprentice Delphine? I'm sorry we didn't do proper introductions. My name is Sarn."

"I wish I could say it was nice to meet you," Amara said, "but that doesn't seem quite appropriate in the circumstances."

He flinched, and I took pity on him. "Is there somewhere we can sleep tonight? And somewhere we can put our horse?"

"Of course!" Sarn leaped into action, seeming much more comfortable with something to do.

Whether because of Amara's status, or because they were trying to win us over, the villagers decided we should have a house to ourselves. The residents vacated it before we arrived, leaving a clean home with two bedrooms for our sole use. I expected Amara to protest since she didn't usually stand on ceremony, no matter who she was dealing with. But she accepted the empty house without comment, even allowing Sarn to care for and feed Acorn in her stead.

As soon as we were alone, I put my hands on my hips and stared her down. "Admit it—you're tired."

She laughed and sat down in front of the hot meal that had been left on the table for us.

"You're persistent, I'll give you that."

"Why are we here in this empty house, playing at being grand, important mages, unless it's because you're exhausted?" I sat down across from her, fixing her with an accusing look.

She sighed, chewing slowly before responding. "I have no interest in pomp and formality if the point is to make me feel superior. But this situation is different. These villagers are living such a remote life, they've lost all respect for the crown. But as you've seen today, there's a very important reason why mages have to be involved in all major public construction. As well as a plants mage to help with the dam's construction, there should have been an elements mage to assess the impact of a dam in this location. The reason the Triumvirate is given an almost equal footing in governance as the king is because the services the Guild renders the kingdom are so essential. Guild mages might be hidebound and self-important—but that's because they *are* important, and they know it."

I blinked. "Was that a compliment or criticism? I'm not sure."

Amara took another large bite, a smile tugging at the corners of her mouth. "The Mages' Guild can't be all bad. I'm a member, after all."

I snorted but left her in peace to eat, keeping a close eye on her while she did so. She might be claiming she had no excessive fatigue, but her actions told a different story. After eating slowly, she announced she was going straight to bed, despite the early hour. I followed her lead, and we both slept solidly, glad for the proper beds.

In the morning I woke to an older lady delivering a breakfast feast. Amara slept through the noise, so I ate quickly and slipped outside into the morning sun with only Ember for company.

No one was waiting to greet me, so I wandered through the village alone. It was more of a hamlet than a village, considerably smaller than Tarin. But the buildings were well-maintained and, most importantly, the animals all looked well cared for and plump.

I greeted several donkeys, half a dozen horses, five cows, and an untold number of chickens as I strolled from pen to pen. The birds reacted to my presence with alarm, despite my ability, presumably because of the fox padding silently beside me. The larger animals were unbothered by Ember, though, coming forward to nudge at me or sniff me.

A particularly proud looking stallion put his head on my shoulder, making me laugh.

"I approve of you, too, fine sir." I patted his long neck.

While I was still standing, mostly obscured by the horse, three villagers walked up to the next pen over.

"What terrible luck that a Guild mage was passing by just when the dam burst," one of them said glumly.

"Hush!" another snapped. "If it had been anyone else, they'd be dead right now, and then we'd really be in trouble. We should be grateful for our good luck that she's an elements mage."

"The important thing is that King Marius is going to find out about us," the third said. "And then his pet mages will no doubt extort every last coin we have."

"Hush!" the second speaker snapped again. "Do you want to get us in worse trouble if someone overhears you? It's bad enough there'll be more mages coming. We should send Callum up to the far pastures to watch the sheep until they're gone."

I frowned, trying to peer around the horse without being seen. Who was Callum and why did he need to be sent away? Was he a criminal they were concealing from the law?

The first speaker sucked in her breath sharply. "Goodness, yes! We need to keep him out of sight completely. I'll speak to his mother today. She's already anxious enough, poor thing. He'll have to go to the Mages' Guild for training eventually, and that's far enough away. She'd be heartbroken if the crown let Calista steal him away forever. How that man can call himself our king when he favors foreigners over his own people, I don't know."

"How many times do I have to tell you not to talk like that?" the second speaker scolded. "At least restrain yourself until the strangers are gone."

I bit my lip. Callum was a youngster, then? One with a strong seed from the sound of it.

Ember growled quietly at my feet, and I looked down to find her staring at the three villagers. I shushed her, afraid she'd draw attention to us, but the trio was already moving off.

I left as soon as they disappeared from sight, returning to the house where I'd left Amara. Concern over what I'd heard sped my gait, and it didn't take long to get there. I found her waiting for me outside, with Sarn in tow, so I had to put the matter aside for the moment. I didn't want to bring it up with any of the villagers around.

Amara surveyed the suspiciously empty village around us with a raised eyebrow. "Scared, are they?" she asked Sarn, but she sounded more amused than offended.

The long sleep had softened her attitude—yet another confirmation that she had been more tired the night before than she'd let on.

"You wanted to examine the dam more closely?" Sarn asked, wisely ignoring her question.

Amara confirmed it, but Sarn didn't move immediately, his uneasy gaze on Ember.

"Don't worry about her," I said. "It's her bedtime anyway."

Almost as if she'd understood my words, Ember brushed against my leg before trotting straight for the door. Amara had left it partially open, so the fox disappeared out of sight inside. Sarn watched her go with a crease in his brow, but he shook it off without speaking and gestured for us to follow him.

It was only a short walk to the artificial lake and the half-destroyed dam wall.

"Did you say the water *told* you the dam was secure?" I asked Amara when we reached it.

Amara chuckled. "Not in so many words, of course. But I pressed the water against the remaining part of the wall with considerable force and not a drop passed through." She got a faraway look in her eyes before nodding once. "It's holding firm today as well. That's good news."

"What do you intend to do?" Sarn asked fearfully.

"I'll inform the Guild, of course." She gave him a compassionate look. "There's no other choice at this point. I'm not a plants mage, and you need one to give this structure a more thorough examination." She hesitated, gazing downstream. "I can include my assessment as an elements mage, at least, so you shouldn't need a second one of those. As the dam stood previously, you were diverting too much of the natural flow. You won't be able to build it as high again. But a smaller dam should be safe for this location."

Sarn's eyes brightened. "You think they'll let us keep a dam of some sort?"

"I can't guarantee it, but I'll speak for you in my report." She looked at the muddy swathe of ground that was still strewn with all sorts of debris. "If I were you, I would clean up the path before anyone arrives from the capital— there's no need to give a bad impression before they even reach the village."

Sarn eagerly agreed, guiding us back to the village where we discovered Acorn already harnessed to our cart. Ember was perched in the back, looking displeased but unharmed.

"You seem in a hurry to get rid of us," I said, making Sarn fall over himself with explanations.

He finished the speech by saying, "Of course if you want to stay, you'd be most welcome," all the while sounding terrified we might actually take him at his word.

I snorted. "Don't worry, we don't want to stay."

"We've added a bag of food to the back in thanks," he said hurriedly, trying to hide his relief.

Once we were back across the mud and on the main road again, I couldn't hold in the chuckles.

"Did you see his face?" I asked Amara. "He couldn't get rid of us quickly enough." Indignation rose inside me, driving away the laughter. "Hardly the gratitude you'd expect given you've promised to help them."

Amara sighed. "There will be consequences from the crown, I'm sure. I can't blame them for being worried and distracted."

I frowned, biting at my lip. "Did you hear them talking about King Marius at all?"

She looked across at me. "Did you? You shouldn't take it too seriously, if so. As I said, it's only human nature to be resentful when you're scared about your future."

I shook my head slowly. "I could understand negative comments about the construction policy, but that wasn't what concerned me. It sounded like the village has someone under seventeen who has tested with a mage level seed. They seemed to think that if the crown sent someone official to the village, that person would steal this child away and send them to Calista."

"What?" Amara stared at me. "Why would the crown or the Guild do such a thing?"

I shrugged. "It was an overheard conversation, and the villagers didn't go into detail. But I'm afraid Grey might have been through this hamlet at some point."

"You think he's been there?" Amara gazed doubtfully back toward the dirt track that led to the hamlet.

I grimaced. It did seem unlikely. "I suppose if he'd been through personally, they would know he's not affiliated with the Guild or its mages. But Grey must have taken this route at some point and visited some of the larger villages nearby. I suppose it's normal that rumors get distorted as they spread."

"So the locals know youths are disappearing, and they think they're going to Calista," Amara said slowly. "Just like you thought back in Ostaria."

I shrugged, feeling awkward. "I don't know if they're going to Calista for sure. I'm just worried they might be. You heard what Halmir said back in Tarin."

"Yes, I heard him." Amara sounded grim. "And now they're saying the same thing in this hamlet."

She fell into silence, and the expression on her face was so dark I didn't dare interrupt whatever thoughts were putting her in such a mood.

CHAPTER

# TWENTY-ONE

Neither of us mentioned the rumors again, keeping more silent than usual for the remaining two days before we reached Caltor. But my spirits lifted at the sight of the city walls, and Amara straightened beside me, as if experiencing a similar effect. We would both welcome a comfortable stay at a large inn.

Caltor was a similar size to Ostaria, and like the more southern city, it also sat on the eastern shore of the Celadon River. However, Caltor was located well above the place where the two northern branches of the river joined into a single flow. And since it was on the western branch, it was more centrally located than Ostaria. Given its proximity to the capital, its streets were even busier than its sister city.

According to Amara, it had seen considerable growth since the restoration of northern Calista, given it lay on one of the popular routes between Tarona and Calista's capital of Calinara. But I couldn't help wondering if its proximity to Calista also put it in more danger from Grey? I could only imagine he'd already visited the city—probably more than once.

The guards at the gate were more diligent than the Ostarian ones had been, eyeing us both suspiciously and examining the back of the cart. The sight of Ember, curled up and sleeping between two bags, made them raise their eyebrows, but neither protested her presence.

When we were finally waved into the city, I looked sideways at Amara. "Have they always been like that?"

She twisted to frown back at the gates. "Not from what I remember. That was a first."

We both lapsed back into silence, and my unease was quickly forgotten as I looked around me, eagerly taking in the sights of my second city. In many ways it reminded me of Ostaria. The houses had a similar design, and the cobblestoned streets were almost identical. But the stone used for construction was several shades darker than in Ostaria, giving the whole city a grimmer feel, and the awnings of the shops were all a uniform forest green.

Amara caught me looking at them and smiled.

"I have to admit, I prefer the cheerful chaos of Ostaria," she said. "Caltor has strict regulations on many things. The city officials like to keep a uniform appearance throughout the city."

"It looks grand," I said slowly, eyeing the gold trim on the closest awning, "and elegant. But I think I prefer all the bright colors of Ostaria as well."

"There are plenty of good people here, though," Amara said. "And even more master mages than in Ostaria since we're closer to the capital. I shouldn't have any trouble finding a healer to help with your learning while we're here."

"Will we be staying long?" I asked, my tone eager given the appearance of an inn of substantial size.

Amara grinned as she directed Acorn into the inn yard. "I've been missing proper beds and hot baths, too. I think we can manage an extended stay."

As in Ostaria, the innkeeper and his wife clearly knew Amara, showing her respect and deference, although they lacked the warmth and enthusiasm of the previous inn's owners.

"Let me guess," I said out the side of my mouth. "You haven't saved this inn from a fire yet."

Her mouth twitched, although she kept her eyes on the landlord. "Not yet," she whispered back.

When the innkeeper's wife bustled away to greet another new arrival, I heard her using the title Master. I twisted to look at the older man but could see nothing remarkable about his appearance beyond the quality of his clothing. Amara had just told me there were more master mages in Caltor, and her words were already being proved true. Their presence made Amara's status stand out less which had to be another factor in the attitude of the innkeeper.

We were still shown to a comfortable room, however, and a box was provided for Ember without protest. When we discussed our next movements, Amara mentioned several mages she knew in the city.

"We should visit the healers at some point," she said, "but I'm not taking you to the hospital yet. Or even to an animal clinic. I know you've been practicing a lot while we've been traveling, but I'm still not sure you're ready for it. For now, we can start with another non-medical aspect of your ability. That should give us a chance to check your progress."

"Another non-medical ability?" I tried to think what it could be.

"Truth telling." Amara didn't look up from where she was unpacking items of clothing from her personal bag.

"Oh yes, of course!" I sat up straighter. "How could I forget about that? It's the one aspect of our ability that even regular healers don't use physical contact for. A useful ability too." I frowned. "I can't say I've noticed it particularly, though. Should I have picked up some sense of it on my own? Everything else has bombarded me, whether I wanted it or not."

Amara glanced over at me, a smile spreading over her face. "I'll take that as a compliment."

I gave her a questioning look.

"If you haven't had any sense of it, it must be because I haven't been speaking any untruths. Don't you think you would have noticed if I was telling you lies?"

A warm feeling crept over me as I considered her words. I hadn't noticed any lies—which meant it wasn't only Amara who had been telling me the truth since our meeting. I shook my head, trying to suppress the pleasure. If Nik had been telling me the truth, that meant he was far away now, and irrelevant to my future. And regardless of his current location, it was pure foolishness to care about whether he'd been honest with me or not. Did it please me to know he had been honest when telling me to stay away from him?

"So how am I going to train in truth telling?" I asked, trying to stay on topic.

Amara turned from her bags, her side of the room neat and orderly. "I've been waiting for us to reach a city again so we could visit a law keeping hall. Smaller towns don't have halls but instead rely on their regular healers for urgent matters. But the cities and larger towns have their own law keeping facilities since they service not only their own area but also adjudicate any official cases brought in from the smaller towns. The law keeping hall of Caltor keeps more than one healer on staff just to truth tell. It's a good job for those with a lower level of power, since it doesn't require mage level strength."

"If strength isn't relevant, does that mean anyone who has the healing affinity can truth tell, no matter how weak they are?" I asked, trying to remember if I'd ever heard anyone talking about it on one of our infrequent trips into Tarin.

"To some extent they can." Amara rubbed the back of her neck. "But it's not entirely true that strength is irrelevant. I haven't experienced it myself, of course, but I'm told that the stronger the healer, the more clearly they can read the truth. It's not always a straightforward process, since the truth is rarely a simple, black and white thing."

I nodded, well able to imagine the sort of situations the law keeping hall might encounter. And even more complicated were the personal issues that would arise in a population where a third of the people had a healing affinity.

Unable to help myself, I wondered what I would have sensed from my father if I had been activated earlier. Did his ignorance about how healers managed squeamishness mean his words would have registered as truth?

"Of course, law keeping can't be achieved only by truth telling, unfortunately," Amara said, bringing my mind back to the present. "For one thing, healers can only detect if a person believes the truth of their own words, not if the words are actually true. Plus you have to know the right questions to ask the right people."

"It sounds like interesting work," I said thoughtfully.

Amara's words made it clear a powerful healing seed like mine would be wasted in the role. It was a pity the things I was more interested in doing— testing seeds and truth telling—were able to be done by those with weaker seeds.

"We'll go to the law keeping hall in the morning," Amara said, breaking through my thoughts. "So get a good sleep tonight."

Of course, since she'd instructed me to sleep well, deep rest eluded me. I tossed and turned for most of the night, my thoughts a jumble of the new town, the promised lesson, and guilt that I still hadn't located Miranda.

The villagers from the hamlet seemed to fear Grey, but did that actually mean he'd passed their way? Nik had tracked Grey south on this occasion, at least, so shouldn't I have found a way to convince Amara to go south as well? Had I placed too much reliance on my own certainty he was moving north?

When morning finally arrived, I got up eagerly, ready for any distraction to chase the fruitless thoughts from my mind. Amara took credit for my enthusiasm and obligingly finished her breakfast and morning routine quickly. In the end, we made such good time that the law keeping hall was only just opening as we arrived.

We entered a spacious marble entrance hall and were greeted by the bored-looking clerk reigning over the lone counter.

"Are you here regarding an existing case or a new one?" he asked, keeping his attention on Amara.

"Neither," she said, making him frown.

"Fines apply for wasting law keepers' time." He spoke in a bored voice, as if reciting from a rule book. "Law keepers may not be used to resolve personal quarrels and are not available to answer questions unrelated to a new or existing case. Unless a crime has been committed, you cannot—"

"Does Anka still work here?" Amara asked, cutting off his monologue.

A gleam of interest entered the clerk's eyes for the first time. He re-examined Amara before turning to me, as if I might hold a clue to our identity.

"You're here to see the head of the hall? Do you have an appointment with Master Anka?" he asked.

"No, we've only just arrived in Caltor." Amara sounded as relaxed as always. "But if you could let her know Amara is here to see her, I'm sure she'll make time for us."

"*Master* Amara?" The clerk's eyebrows shot up to his hairline. "*The* Master Amara?"

She smiled broadly. "I'm not aware of another one."

"If you'll wait right here, I'll be back in just a moment." The man gave us a respectful bow and hurried down a nearby corridor.

I turned to Amara, regarding her silently. It was being borne in on me that I had apprenticed with someone much more important and well-connected than I'd initially realized.

"Don't look at me like that," Amara said without turning. "Anka just happens to be my aunt."

"Your aunt?" My mouth fell open. "Why didn't you say anything?"

"It wasn't relevant before now. Were you expecting me to provide my apprentice with a litany of all my living relatives and their respective positions and affinities?"

"No, of course not. I just didn't realize..."

"That I'd have any important personages in my family tree?" She chuckled. "It does seem surprising given how weak and low ranked I am."

Her words drew out a laugh despite my surprise. "I wouldn't dare think anything so obviously untrue—as you well know. I suppose I hadn't thought about the possibility at all since I only have distant relatives myself. I've never met any of them, so I'm used to it just being Mother, Father, and me."

The clerk reappeared, so we let the conversation drop and obediently followed him into the bowels of the law keeping hall. I had been imagining it as an enormous dungeon, gray and dank, complete with chains hanging off the walls, but it was completely the opposite.

Light and airy, most of the walls were the same white marble as the reception hall, and none of the doors or windows I saw had bars. The long hallway was lined with small rooms, and the whole effect reminded me forcibly of Ostaria's hospital.

I threw Amara a questioning look and found her regarding me with amusement.

"You're thinking it looks like the hospital, aren't you?"

"Of course it does," said the clerk stiffly. "Both are public buildings."

"I haven't decided if reusing the styling and plans was a purposeful choice or merely a cheap one," Amara said. "But the current hospitals and law keeping halls across the kingdom were all built in the same period by King Marius's great-grandfather."

The clerk ignored her words, stopping in front of a thick door with an elaborate handle. With a slight bow, he gestured for Amara to knock. When she did so, a muffled voice bid us enter.

The office behind the door was large but decorated sparsely, the only hint of opulence in the deep red of the carpet and curtains. The older woman behind the dark wood desk stood when she saw us.

"Amara, this is an unexpected pleasure."

Amara swept forward to embrace her. "Aunt. It's good to see you again."

Anka pulled back from the hug and gave me an appraising look that seemed to strip me of every protective layer and pretense. "And who's this youngster?"

I shrank back instinctively, making Amara laugh. "Leave her be, Aunt! She's not one of your criminals."

Anka smiled at me. "Apologies, child. Old habits are hard to shake."

I bowed. "It's a pleasure to meet one of Amara's relatives."

"She's well behaved, at least." Anka bustled over to a low table surrounded by comfortable, padded chairs. As she picked up the teapot from the tea service laid out on the table's surface, she looked back to Amara. "But who is she?"

"My apprentice."

"Your what?" Anka nearly dropped the teapot, succeeding in clanking it noisily against one of the teacups.

"My apprentice," Amara repeated calmly, gesturing for me to approach the tea area at her side.

When I just stood beside the table uncertainly, she sighed. Putting a hand on each of my shoulders, she pushed me into a chair.

"Well, well, well." Anka gave me an even closer look than she had done earlier, making me squirm and wonder what I'd done that might need confessing. "Never did I think I'd see the day Amara would take an apprentice." She looked up at her niece. "But don't tell me you're still roaming here, there, and everywhere, dragging this poor girl with you! Isn't it time you settled down at the Guild?"

"Delphine is as uninterested in *settling* at the Guild as I am." Amara accepted a teacup and saucer from her aunt.

Anka handed one to me next, and I could barely keep my hands steady. I'd been looking forward to coming to the law keeping hall, but perhaps I should have anticipated that law keepers would be intimidating.

"It was proper of you to bring her to me for an introduction," Anka said to

Amara, "but if you're looking for my approval, you won't get it. You're getting far too old for this roaming lifestyle. How in the blazes are you going to find—"

"Aunt," Amara cut her off with a warning look, making me instantly curious as to what Anka had been about to say.

After a look at Amara's face, Anka subsided, however.

"I didn't bring her here because of our connection," Amara said. "I brought her here in the hope you'd be willing to give her some training."

"Training? Me?" Anka sat down, a teacup of her own gripped in one hand. "I've always had a fondness for you, Amara, you know that. But I've no use for elements mages in my hall. You should know that, too."

Amara hid a smile behind her cup. "Really, Aunt! Don't you know me better than that?"

Anka frowned, her brows knitting together as she examined Amara's face, trying to make sense of her words. I could see the moment realization hit her.

She sat back, turning wide eyes to me.

"Don't tell me you've apprenticed a healer!" She didn't wait for our confirmation. "Of all the nonsensical things! And with you flitting about hither and thither, too."

"I don't see the harm in that," Amara said. "She's getting a tour of the kingdom's best healers and teachers. She's already met Clay, and now I've brought her to you."

Anka tried to maintain her stern look, but I could see it was a struggle. Her eyes already indicated she had relented in the face of Amara's flattery.

"You always did know how to make pretty to your elders," she told her niece with a shake of her head.

"Would you like to test me?" I asked. "I can lower my wall, if you'd like to."

Anka leaned forward, raising an eyebrow. "There's plenty to be unpacked in that statement. Have you found an exceptionally humble and polite youngster, Amara, that she would offer such a thing without prompting?" She chuckled. "Or is it actually extreme confidence speaking?" She didn't wait for a reply before continuing. "As to lowering your wall...I have no idea what you're talking about there." Her eyes narrowed slightly. "But it sounds fascinating."

I flushed. "My apologies. It's just my inexperience talking. Everyone of master level strength that I've met so far has wanted to test me, so I forgot it's something that's usually considered rude."

Anka turned to Amara with a look of surprise. "Everyone? What exactly has been going on with your apprentice, Amara?"

Amara took her time answering, her eyes narrowing as she looked at me.

My flush deepened as I remembered that Clay was the only one who had tested me in her presence.

I cleared my throat. "Master Clay was curious, and I had no reason to deny him. I had no experience of mages before meeting Master Amara, so I don't have any prejudice against it."

"Clearly Amara has found you in some remote hole somewhere," Anka said. "It's the sort of thing she would do. But it's equally clear you're more powerful than you have any right to be, given that background."

My face tightened, and I was about to protest that anyone could be born with a powerful seed when she hurried on.

"Oh, I don't dispute that even those from small towns have a chance of being born with a powerful seed. They are not, however, usually still hanging around those small towns once they reach an age to be activated."

I bit my lip, forced to acknowledge she was right. But I wasn't willing to go into my father's history with this stranger—even if she was Amara's aunt. "Why does my willingness to be tested have anything to do with my strength?" I asked instead.

"That's just basic human nature." She gave a self-satisfied smile. "Something I have a great deal of experience with. If those who tested you had subsequently looked down on your strength, you would have rapidly developed the antipathy to the process that most of us feel."

"Oh." I thought it through and was once again forced to concede she was right.

"It is worth pointing out," Amara said, "that my dear aunt is a senior law keeper and therefore has a great deal of experience with the *worst* of human nature. Not everyone is as prideful and ambitious as your standard Guild mage."

Anka chuckled, undaunted by Amara's criticism. "I see your feelings for the Guild haven't softened. It's a pity, especially since you aren't the only one unexpectedly in town."

Amara stiffened, making no move to ask the obvious question as to who else had recently arrived. Anka chuckled, seeming amused by Amara's cold response, but didn't push the matter further. Instead she looked back to me.

"If you're so willing to be tested, child, I won't say no. I may have more insight than most, but I've no less curiosity." She gave me an expectant look.

I rushed to pull down my wall. I'd become so practiced in the last weeks that it barely required a thought to dismantle the whole thing. A sense of her beating heart and steady breathing hit me, as well as Amara's, but my stomach churned only lightly since both of them were in excellent health.

After a moment, Anka sat back in her chair, a contemplative look on her face, and I took that as a signal to put my wall back in place.

"Yes…" she said slowly. "I can see why you took her on, Amara."

"It would have been a waste to allow someone in her own town to activate her," Amara replied, her normal calm returned.

"Who would have thought such an opportunity would fall into your lap?" Anka said slowly. "A strong seed who shares your aversion for the Guild—and a different affinity from you into the bargain. How could you resist?"

"How, indeed?" Amara asked lightly.

"How experienced is she?" Anka asked, turning businesslike.

"Hardly at all. I activated her only weeks ago."

"Weeks?" Anka raised her eyebrows. "And you're already bringing her to me? Law keeping is usually an afterthought for most healing apprentices."

"Unfortunately she's squeamish," Amara said. "So we're starting with testing and truth telling while she develops control."

"Ah. A pity." Anka gave me a considering look. "It's rare we get someone with your potential with a true interest in law keeping."

I sat forward. "I thought weak abilities were sufficient for most truth telling?"

Anka nodded. "Most of my people are of moderate to high non-mage strength, with the occasional weaker mage. But someone of higher strength, such as myself, is needed to run the hall, and I like to have one or two under me with at least moderate mage strength."

"For what purpose?" I asked, too curious to hold in my questions.

"There's more to a law keeper's role than just truth telling," Anka replied. "In extreme cases, where a death has occurred, we have to examine the body for time and cause of death. And, where possible, we like to heal the victims of violence ourselves. That way we can accurately assess the extent of the damage, as well as the likely cause. When we're called in at a later stage—after natural or assisted healing has already occurred—the assessment becomes more difficult."

"But still possible?" I asked. "Even after full healing, you can tell what the damage was and how it was likely given?"

"Some can—those with sufficient strength and skill. Thus why every law keeping hall needs at least one higher strength mage."

"Aunt is the strongest law keeping mage the crown has," Amara said matter-of-factly. "They'd love to have her in Tarona, but for some reason, she insists on working here rather than in the capital. I can only guess she has more sympathy for my dislike of Guild life than she claims."

"Nonsense," Anka said. "This is a retirement, of sorts. Capital life would tire anyone of my age."

Amara snorted. "Nice and slow here, is it?"

Anka sipped her tea with a dignified expression, prompting Amara to turn to me.

"She's famous in law keeping circles. In her first week here, she faced off against a rioting crowd alone. She didn't know any of the inhabitants back then, but she was able to sense and identify the troublemakers who had riled up the sincere townsfolk."

"There was nothing to that," Anka said. "They reeked of deception, the lot of them."

Amara smiled. "No, nothing to it at all. Which is why Master Colton, the Head of Healing, said he couldn't have done such a thing himself—not in the middle of a rioting crowd like that."

"That's hardly surprising," Anka said coolly. "Colton has specialized his whole career in healing people. He'd make a terrible law keeper."

Amara laughed, looking at me. "Clay warned that you'd have human and animal healers competing over your specialization—but there are more than two for you to choose between."

Anka looked up, an eager spark in her eye. "Have you not chosen a specialization? If you're not interested in a settled life, you couldn't ask for a more exciting option than law keeping. You see all sorts of things in this profession."

"Thank you," I said, taken aback, "but I'm not sure—"

"Leave her be, Aunt," Amara interjected. "It's too soon for her to be boxing herself in. We have to deal with her squeamishness first, and then she needs the chance to experience all the different facets of healing before making a decision. Besides, her dislike seems to be of the Guild itself and not of a settled life. She intends to return to her parents' farm after her apprenticeship."

Anka settled back, looking disappointed, while I blinked at Amara.

She was right, of course—that had been my initial intention when I accepted Amara's offer of an apprenticeship. But hearing her say it now felt jarring. Could I really return to my farm as if that life hadn't been a lie?

And even if I put aside the issue of my father, did I even want that life anymore? He had taught me to cling to it so fiercely, fearing anything that might rip me away. But had it ever been more than *his* desire? What did I want for myself?

"Of course I'll be happy to show her the basics anyway," Anka said, cutting through my introspection. "We can avoid the actual healing aspects for now and just focus on the truth telling. I'm busy today, but if you bring her back—"

Angry voices outside made her stop. She stood, turning toward the closed door of her office.

It swung open, banging against the opposite wall as an incensed man strode inside.

CHAPTER

# TWENTY-TWO

Amara rose swiftly, hurrying to her relative's side.

I scrambled up as well, not sure how much help I could be, but ready to assist in providing a united front.

The man, who looked like a prosperous merchant from his clothing, was red-faced with anger. He didn't hesitate at sight of the mages confronting him, striding forward to stand nose-to-nose with Anka.

"Don't try to fob me off this time! I don't care if I don't have an appointment! I want to know what you're doing about this troublemaker—and I'm not the only one. Calista has gone too far, and if the capital doesn't intend to stop them, then Caltor will take matters into its own hands."

"That is enough!" Anka's voice sliced through the tension like a whip crack. "I've told you once, and I'll tell you again. Neither the king nor the Triumvirate are colluding with Calista to steal your precious sons and daughters."

"Then why don't you stop them from leaving?" the man demanded with no abatement in his anger.

Anka sighed heavily. "I can understand your concern, but you know better than this. If our youngsters choose to leave, there is nothing we can legally do to stop them. They may not be fully of age until nineteen, but the law permits a new apprentice to choose their own activator, and once they have been activated, authority over them moves from the parents to the master. If an apprenticeship is offered, law keepers are no more permitted to block a young person's acceptance than family members are."

"Choose for themselves?" the man roared, spit flying. "My son never expressed the slightest wish to leave Caltor until that snake came along and lured him with false promises. I'm telling you, if you won't get rid of him, I will!"

Anka grew taller, the lines of her face somehow becoming even sterner. "If you act against the law, you will be held accountable."

The man finally seemed to remember who he was facing, slowly deflating before our eyes. Anka, clearly extremely experienced in dealing with angry townsfolk, softened her voice to match the change in his posture.

"All accusations are investigated. If Calista is indeed working against Tartora's best interests, it will be brought to light. And you may rest assured that King Marius will not remain idle in that case. But you of all people know the benefit Caltor has reaped from the new trade lanes opened with Calista. If we move hastily, many will suffer."

The remaining bravado seeped out of the man, replaced with an arrested look. I could almost see him weighing his prosperity against the potential danger to his child.

"Naturally we cannot punish before guilt has been proved," he said gruffly. He glanced toward the door, eager to escape now that the fire of his anger had been extinguished. But something held him back. He looked at Anka again. "If anything happens to my son..."

"The safety of Caltor's young people has always been—and will always be —my top priority," she told him gravely.

He hesitated again before giving a perfunctory bow and hurrying from the room.

There was a long moment of silence before Anka let out a slow breath.

"Well, that was interesting," Amara said.

"Feel free to deal with it yourself if you find it so interesting," Anka said sourly.

Amara raised an eyebrow. "The townsfolk have been giving you serious trouble, have they?"

Anka sighed and sat back down. "A subset of them. Basically all the parents of youths nearing or just past activation. They claim some newcomer is riling up the kingdom's children with false promises. Since they all seem convinced Calista is behind it, I thought it was more of the usual nonsense that circulates in any town. But now they're claiming he's actually here..."

She closed her eyes, rubbing the bridge of her nose. "As you've seen, it's not a situation that can safely be ignored any longer. In fact—" She halted suddenly, shooting us a look. "Well, never mind that. Suffice it to say, a law keeper acts as a peacekeeper as often as anything else. Proactive action is better than assigning blame once things go south."

"Very wise," Amara said. "And naturally we shan't pry into the affairs of the law keeping hall."

I was fairly certain I read curiosity in her eyes—it was certainly blazing in me—but I could hardly insist Anka tell us confidential information.

As we rose and exchanged farewells with Anka, my thoughts turned to Nik and what he'd once told me about the youths Grey chose to take with him. If he was right, this merchant had no need to fear for his son. However fascinated the boy was, Grey would never accept a youth from such an influential family.

An uncomfortable feeling filled me as I considered the way the man had given way just at the mention of financial loss. If he wasn't willing to cause trouble for the sake of his own son, did I really think he would continue to make a fuss when his son remained behind and other, unknown, children were taken in his place?

Seeing the man's behavior only confirmed Nik's words. Grey was getting louder and attracting official attention he'd managed to avoid before. It was a good thing, as far as I was concerned, but I was no longer confident it would lead to any actual action.

As soon as we were ushered outside by the clerk from earlier, I turned to Amara.

"Was that merchant talking about Grey? Is he here in Caltor? Should we have said something to Master Anka about him?"

"What would you like to say?" Amara asked. "We can certainly go back if you have anything of value to report." She gave me a challenging look.

My shoulders slumped. She was right, of course. If I'd had anything concrete to report, I would have gone to the authorities before now.

After an extended pause, Amara spoke again. "I hope you may now lay down your sense of responsibility for Grey's behavior. If he has ties to Calista, I don't doubt my aunt will find them."

I muttered something inaudible, not quite ready to agree. I was glad Anka was aware of Grey's existence, but that didn't lessen my sense of personal responsibility toward Miranda. I had told her father I would try to find her, and I'd achieved nothing helpful so far. It was only chance that I'd ended up back in the same town as Grey.

Amara watched me closely throughout the rest of the day, and when evening arrived, she didn't look happy at my request to go out into the streets with Ember. But one look at the unsettled fox made her relent.

"The poor thing clearly needs to get outside to relieve herself and stretch her legs. But I hope that's your only reason for wanting to go," she finished sternly.

"I'm also curious to see more of the town," I said. "It has quite a different feel from Ostaria."

Amara regarded me with narrowed eyes. "You're not going out to search for Grey again?"

I shook my head. "I promised you I wouldn't do that anymore, and I meant it. But poor Ember can't stay cooped up in here all night after already being here all day."

Amara sighed and nodded. "Don't be long."

I escaped with almost as much relief as Ember. The fox pranced down the street with her tail high, sniffing everything she came across. I felt like the human equivalent, my eyes dancing back and forth as I took in the sights of Caltor at dusk. After weeks on the road and in small towns and villages, I was surprised how much I had missed the bustle of a city. There was an excitement in the air that was missing in smaller places.

"Would I get sick of it if we stayed?" I asked Ember as we meandered along without any particular purpose. "Maybe if we're in a city for long enough, I'll start to miss the empty fields and clear sky of home. Is that why Amara likes to always be on the move?"

At first it had seemed natural that she wanted to be as far from the capital and Guild as possible. But meeting Anka had finally forced me to confront my prejudice about mages. An isolated example like Clay was easily brushed off, but none of the mages I was meeting were anything like my expectations of them.

At this point, I didn't even know why I was surprised. My previous impression of the Guild had come from my father, just like my ideas about my own power. He had held up a mirror to show me the world, and I was finally realizing how distorted the reflection had been.

Mages weren't universally self-centered, egotistical beings who lived lives of luxury. All the ones I'd met so far were hard working people, using their strength to benefit their communities as much as any farmer or blacksmith did.

But that didn't mean my father's impression of the Guild was entirely wrong either. Amara avoided it, clearly at odds with its ethos, and she had said Anka chose not to live in the capital as well. So what was it really like? Would I hate it, as I had always believed, or would I find its charms were more than the empty allure I had been raised to expect?

Would the capital have all the life and vigor of Ostaria and Caltor but heightened by its larger size and greater importance? Would I feel the same buzz in the air that I felt here? Part of me longed to find out but the other part wished I could avoid Tarona and the Guild forever.

I shook myself, trying to dislodge a sensation that felt too close to fear. I had once believed myself strong against the wiles of the capital, but now I was afraid to discover not only the true nature of the Guild but the truth of my own heart as well. Far better to stay out here, away from the seat of power, where I could surround myself with mages who were more interested in being useful than important.

Someone brushed past me, catching my attention. They didn't stop, however, busy about their own business. The people in Caltor moved with more purpose than those in Ostaria, walking more quickly and not stopping to chat on the sides of the road. It fit with the more regimented look of the town, but it made me feel more of an outsider given my purposeless wanderings.

I looked up and down the street, seeking a goal. Did they have night markets here? The city was big enough, and I would love to explore one if it existed.

Although I caught no sign of a market venue, my eyes locked onto two youths who walked with their heads together, buzzing with suppressed excitement. I recognized their manner easily—they might come from a city, but at heart they were the same as the youths back home. They were on their way to somewhere or something of great interest.

Acting on instinct, I fell into step beside them. If there was a market, or something similar, they seemed the most likely to lead me there. And if there was some other reason the youths of the city were gathering at nighttime...

I suppressed the thought, feeling guilty. I had promised Amara I wouldn't go looking for Grey, and that wasn't what I was doing. I was equally interested in the girls' destination, regardless of what it ended up being. And if they were on their way to one of Grey's gatherings, then I would leave immediately and go straight back to tell Amara. Surely she couldn't find fault in that?

Before long, the buzz of voices reached my ears. The girls had led me to a square, but I could see no sign of stalls or vendors. Instead, there was a small crowd of young people.

I took several steps into the throng, checking that Ember was close to my side. The many lanterns dotting the crowd cast flickering shadows, and I didn't want her stepped on in the half-light.

I looked back up to see a figure that towered over the rest of the group. The mountain of a man was clearly not a youth, and his eyes roamed over the crowd, as if keeping an eye out for trouble.

I gasped, stumbling back as I recognized one of Grey's companions. He had been the one to grab and hold me during our confrontation, and the sight of him brought back the fear of those moments. It was a small sound, lost in the sea of chatter around me, but somehow it attracted his attention.

For a second we were both frozen, eyes locked. Then we both surged into movement. He pushed people aside, moving toward me, while I spun and dashed back out of the square.

Since I was already on the fringes of the group, I moved more easily than he did, but my lead was small. And I was at a disadvantage given my lack of familiarity with my surroundings.

Running and panicked, I couldn't remember the route I had come, and I was soon lost in unfamiliar streets. I pushed on anyway, aware of pounding feet behind me. But beyond the sound of his footfalls, my pursuer remained eerily silent, not calling out or doing anything else that might attract attention.

Should I call for help? Grey clearly had enemies in the town, so I might find someone willing to aid me. But I was out of breath from the running, and I couldn't shake the fear that I would only come across as a madwoman if I suddenly started shrieking.

Surely I would elude him soon. A man of that size had to be getting tired, given the pace we were moving.

I risked a glance back, and my heart contracted. My original pursuer had gained two companions, both fitter and faster than him. Maybe I needed to call for help after all.

I sucked in a deep breath, but before I could let it out, a fourth person emerged from a side street, barreling into my side. I went flying, the ground knocking my breath violently from my lungs.

For a minute my mind was overwhelmed with panic as I struggled to suck in a breath. Instinctively, I swept away my wall, letting my power surge through my body and force open my airway and lungs.

I panted as the sweet night air flowed into me again. For once I was grateful for the sensations that bombarded me as my four pursuers closed in. Without my wall up, I could use my power against them. But I needed skin contact to achieve that, and all of them were pulling on gloves as they circled me.

I slowly pushed myself onto my knees and then up to my feet, not wanting to precipitate an attack by sudden movement.

"Grey's been looking for you," one of the men said with a grin. "He's going to be mighty pleased with us when we bring you in."

I swallowed. "I'm not going anywhere with you. I'm not interested in Grey's cause or his new land or whatever story he's selling."

All of them except the enormous brute laughed.

"That's no problem. We have our ways with those who are reluctant—if they're valuable enough. And Grey thinks you might be worth the effort."

"I...I don't know why," I said desperately. "There isn't anything special about me."

The speaker laughed again, a nasty sound. "Grey will be the decider of that. And he thinks you're plenty interesting."

I shrunk back but gloved hands were reaching for me from all sides. Ember pressed against my leg, and I silently begged her not to move. She couldn't protect me from four attackers at once, and if she was hurt, they might not give me a chance to heal her.

"Why don't you come along quietly?" the man said again. "Grey's very good at convincing people. You might find you're not so reluctant once you hear what he's got to say."

"Grey isn't touching her." The cold voice cut through the tension around me. Suddenly I could breathe again.

Tears of relief sprang to my eyes as a tall figure stalked down the backstreet toward us. Somehow, impossibly, Nik was here.

"You again!" the large man said, speaking for the first time.

"Me." Nik looked him up and down, clearly unafraid, despite the other man's size and companions.

"This is no business of yours," the first man said, clearly unsure of Nik's identity.

Nik strode through their circle and took a firm grip on my upper arm.

"She's mine," he said.

My heart stuttered and sped up at the confidence in his tone. I knew he was putting on an act for my assailants, but it didn't matter. Everything had changed now that he was by my side.

I straightened, my lips tightening. Examining the two closest men, I looked for cracks in their armor—spots where a reaching hand might find skin.

At some unknown signal, all four of them drew swords and leaped forward at once.

I reached for the closest one, but Nik moved faster, pulling me behind him. He didn't draw a blade of his own, though. Instead he simply stood still, his body blocking their access to me.

I winced, flinching in sympathetic anticipation of the expected blows. But none of the men reached him.

Instead, shouts of protest filled the night as all four of them writhed wildly. I peered around Nik.

Thorny vines had sprouted from the ground and were working their way up the legs of the men, holding them in place and biting into their skin. I turned wide eyes on Nik to find him steely faced, watching the thrashing men.

"I said, *she's mine*," he repeated. "You can run back and tell your master."

One of the men made a strangled sound as a vine wrapped around his middle.

"Oh yes." Nik made a lazy gesture with his hand, and the vines pulled free.

They didn't fall to the ground, however, but remained upright, waving from side to side slightly, as if ready to pounce again at any moment.

The men hesitated, looking at one another.

Nik laughed harshly. "Whichever of you is trying to take control of the vines right now, don't even bother. I can promise you aren't strong enough to take me on."

Confidence seeped from every line of his body, and I shivered. If I were one of them, I would have already run.

Perhaps sensing the same thing I did, the closest man sheathed his sword and dashed off down the street. The others followed quickly, only the large one throwing a reluctant look over his shoulder, as if he would have preferred to take us on.

The vines remained upright until the last of the men disappeared. Only when we were alone did they collapse to the ground and lie unmoving.

I drew in a shaky breath. "I was going to protect myself, you know." I held out a hand. "Deadly assassin, remember?" I paused and then added, "But thank you."

Nik smiled slightly, his gaze roving over my body. "Are you all right? You're not hurt?"

My breath caught at the expression in his eyes. But as soon as our gazes locked, his face hardened, a veil dropping over his emotion.

"Do you think they bought it?" he asked.

"B...bought it?" I asked.

"That act?" He stared into the distance where the men had disappeared. "That we're allies."

"Allies?" I wished I could come up with something more intelligent to say, but I was struggling to follow the abrupt twists in his conversation. "You want them to think we're allies?"

"I want to divert Grey's attention to me." He gave a feral smile. "He'll find me a more difficult opponent."

I frowned. "I thought you purposely didn't use your power in our last clash with Grey because you were trying to keep yourself hidden from him."

Nik looked down at me. The amused expression lurking around the corners of his mouth took me by surprise.

"You have a way of interfering with that plan. Would you have preferred I let those men drag you off to Grey?"

"Of course not," I said hurriedly. "I'm very grateful. I was planning to fight, but they'd clearly come prepared to face a healer." I glared down the dark street.

Ember growled as if echoing the sentiment, and Nik dropped to one knee to offer her a hand, as if she were a dog. She sniffed it elegantly, giving him what looked suspiciously like a gaze of approval.

He glanced up at me. "I've already told you that we don't want Grey getting his hands on you. You're a target, but I'm an opponent. Better for him to be focused on me."

My brows drew together, my eyes narrowing at the implied insult, but could I really dispute his words? He had stopped four men without the least strain, whereas I had been nearly frozen with fear.

"Come on." He straightened, looking up and down the street. "It's best we don't linger here."

I nodded, falling into step beside him as he led me unerringly through the streets. My mind was distracted, though, going over my own actions during the confrontation.

When injured and scared, I'd taken down my wall without thinking and healed myself. It had been easy, and I'd never once felt out of control. Even the awareness of people close around me had hardly been a distraction.

Had I felt nauseous? I couldn't remember it. If the feeling had been there, I must have suppressed it instantly. Or perhaps the fear had done that for me.

I stared at the cobblestones passing beneath my feet, thinking of the difference between how I had faced the men and how Nik had. It was true that my ability required physical contact, but it had been more than that.

I didn't know how to use my ability properly because I was still hiding from it. The night's activities had made one thing clear—I had enough control that I was no longer a danger to myself. How long had that been the case? Why hadn't I said anything to Amara?

I squirmed uncomfortably. I'd been avoiding the whole issue because I didn't want to move on to the next phase of my training. I was afraid, just as I'd been afraid to face the reality of my seed in the first place. But my fear had only made me vulnerable and weak—the very thing I had determined I wouldn't be any longer.

It was time for the wall to go. It was time for me to learn to use my ability properly.

I reached for the wall and realized with a start of surprise that I'd never put it back in place. Cautiously, I focused on Nik beside me and Ember at my feet. Once I was paying attention, a dizzy feeling filled my head. Instinct wanted me to reach for the wall again, but I held back, instead pushing back the nausea.

Within seconds, my head was clear, the night crisp around me. My stomach was settled as well. In fact, my whole body felt light. I imagined the worst farm injury I'd ever heard my mother describe. Her words had once been enough to make me so lightheaded I nearly fainted, but remembering them now, I didn't react at all. Or rather, my ability entirely suppressed my physical response. I imagined the whole scenario in gory detail and without the physical symptoms, I felt only mild curiosity as to how I might approach healing it.

I gave a delighted laugh, earning a confused look from Nik. I shook my head, not wanting to explain, and his brows lowered. He didn't push, however, just watching me with a tightened gaze, as if he suspected me of being affected by the attack.

Perhaps I was since my giddy excitement quickly faded. All this time I had been angry at my father for blocking my power and keeping me weak, but I had been doing the same thing to myself. I thought I had thrown off the fear and timidity he had sown in me, but I had merely peeled back the first layer. How many more still lay undiscovered?

The thought made me shiver, and Nik responded to the subtle movement, his eyes tightening. I met his gaze only to quickly look away. The intensity of his focus on me set my pulse racing in a way that drove out all my earlier musings.

"I thought you were going south?" I blurted out.

He looked away for a moment before looking back, his expression transformed. Gone was the intensity, replaced with a hooded smile. "Did I say that?"

I frowned, trying to remember the conversation back in Ostaria. "I'm sure you did! I remember it clearly."

Amusement played around his mouth. "I believe my words were that I would be leaving by the south gate. Which I did. Before circling the city and heading north. I've been in Caltor for some time."

I turned to face him, my mouth dropping open. "But...why?"

He kept his eyes forward. "I was taught better than to tell a lie to a healing mage."

Both my eyebrows shot up, and I remembered Amara and Anka's words about the complexity of truth telling. It had never occurred to me that Nik might be carefully guarding his words around me, manipulating his spoken truths to conceal a deeper deception.

"But why?" I repeated.

He glanced at me, his brows quirking down. "Didn't you want to keep tracking Grey?"

I nodded, and he shrugged, turning forward again.

"It seemed clear Amara would force you in the opposite direction to me, and it conveniently happened that Grey had practiced the same deception. I tracked him out of the south gate, as I said, and I followed his trail long enough to see it turning north. So I sent you north and also came north myself, keeping behind Grey but ahead of you."

"You did that for me?" I asked, unsure what to make of his confession.

He looked down at me. "As I remember it, you were the one who said a healer might be helpful."

I nodded quickly. "Yes." I spoke as firmly as I could. "I know I didn't show it today, but I will be helpful, I'm sure of it."

The earlier smile twitched at the corners of Nik's lips, and I snuck another glance at him. Was it my imagination or did he seem more relaxed than on our previous interactions? Almost...almost as if he was glad to see me.

I shook my head, shaking the thought loose. I was letting my imagination run away with me. Nik had made it clear I was a nuisance, and I could hardly blame him. On my first night in Caltor, he had once again been forced to reveal himself to Grey because of me.

When we reached the gate of the inn, Nik stopped. I scooped up Ember, ready to carry her inside, only to linger awkwardly, not sure what to say.

"Will you be all right?" I finally blurted out.

"Me?" Nik stared at me.

"Will Grey come looking for you now?" I clarified.

He gave a chuckle. "Let him try."

I nodded, the awkwardness still lingering. I didn't want Nik to end up in danger because of me, but what could I possibly do to protect him?

"Sleep well," he said, turning and striding away so that I had to call my farewell at his back.

Grumbling to myself, I padded up the inn stairs. Would it have pained him so much to give a proper goodbye to my face?

Only at the door of our room did I remember that I had to tell Amara what had happened. It had seemed a simple prospect when I was following the two girls to the meeting place, but the subsequent events of the evening made a less easy story.

She was never going to let me walk Ember again.

Taking a deep breath, I quietly opened the door, easing inside and shutting it behind me. When I surveyed the silent room, I found Amara already asleep in one of the beds.

Breathing a sigh of relief, I put Ember into her box by the fire and hurried into the bed against the opposite wall. I'd still have to talk to Amara, but at least I had a stay of execution until morning.

CHAPTER

# TWENTY-THREE

I thought I would be tossing and turning all night again, but to my surprise I fell quickly into a deep sleep. I must have been exhausted by the evening's events because I slept late the next morning as well.

I awoke slowly, stretching and opening my eyes to morning sun streaming through the window. Remembering the events of the day before, I sat up quickly, looking across at Amara's bed. It was empty.

Taking my time, I got up and prepared for the day, waiting for her to return from the washroom. But as time ticked on, there was no sign of her.

I finally crossed over to her side of the room, only to find a note resting on her pillow. Scooping it up, I read that she was already gone for the day—off on private business—and that I had the day off.

I blinked and read it again. A day off? I hadn't had a day off since I started my apprenticeship, although my tasks had rarely been onerous. What would I even do with a day off?

Ember was no use to me, having already curled up for her day's sleep. And I knew no one in Caltor yet except Anka, who I definitely wasn't going to disturb.

*You know one other person,* a small voice whispered in the back of my mind, but I firmly dismissed it. Even if I wanted to spend the day with Nik, I had no idea where he might be found.

I ate a solitary breakfast in the inn's dining room, and then wandered out to the streets, unsure what else to do with myself. As I meandered around, taking in the sights of the small city, I once again caught myself watching out of the corner of my eye for a tall, dark-haired figure, just as I'd done in Ostaria.

No matter how many times I reprimanded myself, I couldn't seem to shake the instinct—or the hope that leaped up every time I thought I saw him, only to find myself mistaken.

I returned to the inn for the midday meal, pleased I was able to find the way without assistance this time. I planned to return to the streets again in the afternoon but wanted to check on Ember first.

I found the fox still sleeping and decided to lie down for a few minutes on my own bed. Amara hadn't said how long her business would take her, and it was possible she might return at any moment.

Despite my good sleep the night before, I woke to the dim glow of the late afternoon sun. There was still no sign of Amara, but Ember had woken and was demanding attention.

I took the opportunity to hold her, examining her internal systems to make sure there were no lingering issues from her several healings. As I did so, I marveled at my ability to connect with her without any problems. Given the ease with which I'd transitioned, I'd clearly been ready to remove my wall for some time.

My thoughts of the night before had clearly been true. I had left my father physically, but his influence still lingered. Even without his direction, I had been holding myself back.

But now I was free. The ability that I had thought would be a crushing burden was instead an integral part of me. Cutting it off had been unnatural —a constant tension rubbing against my subconscious.

Ember burrowed into my lap. Her warm presence, free from any hint of judgment, soothed my turbulent emotions. For some time I just held her, patting her soft fur, until the aromas of cooking roused me.

Amara still hadn't returned so I once again ventured downstairs alone and ate a solitary meal. Afterward, I returned to the streets, unable to face more time in the inn room. I still hadn't had the chance to tell Amara what had happened the night before, but this time I would stay closer to the inn and away from anywhere I might run into Grey or his people. As long as I stayed on the main roads, I should be safe.

My intention not to look for Grey was sincere, but I still found myself scanning the crowd and peering into every shadow. At first I thought I was motivated by anxiety and told myself to relax, but it didn't make any difference.

Only when my heart leaped in response to the sight of a tall, dark-haired stranger did I realize I was looking for someone else entirely. It wasn't anxiety driving my search at all.

Embarrassed, I sped up, feeling my cheeks redden, although there was no audience to witness my foolishness. Nik might have saved me the day before, but he wouldn't be here on the streets near the inn keeping watch for me. He had no doubt only found me last time because he was keeping watch over Grey's gathering and saw the men run after me.

But even as I thought it, I still kept looking. And every time I saw a flash of a similar build or coloring, I turned to look, my hopes rising and then falling. If only my ability could help me find a specific person in a crowd, but it was useless for such a task.

Turning away from the latest such disappointment, I re-entered the flow of traffic only to catch sight of someone out of the corner of my eye. I turned back to peer down the side street at the person I had glimpsed.

Sucking in a breath, I stepped forward. It was actually him.

But when I reached the mouth of the side street, I stopped. He wasn't alone.

Had Grey discovered him? Was that one of his men? A rush of fear sent me onto the balls of my feet, ready to race to his aid. But something made me pause. The two men were engaged in a conversation, with no sign of any struggle. They were just out of earshot, and Nik was clearly unhappy with whatever the other man was saying, but there was nothing overtly threatening in the stranger's posture.

He couldn't match Nik's height, although he appeared to have a couple decades on him in age. But despite the physical disadvantage, the stranger didn't look in the least intimidated by what appeared to be Nik's increasing irritation. If anything, his manner seemed earnest as he spoke on, all while Nik's hands clenched into tighter and tighter fists.

I was tempted to intervene, afraid Nik might lash out at the older man. But I couldn't bring myself to step closer. I didn't want them to think I was eavesdropping on what was clearly a private conversation.

At last the other man stopped speaking, waiting for Nik to respond. He remained silent, however, the moment stretching out awkwardly. Eventually the stranger gave a visible sigh and spoke again.

Nik snapped something in reply and stalked around him, making the man sigh again. He didn't try to stop Nik, though, instead moving off in the opposite direction, further down the street.

Nik strode swiftly toward me, his head down and his face dark. He had almost reached the end of the street before he finally looked up, finding himself face to face with me.

He froze, his eyes widening slightly as he recognized me.

"Sorry," I said. "I saw you there, and…"

Slowly, as if forcing himself to do so, he unclenched his hands.

"Who was that?" I asked, curiosity getting the better of me.

Nik muttered something under his breath. The words were too rushed and quiet for me to pick up anything but his irritation.

"Sorry," I repeated, "I didn't mean to pry."

I expected Nik to ask me what I was doing there, as he had on previous occasions when we'd met, but he remained silent.

"What were you doing here?" I eventually asked, peering around him down the rapidly darkening side street. "Has Grey been in this area? It seems too near the middle of the city for him."

Nik started slightly, a suspicious red tinging his cheeks. I stared at him in disbelief. Was he flushing?

Slowly it occurred to me that perhaps I was the reason Nik was in this part of the city. Had he been watching for me at the inn and following me ever since? Was that why I kept thinking I saw flashes of him wherever I went?

"Were you looking for me?" I blurted out, making him flinch again.

When he didn't reply, I put my hands on my hips. "Well? You must want something if you left your surveillance of Grey to come find me."

He still looked reluctant to answer, having to force the words out.

"I've found where Grey is keeping them this time. And from the number of youths with him, he still hasn't sent the latest batch away."

"Miranda's here?" I stepped closer, excitement coursing through me. "Can we rescue her?"

He hesitated again before reluctantly speaking.

"That's why I came to find you. I think there might be a chance, but it requires two people."

A different sort of thrill ran through me. Nik really had been looking for me. He needed assistance, and he trusted me for the job.

"What are we standing here talking for, then?" I asked. "Let's go!"

As soon as I said the words, hesitation gripped me. Could I really do this? Hadn't I promised Amara I wouldn't?

I considered my promise. I had told her I wouldn't go looking for Grey alone. I had even joked about how animals didn't count. But Nik was a human —a highly skilled one, at that. So I wasn't actually going back on my word.

It would have been better to talk to her beforehand, of course. But she'd been missing all day, and I had no idea where to find her. I couldn't miss this opportunity. Last time Grey had moved on too quickly, and I couldn't risk that happening again.

"Are you sure?" Nik asked. "It could be dangerous."

"Miranda has been facing that danger this whole time," I said. "I won't turn my back on her now."

Nik examined my face, as if testing my determination, before nodding and leading the way out onto the main street.

He walked quickly, so I had to hurry to keep up, several times glancing back to check Ember was still with us. As I had expected, he led us away from the more populated area of town, eventually stopping at yet another rectangular building with the look of a warehouse. This one wasn't quite against the wall of the city, but it was close.

"They're in there?" I whispered, and he nodded.

"So what do we need to do?" A thought struck me, and my brow creased. My enthusiasm had led me to overlook the obvious question. "I'm all for rescuing Miranda, but why the sudden change in plan? Weren't we just looking for evidence?"

"We're out of time," he said in a grim tone. "Haven't you noticed the mood of the city? The law keepers won't act without proper evidence, but I'm afraid the citizens might take matters into their own hands. And if they do, they won't distinguish between Grey's people and those children. We need to get them out first, and then Grey can face whatever comes for him without a human screen."

I frowned, but memory of the morning before in Anka's office kept me from disputing his words. This was my first visit to Caltor, so I couldn't compare the current tone of the city with its usual air, but Amara had noticed a difference in the guards at the gate. It was quite possible tensions were even more inflamed than I'd realized. It might even be the reason why everyone hurried about their business, not lingering in the streets.

Finally I nodded. Anka clearly knew about Grey, but she and her law keepers hadn't acted. If Nik and I had a chance to rescue Miranda now, I was going to take it.

"What do you need me to do?" I asked.

"The only reason we have a chance at pulling off a rescue is the particular layout of this building," he said. "Grey and his most loyal followers—the ones he lets come and go freely—have been using the main section of the warehouse. They've got the youngsters they lured away in a much smaller office in the back part of the building. It doesn't have a door, but it does have a large window. That's where you come in."

"You want me to get them all out the window?" I eyed him doubtfully. "What will you be doing?"

"I'll be providing a distraction at the front door." His eyes gleamed, as if he was looking forward to it, but I shook my head violently.

"You mean you're going to take all of them on alone? Even Grey? Isn't he a powerful healer? That must mean he's dangerous."

Nik smiled broadly, his hand drifting to his sword hilt. "Only if he can touch me."

I examined him, trying to gauge his mood. I couldn't help but worry he was overconfident, but at the same time, I'd seen him use his ability to take down four men last night with ease. And he was right that his plants affinity had a significant advantage over Grey when it came to a fight, since he could attack from a distance.

"So I smash the window, and I get everyone out," I said.

"You shouldn't have to smash it. I already loosened the wood of the frame. You should be able to knock it out without much more than a tap."

"That's helpful." I looked at him, waiting for him to say more since his manner made it clear there was something else.

"There's usually one of Grey's people in there." He sounded apologetic. "You'll need to climb inside quietly and deal with them before you can start sending people to safety."

I bit my lip, looking down at my hand. It was one thing to try to defend myself in the heat of an attack, but could I really turn my ability against someone in cold blood like that?

"If you don't want to do it..." Nik said, making me look up.

"I'm not abandoning Miranda."

His eyes stayed glued to my face. "Are you sure you're up to it?"

I nodded, resolute. "I'll do it. It's not as if I have to kill them. You can leave it to me."

My confidence had ebbed, however, by the time I found myself standing just to one side of the back window. Light streamed out, indicating the curtains were open, so I kept carefully out of sight.

"You need to stay here," I whispered to Ember, giving her an intent look and hoping she understood my meaning. "You'll just be in the way inside."

She sat, looking off into the night like a sentry, and I hoped that signaled assent.

The seconds ticked by interminably as I strained for any unusual sound. Nik had repeated several times that I needed to wait for his signal, telling me I would know it when I heard it.

A loud shout cut through the silence, making me straighten. It was followed by another and another. Definitely my signal.

Leaping forward, I pushed against the window. Mistrusting Nik's suggestion that a tap would be enough, I put too much strength in. The pane of glass went flying into the room.

Several people shouted as it crashed against a table, breaking into several shards. I scrambled over the windowsill behind it, trying to take in the room and its occupants as I moved.

Most of the young people inside were sitting on a ring of tired looking sofas that sagged with age. Many of them jumped to their feet at my explosive arrival, but it was still easy to identify the older woman guarding them. She stood by the door, clearly having been in position there before my unexpected entrance.

She spun around to face me at the sound of breaking glass, her expression distracted and confused. She had clearly been torn as to whether she should go investigate the shouts from the main warehouse, and her attention was divided. The distraction proved invaluable, just as Nik had hoped, giving me precious extra seconds to find my feet.

By the time she had started toward me, I was ready.

Not bothering to waste time, I launched myself straight into her clutches, my reaching hands latching onto her face. She shrieked, but the sound was muffled beneath my fingers as I pushed my power into her.

I didn't have enough experience to aim for finesse, so I poured my power into her brain, letting my instinct lead the way as I commanded her to sleep. She swayed for a moment beneath my hands and then crumpled to the ground.

I stepped back, panting.

"She's dead!" a girl screamed.

Another girl slapped her across the face, silencing her frenzied cries.

"She's not dead." A young man met my eyes. "You must be a healer too."

I nodded, glad he was strong enough to sense her heartbeat from across the room. His words would be more reassuring to the group than anything I said.

"I'm here to rescue you."

Sudden uncertainty gripped me. I had come this far on faith, but what if these people didn't want rescue? I didn't think I could put them all to sleep before they managed to subdue me.

My eyes searched the silent crowd, looking for a familiar face. I couldn't see any sign of Stefan, the blacksmith's son. Did that mean he had been accepted enough to join the trusted ones in the main warehouse? There was no sign of Miranda, either, although I refused to believe the same could be true of her.

Eventually I spotted Serena on one side of the group. Back in Tarin, my heart always sank at the sight of her, but now it lifted. I opened my mouth to call to her, but before I could say her name, she spoke.

"Delphine?" She stepped forward, staring intently at me. "Is that you?"

I nodded. "Where's Miranda?"

"You're the healer Grey's so worked up about?" she asked, ignoring my question.

I shrugged, uncomfortable, and the boy from earlier spoke again.

"Miranda isn't here. She's the strongest of us healers, so Grey keeps a close eye on her. Especially now, since that friend of yours got them all... jumpy."

"Friend?" I asked, realizing a moment later he meant Nik.

A loud bang, followed by a high-pitched scream, made us all look toward the closed door that led to the rest of the warehouse.

"He's out there, isn't he?" a girl asked, shrinking toward the window.

"He's here to help." I gestured at the empty rectangle where the glass had been. "He's keeping Grey and his people distracted so that anyone who wants to leave has the chance to get away. Caltor is in turmoil and bad things might be coming soon."

They exchanged looks while I held my breath. Serena was the first to step forward, the outspoken boy only a second behind.

"We want out," he said, and the others all began to nod.

"Good." I hurried toward the window. "Climb out one by one, and I'll come last." I looked at the boy. "Once you're outside, lead everyone around the building and all the way down the street. We'll meet in the square at the end."

The boy nodded once and vaulted through the window opening. From the other side, he reached back to help the next person scramble through. Pleased I'd picked the right person to put in charge, I looked around for a chair to help the process.

There were no ordinary chairs in the room, so I had to pull an entire sofa into position. At first it barely scraped across the floor, but a sudden lurch sent it moving and when I looked up, I saw Serena had joined my efforts and was pushing from the other end.

With the two of us, we quickly had it in position beneath the window. Aided by the sofa, the evacuation sped up, the remaining captives easily clambering onto it and then through the window.

"Hurry," I called quietly into the night. "Don't linger here. Get to the square."

There was a hurried conversation and then the sound of retreating steps. But the boy still remained in place, beckoning for Serena and me to come through. We were the only two remaining, apart from the unconscious woman, so I murmured for Serena to go first.

She hesitated. "What about you?"

"Don't worry about me. I need to find Miranda."

"But she's with Grey!" Serena stared at me, eyes wide. "You can't go after her on your own."

"I have to try."

Serena still hesitated, clearly torn.

"Come on," the boy whispered. "Someone could come at any moment."

As if in response to his words, the door creaked, the knob turning. Serena and I both froze, staring at it.

"Come on!" the boy hissed, but we still didn't move.

Swinging open, the door revealed Miranda. She stumbled into the room, as if pushed from behind, and for a single second I couldn't believe our luck.

But a second person followed her, his attention momentarily diverted as he looked back over his shoulder. Grey.

Miranda stifled a gasp when she saw us, but it was enough to alert Grey. He spun around, taking in the situation with one glance and swearing loudly.

"Miranda!" I cried, and she leaped toward us, her hands reaching for Serena and my outstretched ones.

But Grey was faster. He grabbed her from behind, pulling her back toward him so hard that she stumbled and nearly fell.

"Let her go!" I shouted.

Grey slung an arm around her, resting his hand lightly against her bare neck. He held my gaze as he spoke.

"Why should I relinquish my prize?" His eyes ran up and down me. "Are you offering me a bigger one?"

Before I realized what was happening, a foreign power brushed against mine, and I remembered my wall was dismantled. My eyes flew to Grey's, the pleased smile on his face making my stomach turn.

"I thought there must be something impressive behind defenses like that." His eyes grew hungry. "And then there's the defenses themselves. You'll have to teach me how you did that."

I shook my head soundlessly, backing up until I hit the empty window frame.

"Didn't you come all this way for her?" He tightened his hold around Miranda's neck, making her whimper. "Don't tell me you're just going to leave."

I swallowed, not able to tear my eyes away from them. Miranda was looking at me with desperation on her face, and I couldn't bring myself to abandon her and flee.

Grey smiled at my hesitation. "Come over here, and I'll let her go."

I knew what he wanted. Once he had contact with my bare skin, I would be at his mercy. He was a much more experienced healer than me. I would have no hope in a duel between our abilities.

But when I looked at Miranda's face again, my feet stepped forward. At least I had a better chance than Miranda, who hadn't even been activated yet.

"Delphine!" Serena hissed, but I didn't turn.

"Get ready to grab Miranda and go," I whispered, ignoring her wordless protest.

My steps slowed even further as I neared Grey, every part of me protesting against his nearness. But his hand on Miranda's neck left me no other option.

As soon as I was in reach, Grey's hand snapped out and grabbed my bare arm, yanking me toward him.

He didn't let go of Miranda as he'd promised, but I was prepared for that. As Grey pulled me near, I seized her with my free arm and tore her away from him.

Off balance from attempting to hold us both, he released her. Choosing to focus on me, he used his now free hand to get a firmer hold, pinning both my arms.

But Miranda was free.

"Run!" I gasped out, and she stumbled toward the window, looking back at me with horrified eyes but not stopping.

Serena caught her when she nearly collapsed against her, whispering something I couldn't hear.

"I didn't expect you to be such an obedient little thing," Grey murmured to me, making my skin crawl. "That ability of yours is going to be very useful, indeed."

"I won't help you," I said, my voice cracking on the words.

"Are you sure about that?" His power pushed into me again, and I knew, without knowing how I knew, that it was heading for the bones of my right hand. He intended to break one of my fingers to remind me of the power he held over me.

Without thought, I threw up the wall I had been sheltering behind since my activation. It sprang instantly into place, my long practice making it second nature.

Grey's grip on my arms tightened, his face growing stormy as my wall expelled his power, thrusting it out of my body completely.

"What did you do?" he ground out. "How did you do that?"

I glared at him defiantly. He might be more skilled than me, but that didn't mean I was helpless. The skin contact between us worked both ways. Turning the tables, I sent my power into him.

I had vague thoughts of putting him to sleep as I had done to the woman, but the moment he felt the brush of my power, he let me go, dropping his hands and stepping rapidly back.

Before I could regain my balance enough to follow, he dodged around me. Rushing for the window, he reached for Miranda, who was already halfway through the opening, apparently wanting to reclaim his previous hostage.

Serena screamed and threw herself into his path. He barely slowed, his hand clamping around her wrist, and his power shredding through her. She didn't make a sound, dropping limply to the floor as he reached again for Miranda.

This time he managed to grab her arm, pulling her back into the room. She fell backward, and he caught her in his arms. I rushed toward them, but he slung her over his shoulder, one hand wrapped firmly around her wrist.

I slid to a halt as he met my eyes.

"Don't come any closer," he said. "Or she dies. You're a healer. You can read the truth of my words on me."

I froze as I sensed his steely determination. If he was going down, he would take her with him without hesitation.

He stepped forward, his eyes on me as he slowly advanced across the room. I stood in front of the door, but when he reached me, I had no choice but to step slowly aside, Miranda's terrified sobs echoing in my ears.

I didn't move far, and as Grey passed, he paused, turning as if he meant to say something to me. Instead of speaking, however, his hand flashed forward, the concealed dagger in his grasp sinking into my stomach.

CHAPTER

# TWENTY-FOUR

Pain and fire flared inside me, overtaking all my senses as my hands flew to the hilt of the weapon. Dimly I was aware of Grey striding out the door, and I stumbled mindlessly after him.

On the other side, a large space opened out, its shadowy depths hidden by the night. Grey was already heading toward the far side of the warehouse, ignoring the debris, vines, stones, and scattered bodies that littered the floor.

None of the bodies were moving.

Before horror could take hold, a figure loomed out of the darkness, running toward Grey. Nik. He was still alive. My relief was instantly swallowed by a new fear. He couldn't stop Grey or Miranda would die.

"No!" I screamed, but my voice wasn't as loud as I had intended. My diaphragm couldn't seem to contract properly, limiting my breath.

Nik heard me anyway, though, his gaze swinging around to find me in the brightly lit doorway. His eyes dropped to my hands, still clasped around the dagger's hilt, blood oozing between my fingers.

Even across the distance, I saw him falter, saw the horror on his face as he absorbed my state. Changing direction, he ran toward me instead.

Scooping me into his arms, he burst through into the office. Glancing around the room, now deserted except for the two prone forms, he strode over to the closest sofa and laid me down.

Kneeling at my side, his hands reached for the hilt. I batted them away.

"Leave it be," I panted out. "Help her." I gestured toward Serena, my arms strangely weak.

Nik hesitated, but I pushed him away, my strength only just sufficient to make him rock backward.

Grabbing the hilt myself, I pulled it out in one swift motion, screaming with the pain. A healing ability could numb pain, but I didn't have any experience with using my power that way, and I had neither time nor energy to waste. I wasn't the only one needing healing.

Nik leaned forward again at my cry, his face ashen. I ignored him, sending my power racing toward my middle. It burned through me freely, re-knitting the torn places and refreshing the lost blood.

As soon as it was finished, I sat up, gasping at the relief from pain. Nik tried to push me back down, but I glared at him.

"What are you doing? I'm a healer, remember! I'm fine now. We need to help Serena."

He stood, clearly still reluctant, and looked uncertainly between the female guard and the girl lying near the window. Both of them lay still, appearing untouched from the outside.

Exasperated, I brushed past him, falling to my knees beside Serena. As if in response to my presence, she stirred and coughed. Blood sprayed across my dress.

Terrified, I put my hand on her arm and pushed my power inside her. My eyes widened, and I fell back, groaning as I pulled my hand away.

"What is it?" Nik was right behind me. "Did you heal her?"

I shook my head, tears springing to my eyes. "He's literally shredded her insides. I don't know how she's still alive. Everything needs healing. And it doesn't feel...right. My power doesn't know what to do."

Nik looked from me to Serena, determination overtaking his features. "Then we find someone who does."

Leaning down, he picked her up as easily as if she were a child.

"I don't think she'll last long enough," I said, stumbling over the words.

He fixed me with a steely glare. "Then you keep her alive. Keep her alive just as long as it takes."

His words bolstered me, steadying my panicked thoughts. Rushing forward, I put my hand against her and sent my power beneath her skin.

Not knowing what else to do, I focused on her heart and lungs. If her body couldn't keep them going, I would do it for her. As long as her heart kept beating and her breath kept flowing, she had a chance.

I bumped against the windowsill, barely aware of what was happening as Nik passed Serena out to the boy still waiting on the other side. I reached after her, leaning out the gap as I maintained the contact.

I tipped, nearly losing balance, and my feet were swept out from under me as Nik picked me up unceremoniously and lifted me through the window.

When he put me down on the ground outside, I stepped closer to Serena, still not having lost our connection.

The boy who was holding her staggered, nearly dropping her. Nik pulled her back into his own arms, giving the boy a contemptuous look. I shook my head, but I was concentrating too hard to find the words to explain what had made him falter. The boy was a healer, and as soon as he took Serena, he must have felt the state of her insides. It was no wonder he had responded with shock.

Nik hurried around the building, and I followed at his side, pouring my power into Serena, although it seemed to make little difference to her state.

"You're doing well," Nik murmured. "She's still breathing."

As before his words steadied me.

"The others are at the square." The boy hurried past us, moving faster since he wasn't encumbered like we were. "I'll gather the other healers and send someone for help."

He disappeared down the street, running at full speed.

"I don't know if she's going to make it." I felt warm tears on my cheeks, but I didn't have the energy to wipe them away. "The square is too far."

A loud, familiar bark made us both stagger to a stop. Ember raced toward us down a side street, Amara on her heels.

I nearly collapsed in my relief. My master had arrived, and everything would be all right now.

But the relief only lasted a moment before I remembered Amara wasn't a healer. She might be powerful, but she couldn't do anything for Serena.

But more footsteps were coming behind her, two more people appearing on the scene at full speed. It took a moment for my confused brain to recognize the man as the one who had been talking to Nik on the street, and I didn't recognize the much younger girl with him at all.

Nik groaned with relief as soon as he saw the two, however, almost collapsing as he lowered Serena to the ground. I sank down beside them, still maintaining my contact.

Neither of the newcomers paused as they sprinted to Serena's side, both of them dropping to their knees and placing one hand on her.

Instantly I felt her insides change, and I pulled my own hand away, relief filling me. They were healers.

Ember had brought Amara, and Amara had brought healers. I didn't know how she'd known, but she'd brought healers—and powerful ones given the speed with which their power had latched onto Serena's wounds.

Slowly I rose to my feet. Exhaustion filled me, although I wasn't sure if it was from my own healing or the power I'd poured into Serena. If I'd been in a better state, I would have liked to stay connected to her so I could observe what the other healers were doing. But given my current state, I didn't want to risk getting in their way.

Amara glanced at me, but she must have assumed the blood down the front of my gown was Serena's because she immediately turned to the prone girl, concern on her face.

I tried to walk to her side, but a hand gripped my wrist. Unafraid of my bare skin, my captor dragged me down a narrow alley.

Mustering my strength yet again, I was about to send my power into my new assailant when he stopped, spinning me around so we stood face to face.

"Oh, it's you," I said with relief, smiling up at Nik.

He didn't smile back. Instead he dropped my wrist and ran his hands up and down my arms, as if searching for an undisclosed injury.

His breathing was harsh, his eyes strained as they bore into me. "Are you sure you're all right? You don't have other injuries?"

"Don't be silly." I smiled at him, some of my energy starting to return in his presence. "How many times do I have to remind you I'm a healer? I'm fine."

"You nearly died." His face was haunted as his eyes roamed over my face.

I shook my head. "No, that's Serena. We should go and check on her. She's the one who was in real danger."

His only movement was to bring both hands up to cradle my face. My breath caught as his eyes held mine.

"I took you there." His voice was ragged. "I asked for your help, and you nearly died. I nearly killed you."

"I'm really all right," I breathed. "I promise. As a healer, I was never in any real danger from a wound like that. Grey was just being spiteful."

"Spiteful? How can you say...He stabbed you!"

His breathing sounded harsh in the following silence, his eyes burning as they held me locked in place, his hands dropping to grip my upper arms. I swallowed, trying to think of further reassurances, but he swayed forward, and I forgot how to form words. For one breath, we stayed suspended there, and then he pushed me backward two steps, pressing my back against the stone wall and his mouth against mine.

A new kind of fire spread through me as his lips devoured mine, one of his hands returning to my face while the other wrapped around my waist.

I kissed him back, providing the reassurance my words hadn't given. I never wanted to let go.

But somewhere, distantly, a voice was calling my name. He broke off, panting, and our eyes met, both of our gazes slightly wild.

"Delphine!" The call came again, and this time Nik dropped his hold completely, stepping away from me just as Amara appeared at the entrance to the alley.

She looked from Nik to me, her gaze heavy with suspicion.

"What are you two doing in here? What's going on?"

Somehow I found my legs and hurried forward, forcing myself to ignore Nik, although I had never been so burningly aware of his presence.

"How's Serena? Is she healed?"

I burst out into the street, looking around for the other girl. I found her still stretched flat on the ground, her eyes closed, and my heart sank.

Had I been off being kissed while she was dying?

"Don't worry," a man's voice said, his tone warm. "She's fine."

I turned to face the man Amara had brought. Now that I'd stopped panicking, I could sense the truth of his words for myself. Serena's body thrummed with its normal, healthy rhythms.

"We thought it would be best to put her to sleep for a bit," the girl at his side added with a friendly smile. "I've never done such an extensive healing. Her body will need time to regain its energy."

I trembled, remembering how Serena's insides had felt before their arrival.

"Why was it like that?" I asked. "My power usually knows what to do, at least partially, but it was chaos in there."

"That was the effect of healing power." The man sounded grim. "Those weren't ordinary injuries, but ones caused by a healer."

I nodded, my body starting to tremble again. "His name is Grey, and he got away with Miranda."

"Your friend from Tarin?" Amara exchanged a worried look with the man.

The look seemed to convey much more than I could grasp, and it occurred to me suddenly that here was the reason for Amara's absence during the day. She hadn't known to bring a healer, she had already been with him when Ember came looking for her. Or perhaps the three of them had already been looking for me after finding me absent from the inn.

"This is Hayes, by the way," Amara said. "He's a master healer visiting from the capital. And this is his apprentice, Luna."

The girl smiled at me again. "It's a pleasure to meet you, although I would have preferred to do it under less dramatic circumstances. Amara has told us all about you, and I'm excited to get a classmate."

Her warm words confirmed my speculation about Amara's day, although they let loose a host of other questions. Foremost was what she meant by classmate, but Anka's words at the law keepers' hall also flashed through my mind. She had said Amara wasn't the only unexpected visitor to Caltor, and she had seemed to be referring to someone of importance to Amara. Had she meant this man, Hayes? Were Anka's words the reason for Amara seeking him out the next day?

I looked at him speculatively, noting they appeared to be a similar age. Had they studied at the Guild together back during their own apprenticeships?

Hayes himself was looking at something over my shoulder. Before I could question him, he gave a slight bow, his gaze unreadable.

"Your Highness."

I stiffened. *Your Highness?* When had one of the royal family arrived, and what could they possibly be doing here? Surely Hayes and Amara hadn't brought them.

I turned slowly, preparing to drop into a curtsy, but the street was empty of any new arrivals. Only Nik stood there, his gaze fixed on Hayes, his eyes angry.

As I stared at him, he slowly looked from Hayes to me, his expression torn between defiance and apology.

I gasped.

No, it was impossible. Nik—my Nik—couldn't possibly be Prince Nikolas, Princess Morgiana's younger brother.

I had seen a royal portrait many years ago, painted when the twins were children. I struggled with my memory, failing to bring up a clear image of the prince's features. But the one thing I remembered was the startling contrast between the princess's dark brown curls and her brother's straight, fair hair.

"I told you the dark hair looked good on him," Amara said to Hayes, sounding amused.

I couldn't find anything humorous in the situation, however. I felt like a fool. I had sought him out, had trusted him with my life, had *kissed* him—but apparently I was the only one who didn't know his true identity. His *royal* identity.

What was he doing roaming the kingdom? Was this all just some game to him? A temporary escape from the boredom of court life?

I wanted to deny his title, but the look in his eyes and his silence confirmed Hayes's words. And now that I thought about it, I could see how the pieces fit. He had seemed defiant toward authority from the beginning, and yet my criticism of the king—and especially the princess—had enraged him.

I swallowed as I realized I had spoken against the royal family to one of their own. Was he going to return home and report what I'd said?

"Delphine," Nik whispered, but I shook my head savagely, and he fell silent.

Whatever bond had just forged between us in the warehouse and the alley had already been shattered.

CHAPTER

# TWENTY-FIVE

"**S**o it really is you," Luna said cheerfully, oblivious to Nik's mood. "Their Majesties will be very pleased to know where you are."

His eyes finally left mine, flashing to her face. His own expression set into a threatening glare.

"Don't you dare tell them I'm here."

Hayes sighed. "I already told you that we can't possibly—"

"And I told you that if you send word, I'll be gone before they can send anyone back for me." Nik turned his glare on Hayes. "I've been gone for over a year. I'm not the prince you used to know. I'm far more familiar with the streets than you'll ever be."

Hayes sighed again. "Is this all really necessary, Nikolas? Your parents and sister miss you."

"Do they?" Nik's face didn't soften at all at mention of his family. "I can't imagine why. They never had any use for me when I was with them."

"That's not fair," Hayes said softly, compassion on his face, but the emotion only seemed to stir Nik further.

"Isn't it? I suppose next you're going to tell me the Triumvirate miss me too?"

I didn't understand the significance of his words, but something in them made Hayes back down. He broke their locked gazes, looking helplessly toward Amara. She looked equally burdened, but she shook her head slightly, as if letting him know to let it go.

Nik looked back at me, but a groan from Serena made me hurry to her side.

"How do you feel?" I supported her arm as she struggled to her feet.

"Like I ran into a wall and then stumbled off the roof of a building." She groaned again.

Luna hurried to join us, her hand reaching for Serena's. "You have pain somewhere? You shouldn't have pain."

Serena evaded her grasp, grinning at her. "That might have been a slight exaggeration. It's more like extreme exhaustion."

"That's unavoidable after an attack like that from such a powerful healer." Hayes sounded apologetic, as if he bore some responsibility as a member of the same affinity.

"Grey!" Serena spat out an insult that made Luna gasp and cover her ears, although her eyes danced.

"He was always threatening to do something like that," Serena added, "but I was never quite sure if he really meant it." She grimaced. "Apparently he did. So I guess I was right to take him seriously and not make an escape attempt myself."

"You were wanting to leave for a while?" I asked. "I thought you went with them willingly."

"I did." Serena gave me a guilty look. "Life in Tarin was so dull, and Grey offered an adventure. You know how I used to be. I was convinced I was too strong for a backwater like Tarin, but my seed wasn't quite strong enough to get me a ticket out—not even to a city, let alone the Guild."

"What about Miranda?" I asked. "Did she want to go with him initially?"

Serena shook her head. "No, she didn't want to leave her father. Grey forced her to come."

"But why?" I frowned, unable to understand it. "I know she has a relatively strong seed for a non-mage, but she won't be ready for activation for a while yet. I get the impression Grey is taking youths who are already activated—or about to be, at least."

Serena's face twisted. "That's our fault. We'd all talked up her strength, and no one ever mentioned her age. Grey didn't bother to actually check how far she was from activation until he'd already dragged her along with us. He might have abandoned her at that point, but since he'd forced her to come, he couldn't let her free to report him to the authorities. Plus, she was a healer, and he seems particularly interested in strong healers. He must have decided she was worth the wait because he kept a closer eye on her than the rest of us."

I could feel Nik's eyes burning into the side of my face, a silent reminder of all his warnings about Grey's interest in me. I kept my focus on Serena, though.

"What happened with Miranda was the first sign something was off," she said. "I tried to ignore it, but then he threatened that if she escaped, he would kill her father."

I gasped. "Surely that was an empty threat!"

"Miranda decided it was, but then Grey got a report from the person he'd left in Tarin. The report included enough information to prove Grey really did have a person loyal to him there, so he had the means to carry out his threat. Plus the man reported that Halmir had disowned Miranda after her disappearance, saying she was no daughter of his. Poor Miranda was heartbroken and lost the will to escape after that."

"That's all lies!" I cried. "I spoke with Halmir myself, and he never said anything of the sort."

"Really?" Serena looked hopeful. "Does that mean the whole thing was a ruse, and he never had anyone in Tarin? Miranda hasn't been activated yet, and the other healers are weaker, but they all agreed he was telling the truth."

"It was likely a trick," Nik said, finally joining the conversation. "Grey doesn't have the resources to leave people in every town he visits. And, as you know, he's an expert at making anything he says sound convincing. He could talk his way around a healer easily."

"After what happened with Miranda, I wanted to leave," Serena said. "But it wasn't an option. I wasn't the only one, either. Most of us wanted to go home after he revealed the truth behind his promises. But he made it clear he would hold us to the commitment we'd made, and everyone was scared of him."

Amara leaned forward. "And what, exactly, is the truth behind his promises? How were you deceived?"

"He was always talking about the new land, and we all thought he meant Calista," she said slowly. "I'm sure he said as much, but looking back he can't have said it outright, or the healers would have sensed the lie. Going there sounded like an adventure. But he wasn't talking about Calista at all."

"Of course he wasn't," Nik muttered. "That's what I keep saying."

"He claims he's found an entirely new land off the eastern coast," Serena explained. "We've been moving north, gathering others on the way, heading for Grey's base. I haven't seen it myself, of course, but I heard some of his people talking, and I think it's located somewhere in the desert that runs along the eastern coast of Calista. He set himself up there because it's the only spot you can launch from to reach the island safely. Apparently no one sails that coast due to the treacherous shore and the desert, so Grey is the only one who knows about this new land and the route to get there."

She shook her head. "Going to Calista was one thing, but setting sail for some unknown land? Who knows what we'll really find there. And what if we can't come back to visit our families? Are we just supposed to leave our home-land forever?"

"I can understand your hesitation." Hayes voice was gentle and free of judgment. "But there must have been some who still wanted to go?"

"Stefan," Serena spit out the name.

"He wasn't in the back room," I said. "Was he with Grey and his people in the main warehouse?"

"Yes," she said simply, but I could see her seething emotions. She clearly felt betrayed by her fellow townsman.

I looked to Nik, suddenly remembering my one glimpse of the warehouse. "Is he still alive, then?"

He met my questioning gaze, his own heavy, as if I had disappointed him. "Of course. They're all alive."

Running feet sounded from the direction of the warehouse, and we all straightened, spinning toward the approaching group. But our concern was unnecessary since the figures that appeared wore the uniform of law keepers, several of the young people we'd rescued at their head.

"Serena!" one of the girls screamed, running forward to throw her arms around her friend's neck. "I thought you were dead!" She started crying into Serena's shoulder.

Serena patted her awkwardly on the arm. "Don't worry, I'm fine."

"Are you the wounded girl?" one of the law keepers asked. "Our healer is just..."

"I'm here." A trailing law keeper arrived, pushing through the small crowd of people to stand at the front. "Where is the injured..." His words trailed off as he noticed Hayes. "Master Hayes! Thank goodness. The girl was saved, then?"

"Yes," Hayes agreed. "But it sounds like our services might be needed back in that warehouse." He threw an exasperated glance at Nik, who didn't respond.

"Of course." The law keeping healer gestured for Hayes to lead the way.

Hayes stepped forward, only to hesitate and turn back.

"Don't go anywhere, Your Highness. We still have matters to discuss."

"Your Highness?" The new healer did a double take, staring at Nik. "Good-ness, I didn't recognize you at first, Prince Nikolas. Please excuse me." He bowed deeply while Nik threw a poisonous look at Hayes.

Inclining his head slightly, Nik acknowledged the man's greeting, his movements stiff.

The healer looked like he wanted to ask questions, but Hayes bustled him away, Luna herding the rest of the law keepers in their wake.

"They'll take care of the mess you left behind," Amara said to Nik once they were gone.

She looked at Serena and discovered the entire group of rescued young people had followed the law keepers to find us. They were hanging back watching us, uncertainty on most of their faces.

"I know it's late, but I suppose you'd all better come with me to the law keeping hall. Anka will be furious with me if I do anything else."

"And who is going after Grey?" Nik asked. "For every minute we talk, he gets further away."

Amara sighed. "I'm as eager to see him pay for his crimes as anyone, but what do you intend to do if you catch him? You already let him go once because of the threat to his hostage. It sounds like he has need of her, so as long as we stay away, she'll be safe enough. Right now, the most dangerous thing for Miranda would be for us to confront Grey."

Nik stepped forward, his expression incredulous. "You just want to let him go? After what he did?" His eyes flicked back to me.

"I don't *want* to," Amara said, "but I don't see any other choice for the moment. Once these witnesses have recorded official statements, we'll have the evidence we need to mobilize the law keepers. Grey just lost many of his followers, and he won't move as quickly with a hostage in tow. We'll find him eventually."

"Maybe," Nik snapped. "Or maybe he'll go to ground and be lost to us. If he makes it across the border, he's really gone. Even you can't pretend that Tartoran law keepers will scour every inch of the Calistan desert to find him." He turned to me. "Are you really going to let Miranda go like that? I thought you cared about what happens to her."

"I do!" I looked from him to Amara. "Can't we go after him and free her now?"

"If I had no one to think of but myself, I'd leave now," she said. "But Grey himself isn't the biggest danger. You know that, Nikolas—you've said it yourself. You're just too worked up right now to acknowledge it."

"What do you mean?" I asked.

"The real danger to Tartora is what we've seen on the road and here in Caltor," she said. "It's the poisonous seeds Grey has been leaving to cover his tracks. Many Tartorans now believe that their own king is colluding with Calista to steal our young people. It's an outrageous claim, but Grey's been systematically working his way around the kingdom, his words and actions seeming to provide proof. At this point, Tartora is becoming a powder keg. And Serena and her friends are the ones who can defuse the situation. They're what matters most right now."

"Are we really that important?" Serena asked, sounding small for the first time since I'd known her.

"Yes, you are." Amara met her eyes calmly. "Thanks to you, we have the chance to calm the tensions in Caltor immediately, and Anka can then send word out to the rest of the kingdom. That has to be Hayes' and my priority."

"And what about you?" Nik spun to face me. "Is that your decision as well, or are you going to come with me and save your friend?"

His eyes were hard, his face tight, but I read something else behind his icy determination. A hidden note of vulnerability. He'd seen my reaction to his true identity, and now he was asking me to put everything aside and go with him. He was reaching out his hand and waiting to see if I would take it.

I stood, frozen with indecision, my eyes locked on his.

"What are you saying?" Amara snapped, finally losing her cool. "Delphine is my apprentice! Of course she must stay here with me. Do you want her to become a reneger, like you?"

Nik pulled back as if struck, but a moment later he recovered.

"Better to be a reneger and do the right thing, than remain an apprentice and abandon someone you care about."

"Don't twist the situation," Amara said, her calm returning. "Delphine will stay here and help me save the entire kingdom. Staying is how she can do the right thing."

"We have to find Grey," Nik snapped. "If we don't, he'll continue poisoning this kingdom and any other he wanders into. You haven't seen his silver tongue at work or seen the way he charms and manipulates people. We have to go now!"

Amara stared him down silently. For several moments, he met her look for look, but eventually he let out an explosive breath and swung to face me.

"Delphine?" He actually held out his hand this time, and I stared at it.

I had been furious at him after Hayes's revelation, but now I felt only pain and sadness at what I had to do.

"I'm sorry," I whispered. "I can't leave Amara. I have to stay and help Serena and the others tell everyone the truth about Grey."

For a breathless moment, Nik held my gaze, fire leaping across the distance between us. And then he spun on his heels and stormed down the street, disappearing all too quickly into the darkness.

I gasped, swaying on my feet. Serena steadied me, slipping an arm around my waist.

"I'm sorry," she murmured. "I should never have gone with Grey in the first place."

"No, you shouldn't have," Amara agreed, making me wince at her coldness. But she continued on in the same steady tone. "But it has turned out to be fortunate you did. Your testimony, combined with the evidence of your body, will be enough to have Grey declared a criminal across both Tartora and Calista. We'll find him eventually, don't worry."

She stepped closer and took my arm, taking my weight from Serena. Leading me away from the others, she patted my hand comfortingly.

"I'm sorry, Delphine. I don't properly understand—or condone—what's been going on between you and Nik, but I'm sorry I didn't tell you the truth about his identity back in Ostaria. Maybe I could have prevented some of this from happening."

I drew back, reminded of all that had previously passed between her and Nik—and between me and her about him.

"How could you not tell me?" I demanded.

She winced. "As things have turned out, it appears I should have. But I didn't have the benefit of hindsight, then, and the fact that the prince has gone rogue is a royal secret. Those of us entrusted with it have been sternly commanded not to talk about it."

"Are you expected to keep secrets even from your own apprentice?" I asked sadly, but I didn't need an answer. Of course the crown wouldn't think an unknown apprentice should be entrusted with their secrets.

I looked at Amara, suddenly needing to know something. "Would you have told me if it was your own secret?"

I caught the slightest hesitation in her expression and narrowed my eyes as a possibility struck me. "What? Did you think that telling me the truth about his identity would only make him more fascinating to me?"

Amara's eyes shifted, revealing there was at least a kernel of truth in my guess, but when she spoke it was to refute my words.

"I want our relationship to be built on trust, Delphine. If one of my own secrets becomes relevant to you, I will certainly entrust you with it."

"Do you really have that much faith in me?" I asked, my tone conveying my wounded disbelief.

She took my hand again. "If I didn't before, I will in the future. What you did here was incredible given your level of training. I could see Hayes was deeply impressed. He's actually already agreed to help with your training—at least for a while. And I can see you're ready to start that training. It's clear you've completely overcome your squeamishness."

I nodded. "I was going to tell you about it. And about meeting Grey's men and Nik here in Caltor, but you were gone all day."

Amara winced. "I'm sorry about that. I let myself get distracted by…Well, I shouldn't have let myself get distracted. We've only been together for weeks, and we've both failed each other in various ways. But like it or not, we're bound together. Do you think we can start afresh?"

Looking at her earnest face, my frustration with her melted away. My father had tried to control me through secrets and ignorance, but Amara had just declared her desire for openness between us. She didn't even need to use underhanded tactics to manipulate me since she had the authority to control me without such methods. But she chose to walk a different path—to build me up and empower me instead of controlling me. I had been fortunate indeed in my choice of influencer.

"There's no need for starting again on my side," I said in a voice tinged with tears. "You've treated me far better than I expected. Even now, you're treating me like we're part of a team. Thank you, Amara. I hope you know you have my loyalty for far longer than the two years that the law binds us."

Amara looked at me for a long moment before glancing down the dark street in the direction where Nik had disappeared. Turning suddenly back, she swept me into an uncharacteristic hug.

"I've already seen that loyalty for myself. Thank you for gifting it to me, Delphine. I hope that you and I can do great things together in the coming years."

"Starting with getting Grey off the streets of Tartora," I said, squeezing her back.

She pulled away, her dangerous smile making me glad I wasn't Grey. "Starting with that."

# BONUS CHAPTER - NIK

READ THE END OF THE BOOK FROM NIK'S PERSPECTIVE IN THIS BONUS CHAPTER

There was something freeing about letting my power loose. After so long tracking Grey from the shadows, it felt good to step into the open. Defending Delphine from her would-be abductors had given me a taste, but this was even better.

I sent my power reaching into the ground and snaking up into the rafters, continuing on higher into the stone overhead. I held the floor and the roof in my hands, and I didn't intend to let anyone escape.

A man tried to slip out of the main warehouse through the door that led to the children and Delphine. I sent a snaking vine to twist around his ankle, yanking him backward. He tripped and fell, his head hitting the frame of the door as he went down. He didn't get back up.

I smiled viciously and looked for the next person still moving. The first few had come for me in a rush, but when the others saw what happened to them, they'd gone to ground. I didn't mind. I was happy to hunt them down slowly since I was only here to be a distraction.

Grey was the one I really wanted, but he'd disappeared—out of sight from the moment I smashed through the front doors. I was going to find him, though. Grey thought some people mattered more than others, and now he'd set his sights on Delphine. I had no intention of letting him leave this warehouse.

I stepped over a chunk of stone torn from one of the walls and then over the dazed body of the young man it had felled. He looked vaguely familiar, and I thought he might have come from Delphine's village. I hoped she hadn't been fond of him.

Just the idea of it made my chest tight, but I pushed the feeling aside. I needed to stay alert.

Movement in the shadows made me spin around, light on the balls of my feet, ready for action. The largest of Grey's followers—the brute who had once grabbed Delphine—lunged toward me, his blade drawn.

But the attack was only a distraction. The sideways flicker of his eyes revealed the real threat on my left. A dagger flew toward me, carried on a thin, controlled stream of air.

So he had an elements affinity. It figured.

I pretended to be oblivious, keeping my eyes on the approaching man and the blade in his hand. But as the dagger drew close, I sent my power reaching for a small stone that had fallen from the roof as I tore a larger chunk away.

Whipping it through the air, I launched it at the dagger, knocking the weapon out of the thin wind. It fell to the ground with a clatter. Vines sprang from the dirt, wrapping around it and tying it to the ground.

That dagger wouldn't be flying again any time soon.

The man grunted and threw himself the remaining distance toward me. His previous approach had been slow, his attention divided between his movement and his use of his power. But unlike him, I used my power with ease, leaving the majority of my attention on preparing for his physical attack.

Bringing up my own blade, I knocked his aside, sidestepping his attempt at a riposte. He didn't have great skill with a sword, but his height gave him enormous reach, and the confrontation was moving me away from the door I needed to guard. It was time to end it.

Once again pulling my blade up in defense, I kept my eyes trained on the man. But my power reached for the roof, seeking a stone that was already loose from my previous efforts. Wrenching it free, I sent it falling directly onto my opponent.

He sensed it coming at the last moment and sidestepped, but it still caught him on the shoulder. His arm locked up, his sword dropping from his slack grasp. A moment later, he staggered and fell.

A sound distracted me, and I looked toward the internal door just in time to see it swing closed. Someone had gone through to Delphine while I was distracted.

Leaving my dazed opponent, I raced across the warehouse, leaping the fallen stones and vines without looking at them, letting my power guide me.

Just before I reached the door, however, a woman appeared, leaping from my right and colliding with me.

We both went sprawling, a grunt escaping me as my breath was knocked from my lungs. For a second, I couldn't move, too winded by the fall. But the moment my body recovered, I leaped up, raising my blade and looking for my new attacker. She had made it to her feet first, retreating far enough to be out of reach but close enough to launch another attack if I tried to head through the door again.

I dropped into a crouch, considering the best way to deal with her. Before I had decided, the brute reappeared, swaying slightly but back on his feet. He joined her, and a sudden wind picked up the dust kicked loose from the floor, sending it into a whirlwind between us that obscured them from view.

I reached for the ground in their general vicinity, sending countless seedlings sprouting across it. The greenery was short and harmless, unlike the thorny vines I'd exploded from the ground elsewhere, but they brushed against the feet and legs of my opponents, letting me know their location.

A shout of warning from the woman suggested she'd realized their purpose, but she was too late. Reaching for one of the seeds I'd scattered earlier, I pushed my power down to create temporary roots and then up into two thorny vines, each reaching for one of Grey's followers.

Another yell echoed through the space, and the dusty whirlwind between us stilled, the dirt falling back to the ground. The woman was completely trapped, but the man still had his hands free and was trying to hack at the vine with a dagger. I sent new branches snaking out, wrapping around both his arms and pinning them to his sides.

With a wordless bellow of protest, he tipped, falling sideways where more vines sprouted up to tie him to the ground as I had done to his dagger.

Scanning the warehouse, I could see no other moving figures. Had I finally found them all? Either way, I wasn't delaying any longer.

I turned back to the door, but its handle was moving, twisted from the other side. I instantly melted back into the shadows, waiting to see who would come through.

Grey appeared, a girl slung over his shoulder. His hand clamped tightly around her wrist—a threatening gesture in the circumstances. I hesitated for a second while I examined her, making sure it wasn't Delphine he was holding hostage.

It only took a moment to determine it wasn't her, but in that time, Grey had already made it part way across the warehouse, ignoring the mess I had made of both his hideout and his people.

I growled and started after him, ready to end this once and for all.

But while my gaze was focused on Grey, my ears caught a separate sound. Someone had followed him into the warehouse, their gait unsteady.

"No!" The attempted shout sounded breathless and weak, but I recognized the voice anyway.

I whirled toward Delphine, unformed fear tugging at me. She was looking straight at me, and for a moment all I could see were her desperate, horrified eyes. Until my gaze dropped to her middle, and then all I could see was the dagger hilt she was clutching, the red blood flowing around her fingers.

Grey had stabbed her.

Rage filled me, hot and bubbling. But the fear was stronger still.

Abandoning my pursuit of Grey, I sprinted toward Delphine instead. I had sought her out and brought her here. I had asked her to do this, and Grey had stabbed her.

The pain on her face struck me like the blows my opponents had never managed to land, blossoming and twisting inside me. Delphine couldn't die. I wouldn't let that happen.

Reaching her, I scooped her into my arms, barely slowing my momentum. She was light, too light, although I told myself that couldn't be due to her wound.

I barreled straight through the partially open door and took in the empty room in a glance. Spotting a nearby sofa, I laid her down on it and knelt at her side.

I had to get the dagger out and find a way to fix her. I knew I wasn't thinking straight, but it was hard to focus around the white hot rage and ice cold fear warring within me. I couldn't let this girl—somehow fragile and strong at the same time—die because of me. I couldn't let her die at all.

I reached for the hilt of the dagger, still protruding from her middle, but the foolish girl batted my hands away.

"Leave it be." Her words came out on a rough pant, as if she was struggling to breathe. "Help her."

She made a vague gesture toward another girl who lay unmoving near the window. I had noticed her on our arrival, but only to categorize her as a non-threat.

When I stayed in place, Delphine pushed at me, her arms barely strong enough to rock me. I hesitated, trying to understand why she was driving me away.

Before I realized what she was intending, she grabbed the hilt in both her own hands and pulled it out in one smooth motion. Her scream rent the room, her expression twisting with pain.

All the blood drained from my face, my stomach burning as if she had thrust the knife into me after removing it from herself. What did it take to make a healer scream like that?

I leaned forward, but her eyes had lost their focus, her attention on something I couldn't see. For a terrifying second, I thought she was slipping away from me, but instead her color returned, her face relaxing.

Through the fog of my panic, I remembered the way she had healed Ember. Delphine was still a new apprentice, but was it possible her strength was sufficient to handle her own healing?

When she sat up, gasping with relief, the knot inside me started to unravel. Her dress was still a torn and bloody mess, but there was no new red seeping out, and when she twisted, I got a glimpse of smooth, unblemished skin. She really had healed herself.

"What are you doing?" she scolded me. "I'm a healer, remember! I'm fine now. We need to help Serena."

I had no idea who Serena was, and I didn't particularly care, not when I hadn't yet ascertained that Delphine was completely healed and out of danger.

But the stern expression on her face drove me to my feet. I looked between the girl and the older woman, both unconscious on the ground. She must mean the girl, surely?

Clearly out of patience with me, Delphine brushed past me, falling to her knees next to the girl. As soon as she did so, the girl stirred and coughed blood across Delphine's already filthy dress.

I grimaced. I was no healer, but that couldn't be good.

The way Delphine groaned and released her hold on the girl seemed to confirm my suspicion. But perhaps Delphine was merely exhausted.

"What is it?" I asked from over her shoulder. "Did you heal her?"

Delphine shook her head. "He's literally shredded her insides. I don't know how she's still alive. Everything needs healing. And it doesn't feel... right. My power doesn't know what to do."

I had no idea what she meant by that, but I could feel her distress. This girl mattered to Delphine, and I wasn't going to let her watch her friend die.

"Then we find someone who does," I said.

I picked her up as I had earlier done for Delphine.

"I don't think she'll last long enough," Delphine said, sounding distressed.

I gave her a stern look. "Then you keep her alive. Keep her alive just as long as it takes."

I already knew Delphine was stronger than my first estimation. I was certain she was strong enough for this, and I would lend her as much of my strength as she needed on top. I refused to see her spirit broken any more than her body.

She seemed to calm slightly, making contact with the girl again.

A boy waited for us on the other side of the window, and with his assistance, I maneuvered all three of us through. When Delphine nearly tipped through the opening, too distracted by her patient to consider herself, I wrapped my hands around her waist and lifted her through as easily as I might have lifted a kitten.

After relinquishing the injured girl back to me, the boy ran off, planning to gather the other escaped healers. But if Delphine could do nothing for this girl, then the rest of them would have little hope, even working together.

We needed a proper healer and soon.

A bark made me jerk and stop, scanning the nearest cross street. An orange streak appeared, with a woman close behind.

I had been hoping to avoid Master Amara in Caltor, but Delphine's relief at her appearance was obvious. Not that Amara would be much help with a dying patient.

The two people following her were another matter, however. I groaned at the sight of Hayes. I'd barely gotten rid of him once tonight, and I was afraid I wouldn't be so fortunate a second time. But I couldn't deny he was the person we needed right now.

I lowered the girl to the ground, marveling at how heavy she'd grown in the short walk from the building. Delphine sank to her knees beside her, still working to keep the girl alive. She soon had backup not only from Hayes but from the girl following him. She must be the Calistan apprentice he'd mentioned, but I noticed only the vaguest familiarity to her features.

Delphine finally released her hold and rose to her feet. She moved more slowly than I would have liked, and I watched her closely, looking for any sign she might collapse from exhaustion. Her master—who should have been the one most concerned about her well-being—was more focused on the healing underway than her apprentice.

Seized by an uncontrollable impulse, I took advantage of her distraction. Grabbing Delphine's wrist, I whisked her into a narrow side alley, out of the line of sight of the others.

She tensed, as if she meant to fight me, but as soon as I spun her around to face me, she relaxed.

"Oh, it's you." She smiled sweetly up at me.

The combination of her smile and her proximity made my heart race faster than it had done during the battle in the warehouse. But I couldn't smile back until I was sure she was fully healed. I ran my hands up and down her arms, half expecting to find some new injury hidden from my sight.

"Are you sure you're all right? You don't have any other injuries?" I kept seeing the dagger sprouting from her middle and needed physical contact to drive the image away.

"Don't be silly." She seemed to think I was foolish, and I dimly registered that would have once infuriated me. But all I could think of now was the memory of the blood flowing from her. "How many times do I have to remind you I'm a healer? I'm fine."

"You nearly died." The words were flat and hard.

She shook her head. "No, that's Serena. We should go and check on her. She's the one who was in real danger."

"I took you there." My hands rose of their own volition, cradling her face. "I asked for your help, and you nearly died. I nearly killed you."

"I'm really all right." She sounded breathless, reminding me of the horrible moments before she healed herself. "I promise. As a healer, I was never in any real danger from a wound like that. Grey was just being spiteful."

"Spiteful?" The word exploded from me, bringing a wave of the earlier fury with it. "How can you say...He stabbed you!"

I let go of her face, only to grasp her arms instead, still craving the contact although I now knew she was fine.

She was so close—too close for my self-control. I swayed toward her. How long had I been fighting this impulse, telling myself it was only a passing fancy? But after feeling her half dead in my arms, I could no longer restrain the impulse.

My control snapped, and I pressed her backward. She collided with the stone wall of the alley, and I collided with her. My lips dropped to hers, tasting their sweetness as fire burned through me.

One of my hands cupped her soft cheek while the other wrapped around her waist, pulling her closer against me but wanting to be even closer still. She kissed me back, matching my desperate passion, and the fire inside me roared higher.

I had been lying to myself when I pretended this girl was nothing but a useful and temporary ally.

She was the only person who had ever sought me out and valued me not for my title or influence, but for me. She had looked at my ability and seen strength—had even lectured me about the importance of the plants affinity despite being a healer herself. And she had approved of what I chose to do with my ability, even trusting me enough to risk her life at my side.

I needed her beside me, where I could keep her safe. I needed to keep her with me and never let her go.

I pressed deeper into the kiss. But in the distance, I heard someone calling for her. Her master.

The thought speared through me, and I broke off, my breath ragged. Delphine wasn't mine. Not yet.

She stared back at me, the brightness in her eyes changing to confusion.

When the call came again, I let her go and stepped back, just in time to keep Amara from seeing our embrace. She still regarded me with suspicion, though, her eyes flicking between us.

"What are you two doing in here? What's going on?"

Delphine hurried toward her, leaving me behind.

"How's Serena?" she asked. "Is she healed?"

My lips tightened. How could she put me and our kiss aside so easily, her mind moving on to other things?

She hurried away from me, and for a moment my feet refused to follow. But as soon as she was out of sight, I felt an itching discomfort. I couldn't just leave things like that. I needed to talk to her properly.

I followed slowly, listening to the introductions going on ahead of me. When I neared the huddled group, Hayes looked up, meeting my eyes over Delphine's shoulder.

He gave a slight bow, more respectful than he'd been at the end of our earlier conversation.

"Your Highness," he said in a flat voice.

Delphine stiffened at the words, and my eyes widened as I realized my mistake. For some reason, Amara had chosen not to reveal my identity to her apprentice, but she obviously hadn't instructed Hayes to do the same.

Delphine turned slowly toward me, her brow furrowed in confusion and her hands gripping her skirts, as if she was preparing to curtsy to my parents. Her eyes landed on me, but I couldn't bring myself to meet her astonished gaze, keeping my glare fixed on Hayes instead.

Delphine couldn't know the details of the rejections that had driven me from the capital—unwelcome among my own family. But she must have heard rumors, at least, of the disgraced prince who had been cast aside. How would she see me now that she knew I was him? Would she regret seeking out someone who had been deemed unworthy?

As the seconds ticked by, my eyes were drawn irresistibly toward her. I remained silent, although inside I willed her to understand why I had kept my identity hidden.

Amara said something to Hayes, but I wasn't listening, my whole focus having narrowed to one girl. She looked horrified and distressed as she stared back at me, and I realized I had been a fool to forget my status in her presence, even for a moment. I was a disgraced prince and a reneger, and a girl like Delphine would never belong with me.

Her expression transformed again, fear creeping into her eyes. What stories had she heard? Was it me she feared? The sight of it was too much for me, and her name escaped my lips. She shook her head savagely in response, though, and I fell silent.

Another voice piped up, slicing obliviously through the tension. "So it really is you." Apparently Hayes's apprentice remembered me better than I remembered her. "Their Majesties will be very pleased to know where you are."

I turned my harshest glare on her, recognizing yet more of the dangers that awaited me. "Don't you dare tell them I'm here."

Hayes sighed. "I already told you that we can't possibly—"

"And I told you that if you send word, I'll be gone before they can send anyone back for me." I stared icily at Hayes.

I had no intention of returning to a place where I was unwanted and unappreciated. If I was always going to live in the shadows, it would be on my own terms.

"I've been gone for over a year," I continued. "I'm not the prince you used to know. I'm far more familiar with the streets than you'll ever be."

If they tried to stop me, I would disappear right now.

Hayes sighed again. "Is this all really necessary, Nikolas? Your parents and sister miss you."

"Do they?" I almost scoffed at the suggestion. "I can't imagine why. They never had any use for me when I was with them."

"That's not fair," Hayes spoke softly, his pity more abrasive than contempt.

"Isn't it? I suppose next you're going to tell me the Triumvirate miss me too?"

Even Hayes couldn't deny the rejection I had faced from his superiors. He looked away, seeking comfort in Amara's face, as he always did.

I looked back at Delphine, the only person here I wanted to speak to, but her attention was on her friend, Serena. She fussed over the other girl until their conversation turned to Grey and Miranda. I gathered the missing Miranda was the girl Grey had carted off like a sack of potatoes.

When Serena mentioned Grey's interest in strong healers, I stared at Delphine, wondering if she would finally take my warning seriously. I had failed and let Grey escape, and now he would be coming for her more determinedly than ever. I didn't doubt he would want her after seeing the way she liberated all his new acolytes from under his nose.

My insides tightened at the thought of Delphine under Grey's spell. I wouldn't let that happen.

Serena mentioned something about Grey having left a spy in Tarin, and I joined the conversation. I needed to dispel such a ridiculous notion before it took root. Grey was tricky and deceptive, but his reach was limited. If he had been leaving people behind in every town, I would have noticed.

Serena accepted the news of Grey's deception, but when she confirmed his new land had never been Calista, I didn't feel the expected vindication. It was hard to feel anything so victorious when Delphine still hadn't looked at me with anything but betrayal in her eyes.

Serena mentioned the boy from their hometown, saying he had been with Grey in the warehouse, and Delphine looked at me, uncertainty on her face.

"Is he still alive, then?"

Disappointment sunk like a stone in my stomach. Did she think I was a bloodthirsty killer?

"Of course," I said heavily. "They're all alive."

The law keepers arrived before I could engage further, but they didn't stay long. Hayes took the opportunity to betray my identity, ensuring I would have to leave Caltor immediately. I would have resented him for it, but there was no way Grey would linger around the city anyway, so it made no difference.

We would have to move quickly if we meant to catch him. But to my shock, Amara spoke not of pursuit but of taking all the rescued youths to the law keeping hall.

"And who is going after Grey?" I asked, incredulous. "For every minute we talk, he gets further away."

Amara sighed. "I'm as eager to see him pay for his crimes as anyone, but what do you intend to do if you catch him? You already let him go once because of the threat to his hostage. It sounds like he has need of her, so as long as we stay away, she'll be safe enough. Right now, the most dangerous thing for Miranda would be for us to confront Grey."

I stepped forward, unable to believe what I was hearing. "You just want to let him go? After what he did?" My eyes flicked to Delphine, once again seeing the dagger emerging from her middle.

"I don't want to," Amara said, "but I don't see any other choice for the moment. Once these witnesses have recorded official statements, we'll have the evidence we need to mobilize the law keepers. Grey just lost many of his followers, and he won't move as quickly with a hostage in tow. We'll find him eventually."

"Maybe," I snapped, my frustration boiling over. She had no idea how difficult Grey was to track. "Or maybe he'll go to ground and be lost to us. If he makes it across the border, he's really gone. Even you can't pretend that Tartoran law keepers will scour every inch of the Calistan desert to find him."

I turned to Delphine, shamelessly appealing to her concern for her friend as I fought to keep her by my side. "Are you really going to let Miranda go like that? I thought you cared about what happens to her."

"I do!" Delphine looked pleadingly at Amara. "Can't we go after him and free her now?"

"If I had no one to think of but myself, I'd leave now," she said. "But Grey himself isn't the biggest danger. You know that, Nikolas—you've said it yourself. You're just too worked up right now to acknowledge it."

I narrowed my eyes at her insult, but her words had given Delphine pause.

"What do you mean?" she asked.

Amara spun an explanation that sounded both smooth and reasonable, swaying both girls. My desperation rose as I saw Delphine's expression change.

I put my whole focus on her, blocking out the others. My desire for her to remain with me surged up, overpowering my earlier acknowledgment that she would never belong at my side.

"And what about you?" I asked. "Is that your decision as well, or are you going to come with me and save your friend?"

She stood still, her eyes on mine, panicked and uncertain. But I had already lost her. I could read it in her hesitation.

"What are you saying?" Amara snapped, breaking through my focus. "Delphine is my apprentice! Of course she must stay here with me. Do you want her to become a reneger, like you?"

Her words hit me like a physical blow, only confirming my earlier realization. I was an outcast—as I had always been in one way or another—and someone like Delphine would never fit that role.

Still, a part of me fought, desperate not to lose her at the very moment I realized how much I wanted her presence. "Better to be a reneger and do the right thing, than remain an apprentice and abandon someone you care about."

"Don't twist the situation," Amara said. "Delphine will stay here and help me save the entire kingdom. Staying is how she can do the right thing."

"We have to find Grey," I snapped, my desperation leaking through. "If we don't, he'll continue poisoning this kingdom and any other he wanders into. You haven't seen his silver tongue at work or seen the way he charms and manipulates people. We have to go now!"

Amara held my gaze, her own rock steady. I stared back, but as the seconds passed, my momentary defiance leaked away. Why would Delphine choose to abandon everything for me?

I let out a breath. "Delphine?" I held out my hand to her, wishing I didn't already know she wasn't going to take it.

"I'm sorry," she whispered. "I can't leave Amara. I have to stay and help Serena and the others tell everyone the truth about Grey."

I held her gaze, letting all my emotions loose, the fire from before leaping briefly inside me again as I tried to remember this moment and what it felt like to stand beside her.

Then I turned and strode down the street, already feeling the looming darkness closing in around me. I had chosen my solitary life, and I would be wise not to forget it. I would always be alone, and this was why. I would never be enough for anyone.

But I still had a purpose.

The fire in my gut shifted, burning brightly again as I thought of Grey. He was out there, his greed set on Delphine, and I would hunt him to the ends of the kingdom if I had to.

I might never be able to keep Delphine with me, but I could still protect her from afar—her and all the other people Grey had touched, the ones discarded by their kingdom.

# Acknowledgments

At the end of my Mage's Influence series, I knew Nik's story was really only beginning. And while Delphine gets to be the point of view character in this new adventure, Nik has always been a central part of this story. That's why I decided to include the bonus chapter from his perspective at the end of the book, instead of just on my website like I usually do. I hope you enjoyed getting a glimpse inside his head.

Like so many of us in the wake of 2020, I've been battling burnout, and in particular, creative burnout. Given my need to fill my creative well, I'm grateful for the author friends who pushed me into the (belated) discovery of kdramas, and to my long-suffering husband who carried the household responsibilities while I watched way too many of them.

Although those countless hours let me come to this book with a renewed sense of creative interest, I'm still working on recovering my old productivity, and so I'm excessively grateful to my ever-patient team for helping push me across the finish line.

An enormous thank you to my betas, Rachel, Greg, Priya, and Ber. To my editors, Mary, and Dad, and my new proofreader, James. To my cover designer, Karri, who always shows superhuman patience with me, and my map artist, Rebecca. You are all stars, every one.

Thank you also to Marina for writing sprints and general encouragement, and to the Indie Bunch ladies for always having my back (and front and side) in this crazy publishing world. And, of course, my gracious assistant Lyra who makes a continued valiant effort to keep me from forgetting any important pieces of admin. She's struggling against the tide on that one.

And thank you to God who is the king of turning weaknesses into strengths.

# STORMS OF ALLEGIANCE

*For Jitske*
*the perfect companion on many fun adventures*

CALINARA
LAKE ATERRA
ELDRIDA
CELADON RIVER
CEPSON RIVER
VIRIDIAN RIVER
CALTOR
TARONA
KINGDOM OF TARTORA
OSTARIA
TARIN

CHAPTER

# ONE

I ran up the shallow steps leading to the grand entrance of the law keepers' hall. I hadn't intended to be late, but the most recent group of guests at the inn had taken a liking to Ember. They had kept me over breakfast, admiring and patting the fox while they fed her choice scraps of their meal. Every attempt to escape to our room had been blocked until Ember had finally gorged herself so completely that she fell asleep in my arms.

I had been running ever since, depositing Ember in her box by our fire and hurrying straight to the hall. Even so, I was later than the time specified in Amara's note.

My tardiness looked even worse against her early morning activity—she had been up and gone from the inn before I even woke. Of course, based on the contents of her note, she had forgotten it was a special day. Perhaps she would take pity on me when she remembered.

With that thought in mind, I pushed through the double doors and rushed into the spacious entrance hall. My footsteps echoed on the white marble beneath my feet, but no one looked my way.

I focused on the small knot of people around the lone counter and immediately wished I hadn't. If it wasn't for my distraction and hurry, my ability would have given some warning of the disaster waiting for me. But taken by surprise, my body reacted before my mind could.

One look at the unnatural angle of the man's leg was enough to send darkness rushing across my vision. My ears rang as my stomach heaved, an unpleasant reminder that I still hadn't completely conquered my squeamishness. Sinking onto my knees, my head lowered of its own volition, only stopping when it met the cool marble of the floor.

Excellent. I had embarrassed myself before even making it across the entrance hall. At least I hadn't actually lost consciousness.

Sucking in a deep breath, I sent my power spreading through me. Like a wave receding, my nausea settled and my eyes and ears cleared, my breathing slowing to a normal rhythm.

I remained in place for several more seconds, however. As I focused on my breathing, I tried to convince myself I hadn't just completely humiliated myself in the middle of the law keepers' hall. It wasn't working.

"Delphine?" The concerned voice of my influencer made me groan and lift my head.

Amara was reaching a hand down to me, her face concerned. I took the offered assistance and hauled myself to my feet.

"Are you all right?" she asked, her brow still creased. "I thought you'd moved past the squeamishness?"

I sighed. "It's still there. I have enough control now that I can suppress it, so it isn't usually a problem. But if I'm caught by surprise..."

I gestured toward the group by the counter, forcing myself to look at them without flinching. Now that I was prepared, it was a simple matter to keep a firm hold on my reactions, driving away both my mental and physical response to the sight of someone with a significant injury.

Amara grimaced. "An unpleasant business—and unfortunate timing. I should have met you at the door."

I shook my head. "You had no way of knowing I'd rush in here headlong, like a fool. If it had been the hospital, I would have been more circumspect." I looked at the injured person again, squinting to see them better across the remaining distance. "But what are they doing here? They seem strangely composed given..." I swallowed, feeling the faint brush of my mastered squeamishness.

There was something disconcertingly unnatural in the scene before me. The injured man was gesticulating wildly, his primary emotion anger, none of his attention on his horrific injury. His two companions seemed equally irritated, one of them constantly interjecting over the man's words, although from her manner, the woman seemed to be backing him up rather than disputing his words.

The fourth person stood apart from the other three, his position suggesting he was on the opposite side of whatever dispute was underway. He wasn't speaking, but not from any lack of engagement. Instead he appeared too enraged to speak, his face growing redder and redder whenever he looked at the injured man.

"He has already been attended to by a healer," said a new voice as a man almost two decades my senior strolled toward us. "He isn't feeling any pain, and he's in no danger, either."

"Not just any healer," Amara added. "Hayes did it himself, so I'm sure the injured man doesn't feel a thing."

"You did it?" I asked my master's close friend and my sometime instructor. Given Hayes's strength, I was surprised he hadn't completed the healing fully.

"Thankfully I happened to come across the patient within minutes of the injury occurring. In normal circumstances, I would have healed him fully on the spot, but he claimed it was a deliberate attack." Hayes threw the man a look that suggested he doubted the story. "So naturally I didn't dare cross Anka by doing anything other than alleviating the patient's discomfort and ensuring he was in no danger."

"But you're not a weak or inexperienced healer," I protested. "Surely you could have healed him and Anka could have questioned you about the injury later?"

"Thank you for your high praise," he said gravely, despite the twinkle in his eyes. "But I assure you Anka doesn't hold me in such high esteem. In her eyes, I'm as green as any apprentice when it comes to matters of law keeping. I wouldn't even know what it is they're looking for when they examine an injury, so how could I report on it later?"

Amara snorted at this assessment of her aunt, the head of the Caltor law keepers' hall. I gave Hayes a grin of solidarity, though. The older woman was a formidable presence, and I wouldn't want to get on her bad side either.

"So he's claiming it wasn't an accident." I looked at him thoughtfully. Would he have been so quick to insist on going to the law keepers' hall instead of the hospital if there hadn't happened to be a healer on hand to almost instantly relieve his pain?

Before either Amara or Hayes could respond, a new figure appeared in the entrance hall. The law keeper faltered slightly as she saw the injured leg. She quickly regained her stride and hurried over, however, remonstrating with the small group before she'd even reached them. All four of those in front of the desk turned on her immediately, their voices rising again.

"I should have left him a sliver of pain," Hayes muttered in obvious solidarity with the beleaguered law keeper.

When Amara turned a stern look on him, he gazed at her innocently.

"Just to ensure he doesn't forget and try to use the leg, of course."

"Of course," she said with another snort.

The female law keeper, who I recognized as a healing mage—soon had the matter in hand, however. The regular law keepers who had trailed in her wake lifted the injured man, and with a few choice words and a warning about not jostling the man's leg, she had them all out of the entrance hall. I knew enough about the law keepers' processes to know she would be taking them all to a smaller assessment room. Once there, she would complete the healing and any other investigation necessary.

I breathed a soft sigh of relief once they were gone, releasing my hold on my own body.

"I'm sorry for embarrassing you," I said to Amara. "And in the middle of the law keepers' hall, too. I'll be more careful next time."

"I hope you will be." She narrowed her eyes as she examined me. "But for your own sake, not mine. Your squeamishness isn't your fault."

"Maybe not, but I'm not newly activated anymore. I'm a healing apprentice, and I should have better control over myself."

"I didn't realize it still affected you so badly." Hayes sounded intrigued rather than censorious. "I would have expected it to have faded by now through exposure. You've certainly seen far worse injuries while training at the hospital with me—and connected with the injured bodies in those cases as well."

I shrugged, not sure what to say. My squeamishness had abated somewhat, but it definitely hadn't disappeared.

"Hmm..." Hayes rubbed the side of his jaw. "If it's still there at this point, I'm afraid you may be dealing with it permanently. It's unusual for a healer not to overcome it, but as you've already experienced, it won't stop you from completing your duties as a healer."

I groaned. "A squeamish healer. It's bad enough being a squeamish apprentice, but you're saying I'll still be like this after I graduate and become a proficient?"

"Sorry," Hayes said seriously, but I could see the amusement around his eyes.

"You're laughing at me," I grumbled, and he gave a full chuckle.

"You're powerful, Delphine, and a quick learner too. You have excellent control for someone only months into their apprenticeship. You can't blame us seniors for being grateful when we discover the young upstarts have some weaknesses."

I laughed. "You're not fooling me, *Master* Hayes. You're strong enough to hold your head up regardless of any new arrivals in the healing affinity."

"Ah, but that's what old Drake and the others thought until Airlie arrived," Hayes said, referring to the head of the Elements affinity and the young arrival who had shaken up not only the Guild but the whole kingdom with her unprecedented power. She was not only part of the royal family now, but also sister to the queen of neighboring Calista.

I shivered slightly at hearing myself compared to the princess, even in the most casual way. I wasn't like her. I didn't have unprecedented new levels of power. The only unusual thing about my healing ability was that I hadn't been born into a family with an established lineage of strength. And that was by no means unprecedented. The very Master Drake mentioned by Hayes had been born into a family of blacksmiths.

"So Master Anka wants that injured man healed by one of her own healers as part of their investigation of the crime," I said, getting the conversation back on track. "Is that why we're here?" I directed the question at Amara.

I'd been doing a lot of training at the hospital under Hayes's tutelage, since Amara's elements affinity meant she couldn't give me direct training in healing. But she'd mentioned recently that Anka wanted me to do some more training at the law keepers' hall. Apparently the experienced law keeper was always on the lookout for any healing apprentices who showed even the faintest interest in law keeping.

"Actually I didn't know anything about the case when I planned our day," Amara said, reminding me of her early departure.

"I'm so sorry I'm late," I hurried to say, trying to remember if I'd already apologized amid the distraction of my embarrassing collapse. "There was a group swarming Ember in the dining room, and…"

I let my voice trail off, suddenly worried that it sounded like I was making excuses. But Amara just rolled her eyes and smiled.

"That fox. She attracts attention wherever she goes."

The affection in her voice was obvious, despite her complaints. Over the weeks we'd spent in Caltor, Amara had grown almost as fond of Ember as I was. We'd both be sorry if she ever chose to go back to the wild.

"Is there another case going on, then?" I asked, looking around for any sign that something out of the ordinary was happening in the hall. There was no sign of anything, however, the open space now empty except for the usual clerk behind the counter.

A glaring absence suddenly caught my attention, and I looked to Hayes. "Wait, where's Luna?"

The second-year apprentice was usually glued to her master's side, her enthusiasm for learning making her tireless, despite the sometimes long hours of our shared training.

"She's already inside." Hayes gestured at a different corridor from the one taken by the earlier group.

I frowned in the direction he was indicating. I had to be even later than I'd realized if Luna was already deep in the bowels of the hall. But why were we all gathered here? If we weren't assisting with the injured leg, was there a more substantial injury that needed investigation?

As I hurried down the corridor behind Hayes, I braced myself for the possibility of an even more shocking scene. I was determined not to embarrass myself again, regardless of what was about to confront me.

When he opened the door to one of the small rooms lining the corridor, I paused for a beat to steel myself. Preparing to act swiftly and suppress any reaction, I took a deep breath and stepped through after him.

I scanned the room quickly, looking for either a victim or perpetrator. I saw neither.

Instead, an explosion of noise and color made me rock back on my heels as Luna launched herself in my direction.

"Happy birthday!" she squealed as she thrust an enormous bouquet of vibrant flowers into my face.

"Happy birthday, Delphine!"

"Happy birthday!"

A chorus of voices rang out, making me peer around in bewilderment, my vision obscured by the mass of petals and leaves.

"Luna? What's going on?" I took the flowers from her, lowering them so I could see the room.

"You look so surprised!" My friend was grinning with joy at having caught me off guard. "Did you really think we'd all forget your eighteenth birthday?"

Warmth suffused my face as I finally realized what was happening. I twisted around to look at Amara who was watching from the doorway with an amused expression.

"You didn't have to do this," I said.

"I didn't," she replied. "It was all Luna's doing. I was just responsible for getting you here."

"I'm glad you're pleased," said a vaguely familiar voice. "I was afraid that rousing you from your bed at the crack of dawn might not be the friendliest birthday gesture."

While several people exclaimed that it was hardly dawn, I located the speaker and gasped.

"Master Clay?" I stared at the animal healing specialist, who lived in Ostaria. "What are you doing here?"

"How could I stay away when it's the birthday of my favorite healing apprentice with a pet fox?"

"She's not a pet," I said automatically before shaking my head. "You're as outrageous as ever, though! You can't possibly have come to Caltor just for my birthday!"

"I may have had one or two additional reasons," he acknowledged with a suppressed smile.

Hayes snorted. "I can see you haven't changed a bit, Clay."

Stepping forward, he greeted the other man with a firm handclasp and a slap on the shoulder. Clay grinned back at him, the two of them exchanging the greetings of old friends.

Even though Clay specialized in animal healing and Hayes in healing people, it wasn't surprising they knew each other. Not only were both master healers—a small group—but both knew Amara from their apprentice days. They must have all been at the Guild at the same time.

I looked past them, taking in the rest of the room. A small table against one wall had a cake with crisp white icing decorated with yet more flowers. But my eyes were immediately drawn to the girl standing next to the table. She looked uncertain, hanging back with a hesitant smile.

"Serena?" I gasped and hurried toward the older girl. "What are you doing here? I thought you returned to Tarin to finish your apprenticeship? You can't be done yet. It's only been a matter of weeks. Surely your old master didn't refuse to take you back?"

"No, no, thankfully he's been more than considerate about the whole thing." She hesitated before giving me a bigger smile. "Happy birthday, Delphine."

"Thank you." I smiled back, my old animosity for the plants apprentice long gone.

After facing Grey together with me, Serena's previous resentment of me had completely disappeared. I had even been disappointed when she had to rush straight back to Tarin to resume her broken apprenticeship.

I had admired her bravery in facing the issue head on, however. She must have been nervous since her master hadn't been required to take her back. And even if he did accept her, a stigma would still have remained. Once her apprenticeship resumed, it lifted her status of reneger—and relieved the complete social ostracization that the whole of Tartoran society was required to show those who abandoned their apprenticeships. But that didn't mean people would welcome her back with open arms.

"When I heard your old friends were going to be in town, I knew we had to have a party." Luna slipped her arm around my waist and gave me a squeeze before throwing herself at Serena for an enthusiastic embrace.

Serena accepted the hug, blinking at me over Luna's shoulder.

I chuckled. "Sorry, she's just like that."

"Like what?" Luna disentangled herself, giving both of us a cheeky grin. "Kind, thoughtful, and friendly?"

"Yes, that." A smile tugged at my lips, the disastrous start to the day fading from my mind.

"Sorry, did I overstep?" Luna grimaced at Serena. "You feel like an old friend, and not just because of Delphine. It's a strange sort of bond, healing someone when they're close to death. I sometimes forget that the patient doesn't always feel the same way. Especially since you had to leave Caltor so soon afterward."

Serena's and my eyes met, and I knew we were both thinking the same thing, remembering the extensive injuries she'd suffered at Grey's hands.

Luna broke me out of the moment, bumping my shoulder with hers.

"Today is supposed to be a happy day! No thinking sad thoughts!"

I laughed and reached for the cake, digging one finger into the icing. As I tasted the sweet confection, I gave a hum of pleasure.

"Delicious."

"Delphine!" Luna tried to look reproving but failed when she broke into giggles. "I guess you are the birthday girl, so you can do whatever you want."

Serena smiled as well, the expression more hesitant as she glanced between Luna and me.

"I hope *you're* not going to try to claim you came all this way for my birthday," I said to Serena. "Did you come with Clay?"

I glanced across at the older man who was still deep in conversation with Hayes and Amara, the expressions on their faces suggesting the topic had turned more serious. Clay lived in Ostaria, which was the closest city to Tarin, but it wasn't close enough for me to think he and Serena would know each other—especially given Serena wasn't a healer.

Serena shook her head. "I met him five minutes ago while we were waiting for you to arrive."

I winced. "Sorry I was late."

"You don't have to be sorry on your birthday," Luna said. "I'm pretty sure it's a rule."

"I had no idea you were so into birthdays." I shook my head. "If I had, I would have been more prepared."

Luna grinned unapologetically. "We didn't have a lot of access to new things in my settlement growing up, but my mother always made an effort with our birthdays. I don't know how she managed it, but she always found enough ingredients for a feast, and she would make us presents herself."

Her words brought up thoughts of my own mother and the small celebrations we would have every year on my birthday. Tears pricked at my eyes as I realized it was my first birthday without her.

But I didn't wish myself back home. Despite the passing months, I still hadn't worked out my complicated feelings toward my father. He had always been a warm presence on my birthdays, and yet, the whole time, he had been secretly holding me back, letting his fear hold sway over my life.

I shook my head, forcing my thoughts back to Luna. She talked about her parents often since she clearly missed them both. She had supported their decision to move to Calista six months before, however. They had only stayed in Tarona for so long to support her, and she had grown comfortable enough in the Tartoran capital not to need them anymore.

She had assured me it was better for them to go on ahead so many times that I could tell she had mixed feelings about it. But since she would be joining them after her graduation, it wouldn't be a long separation. She had never wavered in her loyalty to Calista, so I knew we would be losing her to the newly created Calistan Mages' Guild once she became a proficient.

Luna was one of the members of the secret settlement who had remained across the border during Calista's years of devastation. They had survived in the wasteland by raiding Tartora, but all had now been forgiven. The Tartoran Mages' Guild had even agreed to train many of the settlement youngsters on behalf of the new Calistan Guild in exchange for the influx of new power the settlers brought to our Guild and Tartora in general.

I had heard people speak of the recent changes in the Guild, but getting to know Luna had made it seem possible those changes were real. If the Guild was now overflowing with young people like her, how could it possibly stay the same?

"Will your clinic be all right without you?" Hayes asked from across the room.

There was an odd tone to the otherwise friendly question that caught my attention, making me look across at the small huddle of master mages. Hayes was looking at Clay with an expression I couldn't interpret.

Clay responded with his usual smile, however, giving no sign he had picked up the underlying discordant note.

"I think Tara is relieved I won't be there to cause her any problems. She's convinced I'm the root of all the clinic's problems, and I'm sure my absence will only prove her right. I'll no doubt return to find everything in absolute order."

I grinned at the memory of the woman who ran Clay's clinic for him. I'd never met anyone who gave such an impression of competence and order.

Amara laughed, and after a moment, Hayes chuckled as well. Whatever I had picked up from him earlier seemed to disappear, his usual good humor returning. He looked our way, his eyes catching on Luna, who was trying to silently signal to him.

For a moment he looked confused, but then his brow cleared, and he gestured for the other two with him to join us by the table.

"I think my apprentice might burst if we don't sing now."

"Sing?" I cried, horrified, but it was too late.

Luna burst into enthusiastic notes, the rest of them following in a ragged chorus. I pressed my hands to my burning cheeks, laughing despite myself.

"Thank you," I said as soon as they'd finished. "But please don't ever do that again."

"Was it really that bad?" Clay pretended to look hurt. "I've previously been told I'm an excellent singer."

I stared at him until Amara's chuckles clued me into the joke. I let out a breath of relief which made him start chuckling as well.

Hayes cleared his throat. "I hate to hurry along your celebrations, Delphine, but Anka will be waiting if we take much longer."

"Anka?" I looked between them all. "So there is a reason we're in the law keepers' hall of all places?"

Luna grimaced. "Obviously it wasn't my first choice. But I really wanted Clay and Serena to be here, and we don't know how long the law keepers will keep them. The only safe option was to meet before they're all due to report to Master Anka." She gave me an apologetic look. "First thing in the morning wasn't my preference either. But you and I, at least, will be having a celebratory meal later, whether you like it or not."

I smiled back at her, but my attention was on the reason for Clay and Serena's presence.

"So Master Anka called you both here?" I looked between them. "Something's going on." It wasn't a question.

I turned to Amara. "Do you know what it is?"

She exchanged a look with Hayes which made me raise both eyebrows.

"You're both involved in these meetings, too?" I asked with a sudden sense of certainty.

Amara hesitated. "For now, she doesn't want apprentices included."

"Except Serena, who's still an apprentice," I said slowly. Meeting Amara's eyes, I gave her a disappointed look. "It has something to do with Grey, then."

"Sorry, Delphine," she said. "We can't say anything more for now. And I'm especially sorry it's happening on your birthday. But Luna has promised to spoil you in my absence."

I managed to dredge up a smile despite the burning curiosity that was now surging through me. After all these weeks of silence, what had Grey done to merit Anka calling in people from other parts of the kingdom?

"I'm grateful to Master Anka." Luna had a determined light in her eyes. "It might not have been her intention, but she summoned some of your new friends just in time for your birthday, and now she's providing you with a day off. It's perfect."

I couldn't help smiling at her spin on the situation. When she put it like that, I had no justification in being disappointed.

*She didn't summon all my new friends.*

The errant thought hit me from nowhere. I squashed it back down, careful to keep my face neutral. I had once thought Nik and I were becoming friends, and he had even kissed me, suggesting he was interested in something more. But he hadn't been honest with me, and he'd chosen to leave. I hadn't heard from him in all the weeks since he left to chase after Grey, and I had no business thinking of him now.

I summoned a smile, linking my arm with Luna's as she waved off the others. "Well then, what did you have in mind for the day?"

CHAPTER

# TWO

Despite it not being long since breakfast, Luna insisted we both eat a slice of cake before leaving the law keepers' hall.

"Master Anka will surely give the others a break at some point, and they can have some then," she said, leaving the rest of the cake behind on the table.

She scooped up the bouquet, however, and pressed it on me. "You can't leave this behind! I went to a lot of trouble to source those flowers for you."

"It's beautiful." I sniffed at it appreciatively. "It reminds me of all the window boxes they had in Ostaria. I miss those."

Luna led the way outside, nodding in easy agreement, although she'd never been to Ostaria herself. "It's such a pity window boxes are against regulations here. But people still have gardens behind their houses. I visited some of the patients you've healed while we've been training here and asked them to let me raid their gardens. They were all more than happy to help. So they're not just flowers—they're flowers grown and picked with love."

My spirits lifted in response to her beaming smile, my hand tightening around the bouquet. Learning how to control my squeamishness enough to actually help people had been the best part of our extended stay in Caltor.

Luna pulled me out into the flow of foot traffic on the street. I fell into step beside her, guessing we were on our way to the nearby marketplace.

"Do you have any idea what that's all about?" I asked, tipping my head back toward the law keepers' hall. "I don't suppose Hayes dropped any hints?"

"Sadly, no." She tugged me out of the way of an approaching cart, continuing once we were safely past the large wheels. "I'm not sure when he would have told me any secrets. You and I spend so much time together, I barely managed to organize your birthday surprise."

Her grin took any potential sting from her words. Luna had already told me many times that she liked having another girl her age to share her apprenticeship. It was fortunate we got along so well since she was right about how much time we spent together.

After Amara had agreed to Hayes and Anka's combined request that we stay in Caltor for the time being, we had made some adjustments to our accommodation arrangements. Amara had moved out of our shared room into a smaller room of her own, Luna taking her place. I had been surprised at the change but not unhappy. Amara and I got on well, but she was significantly older than me and was a master besides. Swapping Amara for Luna felt like receiving a sister in exchange for a mother as a roommate. I had never had any actual siblings, but if I'd had an older sister, I would have liked one like Luna.

My early fears that I would have nothing in common with an apprentice from the Guild had soon faded in the face of her friendliness and my growing understanding of her background. Luna had grown up isolated like me, even if it was in a different way, and she had known nothing about the ways of mages or the Guild before Hayes activated her.

"It's strange to have a complete day off," I said, trying to remember the last time I went a whole day without using my healing ability.

Luna groaned. "Right? They've been working us without mercy! At least at the Guild we had regular days off. I don't know how you cope with life on the road all the time!"

"We've hardly been on the road," I pointed out with amusement.

"You know what I mean. It's the same thing, just without the travel. And Amara is a hard taskmaster!"

I shook my head, a smile on my face. I was used to Luna's lighthearted complaints by now. She had been apprenticed to Hayes for more than a year when the Triumvirate sent them to Caltor, so she found it an adjustment to leave behind the more structured Guild schedule for the chaos of our ever-changing life.

"But she's kind," I pointed out, as I always did. "And I prefer a master who includes me and views us as a team over one who treats me like a schoolchild."

"Hayes is the kindest person I've ever met!" Luna exclaimed, following the predetermined script. She could never hear even the vaguest allusion to an insult to her influencer without leaping to his defense.

"I know, I know," I said hurriedly. "He saved your whole settlement and negotiated you a place in Tartora. He's a paragon of every possible virtue and an excellent healing teacher. Look! We've arrived."

I steered her off the street and into the large square which hosted the daily market. Despite my cavalier attitude, I meant my words. During our stay in Caltor, Hayes had included me in all the lessons he gave his own apprentice, leaving Amara free to work with Anka on matters they both kept close to their chest. And he had never once made me feel like a burden.

Of course, Amara was still involved in my training—the law required her to be. She visited our sessions daily and took charge of our training on general matters such as mental discipline and control. She had also taken both of us for several sessions on the elements affinity. Although Luna wasn't cross-influenced, all mage apprentices spent at least some time familiarizing themselves with the capabilities of the other affinities. And in my case, it was extra fascinating since I had healing cross elements, thanks to Amara's elements ability.

Watching her use her power was like feeling an itch somewhere just out of reach. I couldn't actually connect with the elements like she could, but they felt achingly familiar, as if touching them might be possible if I just stretched out a bit further.

"Look!" Luna tugged me over to a stall selling ribbons, buttons, and lengths of material. "Have you ever seen anything so beautiful?" She lovingly stroked a length of shimmering blue silk which looked remarkably like a living stream.

The stall keeper glared at her, and I shook my head, tugging her away.

"What would I do with something like that? Do you think I have time to sew myself gowns? The hospital is happy to provide basic clothing, and that's more than sufficient for me."

"Delphine!" Luna groaned despairingly. "It's your birthday! You have to buy *something* that's beautiful, not just practical. Don't pretend Amara didn't give you a pouch because I know she did."

My hand went to my pocket where the small pouch sat concealed. Amara had slipped it into my hand with a warm smile and murmured birthday wishes. I'd wanted to protest, but she'd been gone out the door before I could, and once on the street myself, I'd remembered that gifts of coin were common from masters to apprentices on their birthdays.

Relieved of my momentary discomfort, I agreed with Luna on the matter of a birthday purchase. But I wasn't going to buy material that would just sit in our inn room untouched.

"There!" This time I was the one tugging Luna through the crowd.

She smiled, pleased by the stall full of beautifully worked leather. But when she saw what I picked up, the smile fell from her face.

"Really, Delphine?" She groaned again. "You're hopeless! Won't you even look at that bag? The leatherwork is gorgeous, and it would be perfect for carrying your healing supplies. You heard the conversation between Amara and Hayes yesterday. You might be strong enough to heal almost anything completely, but she still wants you to be fully versed in the ways of weaker healers, including carrying bandages and tinctures and other supplies."

"I know." I glanced absentmindedly at the bag she was holding out. "She and I have talked about it a lot. When we're on the road, we travel through a lot of smaller villages and towns, and she wants me to be able to train the locals who have a healing affinity, like she does with those with an elements affinity. So I need to be able to demonstrate the techniques." I ran a hand over the detailing along the strap of the bag. "Plus, if we ever encounter a large scale disaster, I might need to spread my ability out, saving it for the more serious cases."

Luna shook her head. "You really are embracing life on the road." She held the bag out toward me and shook it slightly. "So wouldn't you like this beautiful bag?"

I laughed, returning my gaze to the thin, elegant collar in my hands. The polished green stones that dotted its length winked up at me. They weren't expensive gemstones, but they would still serve my purpose.

"An excellent choice," the stall keeper said hopefully. "It would look very fine on a large cat or small dog."

"How about a fox?" Luna grumbled under her breath, earning a confused look from the man.

I ignored her, beginning to haggle with him over the price.

"This doesn't count, you know," Luna said. "Buying something for Ember isn't the same as buying something for yourself."

I gave the bag she was still holding a closer look.

"What price could you give if I bought the bag as well?" I asked the stall keeper, causing Luna to instantly brighten.

After several more minutes of haggling, we left the stall, my new bag slung over my shoulder with the collar tucked safely inside and several coins still left in my pouch. Amara had been generous.

"Are you really going to put a collar on Ember?" Luna wrinkled her nose.

"I don't have any interest in collaring her in the traditional sense," I replied, busy looking around for the source of a particularly appealing, sweet aroma. "I won't be attaching a lead or anything like that. But she likes to wander the streets at night, and I worry that someone is going to mistake her for a wild animal and a pest and attack her. I want anyone who encounters her to know she isn't a wild fox."

"I suppose that makes sense." Luna sounded disgruntled at having to acknowledge the value of my purchase.

"Ooh, it's those hot cakes making that smell." I pointed to the line in front of a small stall, instantly distracting Luna.

"You've still got coin left, don't you?" She gave me a cheeky smile. "Feel like buying us a birthday treat?"

"Of course," I said promptly. "As many as we can eat."

We joined the end of the line, Luna rising onto her toes to try to peer ahead at the stall.

"I hope they don't run out before we get to the front," she said. "I don't have the patience to wait for them to bake a second batch."

"I'm sure they've prepared plenty," I said absentmindedly.

My mind was going rogue again, reminding me of the early days in my travels with Amara when my heart would leap every time I caught a glimpse of any tall, broad-shouldered, and dark-haired figure. Over the weeks, I had grown used to Nik's permanent absence, but apparently my morning's wayward thoughts had brought my old bad habits back to the surface.

In a large marketplace, there were plenty of tall men, so I hoped I would get on top of the instinct quickly. I was going to develop a twitch otherwise. I forced myself to focus on Luna, who also seemed to be having trouble standing still.

"You've been so focused on me, but is there anything you need to buy?" I asked.

"Only some practical things." She quickly added, "But I can get those later."

"No, why should you? We're here now, so we should get everything done while we have the chance. Why don't you go now while I wait in line for our cakes?"

Luna hesitated, her eyes flicking toward the far end of the market and back.

"Are you sure?"

"Of course I'm sure! Go, go." I pushed her lightly, propelling her out of the line toward the direction of her gaze.

"Thanks, Delphine. I won't take long." She flashed me a quick smile and disappeared into the crowd.

I readjusted the bag on my shoulder and shuffled forward as the line moved. The baker served more quickly than I expected, and I soon had a bundle of hot cakes wrapped in a length of clean material and tucked into my new satchel.

Congratulating myself on the usefulness of my recent purchase, I tucked myself out of the way of the crowds, between the baker's stall and the neighboring one selling metalwork. From this vantage point, I would see Luna as soon as she returned—an unexciting option but one much less fraught than plunging into the crowd in an attempt to find her.

I watched the people lining up for the cakes, idly guessing at their stories and trying to tune out the overwhelming awareness of so many beating hearts and pumping lungs. Hayes had said I would always have to live with some level of squeamishness—an unwelcome prospect. But at least the mere presence of other people no longer made me feel ill. I didn't even have to suppress symptoms unless I touched someone who was actually injured or ill —or else was taken by surprise like I was at the law keepers' hall.

I eyed a man in line whose breathing was slightly labored, trying to guess at the cause, when a hand grasped my upper arm and pulled me backward. Caught completely off guard, I stumbled into the side alley behind me, defenseless. I would have fallen if I wasn't supported by strong, steady hands that deposited me against a wall.

As soon as I caught my balance, I thrust out one hand, seeking any inch of my attacker's skin. It didn't matter how large he was, the moment I touched him, I would have the upper hand.

But a second before I made contact, my eyes flashed up to his and my hand froze, just short of touching him. It wasn't a stranger or thief attacking me, but a familiar figure who had haunted more of my thoughts than I wanted to admit.

Nik. Also known as Prince Nikolas.

CHAPTER

# THREE

"Nik?" I gasped, too shocked to use the proper form of address. "How are you here?"

But a moment later my body stiffened as I remembered myself.

"I mean, Your Highness." I bowed, but it was hard to manage more than a slight incline when he was standing so close, trapping me between his body and the alley wall.

He watched me with an unfamiliar look—a dangerous mixture of amusement and affection. But at the sound of his title, he drew back, his face darkening.

I sighed. Everything about this scene was familiar. His unexpected proximity rolled back time, forcibly reminding me of the nighttime adventures that had marked the beginning of my apprenticeship. Those days had been lost in the sea of endless training since, but suddenly they seemed so close I could touch them. It felt like only yesterday when I had stood like this—too close and yet also too distant from the searing blue eyes that seemed to see straight through me.

"Don't call me that," he said, his voice rough.

I arched one eyebrow. "Why not? It's your title." I left the statement hanging between us like a challenge, and he was the first to look away, running a hand through his hair, the lines of his body taut.

The silence between us grew heavy.

My mind spun through the various questions I wanted to ask him. I should start with Grey and whether Nik had located him. I should ask about where he'd been all these weeks.

I did neither.

"Why didn't you tell me?" The words came out more angrily than I'd intended, bearing a load of emotion I hadn't intended to reveal. "Why did you hide your real identity?"

"That's not my identity anymore." The tone was harsh, and he wouldn't meet my eyes.

I laughed darkly. "You mean because you're a reneger?"

He pulled back as if I'd hit him, but I couldn't tamp down my rising anger.

"You might not be wielding the authority of a prince right now, but that doesn't change your birthright. You grew up in a palace, Nik! Your father is *King Marius*. How could you not tell me something like that?" The next words hung unspoken on my tongue. *You saved me. You kissed me. But you didn't tell me who you were.*

"I…" He ran his hand through his hair again, and I realized I'd never seen him so hesitant, so unsure.

Some of my anger deflated. It felt pointless being angry at someone who was clearly lost and alone. Whatever choices Nik had made that had led him here, he had left himself nothing but his ability and the strange determination that drove him.

He had chosen to cut himself off from everyone and everything, so who was I to think I should be an exception? He had made me no promises.

"Never mind," I said. "The important thing is Grey. Did you find him? What about Miranda?"

I rose onto my toes as the questions poured out of me, my eyes fixed urgently on his face. A hot wave of worry and guilt was rising inside me. Grey had fled with Miranda as a captive, and we had all abandoned her.

We might have had our reasons, but for Miranda, at least, those reasons meant little. Nik had gone after her, though, and I hadn't realized how much of my peace had been built on that knowledge. But now he was back here in Caltor, apparently alone. Had something happened to Miranda?

Nik gazed at me for a moment, absorbing the change of topic. Emotions raced across his face too fast for me to read before he shut them all behind a wall, returning to his old closed-off expression.

"Miranda is fine—physically, at least. Or she was when I left to come here."

When I flinched at his final words, his voice softened.

"I saw no indication that situation will change. Grey wants to use her, not harm her."

I sank back, both relieved and disappointed by his words. I was glad to know she was safe for now, but my earlier sense that I had betrayed her was growing. Until now, I had been able to cling to the hope that Nik would find a way to free her. Now I could no longer deceive myself.

"Why are you here?" I asked, my voice dull and my eyes trained on the ground.

A gentle finger under my chin lifted my face until my eyes met his.

"Happy birthday, Delphine," he said in the gentlest voice I'd yet heard.

Something pressed into my palm, and I looked down to see an object wrapped in a length of plain material.

"A present? For me?"

He didn't bother to answer the obvious question.

I looked back up at him, but he was looking away, one hand rubbing the back of his neck.

I unwrapped the object, exposing a thin, elegant dagger, possibly the smallest one I'd ever seen. I looked at him again, and this time he was watching me.

He cleared his throat. "If you're going to worry about everyone else all the time, you need a way to protect yourself."

I quirked one eyebrow, lifting one of my hands and waggling my fingers.

He shrugged. "I don't care how powerful you are, there are some situations and people that should be approached with a sharp blade, not bare fingers."

I looked down at my hand and frowned, thinking of Grey. He was a healer like me, and Nik was right. When it came to a fellow healer, making physical contact gave them the same access to me as I had to them. Not to mention Nik's own trick of covering all patches of exposed skin.

I shivered, trying not to think about the kind of situation that might require the use of the blade. I hoped I was never going to find myself in such a position again.

"Thank you," I said softly, strapping the dagger and sheath to my belt. "I'll keep it close."

Nik nodded, looking satisfied, and I considered his choice of gift. It was a good reflection of him—dangerous and unhelpful on the surface but surprisingly thoughtful underneath.

"How did you know it was my birthday?" I asked.

He shifted uncomfortably, and my eyes narrowed.

"Have you been following me?"

"I needed to speak to you—alone."

I flushed. He couldn't possibly have been inside the law keepers' hall, could he? Surely there was no way he could have seen my embarrassing start to the morning.

A moment's reflection reminded me of the more important point. Nik had been off searching for Grey and had apparently found him—and now he had something to tell me. That was far more important than my foolish embarrassment.

"How have you been?"

His question caught me off guard, and I just stared at him. There was no way Nik wanted to speak to me alone just to ask about our time apart. He did seem different, but not that different.

The memory of our last encounter made my heart speed up, my awareness of his current nearness heightening. We had been standing very similarly before he had kissed me, and my eyes were drawn irresistibly to his lips.

He cleared his throat and took a step back, giving me room. My rebellious heart sank at his movement. Surely I wasn't foolish enough to hope for a repeat of that particular encounter? Nik was a prince and a reneger—a combination that was still hard to process—not to mention arrogant, condescending, and dangerous. As the enemy of Grey, I could appreciate him as a formidable ally, but I couldn't let myself see him in any other light.

But all my sensible lectures did nothing to change the way the air turned cold around me or to still the fluttering in my stomach that was uncomfortably similar to my squeamish reaction to blood. My mind could pretend I didn't react to Nik's presence, but my body wasn't as easily deceived.

I had never been immune to the prince, and his lengthy absence had apparently changed nothing.

"You've been training hard," he said to fill the silence when I didn't respond to his earlier question.

I started, staring at him again. Exactly how long had he been watching me?

"I see Hayes really did take on that Calistan girl." Now he sounded like he was talking just to cover my awkward silence. "I can't remember her name. Something to do with the sky..."

"Luna," I said, finally finding my voice again.

"Oh yes." He sounded entirely uninterested. "That was it."

"You've met her before?" I couldn't help feeling intense interest in his past. What had led him to reject his life of privilege in favor of becoming an outcast?

He shrugged. "Briefly."

I fell silent when my mental calculations told me Luna's apprenticeship must have started at a similar time to Nik's disappearance. After our confrontation with Grey and Nik's departure, Amara had told me what little she knew about Nik's situation, but it hadn't been much. Because Amara was the most senior traveling mage in the kingdom, the king and queen had taken her into their confidence, hoping she might encounter their son. But even so, they had been short on detail, which was hardly a surprise. The last thing they must have wanted was for the kingdom at large to discover their son had chosen to exile himself from both them and society.

I examined his face, and Nik met my eyes steadily. Ever since he'd pulled me aside, he'd been behaving more gently and considerately than in any of our previous interactions. But I could still see traces of defiance behind his expression, and it made me uneasy.

Whatever had caused the changes in Nik, plenty of his old attitude still remained.

As if reading the mistrust in my eyes, Nik stepped closer again, capturing one of my hands in his.

"I'm sorry about last time," he said in a low, husky voice that was nearly my undoing. "I never should have asked you to become a reneger. I wouldn't choose that life for anyone, let alone you."

My mouth dropped open.

"Careful, Nik," I said playfully. "It almost sounds like you care about me."

He flushed and looked away, making the joking smile fall from my face. I had been half teasing, half probing, hoping to expose the simmering emotions I could see beneath his surface. I hadn't expected him to take my words so seriously.

Awkwardly I cleared my throat. A heedless part of me wanted to believe that Nik had thought as often of me in the weeks of our separation as I had thought of him. I wanted to believe he had truly softened when faced with my absence.

But the more realistic part of me fixated on the reasons for his return. Nik had been unable to convince us to join him and had been forced to follow Grey alone—just as he had always done. His brief experience of allies had ended in a betrayal of sorts—at least from his perspective—and now he was back for reasons I still didn't know. My instincts told me he needed something from me, and I would be wise not to read anything more into this interaction than that.

"Why are you here?" I repeated the question in a firm voice, trying to let him know that I wanted the truth this time instead of distracting comments that made it sound like he'd come back for me.

Nik leaned forward, putting one hand on the wall beside my head, his eyes trained on mine.

"I need you." His low voice sent a thrill through me, sending my thoughts into free fall.

What had he just said? And what could he possibly mean by it? My mind struggled to form coherent thoughts as my pulse spiked dangerously high and my eyes once again dropped to his lips.

But his face remained maddeningly still, just too far away for me to be sure of his intentions, although he was close enough for me to feel his breath against my skin. Whatever Nik had meant, it wasn't what the treacherous part of me wanted it to be.

"What…" My dry mouth failed me, and I licked my lips and tried again. "What do you mean?"

"I think I know a way to rescue Miranda and to take Grey down for good. But my plan requires you." He swayed closer, speaking against the curls beside my ear, his breath making them move and sending goosebumps down my arms. "It involves danger."

His words reached the faltering parts of my brain like a jolt of lightning. I reared back and hit my head against the wall behind me.

Wincing, I reached up to rub the sore spot, but his hand was faster, cupping the back of my head and massaging it gently while his eyes sent me an apology. I gulped and tried to pull back, but his free arm had somehow found its way to my waist, holding me firmly in place.

I tried to ignore the searing effect of his touch and forced my tongue to resume function.

"Why would you need me? There are plenty of healers as powerful as me, and most of them must be better trained."

"I need you precisely because you're young and new to training," he said. "You fit the profile of Grey's targets. He wants people young and malleable— ones who can be bent to his will. And, in particular, he's already intrigued by you. He's tested your strength, and he's curious about your ability. Not many people would be capable of fending him off like you did. He wants you, Delphine, and that's why it has to be you."

For a long moment I stared at him, my eyes trapped by his, something unspoken and charged hanging between us.

But the longer Nik looked into my eyes, the darker his became. "I've spent weeks trying to think of a different plan. I would never suggest this if I could think of any other way. But I believe in you, Delphine. You're strong enough for this."

"You've changed your tune," I said weakly, remembering how often he had rejected me as useless after we first met.

He released me so suddenly, I almost staggered. As he stepped back to put space between us, his eyes dropped away from mine.

"I've already acknowledged your usefulness—I was the one who suggested we work together to capture Grey, remember? And I'm the one who asked you to chase after him with me."

I slowly nodded, confused by his seesawing manner.

"I'm not running away with you, Nik," I warned. After everything she'd done for me, I couldn't abandon Amara like that—not even for Miranda. "If you really have a workable plan, you'll need to convince Amara of that, not just me."

He nodded once, the movement abrupt and the shadow in his eyes at odds with his apparent agreement.

"Delphine!" A distant call from inside the market reached my ears, bringing the rest of the world rushing back to my awareness.

"Luna." I looked toward the end of the alley where I could see a glimpse of the back of two stalls and the crowd beyond.

When I turned back, Nik was staring in the same direction.

"Tonight," he said abruptly. "At the inn. After your birthday meal. I'll be there to convince Amara."

"Wait, what?"

I heard my name called again and glanced back toward the market, frustrated. I needed longer to question him. He couldn't say all that and then just...

Disappear. I sighed as I surveyed the place he had been standing. I couldn't see his exit route, but somehow Nik was already gone.

CHAPTER

# FOUR

I emerged into the market feeling dazed. Luna immediately pounced on me, her face creased with concern.

"There you are! What happened? Where did you go?" She clutched my arm as if she was afraid I'd disappear again if she wasn't holding onto me.

I leaned a bit closer so I could lower my voice in the noise of the crowd. "Nik."

She reared back, her eyes wide. "Here? In the market?" She looked wildly from side to side.

I shook my head. "I think he's gone now."

But even as I said it, I snuck a glance around myself, remembering my unanswered question about how long he had been tailing me. Was it possible he was still here, just keeping out of sight? I couldn't imagine a reason why he would hang around, but I felt certain I wouldn't see him if he wanted to stay hidden.

We continued to wander around the market, pretending to look at the stalls, but it was hard to muster any interest in shopping after the shock of Nik's return. And even the celebratory evening meal Amara had organized at the inn struggled to hold my attention.

The others had returned from their day at the law keepers' hall early enough to join us for the meal, but there had been no time for me to pull Amara aside before it began. As we ate, I caught Amara sending me a series of concerned glances. I couldn't explain my mood to her, though, not with Serena and Clay present.

Clay didn't know anything about Nik's involvement in our fight with

Grey, and while Serena knew the prince had helped rescue her, I didn't think I should tell her he was back. But although I kept quiet, I couldn't stop myself constantly glancing at the door and even the windows. I knew logically that Nik wasn't going to come bursting through one of them into the inn dining room, but I couldn't seem to keep still.

When Amara caught me looking for the twentieth time, she leaned closer, her brow lined.

"Delphine?" she murmured. "Is something wrong?"

I shook my head slightly, keeping a smile pasted on my face. "Later," I breathed back. "I'll tell you after."

Amara sat back, accepting my words, although she still watched me with a curious gaze. At least Serena seemed oblivious, too impressed with the feast to notice my odd behavior.

"The inn in Tarin doesn't cook anything this fancy." She poked at an elaborate roast duck with a serving fork.

"Will you have to head straight back?" I asked, unable to think of a more interesting conversation topic when half my mind was on what would happen after the meal.

Serena nodded, something in her face catching my attention. "After going reneger, I don't have a lot of leeway. Of course my master agreed to this trip given Master Anka had sent for me specifically, but I have to return in the morning."

I glanced from her to Amara, real curiosity flaring. Did that mean the issue that had occupied them all day was resolved? Or just that Serena's part in it was done? From the somber faces of the three older mages, I was afraid it was the latter.

"Do you not want to return?" I asked, wondering about the reluctance I had seen in her face.

She sighed. "Tarin isn't the most comfortable place for me right now. But I know it's my own fault. I just have to win back people's trust. And to do that, I have to return as quickly as possible." She brightened. "I don't know how I'll move a step after stuffing myself so full, though."

I smiled back and put an extra honeyed carrot on her plate. I had been right to label her brave, although I'd never thought of her that way during our shared youth in Tarin.

Eating herself into somnolence, Serena was the first to finish and head for her room. We exchanged goodbyes before she left since she would have an early start in the morning, and then I took my seat again. I waited for Clay to also take his leave, my impatience growing when he made no move.

Instead he sat back in his chair, looking relaxed as he chatted with Amara, a wine glass in his hand and his long legs stretched out beneath the table.

Even when Hayes began to make murmurs about wrapping up for the night, he remained in place, merely raising his glass at the other man in a casual way, as if bidding him goodnight without any intention of following suit.

I frowned between the two of them, wondering if there was any way for me to send Clay on his way while hinting at Hayes not to leave. I would prefer him to be present for the meeting since I felt sure Amara wouldn't agree to anything involving Nik without consulting Hayes first.

My worry regarding Hayes was unfounded, however. As soon as he saw Clay intended to stay, he also remained in place. Apparently he didn't want to leave before the party broke up for the night.

He didn't seem to be in a celebratory mood, though, sitting straight in his chair on the other side of the table and making no move to eat or drink. My attention was distracted, wondering where and when Nik was going to show up, so it took a while to realize Luna was trying to signal me, her movements somehow both frantic and subtle.

My first instinct was to look around the room for some hint of Nik, but when I saw nothing, I looked back at her, frowning a silent question. Her eyes were gleaming as if she was bursting with news she couldn't verbalize.

Once she saw she had my attention, she inclined her head sideways at her master. I glanced at Hayes beside her, but he looked just as he had a minute ago. I frowned back at her, and her eyes widened. She gestured at Hayes again before tilting her head across the table and raising her eyebrows.

I blinked, looking from Hayes's stiff posture and watchful eyes across to the object of his attention. Clay still leaned back, relaxed, laughing at something Amara had just said. His body was angled slightly toward her, giving her all his focus.

My mouth fell open as I looked back at Luna. It was easy to read her delight that I was finally receiving her message.

Had I been too distracted all evening to notice the dynamics between the older members of the group? It seemed likely.

But now that I was paying attention, it was hard to dispute Luna's obvious interpretation of the situation. Hayes seemed uncomfortable at Clay's presence—even...territorial.

But weren't they all old friends? I remembered his strange manner in the morning, and my curiosity grew.

I could see Luna was bursting with interest, but after a moment she glanced once at the door and then at me, tilting her head toward Clay with a question in her eyes. She was obviously fascinated by whatever dynamic was going on between our two masters and the new arrival, but she was also the only other one at the table who knew Nik was coming.

"Enough conspiratorial glances, you two," Amara said suddenly.

Hayes's eyes snapped to hers, a hint of guilt showing in his expression, and Clay straightened, his hand tightening around his wine glass. But Amara's attention was on me and Luna.

I winced, but Luna didn't look in the least abashed at being called out. She seemed more curious at where the conversation was going to go, looking from Amara to Clay and finally to Hayes.

But Amara's eyes had landed on me and stayed there, her expression commanding. It took me a moment to realize that while she had been speaking to me and Luna, she hadn't been referring to our silent conversation about the three of them.

"I don't know what happened in our absence and what you have to tell me, but you don't need to be so jumpy. Anything you can say to Hayes and me, you can say in front of Clay. I promise he knows far more state secrets than either of you."

Clay chuckled lightly at this endorsement and even Hayes nodded, whatever earlier antagonism he had been feeling swallowed. It seemed that if Hayes had an issue with Clay, it was definitely personal and didn't cause him to doubt the reliability of the other healer.

I cleared my throat, unsure what to say now I had everyone's attention. After a moment, I glanced around the dining room, which still held a couple of other groups of diners.

"Let's go up to our room," Luna said. "Since it's the biggest."

Amara looked once more between us, her eyes narrowing, but she ended by nodding agreement. Rising to her feet, she signaled to the rest of us to follow, leading the way to the stairs.

At the top of them, she glanced at me, a smile in her eyes.

"Why do I have a terrible feeling about this?"

I grimaced. "It wasn't my idea."

Both her eyebrows shot up. "You know that only makes everything seem worse, right?"

I chuckled reluctantly, unlocking my door and ushering the small group inside. The room had always felt spacious, but so many bodies inside made it shrink. I cast a quick glance around, hoping not to see any mess I might have left out, and instead encountered a dark shadow in one of the corners—a hulking figure that couldn't entirely blend with his surroundings.

Hissing, I slammed the door shut behind us, making the rest of the group start and look toward me. When they saw me staring into the corner of the room, they all followed my gaze.

Amara immediately stepped forward, one arm raised in a protective gesture, holding me and Luna back. But the figure stepped forward into the light, a provocative gleam in his eyes.

"Prince Nikolas!" Hayes exclaimed as Amara sucked in a breath and slowly lowered her arm.

Clay whistled slowly, raising his eyebrows as he looked first at Amara and Hayes and then at me, his gaze both curious and calculating.

Ember trotted out of the same corner where she had clearly been sitting at Nik's feet, her new collar winking in the light. I stooped to pick her up, murmuring "traitor" against her fur.

"I didn't expect such a crowd," Nik said, still with that superior look that made me want to smack him.

He focused on me. "You didn't warn them?"

Now it wasn't just Clay and Nik looking at me. Feeling the weight of five sets of eyes, I stepped past the others, facing Nik.

"I didn't get the chance. We weren't alone until just now."

"I wouldn't call this *alone* exactly." His eyes gleamed at me, suggesting he wouldn't have minded the two of us being alone.

Amara cleared her throat, giving him a quelling look as she stepped to my side and pulled me back. Whatever else Amara thought of the renegade prince, she did not approve of her apprentice having any involvement with him.

*Involvement.* My lips burned as I remembered the kiss Amara had nearly witnessed after we fought Grey. She hadn't seen enough to be sure, but she'd clearly been suspicious.

She didn't need to worry now, though. Nothing like that was going on. How could it when I knew the full truth of who he was?

I glanced behind me and saw Luna's excitement and Clay's bright curiosity. I sighed. "Why don't we all sit down? Somehow I don't think this is going to be quick."

Amara raised an eyebrow but helped everyone find somewhere to perch. I deposited Ember back into her basket, with a firm command to stay there. I didn't want her injured underfoot with so many people in the room.

Amara gestured for me to sit beside her, conspicuously far away from Nik. And he seemed to have noticed based on the less-than-friendly look he was giving her.

I glared at him. He was here to convince Amara, Hayes—and now Clay— of a plan they would probably all violently disapprove of. So the least he could do was try to play nice. I didn't think Nik knew how to be subservient, though —even before three master mages. And now that I knew his title, I knew why.

I ran a hand over my face. He hadn't even started talking, and I was already tired.

When I opened my eyes again, he was watching me. Was that concern in his eyes? I shook my head at my own fancy. It wasn't likely.

Amara cleared her throat, giving Nik a disapproving look. "I suppose I should start by asking why you broke into the bedroom of my apprentice."

Nik gave her a cool glance. "We needed a private place. This isn't a conversation we want overheard, and I'd rather not be seen by anyone outside this room." He glanced briefly at Clay, as if he would have preferred not to be seen by him either.

"That's Master Clay," I said quickly. "He's a friend of Amara and Hayes and a master healer. And he's also a trusted advisor—"

"I know who he is," Nik's cool voice cut me off. He gave a curt nod in Clay's direction, and the man responded with a half bow from his sitting position.

"This is a great surprise, Your Highness," he said in a level voice that revealed nothing.

I sighed and sank back. I should have known Nik would be familiar with Clay, given he knew Amara and Hayes. Nik might have been a young child when the three of them were apprentices at the Guild, but that didn't mean they hadn't been back since. And as a prince it was probably part of Nik's role to know all the master mages in the kingdom.

I would do well to remember that I was the outsider in this room, not Clay.

Amara had ignored the attempted introduction, her attention never wavering from Nik. "So you're telling me you expected me to enter this room with Delphine?"

He shrugged. "That was the point of the meeting."

"Meeting?" Amara turned to me with a raised eyebrow. "So you really were expecting him to be here?"

"Not exactly here." I glared at him. "Nik didn't bother telling me *where* we were all going to meet after the meal."

"It seemed the most logical place, since it's the largest room," Nik said, unflustered.

Amara sighed and rubbed her eyes. "I'm not going to ask how you know that. I don't want to know. Let's focus on the more important points. What have you discovered about Grey in all these weeks, and why are you here now?"

"I've learned Grey is a bigger threat than we realized and where his base is," Nik replied promptly. "And I'm here because I need Delphine."

Everyone in the room responded to his final words, their reactions covering the full spectrum. Luna looked delighted, as if we were enacting a play purely for her entertainment. Hayes looked pained. Clay looked shocked, his eyes traveling back to me and staying focused on my face in a way that made me squirm with embarrassment and glare at Nik, who looked entirely unmoved by the reactions he'd just unleashed.

Amara, however, straightened, and spoke. "No. Absolutely not. You cannot have my apprentice."

"Obviously you would come, too." Nik met her eyes, his face utterly serious, and her demeanor changed slightly, her expression becoming less determined and more inquisitive. Whatever else she was feeling, Nik had successfully captured her curiosity.

"I mean it, Master Amara," Nik said quietly, and neither Amara nor I missed his use of her title. "Delphine cannot become a reneger."

Amara nodded once, her movement slow. A single crease appeared between her eyes, and when she finally broke gaze with Nik, it was to glance at Hayes.

I couldn't read everything that passed between them, but I could tell they were both surprised. Something had changed in the weeks Nik had been away, and I wasn't the only one to recognize it.

"I think someone had better fill me in," Clay said in his usual good-natured tone. "It's becoming clear that your report on your encounter with Grey was missing some key facts." He sounded amused rather than resentful.

Amara grimaced. "Apologies, Clay. Naturally we gave the full report to Anka, but the instructions from court were to keep the prince's involvement quiet." She glanced at Nik. "I have to confess that after all this time, I wasn't expecting to see His Highness back again."

Nik narrowed his eyes. "I'm not going to ask what you mean by that statement."

His tone sounded vaguely threatening, and both Hayes and Clay bristled, a fact Luna noticed with yet more delight. I rolled my eyes at her, but at least someone was enjoying this painfully awkward interaction.

Amara was entirely unfazed by the animosity in Nik's words, continuing her explanation to Clay.

"Apparently Prince Nikolas had been tracking Grey for some time before Delphine and I crossed paths with him in her hometown. We unknowingly trailed him all the way here, and along the way I discovered my apprentice and the prince had been spending their nights hunting Grey."

She threw me a disapproving look. "I still don't know the full extent of every interaction, but it culminated in the fight you've heard about. Delphine rescued the young people while His Highness dealt with Grey's people."

"Ah!" Clay smiled, apparently pleased. "I did think that story didn't quite add up."

The healing master might run a clinic for pets, but he clearly had his share of experience with court. He'd known something was missing from the report, but he had also known not to question the official story.

"As you know, Grey managed to escape," Amara continued, "and His Highness was...displeased with our response. He wanted us to chase after Grey instead of taking the freed captives to Anka. In the end, he chose to go after Grey alone."

There was the slightest emphasis on the final word, making me squirm a little. At least she hadn't told everyone how Nik had tried to convince me to go with him.

"That was some time ago." Clay leaned forward, his eyes alight as he watched Nik. "But you're saying you succeeded in tracking him to his base? He's there now?"

Nik nodded. "I have reason to believe he's still there, yes."

"That's excellent news." Hayes straightened. "We should lose no time in riding for the capital. King Marius can assign us enough troops to confront Grey head on and end this whole thing."

He met Amara's eyes, another unspoken message passing between them.

Nik smiled slightly, as if he'd expected that reaction.

"I assume from your response that you've finally caught on that there's something suspicious about this blight," he said calmly. "But bringing in troops is exactly what we can't do."

If his earlier pronouncement had caused shock waves, this statement was more of an explosion. My own confusion and curiosity was nothing compared to the reaction from the others.

Hayes surged to his feet, his eyes wide, while Amara sucked in her breath loudly. Clay also rose, striding over to the door and wrenching it open to peer up and down the corridor. When he had satisfied himself that there was no one outside in hearing distance, he closed it again, turning the key that sat inside the lock and exchanging glances with Amara.

Even Ember had responded to the sudden shift in the room, scrambling to her feet in her basket and letting out a terse yip. I hurried over to reassure her, keeping a hand on her soft fur as I exchanged confused glances with Luna. At least I wasn't the only one who had no idea what was going on.

But one glance at the burning expression in Amara's eyes made the confusion sour in my stomach. Whatever was going on, it wasn't good.

"What blight?" I asked slowly. "What is he talking about?"

CHAPTER

# FIVE

"How do you know about that?" Clay asked in a hard voice, his eyes boring into Nik.

I expected Nik to make some half-mocking response, but when he remained deadly serious, my stomach sank even further. Was there really a large-scale blight I hadn't heard about it? And if there was, what could it possibly have to do with Grey?

I sucked in a breath as I realized it had to be related to the meeting that had brought Clay and Serena to Caltor.

Hayes held up a hand to prevent any further words, looking uneasily at Luna and me. I tried to look as harmless as possible, desperate not to be kicked out of the meeting at this juncture.

Amara came to our rescue, however. "I don't think there's any point trying to hide things from Delphine and Luna any longer. Given His Highness is in possession of relevant information—and clearly intends to involve Delphine in the matter—our participation is no longer purely advisory. Involving our apprentices is only natural."

Hayes hesitated a moment longer before nodding and sinking back into his seat.

"I hope you haven't been speaking of this to others," Clay said sternly, his focus still on the prince.

Nik actually laughed, his expression wry. "Who would I be telling?" My heart contracted as I thought of his lonely life, but his eyes hardened as he continued. "You don't need to be afraid. I may be a reneger, but I'm still loyal to this kingdom. I know how to keep state secrets."

To my surprise, it was Clay who backed down, looking away and nodding. It was a strange thing seeing these older, powerful mages navigate their interaction with a prince who was now an outcast. No one seemed quite sure where Nik should be ranked within the group.

"This blight was what you were meeting with Anka about all day," I said, no doubt in my mind. "And you had Serena there, so you already knew there was a connection with Grey."

Amara's expression tightened slightly. "It would more accurately be called a suspicion than knowledge. We have no proof." She looked at Nik. "Perhaps that is about to change?"

"How far has the blight spread?" I leaned forward, my past as the daughter of farmers rising to the fore. "How many different crops can it infect? Is it a new one?" I couldn't quite keep the panic from my voice.

Blight was rarely an issue for farmers—not when the kingdom was full of people with a plants affinity. But every now and then a new blight arose, one resistant to plants power. Guild mages were always called in for such cases, and thankfully they had always been able to get it under control in the past. Once they had properly studied and defeated the new blight, they would train the less powerful members of their affinity in techniques that would keep it away. Acts of service such as these were among the many reasons the Guild was able to adopt such a high and mighty attitude. I might resent them, but I couldn't deny that the kingdom needed their power.

But Clay, Hayes, and Amara weren't plants mages. And neither was Master Anka. If they were being called in for consultations with her on the topic, then this wasn't just a simple blight. How many farmers had already been affected? And what did Grey have to do with it?

If there really was a blight beyond the control of the plants mages, then the whole kingdom could be in dire trouble. An untamed blight could sweep through vast stretches of crops.

I caught Nik watching me, a hint of concern in his eyes. I took a deep breath and forced myself to relax, loosening my shoulders and unclenching my hands. Whatever was going on, there were clearly far more powerful mages than me worrying about it. I had to trust they would find a solution.

"So far it's contained to the north," Amara said. "But it isn't acting like a usual blight. It's been appearing on unconnected farms, and no one can identify a link. The plants mages can't see any obvious signs of tampering, but they also haven't been able to drive it out."

I put my hand to my mouth, my eyes wide. "What do you mean they haven't been able to drive it out?"

It was one thing for the Guild to still be working on a method of suppression that could be implemented by someone with a weak ability, but it was another thing not to be able to do it themselves.

"Enough fields have had to be burned that the king and Triumvirate are getting worried," Hayes said. "We're too close to harvest for there to be time for replanting, and the kingdom could find itself short on food over winter if we have to burn any more."

"It's that bad?" Luna whispered, her face pale.

"Normally the plants affinity would handle blights on its own, and we wouldn't be involved," Amara said. "But ever since Grey left Caltor, Anka has been gathering any hint of his movements, however small or unreliable. And one of her law keepers noticed a correlation between sightings of Grey and the locations where the blight has been appearing."

I gasped. "Grey is somehow causing the blight? But he's a healer! How is that possible? And shouldn't the plants mages be able to tell if it's an unnatural phenomenon?"

"It does seem impossible." Clay steepled his hands and used them to prop up his chin. "We discussed it in extensive detail yesterday, and Hayes, Anka, and I are all in agreement. A healer couldn't possibly use their power to spread a blight among crops. They could possibly unleash a disease in an animal population, but even that is by no means certain. And with plants, it's simply impossible."

I nodded slowly, processing his words. At least now I knew why Clay of all people had been called in. He might have chosen to set up a pet clinic in a small city, but he was clearly powerful and well-respected in our affinity. And from the way he spoke of Anka, I suspected he knew her well—and might even have trained in law keeping beside her at some point.

"So it's not Grey," I said, strangely disappointed. I preferred an enemy we could fight to a natural blight that was beyond our control.

"Not directly, it would seem," Amara said. "And unfortunately Serena never heard Grey or his people make even the smallest allusion to a blight. But that doesn't mean there isn't a connection." Her shrewd eyes dwelt on Nik. "We weren't willing to discount it earlier today, and now it seems we were right."

"I believe you are," Nik said. "On both counts. Grey hasn't been spreading the blight. He couldn't possibly be. But I'm convinced he knows something about it."

"You have a plants seed," Clay said. "Have you examined the blight for yourself? Did you notice anything odd about it? I know some of the most powerful mages of your affinity have been sent out from the capital, but..."

Nik shook his head. "I haven't had the chance to see it for myself. I was following Grey, and he always arrived after the fields had been burned and the capital mages had departed."

Amara and Hayes exchanged a frustrated glance.

"Then it's possible there isn't a connection after all," Amara said. "Grey may have merely been tracking reports of the blight for his own purposes. Perhaps he thought anyone touched by the blight would be more susceptible to his message?"

Nik frowned. "I don't think that could be the case. When I say we arrived after the fields were burned, they were usually still smoldering. And I heard astonishingly few rumors about the situation on my travels. The crown might not be succeeding in defeating this blight, but they've been successful at keeping tight control of the news about it."

That made sense. With a blight this concerning, I should have already heard about it on the streets of Caltor. But if the winter food supplies were in danger, it was no surprise the crown wanted to keep the news quiet until they had a solution. A scared and angry populace wouldn't help matters.

"What are you saying?" Amara asked.

Nik frowned. "I can't be sure, but it felt like we weren't following the blight itself but something else. Something that arrived at each location just before the blight broke out."

Amara sucked in a breath. "You think Grey wasn't causing it, but he knows what—or who—is, and he was following the cause? How is that possible?"

Nik shrugged. "I have no idea. I'm just reporting what I saw."

"It sounds like you followed him across half the kingdom." Hayes's voice was hard to read.

"I did." Nik glanced at me and then away. "It seemed more important to finally find the location of his base than attempt a lone rescue."

I now knew why he suddenly wasn't meeting my eyes. He knew I cared about Miranda and wanted to see her rescued. He thought I would be angry he hadn't charged in alone and liberated her while Grey was separated from his remaining followers.

But my concern for Miranda didn't mean I was heedless about the rest of the kingdom. This matter was too big to ignore.

"So you did find the location?" Amara asked. "Where is it?"

"It's in the desert."

"The desert?" Everyone in the room exchanged surprised looks.

"Over the border, then?" I asked, trying to imagine how anyone could survive for long in the low dunes of the Calistan desert.

"Yes, which is why we never found any sign of him here in Tartora. But since the desert is on the coast, it barely counts as part of Calista. It's too barren to support any population, and the coast along that stretch is too treacherous for boats. The Calistans use the rivers to get north to the nomad lands and south to Tartora, so the desert is untouched. It would be a perfect place to hide if it wasn't so dry and barren."

"So how is he living there?" Amara asked. "I know he spends much of his time in Tartora, but still..."

"The Calistan shoreline is rocky and steep," Nik said, "but at one point a crevasse juts into the desert. And given how green it is, it must contain a freshwater oasis. The crevasse isn't big enough to support a proper settlement, and it's surrounded by desert on three sides and treacherous rocks and reefs on the fourth, so it doesn't appear on any maps. I don't even know if anyone has found it before."

"So how in the kingdoms did Grey stumble on it?" Luna asked.

"He didn't happen to mention the matter to me." Nik's response made her roll her eyes.

"So that's where Miranda is now?" My hand tightened around Ember until she squirmed and I forced myself to relax it.

"This news only makes it more imperative that we ride for the capital immediately," Hayes said. "There can be no question King Marius will support us now. Once we capture Grey, we can find out exactly what is causing this danger to our crops."

"Perhaps we would find out, and perhaps we wouldn't," Nik said. "It would be a chancy business."

"You don't think he'd talk?" Clay asked, his expression thoughtful.

"I think he most definitely wouldn't," Nik replied promptly. "I might hate the man, but I can recognize his strengths. He has a rare determination and focus. We might be able to tell when he's lying, but we can't force him to tell the truth. I'm not convinced anything could."

"Then what do you suggest? We just leave him be?" Amara gave Nik a disparaging look.

"If we can't force him to talk, we need to trick him into it. That's where Delphine comes in."

"Me?" I gasped. "How could I trick Grey into telling us anything?"

"I overheard him talking about you more than once." Nik's voice remained calm, but his hands balled into fists at his sides. "He's fascinated by you, just like I predicted." He met my eyes, his gaze steady, clearly concealing some deeper emotion. "He didn't choose Miranda to take with him by accident. He clearly has an interest in healers, and she'll be a reasonably strong one once she's ready to be activated. But you're on another level. You don't just have mage level power, but master level."

"I'm no master mage!" I exclaimed.

"Not yet," Amara said softly. "Mastery requires more than just raw strength. It requires great skill and control as well. But you have the necessary power to take the mastery exams one day if you wish."

I gaped at her, trying to process her words. I had always known I had strength, but somehow I had never considered a future where I actually became a master.

"You've spent too much time with Amara," Hayes said with a hidden laugh in his voice. "It gives a person a skewed perspective on strength."

Amara gave him an exasperated look, but he continued. "Neither you nor Luna were raised at the Guild, so you're probably not aware of the significance of Amara's very early ascension to mastery."

"Back in Ostaria, someone mentioned she was one of the youngest masters in generations," I said slowly.

Hayes nodded. "Only an exceptional combination of both strength and skill allows someone to take the exam so early. I, myself, only took it recently."

"And what Hayes isn't adding," Clay said with a smile, "is that there's every likelihood he will end up as the next head of our affinity after Master Colton. So it's a significant comparison."

"Are you saying Amara could be Master of the Elements one day?" I stared at my master with new eyes.

She scoffed and shook her head. "Of course not. I have no interest in such a position. And, Hayes, I am well aware you could have taken the mastery exam sooner if you hadn't chosen the route of being a second first." She turned to me. "All three affinity heads and the Royal Mage have seconds. They're always proficients, but only the strongest are chosen for the role. It's considered training ground for future masters. Those who dream of one day becoming head of their affinity almost always choose the path of being a second before they take the exam."

Clay chuckled. "Yes, while Amara has the skill and strength to head her affinity, she lacks the necessary interest in politics."

Hayes drew a breath only to slowly expel it, his eyes narrowing as he looked from Clay to Amara and then away. But it was Amara's expression that caught my attention. She seemed to be showing something akin to guilt and sorrow as she averted her eyes from Hayes.

I had now spent many weeks in close companionship with both of them, and I knew they were old friends. But whatever was going on between them—exacerbated and stirred up by Clay's arrival—was obviously more complicated than I'd realized.

When I glanced at Nik, I found him watching the two of them thoughtfully.

Did he know more about their history than I did? When he turned to look at me, I drew back, however, all thought of asking him forgotten. A discomfort blazed in his eyes, and I couldn't shake the feeling that if I touched it, I would be burned.

"The relevant point here is Delphine's strength." Nik stressed my name slightly. "Or, more accurately, that Grey is aware of her strength. He hasn't been able to access anyone as strong as her. And it's more than that, too. He's also intrigued by her wall."

"He knows about that?" Amara looked at me with concern.

I winced. I had freed myself from the fears that had kept me hiding behind the wall before confronting Grey, but when he tried to attack me, I had still reached for it instinctively. And it had successfully driven his power out of me.

"I had to use it to protect myself in our fight."

"This is the wall you had in Ostaria?" Clay asked. "You were able to use it to protect yourself against Grey's power?"

I bit my lip as I nodded, realizing that was a point I probably should have shared before now.

"I guess that's significant. Sorry I didn't say anything earlier. There was so much going on, and I just didn't think of it."

"And of course I didn't ask," Hayes said ruefully.

He threw Amara a glance. "Yes, yes, I know this is the problem with how we train. There isn't a lot of room for innovation."

Clay sat back, rubbing his chin as he thought. "If the effect could be replicated, it would be significant. I was curious after meeting you in Ostaria and tried to do it myself, but I couldn't manage it. I was thinking it might be helpful for other apprentices in your situation, but healer assassins are a much greater threat. While rare, thankfully, they're extremely dangerous. Having a way to block them..."

I shifted uncomfortably, making Ember whine. Murmuring an apology to the fox, I slipped back to my original seat.

"Sorry," I said again, not sure what else to say to the shocking news that Clay had failed to do something I could do with ease.

Not that I'd used my wall in weeks.

"It's not your fault," Hayes said. "I should have asked more questions about your encounter with Grey. I'm the teacher, so it's my responsibility."

"No." Amara sighed. "Delphine is my apprentice, so it's my responsibility."

"Regardless of who has failed whom," Nik said coldly, "the important point remains. Grey knows she's strong, and for some reason he's been trying to gather strong healers. And he knows she has an ability he hasn't encountered before as well. To put it simply, Grey wants Delphine. Badly. And that's where our opportunity lies. We use his greed against him."

Amara stared at him with narrowed eyes. "You can't possibly be suggesting we hand Delphine over?"

"That is precisely what I'm suggesting." Nik said it calmly, not breaking gaze, but I could see the subtle shift as his jaw tightened, and the muscles across his shoulders flexed. He was pretending coldness and indifference, but something else lay underneath.

Amara stood in one fluid motion. "This meeting is over."

CHAPTER

# SIX

"Amara." Hayes spoke softly, his eyes pleading with her. "We should at least hear the prince out. I'm certain he doesn't want any harm to come to Delphine."

"I've spent a great deal of time considering the matter," Nik said. "If I could go in there myself, I would, in a heartbeat. I would have already gone. But Grey is cautious now in a way he wasn't before. Delphine is the only one he wants badly enough to take the risk."

"Even if he does want her," Clay said slowly, "why would he ever trust her? Didn't he stab her during their last encounter? Surely he's not such a fool as to think she would want to join him after that?"

"Not willingly, no." Nik looked to me. "That's where Miranda comes in."

"Ooh." Understanding slowly bloomed. "You want me to offer myself in her place. Like a prisoner exchange."

For the first time I could see the appeal of his plan.

Nik nodded. "It's the only believable reason you would go to him. And once you're inside his camp, you can find out the information we need—even better if you can get him to trust you."

"Even with an exchange..." Clay shook his head. "He'll be on guard around her all the time, surely? Will she really be able to learn anything of value?"

Nik leaned forward, his manner indicating he had thoroughly thought through every aspect of this plan. "Grey is a very confident man. I would write it off as foolish arrogance except that he really does manage to win people and situations over—even when it seems like they should be beyond his reach. Take Miranda as an example. She tried to escape him here in

Caltor, and yet she now seems to have accepted her lot completely. She didn't make a single attempt to fight him or escape in their whole journey north. Grey believes in his ability to convince people, and that will work to our advantage. He might be suspicious of Delphine at first, but I don't believe he'll stay that way. If she makes it look like he's won her over, he'll believe it."

"How long is she supposed to stay there?" Luna asked, sounding horrified.

Nik's eyes lingered on me again. "As short a time as possible."

"And we're just supposed to let an eighteen-year-old face that kind of danger alone?" Amara asked.

"Of course not. We'll be there, too, as close as possible without being discovered." He hesitated, his jaw tensing again. "But there will be some risk. I can't deny that. And if I could think of any other way, I would never suggest this."

Something in Nik's expression made my stomach flip over. How long had it been since he'd found Grey's base? How long had Nik been resisting bringing this idea to us?

"And you think your father will agree to this strategy?" Hayes asked.

Nik was silent in response, and I snorted. "Telling the king wasn't part of your plan, was it?"

His eyes flicked between the three master mages. "If you all insist on involving him, then yes, I think he'll agree. After all, we're only risking one apprentice mage in exchange for saving the whole kingdom." The derision in his voice made me flinch.

"That's not fair," Amara said in a softer voice than I'd yet heard her use with Nik. "Your father cares about his people."

"But he cares about his kingdom more." Nik's eyes were like stones, cold and unreadable.

A question flashed through my mind. Did Nik have experience with what —or who—his father was willing to discard for the good of the kingdom?

"That's his job," Hayes said. "He couldn't be a good king without that quality."

Nik stood, every line of his body taut, his eyes alight. "If you have something to say, just say it," he ground out.

Hayes continued to regard him with compassion on his face. "All I'm saying is that consulting the king is a necessity. We can't go racing off to attempt something like this on our own."

My brow furrowed. Where were the royal family in all this? Why were they only being consulted now?

"If this problem is so big," I asked the room at large, "why aren't the royal family coming themselves? Where's the king? Aren't they the most powerful mages we have? Maybe one of them could stop the blight without needing to involve Grey."

Hayes hesitated for a moment, casting a glance at Nik that was so quick I wasn't sure I'd really seen it.

"It's true they have great personal strength," Hayes said. "But the royal family are traditionally elements mages. And what is needed in this crisis is plants mages. I'm sure if one of them was a plants mage, they would send him."

The silence after his words vibrated with something unspoken and weighty, something I didn't understand. I looked at Nik and found him completely still, his eyes riveted on Hayes.

"Is that true?" he finally asked, in a voice I didn't recognize. "Do you really believe they would have trusted me with this if...?"

Hayes held his gaze. "You would have graduated by now if you'd never left. You'd be a proficient—a powerful one, on your way toward mastery. I have no doubt they would have sent you. Although naturally, you wouldn't have been alone."

For a second Nik looked so tense I feared he might physically lash out. But instead he swung around, turning his back to us and striding toward the door. Once he had it open, he paused, speaking without looking back over his shoulder.

"Talk in your endless circles if you must. You'll see my plan is the only way that makes sense. When you're ready to take action, I'll be waiting. The rest of you can go to the capital if you insist on groveling before the throne. But Master Amara and Delphine must continue on in their usual way. We don't know what spies Grey may yet have, and we can't tip him off to our plan."

He finally glanced back, his eyes somehow both cold and alight. "Consult whoever you must, but don't put Delphine in danger by doing so."

Without waiting for a response, he stepped out of the room, shutting the door firmly behind him.

Hayes watched him go sadly. "So much potential wasted," he murmured under his breath.

"What happened?" I asked, finally mustering the courage to voice the question that had been burning inside me ever since I found out the truth about Nik. The question I knew I didn't really have a right to ask. "Why did a royal prince become a reneger?"

Hayes opened his mouth only to close it again and shake his head. When his eyes met mine, they were tired and sad.

"I think that's information he should tell you himself. When he's ready. If he wants to."

I flushed, looking away. Spending time in the company of master mages and royalty made it surprisingly easy to forget who I really was—nobody of any particular importance. There was no reason for a farm girl from a remote part of the kingdom to be given information on the private matters of the royal family. It was only by chance I had even been included this much.

"Are we really considering it?" Luna asked. "Will we send Delphine to Grey?"

"His plan does have some merit," Clay said softly.

"Clay!" Amara glared at him.

He held up both hands placatingly. "Just think about it, Amara. We don't know why Grey wants powerful youngsters, but it's clear he has no interest in causing them any immediate harm. And Delphine is a healer—one who knows how to protect herself from other healers. I wouldn't consider it if she was defenseless, but she can both protect herself and heal herself if needed. Grey wants to use her, not hurt her."

"I can't believe we're considering this." Amara threw up her hands, but I could see she was starting to think about it.

But could I do it? Could I voluntarily walk into Grey's hands and turn myself over? I shuddered at the idea, remembering the feeling of his blade plunging into my middle.

More powerful still, however, was the image of Miranda's face as Grey dragged her away. I had rescued everyone else, but I had failed her.

And then I thought of my parents. The usual conflicting emotions surged immediately to the surface. But as soon as I pictured our fields covered in blight, the roiling confusion settled. I might not know how to feel about my father, but I couldn't bear the idea of our farm ruined in such a way. If I was the only one who could help the farmers of Tartora—and my friend along with them—I had to try.

"I don't know if I can do it," I said. "I don't know if I can convince him to tell me his secrets. But I'm willing to try."

"Delphine..." Amara put a gentle hand on my knee. "It isn't something you need to decide right now."

I smiled at her. "I'm not going to change my mind. Not unless the situation changes. We have to do something, and this seems like the best option."

I didn't add the rest of my thoughts. Nik didn't wish me harm. He was another person I had conflicting emotions about, but I was certain of that. If he truly believed this was the only viable option, then I believed it had at least a chance of working.

"Amara's right," Hayes said briskly. "There's no need to make any final decisions right now. Prince Nikolas himself said it's essential that Amara and Delphine head northeast in their usual way. That gives us time. Clay, Luna, and I can go to the capital and consult with King Marius and the Triumvirate. If they endorse the plan, they'll assign us guards. We can meet in Eldrida and make our final decisions there. If the situation has changed, or if you don't want to take the risk, Delphine, you can say so then. No one will force you to do this. If necessary, we can take Grey by force and find a way to make him talk afterward."

I knew my mind wasn't going to change, but I nodded. It was obvious the adults weren't going to accept my certainty until they'd had a chance to put it to the test.

"That means we have to split up." Luna gripped my hand, her face drooping. "I thought we were going to stay together for several more months."

"We'll see each other again in Eldrida," I said, patting her hand.

She scrunched up her nose. "Where even is that?"

I stared at her for a moment before remembering she hadn't been raised in Tartora. It was understandable she didn't know our kingdom's geography in great detail.

"It's our north-easternmost city," Hayes said absently. "On the coast, close to the border with Calista. North of Eldrida, the coastline is unnavigable, but south is safe to sail. There are limited safe harbors, though, and Eldrida is the largest of those. It serves as both a fishing center and a trading hub for the towns of the eastern hills. The eastern section of Tartora is good grazing land, but it's isolated from the rest of the kingdom by both the Viridian River and the dense forest that runs along its eastern bank."

Luna nodded, but I could tell from the glazed look in her eyes that she hadn't absorbed the impromptu lesson. No wonder she still didn't know Tartora's cities.

"The important point is that it's as close to Grey's base as we're going to get this side of the border," I said. "At least in terms of a large enough population that we won't draw attention."

Amara sighed. "I suppose I'll have to accept that plan. But make sure the king and the Guild know I won't be pressuring my apprentice into anything. And even if she's willing, I may still choose to withhold my permission."

I clenched my teeth, trying to read her expression. Would she really do that? I wanted to go, but if she refused me permission to leave, then going anyway would make me a reneger, like Nik.

I slowly relaxed my jaw. Nothing was happening immediately. I had time to convince her.

"In that case, Luna and I will leave for the capital in the morning." Hayes gestured for the door. "The rest of us should leave so our apprentices can get some sleep."

Clay nodded. "I'll head to the capital with you, of course." He followed Hayes out of the room, the two of them making travel plans as they walked.

Amara stood as if to follow them but stopped to give me a stern look. "No lying awake all night stressing, Delphine! We'll leave tomorrow as well, after I've consulted with Anka. So get as much rest as you can. You know what it's like when we're traveling. It might be a while until you find a bed as comfortable as this one."

I stood. "We're leaving just like that? But what about Nik? Don't we need to talk with him further? He's the one who knows where Grey's base is located."

Amara gave me an exasperated look. "Don't worry. If there's one thing Nikolas is good at, it's taking action. You heard him—he'll be ready. And there's no way he'll be going to the capital with the others, so I have no doubt that—like it or not—we'll be seeing him on the road."

She gave me a look that was too knowing—as if she was well aware which of those two categories I fit into—and then departed. Ember slipped through the closing gap in her wake, escaping for her nightly hunt before Amara closed the door.

"I know he's a reneger, but he's devastatingly handsome, isn't he," Luna whispered, punctuating her words with a giggle.

I hurried into my nightclothes to hide the flush in my cheeks.

"I don't know what you mean," I said, voice muffled by my clothes.

Luna laughed again. "You're not fooling anyone, Delphine! I saw all those loaded glances between you. The two of you were just as bad as those other three."

I emerged from my battle with my garments and sat on my bed, my eyes fixed on her.

"Do you know about the history between Hayes and Amara? There's something there, right? It's not just my imagination?"

Luna slid into her bed but lay on her side, her head propped up on her elbow and her eyes conspiratorially bright.

"Hayes has never spoken about her as anything more than an old friend, but I know there's more to it than that. I have eyes, after all."

I slipped between my sheets, also turning onto my side so I could look across at Luna with wide eyes. "Are you saying he feels more for her than friendship?"

She dropped her voice to a whisper although we were the only ones in the room. "No one has told me directly, but I heard rumors at the Guild. Apparently they were apprentices at the same time, and Hayes was wildly in love with her!"

"What?" I gasped, clutching my blankets. But even as I felt the thrill of it, my more sensible self questioned Luna's excited interpretation.

It seemed hard to imagine anyone whispering such things about Hayes. But even if it wasn't quite the dramatic love story she was imagining, it seemed possible Hayes could have cared for Amara when they were young.

"Apparently lots of them were in love with her," Luna said, "since Amara was so outstanding. But she didn't have any patience for most of them, or for the Guild itself even. She was always speaking up against the way things were done. She only had time for two of her peers—" She paused in what was clearly meant to be dramatic tension before announcing, "Hayes and Clay!"

"Are you saying Clay was in love with her as well?" My mouth fell open.

"Apparently he wasn't as obvious about it, but most people think he must have been."

"So what about Amara? Did she have feelings for either of them?"

"She was good friends with Clay, but apparently she was closer to Hayes. According to the reports, they spent most of their time outside of class together. Some people even say that's why Clay left the capital and settled in Ostaria."

I gasped. "Because he was so heartbroken?"

"Maybe?" Luna looked delighted at the idea that our masters had such a thrilling history. "Or maybe he moved there because Amara never goes to the capital. At least in Ostaria, he gets to see her whenever she passes through."

I shook my head, not quite able to believe this flight of fancy. "But what about Amara and Hayes? What happened with them?"

"Everyone thought they would get married after they graduated, but instead Amara left her old master and the Guild behind and took up a traveling life."

"She just left Hayes?" I asked. "Why didn't he go with her?"

Luna grimaced. "That's the bit that everyone has a different theory about. I don't think anyone really knows what happened for sure. Amara just left, and Hayes was *devastated*."

She looked at the door which remained firmly closed before continuing. "Apparently, at the time, everyone thought it was such a pity and a waste— the general consensus was that her potential would be lost away from the Guild. They thought that on her own she'd never develop her skills much further. But then she reappeared in the capital only two years later, asking to sit the mastery exam. Everyone thought it was a joke until she actually passed."

My eyes widened and my lips curved upward as I imagined Amara's triumph. I wished I could have seen it myself.

"Hayes was the only one who believed she could pass from the beginning.

So then everyone was convinced this time they would get married." Luna's shoulders slumped. "But she just left again. And all these years have passed, and Hayes has never been romantically linked to anyone else."

She flopped over to lie on her back. "At least that's what the people at the Guild say."

"He still loves her," I breathed, also lying down and staring at the ceiling.

Luna turned onto her side again, her grin back in place. "He must, right? Isn't it thrilling? And don't you think Clay still likes her, too? Why wouldn't he?" Her voice grew wistful. "I wish I could grow up to be half as amazing as she is."

"You will," I said firmly. "I know it. You'll be the Amara of the Calistan Mages' Guild."

"Do you think so?" Luna covered her face and giggled. But when she looked back at me, she wore a more thoughtful expression. "It feels surreal sometimes. All those years in my home settlement, I never dreamed I could have a life like this."

I nodded, knowing what she meant. "It feels surreal to me too—all the time. I was convinced the rest of my life would be spent on my parents' farm. And now I don't know if I'll ever live there again."

Even as I said the words, I knew they weren't true. I did know the answer to that question. Even without my issues with my father, my life had grown past the farm and there was no going back—not to live anyway. I had seen the way Amara and Hayes helped people, and I wanted to do the same thing. I had been given power when others had almost none, and I owed it to them to make use of my gift.

Luna sighed wistfully. "I just hope one day someone loves me enough that they would wait for me for fifteen years."

I sighed, imagining the love Amara had apparently given up all those years ago. She had told me once that she was alone on her travels but not lonely. I only hoped that was true and she didn't regret what she had given up when she chose the traveling life.

# CHAPTER
# SEVEN

As we prepared to leave the city, I kept a close watch for any sign of Nik, but I didn't catch so much as a glimpse of him. Unsettled and disappointed, I had no choice but to leave without speaking to him, trusting that Amara was right and he would also be making his way northeast.

Much of our travel thus far had been following the Celadon River. But when Amara and I left Caltor, we struck out northeast, moving away from the water. Our intention was to pass north of the capital and through the kingdom's northern farmlands. This was the part of the kingdom marred by the blight, and I was already steeling myself for the sight of burned-out fields.

We didn't encounter any until our second day of travel, however, and by then, I had almost forgotten to look for them. The stretch of black hit me hard, a stark difference compared to the waving green stalks on the other side of the road. Even the air had a faint acrid stench, although I wasn't sure if that was just my imagination, since the burning looked old.

The more I gazed at the ashy, blackened fields, the more my stomach churned, until I had to reach for my power to settle it. Beside me on the front bench of our cart, Amara sat still—unnaturally so. I glanced at her face and caught the sorrow and concern in her eyes.

She met my gaze and managed a small, sad smile.

"I bet it hits you even harder," she said. "Since you grew up on a farm. So much effort wasted, and so much food lost."

I nodded, not ready to put my feelings into words.

"I've never lived on a farm," she continued, "but I've traveled among them for long enough that it's horribly jarring to see burned fields."

I kept my attention on her face, trying to ignore the glimpses of black in my peripheral vision. For the first time, it occurred to me to wonder where Amara had grown up. Somehow I'd never thought of her as a child. I knew a little of her apprentice days, but I hadn't thought further back than that, as if she had sprung into existence already experienced and powerful.

"Were you born in Tarona?" I asked, suddenly curious.

Her eyebrows quirked slightly, as if taken off guard by the question.

"I just realized I don't know anything about your childhood or family," I said. "Except that Anka is your aunt. Given both of you are strong mages, I'm assuming your family is a mage family based in the capital?"

She took a moment to answer, my curiosity rising further with each second of silence. Was I wrong? Was it possible that two powerful mages had come by chance from the same weak family?

"Yes," she said at last. "I come from Tarona."

I nodded, examining her face for any hint as to why that history gave her pause. It was the most common story for mages, especially master mages.

"Do you have any brothers and sisters?" I asked. It was the one part of her childhood I would envy her, if so.

She shook her head. "My mother wasn't the maternal sort."

I frowned, trying to parse out the layers of meaning in the statement. Did she have a bad relationship with her mother?

"She was an elements mage, like me, but not a master. She resented that."

"Did she resent your passing the exam, then?" I asked in a small voice.

"Resent it?" Amara laughed. "Quite the opposite. I only took it so early at her endless insistence. She was convinced I could achieve everything she had failed to achieve herself."

From her expression of distaste, it was obvious a young Amara hadn't appreciated the pressure.

"You keep saying *was*," I said tentatively. "Has she changed, or is she...?"

"She passed away many years ago," Amara said, matter-of-factly.

I blinked, trying to process that information. It was rare for a mage to die so young given their access to powerful healers. Even the regular populace rarely passed away so young unless they had a sudden accident or a chronic condition that required constant healing.

"I'm sorry," I ventured at last.

She closed her eyes for a moment, but when she opened them, there was no sign of moisture.

"It was a tragic waste of both a life and a gift that could have helped so many." She sighed. "But my mother was never interested in helping others.

Her whole life was consumed by bitterness at the status and power she wasn't able to achieve. She married my father, a healing mage—despite looking down on healers—because he was a master. Something he didn't realize until after they were married."

She shook her head, whether at her mother's coldness or her father's foolishness in falling for it, I wasn't sure.

She gazed ahead, her eyes fixed on Acorn's ears as she continued her story. "When he first tested me and discovered I had her affinity and his strength, she was triumphant—she'd achieved her aim, and she was determined I would be her pass to power and influence."

"That's awful," I whispered.

I knew what it was like to have a parent who twisted themselves with bitterness, but at least my father had always treated me with affection. Even his betrayal had been because he wanted to keep me with him.

Almost against my will, I felt a crack in the wall of my own bitterness and resentment. My father had done something terrible, but did that mean I had to poison all my memories of the good moments?

Amara looked sideways at me, a wry smile twisting her mouth. "You can see why I don't talk about my parents much. My father, at least, is warm and loving, but he never knew how to stand up to her. I've been telling him for years that he should marry again, but I think he's lost trust in himself after making such a terrible first choice."

I nodded, not sure what to say. Everything she was describing was entirely outside my experience.

"Since you're too polite to ask, I'll just tell you how she died," Amara said after a protracted silence. "It was after I'd left Tarona, so I only heard about it afterward. I wasn't surprised, though. She was always pushing her ability, convinced she was capable of more than she really was. She knew she couldn't win renown by being the strongest, so she was always attempting experiments, trying to discover something new."

She paused to shake her head, and I thought uncomfortably of the strange way I used my healing ability. It had never been my intention to win any sort of renown by being different.

"She was out on the Viridian River, apparently," Amara continued. "I don't know exactly what she was attempting, but she pushed herself too far and lost consciousness. When she toppled into the water, some fishermen saw her, but by the time they fished out her body and got it to a healer, it was too late for resuscitation."

"I'm sorry," I repeated again, and she merely nodded in reply.

Amara had clearly had a complicated and acrimonious relationship with her mother, but that didn't mean she'd wanted her to die. How had she felt when she got the news? I didn't dare ask.

"So now you know why I've never had any interest in politics," Amara said in a lighter voice after the silence had lengthened and softened. "Being hungry for power doesn't serve anyone—not even yourself in the long run."

"Do you think everyone interested in a position of authority is hungry for power?" I asked, thinking of Hayes.

She hesitated for a moment before sighing. "Perhaps not. I hope not. But it was what was modeled for me growing up, and I swore to myself early on that I would never be like my mother."

"So did you grow up living at the Guild?" I asked, hoping to steer into a less fraught conversation.

Amara nodded. "As a master healer, Father had a suite at the Guild big enough for my mother and me as well as his endless stream of apprentices. I'm glad for it since it means he's not alone now."

"He doesn't work in one of the capital hospitals?" I asked.

"No, although he'll assist on occasion if there's a special case. In general, he much prefers teaching, though. Now that my mother and I are gone, he has more apprentices than ever."

She gave a more natural-looking smile, and I tentatively smiled back. Her story had taken us past the edge of the burned fields, and despite the heaviness of what she had shared, it felt easier to breathe now.

"I can't imagine having apprentices of my own one day," I said, twisting to pat Ember's fur where she lay curled just behind us in the bed of the cart. "One fox seems to be more than I can look after."

Amara laughed. "Don't worry. I used to find it equally hard to imagine and look at me now."

I smiled back, but it was impossible to see myself ever having the same poise and confidence as Amara.

"Will we be making camp by the road again tonight?" I asked, glancing at the lowering sun.

"I'm hoping for a proper bed, but no promises." She signaled for Acorn to increase her pace, but the mare merely flicked her tail and continued plodding on at her usual pace.

I stifled a giggle as Amara frowned affectionately at the horse.

"There's a village close by, then?" I asked.

She nodded. "It's a small one, though, so they don't have a proper inn. With so much of the kingdom's traffic using the rivers, the roads through this section aren't heavily enough traveled for regular, large inns."

"It's the same if you head east from Tarin." I glanced at the sun again, and then reached forward with my power, trying to sense if there were people ahead of us. "Will we reach the village before nightfall at this pace?"

Amara smiled ruefully. "I'm afraid there's not much we can do about it if not. Unless you think you can convince Acorn to speed up?"

"I wouldn't dare!" I grinned at the unbothered horse. "She might like me because of my healing affinity, but I don't think she likes me that much."

Ember stirred enough to let out a soft bark.

"See. Ember agrees."

Amara chuckled. "I'd almost believe that fox understands us at this point. She seems unnaturally canny."

I smiled affectionately at the curled ball of orange, black, and white in the back of the cart. "I couldn't ask for a better companion."

We lapsed into silence as the miles fell away. On our previous travels, Amara had pushed me to use the travel time to work with my ability. I had much better control now, and I was no longer a danger to myself, but I still fell into the old habit.

I could feel the upcoming village, a distant cluster of beating hearts and pumping lungs, and I monitored the distance, matching it against the setting sun.

"We're going to make it," I eventually announced with satisfaction.

Amara smiled, pleased. "You can feel the villagers? Are we getting close?"

"I think we'll be there in less than an hour."

Satisfied with the location of the village, I turned my attention away from the villagers and monitored the surrounding wildlife instead. There was an unexpected exhilaration in the ease of using my ability compared to those first few days and weeks of my apprenticeship. I really was gaining skill and control.

I breathed deeply, enjoying the endless stretch of sky around us which was showcasing the beginnings of sunset. Even the air felt clearer out here without buildings hemming us in. I had enjoyed the novelty of the bustling city, but these wide-open spaces carried the familiarity of home.

The whole atmosphere seemed designed to lull me into a state of calm and peace. Even the late summer air was pleasantly warm without being stifling. But I couldn't quite relax into the moment. Overlaid over everything was a sense of urgency that I couldn't shake. Miranda was out there right now with Grey, and we actually knew where she was at last.

My mind knew the reasons we had to move at our usual pace and understood she wasn't in any immediate danger, but I couldn't shake the desire to mount a swift horse and ride at full pace. How could we meander through the fields when the kingdom was in danger? How many more fields would end up burned before we got answers from Grey?

I forced myself to focus on a nearby flock of sparrows. Their darting bodies were always hard to track, and the concentration required distracted me from the sense of helplessness.

"Delphine." Amara's voice was quiet, but it carried an edge that broke through my focus.

After a brief glance at her tense face, I darted a look around but could see nothing out of place.

"Do you hear that?" she asked.

Now that I was paying attention, I caught what she was referring to—the distant sound of hoof beats pounding along the road at a gallop.

Amara was clearly waiting for something, so I reached out with my ability, trying to pick up as much information about the approaching person or persons as possible.

"It's a lone rider," I said after a pause. "Their heart is beating hard—even for riding at a gallop—but they don't seem to have any injury or illness."

"They're close, then?" Amara tightened her hold on the reins and guided Acorn away from the middle of the road.

"They must have come from the village."

While I had been distracted with the surrounding wildlife, we had nearly reached it. Beyond the approaching rider, I could sense a dense clump of people, although most of my attention was on the rider.

A slight bend in the road revealed a man racing toward us. He was bent low over his horse's neck, as if he hoped to marginally increase their pace by reducing his wind resistance.

Amara's eyes narrowed as she took him in, and she pulled Acorn to a gentle halt. The horse slowed agreeably, always happier to stop than to increase her pace.

The man was slower to see us, but as soon as he did, he shot bolt upright, also pulling on his horse's reins. The animal reduced his pace, dropping to a walk by the time he approached within easy speaking distance of the cart.

The man was dressed in a typical fashion for a farmer, but the quality of his horse told me he was a prosperous one. His eyes swept straight over me, discounting me because of my age, I assumed, and latched onto Amara.

"I don't suppose you're a healer?" he called in a rough voice.

Her shake of the head made him slump in the saddle, his expression that of a man who had been holding onto hope, however unlikely, and was starting to lose it.

He moved to spur his horse back to speed again, but Amara held up a hand to stop him.

"You're in need of a healer?"

The man pulled his horse to a complete stop, now nearly level with our cart. The hope had sprung back into his eyes at her question.

"Do you know where one can be found? Are they nearby? If I have to go all the way to Caltor..." He didn't have to finish that sentence for us to read on his face what a journey of that distance would mean.

"I'm an elements mage, but my apprentice is a healer." Amara gestured at me, and I tried to look less terrified than I felt.

If someone needed me, I would try to help—I had to. But the man's question reminded me there was no backup within reach, no more experienced healer to guide me.

For a moment the man looked taken aback and unsure, looking me up and down and no doubt noting my age. But it was a sign of his desperation that the hope had returned to his eyes.

"You're a mage, you say? So she is, too?"

He started suddenly and bowed awkwardly from the back of his horse as if he had only just remembered the formalities.

When Amara confirmed our status, he bowed again, the hopeful look in his eyes growing as he clutched at whatever straws he could. Clearly he hoped my strength would make up for my lack of experience.

"Are you in need of a healer yourself?" Amara asked, giving no indication she already knew the answer to the question from my earlier information.

"No, not me. It's my daughter. Back in the village."

"Your village doesn't have its own healer?" Amara asked with a frown.

"She doesn't have the strength," the man said as he slid from his horse's back.

I frowned at him, wondering why he was dismounting until he circled around to my side of the cart and held up his hands as if he intended to help me down. I turned wide eyes on Amara.

He gestured for me to hurry. "You take my horse. He's a strong one, and he can gallop a bit longer, but he'll go faster with only one of us."

"You want me to go on alone?" I asked, my fear rising even higher.

"Follow the road into the village," he said. "You can't miss it." He swallowed. "Or her."

I looked at Amara again, and she indicated for me to climb down.

"Amara," I whispered.

She held my eyes in her gaze, which was strong and calm. "You can do this, Delphine. And if you can't, that's not your fault. From the sound of it, you're this girl's only hope, so you certainly can't do any harm. You have to at least try."

I swallowed hard. "I have to try." Parroting her words let me pretend I could also mimic her strength.

Accepting the help of the villager, I scrambled inelegantly down from the cart and raced around to the saddled horse, who was breathing heavily and tossing his mane.

The stranger followed me and before I could ask for help mounting, he put both hands around my waist and threw me up into the saddle. I gathered the reins and paused for a moment to look at Amara.

She nodded. "Go, Delphine. We'll follow as fast as we can."

I took a deep breath, leaned low over the horse's neck and kicked my heels into his flank.

CHAPTER

# EIGHT

The horse shot off faster than I expected, and I had to grab handfuls of his mane to keep my seat. I wasn't an elegant rider, but my childhood around farm horses had made me a functional one, and since my activation my skills had improved. I was more in tune with the animal beneath me now, able to sense the shifts in his muscles and adjust my own position accordingly.

Even so, we flew down the road at a breathless pace, and I wondered if the horse had picked up that I was scared. He was responding by racing home, unaware he was carrying me closer to the source of my fear.

My heart pounded in my ears, and it took all my self-restraint not to use my ability to slow it down. I knew better than to try that, though. Amara hadn't known the safety lectures usually given to new healers, but Hayes had been quick to fill in where she had lacked.

Within an impossibly short time, the outlying buildings of the village came into view. As promised, the main road ran straight through the center of the village, and at this hour it was clear enough that I barely had to check my pace.

But as we neared what looked like a central square, the edges of a small crowd came into view. I frantically pulled back on the reins, and the horse responded instantly.

The sound of our arrival caught the attention of those nearest us, and their curious gazes fixed on me. Someone recognized the horse and set up a shout, and within moments everyone had deduced the meaning of an unfamiliar person riding a horse that had just left town in search of a healer.

By the time I slid down from the saddle, hands were reaching for me, propelling me through the press of people. I barely had time to ready myself for an unknown situation before I was thrust into the small space at the center of the crowd.

For a second, all I could see was blood. The red seemed to be everywhere, coating everything, and my vision swam, a roaring sound filling my head. But I was prepared for it. Pushing my power through my own body, I ruthlessly suppressed the reaction, washing it away.

Fear was still left in its wake, however. There was so much blood. Too much blood.

I forced myself to push the fear away as well, using my own determination instead of my power this time. Focusing on what mattered, I tried to assess the situation.

A young girl—not more than twelve—lay on the paved street near a small fountain. Mercifully, she had passed out because I had never seen a leg mangled as badly as her left one. I could only imagine how bad the pain had been while she was conscious. Had she had a run in with her father's farm equipment? If so, he must have carried her all the way into town. No wonder she had lost consciousness.

It took me another second to take in the older woman kneeling beside the girl. For a moment, I thought it might be the mother, but she was too old.

The woman looked up at me with wild eyes. "I can't get it to stop," she gasped out. "It won't stop."

Her hands and clothes were coated in the red, her face almost as ashen as the girl's. She kept her eyes trained on me, and I saw the moisture in them.

"All I could do was help her sleep." The tears welled enough to fall from her eyes.

I drew a shuddering breath, trying to make sense of the situation. That this older, experienced healer was looking to an eighteen-year-old with such desperation, her face pleading for help, told me more about the situation than I wanted to know.

It didn't make sense, though. A small village wouldn't have anyone with mage level power, but no one would qualify for the title of village healer unless they could at least staunch blood loss. She might not be able to heal the leg, but she should at least be able to keep the girl alive until she could be taken to a more powerful healer.

I dropped to my knees on the other side of the girl. Gripping her wrist, I thrust my power into her. My studies hadn't progressed as far as the level of reconstruction needed for her leg, but I had brute-forced my way through healings before. I would just have to do the same thing here, trusting in the instincts of my power to heal her.

But as soon as my senses reached her leg, the fire of my power quenched, slowing and dimming. I frowned and pushed more power into her, but where my ability should have blazed through her, it instead moved sluggishly, like a fire dimming and flickering from lack of air.

I rocked back on my heels, looking up at the other healer while keeping my hand on the girl's wrist. Now I understood the healer's desperation, even though I didn't understand how a young girl's body could fight me in such a way. I could barely make headway with all my strength; a regular healer wouldn't have been able to do anything at all.

*All I could do was help her sleep,* echoed in my head with the same tinges of horror as when it was first said.

I gritted my teeth. I refused to give up.

Leaning forward, I grabbed her wrist with both hands, pouring power into her. My fire burned and flared, pushing back against the resistance, making slow headway into her leg.

Beads of sweat popped up along my hairline and behind my ears. Gasping for breath, I kept pushing. I could feel the scope of the injury now, and I could already tell that even with the best will in the world, I couldn't pour enough raw power into her to fix her leg. I was fighting the tide.

I loosened my grip, thinking quickly. I wasn't a weak local healer, but the same principle applied. I only needed to stem the blood loss and keep her alive until she could reach a stronger healer—or in this case, a team of strong healers. I didn't have to heal her leg immediately, I just had to stop the bleeding.

Changing focus, I sent my power searching for broken veins, sealing each one as I found it until, at last, I sensed that no more was flowing out of her. With a final burst of effort, I helped her body produce new blood—just enough to stabilize her. As soon as I'd finished, I groaned, letting go of her and collapsing backward.

I lifted a hand to rub my face but stopped when I saw the red coating it. Lowering it again, I looked across at the healer.

Before either of us could speak, a higher, weaker groan sounded. We both turned to see the girl's eyes fluttering open. Lunging in unison, we reached for her arms, gripping a wrist each. But when the local healer saw I had taken hold of the girl, she released her, leaving the job to me.

Within seconds, the girl was returned to a deep sleep.

"Easier, in the circumstances, than blocking the pain and keeping her calm," I said in a breathless voice.

The woman nodded, and another woman stepped forward from the crowd. Sinking down to take the girl's head in gentle hands, she sat and rested it in her lap, heedless of her gown. This woman looked a similar age to the man who had fetched me, and I suspected I had now found the girl's mother.

I looked from her to the healer, gesturing at the motionless child.

"Why…why is she like that?"

"You haven't felt it before?" The older healer understood immediately that I wasn't talking about the injury, but she looked surprised, peering at me in concern. "How old are you?"

"Eighteen. But I started my apprenticeship late. I was only activated a few months ago." I tried not to look self-conscious at the words.

The woman let out a huff of air. "A new apprentice? Then you have a master nearby? What brought you riding in here alone?" She looked up hopefully, trying to peer through the crowd, although she was still sitting on the ground.

"My master is coming in our cart with the girl's father." I glanced at the mother and then away. "But she's an elements mage. That's why they sent me on. I wouldn't usually try a healing like this on my own, but…"

The healer deflated, her shoulders slumping in defeat. After a moment, she took a fortifying breath, her manner turning brisk.

"If you're a new apprentice, you did well to manage as much as you did. You obviously have strength—which makes sense if your master is a mage. But cross-influenced…" She sighed and shook her head. "Still, we can be grateful for what we have because it's more than we looked for. This is Marla, Josie's mother, and I'm Esme. I'm the local healer here. I have rooms nearby, so I'll put some of this crowd to use and have Josie carried there."

"I…I'm Delphine," I said, still reeling from the strangeness of everything.

"We're mighty glad to meet you, child," Esme said. "You came along in perfect timing. I just hope you have strength left for what's next. At least we can do the next part less hurriedly. I have the tools we'll need in my rooms, and once I've caught my breath, I'll be able to guide you through the process. You won't have any experience with this, but you'll only have to provide the strength. I'll provide the skill. I assume you've worked in tandem before?"

I nodded, since that was the way Luna and I worked with Hayes when we learned techniques we hadn't tried before. But even as I was nodding, I held out my hands to stop her.

"Wait. What are you talking about?" I was still struggling to make sense of the situation.

"How can we?" The mother sobbed. "Oh, how can we?"

"Steady there, Marla." The healer clapped a hand on her shoulder, her voice at once bracing and gentle. "We thought we were going to lose her altogether. This is better than that."

"What exactly is better than death?" I projected my voice more forcefully, determined to get an answer.

The healer frowned at me and gestured at the injured leg. "We have to take it off, of course. Healing it is out of the question. You saw that for yourself. But I'm hopeful you have the strength to heal an amputation site, at least."

"Take off the leg?" I stared at her, appalled. "But she's only a child!"

I had heard of the phenomenon before but had never actually seen someone without a limb. It was only those whose limbs were crushed in the remotest locations who needed such drastic treatment. Usually healers could keep the person and the limb alive long enough to reach a hospital.

"It's true I've never done it before," the healer admitted, "but those of us without the strength to heal wounds outright learn wound management you mages don't need. Many of the same principles will apply."

"Wise mages learn all aspects of their ability," said a familiar voice, and my shoulders slumped with relief.

Amara had arrived, and I no longer had to bear the burden of this situation alone. I turned to her with a look that felt as wild as the other healer's expression when she couldn't stem the blood loss.

"They want to remove her leg!" I exclaimed.

"So I deduced." Amara frowned, taking in the situation more fully. "You weren't able to heal the leg?"

There was no judgment in her voice, but I felt guilt all the same.

"I don't understand why not. It was like her body was…resisting me."

I modified my language, avoiding mention of my power burning through the girl like fire. I had learned in Caltor that other healers didn't sense their power in the same way, and some were unnerved by such language. Amara would understand, since it was the influence of her elements power that had likely made me this way, but I didn't want to confuse Esme, who was listening intently.

"I didn't realize Delphine was such a new apprentice, or I would have warned her when she arrived," Esme said, interjecting into the conversation. "If she had started training on elderly patients, she'd have recognized it easily enough. But that's usually left until second year."

Amara's face crumpled, compassion filling her eyes. "She's been sick?"

The mother gave a soft, hiccupping sob. "From when she was three until she was eight. A blood disease. We had to travel to Caltor so many times because it kept coming back. But she's been clear for four years, and the doctor said it was finally defeated. It took three of them working together the last time, though. When she gets ill with all the normal childhood ailments, we have to keep her home instead of sending her to the healer like the other parents do. She can't do anything for her..." Her words dissolved into further sobbing.

I swallowed, finally understanding what I had been so slow to grasp. Although Luna had done some work with the elderly in Tarona, Hayes had planned those lessons for when I was occupied with Amara. New apprentices didn't work on the elderly because over time the body developed resistance to healing power. It was that resistance that meant even the most powerful healers eventually died. And the same effect could be caused by excessive healings.

The more a person had been healed—and the more extreme the healings—the harder it became to heal them. It was usually only a problem for soldiers who had experienced many years of training injuries and battle wounds, and for those who suffered from a small number of deadly illnesses that couldn't be cured by a single healing—the type that kept recurring as had happened to this girl.

Still...I shuddered to think how many healings she must have had to develop such intense resistance at such a young age.

"Is amputation really the only option?" Amara directed the question at Esme.

She pulled herself to her feet, groaning slightly as if she was too old to be kneeling on a hard road.

"When Delphine arrived, I briefly hoped...But it can't be helped. Better to lose her leg than her life."

I expected Amara to argue, to come up with some solution none of us had thought of. But instead she merely nodded, her lips thinning as she cast a sorrowful glance at the girl lying in her mother's lap.

"No!" I said stubbornly. "We can't! There has to be a way."

Amara sighed. "Perhaps there is. But I'm no healer. If there's an answer, I don't know what it is." She moved closer, her voice dropping lower. "I'm sorry, Delphine. I truly am. But this girl still needs saving, and the local healer clearly can't do it on her own."

Her eyes were sympathetic and understanding, but there was no give in her gaze. I had to be part of this whether I liked it or not.

I looked to the mother, thinking I'd have an ally in her, at least. If she protested, refused to give her permission, insisted someone ride for Caltor...

The father pushed through the crowd, his eyes leaping from his daughter's face to his wife's. She looked up at him with a tremulous smile, tears still streaking down her face.

"She's alive. This girl saved her."

The father almost collapsed in relief, the healer catching him under one arm and steadying him.

"We'll need to organize some of the men to carry her to my rooms. I believe this apprentice has sufficient strength to keep her alive once I remove the leg."

I expected the father to exclaim and reject the idea, and his face did flicker, his features sagging. But a moment later, he forced a smile, giving his wife what was clearly meant to be a look of strength.

"Josie will be all right. We'll help her adjust to it. She'll be alive, that's the important thing."

"No!" I shouted, unable to contain myself. "How can you say that? How can you restrict her life like that? How can you accept anything less than her full potential?"

Hands gripped my shoulders, shaking me until I fell silent, the whole crowd hushed in the wake of my outburst.

I was shaking all over, unable to calm my emotions. Defiant, I gazed at Amara's face.

"Delphine, control yourself!" she snapped. "This isn't about you!"

I refused to back down, though, glaring at her with all my overflowing outrage. How could they all agree to this so calmly?

Amara sighed, her grip on me softening.

"We can take her to Caltor," I said, reaching desperately for any option. "I can keep her alive long enough to get her there. They can heal the leg. She doesn't have to lose it."

Amara glanced at Esme, who slowly shook her head.

She didn't quite meet my eyes when she spoke. "You had to stop all the blood flow to her leg to prevent her bleeding out. Maybe you're too new to have learned yet, but a leg without blood can't last more than a few hours before it dies. Caltor is two day's ride. Even if you don't stop overnight and get there in one day and one night, the leg will be past salvaging."

I flushed, finally looking down. I did know that. I had read it in one of the anatomy books Amara bought me. I was talking wildly, from emotion and not reason, and everyone here must know it. I was reflecting badly on both myself and my master, but I couldn't seem to rein myself in.

Esme moved closer to Amara, giving me a sideways look as she lowered her voice.

"If she can't do it…If she's not in a fit state, or if she doesn't have the strength…" She grimaced. "I can't do it on my own, not with the patient's level of resistance."

"Don't worry," Amara said in crisp tones. "Delphine can do it. She just needs a moment."

I wanted to be grateful for her belief in me and proud of the strength she thought I possessed, but anger still raged through me, my embarrassment only adding further force to the tossing waves of my emotions. Everyone was so calm and rational—didn't they care? Did no one care that this young girl's life was going to be made small?

"Is there time?" Amara asked the healer. "Can you keep her sleeping for a while?"

The healer scratched at the side of her face, her eyes distant as she considered. "I can at least keep her asleep. That much I can manage. And it will take us time to get her moved and for me to get everything set up. You can have an hour, even two, if you must. There won't be any lasting damage in that time."

She glanced at the two parents, and even through the fog of my fury, I could read her expression. She and Amara believed that a longer wait would only be delaying the inevitable—a cruelty to the parents who were in great distress.

I tore out of Amara's hold and dove into the crowd. I thought I would have to push through them, but people parted before me, melting away to give me a clear path. When I looked at the wide-eyed stares and then down at my gown, now streaked with blood, I could see why. I seemed like a madwoman, beyond reason or sense.

I ignored them, breaking into a run as I dashed toward the edge of the crowd and the open fields beyond. I needed to get away, I needed to feel my legs pounding and my breath rasping harshly in my lungs. I needed to stop thinking, stop feeling, stop—

A hand grabbed at my arm, pulling me back so abruptly that my momentum carried me around in a half circle. I almost collided with Amara who had firmly planted her feet, a solid presence in the middle of my storming sea.

"Go," she said once I had steadied. "Run it out of your system if that's what you need. You have an hour." She took my chin firmly in her hand and forced me to look her in the eyes. "But you have to be back in an hour. I know this isn't easy for you. I know you haven't properly processed your own pain yet. But this girl's future has nothing to do with the choices your father made for you. No one is reducing this girl—they are saving her life. And they need you to do it. Delphine, do you hear me? You cannot leave this girl to die."

I stared at her, and she continued, unbending. "Promise me. One hour and you'll be back at that square."

I jerked a nod. "I'll be back."

As soon as I spoke the words, she released me, and I fled from the village as if wolves were chasing me.

# CHAPTER

# NINE

For a short time I could see nothing but the field beneath my feet and hear nothing but my rough breath grating in my ears. Everything else had disappeared.

But as my legs began to burn and my breathing became more labored, the world slowly returned. My first awareness was of the animals around me. The wild ones had scattered at my frantic approach, but I could feel one familiar presence behind me, her heart pumping as she matched my speed. Ember.

Without conscious intention, my feet slowed. I wasn't alone. Faithful as always, the fox had followed me, expending the effort she would usually reserve for short dashes after prey. She knew nothing of the situation, she only recognized my distress. Just her presence brought a small measure of calm to my fevered mind.

But as soon as I slowed and started paying attention, I realized Ember wasn't the only one following me. A human was behind me as well, carefully keeping pace so as not to overtake me.

I kept my jogging steps steady, resisting the urge to look around as I reached out with my power. Out here in the fields, running through the crops, there could be no mistake. Someone was following me.

My heart rate, which had finally started to slow, instantly spiked again, my already ragged breathing becoming frantic. Who had followed me out here and what was their purpose? I knew it was a man, which meant it wasn't Amara, but who else would have any reason to follow me?

If it was related to the injured girl, did they intend to force me back immediately, not trusting me to return on my own? Surely no one would want to block Josie's healing, so they couldn't wish to prevent my returning.

Or could my pursuer be unrelated to the incident? Had someone seen me running alone and thought I was weak prey?

Determination filled me. My hands clenched into fists and then stretched out again, my fingers extending to their fullest reach. As soon as my pursuer felt my touch, he would realize his mistake.

Steeling myself, I prepared to make a move. Better to take him by surprise than allow him to dictate the interaction. Readying my muscles, I jerked to a sudden stop, whirling in the middle of the field to face my pursuer.

It took the man several strides to process my abrupt halt, and by the time he slowed his forward momentum, he was close enough for me to grab his wrist. But at the same instant I made contact, I recognized his features.

"Nik!"

I let him go, my legs collapsing underneath me at the sudden release from tension. Cramping pain shot through my calves as they protested my recent intense and unusual activity.

"Whoa there!" Nik caught me under the arms, supporting my weight. "Are you all right?"

The pain in my legs made me wince and shake my head, even as my power reached for the seizing muscles. Within seconds, the pain had stopped completely, but I couldn't bring myself to take my own weight again. The reality of the situation was crashing over me, and the strength I'd feigned only moments ago was already being sucked away.

Nik stared into my face, his brow creased. When I didn't respond, he grunted and swept me into his arms, carrying me like a baby.

For a second, I considered protesting, but I didn't have the will. Instead, I wrapped my arms around his neck, burrowed my face into his chest, and shamelessly let him carry me. For a short while there was only the soothing warmth of his body and the rhythmic fall of his steps.

But all too soon he was lowering me into a sitting position on a large, sawn-off tree trunk. I blinked and looked around.

He had taken me to the edge of the field, aiming for a small cluster of trees that provided an area of shade. Someone had cut down this tree, but for some reason, the others had so far been spared.

I glanced from the grain in the nearest field to the low-lying crop in the next one over. Did they belong to different farms? I knew I was letting my mind wander to avoid the real issue, but I couldn't seem to muster the energy to stop myself.

An orange blur leaped from the ground into my lap, curling up and pressing her head against me. Tears immediately pricked my eyes as I wrapped my hands gently around the fox's body. Her soft fur was familiar and comforting in a way beyond words.

Nik knelt on one knee in front of me, his eyes worried as he examined my face.

"I saw Ember running, which is how I found you," he said after the silence grew too long. "I thought you might be in danger at first, but..." He trailed off, tactfully not mentioning that there had been no pursuer to fuel my desperate sprint. "What happened? What's wrong?"

"I...There was an accident..." It was all I could manage.

"An accident?" He went taut, his face tightening as his fingers slid up and down my arms, looking for an injury not visible to his eyes.

I shook my head. "Not me. A girl. In the town..." Again I struggled to go on, and he waited silently with a patience I hadn't realized he possessed. The same patience he must have used all those times when he watched Grey.

Taking a deep breath, I forced myself to speak, quickly relating what had happened as we approached the village and what I had found when I tried to heal the girl.

He listened silently, showing neither sympathy nor judgment, simply allowing me to get it all out. When I finished, he sighed, maneuvering himself onto the stump beside me and running a hand over his face. Instinctively I knew it was the sort of situation he hated—a life was hanging in the balance, but there was nothing he could do and no one he could fight.

It was the sort of situation that was supposed to provide a moment of glory for a healer, not a warrior. Except when it didn't.

"So there's nothing you can do to save her leg," he said at last.

"How can you say that?" The words exploded out of me. "How can they all just accept that such a young girl should lose a leg? She won't be able to walk or run or dance or..." My words broke off in a choking sob.

He took one of my hands in both of his, seeming to understand that my anger wasn't really directed at him. I looked up at him, my tears making his image watery.

"How can her parents do that to her? They should be fighting for her! It's their responsibility to save her!"

"Her parents..." He repeated the words softly, the look in his eyes impossible to read. For a moment there was silence, and then he squeezed my hand. "Your parents didn't protect you." He didn't say it as a question.

I heaved a shuddering sigh, my whole body trembling. There it was—the thing I had been trying to flee from. The quivering heart at the center of my raging emotions. And just like Amara, Nik had seen straight to it.

I looked up at him, struggling to comprehend this Nik who was both like and unlike the one I knew before. It was like him to see straight to the heart of the issue and to name it without prevarication or softening. But the sympathy in his voice and eyes was entirely new.

The two aspects combined defeated me completely. I deflated, my whole body collapsing inward, my shoulders sagging.

"It's not that they…" I tried again. "No one ever hurt…" I groaned. Trying to dance around the truth was hopeless. "My mother never did anything wrong, but my Father…"

Nik's hold remained gentle, but I could feel his body tense as he waited for me to continue.

"He tried to keep me small so that I would never leave our farm," I said. "He had his reasons for being afraid, but those reasons don't change what he did. He convinced me I should never be activated—telling me my squeamishness would cripple my ability to use my power. I thought it was a horrible joke that I, of all people, had been given a strong healing seed but no way to ever use it."

Nik's mouth fell open slightly, but he quickly recovered himself.

"You're squeamish?"

I blinked. "I never mentioned that?"

"I'm fairly sure I would remember," he said dryly.

"Oh, sorry." I considered. "I guess even after I discovered the truth in Ostaria, it was hard to shake the old habit of finding it shameful."

"I've heard it mentioned occasionally at the Guild. It didn't seem like something to be ashamed about."

"No, I realize that now. Once I had control of my power, it became easy to manage. And before that I had my—"

"Wall!" His eyes lit up. "So that's why you had one. I've wondered about that."

"Really?" I frowned at him. Did he really think about me when we weren't together?

He shrugged. "It's an unusual use of your ability. I don't think I've ever heard of healing power being used that way—and it seems like the kind of thing I would have heard of."

"What?" I asked, managing a light tone I didn't feel. "Did you think you were the only one who could come up with new uses of your ability?"

He looked uncomfortable enough that a real laugh escaped me. "Oh, don't tell me I'm right? You really did think that!"

He shifted slightly on the tree stump. "Of course I didn't think I was the *only* one. But you were a fresh apprentice, then. It didn't make any sense."

I shoved him lightly with my shoulder. "So you're relieved now that you realize I did it by accident because I'm weak, not because I had some kind of unparalleled strength?"

He met my eyes, his own serious. "I don't think you're weak, Delphine."

My stomach contracted, the momentary amusement dissipating.

"Well, that's a new tune," I managed, my fingers twisting in Ember's fur. "I thought you only valued me for my fox."

Nik looked away, and I suddenly, desperately wanted to know what he was trying to keep me from seeing in his eyes. For several silent seconds, I thought he would remain silent, but he finally spoke.

"I've been alone for well over a year now—first roaming the kingdom at will, and then pursuing Grey. For most of that time, I didn't mind the solitude—in fact, I preferred it. I was convinced that my own strength was the only safe thing to be relied on."

He turned to look at me at last, but his eyes were veiled and hard to read. "I was even arrogant enough to think I could keep you safe as well as myself."

"Me?"

I frowned. Did he think he'd failed me somehow?

"I used to be furious that my family wouldn't acknowledge my strength," he said quietly. "But when I looked at you with Grey's knife coming out of your middle, I knew there was absolutely nothing I could do to save you. All my plants strength meant nothing."

"But it didn't matter," I said. "I could heal myself."

He sighed. "And I'm grateful for that. But what if you weren't a healer? I took you in there, and you could have died. Sometimes, our strength just isn't enough. You have a strong seed, but even the strongest healers have limits. Real ones—not the false ones your father tried to impose on you. You've thrown off his limitations, but that doesn't mean you don't have any."

I blinked, considering his words. I wanted to protest, but was it possible he was right? Did I think that by breaking free of my father, I could now do anything and save anyone?

If I truly accepted that nothing could save Josie's leg, it changed everything. Esme's face appeared in my mind, filled with desperation and grief as she knelt beside Josie. Unlike me, she knew this girl and her family. She clearly wanted to save her, and she had far more investment than I did. She also had far more experience as a healer—especially a healer far from a hospital. If she said this was the only option in the circumstances, I was sure she was right. No one was trying to manipulate or limit this girl. All they wanted was to save her life.

Guilt flooded me, followed by shame at my ridiculous behavior back in the village. I was a healer, and healers were supposed to help, not make an already tragic situation more difficult.

I jumped to my feet. "I have to go."

Esme had been right—the sooner we completed the healing, the better it would be for everyone. I couldn't dally out here in the fields. I had to get back quickly and help save that girl's life. And then I would have to apologize to Esme, to Amara, and to Josie's parents. At least Josie herself had been unconscious and oblivious to my outrageous response.

Nik stood as well, grabbing my arm.

"Delphine, I'm sorry. I didn't mean to offend you. I—"

I let him pull me toward him, smiling up at him. His words faded as he took in my expression.

"I'm not upset with you," I said. "I'm upset with myself because you're completely right. And that means I have to go back and face the mess I made."

I swayed toward him, wanting to lean against his chest and soak in his strength and warmth. I was just pulling myself together and straightening when his arms swept around me and clasped me against him.

I melted into him. His chest and arms tightened, squeezing me closer, and my name escaped his mouth on a breath, as if he hadn't meant to utter it. For one second, my eyes fluttered closed, and I allowed myself to relax and imagine staying here forever.

But then I forced my eyes back open and pushed against him. For a brief moment, he held on tightly, not letting me go. But with a quiet groan he released me.

"You have to go." His eyes sparked in the gloom of dusk, and my heart quickened.

"I have to go," I repeated, as much to myself as to him. But I hesitated for one last question. "How are you here, turning up just when I need you most?"

"I told you back at the inn that I would be waiting and ready to act. I've been with you since before you left Caltor."

"You have?" I shook my head. "Amara said something like that. She was expecting to meet you somewhere on the road. You should have joined us instead of lurking behind."

But even as I said it, I remembered why he couldn't. We didn't know what eyes Grey had watching us or what tales he might be receiving. Amara and my travels had to look natural.

I looked around, suddenly alert in the way I should have been all along. But I could see no one else in the rapidly gathering darkness.

"Go," Nik said softly, giving me a light push in the right direction. "And don't worry. I'll be watching over you until you're safely back in the village."

I nodded, wanting to say too many things but not having time for any of them. Glancing at the setting sun, my feet took off of their own volition. Anything I had to say would have to wait. I was needed to save a life.

CHAPTER

# TEN

"You need to rest." Amara's firm but gentle voice reached through the haze of my exhaustion.

"But I need to—" I looked at Josie, still unconscious in the bed, and realized there was nothing left to do.

Had I been working for hours, or did it only seem like hours? A glance at the window told me it was dark outside, but I didn't know how late.

They had all been waiting for me when I returned, the anxious look on Esme's face bringing back the uncomfortable feelings of shame. After my behavior, she hadn't been sure I would return. But Amara's expression told me she, at least, had never doubted me. And her confidence filled me with determination. I wouldn't let her down again.

Her clasp on my shoulder told me she understood the remorse in my face, but I wasn't selfish enough to start my apologies immediately. I had an important task to do, and seeking forgiveness would have to wait until no one's life was in danger.

Josie's parents had wanted to be present, but thankfully the healer had convinced them to leave with several of the villagers. Since Josie was still safely ensconced in assisted sleep, she had no need of their comfort, and once Esme removed the cloth covering her tools, I was grateful no family members were present.

If I hadn't been fully prepared to squash my squeamish reaction, I would likely have collapsed myself just at the sight of them. And I had further reason to be grateful to Esme as she took me through the operation with a calm professionalism that grounded me. She talked me through everything she was doing as she removed the damaged limb, at the same time using her power to demonstrate what she needed me to do inside Josie's body.

She didn't have the strength to change anything inside Josie—not with the level of Josie's resistance—but she went through the motions, her power guiding mine. Following her direction, I provided the strength to actually complete each step of the healing.

We sealed her leg just above the knee, regrowing the skin and burning out the infection that had already crept its way into her blood. As we worked, I sank so deeply into the healing that I didn't realize how tired I was until I finally pulled free. I had been so determined to redeem myself that I had freely poured in my strength, fighting against Josie's natural resistance. Only once I felt Amara's hand on my shoulder did I realize I was swaying, barely left with the energy to stand.

"It's time to rest," she said again. "Josie is healed."

I gazed down at the girl, who looked so painfully small beneath the light blanket covering her. Her face was peaceful in sleep, but how would it look when she awoke and discovered what we'd done? I had helped save her life, but I wouldn't be the one to guide her through all the grief and adjustments to come. It felt like I was walking out on the hardest part of the journey.

"Do you ever feel bad?" I asked Amara. "Changing someone's life and then just walking away? Adjusting to change isn't easy."

Amara put her arm fully around my shoulders, helping to support my weight.

"Sometimes I do," she admitted. "Sometimes I feel a pull to stay some-where just a little longer and a little longer again. But if I did that, those would be the only people I ever helped. There are certain things I can do that most others can't, so I have to use those skills in a strategic way. I can't do everything for everyone."

I shivered, hearing the echo of Nik's words in hers. I couldn't deny their truth, but they still hurt. I didn't want to face the reality of situations my healing power couldn't fix.

"You did well," Amara said softly. "I'm sorry I couldn't go with you earlier to help you process your emotions. I should have been there for you, but if we'd both left...But you obviously did well on your own."

I shook my head. "I had the help I needed." She looked at me oddly, but I pushed on. "I'm sorry, Amara. My reaction was childish and inappropriate, and my accusations were untrue. I let my response to Josie's situation become tangled up in my feelings about my father when it was never the same issue. Please forgive me."

"Of course." She pressed her cheek against the top of my head, the uncharacteristic motherly gesture making tears leak from my eyes and down my cheeks. "You were already forgiven. In the first few months of your apprenticeship, you've been put into far more stressful situations than most Guild apprentices see in their whole two years. And you're still dealing with deep hurt from what happened with your father. The wounds we received from our parents are hard enough to process at thirty-five, let alone eighteen. I don't expect you to be perfect, Delphine." She shifted me slightly so she could look me in the face, her eyes grave. "But you will need to apologize to more than me."

"Of course!" I looked around, but Esme had already disappeared. "Did Esme go to get the parents? I could talk to them all now..."

Amara shook her head. "First you need to sleep. Everyone will be here in the morning."

I wanted to protest, but one look at the dark night sky told me she was right. I let her lead me to one of the nearby houses, too exhausted to take note of its features. Someone had prepared beds for us, and I sank into the clean sheets, merely grateful for a soft pillow and proper mattress.

When I finally woke again, I was more aware of my surroundings, but there was nothing to distinguish the neat home from any other village dwelling. Neither was there anyone else present. Food had been left out on the table, however, and I wolfed it down ravenously. Only once I'd filled my belly did I grow alert enough to realize why I was alone—I'd slept away half the day.

I washed my face even more quickly than I'd eaten and hurried outside. I expected to have to search the village for Amara, but the house sat only one street from the central square. Like the day before, it was filled with people, although the atmosphere was very different.

I hurried into the crowd, noting that all evidence of the previous day had disappeared. Even the cobblestones had been cleaned by some compassionate hand, and the mood was one of good cheer.

In the center of the group, sitting on the edge of the fountain, was Josie. She was perched on a cushion, a plate full of fruit beside her, and a smile on her face.

I stopped, staring at her in confusion, and Amara appeared at my side.

"The whole village is feting her today," she murmured quietly. "So there's little room for grief or sadness. Although that will come, I'm sure. But clearly she has people to support her, and that will make a difference. She'll have sorrow, but she can still have moments of happiness as well—just as we all do."

"Today the village wants to remind her that her loss doesn't have to define her or steal her future," Esme said from my other side, having approached close enough to hear Amara's words. "The hardest part will come once the attention and sympathy dies down. But Josie's a strong lass, and I have no doubt she'll find her way through it."

I nodded, wondering uncomfortably if I had that same strength. I hadn't shown it the day before, but I wanted to in the future.

"Thank you, Apprentice Delphine," Esme said suddenly, filling me with fresh embarrassment. "I'm well aware I couldn't have managed yesterday without your fortunate arrival."

I shook my head rapidly. "Please don't thank me! I'm more than aware I owe you an apology instead. I acted as if you wanted to do something terrible when you were only doing your duty as a healer. I let my own history and issues overcome me. Please don't count my disgraceful behavior against my master. She's trained me better. I was the one to fail."

Unsure what else to do, I gave a respectful bow.

"Goodness, all of this isn't necessary, child." She placed a comforting hand on my shoulder. "You don't spend a lifetime as a healer without learning that some wounds can't be seen by the eye or felt by our power. What matters is that you came back, and you did what needed to be done. You were an excellent student, in fact. I didn't expect it to be so easy to guide you, given how new you are." She hesitated, as if she'd intended to say something more but thought better of it.

"And given how strong she is?" Amara asked in an amused tone.

The healer gave a reluctant chuckle. "Aye, that's right."

"What do you mean?" I looked back and forth between them. "Surely my strength made it easier. And as for following healing instructions, Master Hayes has me well trained by now." I grinned at the woman, confident that even a country healer would know Hayes's name.

"Ah, that explains it!" The woman smiled. "He was never one to stand for any nonsense."

"I am not one to favor nonsense either," Amara said, clearly still amused. "Plus Delphine has never even been to the Guild."

"Never been to the Guild?" The healer stared at me in astonishment.

"She was born to southern farmers and signed up for a traveling apprenticeship with me directly from her home," Amara said.

"Well, well, well." The woman clucked her tongue. "I know apprenticeships outside the Guild aren't much in favor, but clearly they should be if they produce students like Delphine. I'm due for one of my annual visits to the Caltor hospital soon, and you can be sure I'll put in a good word on the matter to the healing mages there."

"I'd appreciate it," Amara said with a genuine smile. "The more voices, the better. Change is slow to come, but I'm hopeful we're in a season of it at the moment."

"I'm still not sure why my strength would be a detriment," I said, not entirely following their conversation.

The healer chuckled and clapped me on the shoulder again. "You're one of the good ones, Delphine."

She wandered back into the crowd, leaving Amara to give me actual answers.

"Unfortunately, strength often comes with arrogance," she said. "And arrogance doesn't pair well with learning."

"Oooh!" I felt dense for needing it pointed out. As soon as she said it, I could picture exactly the sort of mage student I'd always imagined the Guild filled with. My old expectations had been so different from the actual mages I'd met that I'd started to forget them—especially since so much of my thinking had been shaped by my father. But clearly my preconceptions hadn't been entirely wrong.

"Of course not all the Guild students are like that," Amara said, "even the strong ones. Just look at Hayes. It's easy to see he was never that kind of student."

"Not to mention you," I said, shaking my head at her humble focus on Hayes. "You're the very opposite of everything I imagined powerful Guild mages to be."

"We can't express how grateful we are that a Guild mage was on hand," a new voice said, making me start.

I whirled around to find both of Josie's parents standing hesitantly to one side.

"Thank you so much for saving our daughter," Marla said. "I don't know what your fee might be, and I'm afraid we might not be able to…" She trailed off before rallying quickly. "But of course we'll find a way to pay it, whatever it might be."

"Oh no, no!" I held up both hands. "I'm only an apprentice, and I couldn't possibly…" I stopped as I suddenly remembered that as an apprentice, it was my master who set the fee for my services. It was how they paid for the expenses of housing, feeding, and training us.

I glanced at Amara to find her watching me with amusement.

"Given the circumstances, I don't think there's any need to talk of a fee," she said. "It was a valuable learning experience for my apprentice."

"Oh yes!" I agreed gratefully. "And please allow me to apologize to you for my behavior yesterday in the square. I allowed myself to become emotional and to unfairly accuse you. I want you to know it was never about Josie or her leg. It was my own issues, and it was terrible of me to allow those to intrude on such a difficult moment. Please accept my heartfelt apology."

"Did you behave terribly?" The mother turned her blank expression on her husband who looked equally clueless. "To be honest, it was all so traumatic, I remember almost nothing. From the moment of the accident through until I had my baby healthy in my arms again, I can only remember snatches. I was certain that..." She stifled a sob, and her husband put an arm around her shoulders.

"From what we've been told, she would have died without you," the father said. "You saved her life, and that's all that matters to us."

"Thank you." I gave them the same half-bow I'd given the healer. "I'm most grateful for your understanding."

After a few more protestations on both sides, someone appeared to take their attention, and I turned to Amara.

"Everyone here seems to be excessively understanding."

She smiled. "I've noticed that happens after you save someone's life. Especially a child."

"I'm sure you've had plenty of experience with that, even if you aren't a healer," I said, remembering the way she had held back the flood that nearly swept us both away.

"You'll soon have grateful friends of your own across the kingdom." She grinned at me. "Maybe you'll even decide you like a roving life yourself. I hope you do. Tartora could do with more traveling masters."

I shook my head. I wasn't ready to think about a future as a master.

"I'm just glad everything worked out this time. If the poor girl is ever injured again..." I winced.

Amara looked across the square at where an older lad was doing a jig, making the girl laugh.

"I spoke to the parents earlier. This was the final straw for them. They did everything they could to hold onto their farm, but they're going to sell it now and move to Caltor. If their daughter is injured again, she'll be able to be rushed to the hospital there where a team of healers can work on her."

I nodded, relieved at the news. After yet another major healing, I suspected Josie would be beyond the efforts of any single healer, no matter how powerful. Moving to the city would be a difficult adjustment for the family, no doubt, but it was the only safe course.

"Will we stay here long?" I asked, hesitant but trying to keep it from my voice. I had already made enough of an emotional fuss.

Amara smiled at me knowingly. "Of course we've had several offers of accommodation for as long as we want it, but I think this village is in enough uproar. I thought we would move on as soon as I've finished some consultations with the village leadership over the pathway of a nearby stream. And once you've recovered your energy, of course."

"Oh really?" I brightened. "I already feel fine after that enormous sleep. We can leave as soon as you like."

Amara grinned at my hopeful expression, and I tried to school myself into neutrality. It was probably cowardly of me to run away, but it was painful to be so conscious of my bad behavior while everyone kept plying me with gratitude and praises.

"I should be done within an hour or so," she said.

I gazed toward the edge of town. "Would you mind if I went out walking while you finish your business? I feel out of place here."

Amara gave me a piercing look, but after a moment she sighed and nodded. "Try not to get into trouble while you're out there."

I frowned at her. She didn't usually worry about me being a troublemaker. Had her view of me changed after my foolishness the day before? But she threw me a knowing smile that didn't seem to match that thought.

I was still trying to work out what she meant as she moved away toward a small clump of village elders. I turned my own feet toward the edge of town, nearly making it to the edge of the first field before I remembered what I had let slip the night before. I had told her that someone else helped me process my emotions. Given her smile, she must have had a good idea who that person was.

My cheeks heated although there was no one left near me to see it. I didn't stop walking, though. My last conversation with Nik had been cut short by the urgency of the moment, and I would far rather continue it than linger awkwardly with the villagers.

# CHAPTER
# ELEVEN

This time I didn't run, but I did hurry straight to the clump of trees we had sheltered under previously. The sawn-off tree stump stood waiting, but I skirted around it. Casting a lingering glance at the apparently empty fields around me, I pushed into the middle of the trees. There were just enough of them to provide screening from watching eyes, something I had foolishly not thought about the day before.

I just had to hope Nik was on the lookout again today and had seen me arrive.

The minutes ticked by, and I tried to restrain my growing impatience. What if he hadn't seen me? I could spend hours waiting fruitlessly among the trees. Should I go somewhere more visible?

"No Ember today?" a deep voice asked, making me jump.

"Nik! You startled me!" I put a hand on my chest, tracking my racing heartbeat.

"Sorry." His expression didn't match the apology. Was he amused by my fright?

"Ember sleeps at this time of day usually." I paused. "I wasn't sure if you were coming."

"Of course." He said it simply, as if it was the sort of fact that required no further explanation.

Something warm grew inside me, wiping away the irritation at his earlier amusement. I had come trusting Nik was watching for me, and I had been right.

"What happened?" he asked. "With the injured girl."

I rubbed my eyes with remembered exhaustion. "It was a long operation —I'm sure my inexperience didn't help with that. But it was successful. Her health is stabilized now, and she's not in any more danger—at least not from this injury. Her resistance will have grown even further though, unfortunately."

He nodded, but something in the way he looked at me gave me the impression he was more interested in how the healing had affected me than in the future of a girl he didn't know.

"My great-great grandfather did a good thing building the hospitals," he said after a moment. "But there's a shortage of healers in the towns and villages."

I raised my eyebrows. "I didn't realize you noticed that sort of thing."

"What's that supposed to mean?" He sounded stung. "Just because I operate alone doesn't mean I want everyone else to die."

"No, of course not." How had I managed to get off to such a bad start? "I didn't mean that. It just seems like the kind of detail that..."

"Those with a plants affinity are most drawn to farming," he said, not meeting my eyes. "They suffer disproportionately."

I considered his words, slowly nodding. It was true the affinities weren't evenly spread across the kingdom. There were always people of all three affinities in any village, but villages located in farmlands always had more with a plants seed.

"Someone has to think of the people the crown has forgotten," Nik muttered, and my eyes snapped back to his.

What was lurking behind that comment? Gathering my courage, I blurted out the question Hayes had refused to answer in Caltor.

"Obviously you don't travel alone because you hate all people, but I have no idea of the real reason. I can't make any sense of why a royal prince is roaming the kingdom alone."

Nik's eyes tightened, and I stood in silence, wondering if I'd gone too far.

"I've had my share of traveling with others," he said finally. "And I prefer it this way. There's no one to let you down if you're alone."

My heart sank at his words, and it took all my willpower not to reach my hand up to cup his cheek. He looked so strong, but his words told me how much pain was hiding behind his appearance.

Stepping forward, I took one of his hands in mine. "I know people can let you down." I only had to think of my own recent behavior to remember that. "But is it really better to always be alone?"

Nik hesitated, looking down at our clasped hands with an expression I couldn't read. "I used to think so," he said quietly.

"But not anymore?" I struggled to keep my voice even.

He looked up at me. "I found an ally. And then I went off without her, and it was different from how it was before. I used to be satisfied with protecting people from the shadows—I preferred it even. But this time..." His hand shifted, twisting so that now he was the one holding onto me. "I missed having her beside me."

"Your ally..." I murmured. The word felt cutting—someone useful for his mission and nothing more—and I needed that reminder given the way my heart leaped at his other words.

I looked away, afraid of what he would see in my eyes. If I was honest, I had felt an attraction to Nik almost from the beginning, but this new sympathetic, almost vulnerable side of him was appealing in a whole different way—dangerously appealing, considering he was a prince who viewed me only as an ally.

"Sometimes allies don't let you down," he murmured. "Sometimes they make you stronger."

"I want to be that kind of person." I tried not to relive my recent lesson in humility. "But you've known from the beginning how weak I am."

"I don't think you're weak, Delphine." His words pulled my gaze back to his. "When I said you were strong yesterday, I didn't just mean your seed. Everyone has weaknesses, but that doesn't have to mean you're weak. Sometimes weaknesses can turn into strengths. Like with your squeamishness causing you to create the wall. You achieved something amazing, and you only did it because of your weakness."

"So what about you?" I asked, hoping to distract him from the rising heat in my cheeks. "Have you accepted your own weakness?"

His eyes stayed steady on mine, his expression piercing. "Didn't I already say that? I long ago realized that what I thought was my weakness was the most valuable thing to me."

The warmth in my cheeks heated to burning, and no words came. He couldn't possibly be talking about me, could he?

"Your father was fighting the tide trying to suppress you, Delphine," he murmured. "He was never going to succeed. After all, you even managed to win me over."

He flashed me a smile that hit my heart like a thunderbolt. I drew in a gasping breath of air, and his eyes dropped to my lips.

A feeling of panic engulfed me, and I stumbled into speech.

"You now know what my father did to me, but what about yours? How did he fail to protect you?"

He managed to keep his face still, but his whole body stiffened, his muscles snapping tight, as if ready for combat.

"What are you talking about?" he asked stiffly.

I gulped. I hadn't meant to say anything, but I was committed now.

"Last night you saw straight through the nonsense I was spouting to the heart of my real issue. I guess it seemed like you understood me so quickly because you knew how it felt. And since you chose to leave your title and family in favor of roaming the countryside alone, I thought…If I'm wrong, I'm sorr—"

"My parents might be king and queen," he said abruptly, "and they might have power most other families don't, but in some things their hands are tied. They never lied to me. I don't claim my situation is the same as yours."

"But they still hurt you." I examined his face, trying to read the emotions hidden in his eyes.

He shrugged and looked away. "Everyone gets hurt sometimes."

His words were clearly a dismissal of the topic, and it stung after his earlier moment of vulnerability. I looked down, wondering if I should pull my hand free. I shouldn't have pushed so hard.

When I looked back up, Nik was watching me. He had clearly caught my reaction to his words, and his face had softened in response.

"Sorry," he said quietly. "Like I said earlier, I've gotten out of the habit of accommodating other people. You're right that my family let me down, but it's a complicated situation. They weren't the ones to act against me." He paused, pulling his hand free and turning completely away from me. "But perhaps if they'd ever believed in me…" He sighed in frustration, running a hand through his hair.

I watched him from behind, taking in the lines of his straight back and broad shoulders. It was hard to imagine Nik ever feeling weak and helpless, but something in his manner told me he knew how those emotions felt. And I didn't need him to tell me to know he'd hated them.

His shoulders straightened, and he turned back to me. Seeing my expression, his lips curved upward. "I can read all your emotions on your face, you know." He said it humorously, but the tender note beneath nearly undid me.

I needed to extract myself from this situation before I did something even more outrageous.

"I need to get back," I said hurriedly. "Amara and I are planning to continue traveling this afternoon, and she's probably finished her meeting by now."

Nik took a step back, nodding. His face closed off, the moment of openness between us over.

"I guess I'll…I'll see you on the road. Maybe. If we can—" I gestured vaguely at the trees around us before finally cutting off my stumbling words.

"Goodbye, Delphine." There was a shadow in his eyes I didn't want to interpret.

I fled back across the fields, telling myself I wasn't running away. But even I didn't believe it.

And as I went through the motions of saying our farewells to the villagers, the feeling of having disgraced myself grew. Why had I panicked and rushed off? What was Nik thinking of me? It was hard to contain my roiling thoughts while accepting a second round of thanks and polite niceties.

When our cart rolled past the last of the houses, I let out a long breath of relief.

"Are you that happy to be gone?" Amara asked.

I gave an embarrassed grimace. "I know I shouldn't be. And if we'd been needed, I would have stayed. But being there with the villagers, it was hard not to think about the scene I made yesterday evening."

A dreamy, reminiscent look came into Amara's eyes. "I remember a south-eastern village where I thoroughly disgraced myself in the early days of my travel. I still haven't been back there."

"You disgraced yourself, too?" I asked.

Amara laughed at the enthusiasm in my voice. "Don't worry. We're all fools in our youth, one way or another. There have to be some advantages to aging. I just hope your experience will leave less of an enduring stain than it did for me. I wouldn't want to have to avoid this village in future, given its position on this road. I suspect we'll be back within your apprenticeship, let alone after."

I smiled, my mood rising now we were on the road. "I'm sure time will help. My mistakes won't sit so heavily on our next visit."

"Ah, optimism—another characteristic of youth." Amara's eyes danced as she surveyed the road ahead.

"You're not actually that old, you know." I narrowed my eyes, considering adding a comment about what Hayes and Clay would have to say about the matter but decided to refrain. I felt comfortable with Amara, but I wasn't sure I felt that comfortable.

We fell into a companionable silence, and my attention moved to our surroundings. Once the village fell from view behind us, I looked for any sign of another traveler shadowing our progress, but I could see no sign of Nik. When I reached out with my power, I could sense no one behind us on the road. An occasional person was located in the surrounding fields, but I couldn't distinguish between the local farmers and Nik, so I couldn't identify which one was him.

I refused to consider the idea that none of them were. He had to be out there. He had promised. And I needed to show him that I could behave normally again.

When we set up camp for the night, well short of the next village, I half expected him to appear. But again there was no sign of him. I could sense another traveler out of sight, but I couldn't be sure it was Nik. Especially given he gave no sign of stopping for the night. If it was him, he should be resting and not roaming around in the dark.

I would tell him so the next time I saw him.

"You seem unusually jumpy." Amara looked at me with suspicious eyes. "Are you expecting someone?"

I quickly refuted the suggestion and decided to stop reaching out to the countryside around us. Ember had already disappeared into the darkness, but Amara wasn't going to let me follow her, and there was nothing I could do to make Nik appear. He would show up when he was ready.

CHAPTER

# TWELVE

I slept fitfully, but my dreams were about accidents and mangled limbs rather than the absent prince, so I couldn't blame him for my poor rest. Amara took one look at my face when we woke and thankfully refrained from any questions.

We packed up quickly and got back on the road. As the sun rose higher in the clear blue sky, my lingering exhaustion fell away, and my mood lifted.

I took a deep breath, stretching my arms high. "There's something about clear skies and broad, open spaces that's freeing."

Amara looked sideways at me and smiled. "Whenever I leave a town and get back on the road, it's always such a relief. But strangely, whenever I ride into a town, heading for a proper bed and a hot bath, I feel the exact same relief."

She chuckled, and I joined her. I had been on the road for a much shorter time than Amara, but I already knew the phenomenon she described.

"I used to think I was happy at home on our farm, but now I wonder how I endured the monotony."

Amara launched into some lighthearted stories about her own childhood adventures in the capital, and before I knew it, we were stopping for a midday meal. We decided to take the time to prepare a warm meal since we had several nights on the road ahead of us, meaning we had no particular destination that needed to be reached that night.

While Amara established the fire and heated the food, I wandered away in search of the brook I could hear burbling nearby. Amara's elements ability could probably have told me exactly where to find the water, but I preferred to stretch my legs and find it myself.

We had stopped on the edge of a small stretch of trees in order to make use of the shade, but the trunks grew densely enough to conceal the water from my view. Following my ears proved successful, however, and the narrow stream had just come into view when a different sound caught my attention.

Although the cry wasn't especially loud, the series of sharp, rapid notes clearly indicated distress, the intensity of the sound rising as I stopped to listen. Reaching out with my power was instinctual, but it took me a moment to identify the source of the strident call: a bird—and a big one from its feel.

I changed course, moving as quickly through the trees as the undergrowth allowed. Ember, who had roused from her usual daily sleep when we stopped, stayed near my heels, her ears pricked and her nose raised to the wind.

When I finally reached the location of the distressed creature, I realized I had struggled directly through the heart of the thicket and come out the other side. It would have been faster to skirt the grove and avoid the undergrowth altogether.

All such thoughts fell away when I spotted the bird trapped in a dense section of bush. Interlocking branches and long thorns had entangled the wings and feet of the enormous creature, holding it captive.

My early studies, under Hayes's guidance, had focused on human anatomy, so I had yet to learn all the different species of animal found in Tartora. However, I knew enough to recognize the bird as some kind of eagle. I had rarely seen one with such a large wingspan, however.

At the sight of me, the eagle let out another series of harsh notes and flapped its wings. I fell back a step, awed at the bird's size. At full stretch, it would be wider than I was tall.

But the movement only caused thorns to tear into its wings, and the bird fell still again, letting out another, more desperate call. I hesitated, but my compassion soon drove me forward. There had to be a way to free the bird.

Ember hung back, letting out a low whimper.

"Don't worry, girl," I said softly. "I won't let that beak near me."

Even as I said it, I eyed the sharp, curved beak warily. The claws were even more worrying, but with the bird's legs caught in the undergrowth, it would have little chance to use them.

Streaks of red marred the luxurious feathers, but there was no use healing the bird if I couldn't free it. I bit my lip as I examined the tangle of greenery. How had a high-flying creature like an eagle gotten caught in the first place? It wasn't likely to have come zipping beneath the canopy like a smaller bird.

I put the matter from my mind as I focused on the more immediate issue.

"How am I going to free you, good sir?" I asked aloud, tapping my fingers against my belt.

They brushed against the leather of my dagger's sheath, making me pause. Drawing the thin blade Nik had gifted me for my birthday, I smiled at the sight of its sharp edge. I had worried about the sort of circumstance that might require me to use the weapon, but this was a use that made me glad to have it—even if Nik scolded me later for dulling the blade against branches and vines.

"Now just hold still, good sir," I murmured, trying to reinforce my calming tone with overlays of my power.

I had no idea what I was doing in that regard, however. I had heard of healers who managed to attract animals to them with their power, but I didn't know how to do it. Without physical contact, I could identify the bird's presence, but I didn't know how to affect its mood.

I pushed my power outward, attaching to the sense of the bird and hoping that somehow it would sense me back. All I needed was for him to recognize me as a friendly presence and stop fighting.

At first, I thought it had worked. The eagle stilled, regarding me through one beady eye. But as I stepped closer, he resumed his thrashing motion, letting out a cry that was louder than the reedy calls I'd heard so far.

I held out both hands, letting loose a flood of pleading words in my most gentle voice. But it made no difference. The bird, too dazed with pain to recognize my intent, only thrashed harder.

Tears ran down my cheeks as fresh red appeared along his feathers, and I fell back several steps. The bird instantly calmed again, and I took a deep breath. I needed to think of another way, but my mind was coming up blank.

I grunted in frustration, kicking my foot against the ground. What use was all my power if I needed physical contact to use any of it? I was sure if I could just get a hand on the bird, I could calm him.

I continued to push out my power, blanketing the whole area in it, as if that would make a difference. After a while, the eagle seemed to calm further, so I risked moving forward again.

As before, he waited until I was close before launching into frenzied movement, this time swiping his head forward and nearly catching me with his sharp beak.

I leaped back with a quiet shriek that slipped out without my intending it. Ember whined her protest, pressing herself against my leg. I sighed and crouched down, resting a hand against her back.

"What are we going to do, girl?" I asked. "We can't just leave that fine fellow there, trapped like that. He'll die for sure if we can't rescue him."

Ember growled quietly, and I scolded her.

"I'm sure he's never eaten any of your relatives, so you needn't talk like that."

With a sigh, I straightened again. I had to find a way to get close to the bird.

A sudden shrill, chattering call pierced the air as a blur fell from the sky. On instinct, I threw my hands up to protect my head. We didn't get many eagles down south, but we had plenty of merlin falcons, and I recognized the cry, although I had no idea why one would be attacking.

As my mind caught up with my body, I pulled my arms down, my eyes flying to the trapped eagle. Had the falcon perceived his cries as some kind of threat? They were remarkably agile and aggressive birds, and even in the air they wouldn't be discouraged by the larger size of an eagle, let alone now, when its opponent was trapped and helpless.

"Wait! Stop!" I cried, jumping forward and throwing out my arms, as if to shoo the newcomer away.

Even as I moved, I recognized the futility of my actions. But to my surprise, the falcon had already pulled up, flying out of reach of the eagle's snapping beak without having touched the other bird.

My mouth fell open as the falcon swooped in a second time, flying fast and low as it sped toward the eagle, only to pull up at the last moment and fly away, once again with the same chattering call. I tried to remember when I had last heard such a noisy falcon and failed. Something about this bird's behavior was extremely strange.

As I watched, still frozen in shock, the falcon swooped a third time. The eagle waited until the smaller hunter was close, snapping its head forward at the last moment and nearly catching it. The falcon swerved out of reach, however, pulling back out from under the trees.

Staring at the eagle, I realized all of his attention was now focused on the falcon as it dived in and swooped back out, constantly threatening attack, although it never actually touched the eagle. For a startling moment, an impossible thought ran through my mind. Was the merlin doing it on purpose to distract the eagle for me?

Surely that couldn't be the case, but the opportunity was there, all the same. I hurried forward, making sure I approached on the opposite side to the merlin, who was in the process of diving back toward the eagle.

The trapped bird was still, waiting for the right moment to strike, and I lunged forward, grabbing the largest vine trapping it and sawing at it with my dagger. As soon as it gave way, I seized another, sending a silent apology to Nik as I continued to misuse his blade.

When the second vine gave way, only a small branch remained. As the falcon chattered and dove, I gripped the branch in both hands and snapped it cleanly in half.

The moment the wing was free, the eagle swept it forward, nearly knocking the merlin from the sky. Dodging at the last second, the falcon escaped.

The eagle flapped, off balance now that it was partially free. He couldn't go far, however, since his legs were still held in place. I scrambled forward, trying to crawl beneath the freed wing. Red dripped on me as I did so, and my breath caught. How injured had the eagle become in his time in the bush?

I considered stopping and grabbing his wing, taking the time to heal the scratches and tears, but he was further damaging himself with each flap as he tried to pull free of the undergrowth. And the merlin might disappear at any moment, taking away my opportunity.

Gripping the dagger more tightly, I reached for the tangle of thin, thorny branches that trapped the eagle's legs. The seconds stretched out as my sweaty hand slipped on the dagger's hilt. It wasn't designed for a sawing motion, but I eventually managed to cut through the last of them.

As the final whip-like branch gave way, the eagle lurched free, tearing his other wing out of the ensnaring vines. His sudden movement knocked me over, sending me sprawling across the ground. I barely managed to fling the dagger free before I landed on top of it, the breath momentarily knocked out of me.

As soon as I could move, I rolled over and scrambled backward across the ground, gazing at the eagle in consternation. I had intended to grab hold of the final wing and heal the bird before freeing him completely. I hadn't realized the second wing was less ensnared than the other limbs.

He turned on me, his eyes unnaturally bright as he made a flying hop in my direction. I scrambled further back, trying to work out why he wasn't taking off now he was free.

He gave the same alarm call I'd heard previously, but it was even quieter and more reedy than before. And the flow of red had become heavier instead of tapering off as I'd expected in the absence of the thorns.

Staring at his body in horror, I realized I'd misunderstood the situation. His bleeding hadn't been caused by the minor scratches from his captivity. He had clearly sustained major wounds—most likely in a fight with another eagle—and his struggles had merely been exacerbating those wounds.

My hand flew to my mouth as I realized I'd made a grave error. When the falcon distracted the eagle, I should have used the opportunity to heal the trapped bird instead of focusing on freeing him. But since I hadn't made direct contact with him, I'd failed to realize the extent of his injuries.

I instinctively tried to move toward him, but he beat his wings powerfully, driving me back again. Tears sprang to my eyes as more blood flowed from his body. No wonder a majestic eagle had ended up trapped in the underbrush. He must have been driven down during the fight, perhaps even unable to fly. It also explained why he was still on the ground now.

He hopped toward me again, and I scrambled back even further only to collide with a tree trunk hard enough to make my head spin. I gasped and rubbed at the back of my head, staring into one of the bird's bright eyes. It wasn't a natural expression, and with a sick feeling I realized his behavior from the beginning had been the fevered madness of a dying animal. If he'd been merely trapped, my power would likely have calmed him. But he certainly wasn't going to let me near him now.

Tears dripped down my face, but before I could give way to the grief, he stumbled even closer, and a more primal fear swept over me at the sight of his sharp beak and claws.

He lurched forward, swiping at me with his beak, but a blur raced through the air, spearing straight for the eagle's head. Rearing back, the larger bird swept his wing around and finally caught the falcon. Knocked from his path, the bird was flung against a nearby tree, falling like a stone to lie at its base.

"No!" I screamed, trying to scramble toward the collapsed falcon.

But the eagle moved to block me, managing to lift itself off the ground so it could reach for me with its talons.

I flung up my hands to protect my face, but a growl from the ground beside me made me scream.

"Ember, no!" I flung myself sideways, landing protectively over the small body of the fox.

She tried to slither out from under me, but I clasped her in both hands, curling over her and leaving my back exposed to the eagle. I braced myself to feel slicing pain across it, but instead I heard running feet, a thud, and then unsettling silence.

Pushing off the ground, I peered back at the eagle. It was no longer standing or hovering but lay still on the ground, one wing spread out and the other trapped beneath it. It wasn't moving.

I scrambled up and raced over to it, pressing my hands against the closest feathers. But my power didn't respond when I tried to push it into the bird. There was no life left for me to connect with.

"No, no," I sobbed, trying again. But I was too late.

I looked up at Nik, the source of the running feet. He stood beside us, sadness in his eyes as he looked at the broken bird.

I scrambled up and threw myself at his chest, beating it with my fists.

"What did you do? How could you? You killed him!" Tears streamed down my face.

He captured my hands, stilling me. "It was a mercy."

I shook my head stubbornly. "I could have healed him."

"You had to be touching him for that. Were you going to let him kill you while you worked on him? He was too far gone to see you as anything but a threat."

I pressed my face against his shirt and sobbed again. A gentle hand stroked my hair, and somewhere in the back of my mind I remembered our first few meetings and wondered how we'd ended up here.

"Even if it hadn't been a mercy for the animal, I would have acted to protect you, Delphine," he murmured against my hair, and a shiver ran through me.

A moment later, a sudden thought made me push against him, staggering backward and staring around. Before Nik's arrival, someone else had protected me first.

My eyes found the falcon, and I raced toward him, Nik only half a step behind. As I dropped to my knees beside him, I held my breath, desperate for him to still be alive.

"Please, please, please," I murmured to myself as I laid a gentle hand against his feathers.

My power connected with him, and I nearly collapsed with relief. But the relief didn't last long.

I had never healed a bird before. I'd never even connected with one, and his system was unfamiliar and strange. Too much of him seemed to be lungs, his hollow bones structured around air sacs that seemed to fill most of his body. Vaguely I remembered a comment Clay had once made about birds. They didn't breathe like a human or a fox, with their lungs inflating and deflating. They should maintain constant volume, not lie still like an empty balloon.

Grasping the thought, I let my instincts take over, pushing air through the falcon. As it moved through his body, my power followed, healing the crushed airways and sacs.

He twitched beneath my hands, the movement growing until he shook his head and hopped to his feet, regarding first me and then Nik with one beady eye. I pulled back and gazed at him in return.

"Is he healed?" Nik asked, sounding equal parts fascinated and wary.

"I think so," I said cautiously. "I don't know much about birds."

For several seconds of silence, the three of us continued to regard each other.

"But I do know there's something strange about this one," I added.

Quickly I explained his behavior to Nik, detailing how he had helped me, first by distracting the eagle and then by launching a true attack to protect me.

"I've never seen a falcon act like that," I finished.

Nik rubbed at his jaw. "It's unusual, certainly, but not completely beyond the scope of what I've seen before."

"You have?" I stared at him.

He leaned forward, and I expected the healed falcon to dodge back, but the animal held his ground, one of his eyes glued to Nik.

"Aha! I'm right!" Nik sounded smug as he pointed at the merlin's legs. "Do you see how one is darker than the other?"

I examined the yellow coloring, quickly seeing what he meant. One leg was definitely darker than the other.

"That's strange." I frowned. "I've never seen a marking like that before. Does it mean something?"

Nik nodded. "There are a couple of healing mages at the palace who raise and train falcons. I don't know how they do it, but they somehow change the color of one leg so that anyone who comes across one in the wild knows it's a trained bird."

"They change the color of its leg! How is that possible?"

Nik shrugged. "You're the healing mage."

"Apprentice," I grumbled, once again feeling my ignorance acutely. "And I've barely learned anything about animals."

"They're intelligent birds, and the ones raised by healing mages are even more so." Nik gave the falcon in front of us an even closer examination. "Did you send your power out seeking animals to help you?"

"Not intentionally." I grimaced. "I don't really know how to do that."

"If he was raised by a mage, he probably responded to your power, regardless of your intentions. You probably feel familiar to him."

"But does that mean he belongs to someone?" I asked tentatively, reaching beyond the trees for any indication there was another human nearby.

"Not if he's all the way out here." Nik held out his arm, bent slightly and parallel to the ground. The falcon responded immediately, hopping onto it and preening. "I'd guess his trainer died while this bird was still young, and he's been on his own for a while. You can see he has a different look from a kept bird."

"I'll have to take your word for it since I've never seen a trained falcon before." I slowly climbed to my feet, shaking myself off.

Looking down at my traveling gown and bedraggled hair, I grimaced. I looked a complete mess.

Ember trotted over to us, growling quietly as she watched the falcon on Nik's arm.

"Stop that," I told her sternly, accompanying the words with a glare. "Phoenix is one of us now." I glanced at the bird. "If he wants to stay that is."

"Phoenix?" Nik raised his eyebrows.

"You know, rising from the ashes and all of that. It seems fitting." I ran a hand along the soft feathers of the bird's back. "He will want to stay, won't he? If he was raised by a person and lost them?"

"Given you just did a major healing on him, it seems likely." Nik glanced down at Ember. "At least if she's anything to go by."

Ember gave a small whine and trotted off around the edge of the grove, heading back toward our makeshift camp.

"I think she has the right idea," I said wearily. "I'm sure we could all do with some food, and Amara must be wondering where I got to. But we can't just leave..." I looked at the motionless eagle, fresh tears welling in my eyes.

I gave Nik a pleading look, and he nodded gravely. He didn't say anything, but a moment later the earth beside the eagle began to move. Within seconds, the remains of the magnificent bird had disappeared, swallowed by the ground. Only a patch of disturbed dirt showed the location of his grave.

"I couldn't just leave him to be..." I faltered. "It's my fault, you know. If I'd just paid more attention, I could have healed him while he was still trapped. I'm supposed to be a healer, and I didn't even realize how badly he was injured."

Nik placed a hand on my shoulder. "Don't do that to yourself, Delphine. What happened wasn't your fault. You put yourself in danger to try to save him which is more than anyone could ask of you."

He held my gaze, his expression compelling me not to look away. "Do you think the limitations of circumstance are any less real than the limitations of your strength? No healer has ever lived who could heal everyone of everything. And we would know," he added sardonically, "since they would still be alive, healing themselves into immortality."

I drew a deep breath, holding onto his words as I pulled myself together. He was right. Animals died all the time in the wild, and there was nothing I could do to change that. It was a fact I'd always known, but even as a child I'd struggled to reconcile myself to it. Clearly, I was going to have to learn, however.

Phoenix ruffled his feathers, eyeing me from his place on Nik's arm. I managed a smile for the proud-looking bird. At least I could take comfort in having managed to save him.

Once I was sure I had myself under control, I followed in the direction

Ember had taken, planning to circle the trees this time. But I halted when I realized Nik wasn't keeping pace.

I looked back at him. "You are coming, aren't you?"

He hesitated, and I walked back to grab his free arm and pull him along.

"We haven't passed anyone on the road all morning. There's no one to see you with us. You can at least have some hot food."

"I'm fine. I can—" A rumble from his stomach made him fall silent.

"See, your belly knows what's best for it," I said in my best imitation of Amara's firm manner. "You can go skulking off on your own once you've eaten."

"Skulking?" Nik murmured under his breath in disbelieving tones, but his feet followed me, so I let it go without comment.

As we rounded the trees, he picked up his speed until we were walking side by side, Phoenix between us. He looked from the bird to me and sighed.

"What would have happened to you if this gentleman hadn't been on hand? Why do you insist on throwing yourself into danger whenever you see the opportunity?"

"I couldn't just leave that poor creature. He would have died—" A shudder passed through me. But even knowing the eagle's end, I couldn't have just walked away and left him there.

"Didn't you even think about your own safety?" Nik asked sourly.

I looked at him, warmth filling me.

"No," I said simply. "I didn't need to think about it because I knew you would."

"Me?" He looked sideways at me, a guarded expression in his eyes.

I nodded. I hadn't thought about it in so many words, but ever since Nik had appeared in the fields near the village, I had been conscious of his watchful presence, just out of sight.

"It might have seemed like I was walking alone in the woods, but I felt safe because I knew you were watching over me."

"I nearly didn't get there in time." Nik's words came out low and gravely, as if he was judging himself.

"But you did arrive in time," I replied with a smile. "You always do." I patted the sheath at my waist, my smile brightening. "And I found a good use for this."

"That's not why I gave it to you," he grumbled, but a small smile played around the corners of his lips.

"Delphine! There you are!" Amara's exclamation made us both stop. "I was about to ask Ember to lead me to you. What took you so..." Her mouth fell open as she saw the state of my dress and hair. "What in the kingdoms have you been—" She cut herself off for a second time when she finally noticed Nik, Phoenix still perched on his arm.

"It's a bit of a long story," I said. "But we have two extras for the meal."

"A prince and a merlin falcon." Amara shook her head. "I should be surprised, but somehow I'm not. Sit down and tell me from the beginning."

CHAPTER

# THIRTEEN

Amara had prepared a simple stew, but she made me scrub my hands and face before she let me taste any of it. I could see the concern in her eyes, so I told the story as simply as I could, pausing only to shovel in mouthfuls of bread and stew.

"And so you've been following us," she said to Nik at the end of my tale. "I wondered."

He gave her a closed look. "I told you I would."

"Not in so many words!" I protested, nudging his shoulder with mine.

He didn't respond at all to my attempt at playfulness, eating with quick efficient movements.

"His Highness clearly didn't see any value in going to the capital," Amara said dryly. "I surmised the rest."

Nik met her eyes, his expression hard. "I don't have patience with wasting time."

"But you do want to see Delphine protected."

He continued to meet her gaze without flinching. "I will ensure it."

For a moment, the crackle of the fire was the only sound.

"Because she's essential for your plan," Amara eventually said lightly. But her eyes remained serious, as if she were probing him.

"I will always make sure Delphine is protected," Nik's voice sounded like granite, certainty in every line of his face, but I still struggled to make sense of his words.

They hadn't exactly been a denial of Amara's statement. But there was something so sure in the way he spoke about me.

I shoved another spoonful into my mouth, glad of an excuse to look down at my bowl. Since his return, Nik seemed like a different person—but only when we were alone. Around others, the old hardness and arrogance were still there.

I didn't know what to make of it. Why was he so different with me? He had told me he thought about me during his absence, had even suggested he missed me. And I couldn't ignore the new softness in his manner toward me. But neither could I be sure what it meant.

"So you intend to join us now?" Amara raised an eyebrow, her manner still challenging.

Nik shook his head. "As I said in Caltor, you need to make your travels toward the border look natural. Having me with you would destroy that impression."

"And yet, here you are."

"That was me," I said quickly. "I insisted he come for a meal. We haven't passed anyone on the road this morning, so there isn't likely to be anyone overtaking us while we eat."

"I'll be leaving as soon as I've finished," he said.

"Not straight away!" I protested.

When both of them gave me a surprised look—Amara's with a hint of censure and Nik's a spark of amused pleasure—I hurried on. "You clearly know something about caring for falcons. You need to instruct me before you disappear!"

"So this one is staying permanently?" Amara reached out a cautious finger to stroke along Phoenix's back. "I suppose I'm going to have to resign myself to accumulating a menagerie by the time your apprenticeship is finished."

I gave her a guilty smile. "I'll try not to adopt any more wild animals into our ranks, but Phoenix is different. According to Nik, he was bred and raised by a healing mage, so I couldn't just abandon him in the wild for a second time. Not if he wants to stay with me."

"A trained falcon?" Amara looked at Nik who nodded confirmation.

In short tones, he outlined the reasons for his assumption, including his guess that Phoenix had lost his master during the bird's adolescence.

"Oh yes! I'd totally forgotten about the legs." Amara leaned closer to peer at the different tones of yellow between Phoenix's two legs. "I used to see the falcons around the Guild sometimes when I was a child and apprentice. It seems like a long time ago now."

"So he can stay with us?" I asked eagerly.

She smiled indulgently. "How could I turn away such an aristocratic fellow?"

Phoenix chose that moment to preen, as if he'd understood her words, and we both laughed.

"Welcome to our makeshift family, Phoenix." I pointed first to Amara and then to Ember. I didn't know what I was doing, but I tried to put the weight of my power behind my words when I added, "The fox is not for eating. And that goes for you, too, Ember. No bothering your new brother."

Phoenix blinked, training one eye on Ember. After an extended tense moment, he ruffled his feathers and placed his head along his back as if he meant to sleep.

"I think that's agreement," I said with a laugh.

"He reminds me of someone," Amara muttered, glancing at Nik, who pretended not to hear her.

We each had seconds, no one seeming to want to hurry the end of the meal, and Nik waited while I changed my gown and tidied myself up before he told me the little he knew of caring for a falcon.

"Since we'll mostly be traveling through open countryside, he shouldn't need much care," Amara said. "He can hunt for himself and otherwise engage in activities normal for a wild falcon."

"Like Ember." I placed a hand on the fox, who was still regarding our newest arrival with displeasure.

"It's fascinating how they bond with you," Amara said. "I'm only now realizing how little I know about a healing mage's connection with animals. Since most mages live in the capital, or at least one of the larger cities, I'm not used to seeing them interact with wild animals. I regret not finding the time to ask Clay more questions about it."

"I'm not sure Phoenix truly counts as wild," I said. "And both of them were near death when I healed them. I don't think I could just bond with any wild animal I came across."

Tears pricked my eyes as I thought of the eagle. If I could only have formed even a loose connection with him, I could have calmed him enough to save him.

"It's not your fault." Amara put a hand around my shoulders and squeezed. "You can't save every animal any more than you can save every person."

I glanced at Nik. They both kept saying it, and I knew they were right, but I was still dreading the day I experienced losing a person. Every healer eventually had to deal with patients they couldn't save, but thankfully they didn't put new apprentices in those situations.

"If you start accepting it now, it'll make it easier later," Amara said softly, as if reading my thoughts.

"Can something like that ever be easy?" I asked.

"Not easy." Nik reappeared from where he'd been making Phoenix a makeshift perch in the back of the cart. "Death is never easy. But healers and warriors both have to find ways not to be crippled by it."

I looked at the ground. I didn't want to think about what experience Nik had with death, or about the deaths to come in my own future. Today's had been hard enough.

"You're still young," Amara said softly. "You'll learn." She turned to Nik. "I suppose you'll be close by, Your Highness, even if you're out of sight?"

My head snapped up. "You should join us at night."

Amara gave me a quizzical look, but I kept my attention on Nik, remembering the person I had sensed roaming through the darkness the night before.

"Once we set up camp for the evening, if there's no one else around, it would be safe for you to join us, wouldn't it? I know you can't in the villages, but when we're camped by the road…"

Nik glanced at Phoenix, perched in the cart bed, and then back at me. I noticed he didn't look at Amara.

"I suppose that would be safe enough."

I turned a pleading look on Amara. "It makes more sense than setting up two camps and preparing two meals, don't you think?"

"I think…His Highness is welcome anytime we're alone."

I breathed a sigh of relief, but she took a step closer to Nik and continued in a stern tone. "As long as I'm around, that is. I overlooked the other evening because Delphine was in crisis, and it's obvious you helped her, but I think the two of you have done quite enough meeting up alone at night."

I gulped. "So you did know I saw Nik then?"

She gave me an exasperated look. "I'm neither inexperienced nor foolish. I didn't say anything because whatever he said seemed to help you. But I haven't forgotten the damage done back in Ostaria and Caltor. I'm responsible for you during your apprenticeship, Delphine."

"I understand," I said quickly. "I didn't mean to do anything behind your back. I had no idea Nik was watching us so closely, so I didn't even think of it, but he saw me sprinting through the fields and thought I was in trouble."

"If it's safe, I'll reappear tonight." Nik gave me a half smile, the warmth in his eyes sparking an answering warmth in me. But his fire cooled to ice as he turned to Amara and gave a barely respectful half-bow. "Tonight, then."

Before either of us could respond, he strode away, disappearing into the trees.

"I can't work him out," I said quietly, staring after him. "Sometimes he seems to have changed completely, and then other times…"

"His manner masks it, but he's still young," Amara murmured back. "You've shaken him, Delphine, and he's not used to that."

"Me?" I turned to her. "What do you mean?"

She gathered the last of our things, checking the fire had been fully extinguished.

"Prince Nikolas has always been overly confident. From what I've heard, his twin sister is the only one of his peers he ever liked or respected. And his relationship with her has always been...complicated."

"Complicated how?" I climbed onto the bench seat of the cart beside her.

She flicked the reins, sending Acorn into lurching motion. "It's always complicated between older and younger siblings when a title is involved, let alone a crown. But it's more complicated with twins when it's only a matter of minutes between them."

"Princess Morgiana is the older sibling," I said, remembering my lessons. "But she isn't the crown princess anymore. And Nik isn't heir either." I frowned. "I'll admit when the news of the change in succession reached Tarin, I didn't quite understand what had happened. I don't think my parents did either, but we didn't pay it a lot of attention. My father insisted it didn't matter who wanted to sit in a fancy chair and lord it over the capital."

Amara raised an eyebrow. "Who sits on the throne has an enormous impact on all Tartorans—which is why we can be thankful there are mechanisms in place to try to ensure the best successor."

"And that isn't Nik?" I asked, offended on his behalf.

Amara hesitated. "I think only the royal family and the Triumvirate know the truth of how and why the change in succession happened as it did. If you want that story, I think you'll have to hear it from your new protector."

I flushed. "I can hardly ask him why he isn't the heir!"

"Why not?"

"What...But..." I spluttered, trying to put into words what seemed obvious. "He's a royal prince. And he's Nik!" I rolled my eyes. "He's not exactly what you would call open."

"You said he seems changed at times—I can only assume you mean when he's alone with you. So next time you have the chance, ask him about his history. I don't think you'll be able to make sense of him until you know it. And if he's not willing to share it with you...Well, that will tell you something important about him and your relationship as well."

"Relationship..." I muttered under my breath. "What relationship?" But I couldn't get her words out of my head. Could I really just come out and ask Nik about his history as a prince? Usually when it was just us I tried to forget about his royal status, and the one time I'd asked, his answer hadn't exactly been forthcoming. But Amara was right. It was better to be direct and know the truth of where I stood with him.

"All right," I said at last. "I will."

---

True to his word, after we stopped to make camp in the dusk of evening, Nik appeared from out of the shadows. He silently greeted Phoenix and helped gather water and firewood, keeping his distance from the road until true darkness fell.

"Tomorrow we'll look for a more secluded spot a little further back from the road," Amara said, and Nik nodded his thanks.

My earlier conversation with Amara was ringing in my ears, but Nik was obedient to her instructions and made no attempt to separate me from her. I wanted to respect my master's instructions, but I couldn't help a pang of disappointment. If I was going to bring myself to ask Nik questions, it would only be if I could talk to him without an audience.

When I woke in the morning, sometime after dawn, Nik had already disappeared. But after that, he joined us every night we were on the road, sometimes even appearing for the midday meal if we'd stopped in an out-of-the-way location.

We continued northeast across the kingdom, and I began to look forward to our makeshift camps more than the proper beds we were sometimes offered in the small villages we passed. And as my preference for days on the road grew, so did my impatience at our meandering route through every nearby village.

It was one thing to respond to any immediate need we encountered, but it seemed unnecessary to go out of our way, detouring to villages just so Amara could conduct training sessions for those with an elements affinity. It galled me not to move more quickly when Miranda needed us.

Eventually Amara lost patience and remonstrated with me. "I realize it's disconcerting that Miranda seems to have fallen for Grey's charm. But that's exactly what will keep her safe until we can extricate her."

"And what about the blight?" I asked. "If Grey knows something about that..."

"The blight is a matter of serious concern," she said with her usual unflappable and slightly infuriating calm. "But harvest is underway now. If we haven't discovered the root of the problem by the next planting season, then Tartora will have a significant issue. But for right now, these particular villagers will be without clean water soon if I don't show them how to keep contamination out of their dam."

When she put it like that, I couldn't protest further. I might have preferred to be sleeping by the fire with Nik in the next bedroll, Ember patrolling outside the firelight, and Phoenix only a foot away, but I couldn't deny that these people were isolated and in need of assistance.

And once I began to pay attention, I found the variety of problems we encountered fascinating. It was a pity Nik couldn't travel openly at our side since many of the farmers we encountered would have benefited more from a plants mage than an elements or healing one. And I especially wished for his assistance when we came upon the blackened stretches of burned fields.

One night on the road, I finally asked him if he had examined any of the blighted fields. He shrugged and said there was nothing left to examine.

"The fire completely destroys the blight—that's the point of it. What I need is to find a contaminated field before it's burned. But I always arrive too late."

The topic put him in a silent mood all evening, so I didn't bring it up again. I could only imagine his feeling of helplessness in the face of the growing crisis. For a plants mage, it had to be similar to my emotions when I failed to heal the eagle.

As both the days and the miles passed, Nik seemed to relax around Amara, losing some of his stiff coldness in her presence.

"You truly care about all these people," he said to her one night as we sat together around the fire after our evening meal. "I could see it out in the field today. How do you do it?"

"You were there?" I stared at him, wondering where he'd been concealed. I hadn't seen any sign of him.

He gave me a single, piercing look, his expression reminding me that he'd promised to always watch over me. I flushed and looked away, falling silent.

Amara replied, seeming oblivious to the short moment between us.

"It isn't something I have to consciously do. Caring is easy for me."

Nik snorted. "Criticism duly noted."

I gave him a light shove, but he didn't take back the words.

"I didn't mean it as a criticism of you," Amara said, sounding sincere. "But it's interesting you take it that way. Do you consider yourself uncaring of your kingdom's people?"

He was silent for a moment, considering her question, and I noticed he didn't refute the sense of responsibility her phrasing had implied.

"I don't care like you do," he said at last. "You seem to be genuinely interested in each individual and care about their state and their emotions."

Amara nodded. "I do. But that's because connecting with people comes naturally to me. It isn't the only way of caring, though." She paused. "Tell me,

Prince, after choosing to leave the capital, why have you spent a year and a half roaming the most remote regions of the kingdom?"

Nik looked away, either unable or unwilling to answer the question. But whether or not he realized it, he had already told me the answer. He thought the people of regional Tartora were forgotten by the crown. He might not think about it the same way Amara did, but he clearly cared—for some people, at least.

"How about this question, then," Amara said. "Why have you tracked Grey so single-mindedly?"

"He's abducting children and creating a threat to the entire kingdom. And now he might be involved in poisoning our food supplies. How could I not work against him?"

"Exactly." Amara nodded in satisfaction. "You do care. You're just motivated in a different way from me. We don't all have to approach situations and people from the same perspective—different motivations can lead to the same outcome. What matters, at the end of the day, is that you're helping people, not hurting them. Not everyone loves in the same way."

"Love?" Nik scoffed, looking away into the darkness.

"There are different kinds of love," Amara said, her words a rebuke. "For example, the love a king has for his people."

Nik's head whipped around, and he stared silently at her for an extended period. I held my breath, wondering if one or both of them was going to bring up the mysterious reason for his current status. But neither spoke, the popping of the fire the only accompaniment to the more distant sounds of the night.

Eventually Amara suggested sleep, and we all spread apart, banking the fire and preparing the camp and animals for the night. I stepped out of the firelight to check on Acorn's tether and arms encircled me, pulling me close.

My squeak of surprise was muffled by Nik's chest, and I fell silent, letting him hold me tight. My arms were trapped at my sides, but I didn't try to free them, merely resting my head against him.

His body was tense, and I could tell without needing to see his face or hear him speak that he needed comfort in this moment. The longer we stood there, however, the faster my heart began to race. When I heard his heartbeat meet mine, he abruptly let me go and stepped back.

"I'm sorry." His voice was low and gruff.

"No." I put a hand on his arm, stopping him from escaping. "I can't promise to watch over you or protect you from any danger, but I can do this much, at least. If you need someone, I'm here for you, Nik."

He hesitated for a long moment before speaking again, even lower than before. "Thank you."

He swept me abruptly into a second embrace, this one even tighter, but far shorter, than the last. When he released me, it was with a low growl, thrusting me away before striding off into the darkness.

I peered after him, my eyes finally adjusting after the brightness of the fire, but he was already lost to the shadows. And he didn't return that night.

CHAPTER

# FOURTEEN

Most of our journey had been through farmlands, with farmers busying themselves with the harvest. Their industry only high-lighted the tragedy of the empty, still sections of blackened earth. And although talk of the blight had been severely contained by the efforts of the crown and Guild, the issue couldn't be concealed from the villages at its center. As we moved further from the capital, the villages became more and more unsettled. All conversations circled back to the blight, and endless debates raged on what the response from Tarona should be. Some blamed the king, some blamed the Guild, and others declared that a disaster had struck the kingdom beyond the ability of either to fix.

The worst were the empty houses, where families had packed up and gone north into Calista, with no one new arriving to take their place. Since Calista had so far been spared from the blight, those who remained talked of it in suspicious tones that matched the way the southerners had viewed Grey's influence.

Nik's mood grew grimmer by the night, and Amara wasn't far behind him.

"It's worse than I realized," she finally admitted as we camped on the western bank of the Viridian River. We had passed the last of the farmlands, entering the hilly grazing lands of the northern border region.

"Why do you think I proposed such a desperate plan?" Nik's eyes lingered on me, discomfort in their depths.

As the weeks had passed, he had grown more and more reluctant to speak of the plan he'd suggested or of what might await me in Grey's camp. No amount of reassurance seemed to convince him that I wasn't going to change my mind, or that I was perfectly capable of healing myself if something unpleasant befell me.

"I'm sure Amara will agree to my going," I said. "Now that she's seen the state of things up here. You will, won't you, Amara?"

Amara grimaced. "I find myself growing anxious to meet up with Hayes and Clay and hear their report from the capital."

"How much longer will it take us to reach Eldrida?" I asked, trying to picture the coastal city and failing.

"We'll cross the river in the morning," she said. "We've chosen to cross far enough north that we'll be able to head directly east for the coast, skirting just above the northern tip of the forest. The crossing itself will take some effort, so I would normally say we should take our time and do the journey to Eldrida in three days. In the past I've even taken a week, veering south to pass through one of the hill villages. But given the situation, I think we'll take the direct route, and push ourselves. We should be able to make it in two days."

I nodded a quick agreement, glad to finally be moving with some urgency.

"Don't expect to see me tomorrow night," Nik said. "You won't need my protection on the open land between the river and the city. The direct road is well traveled."

I tried not to let my dismay show on my face. I had become accustomed to his constant presence—either seen or unseen. But while I might like knowing he was nearby, I didn't actually need him. Amara and I had enough strength between us to keep ourselves safe.

"You're planning to head straight for Eldrida, then?" Amara asked shrewdly. "You'll travel through the night?"

Nik grunted confirmation.

"Careful," she said lightly. "Traveling in the dark can be dangerous."

"Not for a plants mage," he said with a smirk. "And besides, I'm used to it."

She fell silent, unable to argue the point. A plants mage didn't need light to know the ground beneath his feet.

I slept fitfully after his words, though, and when he slipped out of bed in the morning, I woke as well, sitting upright in my bedroll. For a moment our eyes met, and we both stayed frozen in the early dawn light. Then he looked away and resumed his movement, gathering his things and slipping from the campsite.

I scrambled up and hurried after him, stopping him with a hand on his arm, just far enough away that we wouldn't wake Amara or the animals.

"You're really going ahead?" I asked.

He looked down at my hand, which was still resting on his arm, and nodded. "I want to get a feel for the state of things in Eldrida and see if I can find any word of Grey. Even when he's not gathering more followers, he and his people sometimes travel there for supplies."

I let my hand slip away, slowly nodding my understanding. I had no real reason to ask him to stay near us, and I wasn't ready to confess that it was just because I appreciated his presence.

He didn't immediately leave, however, instead stepping closer and erasing the small distance that lay between us.

"Amara is an experienced traveler and a strong mage," he said. "She'll keep you safe."

"I know," I said quickly. "It's not—" I stopped, dangerously close to the confession I didn't want to make.

Nik slung his pack over his shoulder and gripped my elbow, somehow maneuvering himself even closer.

"Delphine..." he breathed.

His eyes dropped to my lips, and I stiffened, my breath catching as I swallowed.

"I'll miss you," I said in a rush, and his grip tightened, his eyes darkening.

"Delphine, I—" He swayed toward me, his head tilting toward mine.

But a dark rush of movement through the air made us jerk back, springing apart to avoid Phoenix's hunting flight.

"Traitor," Nik muttered after the bird.

For a moment it looked like he was going to step toward me again, but a sleepy groan and the sound of movement back by the campfire made us both peer toward Amara.

"I'll see you in Eldrida," Nik murmured and was gone.

I wandered back toward the fire, feeling disgruntled and out of sorts. Amara greeted me with suspicious eyes, but she mercifully refrained from questioning my uncharacteristic early morning rising.

We packed up more quickly than usual, both driven by the previous night's decision. At last we were free to move at speed, and I could sense us both transitioning from the forced meanderings of the previous weeks into the more natural urgency that now drove us.

"I'm coming, Miranda," I whispered as we led Acorn the short way to the edge of the river.

Most westbound travelers and traders took the direct road from Eldrida to the river. There they either crossed it and took the river road southwest to the capital, or they boarded a boat and floated downriver to the capital. To aid those wishing to cross the river, a barge operated, run exclusively by those with an elements affinity.

Amara had brought us to the river slightly south of this popular crossing point, however, which was the only reason Nik had been able to join us the night before. There was often more than one group camping by the crossing, waiting for the barge to begin daylight operations. Now that we were alone again, I had expected us to move northward to meet the road and the barge, but apparently Amara was happy to facilitate our crossing herself.

When I saw the breadth of the river, however, I had second thoughts. Glancing back at Acorn, who was hitched to the cart, I looked doubtfully at the swiftly moving water.

"It won't take us long to go north to the barge," I said hesitantly.

Amara chuckled. "Have some faith, my apprentice."

"Oh no, no, it's not..." I let my clearly insincere protestations die out.

"The forest on the other side will force us to head north to the main road anyway," she said. "But Nik was right that it's a well-traveled road, and the barge berths on the eastern side of the river. It will load up on that side first, so there can sometimes be an extended wait for the barge on this side. We're in a rush and are able to cross with our own power. But I would prefer to complete this spectacle without an audience."

I raised my eyebrows. Spectacle? Exactly how was Amara intending to get us across?

"Climb up," she said, hopping up onto her usual seat on the cart.

I opened my mouth to ask if she was sure but clamped it shut again before I could say something so foolish. Clearly she was sure.

I perched on the edge of the bench, trying not to look like I was on high alert. Ember picked up on my mood, slinking over the back of the cart to curl up on my lap. Phoenix responded to the fox's movements by taking off, ringing upward and then flapping his way directly across the river.

"It's easy for some," I muttered, watching him go.

"Don't worry," Amara said in amusement. "It will be easy for us, too. At least as far as the rest of you are concerned."

She flicked the reins, and Acorn started forward, walking calmly toward the river. She had clearly been with Amara for a long time because she didn't halt when she reached the shallow stretch of bank, clopping into the water, the cart dragging behind her.

"What is she—?" I cut myself off, biting my tongue to keep myself from speaking. I needed to have faith in Amara.

My hands were white where they gripped the edge of the seat, however, as Acorn made it all the way into the water. She set off swimming, moving unconcernedly forward as if there was no current and she wasn't harnessed to a fully loaded cart.

"How...?" I gasped, but the answer was obvious the second our cartwheels left the riverbed, the whole cart floating in the water as if it were a barge itself.

I whirled around to peer into the back of the cart, expecting to see water flooding our bags and crates, but it was just as dry as before. There was only one way such a thing was possible, and remembering the unnatural wall of flood water, I knew the source of our impossible passage.

Amara was using her power to float both Acorn and our cart through the water, keeping us cocooned in some sort of bubble, so that the water didn't flood in.

I gazed at her in awe, once again shocked at the easy way she used power most people couldn't dream of.

"You needn't look at me like that, Delphine," she said with a small smile. "I assure you that any elements mage from the Guild could manage such an easy feat as this."

"Perhaps so," I said in a slightly strangled voice. "But I don't come from the Guild. No one I know with an elements affinity could possibly do this."

Acorn's feet hit the ground on the other side, her movement making the cart sway as she clambered out of the river, dragging us behind her. As soon as the cart had been dragged fully clear, water streamed off the outside of the wood and the horse until everything was completely dry, including Acorn's coat.

"Now that is a handy skill," I said, nodding my approval.

Amara grinned. "One of the first I perfected. The air is getting too cold at this time of year for Acorn to be wandering around wet."

On this side of the river there was only a dirt track following the curve of the river north, but it was wide enough for our cart. We moved off at a brisk pace by Acorn's standards, the horse apparently invigorated by her unlikely swim across the river.

Further south, the forest pressed close to the river, but here we had a bit of room to breathe as the forest tapered off to its northern tip. I could see the trees in the distance, however, and I reached for them, encountering a wealth of animal life beneath their sheltering boughs.

"Here comes the main road," Amara murmured, pulling my attention back to my immediate surroundings.

Phoenix dove from above us, spreading his wings to land in the back of the cart. Ember, startled awake, barked in protest, leaping forward to join me on the front seat once again.

I gave Phoenix a disapproving look but didn't have the heart to actually scold him for his dramatic entrance. Instead I petted Ember back to sleep as I watched the approaching road grow closer.

As warned, a slow but steady trickle of travelers moved along it, ranging from single walkers and riders to chains of several wagons, clearly bearing goods toward Eldrida.

"It looks like a barge has just disembarked," Amara observed, directing Acorn to swerve right and join the road, heading east.

We fell in behind a small group of riders, but without the encumbrance of a cart or carriage they drew ahead, eventually disappearing from view. I thought the carriage behind us might overtake us as well, but Amara somehow inspired Acorn to a faster than usual pace, managing to stay just ahead of the travelers to our rear.

Our stop for lunch was also shorter than theirs, but several individual riders overtook us over the course of the afternoon, and one carriage pulled by a team of four went thundering past, causing Amara to draw our cart off the road entirely.

"Is that how Hayes, Clay, and Luna will be traveling to Eldrida?" I asked, watching the carriage disappear into the distance in a cloud of dust.

"Not if they're trying to avoid attracting attention," Amara said dryly. "And there's not much point in their hurrying if they're only going to arrive in the city and then sit around waiting for us."

I remembered our meandering path through the mid-north of the kingdom, our road taking us through all the villages.

"I suppose they'll be in Eldrida already."

"Perhaps." Amara gazed ahead, although the carriage was almost gone from sight. "That depends on exactly what happened in the capital and how many soldiers King Marius decided to send with them."

"You don't think he'll have forbidden them from leaving at all?" I asked, dismayed at the sudden thought.

"No, I can't imagine he'll do that," she said thoughtfully. "Even if he wishes to block our plan, he'll let one of them, at least, come to inform us of it."

"He must want Grey stopped, though."

"Of course. But he may prefer to take his chances with a more direct route." Amara glanced at me but said nothing further.

"He might not trust me, you mean," I said slowly, catching on.

"That is one possibility."

I drew a deep breath, glad she hadn't denied it. I preferred that she was honest with me, even if it wasn't the most pleasant thing to hear. But the king didn't know me, so I couldn't blame him if he didn't want to commit to a plan that relied solely on me.

And then there was Nik. I had no idea if his son's involvement would turn the king toward or against the plan. Was it possible he'd send Hayes and the soldiers to Eldrida only so they could collect the prince and take him forcibly home to the capital?

Once the thought had entered my mind, it was hard to dislodge. Was that why Nik had left early, planning to slip surreptitiously into the city to gauge what was going on there? Did he worry that he would be more easily apprehended if he stayed near us?

I shook my head. King Marius had the whole Guild at his command. If he'd wanted to find Nik and force him home, he could have done so before now. The fact that he hadn't suggested he wanted to deal with the matter quietly—even if that meant allowing his son a time of freedom.

Unless this new crisis had changed his mind.

I shook my head, pushing away the circular thoughts. There was nothing I could do about it either way except wait and see what we found in Eldrida.

We camped at a place with a large wooden shelter, open on one side but providing protection from the wind and rain on the other three. Several other groups had also gathered there, arriving before or after us, and we ended up gathering around one large bonfire, the atmosphere bright and cheerful. At the halfway point, it was a stopping spot for those making the journey in two days, and everyone was anticipating a warm bed and proper meal the next night.

Ember slipped out early on, and Phoenix remained outside the shelter in the bed of the cart, with Acorn tethered nearby. That left only Amara and me from our usual small group, and it felt lonely, despite the crowd of people around us.

It took me a long time to fall asleep, thoughts of Nik circling in my mind. Was he still hurrying on through the darkness? Surely he would need to snatch some sleep at some point.

I awoke the next morning with a jerk to the sound of one of the groups pulling away onto the road, calling a cheerful farewell as they made an early start. I couldn't remember when I had fallen into sleep, but from the aches of my body, I had slept in a strange position, my muscles tense.

Amara and I ate a cold breakfast, hurrying out not too far behind the first group. Ember had returned sometime during the early hours, curling up beside me in my bedroll, and she happily settled into the back of the cart. But Phoenix, preferring to hunt at dusk and dawn, was off chasing smaller birds as soon as we hit the road.

We spent most of the morning in silence, and I suspected Amara's thoughts were in the same place as mine—what awaited us in Eldrida and, beyond that, in the desert.

When we stopped for a midday meal, Amara assured me we were making good time and should arrive in Eldrida well before dark. We continued on our way, again mostly in silence, until sometime in the middle of the afternoon.

Amara, who had been sitting with a distant expression, the reins slack in her hands, suddenly straightened, her eyes going wide. I began to ask a question, but she whipped up a hand, indicating I should be quiet. It was such an uncharacteristic gesture that I fell instantly silent.

When she turned to look north, I mimicked the movement, but nothing looked out of place, the green hills stretching away toward distant clouds. Whatever had alarmed her, I didn't think she had sensed it with her eyes.

I threw out my own power, searching for an unusual group of people, but I could feel nothing beyond the normal wild animals, the travelers ahead and behind us, and a distant shepherd with his flock.

The cart jolted, making me let go of my power and grip the seat instead. Amara flicked the reins again, calling for Acorn to pick up her pace, and I added my own voice of encouragement, trying to reinforce it with my power.

I didn't know if I succeeded, but Acorn's speed increased. I remained silent, afraid to disturb Amara in case she was concentrating. Instead, I focused on the group who had left the shelter ahead of us.

We had remained close behind them, just out of sight, for most of the day, but we quickly gained on them at the faster pace. When we reached their rear, Amara guided Acorn to one side of the road where a flat patch of ground gave us the opportunity to overtake them.

As we drew level, she leaned over me, calling to the closest driver.

"Do you have anyone with an elements affinity among you?"

The man looked surprised, distracted by our unexpected appearance, and she called the question a second time. This time he blinked and nodded slowly.

"A couple, but not of any particular strength. Just the usual weather trackers. Why?" He glanced uneasily at the sky, and I did the same.

With a start, I realized the distant clouds in the northern sky were much closer than they had been before, their color an ominous dark gray.

"Get off the road, now," Amara shouted. "And form a storm huddle."

"Storm?" The man called, but we were already passing him.

The next driver had heard the shouts, though, and took up the conversation.

"Our weather trackers didn't say anything about a storm coming." He looked at us both with suspicion.

"Ask them again," Amara yelled with uncharacteristic irritation.

"She's a master elements mage from the Guild," I bellowed at the man. "If she says get in a storm huddle, I'd listen if I was you."

"Master mage?" The man's eyes widened, and he immediately turned to call something to someone on his other side.

Amara nodded once, returning her focus to the front, satisfied her message had been received. Within a short time, we had passed the entire group and pulled back onto the road.

Twisting, I looked behind us and saw the wagons were rapidly falling away into the distance as they slowed to a stop and pulled off the road.

"They're doing it." I turned back around. "But what's a storm huddle?"

Amara replied without looking my way, her focus flicking between the road ahead and the storm clouds to our left.

"There's no proper shelter nearby, so they'll have to do the best they can on their own. They'll turn the wagons with their backs to the wind and get the animals calmed and protected as much as possible." She sighed. "If they'd had any warning, they would have stayed at the overnight shelter. Everyone will have left there by now, and most of the others are still behind us."

A single rider, approaching from the direction of Eldrida, caught her attention and she fell silent, waving a hand to flag him over. He slowed, both of us coming to a halt so they could exchange words.

"Good afternoon," he began, but Amara jumped straight in, ignoring the usual pleasantries.

"There's a bad storm coming."

The man's eyes immediately flicked to the clouds, indicating he'd been aware of them already.

"It's a severe one, then?" He frowned. "I'm a plants mage, so I wasn't sure..."

"There's a group of wagons who've just pulled over not too much further along," she said. "You should wait it out with them. The next proper shelter is too far."

The man's hand went to his horse's neck, and I wondered if the gelding was especially jumpy in storms.

"Are you certain?"

"She's a master elements mage from the Guild." I jumped in, hoping to save us some time.

"Oh, well in that case..." The man bowed from his saddle. "I appreciate the warning, Master."

Amara nodded distractedly. "Hurry on, then. If we encounter anyone else, we'll send them to join you."

The man kicked his horse's flank, and Amara flicked the reins, each of us starting off in opposite directions.

"If the storm is so bad," I began hesitantly, "should we be...?"

I trailed off when Amara began to shake her head.

"I can protect us. We need to get to Eldrida."

"We do?" I asked, still confused about what was happening.

"It's not just a bad storm, it's really bad," she said in clipped tones. "And more importantly, it's come on with almost no warning. Anyone with an elements affinity—from medium non-mage strength upward—should have been able to track a weather phenomenon that big from hours ago.”

“What does that mean?” I asked, but even as I spoke, I remembered the preparations we would make on the farm if we got word from Tarin that there was a big storm due the next day. “No one’s going to be prepared.”

“That’s right,” Amara said grimly. “The fishing fleet will have left this morning as usual, and trading ships will be out at sea as well. Not to mention any damage the actual city may sustain.”

I gasped. I hadn’t even thought of ships at sea.

“And once the initial chaos dies down,” she continued, her voice dark, “people are going to start asking questions.”

“Questions? Will they blame the elements mages?”

“Not ours.”

“What do you mean, not our—oh.” My eyes widened as I caught on to her meaning. A large and dangerous storm had come in too quickly, and it had come from the north.

“Do you think it’s possible some Calistan mages drove the storm south?” I asked in a small voice.

“I would like to think no one with the strength and control to do so would be so reckless,” she said savagely. “But I can’t absolutely guarantee it.”

Her shoulders sagged. “Everyone knows Calista is still in the process of rebuilding, and that includes their Mages’ Guild. They lack the structure and experience that governs our own mages. Even if they didn’t do it, people will suspect they did. And when the whole countryside is already on edge...”

“Plus, if they didn’t do it, and this storm isn’t natural...” I didn’t need to complete the question because we were both already thinking it. If the Calistans hadn’t sent this storm, who had?

CHAPTER

# FIFTEEN

The winds reached us first, followed quickly by a sheet of driving rain. The wind alone might have been enough to knock us from our seat, but it never had the chance to touch us.

An invisible bubble sprang up around us, an unnatural circle with neither wind nor rain. And when lightning began to arc down from the sky, none of the branches came near us.

The storm spooked Acorn, however, and she picked up her pace again, speeding us toward the shelter of the city walls. Ember was equally unhappy, huddling in my lap and shivering almost constantly while Phoenix sat unusually still on my shoulder.

"How long can you keep this up?" I asked Amara, lifting my voice above the storm. "How long can Acorn?"

"For me, as long as we need." She peered at the horse. "As for Acorn—shouldn't I be asking you that?"

I grimaced. "She's in good health, but this is a fast trot for her given she's pulling the cart. I'd have to touch her to know how her energy levels are going, though."

"For now she should be fine. She and I have been together for a long time, so I think I have some idea of her limits."

We both lapsed into silence, which was easier than trying to be heard above the beating rain, roaring wind, and unpredictable cracks of thunder. It didn't scare me, though, which surprised me until I remembered I was healing cross elements now. Storms would probably never scare me again.

Thoughts of the people in Eldrida did worry me, though, so it was an uncomfortable ride. After some time, Amara eased Acorn to a stop, directing me to climb down and check on her. I did so quickly, almost collapsing when I landed on my stiff legs. But it only took a moment to recover and rush forward to place a hand against Acorn's flank.

She was tired, that much was easy to tell. I sent my power into her, easing her aching muscles and refreshing her fatigue. I'd never done it to a horse before, but Luna and I used to secretly practice on each other when Hayes's lessons went long. We knew if we told him we were doing it, he would lecture us on the difference between a healer easing our fatigue and true rest. But this wasn't a time to worry about the difference.

When I climbed back into the cart, I nodded at Amara. "She's ready to go again."

Amara smiled tightly. "I knew it would be handy to have a healer along."

We pushed on, the sky unnaturally dark for the hour, and the rain blocking visibility for more than a few feet. It felt as if we were alone in our small cocoon, the rest of the world a raging storm of wet and cold and noise.

Given the visibility issues, we were nearly at the gates of Eldrida before the walls loomed out of the storm in front of us.

"We're here," I gasped, rubbing warmth and life into my cold fingers. "We made it."

"Now the real work begins," Amara said, immediately dousing my momentary joy.

Silently, we continued through the open gate, exchanging looks as we noticed the absence of the normal gate guards. We hadn't made it far into the city when I realized why.

Out on the open plains, the winds had been terrifying and fierce, and at first I had been relieved by the shelter of the city walls. But once we moved past their immediate vicinity, the wind picked up its tempo again, even scarier than before. The streets only served as wind tunnels, channeling and strengthening the trapped wind.

Everyone must have sought shelter inside because the cobblestones were deserted. Amara seemed to know where she was going, though, directing Acorn with confidence.

"The harbor," she said when I gave her a questioning look. "That's where the elements mages will be, trying to keep the ocean from flooding the city and bringing in any ships close enough to reach land."

I shivered, picturing the terror of being out on the open sea in winds and rain like this. If ships did make it to harbor, they might be in need of a healer. It was the most logical place for us to be.

Before we made it there, however, we turned a corner and came to a stop, our passage barred by absolute chaos. Large buildings lined what appeared to be the city's central square, standing firm against the weather. But the square itself was a litter of broken wood, scattered wares, and terrified animals. And between the cracks of thunder, I caught screams. My eyes found the evidence of trapped people who must have attempted to shelter beneath the market stalls when the rain started.

Amara's face paled as she looked from left to right, struggling to know where to settle her gaze. We couldn't drive through the square, but how could we turn our backs on this disaster to take a different route?

While we lingered on the street, shocked and uncertain, the creaking of wood sounded, and an enormous wooden gate swung open. It appeared to be the entrance to a small stables—whether of an inn or private property, I wasn't sure—located just down from the square.

"In here!" a voice yelled. "You'll have to leave the cart, but there's room for you and your horse."

Startled, I peered inside to see a mass of huddled, frightened faces gazing back.

A grizzled, elderly man stumbled out, passing through the rain briefly before entering the bubble that surrounded us and starting to unhitch Acorn. Amara slid down and hurried to join him, me at her heels.

"I thought I heard hoof beats just before that last thunder," the man said. "Couldn't think who would be out riding in this, though. But mighty handy that is." He pointed upward at the invisible barrier holding back the rain. "You'll be a mage, then, which explains it. But mage or not, you'll want somewhere safe for this lady." He patted Acorn's neck.

"Have you seen what's happened in the square?" Amara asked in a stern tone.

The man nodded, his expression serious. "That's where all them came from." He gestured over his shoulder with his thumb. "It came on so quick there wasn't much warning, so I opened the doors for anyone fleeing this way. Best not to be out traveling in this."

Amara nodded, her expression softening. Meeting my eyes, she gestured at the cart, and I hurried back to it. Scooping up Ember, I pointed at my shoulder, waiting for Phoenix to give a flying hop into position there. When I had realized he preferred that spot to my arm, I had added leather padding to the shoulder of several of my dresses, and we had become practiced at the movement.

Looking at the remaining bags, I scooped up two of the most precious— all I had room to carry in my remaining arm. Amara appeared at my side and took several more before we followed the elderly stable master and Acorn into the dark building.

The man led Acorn toward the only empty stall, the crowd squeezing together to allow enough room for them to pass. Amara watched them go, but as soon as she was satisfied that Acorn had a place to go, she turned back to the crowd.

"I don't suppose there are any mages among you?"

A sea of shaking heads confirmed her guess. "What about those with medium or high strength?"

This time, a number of hands were hesitantly raised.

"Any healers?" Amara asked, but all of the hands went down.

"The healers stayed in the square," the woman nearest to us volunteered. "There were a lot of injured."

"You're right," Amara said coldly. "There are many in need. Are you telling me only the healers went to help? I didn't expect to be ashamed of my own affinity."

Silence spread through the group, people shifting uncomfortably and exchanging glances.

"What would you have us do?" the woman asked, half defiantly, half curiously.

"Since you didn't put your hand up, you must have a weak seed," Amara said. "That means you're exactly where you should be. We don't want to create more victims. But those with sufficient strength and an elements affinity should come with me to the harbor."

"The harbor?" several voices called, followed by someone exclaiming loudly, "The ships!"

Amara nodded. "I'm an elements mage, and that's where I'm going. I'm sure that's where I'll find others with an elements affinity. Who will join me?"

After a brief hesitation, several people stepped forward, about half of the group who had raised their hands. The rest were probably plants affinity, and it only took me a moment to realize what Amara wanted them doing.

I raised myself as tall as I could go and tried to project my voice. "As for those with a plants affinity of reasonable strength, you'll be with me. I'm a healing mage, so I'll be staying here at the square. But people are trapped, so I'll need help with all that fallen wood and stone."

Amara took my arm, pulling me slightly aside. "Are you sure?" she whispered. "These are all adults, but officially you're still underage. By rights, I shouldn't be abandoning my apprentice in a dangerous situation like this, but I'll be needed at the harbor, and your strength could make a real difference out there."

"Don't worry about me," I said with more confidence than I felt. "I'll have these people to help me." I gestured at the remaining people who had stepped forward. From the look of it, Amara had successfully roused all of those with high enough strength to be useful.

A girl who looked about twelve watched me with sorrowful eyes. "I have a high strength seed," she said. "If only I was older, I could help."

"You can help now." I cradled Ember, whose body trembled in response to another peal of thunder, and held her out to the girl. "Could you look after my fox for me?"

"Your fox?" The girl took her, sheltering her against her body and stroking her fur with an amazed expression.

"Her name is Ember, and she doesn't like the storm."

I glanced upward to where Phoenix perched on one of the stable rafters. He had taken off from my shoulder almost as soon as we stepped inside and would be fine up there until I returned.

"I'll take care of her," the girl promised, still focused on Ember rather than me.

Managing a small smile, I murmured thanks and turned for the door, bracing myself for what was to come. We all stepped outside together, Amara's bubble still keeping the rain off. But we were about to part ways, which meant I would soon be wet.

Amara hesitated for a final second, looking at me with concerned eyes. But I shooed her away, calling for the plants people to follow me. Taking a deep breath, I jogged out of the protective bubble, gasping as the freezing rain hit my face.

Almost immediately I was soaked, the enormous drops quickly permeating my layers of clothing. But within a few steps we were inside the square and the chaos around us drove out thoughts of my own discomfort.

Other people scurried around, pulling at fallen structures or kneeling over injured people, but with the rain affecting visibility, it was hard to see how many or how organized they were.

*Don't look at everything,* I told myself. *Just focus on one thing you can fix.*

I looked at the closest collapsed stall and then the next one down. No one was at the nearer one, but at the further one, a man knelt beside a trapped woman. From the way he held her wrist, I guessed him to be a healer.

"Two of you go help him." I pointed at the healer. "The other two, help me lift this."

I hoped they didn't need more detailed instructions because I had no idea how to direct someone to use their plants power. Nik would be helpful in the situation, but he could be anywhere in the city. I didn't doubt that wherever he was, he was helping, though. And with his strength, he would be making a difference.

Thankfully, the young lad and older woman who had stayed with me got to work on their own, calling out words to each other that I couldn't clearly hear over the sound of the storm. Their coordination worked, however, and the jagged planks of wood slithered to the side, as if moving of their own accord.

The man beneath was soon uncovered, but as they were about to move the last piece of wood, I screamed for them to stop. Both of them froze, staring at me wide-eyed.

"Wait a moment," I shouted and dropped to both knees beside the man.

I had nearly missed that the wood, shorn in half and turned into a spear, had impaled the man in the side. I'd never dealt with an injury like that, but I knew you needed a healer ready before you removed any object still piercing a person. The blood loss when the wood came out could be immense.

"It's all right," I yelled at the man, trying to sound reassuring despite my volume. "I'm a healer."

The man instantly relaxed, although his eyes remained wide and wild.

I pushed my power into him, masking his pain as I tried to ignore the discomfort of feeling something foreign that didn't belong. He had several broken bones as well, but I bypassed those, focusing on the severed veins and seeping blood.

My two assistants approached, kneeling beside me and staring at the man in horror.

"It will be all right," I said when the wind quieted slightly for a moment. "Just be ready to pull the wood out when I say so."

The older woman nodded and gripped it with both hands, watching me closely.

I sent my power to wrap around the organs closest to the wood, nodding my head as soon as I was ready.

"Now!" The woman pulled and the wood slid out, the patient screaming in response, although his pain was only a shadow of what it had been before.

I let my power guide me, instinct taking over as I restitched veins and sealed organs, sending a tendril to calm the pain that still darkened his brain. He immediately quieted beneath my hands, his breathing steadying as I knit the wound in his side, sending my power blazing along his bones, reforming those that had cracked under the weight of the stall.

As soon as I was finished, I let go and sat back, taking deep, gasping breaths. If I had been Hayes, I could have done that with much less energy. And for the first time I fully understood the value of that. How many more people in this square still needed my help?

"Come on," I told my two assistants as I lurched to my feet. "There will be others."

The man called out his thanks, and I stopped to look at him. "What's your affinity?"

"Elements, but I had no idea...I didn't see this coming when I can normally sense—"

"What's your strength?"

"Weak," the man admitted reluctantly.

I pointed out of the square. "There's a stable just down that road. If you knock on the door, they'll let you shelter inside."

Without waiting for a reply, I hurried further into the debris field, picking my way over fallen wood, torn material and what seemed to be several spilled baskets of potatoes.

The group at the next stall had already freed the trapped woman, although the healer was still working on her. I left them to it, continuing on in search of more victims. A piercing scream pulled my attention to the right, and I hurried in that direction, trying to peer through the heavy rain. I kept wiping the drops from my eyes, but they were coming down so hard it did little good.

A woman staggered toward me, blood streaking her already soaked gown. Before she could reach me, though, someone else responded to her yell, catching her as she collapsed. For a moment, I didn't recognize the sodden figure assisting her, but something in the way he laid her down and knelt beside her was familiar.

"Hayes!" I cried, and he glanced up briefly, meeting my eyes with a shock of recognition.

I waved his attention back to the woman, though, turning to look back into the square. If Hayes had charge of her, then she was in good hands and didn't need me.

Several steps brought me to another collapsed stall, this one surrounded by scattered items, all made from leather. Two people seemed to be beneath the pile of broken wood, but a man and a girl were already pulling planks aside, working to free them.

These two were also familiar. Clay and Luna.

I nearly called a greeting before thinking better of it. They didn't need a distraction, and there were more people in need. I continued deeper into the square, passing several more injured people who sat or lay on the ground. Those with significant injuries had someone kneeling beside them wearing the focused, slightly absent, expression of a healer at work.

A hysterical woman who grabbed at my arm turned out to be fine, but her young daughter had been struck in the head by a flying piece of stone. I paused to heal her, sealing her gash and pushing out the pressure threatening her brain.

The girl brightened as soon as I'd finished, putting a hand to her head.

"My headache is gone!" she exclaimed. "Thank you!"

I could barely hear her high voice over the wind, as much reading the words on her lips as hearing them.

I nodded, hurrying on to where my two assistants were already pulling the wood off another trapped stall keeper. This one had escaped with a single broken bone and a deep gash, so it didn't take me long to burn through his injuries.

Both my assistants were now shivering uncontrollably, so I took a moment to give them a burst of warmth and energy. They smiled their thanks, the woman grasping my arm and leaning close to talk into my ear.

"Don't forget yourself, child!"

I nodded and sent a spark of power through my own body, just enough to drive away the uncontrollable shaking. I didn't want to waste too much, though. I already felt worryingly weak and tired, and people still needed me.

The next few stalls were already deserted, the people around them having fled before the wind hit or else having been rescued already. I almost began to hope the square was nearly cleared when we reached the west side and found an entire building had collapsed.

Stone and wood lay everywhere, and from the moans and cries, there were still people trapped beneath.

An arm appeared from the rain, and I grabbed it. "What happened here?" I shouted.

"A building was still under construction," the man yelled back. "It wasn't sturdy enough to withstand the—" He broke off. "Delphine?"

"Nik?" I stared up at him, blinking against the hard drops of rain and sputtering slightly.

I swayed, and he grabbed both my arms. "How many people have you already healed?"

"Never mind that! How many are still trapped?"

"I'm not sure. I just arrived. I was working on the other side of the square."

I glanced in the direction he was pointing and saw a far more orderly stretch of ground, the various collapsed stalls swept out of the way, as if by a giant's hand. Nik at work, no doubt.

"Don't worry about me, then," I said. "Tell these two how they can help you." I gestured for my assistants to come forward. "They both have plants seeds, like you."

Reluctantly, Nik let go of my arms, turning to the woman and the boy. He began issuing rapid fire instructions that I tuned out, glad not to have to take responsibility for something outside of my field.

Within a minute, the three of them were at work, several other people appearing out of the rain to help them. Under Nik's guidance, the fallen stones and broken planks of wood lifted into the air, flying in neat formations to form piles against the base of the closest sturdy building.

Nik seemed to be the one actually lifting the stones, but from the expressions of concentration on the faces of the others, they were using their power to assist in some way. Working as a team, they soon had the first person exposed, and I dropped to my knees, feeling the jarring thud all the way through me.

It was a young boy, looking terrified and in pain, so I sent my power into him, blocking off the pain before I even examined his injuries. He drew an immediate, gasping breath, stuttering out a thank you.

"Just lie still," I called, closing my eyes against the water that streamed down my face.

One of the boy's feet was twisted at an unnatural angle, and I sent my power racing through his ankle, popping it back into place and fusing the bones back together.

When I opened my eyes, he was watching his foot with curiosity, apparently undaunted by the process now that he was no longer in pain. As soon as I checked the rest of him and let him go, however, he pointed back at the still shifting mound of debris.

"I'm Coby," he said inconsequentially, his face twisted in an expression of worry that was out of place on a young child. "Have you seen my mother? I think she might be under there still."

"We'll get to her," I yelled as the wind picked back up. "But you should move out of the way." I looked around until I saw a small group huddled against a stretch of wall some way from where Nik was piling the rubble. "Over there. I'll send her there to find you as soon as she's free."

He hesitated, but when a stone came floating past our heads, he nodded agreement and hurried off. I turned back to the building, hoping desperately that his mother was still alive under there.

The next stone to lift revealed a leg, followed by a second one. Something about the look of them made my stomach turn, although I wasn't sure why. The urgency and chaos of the crisis had so far suppressed my nausea almost as effectively as my power could.

The sight of the person had an effect on Nik as well because all the remaining stones covering them began to lift at once. I didn't wait to see who the legs belonged to, however, wrapping my fingers around one ankle.

I tried to push my power into the person, but it wouldn't move. I had experienced the effect only once before, but I refused to accept it, trying again and then again.

"No, no, no, no, no, no," I muttered over and over until a loud moan broke through my daze.

For a heady moment, I thought the groan was evidence I'd been mistaken, but it wasn't coming from the body in front of me but from someone deeper in the rubble. I hadn't been wrong. The owner of the leg was beyond my help.

The last of the rubble lifted off the body, and I steeled myself to look at their face. It was an elderly man, lying still, his eyes closed.

It wasn't the boy's mother, then. Guilt washed over me at the spear of relief I felt. This man had just lost his life, and someone, somewhere would soon be crying over it.

Nik's voice echoed in my memory. *Death is never easy. But healers have to find ways not to be crippled by it.*

It had seemed unthinkable and almost cruel at the time, but I understood what he'd meant now. I couldn't let myself think about this man or his family. Someone nearby was still moaning, which meant that person wasn't beyond my help. I couldn't fall apart now.

I crawled around the man, not bothering to push myself back up against the wind and rain. Gradually it filtered through to my awareness that the storm seemed to be lessening, the wind no longer so strong and the rain starting to ease. I couldn't think about the weather, however.

More rocks lifted into the air, and I crawled along in their wake, seeking the owner of the moans. When the floating rubble finally revealed a woman a similar age to Amara, it was clear she was in bad shape.

But when I crouched beside her, I realized she wasn't giving wordless groans of pain but was saying two garbled words over and over again.

"My son. My son. My son."

I grabbed her hand, squeezing it as gently as possible. Sending my power into her, I first eased her pain. "Is your son young? Maybe eight?"

"Coby! He's nine!" The words came out clearer now that her pain had lifted, although from the sound of her breathing at least one of her lungs was in trouble. "Have you seen him?"

"I healed him just earlier," I said in my most soothing tones. "He told me his name was Coby, and I sent him somewhere safe. I also told him I'd send you after him, so I need you to work with me and stay strong."

The woman collapsed, her tense muscles loosening now that she was freed from both pain and fear. But as my power raced through her body, I sucked in a breath. Her internal damage was severe, far worse than any of the others I'd so far healed.

My head spun, and I shook it, trying to get a hold of myself. I was already so drained from the previous healings, but I couldn't lose focus now. This woman didn't have much time, and her son was waiting for her.

I sent my power into her, wishing I knew more about the parts I needed to fix. Pages from my anatomy books swam before my eyes, and when I touched her collapsed lung, I tried to remember everything Hayes had ever told me about the organ.

But I was too tired for finesse. I would have to do what I'd done too often before and rely on strength and instinct to force a healing. The fire that spread out from me seemed to flicker instead of burn, though, nearly exhausted. I coaxed it brighter, pushing it onward through her body. From her lungs, it traveled to her ribs, her kidneys, her liver, her stomach, mending and repairing and regrowing as it went.

The woman gasped. "The sensation! It's so strange!"

I frowned. Patients didn't usually feel our healings. They found it distressing, so we blocked the sensations. I knew how to do that. Didn't I? Wasn't I doing it right now? I thought I was. My thoughts flew out of my grasp, fuzzy and indistinct. I tried to grab hold of them, tried to remember what I was doing. Blocking the sensation! That was it. I told my power to do it, but nothing happened. I reached deeper and finally it responded.

The woman calmed, and I pushed on. How it felt wasn't important anyway, as long as she was healthy at the end of it.

Her bones came after the organs, then the veins and finally the single patch of torn skin. I knew I should do a final sweep to be sure I'd fixed everything, but my power didn't seem to be responding to me anymore.

"Make sure you see a healer soon," I gasped out. "To check..."

The woman pushed tentatively to her feet, looking down at herself in wonder.

"I thought I was dying. Absolutely everything hurt, and I couldn't breathe. But now I feel fully healed." She peered into my face. "You're so young!"

"Promise you'll check," I whispered and realized the wind had nearly stopped completely because she could hear me.

"I will, I will!" She reached down a hand to help me to my feet. "Thank you! Thank you so much."

As she hauled me upward, I noticed the rain had also stopped. I knew I should be relieved by that, but I felt too numb to care.

I couldn't seem to feel my feet either, which must have been why I was swaying, but the woman didn't seem to notice, distracted by her visual search of our surroundings.

"Over there." I somehow managed to raise my arm and point. "Coby is waiting for you."

"Thank you!" the woman cried again, spinning and dashing off across the wet ground.

"Careful," I tried to call, but the word wouldn't fully form, my voice strangely quiet.

What was wrong with me? I tried to lift a hand to my head, but my limbs weren't responding now, like my power hadn't earlier.

A roaring filled my ears, although the wind didn't seem to have picked back up. My legs gave out completely, and I collapsed.

Strong arms broke my fall, and I thought I heard a familiar voice frantically calling my name. But my eyes were closing against my will, and all sounds faded away, replaced with deep, refreshing, nothingness.

CHAPTER

# SIXTEEN

The first thing to reach me was noise. But it wasn't the wordless roaring of the wind or the pounding of heavy rain. A babble of voices overlapped each other, mingling with footsteps and the various bumps and bangs of industrious activity.

The next thing was the soft fur of a familiar, sleeping animal, her warm body tucked under the blankets by my side.

I tried to open my eyes, but they resisted. I reached a hand up to my face and found a cloth lying across my eyes. From its stiff feel, it had once been wet, although it had long since dried.

I pulled it off, opening my eyes, only to quickly close them again. Without the protection of the material, the bright daylight speared at me even through my eyelids. Taking several deep breaths, I waited for my eyes to adjust to the daylight filtering through my closed lids. Only once it reached a comfortable level did I try cracking my eyes open again.

For a second time I had to wait while they adjusted to the new level of light. How was it already full day? How long had I been sleeping?

"She's awake!" A jovial but unfamiliar voice called out the news, and a renewed flurry of footsteps sounded.

I barely had time to take in my surroundings—a row of beds in a suspiciously familiar looking room that had a bright, airy feel—before a small crowd of people surrounded me. They all beamed down at where I lay flat in bed.

"Our sleeping beauty awakens!" the original speaker cried, in the same beaming tones. "Which means we can officially discharge our last storm patient."

A resounding cheer went up from those gathered around my bed, although I couldn't spot any familiar faces among them. The speaker seemed to be the one in charge as well as the oldest, a round-faced, matronly woman who regarded me with the affectionate indulgence of a grandmother. I wanted to ask who she was, but that seemed rude. My second thought was to ask where I was, but I was fairly sure I already knew the answer to that.

"Where's Master Amara?" I asked instead, hoping she would have answers for me.

"Ah yes, someone must inform the girl's master!" The woman turned to the group around her, and the youngest of them jumped to attention, hurrying out of the room, presumably to search for Amara.

In the wake of his departure, the older woman shooed most of the others away as well, directing them to return to their regular tasks or seek rest of their own. From the way she addressed them, it appeared they had been working hard for an extended time and were now reaching the end of their labor.

"Don't worry," the woman said to me in comfortable tones when she turned her attention back to me.

I felt more confused than concerned, but I remained silent, hoping she would continue.

"Master Amara is perfectly well." She folded her hands across her belly and beamed at me. "She would have liked to be here at your bedside, I'm sure, but she's a woman much in demand." She chuckled to herself before continuing. "She visited briefly, of course, and confirmed your identity and condition, but she barely had the chance to leave the harbor until this morning, and the city's leaders and mages have all been clamoring to consult with her."

I tried to sort through this flood of words for the important points.

"Confirm my identity? How did I get here?"

I didn't bother to ask where *here* was. Now that I'd had a more complete look at the room and its occupants, I was utterly certain I was in the Eldridan hospital. My training with Hayes in the Caltoran hospital made it a familiar space since all the hospitals in Tartora had been built with the same design.

"You arrived just after the end of the storm, unconscious," the healer said. "It was true chaos here, then, so I didn't get the name of the person who carried you in. But he was the whole package." She leaned forward and winked broadly. "Tall, dark, and handsome, so you're a fortunate young lady."

From the matron's satisfied beam, it seemed she thought a mid-storm rescue was the immediate precursor to a betrothal announcement. I groaned and rubbed my head, but I didn't ask any more questions about my rescuer. The healer's description gave me a good idea who it had been, and hazy memories were starting to return of a familiar voice calling my name and strong arms scooping me up and holding me close.

Gingerly, I sent my power around my body, searching for any sign of illness or injury or even of recent healing. I found nothing. Every part of my body seemed perfectly normal.

I looked again at the broad daylight outside the closest window and frowned.

"How long have I been here? How many hours has it been since the storm finished?"

"Hours?" The healer rubbed her chin. "I'm not sure I could tell you that. I've been on my feet for too long to be worrying around with numbers and sums."

"Sums?" I pushed myself up to sitting, making Ember stir in protest. "How long has it been?"

A younger man, maybe a decade older than me, joined us. "It's late afternoon, the second day after the storm."

"Two days!" I shrieked, swinging my legs out of the bed.

The man immediately put his hands on my shoulders to stop me. "Slowly now, Apprentice. You've been lying down for a long time. No need to rush things. I'd rather not have you collapse for a second time."

I didn't fight him, sitting on the side of the bed, my mouth hanging open. "It's really been two days? And I've just been lying here the whole time? What in the kingdoms was wrong with me that it took that long for you to heal me?"

I could imagine many of the injured and ill had been forced to wait in the immediate aftermath of the storm, but I was the only one left in the room now, and the older healer had declared me the final storm patient.

"We didn't heal you at all," the matron said in the same hearty tones as always. "Didn't use a lick of power on you, in fact. All we did was provide a bed and keep an eye on you."

A nose appeared from under the crumpled blankets, followed by a lithe body moving sleepily. I put a hand around Ember's middle, guiding her as she curled back up at my side, this time on top of the blankets.

"We don't normally allow pets in the hospital," the male healer said. "But every time someone shooed her out, we would turn around to find she'd snuck back in again. I've never seen such devotion from a wild animal—even to a healer. We gave up in the end, since everyone was too busy to keep watch for one small fox."

"I'm sorry. I seem to have caused you a lot of unnecessary trouble." My fingers brushed over the stiff cloth that had been covering my eyes.

"Ah, now, that wasn't one of us," the matron said, her smile hinting at an intriguing secret.

"No one will swear they saw anything for sure, given the crowds that were coming and going," the man said with an amused smile of his own. "But given the legends already springing up about you and your master, the younger ones have been talking. They all swear they haven't had time to come near your bed in the busyness, but at least half of them claim to have seen glimpses of a tall young man slipping in and out among the crowd."

The matron chuckled, and I realized her earlier comment had been based on more than just Nik's supposed rescue of me. Warmth rose up my cheeks, and I cleared my throat uncomfortably.

"Nothing like a bit of mystery to add to a legend in the making," the matron said. "It's good for the youngsters to have something to focus on other than where that storm came from."

She exchanged a weighted glance with the man, and I remembered Amara's words on the road as well as the matron's assertion that Amara had been in demand among the city's leaders. What had been happening in Eldrida while I slept?

"But why was I here?" I asked, trying again for a straight answer. "Why did I sleep so long? And what do you mean by legend?" My head was starting to spin almost as much as it had in the square at the end of the storm.

The man, who had a much brisker air than the matron in charge, answered my questions in order.

"You're here because you overextended yourself in the square and collapsed. That's what happens when you push your power too far." He gave me a censorious look. "And you weren't just sleeping but unconscious, regaining your energy. For two days. That's also what happens when you overuse your ability. There's a reason people try to avoid doing it."

My flush deepened as I realized I hadn't been injured at all. I had just humiliated myself by making the rookie mistake all apprentices were sternly warned against. I hadn't known my own limits.

Looking back, all the signs had been there: the flickering fire of my power, the fuzzy thoughts and confusion, forgetting to include basic elements of a healing. I had ignored it all and pushed my way onward without thought.

And once again, Nik had saved me. It had been a dangerous risk, though. Given my location, I could easily have fallen and hit my head—even killed myself, as had happened to Amara's mother. And I had certainly rendered myself unable to help anyone else—a patient taking up the hospital's resources instead of another healer to help finish off the less severe cases the following day.

I could still feel the lingering sensation of Nik's arms around me, carrying me, but I could also hear his voice in my mind. *Even the strongest healers have limits.*

I had once again tried to ignore that truth, attempting to heal based on the need before me, without considering what was possible.

I tried to look at the matter objectively. The last woman I healed had been badly injured. Should I have left her to die, saving my power to heal multiple other people with dangerous, but less complex, injuries? Could I have done so?

Remembering Coby's face, I didn't think I could have. It was only natural to respond to the known need in front of me. But that didn't mean I had to burn myself out until I sputtered and died. I could have done enough to save her life and then stopped, saving my energy for other patients. And I should definitely have stopped once I felt myself reaching my limits. If I had fallen and died, unnoticed in the middle of the storm, how many future Cobys would have lost their mothers as a consequence?

I never wanted to become a person who refused to give what they had to give, but neither could I act foolishly and rashly, as if I was invincible. That was the action of a child. Part of the gift I had been given involved using my resources wisely.

I looked up, meeting the matron's eyes. She smiled at me kindly.

"Don't worry, Apprentice." Her voice was gentle. "You're not the first, and you won't be the last. Some things have to be learned through experience. You'll know better next time."

I managed a smile, grateful for her words. Tentatively I glanced at the younger healer to find his face had also softened.

"To tell the truth, you weren't even the only one in the storm. Although you did need to sleep the longest. The other apprentices seem to think it means you won some sort of contest." He exchanged a long-suffering look with the matron. "And of course that only adds to the mystique."

"Mystique?" I asked uneasily, remembering his earlier talk of legends.

"Well, as to that..." He hesitated. "A boy and his mother came looking for you and had to be turned away. They were very insistent about needing to thank you."

I smiled, tears pricking my eyes. So Coby's mother had found him. That was a relief.

"They say you're only an apprentice like us," a young man of seventeen or eighteen said from the end of the bed. Three others of a similar age clustered around him, eight eager eyes trained on me.

"Even newer than us, I heard," one of the girls added. "But that mother said she was on death's door when you got to her."

"I heard you'd already healed half the injured in the square before her," a third said. "They say you rode into the city in the middle of the storm, mustered a rescue party, and healed everyone."

"You pulled them out from under the stalls, and then moved on to the next one like it was nothing," the fourth added.

"Me?" I gaped at them. "People are saying *I* did that?"

"Not alone, of course," the first one said, and I relaxed for a second before he continued. "You had your master with you, naturally. And while you were fixing the square, she was at the harbor."

A new layer of awe settled over the group at the mention of Amara.

"They say she single-handedly stopped the waves breaching the harbor."

"And she saved five ships as well as countless sailors who'd gone overboard."

"My cousin was there, and she saw a ship sailing into harbor like they were in a bubble—the sea at their prow and stern as calm as if there wasn't any storm raging at all."

"It wasn't just the ships everyone could see either," the first boy assured the second. "She saved ships too far out for the other mages to even sense."

"I heard the winds quieted, and those who'd gone overboard flew through the air until they reached the dock, like a bird coming in to land," said one of the girls.

I clapped both my hands to my head. Now I understood what the older healers had meant about a legend. In the chaos of the unexpected storm, many people had helped rescue the trapped and injured—most of the helpers being local Eldridans. But in the wake of the tragedy, people wanted heroes, and powerful and mysterious strangers made much better fodder for legends than the person next door. Especially when Amara was such a compelling figure. I had no doubt she really had achieved impressive feats at the harbor —even if not quite to the level of the stories circulating among the apprentices.

Hayes and Clay must have done more than me in the square—just to name two—but they hadn't come in the company of a mage who could make sailors fly.

"What I want to know," one of the girls said, "is who's the man who carried you in? Because I heard some things about him, too."

My eyes snapped open, but I stayed in position, my face lowered and hidden from their view. Apparently Nik was another reason for my so-called mystique.

The other girl giggled. "I heard he's terribly handsome." She sighed. "And powerful, too. They say he cleared half the rubble in the square single-handedly, but he disappears whenever someone starts asking questions."

Even without seeing it, I could feel her eyes boring into me.

"Do you know who he is? Why doesn't he want anyone to know his identity?"

"I heard," the first girl said, her voice dropping to a whisper, "that he's a *prince*."

My head whipped up, my hands falling away. They couldn't possibly know the truth of Nik's identity. Their imaginations were simply taking them to the furthest reaches of romanticism. But whereas the other rumors led them to painful exaggeration, in this case, their flights of fancy had brought them dangerously close to the truth.

"This is all ridiculous!" I snapped. "Of course I did my part and healed as many as I could, but I didn't do anything outstanding. And while Master Amara is strong, she's still just one mage. I'm sure she had a whole team of people helping her bring in the boats."

The two girls exchanged disappointed looks.

"Are you sure you don't know who he is?" one of them whispered. "Because I got a glimpse of him putting that cloth on your eyes, and the way he looked at you—"

"That's enough," the male healer said sternly. He gave the girl an exasperated look. "You saw him, did you? Because when I asked, you all said that none of you got a good look at anyone who didn't belong in the hospital."

"Well, of course, I didn't get a *good* look," the girl muttered, flushing. "But I'm sure I saw *someone*."

"Someone!" The man threw his hands up in the air and gave the apprentices a look of such exasperation that they all scattered, mumbling about urgent tasks that needed their attention.

The healer shook his head as he watched them flee. "A prince? Really?" he murmured. "Anyone would think we hadn't just run our apprentices off their feet."

The matron, who had watched the whole thing in silence, chuckled. "Leave them be. They're young, and the young need something to talk about."

"Not just the young." The man eyed two older healers who were murmuring together on the far side of the room, casting frequent glances our way.

The matron shook her head, her smile dropping from her face. "With so much lost and so much to grieve, they need something thrilling to provide moments of relief."

"But why me?" I asked. "I'm sure you both healed more people injured by the storm than I did."

"Aye, that we both did." The woman's belly swayed with her laughter. "But we did it from within the walls of this hospital, which is much less romantic."

"I saw lots of healers in the square," I continued stubbornly. "Most of them must have been yours."

"They were, of course," the man said. "We sent everyone we could possibly spare when we heard of the disaster. But we didn't send out our apprentices, so you were probably the youngest there—and you held your own despite your age and lack of training."

"Luna isn't that much older than me," I muttered rebelliously. "Why don't they make legends about her and Master Hayes, instead?"

"Oh, you know Master Hayes, do you?" the matron asked. "We were most grateful for his assistance, along with his apprentice and Master Clay, as well, of course. And I'm sure people would be talking about them if they'd ridden into town with someone who spent the storm flying ships through the air. Don't go getting a big head, child. It's your master who caught the crowd's attention. It merely made the story even better for her apprentice to be a prodigy as well, saving the city in a different way."

"Now the *ships* are flying, I see," the man said caustically. "You're as bad as the apprentices."

The matron winked at him. "We were all apprentices once. And I've received enough laurels in my time not to be hungering after recognition at my age. By the time you're weary from running this hospital for two decades, you'll be more tolerant as well."

"Delphine!" The shout from the doorway was half-enthusiastic greeting, half wail.

Luna shot across the room and threw her arms around me, nearly knocking me back onto the bed. Ember stood and shook herself, growling slightly until I reassured her with a quick hand on her head.

"You're awake!" Luna cried in my ear, making me wince.

"You're here?" I asked, in unenthusiastic tones. "Come to laugh at me for making a fool of myself?"

Luna pulled back and grinned. "Don't worry about that. I would probably have been in the bed next to you if Master Hayes hadn't stopped me in time."

"A salutary reminder to the person who actually deserves the scolding." Amara entered the room much more calmly, Hayes a step behind.

She stopped at my bed and looked down at me with a guilty expression.

"I'm sorry, Delphine. I failed in my duty to you, and I wasn't even here when you woke up."

I struggled to my feet, fighting against Luna's weight. I could see the shadow in her eyes, and I wondered if she was thinking of her mother. Amara, of all people, knew the dangers of pushing yourself to the point of losing consciousness.

"You don't need to worry about that. Of course you needed to be at the harbor saving lives during the storm, and I can understand them wanting your help in the aftermath as well. I'm the one who made the foolish mistake."

"I'm sorry as well, Delphine," Hayes said. "Unlike Amara, I was in the square, and I even saw you'd arrived. I should have kept an eye out for you, like I did for Luna. You might not be my apprentice, but you are my student."

"Don't worry," I repeated. "I've finally learned my lesson. No more attempting to do the impossible for me. Next time I feel like I'm getting close to the end, I'll pull back. And sit down. That would have been a helpful move in the circumstances."

Amara laughed. "The lesson you learned is that next time you should sit down?"

I scrunched my nose. "When you put it like that..."

Amara stepped closer, and Luna and the local healers moved back to give her room. She put a hand on my shoulder and smiled at me.

"In all seriousness," she murmured, "I'm proud of you. It isn't an easy lesson to learn. And you shouldn't expect yourself to suddenly be perfect at it. But it does you credit that your desire to help others is so strong. I hear you saved a lot of lives."

I grimaced. "Unless you actually did single-handedly bring five ships flying in from the depths of the ocean with a singing chorus of mermaids to accompany them, I wouldn't believe everything you hear about my supposed feats."

She laughed. "Well, there weren't any mermaids..."

"Amara!" I stared at her, and she chuckled again. "The rest might be a little exaggerated as well."

She leaned closer, her voice dropping to a whisper. "I may be proud of you, but I would prefer not to repeat this particular scenario for more reasons than one. A certain someone has already reminded me of how I failed in my responsibilities where you're concerned. And since he's not the most responsible person himself, I'd prefer never to find myself on the receiving end of that particular lecture again, please. Especially when I don't have a word in my own defense."

I pulled away, flushing. But a moment later, a horrible thought occurred to me.

"Wait, does that mean you're going to refuse my going—?"

She put up a hand to silence me, her eyes sending a warning. "Not here," she mouthed, and I quickly stopped talking, my flush deepening.

"Does she have your official permission for discharge?" Amara asked the matron who was still standing nearby, an expression of interest on her face.

"Of course, of course," the matron assured her.

"Properly speaking, you didn't need to be here at all," Hayes said, "since healers can't do anything to speed recovery from ability overuse. But since you were brought here in the first place, and we've all been run off our feet without break, it seemed sensible to just leave you here. No one wanted you lying alone in our accommodation without anyone to watch over you."

"It certainly relieved my guilt to have you here," Amara said with another apologetic smile at me.

"I'm grateful for your care," I told the healer. "Please pass on my thanks to all the other healers as well."

"We should be thanking you for being by far our easiest patient," she replied with a laugh at her own joke. "You can never tell with healers. They're either the best or the worst patients."

"Do I want to know which you are, Hayes?" Amara murmured, and Luna broke into giggles.

"I can tell you all about that if you want to know," Luna said.

Amara stepped closer to her with a broad grin, but Hayes cleared his throat loudly.

"There's no time for such things now. There are people waiting for us."

All three of us laughed at that blatant attempt at distraction, but his words still caught my attention. I glanced at Amara, and she nodded confirmation of the question in my eyes.

Whisking Ember off the bed, I declared myself ready to depart, ignoring the knowing look in Amara's eye.

As we left the hospital—which really was eerily similar to the ones in Caltor and Ostaria—I directed a question at Hayes.

"What about Master Clay? I saw him at the square as well. Is he one of the ones waiting for us?"

"He should be, although he's been busier than the rest of us in the aftermath of the storm."

I directed a questioning look at Amara, who explained.

"Given the scale of the disaster, the injured humans got all the initial attention from the healers, regardless of their specialization. But now that the hospital is cleared, the animal healers have been in great demand. Sadly, many animals were also injured during the storm."

Her words made me look up into the clear sky. Surely Phoenix had been safe in the stables where I'd left him and wasn't one of the casualties?

Before I had time to ask, a speck appeared in the now cloudless blue, growing larger rapidly. A blur descended toward us, pulling up at the last minute to reveal a bird twice the length of my hand with a blue-gray back and an underside speckled orange and black. Phoenix.

I flicked my hair off my shoulder just in time for him to execute a neat landing.

"Other than hunting flights, he's been waiting near the hospital," Amara said. "I think he was keeping watch for you to emerge."

"Thank you, kind sir." I ran a finger along the feathers of his underside.

"Even I wasn't able to lure him back to our lodgings," a cheerful voice said from the other side of the street.

We all smiled at Clay's arrival, although I noticed the expression was more strained on Hayes than the rest of us.

"You're finished for now?" Amara asked Clay, her expression concerned. "Have you eaten anything today?"

"Yes, far too much, in fact," he assured her with a wide smile. "Everyone I visited plied me with food. I've been treated like a king."

"I should hope so, given you've been working for free for days," Luna said. "At least we ran out of patients yesterday when the local healers kicked us out of the hospital, saying they could handle the remaining injured themselves."

"How could I deny my help, given how the injuries came about?" Clay gestured for me to mount four shallow steps to the front door of an elegant, narrow home.

I blinked at it in surprise, pausing long enough that the rest of the group stopped as well.

"This is an inn?" I asked doubtfully.

"We have proper lodgings this time," Luna exclaimed in glee. "Apparently no one wanted to see the heroes of the disaster forced into ordinary inn rooms."

I groaned. "Please tell me you're talking about yourselves."

"Of course not," she said, her grin turning wicked. "I only healed a very average number of people in the square."

I groaned again but let her push me up the stairs and through the door. She guided me immediately left, through an internal doorway and into a large, bright sitting room furnished in light wood and elegant brocade.

A tall figure turned from the mantelpiece at our entrance, his eyes fixing on me. I stilled, and Nik and I regarded each other in silence for several seconds before he moved, striding across the room to meet me in the middle.

"You're fully healed?"

I covered my eyes with my hand. "I didn't need healing, just a long sleep —like a total novice. Please don't remind me."

He pulled my hand away with gentle fingers.

"Next time, please spare a single thought for yourself."

"I'll do my best," I murmured. "No more overreaching for me. But thankfully on this occasion I had you there. I only remember it vaguely, but you were the one who carried me to the hospital, weren't you? Thank you."

He shook his head, looking frustrated. "I hope you really mean that about the future. It was only chance I even knew you'd arrived in Eldrida. And there I was, foolishly thinking you couldn't run into any trouble in your two days on the road." He shot an accusatory glance at Amara, reminding me of my earlier fear about her withdrawing her permission for the plan against Grey.

"Never mind that." I put a hand on his arm and turned to my master. "The important thing is what happens next. If the storm wasn't natural, could it have been sent by Grey?"

"I've been wanting to ask the prince's opinion on that question myself," Hayes said. "He's our expert on Grey."

Nik's face twisted at the unwanted title, but he didn't deny it.

"Grey himself is strong," he said, "but he has a healing affinity. He couldn't direct a storm. And while he does have elements followers, he's been forced to take untrained youngsters from the fringes of society, so none of them are mage strength. And it would take several skilled mages working together to drive a storm that large."

"So it wasn't Grey," Clay muttered. "I wish that was better news. But that storm came from someone, and if it wasn't Grey—who?"

"There's no way it was Calista," Hayes said with confidence. "Not unless it was a group of mages gone rogue. And honestly, I don't think they have the capacity for that to be an option yet. They still have so few strong mages that they're all gathered in the capital where most of the rebuilding work has been done."

"You have that much confidence in the integrity of their new Mage's Guild?" Amara asked. "They wouldn't consider it worth the consequences to push their problems south to us?"

"My confidence is in their king and queen," Hayes said. "As the strongest two mages in the kingdom, they work very closely with their fledgling new Guild, and they would never sanction such a thing."

"No, I suppose not," she murmured. "Not given Queen Cadence's sister's position in Tartora."

"They're not that sort of people regardless," Hayes said firmly. "I would stake my life on it."

Amara raised her eyebrows at that, shooting a glance at Nik. When he slowly nodded his agreement, she let the matter drop.

I spoke into the silence. "In that case, we have two mysteries on our hands. What is causing the blight, and where did that storm come from? Would anyone wager they're unconnected?"

All three of the mages exchanged worried glances.

"Which means we need answers more urgently than ever," I continued, fixing my eyes on Amara. "And we know Grey has at least some of those answers. So when do I leave for the desert?"

# CHAPTER
# SEVENTEEN

It didn't end there, of course. Amara protested about the danger to me, and we all talked in endless circles for over an hour. But we'd all been in the middle of the storm, and no one could deny the new urgency to discover Grey's secrets.

Adding weight to my position was Hayes's report from the capital. After extensive consultation with the king and Triumvirate, they had agreed to back Nik's plan with only a few modifications.

As well as the squad of guards they had brought from the palace, Hayes and Clay had already recruited more from the local barracks—focusing on those with experience of both the local area and the desert. They had even hired an expert desert tracker—a rare breed since no one lived in the desert region.

"I have a friend among the local mages who's helped us with the selections," Hayes said. "I'm confident the ones we've recruited can be trusted, and we've told no one else the purpose of our visit. Officially, I'm here to give my apprentice broader experience."

Luna beamed. "Happy to be of assistance."

"And I'm here consulting with some of the local clinics on new techniques," Clay said. "The clinics in Eldrida have the most experience healing sea creatures."

"You get a lot of those in Ostaria do you?" I asked with a snort.

"I'm sometimes called south to the coast for consultations with local healers," Clay said with dignity before cracking a smile. "It was the best I could come up with, but I have old friends here, so no one has asked too many questions."

"We have no need of the tracker," Nik said caustically, having been mostly silent through the conversation, his eyes narrowed and steely as he watched the mages talk. "Or don't you trust that I can get you there?"

"I think it's getting back that's the primary concern," Hayes said when no one else immediately answered.

"Getting back?" I asked, not quite keeping the note of uncertainty out of my voice at this unsettling comment. I glanced at Nik who had straightened, giving Hayes his full attention.

"If we've really decided to do this," Hayes said, "then there's one other condition from the capital."

He glanced at Amara, but she didn't protest, apparently having been worn down either by their arguments or my determination.

"The condition?" Nik asked when Hayes didn't immediately speak.

"We are all to accompany Delphine part of the way into the desert and set up our own camp in a suitable location, to be determined by you and the tracker. But Your Highness is to accompany Delphine the rest of the way and to stay close enough to Grey's camp to monitor her conversations."

Nik went utterly still.

"Only me?" he asked stiffly.

Hayes cleared his throat. "I believe it was felt that only one person could safely conceal themselves so close to the camp. And since you're the one with both experience of the location and the necessary skills..."

"Necessary skills?" I looked between them. "What do you mean? How can Nik possibly listen to my conversations if he's not even inside the camp?"

"It seems Father has great belief in my ability." Nik's tone was impossible to read.

"Is he wrong?" Hayes asked quietly, not flinching in response to Nik's closed expression.

I threw Amara a desperate look, hoping she might rescue me with actual answers.

"Plants mages with sufficient skill and power can use root systems to listen to conversations happening at some distance." She looked at Nik curiously. "Can you really do it? You'll have to create and maintain the root networks yourself, since they won't exist in the desert."

Nik hesitated for a moment before nodding once. "I can do it."

Hayes smiled slightly, and I wondered if he had been the one to assure the king about his son's growth in skill during his time away.

But my initial uncertainty still hadn't been answered. "What does any of that have to do with needing a tracker to return?" I asked.

Nik's eyes turned dark, although his mouth curved upward in a humorless smile. "I believe there's another reason for sending only one to accompany you. It seems *His Majesty* considers me expendable." He looked at Hayes. "Or is that coming from my dear friends among the Triumvirate?"

I frowned. If I wanted to understand Nik, I really needed to find out what troubled history lay between him and the three most powerful mages in the kingdom.

"Expendable?" I asked instead, knowing it wasn't the time or place for the other conversation.

Hayes didn't seem daunted by Nik's observation, keeping his focus on the prince when he answered.

"That's one way to consider it. I prefer to think that they're giving you a chance."

"A chance?" Nik raised an eyebrow.

"To prove yourself...Among other things." For some reason Hayes's eyes flicked to me, and Nik's followed them, a strange look coming over his face.

What did Nik's proving himself have to do with me? A sudden horrible thought occurred to me. Had Hayes picked up on Nik's protective attitude toward me and reported on it to the *king*? Was King Marius attempting to win his son back by giving the order he thought his son would want—allowing Nik to stay close to me while also demonstrating that King Marius trusted in Nik's abilities?

I shook my head at my foolish thoughts. Surely not. The king would be interested in protecting his son, not pandering to Nik's strange insistence on shadowing me.

"Very well, then," Nik said suddenly. "We'll leave before dawn."

"Wait, what?" I asked, startled out of my thoughts.

"Why?" Nik looked at me with a shade of amusement. "Are you feeling short on sleep?"

"Quiet, you." I narrowed my eyes at him, but he just chuckled at my glare, his whole manner changed from the stoic, icy warrior who had observed most of the conversation. Whatever meaning he'd taken from Hayes's words, it seemed to have shaken him out of his earlier mood.

"That makes me feel better, actually," Amara said. "You should have mentioned it earlier."

"It does?" Nik looked at her in surprise.

"I'm not saying I approve of you, reneger," she said, and his remaining smile disappeared at the word. "But you've proven yourself when it comes to protecting Delphine." She held up a finger. "Which is all I'm giving permission for, mind you."

"Amara!" I cried while Luna cackled into her hands.

Nik ignored them both, turning back to Hayes. "Meet at the north gate just before dawn. With or without your guards and tracker. It makes no difference to me."

Hayes agreed to the meeting place, looking like he would have liked to say more but was refraining. But when Nik strode out of the room, heading for the front door, something else flashed into my mind.

I dashed after him, stopping him with a hand on his arm just as he reached for the door handle. He turned quickly, surprise and something else flashing across his face when he saw it was me.

"Is there a problem?" he asked, but the way his eyes lingered on my face made me think he wanted to ask something else.

I forgot my original purpose, a different question distracting me.

"You barely said a word back there. The plan was your idea in the first place—I thought you'd be the one working hard to convince Amara."

"Does that worry you?" He examined my eyes.

I considered the matter. "More curiosity than worry, I suppose."

"Seeing you in that hospital bed for so long..." His eyes tightened. "Let's just say I've been starting to agree with Amara's opinion on this."

"But it was your plan!"

"Exactly. What was I thinking to suggest such a thing? You might be strong, but even you have your limits."

"Don't worry," I said with a cheeky grin. "Out in the desert there will only be one of me to heal. I won't go collapsing on you again."

He cast his eyes toward the ceiling. "Yourself plus Miranda and about twenty animals, if I know you."

Phoenix, still perched on my shoulder, gave a chattering call, ruffling his feathers.

"Your objection has been noted," I said on a laugh. "I'll try to refrain from attracting too many more animal companions."

"Was that what you wanted to ask me?" Nik's eyes lingered on the hand that still rested on his arm. I pulled it back.

"Actually, it was something else. It might not be a problem, but..."

His brow instantly tightened, his expression turning serious.

"When I woke up, the apprentices at the hospital were full of talk. There seem to be all kinds of outlandish rumors flying around."

His face relaxed, and he laughed. "Oh, that. Don't worry, healer. I don't suddenly think you can heal multitudes or fell armies with a single touch. I won't relax my vigilance out there."

I shook my head. "I'm not worried about me," I said, exasperated. "It's you I'm concerned about."

"Me?" His amusement lingered, sparking with an added hint of warmth.

"You don't need to concern yourself about my safety. I learned to look after myself long ago."

I rolled my eyes and pushed on. "They seemed to be competing with each other for the most dramatic exaggeration on the stories, but unfortunately in your case..."

"Goodness," he said lightly when I fell silent. "Whatever did they say about me?"

"A few people got glimpses of you coming in and out of the hospital." I gave him a reproving look, and he glanced away, apparently uncomfortable at being found out.

"Since you carried me in from the square, someone connected you with the unknown plants mage who was helping there. And from there they kept exaggerating the situation until they accidentally stumbled onto the truth. They were talking about a prince with the power to move stones. One with a connection to me."

I trained my eyes on him, hoping he would understand my concern.

He raised an eyebrow. "Which of those facts concerns you, exactly?"

"Nik!" I whacked his arm lightly. "Be serious! Unless you want the whole city to work out who you are, you'd better stay out of sight until tomorrow morning."

"Thank you for your concern, but didn't you hear Hayes? My father has graciously extended his permission for me to risk my life for the kingdom, so I no longer need to fear finding myself carted off to the capital with a sack over my head."

"Nik!" I cried again.

"Or are you worried the Eldridans will realize my identity, thus discovering I'm a reneger, and form a mob to punish me for trying to mingle in regular society?"

He raised an eyebrow, and I sighed.

"Never mind, then. Go and proclaim your identity from the steps of the law keepers' hall for all I care."

"Delphine." Both his face and voice softened. "Thank you for your concern—truly. But I wish you wouldn't waste any worry on me."

I glared at him. "Isn't it for me to decide if it's wasted?"

"Delphine," he said again, a different note in his voice.

One of his arms snaked around my waist, and my breath rushed out of me, my eyes jumping to his. The expression in them made my middle seize, and I held my breath, keeping still as I waited to see what he was going to do.

But a slight rise in the voice of the speaker in the sitting room made him glance over my shoulder at the closed door behind me. Sighing, he pressed a fast kiss to my forehead.

"Stay safe, Delphine," he said. "I'll see you tomorrow."

I tried to protest, but by the time I'd worked out what to say, he was already out the door and onto the street. I watched the front door swing closed with a sigh of my own.

Nik had now been back for weeks, and it was obvious something significant had changed in his feelings toward me since our unexpected kiss in Caltor. But in other aspects, it sometimes seemed like he hadn't changed at all.

Whenever his family came up in conversation, I didn't know what I hated more—his icy, bitter reaction or the reminder that regardless of Nik's feelings, his complicated status still stood between us. If his family ever did reclaim him, it wouldn't be with a bag over his head, and they wouldn't have any interest in an ordinary farmer's daughter clinging to his side. But if they didn't accept him back, then he would forever remain a reneger, never able to properly interact in normal society and shunned by anyone who discovered his identity. Whether as royal prince or outcast reneger, Nik wasn't someone I should be thinking about. And yet, every time he got close, I forgot all about those concerns. And when he left, I couldn't stop my thoughts from filling with him.

"Are you really going to do this?" a small voice asked from behind me.

I turned and managed to dredge up a smile for Luna. "Of course I am. You were out there in the storm, too. We have to do something."

"Someone has to do something," she agreed, "but does it really have to be you?"

I opened my mouth to answer glibly but stopped myself just before I spoke. She was asking earnestly, and it was a question worth proper consideration.

"I'm just an apprentice from Tarin," I said after a moment. "So, no, I don't think it's my responsibility to work out what's happening with the blight, or even the storm. But Miranda is my friend. I've known her since we were small children, and I promised her father I would look for her. I know where she is right now, and I can't turn away from that. I have to try to reach her."

Luna sighed, reaching out to squeeze me tightly. "Just make sure you come back."

I hugged her back. "I promise I'll do my absolute best."

She stepped away and gave a chuckle. "I'm being foolish, aren't I? Miranda's been safe all this time, and you'll be all right too."

"Exactly!" I said brightly, putting in more confidence than I felt. "We're healers, remember? We don't kill easily."

Amara appeared in the doorway, looking at me steadily. "If you feel in real danger at any point, I want you to just walk out of there. We'll be waiting for you in the desert, and no one is going to blame you if you don't succeed." Her fierce expression told me if anyone wanted to blame me, they would have to go through her.

"Thank you," I said softly. "I want to help if I can, but I don't have any plans for grand self-sacrifice. My first priority is getting Miranda out, and if that means leaving without discovering Grey's secrets, then I'll do that and leave the matter to the Guild mages."

She nodded decisively. "Then we'll depart in the morning as planned. I know you've just slept for two days but try to get a bit of rest before then, please."

CHAPTER

# EIGHTEEN

I tried not to be intimidated by the number of guards waiting for us just outside the north gate of the city. But it was hard to ignore them when most of them were throwing covert glances my way, clearly curious about the girl at the center of our plot.

How many of them had heard the rumors from the storm? It made me uncomfortable to think they might be giving me far more credit than I deserved.

Eldrida soon faded behind us in the pre-dawn gloom, and I was surprised that my mind lingered on the disappearing city instead of the task ahead of me. I had roamed the streets until it grew pitch black, hoping the activity would make me tired enough to sleep again, and I couldn't forget my breathtaking first glimpse of the ocean.

I had known it would be large, but the vastness of it still struck me somewhere deep inside. The seas were shockingly still after the furor of the storm, the blue growing darker as it approached the horizon.

The smell of salt on the air, the call of the seabirds, and the white spray thrown up by the breeze permeated all my senses, immersing me in the moment in a way I'd rarely experienced. And when I returned to our lodgings, the sound of the waves chased me into a light doze.

Even the slate gray of the buildings—those near the harbor specked white with dried salt—seemed different from the buildings I knew from the rest of the kingdom. And the people were different as well, speaking with a lilt to their words that was refreshing and new to my ear.

"This is my first time east of the forest too," Luna had told me after leading me to the harbor and watching my reaction with satisfaction. "But I've heard talk about the people in this eastern stretch of the kingdom. Those in the capital say the easterners have their own ways. They're so isolated from the rest of Tartora that I suppose it makes sense."

I had hoped to find the two locals who had helped me during the storm, but I had no way to discover their names or locations. Even the grizzled stable master—who recognized Ember and Phoenix before he recognized me—had no idea who they were.

I had spent only a short time in the city—and for much of it I was unconscious—but fighting the storm shoulder to shoulder with the locals had given me a sense of kinship with Eldrida that I hadn't managed in months of living in Caltor. I just hoped I would have the chance to come back one day and spend more time here.

At first, we traveled north through the same sort of hilly grazing country as we had traversed from the river to the city. I didn't have much chance to observe it, however, since we traveled in closed trading wagons. Our mode of travel was one of the decisions made before Amara's and my arrival in Eldrida. The decision makers had decided that merchants traveling by an unusual route would draw less attention than a collection of royal guards and mages heading north.

Each wagon was pulled by a team of horses, and we made good time on the little used road that headed north and slightly west, heading for the northeast tip of Lake Aterra, where travelers could skirt the southern tip of the desert and join the fertile land that covered the middle of Calista.

We didn't camp for the night until after dark, when Nik appeared from the front wagon and told me we had crossed the border.

"You mean we're in Calista right now?" I asked.

He nodded. "My father will probably have sent word to Zeke and Cadence since the desert is officially part of their territory, but they have little true ownership over it since it's infertile and uninhabitable."

It took me a moment to realize he was talking about the Calistan king and queen. I nodded silently, reminded that Nik was the kind of person to casually refer to foreign monarchs by their first name.

An old memory suddenly surfaced of him claiming to have helped Queen Cadence restore Calista from its fallen state. I had scoffed at the suggestion at the time, but now I felt foolish for having done so.

Amara appeared, handing out bowls of stew, and our moment of private conversation ended. His words stuck with me, though, as we continued traveling the next day.

Even traveling at speed, starting before dawn and continuing until after dark each day, it took us two more days to reach the tip of the lake. A few settlers had moved into the rundown village there, but they had only restored three of the houses so far.

Our group slept under the stars before parting ways with the wagons and their drivers. They would return home at a more leisurely pace as the rest of us continued into the desert on foot.

I expected it to be burning hot on the desolate stretch of sand, but the pre-dawn cold of harvest season left me shivering as we stepped past the last scrubby patches of grass. As the sun rose, it grew hotter, but never to the blistering heat I had expected.

A comment from Nik told me it had been less pleasant during the summer, and I was glad for the timing that brought us here on the verge of winter. My legs soon grew weary of trudging over lightly packed sand, however, and they would eventually have been burning more than the noonday sun if I hadn't used my power to soothe the ache.

When I saw Hayes and Clay circulating among the soldiers—a soft word and brief handclasp enough to provide the same service for them—I offered my assistance. Hayes agreed, having Luna and me join him in providing relief for several of the guards. Like with our studies in Caltor, he used his own power to complete the task, having us join with him and shadow his activity with our power, amplifying his efforts. His demonstration, combined with a few words of explanation, showed me a more efficient way to target the relevant muscles, a method that required less power than I'd been using on myself to achieve the same end.

It was an interesting process—the only proper stimulation in the whole day—but he warned me that he had only permitted it as a training exercise.

"I don't want you using unnecessary energy from tomorrow onward. Keep it for whatever you encounter in Grey's camp."

I nodded, trying not to show how unsettled I felt at his words. The closer we got to Grey, the more real this whole situation became, and I was dreading the moment when I left the rest of the group behind.

Nik had spent the journey in the lead, accompanied by the desert tracker who consulted with him in low tones. I could only assume Nik was teaching him the route he was taking and the two of them were choosing the best place for the rest of the group to wait.

In the end, they led us to the coast, the sight of the sea catching me by surprise. It had been huge and overwhelming from Eldrida's harbor, but from the desert it seemed vast and wild in a wholly different way.

We all traipsed down a short but steep cliff, finding a tiny hidden cove at the bottom. Gazing out to sea, the water looked tempestuous, roiling over unseen obstacles that occasionally reached above the water level, the jagged points of rock deadly and unwelcoming.

Turning, however, I saw that the small strip of damp sand led to a deep cave that stretched back into the cliff side.

"Even if Grey sends a team south from his camp, they won't see you in here," Nik said with satisfaction.

"How did you find this place?" I asked, gazing back up the invisible path that had led us down the steep incline.

He grinned. "Plants affinity, remember? I made that path. And I felt the cave under my feet when I first passed by. I used it to hide from Grey's people myself last time, so I know high tide doesn't even come close to filling it."

One of the guards gazed uneasily at the turbulent ocean beyond the cove. "That was a different season, though, wasn't it?"

"Don't worry." Amara's smile showed her teeth. "I'll take care of any water troubles we might encounter."

The guard immediately nodded and disappeared back into the crowd of his comrades, eyes wide. I hid a smile. Whether or not they'd heard of my supposed feats, our companions had certainly heard the rumors about Amara.

We all slept in the cave that night, the strange echoing space unfamiliar after the open skies of our nights on the road. Ember was fascinated by it, trotting away to sniff at dark corners until Amara warned her sternly not to wander.

"If you go far enough in, we might never find you," she said, making me clasp the fox tightly.

Phoenix was less impressed, however, opting to leave us for the night in favor of sleeping in the desert above. I tried not to be offended by his desertion, but I would have appreciated his presence in the restless night that followed.

But when I reached the top of the cliff the next morning, he was already flapping his way toward me, landing on his usual perch on my shoulder. He stayed in position as Amara, Hayes, Clay, and Luna gave their final farewells, each giving various pieces of advice that I promptly forgot in the tension of the moment.

Now that the moment had come, I wanted to cling to Amara like I would have to my mother if she was there, but I restrained the impulse. I had told them all that I could do this, and I needed to prove that was true.

But I was incredibly grateful to have Nik at my side as I walked away. The comfort didn't last long, however. We'd barely lost sight of the others when Nik stopped, turning to me with a serious expression.

"You'll need to go the rest of the way on your own. If Grey is going to believe you came looking for him alone, he needs to see you coming."

I swallowed. "How am I going to convince him I came all this way alone, exactly?" All the plans we'd discussed seemed to have disappeared from my mind.

"You heard rumors in Eldrida," he said patiently. "So you came north. You've left your master and followed the coast to his camp. You made a promise to Miranda's father, and you're there to get her out by taking her place."

"I did make a promise to her father," I said.

He nodded. "Exactly. He's a healer so you can't lie outright to him. But he saw you in the warehouse—he knows you want to rescue Miranda. I think there's at least a chance he's been keeping her close in the hope you'll come."

"But surely he'll be suspicious," I said, knowing I was echoing words from our very first conversation on the topic but not able to help myself.

"Probably." Nik shrugged unconcernedly. "But I've never seen anything to match Grey's confidence. He'll trust in his ability to win you over."

I straightened my shoulders. "Well, he's about to meet his match, then. I have no interest in whatever bright future he's claiming to offer."

Nik nodded approvingly. "All that matters is that he believes in his own persuasiveness. Just don't make the mistake of mentioning any of us. He has to believe you came on your own."

I nodded. "I'll tell him Amara thought it was too dangerous for me to seek him out. That's true, even if we did eventually manage to convince her."

"Just remember," Nik said. "You won't see me, but I'll be there. If you need help, shout for me, and I'll hear you."

I managed a tremulous smile. He might hear me, but that didn't mean he'd be close by.

I forced my back to straighten. Nik hadn't helped in my last confrontation with Grey, and I didn't need him now. I could face this.

And I wouldn't be completely alone anyway. I put a reassuring hand on Phoenix, who was heavy on my shoulder. No one had even suggested trying to keep the animals behind, and I had never been so grateful for such loyal companions.

Nik looked like he wanted to say something more, but he must have seen from my face that I was only just holding on to my composure. With a single clasp of my arm, he slipped away, disappearing down another steep incline just as the first rays of the sun slid above the ocean.

I watched the place where he'd been for a moment before turning north. The desert ended at the coast, but there were no gentle, sloping sandy beaches like on the southern coast. Instead the desert ended abruptly, my vantage point allowing me to look down at the crashing waves below.

I had no idea how Nik would keep pace with me down there on the narrow, rocky coastline, but his plants affinity made him far more equipped to do so than I would ever be. I needed to trust he could look after himself and focus on my own task.

I carried a pack, but it wasn't heavy. Someone had carefully crafted it to look like I was near the end of a long journey, my supplies running low, so I was confident I could easily carry it for a day's walk.

As I traipsed along, the desert stretching to my left and the sea extending out to my right, I rehearsed what I would say to Grey. I would need to choose my words carefully, implying any untruths instead of stating them outright.

I had thought the day would last forever, but instead I seemed to blink and something green was breaking the monotony of my view ahead. I stared at it, trying to make sense of what I was seeing when shouted voices made me jump.

After the hours alone with Ember and Phoenix, the sound of human voices sounded strange and jarring. By the time I found their owners, two men had nearly reached me, running heavily across the rocky desert ground.

I stopped, waiting calmly for their approach. They were carrying drawn blades, but as they neared and saw that I was one girl, traveling alone, their posture changed, their weapons dipping.

As soon as they were close enough to hear me without having to shout, I spoke.

"I'm Delphine, and I'm here to see Grey."

"Here to see Grey?" One of them repeated, looking incredulously at the other. "Just come for a social call, have you?"

I tried to keep my tension from my face. "I'll discuss my purposes with Grey, and Grey alone."

"Will you now?" The second man stepped forward with a threatening air, but Ember's growl from near my ankles made him pause, his eyes jumping from her teeth to Phoenix's curved beak. The bird was regarding him with a steady eye, and the man quickly halted his approach.

"I'm not here to fight." I stretched my arms wide. "I carry no concealed weapons. All I want is to speak to Grey."

I had no idea if either of them were healers, but it seemed better to assume they were and watch my words, no matter who I was speaking to.

Once again the two exchanged looks, and this time they shrugged.

"Go on, then." One of them indicated with his sword that I should proceed, walking toward the green patch ahead.

I did so, forcing my head to stay high and my pace steady. The two men fell into place on either side of me, their swords still drawn. Given the careful distance they kept from me, they were either concerned I might be a healer or worried about my animals. Either option worked for me.

As we approached closer, the green ahead took further shape. The cliff side here stabbed inward into the desert, creating a sharp 'v' shape that must have a clean water source based on all the green that grew inside the sheltered area. The green I had glimpsed from afar was the tops of trees, but when I peered over the edge, I saw plants of various types below.

The men directed me to lead the way down an established path that snaked down into the crevasse. It was much easier to follow than Nik's temporary creation, and Ember was even able to walk at my feet.

Our height made us stand out, and by the time we reached the bottom, a small crowd was converging on the path. Many of them were of a similar age to me, but a few stood out from the others, their faces bearing the marks of greater age and their hands resting on sword hilts at their waists. Before I had time to be intimidated by the number of people, however, someone thrust through the middle of the crowd, pushing the others out of the way.

"Delphine!" Miranda screamed my name before throwing herself into my arms.

I clung to her, murmuring her name as I squeezed her tight. So many of the memories of my childhood had been marred since leaving Tarin, but Miranda remained as a bright spot.

I pulled back so I could look at her properly, holding her by the arms and examining her from head to toe.

"Are you all right?" I asked.

"Of course!" She beamed at me, her expression slowly growing confused. "Why wouldn't I be?"

"Well...I..." My words trailed off as I remembered the last time I had seen her.

Had she forgotten being threatened by Grey and carried off over his shoulder? Had she forgotten his casual attacks on first Serena and then me? It occurred to me that Miranda had been half out the window at the time and might not have seen him take out Serena. But she must have seen him stab me.

Her head cocked to the side, and her brow creased, as if she was wrestling with a large and confusing thought.

"I'm so happy to see you, Delphine. But what are you doing here?"

"I came to get you."

"Me?" She gaped at me, as if the thought were unimaginable. "But that can't be right. No one wants me back."

I frowned. "Why would you say that? Of course we do! Your father was devastated when you left."

"He...he was?" She slowly shook her head. "He must be very angry then. I heard he disowned me because of it."

"Don't be silly!" I said bracingly, remembering the lies Grey had told before Serena's departure. "He's waiting for you to come home."

"No..." She frowned, looking lost and confused. "That can't be right. My father never wants to see me again."

I moved my hands to her shoulders, angling her body so her eyes met mine.

"Your father loves you and wants you back at home. That's why I'm here. I promised Halmir that I'd find you and send you back."

She still hesitated, and I shook her lightly. "You have a healing seed, Miranda. I know it's not activated yet, but you must be able to sense that I'm telling the truth. Your father is waiting in Tarin for you."

Her eyes lit up, all her confusion falling away. "He is? And he sent you to bring me home?" She threw her arms around me again, nearly knocking me over.

"Well, well, well," a silky voice said, as Grey strode toward us, the crowd parting before him. "This is an unexpected visit."

"Is it?" I asked, putting my arm around Miranda's shoulders and pulling her close to my side.

His smile widened. "Maybe not entirely."

All the way here I had worried, but now that I was here, confidence settled over my shoulders like a cloak. I had forgotten that the healing power worked both ways. I could sense sincerity or deception on Grey as easily as he could on me. I had felt the lie behind his opening words, and it lent credibility to Nik's certainty. Grey wasn't surprised by my arrival. He had been hoping I would come.

"We've never had a recruit travel so far on their own," he said lightly, his eyes dwelling on me.

My arm tightened around Miranda, drawing his eyes to her, and for the first time I saw a hint of displeasure creep onto his face.

"I'm not a recruit," I said, not wanting to overplay the situation. "But I'm willing to stay on one condition."

"Oh?" He raised an eyebrow. "And what is that?"

"You let Miranda go free."

"Let her go?" He spread his arms wide. "No one is held here against their will."

A murmur of agreement ran through the crowd. I frowned as I examined his face. His words felt like the truth, but I couldn't shake an air of deception that I sensed hanging around him like a shroud.

"Is that true, Miranda?" I asked, turning to the younger girl for confirmation.

"There didn't seem any point leaving when I had nowhere to go." Her eyes shone as she looked up at me. "But now that I know Father is waiting for me, of course I want to go home with you."

"With me," I repeated the words softly.

It had never occurred to me that Grey might let me collect Miranda and walk straight out again. If he really did intend to let her go, should I accept? Miranda was my personal focus for this mission, but I still wanted to help the rest of the kingdom if I could. But if he was going to let us both go, what reason could I give for staying? I had already said I wasn't here to join him.

I looked straight at him, taking a gamble.

"Excellent. In that case we can leave immediately."

Grey tensed slightly at the words, his movement reassuring me. He spread his arms wide, however, keeping a friendly expression on his face.

"Come, come, there's no need to hurry away. You must have had a long journey here, and you'll be needing more supplies, surely?"

I hiked my pack higher on my shoulder, pretending to feel its light weight, as I acted out the process of wavering.

"You'd just give us supplies freely?" I asked.

"Well, everything in life is a negotiation, isn't it?" He grinned. "But I think you'll find I can be reasonable."

My hand moved to my middle, pressing against the place he had plunged his dagger. It was an intentional movement, but I hoped he would take it as an instinctive response.

"Ah yes, you must accept my most sincere apologies for that," he said. "I was under attack and acting out of a most foolish anger. I can assure you that I'm not usually so impulsive."

I raised an eyebrow, but I couldn't deny the challenge in his eyes. They were calling on me to acknowledge the truth of his words, and this time I could sense nothing but sincerity from him. He truly did regret stabbing me.

I remembered my words to Nik at the time. Grey had always known I could heal myself—it had been a petty moment of revenge. Now he was claiming the impulsive moment was uncharacteristic, and I could well believe he usually behaved in a much more calculated manner.

If it was true that Grey wanted me among his followers, he must have realized in retrospect that stabbing me hadn't been a good opening move.

"We'll soon be sitting down for our evening meal," Grey said. "Why don't you join us? That way we can talk comfortably, and any further travel can happen in the daylight tomorrow."

I glanced at Miranda, but she seemed perfectly content with this plan. She even volunteered to show me around the camp, chattering most of the way about the daily business of life in the desert.

I had imagined it as a harsh, sweltering place, full of dirt and heat. But the hidden crevasse teemed with life, an oasis in the desolate land around it. There were even a few proper wooden buildings, although most of the houses were made of heavy canvas hung over wooden frames.

Down here among the greenery, the heat of the day had already faded, the temperature pleasant and cool. A long wooden table sat in the open space between the two rows of dwellings, people already starting to lay out plates and trays of food.

It was simple fare, but plentiful, and I wondered how much they provided for themselves and how much they traded for. While I doubted Grey would have a moral issue with stealing, he knew better than to draw attention to himself with that sort of behavior.

"As you can see, we're an amicable community," Grey said, taking a seat at the head of the long table and gesturing for Miranda and me to sit beside him at the long bench that ran down the right side.

Miranda seemed pleased at the placement. She appeared to harbor no resentment toward Grey for his lies, seeming almost normal as long as the topic of her father didn't come up. When it did, confusion took prominence, and I noticed Grey steered the conversation away from any such discussion.

"So what do you want in exchange for supplies?" I asked as soon as my plate was full.

"Straight to business, then?" Grey gave me an amused smile and a tilt of his eyebrow.

I held my ground, silently waiting for an answer.

He chuckled. "Very well. In all honesty, I was rather hoping I might convince you to stay."

Miranda frowned. "If Father is waiting for me, I can't stay here. He must be terribly worried after all this time."

"Naturally, you need to go. I can see that," Grey said smoothly, his words oozing truth. He understood what I was demanding from this bargain. "But perhaps your friend might like to stay."

Miranda turned wide eyes on me. "But your parents must be worried about you too! I saw you in Caltor, which means you've been gone nearly as long as I have!"

I looked away from her, real pain pinching my chest. "I have no interest in returning to my farm."

"What?" Miranda grabbed my arm, twisting me back around toward her. "What do you mean? Surely you didn't fight with your parents? You always seemed so devoted to them."

"I was." I looked down at my plate. "And then I left Tarin and found out exactly what my father had been keeping from me. I've seen a bigger world than one farm now, and I have no interest in that life anymore."

Despite my continued anger at my father, it hurt to reveal so much painful truth in front of Grey. But that truth was also the best tool I had against him.

Out of the corner of my eye I could see the sharp interest in his eyes, and the small upward curve of his lips. He was trying to look detached and disinterested, but he was delighted to read this particular truth on me.

"I've left everyone behind," I continued, "and I walked across the desert because I heard you might be out here. Unlike my own father, yours always fought for me, Miranda. I promised him, and I couldn't let him down."

"Oh, Delphine." Miranda took my hand, tears in her eyes. "I'm sorry. You'll always have a place with my father and me. You know that, right?"

I forced a smile, nodding my thanks. "And I appreciate it more than I can say. But I'm not ready to go back to Tarin yet." I tore a piece off the chunk of bread on my plate. "But the same doesn't apply to you. You need to get back to your father."

"How could I go without you, though?" she asked.

"It's easy. All you have to do is follow the coast south until you reach Eldrida. From there, you can buy a place with merchants heading west." I glanced at Grey, and he chimed in as I had hoped he might.

"Naturally, I will provide provisions and gold for the journey, since I was the one to drag you all the way out here."

Miranda laughed, as if she hadn't been carted away as a hostage. "I don't know if I should accept, but I will. I can't leave my father waiting."

"I just hope there are no more big storms while you're traveling," I said, watching Grey closely out of the corner of my eye.

"I hope not!" Miranda's eyes widened. "We were lucky to be so sheltered down here, but even so we sustained some damage."

Grey's eyes also darkened at my words, but not with the emotions I'd expected. Instead he seemed genuinely angry, as if the storm had been an attack on him as much as us.

I chewed on the inside of my cheek, trying to decipher what that could mean. Did Grey know who had sent the storm as we suspected?

"The worst storms won't be until the turn of the season," Grey said. "Your journey should be a safe one, Miranda."

"Will you really stay here, though, Delphine?" Miranda asked. "Do you want to go with Grey to the new land?"

I shook my head. "I don't intend to stay here that long. But I'm curious enough to hear more about it. If Grey is going to leave soon, I can always return the way I came."

I turned to him. "Isn't that right?" I challenged, wanting to see his reaction.

A small smile turned his expression smug. "Certainly. If you still wish it."

Truth. I couldn't stop the twitch of my brows as I read it on him. Everything was so smooth, so easy. I hadn't even had to outright bargain with him for Miranda's freedom.

Instead of bolstering me, my success sent a thrill of uncertainty through me. Nik had talked endlessly of Grey's confidence, but this seemed beyond excessive. He couldn't possibly mean to let me wander freely around his camp only to leave again whenever I wanted.

Grey lifted his glass to me in a silent toast, his expression suggesting he could read the wheels turning in confusion behind my eyes. He had to suspect something, but it wasn't giving him a moment's discomfort.

And that made me very uncomfortable indeed.

CHAPTER

# NINETEEN

My half-formed fear that Grey would change his mind at Miranda's actual departure proved unfounded. At least half the camp turned out to see her off, the younger members hugging her in what seemed like genuine affection.

Watching them sent a spear of discomfort through me. Did they have families at home waiting for them like she did? Was it wrong of me to care only about freeing my friend?

But I reminded myself that our end plan was to dismantle the camp completely. At that point, everyone would be returning to their normal life in Tartora, so I wasn't abandoning these others.

Miranda appeared uncertain when it came to actually setting off alone, but the determination that had entered her when she realized her father still loved and wanted her hadn't waned. With an uptilt of her chin, she climbed out of the canyon and disappeared into the desert overhead.

"Will she really be all right on her own?" I murmured to myself, although I knew she would only have to travel for a day before being picked up by Amara and the others.

"You made it alone, didn't you?" Grey asked with a smile.

I nodded, glad for the first time that I'd had to walk alone for the last day.

"Well, not entirely alone," I corrected, making him stiffen slightly. But when I gestured at my two ever-present shadows, he relaxed.

"Ah yes, I never expected to be making recruits among the animal world."

I turned to face him, ready for a more direct conversation now that Miranda was safely gone.

"I already told you, I'm not a new recruit."

"You were here to rescue your friend," he said, speaking more openly than he had since my arrival.

"Can you blame me?" I asked.

"Not in the least. I behaved without circumspection in Caltor, and I hope you will accept my apology." Again his words rang true.

"I don't know what you're planning," Grey said. "But I have no doubt you came here with a plan."

I raised both eyebrows. I hadn't expected him to be that direct.

"And if I did? What do you intend to do about it?" I challenged.

"I intend to change your mind," he said. "After what you've seen of me, your suspicion is perfectly understandable. But I'm hoping that once you've heard more of the story, you'll see things in a different light."

A girl about my own age strolled past, a bundle of chopped wood in her arms. She smiled at us both, her eyes lingering hopefully on me, as if she saw a potential friend.

I smiled back uncertainly. So far Grey's camp had been nothing like I expected. Instead of a military barracks crossed with a prison, it felt more like a village or even an extended family, everyone working together cheerfully to keep the community functioning.

"It's not like you expected, is it?" Grey's ability to guess my thoughts unnerved me, but I smiled back as sweetly as I could manage, keeping silent.

"Other things aren't like what you think either. Like that storm."

"The storm?" I looked quickly at him, not bothering to hide my curiosity this time.

"You might have missed us if not for that storm, actually," he said, making my shoulders tense in retrospective anxiety.

What did he mean by that? We had thought there was no hurry to find Miranda, but had we been wrong?

"You're leaving for the island already?" I asked without thinking.

Both his eyebrows shot up. "You know about the island?"

I managed a weak smile. "I spoke to Serena. She told me she wanted to leave you because your promised new land turned out to be across the ocean."

"You saved her?" He regarded me with fascinated, hungry eyes.

I almost corrected him—it had been the combined efforts of Hayes and Luna that had saved Serena—but I bit my tongue just in time. I was supposed to be making myself an appealing recruit, and apparently Grey wanted strong healers.

"So you spoke to Serena," Grey murmured. "That's how you found me, then."

440

I looked away. My slip had turned out in my favor, giving him an explanation for my sudden appearance here. Serena had never made it as far as the camp, but she'd known it was on the coast of the desert.

"You've shown remarkable loyalty to your friend," he said. "But then I've always found that those disenchanted with their homes are most interested in talk of a new home."

I nodded slowly, easily able to acknowledge the truth of those words, even if they didn't apply to me. My truth the night before had served me as well as my slip just now. Grey wanted to be convinced, and I had given him just enough ammunition to do it. Was this a glimpse of how he worked on others when the roles were reversed?

"Let me show you our main work here," Grey said, gesturing toward the ocean.

I hesitated, but the whole point of my presence was to get him talking, so I followed obediently in his wake. Overnight I had been comforted by Miranda's presence, the two of us sharing her bed before she solemnly handed possession of it over to me.

But now she was gone, and I was alone. I surreptitiously ran my hand over the closest bush, wishing I could send my power along its roots as Nik could apparently do. Was he listening even now?

I clung to the sense of his presence, however false it was, taking what courage I could muster from it.

"Here you are." A note of pride entered Grey's voice. "Isn't she beautiful?"

I blinked at the size of the sleek wooden ship that had appeared past the screening line of trees. It was as large as the largest I had seen in Eldrida's harbor.

"Did you build that?" I asked in astonishment, even as I watched the girl from earlier walk back down the gangplank, her arms now empty of branches.

She waved when she caught sight of me, smiling brightly as she headed back into the depths of the crevasse. Grey watched her go with an indulgent expression before looking at the ship again.

He had a warmth in his eyes when he regarded the wooden vessel that I had never seen when he looked at a human.

"We had to build her here," he said. "That's why preparing for this trip has taken so long, even with a team of people using their plants power to speed the work. It was the only way since the waters are too treacherous to sail up the coast from Eldrida. We can reach the island from here, but only by charting a very particular course, and only from this exact spot."

"So there really is an island." I gazed out at the ocean, which appeared smooth and unmarred by any other landmass. "And you're saying it's some sort of paradise that will provide us all with a better life?"

Grey started to nod only to stop, giving me a calculated look that I pretended not to see.

"That is part of the truth, certainly," he said after a moment.

I turned to him. "And what's the rest of the truth?" I asked boldly.

For a second, I was sure he meant to fob me off, but instead he looked at the people moving industriously around the ship and gestured for me to follow him. I did so cautiously, but he only led me toward the oldest of the wooden buildings, making no comment when Ember and Phoenix followed me inside.

From the outside it appeared to be an ordinary shack, and the inside confirmed that impression. A square room served as sitting room, dining room, and kitchen, with a stove under a chimney along one wall. A door on the opposite side of the room gave a glimpse of a single bedroom beyond, and from the look of the bed, Grey had slept in it the night before.

It was a step above the canvas tent that Miranda had shared with three other girls, but it wasn't significantly more luxurious. And it had a worn, lived-in feel that made it seem as if it had been inhabited for decades, passed down from previous generations.

I looked around openly, trying to work out what this house told me about Grey. But the more I saw of Grey and his camp, the more confusing it became. The ruthless, violent man I had previously encountered had disappeared entirely, and if I had just met him, I would have believed him to be a kindly village head, beloved by his harmonious community.

It was impossible to reconcile the two pictures.

Nik's words echoed in my head, reminding me of Grey's slippery charm, and I put a hand to my middle, the gesture unconscious this time. If I wanted to avoid falling for Grey's story, I needed to remember the feel of his dagger plunging into me.

"Please, sit down." Grey pointed at a simple wooden chair at the worn table in the middle of the room.

I sat obediently, watching as he lowered himself into the chair opposite, stretching out his long legs in a comfortable gesture and smiling across at me. I tried to keep my gaze open and unsuspicious, but the hint of amusement in his eyes made me suspect I had failed.

"To most of my followers, I focus on the new life awaiting us," he said. "But I can see you know more than most." He leaned forward, his voice turning earnest. "Given our protected location here, most of my people don't realize the extent of that storm. But I can imagine what it did in Eldrida, coming on without warning like that."

I nodded, allowing some of the horror of those hours to show on my face.

"I don't know the final count of the dead," I said, "but there must have been many given how many boats were out at sea."

"A true tragedy," he said.

I frowned, trying to make sense of him. I didn't get the impression he particularly cared about the people of Eldrida, but I also didn't read any outright lie in his words.

"Are you saying it wasn't a natural phenomenon?" I asked. "You're saying someone created this tragedy?"

He nodded. "That's exactly what I'm saying. I can see that you're someone with a high sense of responsibility, and I applaud that. You came here to save your friend, but what if I told you that you can help save all of Tartora?"

I blinked. Whatever I'd been expecting, it hadn't been that.

He sat back with a satisfied expression.

"The people on that island live a comfortable life," he said. "And it's a life we can also experience. That much is true. But I have another reason for going."

"Wait." I sat up straight, my sudden movement making Ember growl, lifting up her head from where she lay curled on the floor.

I ignored her, too distracted by Grey's words. "You're saying there's already a community of people on the island—people no one here knows exist—and they're the ones who sent the storm?"

"That," said Grey, "is exactly what I'm saying."

"And the blight, too?" I asked, forgetting to be cautious. "They somehow caused that as well?"

Grey whistled quietly. "You know about that, too? You really have connected the dots."

I shrugged. "Never mind that. Tell me." I trained my eyes on him, determined not to misread the truth of his words.

"Yes," he said simply. "I have reason to believe they have been causing the destruction of Tartora's crops, as well as sending the storm."

There wasn't the slightest shade of deception around his words.

"What are your reasons?" I asked. "Do you have certain proof?"

Grey's expression closed off. "You're a healer. You can read the truth of my statements for yourself."

His manner made it clear I had pushed too hard. I sat back, forcing myself to relax.

"Of course," I murmured. "Sorry. I'm just shocked."

He relaxed slightly. "I can hardly blame you for that. I was shocked myself."

"But why?" I cried. "Why would they want to move against Tartora after all this time?"

Grey shrugged. "They have the power to rule over anyone. They seem to have decided it's time to wield that power."

"Rule?" I glanced down at the wooden planks under my feet. Could Nik hear through the dead wood of a house, or did it have to be a living network of roots? Was he hearing this? "Are you saying they intend to overthrow the king and take Tartora for themselves?"

"It's a supposition on my part, but I believe it to be a real possibility."

"Who are these people?" I asked, horror in my voice.

"They're mages," he said. "Powerful ones who don't answer to any Guild or tribe."

I swallowed. Amara was frustrated with the way the Guild ruled over all the mages in Tartora. But this was the reason Tartora maintained the Guild— the reason Calista was recreating theirs. The nomad tribes, located in the mountains north of Calista and the grazing lands west of Tartora, lacked a guild, but their tribal system had its own ways of keeping their mages under control.

"But where did they come from?" I asked.

"Calista," he replied.

"When it fell?" I asked slowly, trying to work out how they could have split off without anyone knowing.

He nodded. "A century ago, after the attack, most of the ordinary people fled to Tartora or the nomad lands, and some of the mages managed to find sanctuary among the tribes. Others were killed, of course, but not as many as everyone believed. Because of the chaos and destruction, no one ever even knew some were missing."

"So some of them escaped east while the others fled west," I said slowly. "And that was a hundred years ago, so they must have grown in number since."

"I see you appreciate the danger," he said. "They've been living peacefully on their island until now, attracting no attention. But they have never forgotten the route back to the mainland, and the time has come when they've decided to use that knowledge."

I jumped to my feet. "We have to warn the rest of Tartora! We have to warn the king!"

I raced toward the cottage's door, but Grey sprang to his feet, catching my wrist and pulling me to a halt.

"Do you want to see a mage war lay waste to Tartora like it once did to Calista? As you said, it's been a century, and Calista is only starting to be rebuilt now."

I stared up at him, my brain whirling in confusion. Of course I didn't want a war, but we couldn't just let the islanders take over unopposed.

"We have to—"

"We have to stop them, I agree," Grey said. "But we have to do it with as little disruption and bloodshed as possible. Which means I have to do it."

"You?" I stared at him, my brows lowering. "What do you have to do with the islanders?"

"Everything," he said simply, the single word ringing with truth. "On the island, a single family rules over the others. The Constantines. If the islanders are seeking war now, it's at the instigation of this family."

"And what does that have to do with you?" I asked.

"I'm part of that family."

"What?" I ripped my arm free of his hold, but I didn't try to flee again, instead waiting for his answer.

"My father was the oldest son of the family and should have been their next leader. But he wanted to run things differently—to give the people of the island more say in their own governance. He intended to change things, so his younger brothers turned on him. They murdered him while I was still an infant, but my mother escaped with me. She made it to a small boat and set out for the mainland. But she didn't have time to gather proper supplies, and by the time she arrived..."

He lowered his head in grief, and unwilling sympathy squeezed me.

"She was weakened to the point of death by the time the boat washed ashore," he said. "Since I was only an infant, I would have died as well if there hadn't been an old couple here who cared for me and raised me."

"Here? In the middle of the desert?"

"When the group of mages set sail for the island, a small handful chose to stay behind. These two were the last remaining of that group. My mother lived just long enough to tell them what had happened to my father and to sketch out the route to the island. She hoped I would have the chance to return one day."

"And you believe they'll accept you as their true leader if you do?" I asked.

He smiled wolfishly. "I'll make them."

"And that's how you're going to stop their attack?"

He stopped closer, his eyes earnest. "Do you see, Delphine? I need to get to that island—and for that I need people with both plants and elements abilities. We've been working on our ship for so long, but it's nearly finished now. Within a few days we'll have fixed the storm damage and be ready to sail."

I frowned, trying to work out why his words confused me. I finally realized the flaw.

"But I have a healing ability and so does Miranda. Why do you want healers?"

He smiled, placing a friendly hand on my shoulder. "I would never discount the importance of our own affinity! Since I've recruited all these people, I need to keep them safe. And that's the job of healers, isn't it?"

I nodded, pleased with his answer. The niggling feeling remained, but I brushed it aside. I had thought I would never be convinced by Grey, but that was because I could never have guessed the truth. He had never been the one undermining Tartora—he was trying to save it.

"Do you really need my help?" I asked, gripped by a new sense of certainty.

"Of course." He held my gaze. "You and I are the most powerful here, Delphine. I may be the only one who can save Tartora, but I need you by my side. I need you to help me lead these people. Your family may have betrayed you, but I can lead you to a new people and a new home—a home you can reign over like a queen."

His words filled me, warming and lifting me. There was nothing romantic in the way he was looking at me—he didn't want me, he wanted my ability— but there was undeniable truth behind his words. People needed me—both the people of Tartora and this smaller community—and I could provide for them. I could keep them all safe.

"I don't care about ruling," I said. "But I'll do my part to keep everyone safe. You can rely on me."

His smile grew slowly, eventually covering his whole face. "I knew I was right to trust you with the whole story. Recruiting your friend was a mistake —she's too far from activation—but I was right to hope she might bring you to me."

He hesitated. "I'm hoping you can help me in other ways, too. I've never seen someone with your skills before. I'm hoping you can—" He cut himself off with a shake of his head. "No, never mind that. I don't want to overwhelm you. For now, it's enough that you want to help. The whole camp is busy preparing the supplies we'll need for the voyage, and as leader, I'm constantly busy. Could you circulate among my people and give each of them a physical check? I wouldn't want our busyness to mean I miss any illness or injury in any of them."

He shook his head with an affectionate smile. "They're all so devoted to the cause that they're prone to ignoring their own ailments."

I nodded. "I'm only an apprentice, but I'll do what I can."

He smiled at me. "I'm sure I can trust in your strength to make up for any lack in experience."

I nodded. That had usually been my experience so far.

I let myself out of the cottage, my mind whirling. The answers I was seeking had turned out to be far easier to uncover than I expected. But now that I had them, I couldn't follow the plan and leave.

I had seen the devastation in Eldrida from one storm, and I had witnessed the destruction left in the wake of the blight. What would be left of Tartora if it came to all-out war with the islanders? I might not like the way Grey had been luring young people away, but he was the only one who could save Tartora, which meant I had to work with him, regardless of my personal feelings.

I wandered across the camp toward my new bed in Miranda's old tent. How much had I misunderstood of what was going on here, anyway? Miranda hadn't been a prisoner like I expected—no one here was. And Grey really did mean to lead them to a new life in a new land like he'd promised. Maybe we had gotten the wrong idea about him, blaming him for under-mining the king when it had actually been the islanders doing that all along?

I wished I could explain my intentions to Amara before I left, but I couldn't risk making the trip back to find her. It was a full day's trek each way, and Grey would sail soon. I couldn't risk missing the boat, not when I was needed onboard.

Phoenix nipped gently at my ear, and I scolded him lightly. The pain of the pinch shook something loose in my mind, reminding me of the earlier niggle at the back of my thoughts. But the more I tried to work out what my concern had been, the less I could grab hold of it. Eventually, I gave up with a shrug. Whether or not I personally approved of Grey was irrelevant. We had a common enemy, and that was enough for now.

CHAPTER

# TWENTY

It took me the rest of that day and all of the next to examine every one of Grey's followers. No one had any significant health concerns, although there were plenty of niggling issues for me to heal.

I had thought the issues were only natural, given the weak strength of their healers, and it wasn't until the second day that it occurred to me Grey himself was a powerful healer. I stopped halfway through my healing of an older woman named Ida, who had greeted me with a smile despite her pain. Her ailment wasn't a threat to her overall health, but it brought her significant pain, so I was glad to be able to heal it for her.

When I realized I'd stopped, I gave myself a shake and quickly finished. But as Ida thanked me profusely, relief shining from her eyes, I couldn't stop frowning. Why had Grey allowed her to suffer when he could have fixed it more easily than me?

"Why didn't you go to Grey before now?" I blurted out, cutting across Ida's thanks.

"Grey?" She stared at me, her brow creased and her eyes blank as if the idea had never occurred to her. "Why would I go to him?"

"He's a healer, isn't he?" I asked. "He could have healed this for you back when it first started."

"Go to Grey for healing?" Ida's eyebrows rose, and she gave me a curious look before shrugging. "I guess you're new here, so you don't know. Grey doesn't use his power for things like that."

"Things like...what?" I asked. "Healing?" I laughed as I said it, but Ida didn't smile back. My own smile fell away. "You're joking. Grey doesn't heal people?"

She considered my question. "I suppose he probably heals himself. And perhaps there are others, though I've never seen it." She shrugged.

I stared at her, appalled. "But why? He's a strong mage! He could easily heal something like this without straining himself. How could you just live with it when he had the means to offer relief?"

"The healers on the island would have fixed me soon enough." She patted my knee. "Don't worry. I've endured far worse in my past, and I could endure far more to make it to our new life. You'll see. It will all be worth it."

She excused herself with further thanks, and I watched her go, unsettled. Was Grey truly so uncaring about his followers, or were they the ones putting him on a pedestal, not telling him about their needs?

I sat alone for some time, wrestling with the thought, but eventually forced myself to move on in search of the next person. Grey had asked me to check everyone which meant he must have some care for them. Worrying about how far that care extended was purposeless when he was the only chance we had of defeating the islanders. My support for him stemmed from need, not from any admiration of his character.

I had to remind myself of that fact again when I sought Grey out to report my completion of my task. I found him berating one of his younger followers for accidentally smashing a barrel and spoiling the provisions it had contained. The poor boy was cowering before him, although Grey hadn't actually lifted a hand against him.

I could understand the boy's reaction, however. I was only a bystander, and even I felt shaken by the look in Grey's eyes. When he saw me, he calmed, however, his expression changing into a rueful smile.

After drawing a deep breath, he apologized to the boy for losing his temper and gave me a remorseful look.

"With our departure approaching, I fear we're all on edge, and I'm worst of all. But have you had a chance to check on everyone's health?"

Hearing the question calmed my agitation somewhat, reminding me that for all his flaws, Grey did have some consideration for his people. I might wish he had more restraint, but I could accept worse flaws if it meant saving an entire kingdom.

"Everyone is in good health," I reported. "I've just completed my final examination."

"Excellent!" Grey rubbed his hands together, his smile becoming broad and genuine. "In that case, we are clear to sail with the dawn tide."

"Really?" I cried, relieved I hadn't attempted to leave the camp. "Already?"

Even the boy smiled at the news. "May I tell the others?" he asked, and Grey nodded graciously.

The boy hurried away, and a buzz of excitement soon filled the camp as the news spread.

Phoenix, however, seemed unsettled by the commotion, fixing one of his eyes balefully on Grey, his small body tensed, as if ready to launch into flight.

I angled my shoulder away from Grey, hoping he hadn't noticed the bird's attitude. I had been carefully staying quiet about both Ember and Phoenix, hoping Grey wouldn't attempt to bar them passage aboard his ship.

"Can't you try to be a little friendlier?" I asked the bird after Grey hurried off for a final check of the restored ship. "I know he isn't our favorite person, but he's in control of who gets to go to the island."

To my dismay, Phoenix responded by launching himself off my shoulder and disappearing into the sky above the crevasse. I watched him go with a sinking heart. It wasn't a normal time of day for him to hunt, but perhaps he'd spotted some appealing prey.

I only hoped he hadn't decided he was ready to be a wild bird again. I had grown used to his weight on my shoulder and his company during the day while Ember slept—not to mention the way people treated me with increased respect now I came with a sharp beak and claws attached.

As the evening bore down and he didn't reappear, my worry grew. But there was nothing I could do about it. The people around me were all rushing hither and thither, packing their personal belongings now that the ship was finally readied.

I had so little to pack that I was soon at a loose end, my wandering feet taking me deeper into the crevasse, following it all the way to its tip. The greenery grew thicker as I went until I felt entirely ensconced in plant life, separate from the bustling camp that lay behind me.

Once I was sure I wouldn't be overheard, I crouched down and murmured into a particularly lush bush.

"Nik." Just speaking his name sent a pang through me, but I was glad he could hear everything and would be able to take a message to the others. He could explain my disappearance and the danger hanging over us all.

"I'm assuming you already heard about the islanders and the threat to Tartora. Obviously I have to go, but I'll return as soon as I can. Please tell Amara that I'm not abandoning her or my apprenticeship—I'm just completing the task she assigned me." I hesitated again. "I'll miss you," I finally added on a whisper.

The last three words might have been too quiet for him to hear, but I couldn't bring myself to repeat them. I was talking to a group of leaves right now, and I already felt foolish enough. I intended to be back sooner rather than later, and the rest of the conversation could be done in person—if I hadn't remembered by then exactly why it was a bad idea to have this conversation with Nik.

I hurried toward the ocean much faster than I'd meandered away from it, my cheeks burning. But by the time I reached the communal table, I had calmed enough to appreciate the feast being laid out on it. Every scrap of food that hadn't been packed was ready to be consumed by the excited camp of travelers.

Grey signaled for me to sit beside him yet again, patting my hand in an avuncular way when I took the place he'd indicated. He seemed in good spirits now that our departure had arrived, and the rest of the faces at the table matched his. Ida was on my other side, news of the dawn sail having brought a glow to her face and eyes. She had always been friendly, but she had carried a reserved air along with it. That reserve was gone now, and she seemed positively animated.

I expected her to talk about the island, but as one of those with an elements affinity, her immediate focus seemed to be on the voyage. I tried to nod in the right places, not really following her complicated talk of tides and rips and currents, and the other threats lurking beneath the surface of the ocean. I did gather enough to understand it was a dangerous voyage, and we would be relying heavily on the route charted for us by Grey's mother.

A team of powerful elements mages might have been able to keep the ship safe without the detailed instructions, but the underwater obstructions in this region created a series of narrow passages that became a maze without the correct map. Stumbling on the path to the island would require either great luck or endless perseverance.

"Do we really have to sail at dawn?" I asked, leaning back at the end of dessert with a groan. I had overindulged and was considering asking someone to roll me toward my tent.

"Sorry." Ida's excited smile suggested she didn't really regret our early departure. "It's a matter of tides."

I held up my hand, forestalling any further spiels about our upcoming journey.

"Very well, very well, I believe you." I groaned again. "I shouldn't have eaten so much."

Everyone was starting to rise and drift away from the table, still talking animatedly in pairs or small clumps as they started toward the tents. I also rose, wishing I could enter into everyone else's excitement, and wishing I hadn't eaten so much in an attempt to placate the strange, unsettled feeling at the pit of my stomach.

I was doing the right thing. I knew I was doing the right thing because

Grey was the only chance we had of defeating the islanders. He was the only one who could stop them, and he could do it without bloodshed. So why wasn't I more excited about setting sail?

I concluded it was because I was the only one not sailing toward a new and better life. Or possibly it was merely Phoenix's absence. If the falcon hadn't returned by the end of the night, I would be forced to go without him, a thought that set tears pricking behind my eyes.

I sighed as I pushed the tent flap open and prepared for sleep. Given the early start, I wanted everything ready so I could just roll out of bed and go. Ember got an especially stern speech about being back well before dawn—all while I wished she really could understand me as Amara always joked she could. If I was going to have to sail without Phoenix, I couldn't bear to be without Ember as well.

Finally there was nothing to do but climb onto the pallet. I lay on my back, staring at the canvas overhead and thinking about the people I could still hear moving about the camp. The unsettled feeling still continued to niggle at me—hinting at some truth lurking just beyond my reach—but in spite of it, I fell asleep quickly and slept deeply, undisturbed by dreams.

---

When I woke, I woke abruptly, sitting up and blinking in the near darkness. It took me several heart-pounding seconds to remember where I was and what the day ahead held.

I calmed only slowly, and my heart rate picked up again when I realized Ember had not yet returned. From the way the black around me was starting to creep toward gray, it was nearly time for the camp to stir. She should have been back by now.

I slipped out of bed, glad I had everything prepared. I had known she couldn't understand me, so I shouldn't have expected anything else. All I had to do was find her before full dawn arrived. It shouldn't be an impossible task given the limits of the crevasse that housed the camp.

Out of the tent, there was more gray than black, and my tension rose again. But I forced myself to breathe deeply and remain calm. I would find Ember, and everything would be all right.

I knew my anxiety over her absence was getting away from me, rolling into the queasy feeling from the night before and building to unnecessary heights. But even my power could do nothing to settle my stomach this time, the feeling clearly mental rather than physical.

My mind was convinced something was wrong, and it didn't mean to let me forget it. Which meant I had to find a way to calm it and remind it that nothing disastrous was in the middle of happening after all.

"Ember," I called softly, not wanting to wake anyone from any of the nearby tents. "Ember!"

There was no answer or sound of movement. I moved further into the dense greenery at the back of the crevasse since I didn't think she would be likely to lurk near the ocean.

"Ember." I called again as I got further in.

A rustle of movement among the leaves ahead made me freeze. I peered forward, the increased light allowing me a glimpse of orange fur.

"Ember!" I rushed forward, pushing between overhanging leaves.

Strong hands grabbed me. Before I could protest, I was pulled further into the branches, out of sight of not only the camp but also the path leading to the back of the crevasse.

CHAPTER

# TWENTY-ONE

I stifled a squeal as I was wrenched through the leaves. I could see little against the blur of green rushing past my eyes, but something about the hands felt familiar, keeping me quiet.

When I came to a stop, my arms were being gripped in a rough hold, but the face looking at me held no animosity.

I sucked in a breath at the sight of Nik's familiar features, so welcome in this strange place. Tears welled up and spilled over my lids.

He let go of one of my arms to run a thumb across my cheek, wiping away the moisture.

"Delphine," he said in a rough voice that was half angry, half pained. "What's wrong? Did he hurt you?"

I gurgled a laugh, shaking my head. "I'm just happy to see you." I threw my arms around his waist and buried my face in his chest, making him rock back.

He froze for a moment and then his arms came up cautiously around me, gently rubbing my back.

"He didn't touch you?" His voice was low and gravelly in my ear.

"Everyone has been extremely nice, actually." I managed to pry myself away from him, wishing I could hold on forever but already embarrassed at my display.

"*Nice?*"

I nodded. "It's not at all like we were thinking. Grey isn't like we were thinking. I guess you won't have talked to Miranda yet, but hopefully she's met up with Amara by now, so the rest of them will know—"

"Grey isn't like we were thinking." The repeated words sounded different in Nik's hard voice, like an accusation instead of a reassurance.

He grabbed my arms again, his eyes running over my face, as if searching for answers there. I tried not to think about how I probably looked, managing a weak chuckle.

"You're not going to find any hidden bruises, Nik. No one has offered me a harsh word, let alone a raised hand."

The thought of Grey berating the youth ran uncomfortably through my mind, but I pushed it aside. It was true no one had treated me that way.

But my words did nothing to soften Nik's expression. I frowned, doubt creeping in.

"You did hear everything, didn't you? You know why I have to help Grey."

"Help him? Is that what you were talking about when you said you were going somewhere?" His grip tightened, his eyes narrowing. "What hold does Grey have over you, Delphine? Have you found out what's causing the blight? If you're not a prisoner, why didn't you come back to me?"

His words still sounded harsh, angry, but I caught a trace of vulnerability behind the last question.

My heart softened as I realized he hadn't heard the whole story. He had been waiting all this time, confused and worried.

I smiled up at him. "Thank you for coming. I'm so happy to have a chance to see you again. And now you can take the full story back to the others."

"Delphine." There was a warning note in his voice. "Why do you keep talking about leaving?"

I grimaced. "We were wrong about Grey. I'm not saying he's a wonderful person, but he's not the cause of Tartora's problems. He's trying to fix them." I quickly explained how the islanders were behind both the blight and the storm and about Grey's plans to stop the war before it could launch.

Nik looked sufficiently concerned, but his face lacked the shock I expected. Instead his frown grew deeper and deeper.

"Grey told you this spiel, and so you decided you would leave us all without a word, get on his boat, and just sail away!" His voice rose slightly with each word, until the volume made me flinch.

I glanced over my shoulder, frowning into the lightening sky.

"Hush, not so loud. Of course I wasn't doing it without a word." I looked significantly at the tree beside us. "I thought you could hear everything."

Nik groaned. "Delphine! My ability has limits. And it certainly can't hear anything happening inside a closed house. I'm using root systems, remember?"

I winced. I had wondered about that, but then I'd forgotten again, caught up in the urgency of Grey's news.

"At least I came out here and sent you a message." I pointed at a nearby bush.

Nik laughed, looking as if the sound was reluctantly pulled out of him. "Is that why that was so loud and clear?"

I flushed. "I wanted to make sure you heard."

"Well you did a good job of tipping my worry into panic. I was already preparing to come when Phoenix showed up."

"Phoenix?" I peered into the surrounding trees, nearly bursting into tears when I saw the falcon perched on a nearby branch. "I thought he'd abandoned me!"

"I thought all kinds of terrible things when he showed up," Nik said grimly. "You have no idea how hard it was to wait until dark to start moving, or to wait for you to emerge once I arrived. I was about ready to start tearing apart tents looking for you."

Affection welled up inside me, and I put a hand on his cheek. He sucked in a breath in response to the touch, and I let my hand rest there for a second before dropping back to my side.

"I'm glad you didn't. That might have been a bit hard to explain." I chuckled.

"Thankfully I didn't need to. But other people are up and moving about now. We might need to stay hidden here until after the ship has left."

I nodded. "Yes, you should be safe enough here. And after we've left, you can move about freely."

"We?" He grabbed my arms again. "What are you talking about? You can't go with them!"

I shook my head. "Nik! Didn't you hear a word I said? I have to go. The whole of Tartora is in danger!"

"Delphine." He sounded dangerous, driven to the edge of desperation, although I couldn't understand why my words were having no impact on him. "I am not letting you get on that ship."

"Nik—" I tried again, but he cut me off.

"Think about what you're saying Delphine. Even if we assume that everything Grey said is true—that the islanders are the cause of all this and that he's the heir of their deposed leader—do you really think they're just going to bow the knee when he arrives unannounced on their shores?"

"It is true," I said, but my brow creased as I tried to remember the explanation for his question. I couldn't seem to think of a logical one, even though I *knew* they would accept Grey's leadership.

"*How* do you know?" Nik pressed on. "What evidence did Grey provide?"

I stared at him, unable to answer.

"I know healers can sense lies," Nik went on, "but you know Grey is a master at getting around that. He must have worded his story in a deceptive way. There are just too many holes in it for it to be true. If the islanders have been living on that island for a century, why are they suddenly attacking Tartora now? And if all Grey knows about his heritage are his mother's dying words, how, exactly, does he know so much about the islanders and what they're doing?" His voice tightened along with his hold until it grew so firm I winced. "And, most of all, why does he need you, especially? If Grey is going to overthrow the island's leadership peacefully, why does he need more than one powerful healer? If his story is true, you can stay right here with me, and Tartora will be saved, regardless."

"No." I shook my head. "Grey needs me to be able to save everyone. I'm essential."

"Delphine." Nik shook me slightly, his words hard-edged and his eyes terrified. "What has he done to you? Do you even hear yourself?"

"I..." I started, only to stop and frown. The roiling was back in my belly, but I still couldn't put words to any of it. "I'm sorry, Nik. I guess I'm not explaining it well. But please believe me. I'm certain about this."

Nik's desperate grip slowly relaxed, growing gentle. His hands ran down to my wrists and then back to my shoulders.

"I don't know what I mean to you, Delphine, but I'm begging you. Snap out of this madness. You cannot get on that ship."

"Nik." I looked at him, my eyes sad and pleading. "Think of Tartora."

"No!" The word was sharp, his eyes blazing now. "I'm thinking of *you*, Delphine. You cannot do this. I won't let you." His grip tightened again, and it flashed through my mind that he meant to hold me captive here until the ship had sailed.

But instead he pulled me closer and lowered his head, pressing his lips against mine. When I didn't resist, he pulled me closer again, one hand reaching up to cup the back of my head while the other wrapped around me.

Briefly his lips left mine, hovering half a breath away so he could whisper against them.

"Please, Delphine. I don't know what he's done to you, but please break free." He gave a growl. "I won't let him have you."

The last words seemed wrenched from him, and he immediately pressed his lips back to mine, more forcefully this time.

I sank into his arms, my roiling stomach a discordant note from the joy soaring through me at his embrace. Surrounded by Nik, breathing him in and kissing him back, it was hard to remember my earlier sense of urgency. What reason could there be to ever leave this moment?

"Delphine!" Nik pulled back again, his low, urgent voice not leaving me alone. "Please! Break free!"

I reached up to wind my fingers through his hair and pull his head back down to mine. He groaned as he came, his hold tightening as his lips once again crushed against mine.

Nik cared about me, that much was obvious. He claimed to care about me more than the entire kingdom. And standing here in his arms, I knew—down to my bones—that the same couldn't be said of Grey.

My certainty about Grey cracked, snakes of doubt slithering into the gaps. The spinning in my stomach surged, reaching up my throat. It had no place in this moment, and I reached for it with my power. No one belonged in this moment but Nik and me, and I would drive out the lingering whispers of Grey.

It had been months since I'd had need of my wall, but as soon as I decided to drive Grey out, it sprang back into being as easily as if I'd only dismantled it yesterday. It had been the first skill I perfected with my power, and the memory of it was strongly ingrained.

I let it push through me, driving the teeming discomfort with it, succeeding where my regular healing efforts had failed. In its wake, my mind and body felt light and free.

I stretched onto my tiptoes, leaning further into the kiss, finally able to focus on nothing more than the assurance of Nik's presence. But even as my feelings swelled, my mind sprang back to life. I pulled away, panting and staring at Nik.

It took him a moment to register my expression, his breathing ragged and eyes unfocused. But as soon as he absorbed my face, he snapped to attention.

"What?" he asked. "What is it?"

"I think it might all have been lies." I shook my head, confused. "Or some of it any way."

He fell back a step, running a hand through his hair and giving a strangled laugh.

"That's what I've been trying to tell you."

I shook my head. "No, you don't understand. I was *sure* it was the truth." I held his gaze, willing him to understand what I was saying. "I've never been so certain of anything in my life. I was uncomfortable about it the whole time, but every time I tried to think about the issue it was within the context of absolute unshakable certainty. I kept trying to think around my discomfort, but my thoughts couldn't reach a sensible conclusion when I was so sure Grey was the only one who could stop the islanders, and that he would do it without bloodshed—even that, for some reason he *needed* me there to succeed." My voice was trembling. "It's complete nonsense, but I couldn't see that."

Nik frowned, his demeanor growing serious as he tried to process my words. "So what changed?"

I flushed, thinking of his kiss, but it hadn't been the kiss alone. The kiss had only inspired me to...

"My wall!" I cried, realization hitting. "Back in Caltor, when Grey tried to use his healing power to attack me, I used my wall to push his power out of my body before it could harm me. I think I just did something similar. I couldn't shake that uncomfortable feeling, and I wanted to push it—and him—out of me, so I used my wall again. It's the first time I've used it here. I haven't even thought of it since I've never felt attacked."

An entirely different kind of discomfort welled inside me. Was that why Grey had been so unexpectedly pleasant ever since I arrived? The reason he let Miranda go without a murmur? He knew about my wall. Had he worried that it would protect me against—But my thinking stalled at that point. Protect me against what? What exactly had Grey done to me?

As a healer I could sense a lie—that was an innate part of my ability, one every healer possessed. So how had Grey fooled me so thoroughly? He hadn't just gotten away with a lie, he had utterly convinced me of a false truth. And not a single part of the whole business made sense.

"Did he actually lie to you directly?" Nik asked. "I've never heard of someone being able to fool a healer's ability to truth test unless they were using slippery words and evasive talk."

"I...I don't know." I frowned at the leaves, not really seeing them. "I can't explain how he did it. I just know how I felt before and how I feel now. Nik," I looked across at him, horror filling me. "I was just going to get on that ship!"

A muscle jumped in Nik's jaw. "I'm aware."

But now that the wheels were turning in my head, they wouldn't stop, racing forward too fast for me to follow. Everything that had happened in the last couple of days had been false, built on a mirage I still couldn't fathom. And if that was true for me, why wouldn't it be true for the others living in this strange oasis?

I thought of Ida, speaking fiercely of what she could endure for her new life, and of the boy who smashed the barrel, flipping immediately from browbeaten to excited at the mention of our departure. Was everything they'd built their hopes on lies?

I tried to think it through, make sense of it. There had to be an island—that much had to be true. It was the only reason for Grey to be out here, building his ship. And someone other than Grey had unleashed a blight and a killer storm. I had examined every person in this camp, and even combined they didn't have the power to have done either one. The blight and storm were the work of plants and elements mages. They weren't here, so they had to be out there on the island. So perhaps what he'd promised his followers wasn't an illusion at all.

The next logical step took my breath away. I had come here utterly prejudiced against Grey—a man who had once stabbed me with a dagger. I had come here knowing he was clever and slippery and charming, and yet I had still been fooled by him. And not just fooled but utterly and completely taken in. Grey wasn't just charming. There was something far more insidious at play here, and Grey was about to take that strange ability of his to an island full of powerful and unsuspecting mages—an island he wanted to rule.

Icy cold trickled through me, starting at my crown and working its way down until I could no longer feel any warmth in the pre-dawn air. Grey wasn't going to the island to defeat the threat against Tartora, he was going to take control of it. If he sailed away, it would be to trap more people under his false sway, seeking power and his own little fiefdom.

We had to stop him. I had to stop him. I was at least partially responsible for this mess. I had walked into his trap like a fool. If I had reported back properly once I had answers, there would have been time for the king's forces to arrive and arrest Grey before his ship was completed. But there was no hope of them getting here now. There was barely even time for the two of us to…

The distant sound of activity had been growing louder, but it took on a new tone as I tried to think what to do next. Loud shouts were echoing through the crevasse, and I caught several voices calling about tides as well as others that seemed to be calling my name.

Someone, perhaps Grey himself, had realized I was missing. But would they hold the launch for me and risk missing the tide?

If I charged out now and told them not to sail, no one would listen, and Grey would realize his hold on me had broken. I certainly had no way to physically sabotage the boat.

I looked at Nik, whose eyes were swiveling between the direction of the calls and my face, his eyes calculating and his face set. Nik could destroy a wooden boat. I had seen enough of his power to be confident of that. But how long would it take me to explain my thinking and convince him we needed to expose ourselves? Possibly more time than we had.

Because what happened if we succeeded? Our back up forces were a day's walk away, and we would be surrounded by a settlement of angry, disappointed people. There was every chance Nik would consider the risk too great. He had already said once this morning that he cared more about my safety than the kingdom. He would tell me it was too dangerous.

An even more unsettling thought crossed my mind. Even without the danger, would he want to stop Grey? Would King Marius? The king didn't know Ida and her past pain. He didn't know the horrible, slimy feeling of being duped and deluded and not even knowing it. What if he saw a threat—the islander mages—and a solution that required no risk from any of his own people?

Wasn't that the sort of bargain rulers made all the time? Trading the comfort of others for the comfort of their own people, and placing their kingdom's current security above the risk that they were creating a threat for the future?

All I saw was danger—the danger of handing Grey power large enough to destroy a kingdom. But it was possible King Marius would see something entirely different. What if he sent him on his way with his blessing?

"Delphine! Delphine! Where are you?" The cries were getting closer. I had to act now. There was no more time for thinking.

"Nik." I met his eyes, all my feelings for him bubbling up and filling my face.

He saw my expression and stilled, reaching to take my hands when I held them out.

"I'm sorry," I said, anguish creeping in.

He stiffened, but it was too late. The skin of his hands was warm against mine. I sent my power into him, and he collapsed into immediate, unnatural sleep.

He dropped in slow motion, crumpling downward. I only just managed to break his fall, preventing his head, at least, from hitting the ground. There was no time to place him in a more comfortable position, though. I had to get out of here before the searchers found us.

Blundering back through the greenery, I called loudly as I ran.

"I'm here! I'm here! Sorry!"

I stumbled straight into the arms of a small group of searchers, all of them looking tense and irritated.

"Sorry," I repeated, reaching for an excuse for my absence. I didn't find one, but it didn't matter. None of them cared enough to ask, all their focus on getting us aboard the boat.

I hiked my pack over my shoulder and let myself be swept up the gangplank and onto the deck of the ship. Most people were already aboard, but a few other searchers streamed on after us until at last the visible parts of the crevasse were still and silent.

Grey stood beside the wheel, annoyance on his face as he watched the final stragglers. I looked up at him with what I hoped was an appropriately apologetic expression, and he gave me a nod. Apparently I'd succeeded.

I was struggling to catch my breath, though, still swept up in the suddenness of my decision. I'd had no time to think it through and make a measured choice. I'd simply seen one way forward and acted on it. I still didn't even know for sure if I'd be able to stop Grey.

But my instincts told me that, for some unknown reason, I was essential to Grey's plan. His behavior had certainly seemed to suggest it. So if I was necessary for whatever he was planning, then it also followed that I was exactly the person who could most successfully sabotage it. I just needed to continue to play the part of a duped fool and wait for my opportunity.

A shiver ran through me. Alone. I had to wait alone.

All the way here, I'd always known that Nik was in the shadows protecting me. Even when I'd gone to Grey's camp, I'd been aware that he was nearby, tracking my movements. And I'd had Ember and Phoenix with me, as well.

My earlier panic after waking and finding Ember still gone hit me all over again. I had never intended to board this boat without my loyal companions. But neither could I regret leaving them to stand guard over Nik's unconscious body. I was alone, but at least I'd chosen it for myself. He'd been abandoned.

The boat lurched and groaned but didn't immediately move away from the shore. Several unhappy glances were sent my way as mutters passed back and forth about tricky passages and missing the opportune moment. But no-one spoke too loudly, and I caught a number of surreptitious glances sent toward Grey.

Strangely, their antagonism bolstered my spirits. It seemed I was right in assuming I was important—important enough to delay the launch and important enough that Grey's followers dared not criticize me too loudly.

Surely that meant I was important enough to destroy Grey's plan from within. I just needed to fool him long enough to do it.

CHAPTER

# TWENTY-TWO

There were fewer women than men among Grey's followers, and we were assigned a large cabin to share. It had bunks built along the walls, as well as hammocks hanging from the center of the room. By the time I found my way there, only one of the hammocks was left unclaimed.

I took it without complaining, already self-conscious about the ill feeling I had accidentally engendered. At least we had finally managed to get underway, and water was foaming around the prow of the ship as we sailed before an unnatural wind.

I would have liked to be on deck, but almost everyone else was there, and they apparently needed more time to forgive my early morning disappearance. Rather than stay where I wasn't welcome, I'd retreated to my cabin. But there I found two girls I'd barely spoken to previously. From the look they gave me, my presence wasn't wanted in the cabin either, so I fled again.

Without anywhere else to go, I ventured deeper into the ship, holding my skirt as I climbed awkwardly through an open trapdoor and down a rough ladder. Setting sail from the middle of the desert, we'd had no livestock to take other than a large collection of chickens. They were all housed on this deck, along with our supply of fresh water in barrels, and a collection of bags and crates.

I greeted the chickens, checking their health for something to do, although their companionship seemed lacking now that I'd become accustomed to Ember and Phoenix's constant presence. When the chickens could no longer hold my attention, I wandered the hold, exploring its nooks and crannies.

Both ends had a closed trapdoor, and I grew curious enough to pull one open. Another ladder led down into a second hold, this one apparently without portholes, given the darkness. I nearly gave up on the idea of further exploration, but two lanterns had been placed next to the trapdoor, inviting use.

After lighting one, I navigated the climb down the ladder one-handed, wondering what I was going to do with my time for the rest of the journey if I was already driven to this on the first day.

The deeper hold had even less of interest than the top one since it lacked the chickens. All I could see in the circle of my light were more bags and crates. But to my surprise, my power caught the presence of another person and two animals, deeper inside the cavernous space. What were they doing lurking down here without a light?

I held onto the edge of the ladder, not quite willing to let go of the sense of escape it provided, even as I held up the lantern and peered into the depths of the cavernous space.

"Is there someone there?" I called, although I already knew the answer. "Are you in trouble?" Perhaps they had somehow lost their light and were stuck here. Given the way we'd lurched through the first part of our passage, someone down here checking on the cargo might have fallen and been injured.

The faint sounds of movement reached my ears as my now-alert senses tracked the person moving closer to me. Why didn't he or she speak? My hold on the ladder tightened, until I noticed further details about the two animals. They weren't chickens escaped from the upper hold or other livestock either. In fact, they felt exactly like a fox and a bird of prey.

"Ember?" I gasped. "Phoenix?"

Orange fur entered the patch of lantern light, Ember trotting daintily forward to lean against my leg. I stared down at her, too astonished to move.

"What are you doing here?"

"I brought them," said a deep voice as a man stepped into the light, a falcon on his shoulder.

"Nik?" My mouth dropped open, and I left it that way, too stupefied to close it. "What are you doing here? *How* are you here?"

He gave me a stern, disapproving look. "Did you really think I was going to let you run off to try to stop Grey alone?"

I grimaced, too guilty to meet his eyes. "I'm sorry that I...There was no time, and I knew you would..."

"Yes, I would have," he said. "This is an inexcusably fool-headed endeavor, Delphine! What would happen if you got yourself into trouble with all your friends an ocean away? Luckily, your little trick wore off as soon as you ran away. It took me a few moments to regain my wits and work out what had happened, so I was too late to stop you, but in the chaos of the departure, I managed to swim out and climb aboard."

"So you've come along as a stowaway?" I asked, as incensed as him. "And that seems like a more sensible choice?"

He shrugged. "It was the only one you left me. I wasn't letting this ship sail away without me—not when you were on board."

"Nik!" I cried in a half-stifled shout, as the full ramifications hit me. "If you're here, who's going to tell the others what we discovered? They'll have no idea of the danger from the island!"

"We'll just have to find a way to get straight back there," Nik said implacably, showing no remorse.

"Ugh, you're impossible!" I muttered.

He stepped closer, but I noticed he remained just out of my reach. Guilt stirred. He had trusted me, and I had betrayed that trust.

"I really am sorry," I whispered. "I was making decisions under pressure, and....well, it wasn't my finest moment."

He stayed where he was, a silent statue in the flickering light, assessing my face with his eyes. I tried to look strong and trustworthy, while inside I remembered every time he had touched me—grabbing my wrist, cupping my cheek, taking my hand, touching his lips to mine. It had never struck me before just how much trust it showed to touch a healer, especially a new healer in training.

Had I just destroyed Nik's trust?

His face softened, and he stepped closer, coming fully into the circle of my lantern.

"You're right that you shouldn't have done it," he said. "But it's too late to worry about that. We're both here now, and what's more important is what we're going to do next."

I looked upward, into the hold above, an obvious fear hitting me.

"You've just stowed away on a ship with multiple healers!" I hissed, letting go of the ladder to grab his arm and push him further away from the trapdoor. "Someone is going to sense you down here!"

He shrugged, as if he'd already considered the risk and dismissed it as insubstantial.

"They aren't mage level strength which means they can't sense much of anything without physical touch. Their reach won't stretch this far."

"What about Grey?"

"Grey isn't the type to be climbing up and down ladders fetching supplies. He'll be on deck or in the captain's cabin, and from there he'll be feeling people all over the ship. There's no reason for him to take any particular note of someone being in the hold. You're the only one likely to discover me." A smile spread over his face. "And I was hoping you would—sooner rather than later, although you exceeded even my expectations on that one."

"Nik." I rolled my eyes, but I was also laughing.

He stalked closer, his eyes dropping to my lips. "I think we have some unfinished business from last time we talked."

"Nik," I protested again, putting my free hand up to fend him off even as he slipped an arm around my waist. "Be serious."

"I am serious. Down here in the pitch dark, wedged between a sack of potatoes and a barrel of flour, there's not a lot to keep my attention. So I've had plenty of opportunity to think about exactly where we left things." He leaned closer, only stopping when Phoenix ruffled his feathers disapprovingly.

Nik threw him a sideways look that was half amused, half irritated. "If you don't like it, there are plenty of other perches down here."

I put the lantern down so I could use both hands to push him firmly away.

"We need a plan. An actual plan. Not this." I gave him a fierce look, and he nodded meekly, his posture not matching his expression.

I rolled my eyes and crossed my arms. "We're here now—which I freely acknowledge is due to my own foolishness, at least where I'm concerned. I take no responsibility for you following me and compounding all our problems."

"Aren't you even a little glad to see me?" he asked.

I glared at him, hoping it covered my true emotions. Because I wasn't ready to confess to the enormous rush of relief I'd felt the moment I realized he was with me. And he'd even brought Ember and Phoenix. I'd thought I was alone, but I wasn't, and the feeling of lightness was incredible. But those were selfish emotions. I shouldn't want Nik to be here in this trouble with me, and I certainly didn't want Amara, Hayes, and the others to be left with no idea what had happened to us.

"How I feel is irrelevant," I said shortly. "What matters is what we're going to do next."

Nik looked disappointed at my words, and a pang shot through me. Did he really care so much? It was harder and harder to deny it to myself, but I had no idea what to do with his devotion or with my own messy, complicated return feelings. He was both an outcast and a royal prince, and neither of those identities made a future with him possible.

But before I could think of anything to say, Nik's expression hardened, his manner becoming businesslike.

"Clearly Grey found some way to influence your mind which shouldn't be possible. There's not much we can do while we're stuck on the ship in the middle of the ocean, but at least you can try to find out more information from Grey."

"Do you think he'll tell me?" I asked uncertainly, but even as I said the words, I suspected it wouldn't be as difficult as I was envisioning. Grey wanted to use me for something, and to do that, he was eventually going to have to explain what that something was.

"The fox will have to stay down here with me," Nik said. "Too many people saw you come aboard and know she wasn't with you. But you can take the falcon. He'll need a chance to stretch his wings, and he could easily have flown out to you before the ship sailed too far out."

He stepped closer again, but only to align his shoulder with mine so Phoenix could hop across to his favorite position. The falcon did so with alacrity, and I leaned my cheek against the softness of his feathered body. Feeling his weight on my shoulder again made everything else seem a little less frightening and uncertain.

It was still difficult to climb up the ladder, leaving Nik and Ember in the dark, though. I'd hugged Ember close to my chest, whispering all the reasons she had to stay behind, but as always, it was impossible to know how much she understood. At least she accepted my departure silently, watching me go and standing close to Nik.

It felt a little better to know they had each other, but it was tempting to leave the lantern. Nik had refused, saying that a light in the deep hold might attract attention, but it was hard to believe he was really all right without one.

When the trapdoor banged closed, I told myself not to be fanciful and imagine there was any note of finality in the sound. I would be back as soon as I had something to report, and Nik would be fine in the meantime. The ship had been packed in enough of a rush that there were bags, boxes, crates, and barrels everywhere. I'd even seen a number of piles of planks that had no purpose I could fathom. Even if someone came down here for supplies, Nik could easily conceal the two of them among the chaos of jumbled cargo.

I didn't stop climbing until I'd made it all the way up to the main deck. Now that I had Phoenix with me, I couldn't be a coward and skulk inside the whole time.

The crowd had dispersed, although plenty of Grey's followers were scurrying around carrying out the various tasks of sailors.

I considered offering to assist but decided I would be more hindrance than help. I knew nothing about ships, having never been on one before.

Instead, I tucked myself against the railing where I would be out of the way and let my eyes roam over the horizon. The ocean went on and on, no matter what direction I looked, its enormity striking me all over again now that I was out in the middle of it.

The ship—which had seemed large and solid while anchored to Grey's simple dock—felt small and weak in the face of such a powerful force. A wave hit the prow, making me rock and grab for the rail. It didn't take much to imagine what it would be like to be out here in the middle of a storm.

I glanced up at the wheel, Grey still beside it, although he was leaving the actual steering to someone with an elements affinity. Had his claims about the storm been true? Had it really come from the island? It seemed logical, and if it had, it meant the islanders were ruthless and callous. We had to think of a way to stop not only Grey but the islanders as well.

I gripped the rail until my knuckles turned white, overwhelmed by the task ahead. My eyes stared blankly across the expanse of dark blue, the white tops of waves breaking up the monotony where the wind tugged at the water.

The flap of wings drew my eye as Phoenix glided back toward me, angling himself to land on the rail at my side.

"I see your friend followed you." Grey's voice came from behind me, and I barely stopped myself from stiffening. When had he come down from the quarterdeck?

I turned slowly. "Phoenix is very loyal."

Grey smiled, although the expression now sent a shiver down my back.

"It will take us several days to reach the island," he said. "And I want to put our time onboard to good use."

I raised my eyebrows. "What did you have in mind?"

"I'm hoping we can each teach the other a new skill." His voice was light, but the intensity in his eyes suggested this wasn't a minor matter to him.

"New skill?" It didn't take much acting to look confused. "I'm only an apprentice. What skill could I teach you?"

He leaned one hand against the rail, looking out over the ocean. I examined his profile, wondering if it could really be this easy. The ease of it all made me uneasy after the way things had turned out in the crevasse. What fresh deception was he preparing?

He abruptly turned his head, fixing me with his startling green eyes. "I've been fascinated with you ever since we met, Delphine. It's not often I meet someone with an ability that surprises me."

Unease filled me as I realized the obvious—Grey wanted to know about my wall. But I pretended ignorance.

"Me?" I kept my reply short, avoiding any comment that might have the taste of a lie.

"The first time we met, when I tried to test you, I couldn't reach you." He leaned forward, the eagerness in his voice and eyes betraying him. "And then again in the warehouse, when I sent my power into you, you pushed me out."

I drew back, letting one hand float to the place where he had stabbed me.

"The warehouse..." I put all my uncertainty into my voice.

Grey winced before quickly pasting his smile back in place. He took my other hand in both of his, fixing me with an earnest look that struck me as a lot less earnest than it had back on land.

"Let me apologize again for that. It was a terrible error in judgment and a shame that stays with me." He bowed his head in false contrition. "Of course, I never meant you any permanent harm since I knew you would be able to heal yourself."

I left my hand in his, blinking at his lowered head. I didn't feel any of the strange, unquestioning, unthinking certainty of before, just the normal sensations that came from my ability. Grey didn't need to use any special ability because he was telling the truth.

I sorted back through his words. He hadn't actually said he felt guilty. He'd called it an error in judgment and spoken of shame. Was he ashamed of having inflicted pain on another person, or was he ashamed with himself for letting his emotions lead him into a poor strategic decision?

Somehow I felt sure it was the latter. If nothing else, I was getting a first-hand lesson in how to manipulate words in order to avoid a healer's truth telling sense.

"Thank you," I said, thinking of the future value of the lesson in order to give my words the ring of truth.

When he looked back up, he was beaming. "I'm not surprised to find you so gracious."

He let the words stand as an apparent compliment, although I could guess the true meaning behind them. He still thought me in thrall to him, and that knowledge was far more welcome than any of his compliments could ever be.

"I don't know if I can teach someone else how to make a wall," I said. "I've never tried before."

Grey frowned. "Is it difficult?"

I tipped my head to the side, honestly considering his words. "Not for me. But I don't really understand how I do it. I created it almost as soon as I was activated, so at the time I was driven entirely by instinct." I had no desire to help Grey, but I also didn't want to make him suspicious. "Master Clay told me he tried to do it and couldn't."

I met Grey's face openly, keeping my features calm. He would sense the truth of my words, and hopefully they would help prepare him for his eventual failure. I didn't want him blaming me, but neither was I going to put effort into teaching him.

Giving false lessons to a healer turned out to be no easy task, however. There was only so much prevarication I could manage in answer to direct, detailed questions. And what I had thought might be an hour's lesson between Grey's other tasks turned out to be a marathon effort.

Grey might have taken the captain's cabin for himself, but he wasn't actually involved in sailing the ship. Given he was a healer, it made sense, but I had still expected him to be up on deck playing the part.

Instead, he shut us both in his cabin for the better part of two days as he tried again and again to recreate my wall. We didn't even break to eat with the others, instead taking brief breaks to eat the food that was delivered by one of his followers.

The cabin was almost as large as the one which housed all the females onboard, so there was plenty of room for us, but it contained few other luxuries. Apparently there had been barely time to make the basic furniture and no time for extra ornamentation. It made no difference to our efforts, although I soon grew bored of plain brown walls, plain brown floor, and plain brown roof.

We weren't alone, at least, since Grey brought in a steady stream of his followers, usually one at a time. All of them had a healing ability, and he had them attempt to make a wall as well as attempt to breach mine while he gripped my other arm, using his power to watch the interplay of our abilities.

Whether he tried to push his healing power into me himself or watched someone else attempt it, he couldn't find a way past my wall. And when we reversed roles, none of them could put up a wall to keep me out.

"Is this an ability unique to you?" Grey stared at me hungrily as the sun approached the ocean on the second day at sea. "How can no-one else do it? I understand the rest of them failing, given their weaker seeds, but even I can't..." He trailed off, his brow creased in a scowl.

As time had worn on without anyone making any progress, both my confidence and my curiosity had grown. Why were they all unable to replicate what seemed an easy feat to me? Faced with Grey's specific and repeated questions, I soon began to think about it in earnest. But even when I was trying to be helpful, I could think of no way to explain it.

"I had no idea it would be so difficult," I said. "I really don't know what's so different about me."

Grey stared at me, clearly frustrated, but unable to claim I was lying to him. He had failed, but he couldn't blame me. And from the way he was reining himself in, he wasn't ready to risk scaring me by unleashing his true anger and frustration. So far, I had been the only teacher, but he had spoken of both of us learning a new skill, so he still had other uses for me.

"What about my new skill?" I asked. "You said you were going to teach me something as well."

"Ah yes." Grey forced a smile. "It's clearly useless to continue our attempts at the wall for now, so it's time to switch focus." He glanced out the window at the setting sun. "However, it's getting late, and we're both tired. Let's come to it fresh in the morning."

I forced a smile and nodded, although I could barely contain my impatience. But as soon as I stepped out of his cabin, I realized what the early freedom meant. The night before, we had stopped our futile efforts so late that I hadn't had enough energy to do anything but fall into my hammock and snatch a few hours' sleep before starting over again. But now I had time.

I hurried for the open trapdoor that led to the upper hold, swerving away at the last minute when I saw two others approaching. I pretended an interest in the view out the nearest porthole until they had walked on, leaving the passage clear.

Half-tumbling down the ladder, I peered around in the dimness of evening. Was I alone down here?

A quick sweep with my power told me I was, so I hurried across to the closed trapdoor that led further down. Grabbing a lantern, my fingers trembled with my haste as I struggled to light it.

As soon as the flame blossomed, I pulled up the door and started down the ladder. By the time my feet reached the deck, Nik had appeared, Ember at his side.

"Delphine!" His voice was ragged, and he looked exhausted. He swept me into a tight embrace, speaking into my hair. "You're all right."

I let him hold me for a moment before pulling back. For a second, he resisted my efforts before finally letting me go with a low groan.

"Do you know how close I was to sneaking out of here? I thought you would be back much earlier!"

"Are you all right?" I asked, sudden concern filling me. "Are you hungry? I never even thought of bringing you food! I thought—"

"That I was surrounded by stores of food?" He shook his head, impatient. "I don't need you to bring me anything—I just need to know you're safe."

"Oh. Sorry." But the more I thought about it, the deeper my frown grew. "You were thinking of coming out of hiding? Are you serious? You can't do that!"

He ran a hand through his hair, the lantern deepening the shadows on his face and making it look like he hadn't slept at all.

"There are no networks of roots here. I can't hear what's happening to you, and it's driving me to distraction."

I sighed. "You just have to trust me. I can look after myself."

He closed his eyes for a moment before opening them and grimacing. "I know. But there's not a lot down here to focus on instead."

I wrapped my hand around his arm. "I'll try to get down here more often. I promise. But I've spent the last two days locked in Grey's cabin, so I haven't had a chance to sneak away."

He stiffened immediately, his muscles leaping beneath my arm.

"He had you locked up?" From his growl he was ready to go find Grey right now.

"Not literally." I rolled my eyes. "But I'm trying not to raise his suspicions, remember? He's been trying to learn how to make a wall *this entire time*." I groaned dramatically in remembered exhaustion.

"You mean he can't do it?" The news distracted Nik from his dark emotions. "Is it so difficult?"

I shrugged helplessly. "It doesn't seem like it is to me, but apparently other people find it impossible. I have no idea why. But with his ability, I couldn't lie and give him bad instructions. By the end I was doing my truthful best, but we still got nowhere."

"Good," Nik said savagely. "The fewer weapons Grey has, the better."

I nodded my agreement, but I couldn't put the matter aside so easily. Why could I do this thing that no one else could do? It didn't make any sense.

"Did you learn anything else?" Nik asked. "Do you have any idea how Grey fooled you so completely?"

"Not yet. But I think I might get some answers tomorrow. We're due for another lesson in the morning, and this time Grey says he has something to teach me."

CHAPTER

# TWENTY-THREE

"I'm sorry, say that again?" I stared at Grey, too shocked to think about what emotion I should be pretending to display.

"Incredible, isn't it!" His eyes were shining, as if it had been difficult to hold in this secret, and it was a relief to finally talk about it. "It was the first thing my mother taught me after she activated me and taught me control."

His mother? The words pierced my shock, bringing confusion. But for once Grey wasn't guarding every word, and he didn't notice his slip or my reaction to it.

Grey had previously said his mother died just after they washed up on the mainland, but his current claim that she had been his activator had the ring of truth to it. When he'd told me about her death, it hadn't been my own ability that had perceived his words as truth but rather...

My thoughts tangled and stuttered, still struggling to take in Grey's revelation.

"How...how is that possible?" I asked. "You're telling me that anyone with a strong enough healing seed could learn a skill like that, and yet no one has discovered it except those mages out on the island?"

"They discovered it before the island," he said. "Sometimes new developments only spring from desperate necessity. I suppose this particular skill needed a disaster as large as the destruction of an entire kingdom to be discovered. How do you think my ancestors escaped the invaders a century ago—and without anyone knowing about it?"

I massaged my temples. "So, you're telling me that as a healer I can force someone to believe a lie? Any lie at all?"

"Not any lie." Grey sounded regretful. "The certainty will fade in the face of direct evidence to the contrary. For instance, if a traveler gets told they stayed in a red house in the last town they visited, they'll believe it for the rest of their life. But if you tell someone the house they currently live in is red, they'll shake off the mesmerization in a day because they can see with their own eyes that it isn't true."

I considered his words against the examples I'd seen. Miranda had become confused as soon as I showed up, starting to question everything and quickly agreeing to leave. Since Grey had mesmerized her into believing no one from her old life cared about her or wanted her back, that made sense. The simple fact of my arrival had provided evidence that broke the mesmerizing effect.

In my case, there had been no direct evidence available to me about the islanders or their intentions, so I'd had no way to shake off the false beliefs. I'd only managed it because Nik had made me doubt Grey himself strongly enough that I used my wall.

I shook my head at my own foolishness. I should have been using the wall since the moment of my arrival instead of being lulled into a false sense of security by Grey's manner. I had thought that if Grey made physical contact and tried to push his power into me, I would feel it and be able to take action, but it had been so subtly done, I'd missed it completely.

A new thought struck me. "Can you mesmerize someone without touching them, like with truth telling?"

"Unfortunately not. It's the greatest flaw to the skill."

I held in my look of disgust at his disappointment over the limitation. Instead, I tried to remember if Grey had touched me before telling me the story about his history. He must have, but I couldn't recall the exact details of our interaction.

"It's especially a pain if the mesmerization needs to be refreshed," he added.

"Refreshed? I thought it would last forever if it wasn't directly refuted by physical evidence to the contrary."

"You've studied with the law keepers, haven't you?" He sounded impatient. "There are shades of gray between no evidence at all and indisputable physical evidence. With enough circumstantial evidence, the mesmerization can start to fade. That's the mistake I made with the last batch of recruits." His eyes darkened. "I got arrogant and didn't refresh the initial mesmerization. I tried to gather too large a group before returning to the desert, and I lost control of the situation."

From the vitriol in his voice, Grey didn't like losing control.

Had he reinforced his mesmerization on me? I thought back over our interactions, remembering several occasions when he'd found a casual reason to touch me.

I suppressed a shudder, feeling a sudden desire to scrub every inch of my skin. How was I ever going to bring myself to let him touch me again?

"So this is what makes the islanders so dangerous," I said, remembering that I was supposed to be pretending they were my main worry, not Grey. But even as I said the words, they didn't make sense. "But so far they've attacked with a blight on our crops and a storm. Those must have been the work of plants and elements mages and doesn't have anything to do with mesmerizing."

"Doesn't it?" Grey looked amused. "I'll admit, the storm was the work of their elements mages, but are you so sure about the blight?"

"Healing power doesn't interact with plants," I said, still sure of that, even in the face of Grey's revelation.

He smiled slowly, the expression unsettling. "How do you know there ever was a blight?"

"Of course there was! I've seen the aftermath of it myself all across northern Tartora."

"You saw a field infected with blight?" He raised both eyebrows.

I shifted on my feet, impatient. "I saw the fields burned by the Guild mages. You said mesmerizing doesn't work if someone can see the truth with their own eyes, so there must have been blight. This ability doesn't allow you to control someone's actions and force them to burn a field."

Grey chuckled. "Do you really think you can't control someone through manipulation?" He shook his head at my apparent naïveté. "The islanders have a hundred years of practice, remember? Although even I had to salute the elegance of their approach in this instance."

I stared at him, and he instantly modified his expression. "A terrible thing, of course."

His words rang false in my mind. Grey didn't care about the lost crops or the ruined farmers. But I couldn't call him out on it. I wanted all the answers he could give me.

"Are you telling me they manipulated those farmers into burning their own crops?"

Grey frowned. "I think that would be beyond the power of mesmerization. As I said, elegant thinking was required in this case. I tracked them across the kingdom, and from what I've been able to piece together, it was a process of several steps. First, the islanders mesmerized the farmers into believing they'd seen blight and that they should contact the plants affinity at the Guild and stay away from the infected fields in the meantime. When the mages arrived, they found nothing, of course. But the islanders intercepted them on their return journey and mesmerized them into believing they'd not only seen blight but also burned the infected fields."

"But you said the farmers wouldn't have..." I trailed off as I realized the truth. "The islanders were the ones to burn the fields."

Grey nodded. "That is the conclusion I've come to. They burned the fields, and then convinced both the farmers and the Guild mages that the Guild were the ones to do it due to the blight. It's standard procedure in such a case, so it's easy to believe. And once the fields were burned, there was no evidence to break the illusion, so they'll go on thinking it forever."

"There was never any blight..." I shook my head as I fully absorbed the enormity of that.

There was no mysterious blight that couldn't be fixed by the Guild. For a moment I felt relief, but it didn't take long to realize that the effects on the kingdom were the same. There might not be a blight, but the unrest and food shortage were very real impacts of the deception.

It was hard to contain my emotions, but I had to try because Grey's initial lack of caution seemed to have worn off, his eyes tracking me more closely than before. He was worried this news was going to shake me enough to throw off his own mesmerizations.

"Teach me." I thrust out my arm, inviting his touch, although it went against every one of my instincts. "Teach me how to mesmerize."

Grey's eyes lit up, and I knew I'd made the right move. It was easy for him to believe this reaction because it aligned with his own. I was sure he'd been eager to try mesmerizing ever since he first heard of it.

Grey put his hand on my arm, his power snaking inside me. But it was a light, subtle touch that I almost missed since it made no attempt to connect with the various central systems of my body.

"Your tent back in the crevasse was such a beautiful blue," he said, almost casually, and I found myself nodding in agreement.

I could see the gorgeous, deep, peacock blue in my mind's eye. Grey dropped his hold of my arm, but I ignored him, distracted by thoughts of my old tent. But despite the harmless beauty of the image, something about it tickled at my mind, unsettling me.

I gasped as I remembered the feeling and where I'd felt it before. Instinctively I pulled up my wall, pushing Grey's power out of my body and purging the falsity from my mind. My tent had been ordinary canvas.

As soon as I was free of the grip of Grey's mesmerization, I remembered that I wasn't supposed to be able to free myself. I looked quickly up at Grey, but thankfully he'd released his hold before my instincts took over and had no idea what I'd done.

He smiled with satisfaction as he thrust a plain canvas bag into my hands. "This is the canvas we had access to back in camp," he said. "We used it to make a number of bags as well as all the tents. Your tent was never blue."

I stared down at the canvas in my hands, pretending to be struck by his words. After a carefully judged moment, I gaped up at him.

"I was expecting you to do it, and yet I still…"

He smiled broadly. "Powerful, isn't it? Just being on your guard isn't enough."

I shook my head as I remembered how it had felt. "I could remember the tent as blue! I could see it in my mind! How is that possible? How did you plant an image in my mind along with the words?"

Grey shook his head. "I didn't do that. You did."

"Me?"

"Our brains are incredibly clever—too clever for their own good, in this instance. Once you believe something implicitly, your brain cooperates and creates memories that match. That's where the power of mesmerization comes from. Once those false memories have taken root, it takes a lot to dislodge them."

"Incredible," I murmured, despite myself.

There was no denying how horrifying this ability was, but it was equally impossible to deny the curiosity coursing through me. I wanted to understand how it was done.

I didn't try to suppress the feeling, instead letting it show on my face and in my eyes. Grey smiled at my expression, convinced I felt the same way about this as he did. Sticking his head out the door of his cabin, he called for someone to join us.

At first I was just a silent observer, allowing my power to ride along with his as he convinced this new person that their tent back in the camp had been blue. And when he did it again to the next person, and then the next, I sensed the patterns of his power.

By the afternoon, I was doing it myself. The first time I succeeded, I let out an involuntary cheer, buoyed by the satisfaction of success. I couldn't deny the underlying thrill of power.

But one look at Grey's pleased smile brought me down hard. The slimy feeling I had felt when I first understood Grey's deception trickled through me again. I was playing games with people's minds, and while it was harmless deception on this occasion, no one should have that kind of power over someone else.

I couldn't refuse to cooperate, however. Too much lay in the balance for me to alert Grey to my true feelings. I would play along—at least until he asked me to deceive someone about something that actually mattered.

Even knowing the importance of fooling Grey, I was still exhausted by the end of the day. Doing it over and over again had made the slimy feeling fade, and somehow that was the worst feeling of all. I couldn't let myself become desensitized to using this new skill.

Once again Grey had simply handed me the answers I sought, and once again they had turned out to be a poisoned chalice.

Grey must have been pleased with my progress because he called everyone together to eat for the first time since we boarded the ship, his manner jovial and charming. He was delighted, making me conversely afraid. Clearly my mastering this ability was a crucial part of Grey's plan, and the thought made me feel as if ants were crawling all over me.

I managed to sit through the meal, but as soon as people dispersed to either their beds or night duties above deck, I hurried straight for the hold.

# CHAPTER
# TWENTY-FOUR

I almost fell down the ladder, landing in Nik's arms. He held me tightly, and I trembled, grateful he had been waiting for me. He was tense—I could feel it in his muscles—but he said nothing, allowing me to slowly calm at my own pace.

When I finally relaxed into him, his arms tightened even further.

"Do I need to go find Grey?" he asked, but he sounded like it was a joke. Mostly.

I nearly started shaking again but managed to hold it in.

"We should find a spot to sit away from the trapdoor." I glanced upward to where our light must have been leaking through to the hold above. "I don't think this will be a short conversation."

Nik led me through the maze of supplies, taking me to the small corner he had claimed for his own. He had placed the spare planks so that they formed a miniature makeshift cabin, using his power to fuse them together. It was enough to block him from casual view, at least, and inside he'd laid out several blankets into a makeshift bed. Best of all was the orange shape curled in the center of them.

Ember awoke at my arrival, trotting over to me eagerly and allowing me to scoop her up. I kept her in my arms as Nik helped me sit on the blankets. He sat next to me, his arm and leg pressed against mine, rather than facing me as I'd expected. But I couldn't bring myself to comment. I wanted him close as much as he obviously wanted to be there.

I told him everything Grey had revealed, detailing our practice session and my eventual success. He didn't bombard me with questions as I expected, listening in shocked silence instead.

"Show me," he said when I finally fell silent. His fingers wound through mine, holding my hand tightly and providing the contact I needed.

I took a moment to gather myself, not wanting to do it again, especially to Nik. But I understood why he needed to feel it for himself.

I stroked Ember's back as I cast around for an easily broken lie. My hand stilled as an idea came to me. It wasn't as harmless as the color of a tent, but it would be an effective demonstration of both the power and limits of this terrifying skill.

I took Ember out of my lap, putting her beside me on the opposite side to Nik and half covering her with blankets. She looked at me with bright eyes but accepted the arrangement, remaining still beneath my hand. I made no effort to disguise my movements, and Nik watched me with curiosity.

Once I was finished, and Ember was tucked out of his sight, I turned my head to face him. My power snuck gently into him through our still twined hands.

"Ember's dead," I said after a moment, letting my power implant the certainty of truth inside his mind. The ragged emotions of the day leaked out of my voice now that I was no longer trying to control them. "It was her heart. I tried to help her, but I was too late. Just like the eagle."

"Delphine! No!" Nik's eyes filled with horror as he stared back at me, not once questioning my statement or pointing out he had just seen me place Ember out of his sight.

He twisted, pulling me into a hug even tighter than the one by the ladder.

"She was still young, wasn't she?" His voice sounded shaky. Was he crying?

Guilt clawed through me, and I pushed him back.

"No, no, she isn't dead. I didn't mean it."

But Nik shook his head, accepting my rejection of the hug but taking both my hands in his.

"I know it isn't easy to accept," he said, and I'd never heard his voice so gentle. "But denying the truth will only prolong the pain."

"No, she isn't dead." I said it with as much confidence and certainty as I could, but he merely continued looking at me with sad eyes.

Even I was shaken now, regretting my choice of example. This was different from the people standing in Grey's cabin, smiling at the memory of a rainbow of tents.

Ember scrambled out from under the blankets, letting out a sharp yip.

Nik shouted, almost tipping backward in his violent reaction to the shock. Looking from the fox to me, his face was pale even in the light of the lantern.

"She's...she's not dead," he said in a shaky voice.

My instinct was to apologize and comfort him, but I needed him to remember this—to understand the extent of it.

"That's the power of mesmerization," I said. "And that's it's limits."

For a long moment, we just stared at each other, both frozen in place, him still pulled partly back and me stiff and straight. I saw the emotions growing in his eyes, though, the shock replaced with horror and something even worse—fear.

"I'm sorry!" The words jumped out of me. "I should have used a more innocent example. I just wanted you to see...But I shouldn't have done that to you."

More than earlier, I wished I could take it all back. I wanted to turn back time and never have Nik look at me like he was afraid of me.

The increasingly frantic tone of my voice propelled him back into movement. He wrapped me in his arms, murmuring against my hair.

"Shhh. It's all right. It's all right, Delphine."

When I calmed, we both pulled slightly apart so we could look at each other.

"I'm sorry," I said more calmly. "That was cruel."

"No." He shook his head. "I understand why you did it. I still can't believe I just...I didn't even question...But it was true. I felt it with such certainty."

I nodded, letting out a long shaky breath. "That's what it's like. I can't control you directly—if I tried to tell you to kill Ember yourself, you'd never do it. But just think of all the ways I could manipulate you."

Nik went still, his arms still partially around me, his face stricken. "They might not be able to tell me to kill Ember, but if Grey mesmerized me into believing you were dead, someone might die at my hands."

I stilled as well, frozen for a moment, before I pushed him away.

"Nik! How could you say that?" But one look at the dangerous expression on his face made me go quiet.

"I'm not saying I'm proud of it," he said hoarsely. "But I really don't know what I'd do if someone killed you, Delphine."

"Shh." This time it was my turn to comfort him, pulling him close. "No one's going to kill me. I'm a healer, remember?"

He put one arm around my back and tangled the other in my hair, pressing my head against his shoulder.

"They'd better not try."

I shook my head against him. "You should try to be a little less bloodthirsty, you know. No matter what happens to me, it isn't worth making yourself into a monster."

"Why would it matter?" The quiet volume of his words did nothing to disguise their bitterness. "Without you, I would have nothing."

I sat up straight. "That's not true!"

"It isn't?" He arched an eyebrow. "Enlighten me. What would be left to me in a world without you? I spent a year wandering the kingdom alone before I met you, so I know exactly what that life is like."

"But why do you have to be alone?" I asked, finally asking the question that had been burning in me for so long. "You have a family, and from what Amara and Hayes have said, they miss you. And you're a prince. I'm sure your old master would take you back and let you complete your apprenticeship like Serena is doing."

"My family were the ones to reject me," he said harshly. "They've made it clear there's no place for me at court."

"But how can that be?" I asked. "Are you sure—?"

"Of course I'm sure!" He laughed darkly. "The Triumvirate cut me out of the line of succession. It's not something that can be taken back. At least before, when Gia was crown princess, I had a purpose of sorts. I was the spare, in case anything ever happened to her. But now I'm nothing at all. My cousin, Evermund, will be king one day in my place, and there's nothing at all I can do about it."

I knew there had been a change in succession, but I had never understood why or the details of it.

"Your father just let them do that?" I asked, still unable to believe it. "Surely they can't just—"

"Actually they can," he said, cutting me off coldly. "My father can't rule without the Triumvirate, and he can't interfere in this law. It's an old one, from the beginning of both the throne and the Guild. The Triumvirate have always been against me from the beginning. Even when I tried to do everything they asked of me, they always had an excuse for why I'd done the wrong thing. Evermund will be king, and I will be nothing."

"Your parents must have been devastated," I whispered, trying to imagine how it would feel to have your children swept aside by forces outside your control.

Nik chuckled darkly. "That just shows you don't know my family at all."

My brows contracted. "Hayes says—"

"Hayes wants to believe the best of things. He has a positive nature." Nik's harsh tone derided such positivity. "He was always busy at the Guild. He knows nothing of my childhood."

"Tell me," I said, my voice soft. "I want to know about it."

Nik looked at me, unseeing for a moment before my expression registered and his arm tightened around me.

484

"Are you sure you want to know? It isn't a neat, pretty story."

"Of course I do!" I gave him a stern look. "It's a part of you, and I don't only want to know the pretty parts of you."

For a moment, he just looked at me, something reflected in his face that made my insides tremble. But then he tamped it down, hiding the depths of his feelings away as he usually did.

"From my earliest memories, I always knew it mattered that Gia was a few minutes older," he said, and it took me a moment to remember that Gia was his nickname for Princess Morgiana.

"But as small children we were always together, and everyone treated us the same. Sometimes I even forgot we were two separate people and thought of us as a single unit, two who would always be together."

I smiled, but before I could do more than picture the two of them as toddlers, he continued. "But then the rumors started."

"Rumors?"

"All the healers at the palace know not to privately test royal children until their official seed testing when they turn five. But people started to notice we were drawn to play in the gardens, and that after we'd been there, the flowers bloomed bigger and the grass grew lusher. Whispers began to flow around the palace about a plants seed."

"What's wrong with a plants seed?" I asked, indignant.

"Nothing, if you're a regular person." His eyes burned into the closest plank. "All three of the main affinities serve different functions, and all are essential to the well-being of the kingdom. Officially, none of the affinities rank above the others."

"But unofficially?"

He gave a sour laugh. "Elements is the affinity of warriors and kings. Elements controls tempests and tidal waves and brings down lightning bolts. Elements is the affinity of Tartora's royal family."

I was silent, remembering some of his conversations with Amara. This was why he had accused her of believing her affinity superior, although I'd never seen her show any evidence of such thinking.

"So Father brought our testing forward," Nik continued. "He told Mother it was to quiet the rumors and put the issue behind us. But even as I child, I sensed the truth. He was afraid."

"Afraid?"

"Afraid it was true." He swallowed. "I may have been young, but the memory of our testing is still crystal clear. I can recall my father's exact expression—the relief on his face when he discovered it was me, not Gia, who had the undesirable seed. That was the moment I knew."

"Knew what?" I asked, my heart sinking as tears welled in my eyes for Nik's childhood self.

"That Gia and I weren't the same at all. That we had never been one, and we never would be. We were always separate, never equal. I knew in that moment that I was the disappointment. But the worst thing of all?" His voice grew jagged, his volume dropping even lower. "Worst of all was that my being a disappointment didn't even matter."

"Oh Nik!" I threw my arms around him, squeezing his shoulders as tears slipped down my face. "I'm sure that's not true. I'm sure your parents love you too."

Nik leaned into my touch, as if he couldn't help himself, but he continued talking as if I hadn't spoken. "And the irony of it all? The irony is that Gia didn't even want the crown. When we got old enough for that to become clear, it was like constant salt being rubbed in my wound. Gia was the one who mattered, the one with a future, the one with the right seed—and she didn't even want any of it."

I put my head on his shoulder, unable to think of anything to say, and he rested his chin on top of my hair, breathing out deeply.

"My parents always thought she would come around to her duty—that it was just a phase, and she would get over it. But Gia was the one who got what she wanted in the end." His angry laugh sounded again, low in the confined space.

"For one brief moment, when they were forced to accept the truth, I thought they finally cared about what a disappointment I was. I thought maybe they would at last realize that if only they'd ever believed in me, I could have become what Gia never wanted to be. But it turns out there was always a better option than me."

"Evermund." The name fell heavily between us. "So your cousin will get the throne after your father's death. Do you...do you hate him for it?"

Nik ran a hand over his face, his smile bitter. "Sometimes I think it would be easier if I could. Just like I used to wish I could hate Gia. But Gia was always impossible to hate. And Evermund is...Evermund. He's everything Gia is not—focused, disciplined, controlled—and always dutiful. My older cousin has only ever wavered in his duty to the kingdom for one reason. And look how that turned out!"

"One reason?" He clearly expected me to know what he was talking about, but I had no idea.

"Airlie. The strongest elements mage to appear in Tartora in generations —and now sister to Calista's queen. She is the only person or thing Evermund has ever put before Tartora. And in return, he won her heart and secured her loyalty to our kingdom. Winning Airlie as our future queen was a coup I could never compete with—and Evermund wasn't even trying to be strategic. Even when he wavers, he ends up benefiting the kingdom." He shook his head. "Who wouldn't want him to be king?"

I drew a deep breath and let it out slowly, remaining silent because what was there to say? After a moment, Nik spoke again, trying for a lighter tone but failing.

"See? Even you can't bring yourself to say I'd be a better ruler."

I sat up straight, indignation filling me. I couldn't stop Nik from thinking about the other people in his life in any manner he chose, but I wasn't going to let him work me into his twisted narrative.

"Is being a ruler the only future that matters? Is everyone in the kingdom worthless except the best candidate for future king?"

My indignation ballooned inside me. It felt good to let my feelings out instead of having to bottle them inside as I'd been doing all day with Grey. I scrambled inelegantly to my feet and took two steps away before stopping and turning back, my emotions boiling over again.

"I have no interest in a life at court, or at the Guild, or even in the capital. I certainly have no interest in ruling anyone or anything. So I guess that makes me a worthless, useless person, unfit to be loved by anyone!"

"What? Delphine!" He jumped up, striding after me. When he reached for me, I stepped back out of his grasp. "Of course I don't think about you like that!" He looked part concerned, part irritated.

I crossed my arms and glared at him. "Then why are you so determined to assume that everyone else thinks that way about you? You didn't lose something that should have been yours, Nik! You weren't born to rule—that was never your place. So why can't you let it go? Why can't you put your energy into finding what role you *are* supposed to fill?"

"Delphine, I—"

I waited, eyebrows raised, but he didn't finish, seeming at a complete loss in the face of my anger. Spinning around, I dashed out of the makeshift cabin toward the ladder.

"Wait!" he called after me, but I didn't stop. Climbing up to the upper hold, I checked carefully that I was alone before emerging fully and closing the trapdoor behind me with a bang.

If Nik was determined to be pig-headed, he could stew on his own. It had been a long day—a long three days—and I couldn't take any more emotional upheaval.

CHAPTER

# TWENTY-FIVE

I went to sleep with my harsh words running through my mind and woke up to hear them repeated again. But I couldn't bring myself to regret saying them. I had spent plenty of time thinking about how Nik's status as both an outcast and a prince stood between us, but it had never just been his position. His bitterness and anger were also a barrier, a well of darkness that I wasn't willing to be dragged into. If Nik couldn't confront his feelings about his past and move beyond them, then we could never have a future together.

Part of me wanted to run straight down to the hold, but I forced myself up on deck instead. I hadn't had the chance to spend time in the fresh air for days, and I needed it. It was also the move Grey would be expecting me to make. I didn't want him to start questioning why I spent so much time below deck.

He smiled when he saw me and waved from his position next to the wheel. As I neared my old spot by the rail, the ship juddered, swinging sharply left. I staggered and just managed to grab hold before I lost my balance.

I looked quickly up at the helm, but nothing in Grey's face, or the faces of the two men beside him, indicated there was a problem. When I peered over the edge, I saw a section of frothing water, sharp points of rock appearing occasionally among the white bubbles. It looked dangerously close to the edge of the boat and must have been the reason for our abrupt change of direction.

I sighed, wondering why I wasn't used to sudden movements of the boat by now. The whole journey had been a zigzag as we followed an unseen, narrow course, and I was long since glad I'd been forced into a hammock. Several of those in the bunks had been tossed out in their sleep when the team controlling our passage adjusted our direction in the water.

The stiff breeze that filled the sails was unnatural too, always blowing steadily and never from the wrong direction. I couldn't connect with it, but Amara's influence allowed me to recognize it had power laced through it.

I stared across the water, my eyes instinctively looking for landmarks of any kind and finding only the flat expanse of the ocean. I had always longed to see the ocean, but the more days I spent entirely surrounded by it, the less enthusiastic I became. All I wanted now was land beneath my feet again.

We turned a second time, but I felt the wind shift direction first and had the chance to ready myself, gripping the rail with all my strength. Once we settled into our new direction, I considered my last three days. At least in Grey's cabin, I had been too distracted to take much notice of the wild movements of the ship.

My mind skipped past the revelation about mesmerizing and back to the two days preceding it. Had we really worked so long and so hard only to get nowhere? Grey had never managed anything close to a wall, no matter how many times I told him to picture himself building it stone by stone.

But why?

The shock of Grey's lesson had driven the pressing question from my mind, but it floated back to the surface now. Why couldn't anyone else do what I had done as a new apprentice? I was reminded of how I had started out testing children's seeds without touching them when other healers always used contact. My ignorance kept driving me to do things other healers didn't even bother trying. But at least in the case of the testing, other healers of equal strength were able to replicate the feat if they wished to do so. What made the wall different?

"Maybe you need to be squeamish," I said out loud to the breeze, smiling a little at my own foolishness. "A lifetime of fainting and vomiting would be enough to..." My voice trailed into silence as I considered my own words.

What had Grey said about mesmerizing? It had taken a tragedy of epic proportions before someone stumbled on the skill. What if the same thing applied here? Not a large-scale tragedy but a small, intimate one.

My whole life used to feel like a tragedy—a joke I couldn't bring myself to laugh at. It wasn't just my squeamishness, although even Clay had said I had an extreme version of it. My father's teachings had also played a part. From almost my earliest memories I had wished my power away, longing for a different, weaker seed. Activation had been a frightening, impossible prospect, to be refused and avoided.

What if that was the necessity required to birth this skill? Grey was focused solely on the ability to block another healer's power, and that was what we had focused on in our attempts. But that had only been an incidental side effect of my original purpose. I had built my wall not to keep others out, but to block my own power. What if, before you could block away your ability, you had to really, truly want it gone?

Phoenix soared toward me, but I barely registered his presence, my thoughts racing and whirling. The more I thought about it, the more it made sense. I didn't want my power gone now, but I had already created my wall a thousand times. Bringing it up was instinctive and easy. But could I have done it the first time without that desperation to keep my own power at bay?

As I considered the possibility, I could finally believe that I might have been the only one to create a wall. Had there ever been another healer of my strength who had feared their own activation like I had? Given what could go wrong with healing power, there must have been some who came to resent it later, after a tragedy had unfolded. But by then they would have already been taught how to use their power, their minds set in the idea of what was and wasn't possible. Youths with seeds as strong as mine usually traveled to the capital well before activation and began learning the basics of their own affinity.

My wall had kept me safe until I didn't need it anymore, and then it had kept me safe again when Grey reached into my mind and overturned it. And there was a good chance I had only ever created my wall because of my father.

I didn't know what to do with that thought. My squeamishness had been the greatest weakness of my life, and yet it had turned into strength. Was it possible my history with my father could do the same thing? And if it did, did that mean I had to forgive him and let go of the ways he'd wronged me?

I wanted to hold onto my anger, but my words from the night before in the hold reappeared, unwanted, in my mind. I had berated Nik, chastising him for not letting go of his bitterness and anger. So why was I clinging onto mine so tightly?

I claimed I didn't want to be pulled into Nik's well of darkness, and yet, all the while, I was busily at work creating one of my own. My father had trapped himself in his anger and bitterness, and he had nearly trapped me in it with him. I had broken free, but had I seized my freedom only to make the same mistake and become mired in anger and bitterness of my own?

Phoenix gave his brief, chattering call and nipped at my ear.

"Oi!" I batted at him, coming close enough to unseating him that he had to spread his wings for balance.

"You think I should forgive my father, don't you, fine sir?" I ran a finger down his back while he regarded me steadily with one beady eye.

Even as I said the words, I felt a heaviness lift off me. The thought of going home still held little appeal, and I would never regain the closeness I had once shared with my father. But at least the thought of one day visiting the farm no longer filled me with revulsion and confusion.

"When was I reduced to this?" I muttered. "Receiving life wisdom from a bird." I couldn't help but smile, though. I had enough burdens to carry without lugging around an unnecessary one as well.

"If I'd realized all this three days ago, could I have taught Grey to make his own wall?" I mused to Phoenix. "Is understanding it enough to make a difference?"

I wouldn't know for sure without trying, and I had no intention of giving Grey any more tips. But I suspected no explanation from me would be enough. Grey wasn't the sort of person to ever wish away a single portion of his power. If sincerity was required, he would never be able to muster the necessary sentiment.

Someone approached me with a serving of bread and cheese and an apple. I accepted the lunch with a brief thanks and ate it on deck where I stood. As soon as I'd finished, however, I moved toward the door leading below deck.

Forgiving my father had softened my heart enough that I couldn't stay away from Nik any longer. I had at least had the wind and the sea and the sky to aid me in my reflections. He had nothing but darkness and the creaking of the ship's sides.

In my haste, I slid down the ladder into the upper hold, only to freeze at the sight of several people sorting through a section of bags and crates. Two of them looked up at my arrival, nodding a wary greeting.

I nodded back, my mouth suddenly dry. Picking a direction at random, I hurried away from them, stopping at a pile of crates and pretending to examine them.

It seemed to take hours for them to finish their task, hauling away several of the bags. Creating a chain, they passed each of the bags up the ladder while I moved on to another pile of crates, pretending not to have found what I was looking for.

When they finally disappeared from view, I let out an explosive breath. I had gotten careless and was lucky none of them had questioned my presence in the hold. I would have to make sure that I came up with a good excuse for the next time I ran into someone.

Hurrying to the closed trapdoor, I climbed down, stopping awkwardly part way down to close it behind me.

Nik appeared, stepping into the light with a glance upward. "That's new."

"There were people up there when I came down. They've gone now, but I don't know if they'll be back."

He accepted my explanation without comment, and I looked around for Ember. But, of course, it was daytime, so she must have been sleeping back in their makeshift bed. Which left Nik and me to stand and silently regard each other.

I couldn't read his expression, blaming the flickering lantern light for giving him a foreboding look.

"I'm sorry," I blurted out at last. "I shouldn't have spoken so harshly to you when all the time I was carrying around the same bitterness toward my own father. I've known for a while now that he didn't deserve the intensity of my anger, but..."

"It's not so easy to let go of." Nik finished the sentence for me, his words calm and measured.

My eyes flew to his face. What conclusion had he come to down here alone in the depths of the ship?

"I decided to let it go," I said in a rush. "I won't ever go back to resume the life I imagined on the farm with my parents, but I want to be able to see them again one day. And I want to remember their love for me without it hurting."

"And you want me to do the same?" Again his voice was flat, giving away none of the emotion behind it.

I tipped my head to the side, considering his question. "It isn't about what I want. It's about what you want. Because I want you to be free, but that doesn't mean anything unless you want it too."

"I thought I already was free," he said. "When I left my old life to wander alone, I thought of it as freedom. And then I met you."

I shivered slightly at the way he spoke of our meeting, as if I was an axis that his life turned around. Before and after.

"I don't want the freedom to be alone anymore," he said. "And neither do I want to be chained to my past."

"You've forgiven your family?" I couldn't keep the eagerness out of my voice.

"Was there anything to forgive?" he asked in a strange tone.

I moved toward him, reaching for him without meaning to do so. He looked at my outstretched hands, his whole body trembling slightly, as if he was suppressing something that took enormous effort.

I lowered my arms again slowly, my eyes locked on his as I waited to hear what else he had to say.

"When you left last night—" The tremble was in his voice as well, and it took everything I had not to close the last of the distance between us and put my arms around him.

He swallowed. "When you left, and I didn't know if you were coming back, I—" He shook his head as if shaking off an unwelcome thought and glanced sideways.

I followed the direction of his gaze to see a mess of smashed wood and several broken objects I couldn't identify. Nik claimed it had been my departure that had sparked his wild emotions, but I knew it was more than that. I'd stirred up his problems with his family, and they were emotions he needed to face.

"When I came to my senses, I knew you were right," he said. "And so were they."

"Right about what?" I asked cautiously.

"Right that I was never suited to rule. I didn't get on this ship to protect the kingdom from Grey or the islanders. I came to protect you. In that moment, you were the only one I cared about, Delphine. And even now, I would walk away from the rest of them and never look back if you needed me to."

"But I don't—"

"I know you would never ask that of me," he said quickly. "But that isn't what matters. What matters is that I would do it. I thought the Triumvirate rejected me because they doubted my power. Even when they told me it was because I lacked the qualities of a ruler, I refused to hear it. I refused to see any deficiency in myself. But my father turned his back on his own son when the kingdom demanded it of him. And even I have to acknowledge that as far as Tartora is concerned, it was the right thing to do. A king puts his kingdom first—it's the most basic requirement for the role. And I don't think I've ever been selfless enough to do it."

He shook his head slowly. "I was fooling myself the whole time—telling myself I was doing things for the good of the kingdom when I was only ever thinking about myself. I was just like Grey—seeking power for its own sake not because I wanted to use it to help anyone else."

"We all lie to ourselves like that," I said softly. "We come up with admirable reasons for our actions to cover the selfishness or fear that is truly driving us. But this conversation right now is what separates you from Grey. Do you think he's ever peeled back the layers to look at himself as he truly is? Do you think he has any desire to do so?"

"Maybe there's hope for him yet," Nik said with a rough laugh. "A year ago I was no different. And then I fell in love with you."

I froze, staring at him. He finally drew closer, standing a mere step away, although he kept his arms at his side.

"I love you, Delphine. More intensely than I thought I could love anyone or anything. So now I'm selfish in a different way. But at least you make me want to be better."

Unable to restrain myself any longer, I reached out and took his hands. "Maybe you're not made to be a ruler, but you're too harsh on yourself. You do care about the people of Tartora. I've seen it. You were tracking Grey before anyone else cared enough to notice what he was doing. You didn't turn your eyes away from the ones the rest of the kingdom preferred to forget."

"I know what it's like to be unwanted by your kingdom," he muttered.

"And you were out there in the middle of the storm in Eldrida," I continued relentlessly, "putting yourself at risk to rescue people. You didn't have to do that. No one would even have known if you hadn't."

He frowned but was apparently unable to come up with a suitable retort.

"There's more to you than just selfishness, Nik. And without the lure of a throne to lead you off track, you can finally work out what you were made to do. Remember what Amara said? We're all different, and that means we all show our love differently. You might not be well suited to making the strategic decisions that affect everyone, but that doesn't mean you can't make all the difference to some people." My voice lowered. "You've already made a difference to me."

Nik's fingers tightened around mine, his eyes latching onto my face with painful intensity.

"What sort of difference have I made to you, Delphine? I don't expect you to feel the same way I do right now, but do you think there's any chance that one day you might—"

I pulled my hands loose and grabbed two fistfuls of his shirt. For half a second, I stayed paused there, taking in his features. When I had first met him, I had found him simultaneously terrifying and attractive, and even now, the fire burning in his eyes scared me a little, although in a different way. I had no idea how someone like Nik could feel so intensely about me. But I had been fighting my own feelings for too long, and I didn't have the strength to resist any more.

Yanking him downward, I stretched up and smashed my lips to his. For a moment we were frozen there, his shock holding him immobile. Then his arms were around me, his lips were moving on mine, and he was whispering my name in a voice that sent a shiver all the way through me.

Giving up the fight completely, I lost myself in the kiss. But even as I did, an echo of fear lingered. This spark between us might lift us to new heights, or it might burn us to the ground. Even as the flames engulfed us both, I couldn't be sure which it would be.

# TWENTY-SIX

It took all my self-control to fight my desire to spend the rest of the afternoon and all the next day at Nik's side. But I had to stay up on deck, visible to Grey in case he came looking for me. I couldn't risk his discovering Nik at this point.

If I found it hard to leave, Nik found it even harder to let me go. But even he acknowledged the danger.

"He's sure of me, ridiculously sure." I shook my head. "But I still can't take the risk."

"He underestimates you."

"He must." My words grew more heated. "But does he really think I'm so stupid that he can tell me about mesmerizing, and I won't question everything he's ever told me? I've even been using my wall constantly the last few days."

I knew Grey did still believe I was mesmerized, though, because he'd already refreshed his original lies several times since we'd come aboard. I'd become almost used to the horrible process. It didn't matter what he lied to me about. I recognized the feeling of having been mesmerized and knew how to drive his power out of my mind.

"We know where his confidence is coming from now." Nik sounded disgusted. "But I suppose it's working to our advantage in this instance. It must be hard to shake a lifetime of certainty that your words will be believed. After all, you're the first person he's ever told the truth to. But he isn't totally foolish. I notice he waited to tell you about mesmerizing until he had you in the middle of the ocean. From his perspective, if his plan goes awry, there's nowhere for you to run. He's probably trusting that if you show any signs of rebellion, he can find a way to mesmerize you again."

I shivered at the thought, even though I knew it was impossible. Now that I knew the feeling, he would never be able to fool me for long.

I still flinched when Grey called my name on the fourth day, however. But I managed to pin a smile in place before I turned around, and I made no protest about returning to his cabin yet again. I had grown to hate the wooden box, but I kept those emotions from my face and considered each word I uttered carefully.

"We'll arrive at the island not long past dawn tomorrow," he told me, successfully taking my mind off everything else.

"Already?" I didn't care how glad I sounded. Sailing wasn't for me.

He chuckled. "I'm rather anxious to arrive myself. But I need to prepare you before we go ashore."

"Do you expect trouble when we arrive?" I asked, afraid of how he might want me to get involved.

"No, no," he assured me with a forced air, although I could read the words were mostly truth. "I just need to give you a warning. It's different in my case because I'm family, but it might be dangerous if they learn you're also a powerful healing mage and know how to mesmerize. From what my mother reported, her family are obsessed with strength—to the extent that they don't even allow any cross-influencing on the island. But all that strength is carefully controlled. To keep you safe, I'm going to tell them you have an elements affinity. But, of course, you won't be able to use elements power, so it would be best to give them the impression you're weak."

I considered his words. "But aren't they healers themselves? How will you be able to lie about my affinity?"

His lips stretched, revealing his teeth. "Very carefully."

I wanted to protest, but there was nothing I could think of to say. He had framed his suggestion as keeping me safe, and there had been no hint of a lie about his words of caution. If being a healer would put me in danger from the islanders, then it was in my interest to fall in with Grey's plan. Especially since I couldn't let him know I was aware he had a bigger scheme underway.

I would just have to wait and see what request he made of me next.

"Make sure you sleep well tonight."

He still seemed overly pleased, which made me jumpy. But there was nothing I could do except agree and leave his presence as quickly as possible.

Given the tight confines of the cabin, Phoenix had been sleeping on deck, leaving me alone in my hammock. I wished desperately for his company or for Ember's warm, furry body curled at my side. Instead I had to make do with the sleeping sounds of women all around me as I lay and wondered what would happen to us all in the morning.

There was no time to sneak down to Nik after I rose. I could only trust his reassurances that he would find his own way off the ship. At least Phoenix was able to join me, taking up his usual perch on my shoulder.

Those of us not involved in guiding the ship gathered together on deck at first light. Already the island was looming before us, larger than I'd imagined and rising to a single, tree covered peak, the dark green a welcome relief from the blue all around us.

Our ship cut smoothly through the still waters, with no sign of rocks at this end of our journey. We approached not a sandy beach as I'd imagined, but a dock that reminded me of the one in Eldrida. A row of buildings lined the waterfront, although there would be no trade ships sailing in and out of this town.

From the look of the small vessels and fishing nets, there were plenty of fishermen, however, which had to explain the existence of the dock. Murmured conversations were taking place all around me, but no one attempted to include me in their exclamations and excited imaginings. Three days shut up with Grey in his cabin working on experiments the rest of them didn't understand had done nothing to soften the underlying antagonism from the beginning of the trip.

"It's more beautiful than I imagined," someone breathed beside me, and I turned gratefully to smile my agreement at Ida. It was nice to be included by someone.

"That tree covered mountain is like a feast for the eyes after nothing but ocean."

She laughed. "You didn't take to life onboard, then? Personally, I found the ocean peaceful." She lapsed into silence, as if remembering the past hurts that made the emptiness of the ocean so appealing in comparison.

I had no time to say anything supportive since various shouts were rising around us. Some came from among us as those with elements power worked together to maneuver the ship to the end of the long dock. But others came from ashore. Despite the early hour, some people were already up and about on the dock, and all of them had stopped to gape at our arrival.

One of the onlookers set off running, disappearing down a street that looked much like the ones I had seen in Ostaria, Caltor, and Eldrida. In fact, from what I could see, only the natural setting distinguished this island settlement from any city or large town in Tartora.

I glanced at Ida, wondering if she'd be disappointed by the familiarity, but her eyes were shining just as brightly as before. I cast another look toward the door that led below deck. Where was Nik right now? How was he preparing to disembark?

We made the lightest of contacts with the wooden dock, and several people sprang over the edge of the rail to receive the lengths of rope being thrown to them. Within no time they had the ship secured and the gangplank in place.

I had my personal pack over my shoulder, as we all did, but many people had a second bag as well. Clearly Grey's plan didn't include arriving empty-handed.

By the time we were ready to file off the deck and onto dry land, the fruit of the runner's efforts had arrived. A group of people—all of whom looked like they didn't usually spend their mornings on the dock—ran into view, coming to a stop just short of our landing place.

I examined the silk of their robes, and the winded expressions on their faces. These were people whose lives didn't usually require them to dash from place to place. I was surprised they were even awake.

We arranged ourselves loosely, me moving toward the back of the disembarkation line. But as Grey strode down from the helm to take the lead, he brushed past me, indicating for me to follow him. His movement had been subtle, but those around us had picked it up and reluctantly parted to allow me through.

I could have done without the honor, preferring to remain at the back away from the attention, but I had little choice but to obey. Grey ignored his followers, all his attention on what lay before us. He took in the dock and the buildings behind it in a single, comprehensive glance, his attention settling on the people waiting for us.

His usual air of confidence hung about him as he strode down the gangplank and onto the wooden dock. I followed eagerly, only to lurch slightly when I finally reached ground.

Why was the land moving beneath my feet? It felt just like the ship I had been so eager to leave behind.

I looked frantically back at the group gathered on deck, managing to catch Ida's eye. She appeared to be laughing at me.

Taking pity on the frantic look in my eyes, she waved me forward encouragingly, mouthing something I couldn't catch. But when I turned back to face forward again, I noticed there was something different about Grey's gait. He might not show it in his air, but he walked as if he felt lingering effects from being onboard. So perhaps this was normal after all.

I hurried to catch up with him, hoping the unnerving sensation would soon disappear.

A man, taller than the others, stepped forward to put himself at the front of the group. His clothes were the most elaborate, and now that he'd recovered his breath, his arrogant manner made it clear he was the highest-ranking person present.

I couldn't help immediately disliking him, but I wasn't sure if that was his manner or the fact he was likely a relative of Grey's. I hid the emotion, however, keeping myself a couple steps behind Grey. Hopefully all attention would be on him, and there would be none left over for me.

"This is a most unprecedented occasion," the man said, his tone far more conciliatory than I had expected. "You are the first visitors we have ever welcomed to our fair shores."

"It is not, however, my first time here," Grey said smoothly. "I have waited many years to return to my home."

Shock pierced the man's mask, the true emotion making it obvious how false his previous pleasant manner had been. His mind clearly worked quickly, however, as the jarring expression smoothed almost instantly into a smile.

"But surely...It cannot be that you are my missing cousin, Grey?"

"Indeed I am." Grey stepped forward to clasp his long-lost cousin's arm, the two of them slapping each other on the back in apparent delight at the reconciliation.

I tried to keep my eyes from widening perceptibly as I took in the odd scene before me. Anyone would think these two had been parted mere months ago instead of shortly after Grey's birth. I had assumed Grey's claim about being welcomed back with open arms as their leader had been an obvious falsehood—one he had only dared utter because he was mesmerizing me.

But this seemed just the sort of reception he had claimed was waiting for him. These people weren't just going to hand the island over to him, were they?

But no. A reminder of what these people were capable of was enough to eliminate that thought. They must be masters of manipulation, just as Grey himself was, and I should view all their interactions through that lens.

I examined the man again while he introduced himself as Ignatius Constantine, smiling and inquiring about the voyage as though he was genuinely glad to see us. But I suspected the only real emotions I had seen from him were the arrogance visible on his face in its natural, resting posture, and the momentary shock that had broken through following Grey's announcement.

"But what of my Aunt Chloe?" Ignatius asked. "She didn't accompany you?" Something in his expression looked off at this question, as though it carried far more importance than he wanted to reveal.

Grey bowed his head, his face dropping. "I'm afraid to say my mother has been dead for many years. Our crossing to the mainland took a terrible toll."

"A grave loss, indeed," Ignatius said in suitably solemn tones. "My father and Uncle Ambrose will be shocked to hear it. As will Grandmother, of course. She always believed her daughter was living happy and well in another place."

I twitched slightly, but thankfully neither of them noticed. Grey's mother was the one who'd been a member of this family? What about the story of his murdered father, the one who'd wanted to bring about change? Was that a complete fiction?

"It has always been my dream to return to her family and my first home," Grey said. "But it took me many years to gather those who also desired a new life and who could help me build a ship and travel here. I hope we will all find a welcome in this place."

"Of course." Ignatius raised his voice so that all those gathered behind us could hear. "All are welcome here! You have had a long and difficult journey, but I hope here you will find peace and a new beginning."

My lips twitched as I tried to make sense of this man who seemed a mass of strange contradictions. Nothing he had said had carried the feel of a lie, and yet I couldn't shake a profound feeling of distrust.

Ignatius stepped to the side slightly, placing himself directly in front of me. Inclining his upper half, he offered me his hand. For a moment I stared at it, trying to overcome the feeling that I was reaching for a hissing viper.

But Grey's presence loomed beside me, and his warning rang in my ears, so I hesitantly extended my own hand and allowed Ignatius to clasp it in his. He was murmuring empty words of welcome, but I could barely follow enough to nod and smile in the right places.

Most of my attention was focused on the tendril of power he was subtly sending into me through our hands. It took everything I had not to rip my hand from his or throw up my wall to drive him straight back out. But I knew I couldn't afford to reveal myself yet, so I stayed still, allowing him to plant a false truth inside my mind.

His words, which had previously only been a background noise, came into sharp and sudden focus. I wasn't sure why I had been so tense and worried when this family, the Constantines, were ready to welcome all of us into the life of peace they ruled over.

Ignatius let go of my hand promptly, moving to the next in line. Not that I blamed him. He clearly meant to greet us all individually—a truly gracious gesture—so he could spare only seconds for each person.

How delightful that there was no need for the scheming and deception I had expected. Peace and rest sounded perfect after the tension of the voyage.

And Nik could stop skulking in the shadows as well. The Constantines wouldn't care that Grey didn't approve of him.

Of course, Grey himself might be a problem. I would need to tell Ignatius about his true nature as soon as I had the opportunity. Once he was taken care of, I would have no need to worry further. Clearly everything he'd said was lies—these people would never burn the crops of strangers across the sea or send storms to destroy them.

I relaxed, wishing only that the uncomfortable, twisted feeling in my stomach would go away. I was sick of niggling thoughts, and layers to everything. I was ready to—oh!

Pulling up my wall, I pushed it through me, driving out the unfamiliar power that was tainting my thoughts. Within seconds, my mind was clear again, a horribly familiar, slimy feeling taking the place of the peace I had felt moments before.

I recalled my thoughts of only seconds ago and shivered. I had been on the verge of telling this stranger about both Nik and Grey. It was unnerving the way the deception left my other thoughts and memories intact, and yet that one central truth reshaped everything else around it.

I looked behind me and saw Grey's followers had formed themselves into a line, eagerly holding out their hands for Ignatius's greeting. I glanced across at Grey, expecting to see him furious. He must know what his cousin was doing, that he was taking Grey's people and making them his own.

Grey's expression remained calm, however, only a note of speculation in his eyes. He must have been expecting something like this. I supposed it was the only way the Constantines would allow a foreign group to enter their island, so Grey couldn't prevent it.

I did, however, notice that Ignatius made no attempt to take Grey's hand. Even earlier, when they had first greeted each other, they had clasped arms and slapped backs, their hands carefully touching only sleeve and jacket. If Ignatius didn't know for certain, he was certainly aware of the possibility that Grey was a powerful healer who knew how to mesmerize. Apparently he wasn't willing to risk receiving what he so happily dispensed.

Had he not considered the possibility that one of the rest of us might have the same ability? Apparently he couldn't fathom that anyone—even the long-lost Grey—would have shared the skill outside their family line.

Was he checking for affinities, at least? Should I prepare myself for his already knowing I was a healer, and a powerful one at that?

On reflection, I thought he remained unaware. Surely he would have reacted in some way if he'd checked. I'd done mesmerizing myself, and it was a subtle, difficult skill that required concentration. And Ignatius was mesmerizing many people in quick succession, our numbers meaning he could afford only seconds for each person. My experience told me he would be highly focused, not having the time or capacity to check for anyone's seeds.

Not that it would have mattered that I was a powerful healer if I hadn't also been able to make a wall. I might know how to mesmerize, but ten minutes ago, I would have had no desire to use my power against any of the Constantines.

"Delphine." Grey placed a hand on my shoulder, the edge of one finger brushing against the exposed skin of my neck. He lowered his voice before continuing. "I hope you know you're my most trusted follower. If we're going to save Tartora, we'll need to stick close together and trust each other implicitly. The Constantines can't be trusted."

As soon as he finished the words, he stepped back. My eyes flicked straight to Ignatius, to find him looking our way, a frown on his face. It had been a brief interaction, and he was occupied most of the way down the line of new arrivals, but he must have been keeping an eye on Grey.

I wasn't surprised, though. He was a tricky man, and he must view everyone else with the same suspicion he knew he deserved. It was a wonder Grey had come from such an unpleasant family.

Something niggled at the back of my mind, and I jerked back in distaste, throwing up my wall again and purging my mind.

Breathing deeply to calm the disgusted shivers, I considered what I'd just learned. A mesmerization could be broken by hard evidence to the contrary, but it could also be overridden by a contradictory mesmerization.

I worried at the inside of my cheek. Grey had accepted that his followers were no longer his—at least for the moment—but he had taken the risk of reclaiming me immediately. I understood why, of course. I was both his most valuable follower and his greatest weakness. But in taking such immediate action, he had brought me to Ignatius's attention.

Even as the Constantine continued down the line, still clasping the last of the hands in ostensible welcome, I felt his eyes flicking several times back to me. He must have been wondering why I alone was the one Grey had touched.

Would he risk testing me? If his power was equal to Grey's, he had strength to do it. But would he take the risk of my sensing his probing? Testing an activated mage wasn't the same as checking the seed of a child. It could be done without physical touch, but I had always felt it in the past.

I felt no such intrusive probe now, so I could only assume he had decided to bide his time. Instead, he directed his companions to find beds for the new arrivals throughout the city.

"We can accommodate a few of you at the manor house," he told Grey, "but not all of you, unfortunately. Perhaps five or six of you can accompany me."

Grey nodded and gestured for five of us to come closer. I was unsurprised to be one of those selected but disappointed Ida was not. Instead Grey chose an eclectic mix, including some older and some younger. I hadn't seen him showing any particular interest in the other four previously, but they all came willingly enough. Given the way their eyes glowed as they looked at Ignatius, I suspected it was only a matter of time before Grey found a surreptitious way to renew his control over them.

Ignatius gave no visible sign he was aware of the danger, however, his false smile spread across us all equally. The others had started to disperse into the surrounding streets, walking in small groups, each led by a single local. Only our group had three locals at its head, since two of Ignatius's acolytes had remained at his side.

They led us up the largest street which ran in a straight line through the settlement. I would need a higher vantage point to see the settlement's full size, but it seemed to be a large town built at the base of the island's one mountain, cushioned between the slope and the sea.

Already the sensation of the ground rocking beneath me had faded, and I reveled in striding forward, free of the restrictions of one small deck. But I couldn't help glancing over my shoulder several times, straining to see some sign of a man and a fox disappearing from the dock.

I didn't catch so much as a glimpse of Nik, however, and it was hard not to imagine him trapped below decks. I would have given almost anything to have him walking beside me, my hand held firmly in his. But instead I had to keep my head high and walk down the street between two equally treacherous men, both of whom wanted to control me like a puppet.

The town itself was attractive—clean and orderly with houses in neat rows. Most of the structures had been built with dark gray stone, but a different, unfamiliar stone—deep black and glossy—had been used decoratively, giving the whole town an elegant air. Combined with the green mountain rising ahead of us, the lush blossoms that poked from unexpected places, and the hint of moisture in the air, it was easy to believe we were no longer in Tartora.

The central street led us all the way through the town, gently sloping upward until we reached the lush grounds surrounding a house far grander and more extensive than any other buildings I'd seen. It was built of the same stone as the other houses in town, but the similarity ended there. It wasn't a palace, like the one I'd heard tales of in Tarona, but it was clearly home to the leaders of the settlement.

Grey and my four companions looked around, exclaiming in delight at everything they saw. I did my best to mimic their behavior since I could feel the weight of Ignatius's eyes on me at frequent intervals. I was sure I was doing a poor job, however, given I felt far more dread than delight at the sight of the luxurious mansion.

But when we reached the front steps of the house, I realized the true source of my dread. Someone must have come ahead to give warning of our arrival because a formidable line of people were waiting to greet us. The Constantines.

# TWENTY-SEVEN

Ignatius gave a loaded look to the people waiting for us. I half-expected them all to insist on shaking our hands themselves, but apparently there was some trust within the family, at least, because they settled for spoken greetings.

Grey stepped forward and bowed respectfully.

"Grandmother," he murmured to the formidable older woman who stood in the center of the group. Her hair was stark white, but it did nothing to make her look soft.

However a glint of something sentimental entered her eye as she nodded her head in response. "Young Grey. I never thought to see my fourth grandson a grown man."

Ignatius and a man who looked like an older version of him exchanged the briefest of glances, but I was sure I hadn't mistaken their discomfort with the matriarch's reaction. Did they see Grey as some kind of competition?

Seeing them all lined up, it was obvious why Ignatius hadn't questioned the family connection claimed by Grey. Not only had Grey known the route to the island, but he also possessed the same striking green eyes as five of the people arrayed before me.

"It gives me great pleasure to have finally made it here to stand before you," Grey said. "And I must thank you for your acceptance of my people. They have come seeking nothing more than a safe harbor."

The white-haired woman nodded. "That much we can provide."

"Here with me are my strongest elements followers. They're the ones who brought our ship safely to your shores." He gestured at the five of us, and I suddenly realized why he had chosen the other four. On the ship he had said that his ruse about my affinity would have to be communicated carefully, and this was his strategy. It was true that the other four all had an elements affinity, so his words would ring true. And it would only be a natural assumption for me to be lumped in with the rest of them.

The matriarch nodded graciously at us all, and the people ranged on either side of her followed her lead. Only Ignatius remained still, and I hoped I was imagining that his eyes lingered on me.

A round of introductions followed, with a notable lack of physical touch from anyone, including between the Constantines themselves. Did that mean their mutual trust had limits?

From what I could gather, the matriarch—only ever referred to as Grandmother—had three children. From the order of their introduction, her oldest son was Augustine, the father of Ignatius. It made sense since Ignatius carried himself like the oldest son of an oldest son. Second was Ambrose, along with his wife Kendry, and their son Barnabas. And, of course, third was the missing Chloe.

Barnabas seemed an unprepossessing man next to Ignatius, and from the flash of fire in his eyes when he looked at his cousin, he was aware of it. But his mother seemed the most genuinely warm of the group, her weak blue eyes a reminder that she was the only one of them without actual Constantine blood.

No one mentioned Ignatius's missing mother, but a second younger man appeared, his late arrival rounding out their numbers to seven. He received mostly dismissive glances from his family, but someone hurriedly introduced him as Costas, another son of Augustine.

I gazed at the new arrival, wondering how Ignatius and his brother could have the exact same eyes and yet otherwise be so dissimilar. Not only was his coloring lighter, but everything about his bearing was as well. Even his expression displayed only interest and curiosity, without a trace of superiority.

I found myself wanting the chance to talk to him—preferably without the rest of his family around. But from the way he stooped to kiss his grandmother on the cheek, his smile affectionate, perhaps he was only a better actor than the rest. He certainly didn't seem to bear them any animosity, despite their attitude toward him.

After a few more pleasantries, we were invited inside for breakfast. It turned out to be a formal meal held in an enormous dining room with a long wooden table, polished until it shone. Seeing the tapestries on the walls and the fine carpet underfoot, I was glad I had sent Phoenix off to hunt instead of attempting to bring him inside.

To my disappointment, I was seated between Ignatius and Grey—the two people I would have liked to be furthest from. And as the meal progressed, I grew more and more certain I wasn't imagining the suspicion in Ignatius's eyes when they rested on me. Any time now, he was going to decide to test me. I had to find a way to placate his concern.

I racked my brain as his eyes bored into me.

"How did you find the passage?" he asked.

I almost admitted to disliking sailing until I remembered that anyone with a true elements affinity would feel at home on the sea. And it was true my cross-influence had made me comfortable on the waves, without fear of seasickness, but I had found the ship itself restrictive and unpleasant.

"The sea is magnificent, of course," I said carefully. "But I don't appreciate being surrounded by dead wood."

Ignatius smiled thinly. "I understand your sort prefer to be out in the elements directly. I suppose you would have rather swum."

"Not quite that, perhaps," I said with a forced smile, hoping my awkwardness wasn't as apparent to him as it was to me. Talking to him felt like picking my careful way through a nest of deadly scorpions.

Grey was watching our conversation, clearly alert and listening for every one of my words. His attention did nothing to calm my nerves, and I felt my heart rate increase.

Ignatius looked my way, his eyes narrowing, and I realized that as a healer, he would also be able to sense it. I sent my power toward my heart, ready to slow it back down to a normal rhythm only to stop myself at the last moment. If I acted too obviously I might tip my hand and reveal my affinity.

But I had to do something to distract his attention. I wished intensely for Nik's presence and assistance, and just the thought of him gave me my answer. Fear made my heart beat faster, but so did being in Nik's presence. Which meant I had to fake something I had no interest in faking.

Gritting my teeth and forcing a smile, I leaned slightly toward Grey, meeting his attentive eyes with as bashful a glance as I could manage. When he smiled back at me warmly, I tucked my hair behind my ear and smiled into my lap. Waiting one beat and then another, I snuck a sideways glance at him. He was still smiling at me, apparently having picked up on my intention.

By the time I looked back at Ignatius, he had one eyebrow slightly raised, a look of understanding on his face. Apparently my acting had been sufficient for the occasion, and it had even given an explanation for Grey's particular interest in me.

A serving girl appeared at my elbow, blocking my view of Grey, and I smiled at her more brightly than the service required. She was carrying a steaming pot of porridge, a cloth wrapped around its handle to guard her hands from the heat. She clearly intended to place it in the middle of the table, but between the placement of our chairs and the weight of the pot, it was a tricky maneuver.

A memory flashed through my mind of Grey telling me that the Constantines didn't allow cross-influencing on the island. In a flash of brilliance, I thought of a way to give Ignatius the final proof he needed.

Reaching for the metal pot, I wrapped my hands around its base, taking it from the serving girl with another smile. She gasped, but her smile returned when she saw I didn't shout from pain or pull my hands away. I placed the pot on the table in front of me, handing the cloth around its handle back to the girl.

If Grey was right about the islanders' lack of experience with cross-influencing, then they would associate a tolerance for burning temperatures solely with an elements seed. They might even be completely unaware that being cross elements conferred that particular protection.

When I finally risked another glance at Ignatius, he wasn't looking at me at all. Apparently, I had succeeded in shaking his interest. I smiled to myself, although my pleasure at my quick thinking dimmed when I saw the approval in Grey's eyes. But on this matter, if nothing else, our goals were temporarily aligned. Neither of us wanted the truth of my ability exposed to our new hosts.

Released from my worry over Ignatius, I finally paid attention to the rest of the table, only to find another pair of green eyes watching me. Costas sat across from me, and my display with the pot seemed to have roused rather than quenched his interest.

"I had hoped my new cousin might be elements like me," he said with a friendly smile. "But at least he has brought you with him."

I glanced at Grey who looked as surprised by the comment as me.

"You have an elements affinity?" Grey asked, leaning forward.

Costas chuckled. "It's uncanny how much like a Constantine you look right now. Astonished and mildly disgusted is exactly how they feel whenever they consider how they managed to produce a disgrace like me."

"Are you the only one with an elements affinity?" I asked.

His smile grew lopsided and self-deprecating. "In three generations, if you can believe it."

I raised both eyebrows. "But usually—"

"I don't know how it's done on the mainland," he said, "but here, Constantines only marry other healers. I didn't even know we had anyone in our lineage of a different affinity, so I was as astonished at my testing as everyone else."

"Everyone has to marry a healer?" I asked, my astonishment growing. It seems it wasn't only the regular people on the island who had their lives controlled by this family.

"Except for my rebellious Aunt Chloe, of course," he murmured, eyes on Grey. "How ironic that her son is the healer and not me."

His words should have carried a heavy dose of bitterness, but he said everything lightly, as if he had long since accepted his position as an outcast in his own family.

I wanted to question him further about Grey's mother, but I didn't dare do it with Grey sitting by my side. I wasn't sure if he even remembered that he had lied to me about her, or if he was merely trusting his mesmerization to hold regardless, but it didn't seem a good idea to display curiosity over the matter.

The Constantine matriarch abruptly stood, and everyone else put down their cutlery. It seemed the meal was over, whether we were finished eating or not.

I don't know what I expected to happen after breakfast, but the reality turned out to be an anticlimax. Ignatius and Barnabas both descended on Grey, sweeping him off with them for some sort of cousinly bonding or testing—I suspected they would claim the former while actually intending the latter.

The rest of us were shown to our rooms, where our packs were already waiting for us, and were then left to our own devices. I would have liked to explore the house, but I feared it would be frowned on. In desperation, I searched out Grey's four companions since their company would be preferable to sitting alone in my room for a full day.

I found them in the gardens in front of the house, and they welcomed me easily enough. Now that we were in such unfamiliar surroundings, they seemed to have forgotten the feelings they'd harbored on the boat.

"Are we really free to do whatever we want?" I asked, not quite able to believe it.

"I heard there's a market in the center square," one of them said. "Shall we see if we can find it?"

The others all seemed enthusiastic about the idea, so I trailed behind, watching them all in disbelief. I knew it wasn't fair of me—I had felt the power of mesmerization often enough to understand its effects. But it still seemed incredible that none of them felt the creeping sense of danger overlaying this strange place.

Their enthusiasm only increased when we reached the promised market, a bustling place that reminded me of all the markets I had visited in cities on the mainland. But as soon as I was standing among the stalls, I was forcibly reminded of the last occasion I had stood in a similar square. Looking around at the wooden stalls, all I could see was a different market, the stalls splintered and broken, the air full of driving rain and shouts of pain.

It took me a moment to shake off the memories, but it was long enough for me to lose my temporary companions. I spun in a circle, but they had completely disappeared into the crowd.

Instead of searching for them further, I wandered through the market alone. Seeing how established the town was, it was easy to believe a hundred years had passed. But in other ways it felt as if their separation from the mainland must have been recent. Even their style of dress echoed the current styles in Tartora.

A moment's consideration made me realize why. Some of the Constantines must have visited Tartora to enact their sabotage of the crops. They would have needed to blend in, and the new clothing they brought back must have started a trend here. It was easy to imagine that the mesmerized locals would follow their ruling family in everything, hurrying to copy their styles.

I wandered along the closest line of stalls, admiring the various wares while I watched the unfamiliar crowd. I was just leaning forward to examine a beautiful length of cloth when fingers twined into mine.

I jumped, whirling to stare in consternation at a familiar face.

"Nik!" I gasped, but he laughed and shushed me.

Pulling me away from the cloth, he tugged me into a quiet nook between stalls. He was gazing down at me with a happy expression, but I could only manage a horrified response.

"What are you doing walking around like this?"

He grinned at me. "And why shouldn't I walk around?"

"Why shouldn't you...?" I spluttered into silence, and he dropped a kiss on my nose.

I stared up at him in increased shock. I had never seen Nik in such a light-hearted mood.

"Don't worry so much," he said. "Surely you didn't think I would stay away from you?"

"But the risk! You'll be seen by so many people in a crowded place like this."

He shrugged. "And so what if they do see me? Locals will assume I'm one of the newcomers from the boat, and Grey's followers will assume I'm a local."

"What if one of them recognizes you?"

"They won't." He sounded supremely confident. "Those of Grey's followers who encountered me in Caltor are still in custody there. Only Grey himself has seen me before, and he's occupied up at the manor."

I stared at him. "How do you know that?"

He grinned again. "I have my ways."

I started to protest again, but he leaned in quickly and stole a kiss, silencing me with his lips on mine.

"I've been stuck in that hold for days," he said when he pulled back. "I'm going to enjoy being free. And I'm going to enjoy it at your side. For once, I'm free to walk through a market holding your hand, and there's nothing you can say to dissuade me. Please?"

He must have seen my expression soften because he smiled, his eyes flashing as he leaned closer to steal another kiss.

"You never know, you might even enjoy it."

# CHAPTER
# TWENTY-EIGHT

I was too shocked by Nik's unexpected manner to keep protesting. But as we walked through the market side by side, I kept throwing him sideways glances. He caught me looking and flashed me a broad smile.

"Don't worry," he whispered, leaning close to speak into my ear, "I haven't been mesmerized into a different person. I can promise that no one on this island has made physical contact with me. I've been following Grey for over a year now—I have a lot of experience keeping myself safe from healers."

As he said the words, he lightly squeezed my hand where it was clasped in his, reminding me there was one healer he didn't protect himself from.

I shook my head at him, but inside I was smiling. I was used to brooding, intense, focused Nik, but I couldn't deny I liked lighthearted Nik as well. Was the change because we were no longer in Tartora with the shadow of his abandoned position hanging over him? Or was it because he had truly let go of the weight of bitterness he had carried for most of his life?

I still caught glimpses of the old intensity. When someone barreled past towing a hand cart and nearly knocked me down, only Nik's quick reflexes pulled me out of harm's way. And I recognized his look of ice-cold contempt when we overheard a stall keeper trying to cheat an unwary customer. But whenever he looked at me, the warmth I had previously only seen in veiled snatches shone from his face like a beacon.

When he murmured that a hundred similar days wouldn't be enough, it occurred to me that this was the first time we had ever spent time together without having either a focused purpose or Amara's presence with us. And I couldn't deny that it sent a thrill of pleasure up my spine whenever my eyes landed on him or when I thought about his warm, strong hand in mine. I had walked through a hundred markets, but it had never felt like this.

I couldn't entirely relax, however. Nik gave every appearance of having forgotten the danger hanging over us, but I couldn't put it out of my mind as easily.

Except as the morning progressed, I started to suspect he hadn't forgotten about it either. More than once I caught his eyes lingering on a local in a way that told me he saw the same thing I did.

"There's something strange about them, right?" I asked on the third occasion.

He frowned, not needing to ask what I meant or who I was referring to. Instead he tugged me over to the closest food stall and ordered two meat skewers. As they cooked, he tried to engage the stall keeper in the sort of polite, empty conversation Nik usually avoided.

"We're from the ship and just arrived today, so this is all new to us," he said, his openness about his origins making me twitch.

But when I looked around as surreptitiously as possible, I couldn't spot any of Grey's followers in our vicinity. Knowing Nik, he had probably been aware of that before he spoke.

"Aye, I figured as much," the stall keeper said before lapsing into silence again.

I frowned at him as Nik tried again.

"We came from the mainland with the missing Constantine grandson."

"That would explain it, then," the man said matter-of-factly, leaning over to add a pinch of spice to the cooking meat.

Nik exchanged a look with me before making a third attempt.

"We're looking forward to discovering the best food on the island."

The man immediately smiled broadly, his whole manner changing.

"You've come to the right place for that. You won't find anything better than my skewers. And if you want to wash them down with the freshest of beverages, I can recommend the stall across the way. The stall keeper is an excellent fellow who will give you a good deal, and I can assure you he grows the oranges himself, using only the freshest."

We glanced the direction he was pointing where a man of a similar age stood behind a pyramid of bright oranges. When he saw us looking, he gave a welcoming smile.

Nik accepted our cooked skewers while I murmured our thanks. After an exchange of glances, we crossed over to the other stall. The second stall keeper greeted us warmly, his focus on the sale. But once he began squeezing the juice, he fell silent.

"Oranges must grow well in this climate," Nik said conversationally. "Do you get a consistent crop?"

The man stared at him. "Our island has everything we could want and more."

"I'm sure it does," I said. "It's a beautiful place."

"But fruit especially must grow well," Nik said.

The man stared at him blankly.

"Because of the warmth," Nik finished slowly.

"We have all we need," he repeated in apparent confusion, as if he couldn't make sense of Nik's comments.

"What's your affinity?" I asked, trying to understand why the man found the simple conversation so difficult to follow.

"Plants." He held out our two cups, accepting Nik's coin in exchange.

We thanked him awkwardly and hurried away.

"That was odd," I muttered once we were far enough away not to be overheard. "Especially for someone with a plants affinity. It was like he didn't understand the connection between the weather and his crop's growth."

"That can't be true for someone with a plants affinity," Nik said. "Even if he wasn't taught it, his power should sense it naturally."

We fell into silence, drinking as we walked. The earlier light mood had disappeared completely, and I felt increasingly uncomfortable as I looked at the people milling around us.

"Do I want to know how you already have local coins?" I asked when we'd finished our drinks and returned the cups to the boy who came running after us to fetch them.

"I didn't steal it, if that's what's worrying you." Nik gave me a self-satisfied smile. "Unless liberating some supplies from the ship's hold counts as stealing. But since those belonged to Grey, I can't say I feel guilty."

I rolled my eyes but didn't have it in me to protest. My focus was now firmly on the people around us, and we attempted several more conversations with an equal lack of success.

"They all seem so...lifeless," I said after our last awkward attempt. "They aren't curious or interested in anything much. This is an incredibly closed-off community—how could the arrival of an entire ship not set everyone talking?"

Nik frowned, glancing along the closest row of stalls. "My first instinct is to assume they're holding back—that they know it's dangerous to talk about the Constantines, the ship, or anything related to them. But I don't think it's that. You can guard your tongue, but it's hard to keep curiosity from the eyes. And they don't seem afraid or even wary."

"Just genuinely uninterested," I finished for him. "I've never seen anything like it."

We continued wandering along, no longer touching. After seeing several of Grey's followers clustered around a leather worker's stall, I had refused to let Nik take my hand again. The other mainlanders hadn't appeared to notice us, but I could feel the lingering effect of their presence.

We finally reached the edge of the market, stopping at the final stall to buy several sweet buns. I hummed in pleasure as I polished off the first one. Whatever strangeness gripped these people, it hadn't affected their ability to cook.

Before I could take a bite of the second one, I noticed a pair of bright eyes fixed on us—or more specifically on the buns in our hands.

I smiled at the two young children who lingered just outside the edge of the market, as if they knew they would be chastised if they stepped inside. The older one drew back a little at the attention, but the younger one smiled more broadly.

I held out the bun, and he jumped up and down. Evading his older sister's grasp, he scampered forward and snatched it from my hand, as if afraid I would change my mind if he delayed.

"Fergus!" the girl snapped. "That's rude!"

"It's all right." I smiled at her and held out another bun. "We have plenty to share."

She hesitated. "Are you sure?"

"Of course." I waggled it encouragingly.

"See, Lumi," Fergus said around a large mouthful. "I told you they'd be nice."

"Us?" I asked in bemusement.

"Not specifickerly," Fergus said, still speaking with his mouthful. "Just the ship people."

I exchanged a glance with Nik.

"You were talking about those of us who came on the ship?" I asked.

"Of course." Lumi accepted the bun I was offering and took a daintier bite than her brother. "We've never had a ship arrive before. Even our ma says she's never heard of one coming. Not ever."

"And she's *old*," Fergus added.

Both children regarded us with wide eyes, expecting us to recognize the import of this news. I looked at Nik again. I doubted their mother was actually that old, but she was right that they'd never had newcomers before.

"It's natural to be curious," I said, picking my words carefully. "Is everyone talking about us, then?"

Maybe the islanders were better actors than we'd given them credit for, and their disinterest had been a show for the new arrivals.

But Lumi wrinkled her nose in an expression of disgust. "Of course not. The rest of them are never curious about *anything*."

"It's boring." Fergus gave a world-weary sigh that made me hide a laugh behind my hand.

"What about the other children?" Nik asked. "They must be curious at least?"

The nose wrinkle reappeared. "We don't play with them much," Lumi said. "They're just like their parents."

"Boring," Fergus spelled out, in case we were confused.

I considered this information, but it was hard to know what to make of it. What had happened to these people, and what made these two children different?

Fergus, who had finished his bun in record time, began clambering up a rough pile of stone that had been left against a wall in the mouth of a nearby alley.

"Careful!" Lumi called, her voice sounding more anxious than the danger warranted.

"Are the healers in town expensive?" I asked, curious as to the source of her excessive fear.

Lumi hesitated. "Not particularly. But there aren't many of them, and they're too weak to be of much use."

I frowned, exchanging yet another glance with Nik. Costas had told me that Constantines only married other strong healers. Did that mean they were hoarding the healer bloodlines?

"But in a town this size, there must be someone," I mused aloud. "Even if the Constantines are the only full healer family, there should be the odd one here and there—given the way affinities, and even strong seeds, can pop up seemingly out of nowhere."

Lumi stared at me as if she didn't know what I was talking about.

"I used to wonder the same thing," a new voice said, joining the conversation.

I jumped, startled by the new arrival, but the two children exclaimed in delight.

"Costas! Costas!"

Fergus jumped down from the pile of rocks to join his sister in swarming Costas. He smiled at them both, producing sweets from his pockets that distracted them enough that he was able to extricate himself.

"Delphine," he greeted me with a pleasant smile, his eyes traveling on to Nik with a questioning look.

"I'm Nik," the prince said shortly, looking at him with open speculation.

I tried to take a subtle step further away from Nik, remembering that Costas had witnessed my performance with Grey at the breakfast table.

"This is Costas," I said. "He's the second son of Augustine, who is the oldest Constantine son."

Costas cleared his throat awkwardly. "Actually, I'm Augustine's older son. I'm the same age as Barnabas, and Ignatius is the younger one. Thus the name."

I stared at him, and he seemed to misunderstand my confusion.

"I'm Costas now, but once upon a time I was Constantine Constantine." He shook his head. "No little boy needs to be saddled with a name like that."

"But...you're the oldest?"

"I know." He looked sheepish. "I'm well aware Ignatius is the one with *the look*."

"I'm not sure that's such a good thing in this case," I muttered, remembering my impression that Ignatius carried himself like the oldest son of the oldest son—an observation that was even less complimentary now I knew it wasn't actually his position.

"My Uncle Ambrose and Cousin Barnabas agree with you on that, I think," Costas said in an amused tone. "Since the oldest son's oldest son is such a disappointment and clearly cannot be heir, they think the torch should pass to Barnabas as the next oldest grandson."

I raised my eyebrows to hear him speaking so openly about the power dynamics in his family. Just in time I remembered I was supposed to be in thrall to the Constantines and rearranged my face accordingly.

"You seem sufficiently popular here." I gave him a sweet smile as I indicated the happy children.

He laughed. "With Fergus and Lumi, yes. As for the rest of them..." He looked across the market. "They like me well enough, I suppose. They're used to me, at least."

"That's because you actually come here," Lumi chipped in, surprising me with her awareness of the conversation. "Don't the others get bored never leaving their house?"

"Of course they leave the house sometimes, brat." Costas ruffled her hair affectionately. "You know that. They often go to one of the beaches or walk in the lower slopes of the mountain. And they come into the town on festival days."

She wrinkled her nose, an expression I was already becoming familiar with. "Not enough for us to know them like we know you."

"That's true," Costas conceded in a light tone, but something in his face gave me a different impression. I couldn't be sure whether he thought it was a good or bad thing that the townspeople weren't given the chance to get to know the rest of his family.

For the first time it occurred to me to wonder what sort of mesmerizations the Constantines used on their only non-healer son. Was he one of them, privy to all their secrets, or did his affinity make him another subject to be manipulated and controlled?

"I'm still curious about those missing healers," Nik said in a level voice that hinted at something more serious.

Costas turned to give him another interested look, while I glared at Nik from over his shoulder. Nik had done well at staying quiet so far. He should have kept it up. The last thing he needed was to catch the attention of a Constantine.

"The healers aren't missing exactly," Costas murmured, immediately understanding what Nik had meant. "Some of them have the very great honor of marrying into the Constantine family and helping to produce future healers of power."

His tone of voice suggested he considered it the opposite of an honor, and I wondered again about his absent mother.

"And the others?" Nik asked implacably.

Costas withdrew another couple of sweets from his pockets and gave them to the children, indicating they should perch themselves on a nearby planter box to eat them.

Once they were slightly removed, he lowered his voice. "It's a sad thing, but even a strong healing seed will do nothing to help you before activation. And there are so many potential accidents that can befall an adventurous child on an island like this—accidents that end in tragedy before a healer can be fetched." He paused thoughtfully. "Unadventurous children as well, apparently."

My mouth dropped open, and I was temporarily robbed of speech. Was he saying what I thought he was saying?

"That is...unfortunate," Nik said in a savage tone that gave the word a new meaning.

"Yes." Costas met his gaze steadily. "*Most* unfortunate."

I made no attempt to suppress the sick feeling swirling in my stomach. No wonder the Constantines kept to themselves. If their people had enough exposure to their rulers' true natures they would soon shake off their mesmerizations—as had happened with Serena and the rest of Grey's recruits in Caltor.

A sudden thought sent my eyes flashing to Costas. The Constantines were his family, and he lived with them on a daily basis. They might have mesmerized him a hundred times, but how long would those falsehoods ever stick?

The evidence of their true nature would soon reverse the effect of their lies. No wonder he seemed different from both them and the regular islanders.

He looked back at me, his own face as full of curiosity as mine must have been.

"It must be difficult for the people to be without strong healers," I said, unable to keep the challenge from my voice, although I knew the situation wasn't of Costas's making. "Many must die needlessly."

"Not at all," he said. "Anyone needing healing—no matter how mild the ailment—will find an open door at the manor."

"Your family heals them all freely?" I asked skeptically, remembering Grey's lack of care for his followers. I looked at Fergus and Lumi, who were edging back toward us, their eyes moving between my leftover buns and Costas's bountiful pockets.

I handed over two buns, directing my question at Lumi.

"If Fergus had fallen and hurt himself on those stones, would you have taken him up to the manor?"

"Of course not! Ma won't let us go there. That's why he should be more careful." The last sentence was delivered with a glare for her younger brother.

"She won't let you…" I said slowly, processing that.

"She doesn't send us for the monthly checkups either," Lumi volunteered.

"Monthly checkups?" Nik asked, crouching down to her level. "What do you mean?"

"Don't you have those where you come from?" She regarded him with wide eyes. "Everyone else goes up to the manor for monthly health checks."

Nik rocked back on his heels, looking up at me.

"How…generous," I said with dismay, easily recognizing the true purpose of the *checks*. "When does everyone else start going for them? When they're children?"

Lumi shrugged, not overly interested in the topic. "When they're babies, I think."

"Babies?" I repeated slowly, trying to keep my horror from my voice.

No wonder the population of the island seemed so strange—lacking in curiosity and unable to follow a logical, sequential thought process. From the earliest age, their brains had been shaped and warped by mesmerization. How could you develop a normal level of rational thought when your thoughts and experiences had always been forced to bend unnaturally around unshakable truths—truths that needed no logical explanation or evidence to back them up, truths your mind wasn't capable of questioning? The central truths of their lives didn't come from reason, logic, observation, experience, or emotion, and every other strand of their thinking had been forced to twist around those central pillars.

"Is there anyone else who doesn't go for the checkups?" I asked Lumi. "Other than you and your ma?"

She considered the question for a moment. "There was Old Man Terrier."

For a confused moment I considered questioning the name but decided it was probably a title bestowed by the local children.

"He's a hermant," Fergus supplied, making all three of us stare at him.

"I think he means hermit," Costas said after a moment, clearly stifling a laugh.

Lumi rolled her eyes. "He's not a *hermit,* Fergus. He just has no patience for annoying children." Her accusatory look suggested she thought Fergus was the main problem and that she could understand how the old man felt.

"But I saw him at the manor just last week," Costas said.

Lumi shrugged. "He used to refuse to go, but then he got that fever."

"Fever?" I looked to Costas, who winced.

"It went through the town three winters ago. It was a new one, and my whole family had to come down from the manor and go house to house to stamp it out."

Lumi nodded. "Ma took us up the mountain at the first talk of a new sickness, so we escaped. But when we came back, Old Man Terrier was going to the manor for checkups like everyone else." She shrugged again.

I gulped, understanding what must have happened. After a lifetime of quiet resistance, a single illness had forced him into contact with the Constantines.

Without meaning to, my gaze met Costas's, and I read the same sadness in his eyes. Seized by a moment of recklessness, I spoke even more openly than I had so far.

"And your family is all right with Lumi and Fergus and their mother not going for these checkups?" I asked him.

He frowned. "Their mother lives a quiet, secluded life, keeping out of notice as much as possible. I'm not sure anyone in my family even knows they exist."

I stared at him, and he looked back, his gaze direct and open. There was no doubt Costas was different from the rest of his family, and his expression and words suggested he recognized there was something different about me, as well.

But being different on this island was dangerous. And I didn't know how far I could trust Costas. Was he just pretending sorrow over his family's actions in order to win our trust?

An insidious thought snaked into my mind. All it would take was a light touch, and I could make sure Costas saw me as safe and unthreatening. My power could override any suspicious word or action he might have observed.

Would it be such a terrible thing to tamper with a single morning's memories if it meant keeping Nik and me safe? If his family weren't above killing those who threatened their rule, then the danger was real.

But as I pictured myself doing it, every part of me rebelled. If I started down that path, where would it end? Just because I had the power to do it, it didn't give me the right to meddle with someone else's mind.

Instead, I would have to take a risk and choose to trust Costas.

Nik looked down at me with a question in his eyes, but I just shrugged, unable to explain myself. He might not agree with my decision—not when my safety was at risk—but that didn't matter. At the end of the day, this was my ability and that made the responsibility mine. I would not choose to mesmerize someone just to keep myself safe.

# CHAPTER
# TWENTY-NINE

Costas offered to walk me back to the manor, and I put a quick restraining hand on Nik's arm before he could protest. I could see the storm in his eyes, but I glared at him until he sighed, his shoulders relaxing. Nik couldn't go anywhere near the manor.

"Thank you," I told Costas, who had watched the brief interchange with far too much curiosity.

He led me back through a maze of streets, bypassing the market square, and I caught enough glimpses of movement behind us to know Nik was shadowing us. He could do that all he liked as long as he stopped at the edge of the main town, not continuing on to the manor grounds.

But when we reached the edge of the manor gardens, Costas stopped as well, looking at me ruefully.

"You should probably go on ahead on your own from here. It won't do you any good to be seen with me."

I raised an eyebrow, and his self-deprecating smile grew. "They tolerate me because I'm family, but you won't win any points from association."

I wanted to protest and tell him I would rather be associated with him than any of the rest of his family, but I wasn't here for a social visit. Despite the guarded level of openness that had existed between us in the town, I had to remain wary.

So I merely nodded agreement and left him behind, glancing back over my shoulder only once. He was watching me go with the same curious expression he'd worn earlier.

Inside, I had to ask a young woman busy scrubbing the floor for directions to my room. She stopped her task and took me there herself, chattering the whole way about the plans that had been made in my absence. Apparently there was to be a party the next night in honor of Grey's return, and she was to serve at it.

"Wouldn't you rather attend than serve?" I asked.

"Me? Attend?" She threw her head back and laughed, a light, merry sound at odds with her words.

I considered pressing the matter or asking further questions, but after all my interactions in the market there seemed little point. Especially when her continued chatter revealed she had only been working at the manor for a month. Apparently all the staff changed regularly, a necessity if the Constantines wanted to keep the population at arm's length.

I half-expected lunch to be the same formal affair as breakfast, but instead I was served a meal on a tray in my room. I wasn't especially hungry after what I'd eaten at the market, and it wasn't long before I lapsed into severe boredom. I would have thought it impossible to feel so restless given the danger of the situation, but apparently an empty room and nothing to do produced the same effect regardless of any looming peril.

Eventually I escaped to the gardens, my boredom instantly lifting when Phoenix came speeding toward me. He must have been busy hunting or exploring our new surroundings when I left for the market, but he had clearly been on the watch for me since.

Calmed by his familiar weight on my shoulder, I wandered through the ordered, sculpted gardens which circled the manor. When I reached a collection of rose bushes that were surrounded by a tall hedge, I paused and sat on a well-positioned bench. I obviously wasn't the only one to enjoy the artificial haven, but I couldn't deny it felt like a relief to be out of sight of the staring windows of the manor house.

I had barely begun to relax, however, when I heard a rustling in the hedge behind me. Whirling, I saw a bundle of orange and white fur pushing through the leaves.

"Ember!" I scooped her up and held her close. "What are you doing here? You're supposed to be with Nik!"

She looked up at me with her dark, liquid eyes, and my heart melted. But at the same time, I couldn't risk keeping her at the manor. Grey would definitely recognize her and question her presence.

Footsteps sounded on the gravel path, and I jumped to my feet, trying to hide Ember with my skirts. But only one person rounded the hedge, gazing in wonder at the profusion of roses.

"Ida," I exclaimed in relief. "What are you doing here?"

"We've been bringing supplies up from the ship, and someone said we're free to look around the gardens. They're so beautiful!"

She still bore the shining look of hope from earlier in the day, and I wondered what interactions she'd had with the locals.

"How are you finding it so far?" I asked cautiously.

"It's wonderful!" She sighed in deep satisfaction. "Everything is so beautiful and peaceful."

"Has anyone asked you any questions or shown any interest in you?" I asked.

"None whatsoever." She sounded delighted.

My heart squeezed. What had Ida experienced in the past that she found a complete lack of interest from anyone to be a delightful prospect?

But her words gave me an idea.

"Are you staying at the manor for the afternoon?"

She shook her head. "I'm about to head back to my host's house now that I've seen the gardens."

I stooped and picked up Ember, holding the fox out to the older woman. "Would you be willing to look after Ember for me?"

"Your fox?" Ida took her willingly enough, and to my relief Ember didn't protest either. "I didn't realize she was with you."

I nodded. "She came on the ship." I spoke the words matter-of-factly, as if there was nothing interesting about the situation.

Hopefully she wouldn't ask any questions—and neither would her hosts. With everyone so uninterested in the newcomers, I didn't think anyone would make a fuss about a single fox.

Ida wasn't a healer, but I'd had a feeling she would be good with animals, and it was clear I was right. From the way she was already fussing over Ember as she walked away, I should be worried Ember might never want to come back to me.

Phoenix pecked at my ear, and I scolded him loudly.

"Don't worry," I reassured him. "It's only for a little while. We'll get Ember back soon."

He settled slowly, ruffling his feathers, one of his eyes trained on Ida's disappearing figure.

"I didn't know you cared so much," I muttered, secretly delighted that the falcon had grown attached to Ember.

I just hoped I was right about being able to retrieve her soon. I didn't think I could keep up our complicated ruse for long.

The problem was that I had no idea what our next steps should be. How did we extricate ourselves from the situation safely without leaving Tartora open to constant attack?

I walked slowly back to the house, reaching the back porch just in time to see Ignatius and Augustine come striding outside, engaged in heated debate.

"Watch yourself, son," Augustine snapped, too absorbed in the conversation to notice me lingering among the ornamental fruit trees. "You're not the heir, and you won't be for many years to come. I intend to live a long life."

Ignatius, who was slightly taller than his father, looked down his nose at him. "I won't ever be the heir if Uncle Ambrose has his way. He'll push that weakling cousin of mine to the front if he can possibly manage it."

"Which is why I'm telling you that you need to moderate your behavior. You shouldn't have gone dashing off on your own this morning. My brother has been in your grandmother's ear about it all morning, saying you lacked proper respect for your elders and your place."

Ignatius's manner became even more haughty. "I received urgent word that a ship was already in the process of berthing. I could hardly delay to find someone more fitting. We can be glad I was there so quickly, or we might have been overrun before we knew what was happening."

His words sounded like the truth, but it was easy to read on his face that he had been more than happy to receive the message alone.

"Pretty words," his father snapped, clearly perceiving the same thing. "But no one knows better than the Constantines how useless those are."

"Guard your tongue, Father!" Ignatius said with heat, throwing a glance around the garden.

He caught sight of me at once, locking eyes with me before I had the chance to look away. I curtsied, mustering up a smile that must have looked far from relaxed. Ignatius's brows lowered, his eyes dwelling on me for too long.

When he finally looked away, it was to murmur a quiet word to his father, the two of them disappearing around the edge of the building.

"There's nothing to worry about," I murmured more to myself than Phoenix. "He thinks I'm mesmerized, and nothing they just said could possibly have broken through that. Not from one conversation."

But I couldn't shake the feeling that I'd undone my efforts over breakfast, regaining Ignatius's suspicious interest.

I circled the building in the opposite direction to them, nearly colliding with Grey.

"There you are! I've been looking everywhere for you."

"For me?" I asked, relieved he hadn't found me earlier when I was with either Nik or Ember. "Did something happen?"

"No, but we have no time to waste." He smiled, looking far too pleased for my comfort. "The situation is even better than I imagined, but we shouldn't hesitate to get to work."

"What do you want me to do?" I asked with a sinking heart.

He was going to ask me to mesmerize someone, and the moment I refused, it would all be over. He would realize I'd found a way to break free from him, and I would instantly transform in his mind from his greatest tool to an adversary who needed to be eliminated. I would have to at least pretend I meant to comply while I worked out what to do instead.

"I need you to find Grandmother," he said. "She's been careful not to touch me, and the others have been equally careful never to leave me alone with her. She might be elderly, but she still rules this family. You, on the other hand, are just a young girl with an elements affinity. None of them will see you as a threat. Good work at breakfast, by the way."

I thought uneasily of Ignatius's suspicious eyes but said nothing.

"You want me to mesmerize your grandmother?" I asked, feeling sickened.

"Of course I only want to help my family," he said earnestly, as if only just remembering the line he was supposed to follow. "But I can't do that when they don't trust me. All I'm asking you to do is reinforce the emotions that Grandmother naturally feels. Just remind her how overjoyed she is at my return, and that she always loved my mother best. It's only natural she would want to have her daughter's son by her side, especially since I'm both her strongest and most trustworthy grandson."

I stared at him, barely restraining myself from rolling my eyes. Would my mesmerized self really have fallen for this line? Sadly I knew I had previously fallen for more outrageous lies.

And in truth, what he was asking wasn't entirely contrary to his grandmother's natural response. She really had seemed happy to see him again.

That thought allowed me to consider another one. Could I really do it? I had refused to mesmerize Costas, but that had been because I mistrusted the instinct that drove me to do it, driven as it was by my desire for self-protection. But this was different. I would merely be reinforcing an idea the grandmother already had, and by playing along with Grey for the moment, I would ultimately be protecting her and her family from him, as well as all of Tartora from the lot of them. Working with Grey now would give me time to discover his full plan and work out how to undermine it.

"All right," I said. "I'll go find her now."

"Good girl." Grey's eyes glowed, and it was hard to keep my smile in place. I only managed it by thinking of how happy I was to be leaving his presence.

It took me a while to find the Constantine matriarch, sticking my head into room after room until I finally found her in a brightly lit sitting room presiding over a tea tray. She was pouring tea for her daughter-in-law when I arrived, and I saw a flash of something calculating and curious in her gaze before she quickly covered it with a false grandmotherly warmth.

"Welcome, child!" she called. "Would you like to join us for tea?"

I nodded, dropping a belated curtsy.

"I had been hoping one of the newcomers might join us." She patted the sofa at her side invitingly. "I would so love to hear about life on the mainland."

*Yes,* I thought sourly. *Because you haven't had your curiosity and free thought sucked out of you by a lifetime of manipulation.*

On the outside, I smiled and accepted the offered seat. The elderly woman made no move to pour me a cup, however, instead reaching for my hand with both of hers. I braced myself.

After all my practice on the ship, I was confident in my ability to mesmerize. But this would be a challenge—both due to her strength and experience and because she would be trying to simultaneously mesmerize me.

My one hope lay in our deception. She had no reason to be suspicious, and unlike Ignatius on the docks, she wouldn't be in a hurry. Which meant I had a chance to get my mesmerization in first, before she began to confuse my mind. It would be a delicate matter, however, since I would need to watch my words. Ambrose's wife, Kendry, must be a healer as well, and she would sense any lie I uttered from the other side of the small table holding the tea set.

As soon as the grandmother's hands brushed my right one, gathering it up into a warm grasp, I sent my power slithering into her. I threw out only the tiniest tendril necessary, rushing into speech as I did.

"We're so grateful for your hospitality. Especially Grey. He has longed so much to be here with you all. And he's so strong." *The strongest!* my power echoed. "He clearly belongs here with his family." *You can trust him!* "I can only imagine how much you must miss his mother, your daughter, Chloe." *She was your favorite. How glad you are to have her son back.*

The grandmother's face instantly softened. "You're right, my dear. What a thoughtful young thing you are. But it is our pleasure to have Grey back where he belongs. I couldn't be happier to see him again."

Across the table, Kendry watched us with a slight crease between her brows. But her focus wasn't on me or my words but on her mother-in-law. Was she worried about her attitude toward Grey? I had suspected from the beginning that the younger generations viewed him as a threat, and his aunt's expression seemed to confirm it. Her son, Barnabas, already had enough competition from his younger cousin.

I hoped Grey didn't expect me to mesmerize every member of the family, starting with his grandmother and working my way down. I had a sick feeling that might be his plan, however. If he didn't, they were going to turn on him sooner rather than later.

"But I hope you know you are also welcome," the grandmother continued, her words ringing in my mind with truth. "You can trust us to take care of you."

"Of course," I said, the agreement coming easily and naturally. "I feel fortunate to have made it to such an incredible place."

The grandmother smiled in satisfaction, dropping my hand and exchanging a lightning-fast look with her daughter-in-law that triggered a queasy feeling in my middle.

Responding to that feeling had become instinct at this point. I threw up my wall, driving the lingering effects of the woman's power from my mind.

As soon as it was gone, I could think clearly again. As soon as my mind was my own, exhaustion crashed over me. I couldn't stay in this room where I had to watch every word and expression.

I jumped to my feet. "Please don't call for an extra cup," I said in a rush. "I would be embarrassed to interrupt your afternoon ritual." I curtsied again to both women. "You've already done so much by welcoming me into your home." *So much damage,* I added silently.

"You really are a most considerate child," the grandmother said with a smile that showed more of her true calculating nature than her earlier expression had done. "I don't know what my third grandson can have been thinking. He's becoming fanciful in all the excitement."

I kept my expression neutral, pretending not to notice the hint of pleasure on Kendry's face at this criticism of Ignatius.

Curtsying again, I backed out of the room as if they were queens. As soon as I closed the door behind me, I fled down the hall, not stopping until I was back in my own room.

My heart raced, and I didn't even think about slowing it down. Had I really just done that? I had matched wits and power with a woman who had spent decades mesmerizing people, and I had come out on top. It was only because I had been the one with the element of surprise, equipped both to mesmerize and to protect myself against its effects, but I couldn't deny the feeling of power.

I took deep breaths, trying to calm myself. This reaction was what I feared most. I couldn't let myself become enamored with this new and dangerous ability.

I had regained some of my calm before the evening meal, but even so, it was a fraught event. Every look and word was measured—not just by me but by everyone else around me—until it felt less like conversation and more like the thrust and parry of a fencing match.

Costas seemed the most honest and open of the group, but far too often I felt his curious eyes on me. By the end of the evening I wanted to snap at him to stop looking at me—unless he was trying to put a sign around my neck for the rest of his family to see.

The pounding in my head became so bad that I couldn't help massaging it, reaching out with my power to ease it at the same time. My face relaxed as soon as the pain eased, but it tensed again when I looked up to see Costas watching me with an arrested expression, his eyes narrowing. I hurriedly turned to Kendry next to me and launched into speech, but I could still feel his eyes on me.

Even at the end of the interminable evening, Grey insisted on walking me back to my room. Ignatius's knowing look made my skin crawl, and Grey's pleased praise when we were alone had nearly as uncomfortable an effect.

By the time I closed my bedroom door and leaned against it, I never wanted to emerge again.

# THIRTY

Thankfully, breakfast was delivered on a tray the next morning. According to the girl who delivered it, no one had time for a formal meal when they were busy preparing for the party.

I had opened my window the night before, letting Phoenix inside, and with the falcon to keep me company, I hid inside my room like a coward all day.

Eventually I had to emerge, however. I knew that if I didn't give Grey a chance to find me before the party began, he'd come barging into my room, and I couldn't bear to have him inside my one safe haven.

Sure enough, I'd barely stepped out of the house when he appeared. Grabbing my arm, he whisked me off to the rose garden.

"Everything is working perfectly," he said as soon as he was sure we were alone. "You might as well have released a hornet's nest in the manor house. They're all furious."

"And that's a good thing?" I couldn't quite keep the skepticism out of my voice.

Grey shot me a look, and I added, "Aren't you worried they're all going to team up and come after you?"

He relaxed at this suggestion that I was only concerned for him. I hoped he did mean to explain, however, since I was legitimately curious as to what he hoped to achieve by oversetting the Constantines' very fragile balance.

An unnerving smile spread over his face. "That's why we're going to direct their attention and anger elsewhere."

"We?" I asked, my voice squeaking.

"Don't worry, my dear." He patted my hand. "You've proven yourself more than capable. All my lessons have paid off."

Trickling cold started in my scalp and crept down. I wished I could block my ears and not hear whatever Grey was going to say next because I already knew I wasn't going to like it. I had convinced myself that it wouldn't do any great harm to play along with Grey for one mesmerization—that it was even serving the greater good. But in retrospect I could see my mistake. If the results of my efforts pleased Grey this much, then I had greatly underestimated their significance.

I had known it was the wrong thing to do to mesmerize anyone, but I had done it anyway. Now I was learning the lesson again—hopefully for the last time—but was it already too late?

"During the party, I'm going to lure Ignatius away," Grey said. "I'll find a way to keep him occupied just long enough. All we need is to have him out of sight."

"Wh...Why?" I managed to choke out.

"As soon as you see me disappear, you need to find Augustine. Mesmerize him into believing Ignatius is dead and Ambrose and Barnabas were the ones to kill him. That's all you have to do."

"Just...just that," I whispered weakly, and Grey nodded, apparently taking my words as understanding and agreement.

I could barely see him, though, my vision a haze as I finally realized what Grey was planning. He must have been assuming that, in my mesmerized state, I wouldn't understand his intentions. But he didn't know what Nik had said to me back on the ship after I mesmerized him into believing Ember was dead.

Back then, Nik had imagined a situation all too much like this one. He had said that you couldn't order someone to kill, but you could manipulate them into doing it of their own volition—for instance, by claiming someone they loved was dead. Grey intended for Augustine to retaliate against his brother and nephew, ripping the Constantine family apart in the most vicious and violent way, and ensuring that whoever was left at the end was easy pickings for Grey.

I wouldn't do it. However evil the Constantines were, there was no way I would be party to this.

But I couldn't say as much to Grey right now. That would be suicide. I had to at least pretend I meant to comply.

I went through the motions, glad Grey was too distracted by his plan to expect any particular input from me. If only I had come out of my room earlier. At this point, the party was almost ready to start, and I had far too little time to work out what to do.

I trailed behind Grey back to the manor house, racking my brains for a plan. But the harder I thought, the more any sensible ideas escaped me. Instead, my mind whirled in a circle, moving faster and faster and less and less productively.

One of Grey's female followers met me outside my room, gushing excitedly about the beautiful dresses we'd been loaned for the occasion. Her room was next to mine, and she was already wearing hers, a floating yellow concoction that reminded me of a dessert.

She wanted to accompany me inside to see mine, and I let her, my mind numbed by panic. The gown laid out on my bed was a deep forest green, and in normal circumstances, I would have been as excited about its elegant flowing lines as my companion. I had certainly never worn such a garment before.

As it was, however, I stepped into it mindlessly, letting the serving girl who arrived to assist me do up the endless row of buttons. She chattered away the entire time she buttoned, eventually breaking through my fog enough that I recognized her as the girl who had told me about the party the day before.

Her excitement hadn't dimmed in the intervening time, and she enthusiastically offered to arrange my hair. I agreed, glad I didn't have to think about it myself, and she somehow wrestled the tight curls into a complicated pattern of braids that crisscrossed my head.

Even through the confusion and panic, I recognized her skill, marveling at the face looking back at me from the mirror. I looked older, more confident, and more womanly. I just wished the appearance came with wisdom to match it. If only Amara was here to tell me what to do.

If I told the Constantines about Grey's plan, they would be more than a match for him with their numbers and combined strength. But where would that leave me and Tartora? If I did nothing, however, Grey would soon realize my betrayal and do something even more drastic—but this time I would be another name on the list of intended victims.

Far too soon, the serving girl was declaring me finished and ushering me out the door. Phoenix had already been banished outside, and I wished I had a beak and claws of my own so I could scratch and fight, struggling against the inexorable forces sweeping me forward.

But all I had was my words and my power, and I couldn't think what use either of them might be in the situation.

The room hosting the party was a large one I had yet to encounter, almost grand enough to be called a ballroom. The polished floorboards shone in the light of innumerable branches of candles, and a long table bent slightly under the weight of the food covering its surface.

Plants mages had filled the room with blossoms, their vines growing through the open windows and doors or twining upward from large pots placed around the edge of the room. They created a riot of color and scent, reminding me that we were far from home.

I had expected the party to be teeming with people, the room so crowded you could barely move. But while there was a small crowd, they were fewer in number than I had envisioned.

The Constantines themselves stood out, their clothes finer than anyone else's, the gold and silver threads sparkling in a way that suggested they were spun from the actual metals. But besides them, I could see only familiar faces from the ship.

I peered around the room, sure that I had to be wrong. But the more I looked, the more certain I became. When my eyes alighted on the same serving girl, now bearing a tray of drinks, I hurried over to her.

She beamed at me, her eyes shining as she looked around at the sumptuous room.

"Isn't it beautiful?" she breathed. "Even better than I imagined."

"But where are all the people?" I asked.

"What do you mean?" She surveyed the partygoers with a crease between her eyes. "I don't think anyone is missing."

"I mean, where are the locals?"

"The locals?" Her eyes traveled to a clump of Constantines standing close by. "You mean the Constantines? You can see Ambrose and Kendry over there, and just beyond them is—"

"No, no, I mean the regular people. From the town."

She burst out into the same peals of laughter as earlier, and I finally realized why she had found my original question so amusing. The idea of her attendance hadn't been laughable because she was low-ranking or poor within the town. It was because no one in the town had been invited to the party at all.

"Is anyone from the town ever invited here?" I asked. "As a guest, rather than a servant or patient, I mean."

Her laugh trailed off into giggles. "No, of course not. It's a very great honor that you've all been invited. You must be highly favored."

A sinking feeling made my legs tremble. I spun in a circle, taking in the scene again. The Constantines were now moving through the crowd, a handshake here, a light touch there, a pat on the shoulder. We weren't favored: we were new. All of this was designed to bind us tighter and tighter to this family and the strange life they lived on this island.

I caught sight of Ida's happy smile as she bowed her head over the grandmother's hand. I knew it must have been my imagination, especially at this distance, but I thought I could see her eyes growing more vacant and glassy. I shivered, stumbling my way through the crowd to seek the meager relief of the closest wall.

Strong arms steadied me, guiding me behind the closest large pot where the rest of the room was at least partially shielded from view.

I sucked in a deep breath and then another, the overwhelmed panic slowly fading, replaced with a sense of security. But as soon as my mind kicked back into proper motion, I looked up, the horrified feeling returning.

Nik had meant safety to me for so long that my body responded instinctively to his presence. But on this occasion it was betraying me.

"What are you doing here?" I hissed. "You can't be here!"

He smiled down at me like he had in the market, except I could see that this time the expression was masking his concern. He'd just seen the state I was in.

"Of course I had to come. How could I miss the chance to see you dressed like this? Delphine, you look stunning."

I brushed away his words, although some small part of my mind tucked them away to be brought out and treasured later.

"Never mind that. You really can't be here!"

"It was fine in the market," he said with his usual confidence. "And it'll be even easier here since it's more crowded. None of Grey's people will be surprised to see a local man dancing attendance on you—not when you look like that."

"No! Nik!" I grabbed his arm and looked up at him beseechingly. "You're not listening to me. They didn't invite any locals tonight! It's only people from the ship and the Constantines themselves."

I looked around frantically, trying to spot if anyone had already noticed him. At least we were tucked away, mostly out of sight.

"I'm not leaving." His voice was back to its usual steel. "Not when I haven't seen you since yesterday morning. And something has happened. I can see that clearly. I won't leave you. There is no risk I wouldn't take to keep you safe."

I moaned. Yet another reason why I shouldn't have hidden in my room all day.

"How is you being caught by Grey going to keep me safe?" I demanded.

"First tell me what happened," he said, unmoved by my pleading.

Shamefaced, I confessed what I had done at Grey's instigation and what his next step was. Nik shook his head slowly.

"That's extreme, even for Grey. This is his own family we're talking about."

"I don't think he sees them that way. From a few things he's let slip, I think he sees them only as the people who abandoned him and his mother. I'm not sure who he resents more for depriving him of the life of privilege he should have led—them or her."

"And now he wants revenge." Nik looked cold and unsympathetic.

"And even more than that, he wants to reclaim that life—but with no one at the top but him."

I looked through the leaves of a climbing vine and spotted Grey across the room. At least he was talking with Barnabas, not Ignatius, so I still had a bit of time.

When I looked back at Nik, I found him watching me with a horrified, sick expression.

"What is it?" I asked, distracted.

"If he means to rule this island as the only Constantine, he'll be solely responsible for ensuring the family line continues. And as we now know, there are no other strong healers on this island for him to marry."

All the blood rushed from my face as I realized what Nik was saying. Grey may not have intended it from the beginning, but I had no doubt he would be willing to force me into the role of his bride through any means necessary.

"This ends tonight," Nik growled.

I grabbed his arm with both my hands. "Nik, wait, no! What are you thinking? We need an actual plan!"

Nik calmed slightly, giving me his attention. "You have a plan?"

I bit my lip. "No. But we need to come up with one. And I think..." I drew a deep breath. "I think we can trust Costas. I think we should include him in this."

"Costas? But he's one of them."

"By blood, yes, but not where it matters. He's not a healer, and it's clear that's all they care about. He's a complete outsider here."

Nik stilled, and I knew he was thinking of his own family. I only hoped he was seeing how much worse it could have been and remembering the good moments with his sister and parents—the moments I suspected Costas had never had.

"I think he was so open with us yesterday because he sensed there was something different about the two of us. I think he might be hoping for allies."

I peered through the leaves again, but I couldn't see Costas anywhere in the room.

"Where is he?" I whispered, frustrated. "We don't have time for any delays."

"I'll find him," Nik said. "If you leave, Grey might notice."

Reluctantly I accepted his reasoning. "Please hurry," I begged, and he nodded, already slipping away from me.

With a fortifying breath, I entered the crowd again, circulating toward the supper table, although I was sure I couldn't force any food into my leaden belly. All I needed was to be seen, to give Grey the reassurance he might need.

With every minute that passed, my tension rose, but there was nothing I could do to hurry Nik. All I could do was wait, and it seemed like the hardest task of all.

"Delphine!" Costas's cheerful voice nearly made me collapse with relief. Nik had found him.

I turned to greet him, his smile fading as he took in my wide-eyed expression. Grabbing his arm, I dragged him through a nearby full-length window and out onto the porch beyond. Tucking ourselves behind a tall, potted tree, I finally let his arm drop.

"Delphine? Is something wrong?"

I opened my mouth only to close it again when I realized I had no idea where to begin.

But Costas seemed to pick up on what was happening anyway. "Grey is making a move tonight? Even I can sense how unsettled everyone is."

I nodded. "He's planning to turn you all against each other."

"How is that possible? None of us will risk letting him touch our skin. My family are wrong-headed about a lot of things, but they aren't fools."

I took a deep breath. This was it. The moment where I was putting everything on the line.

"It's me. I don't really have an elements affinity. I'm a healer. A strong one. And Grey has taught me how to mesmerize."

Costas sucked in an audible breath, confirming my impression that to a Constantine it was unthinkable that the ability would be shared outside the family.

"I guessed there was something different about you," he said. "I even wondered if you were a healer. But this…"

"I'm so sorry, Costas, but I mesmerized your grandmother under Grey's instruction. I thought it was a small thing to do, just to ensure our place here. I didn't realize it would set off such a disastrous chain of circumstances."

"You've only been here two days. How could you know how deep the animosity goes between my father and my uncle, with the next generation following in their wake? Grandmother has been the only one keeping the peace for a while now, and when she greeted Grey so warmly, and then grew more and more pleased with him…" He sighed. "Even I didn't realize quite how delicate the balance of power had become in my family. But I suppose Grey is to blame for that, as well."

"What do you mean?" I asked. "How could he be to blame for the state of the Constantines before our arrival?"

"I suppose it's possible it might be someone else." Costas peered at me. "Does anyone else on the mainland know about our existence? I thought it was only Grey."

"As far as I know it is only him. Why?"

He hesitated. "Are you aware of some recent attacks on your homeland?"

"The false blight and the storms, you mean?"

"Yes. Ignatius is behind those. Not that he acted alone, of course. But there are plenty of strong plants and elements mages in the town, so he took some of them with him. He even took Barnabas as well to help with mesmerizing. But the two of them came back with very different ideas about what to do next."

"What do you mean? Are they planning further attacks on Tartora?"

"Barnabas thinks the retaliation was sufficient, and that we should go back to our established life as rulers here—with himself as heir, naturally. Ignatius has other ideas, though. He thinks Tartora is ripe for the plucking. He hasn't said it directly, but I think he has dreams of something greater than being the next lord of the manor. He wants a crown and a throne."

I gasped. "He wants to take Tartora by force?"

Costas waggled his fingers, his expression sad. "Not the normal kind of force."

I shivered. "He won't find it such an easy thing to keep an entire kingdom in thrall like he does with a single town."

"Would he really need to, though? Wouldn't it be enough to entrap key people at the capital?"

"Perhaps," I said slowly, unsure of the answer myself. But I was very sure I never wanted to see him try.

"But why is this all happening now?" I asked. "And why is Grey to blame?"

Costas's expression changed to one of surprise. "You don't know? Did he keep it secret even from his followers? He must have had some of them helping him, at least."

"I only came to Grey's camp days before we sailed," I said. "I know very little about his plans and actions before that."

"It's possible I'm wrong," Costas said, "but I don't think so. Someone attacked us first, and there's no one else it could have been but Grey. Of course, originally we had no idea Grey was still out there. We thought the mainlanders must have discovered our existence, so Ignatius convinced the elders to let him take a small boat to the mainland to retaliate. But on their return Barnabas claimed the Tartorans were as ignorant about our existence as ever. And when Ignatius was pushed, he had to agree. So now Uncle Ambrose and Barnabas blame me, saying I made a mistake."

"You? What does it have to do with you?"

"I'm the only one in the family with an elements seed—I'm the strongest elements mage on the island, in fact, although my family doesn't value that. I was the one to tell them that the fire which took our crops wasn't started by lightning but by arson—though it couldn't have been anyone from the town, for obvious reasons. No one here could manage such a deception. And later, after their return, I was the one to warn them that the storm which sank one of our fishing boats wasn't natural. In fact, I was the one to turn the storm around and push it back the way it came from."

He grimaced. "Of course I found out later that Ignatius ordered a whole group of elements mages from the town to combine their power to make it larger and more potent. I had let it go by that point, so I didn't realize until much later when someone mentioned it in passing."

He gave me a shadowed look. "I suppose many lives were lost?"

"I'm afraid they were." I wished I could give him better news. "It hit a coastal city that had many ships out at sea."

He winced.

"But I'm not sure I'm following," I said. "You're saying that Grey came here first in a smaller boat—on a stealth mission—and burned your crops? And then he sent a storm after one of your ships? So everything your family did against Tartora was direct retaliation for what you thought were attacks from us?"

"That's right. Ignatius claims King Marius must know about us and be keeping the information quiet from the common citizens."

"He doesn't," I said. "I'm completely sure about that."

"As soon as Grey arrived, the answer seemed obvious," Costas agreed. "It all came from Grey. He was trying to destabilize the situation before his official arrival, and he succeeded more than he could have dreamed. He has several times referred to having been on the island before, but the others believe he means as a baby."

"How could they not suspect him?"

"Oh, they suspect him of wanting to take their place, but they're blinded in other ways. There are certain things they believe a Constantine would never do. After a century of absolute rule and control, they've bought into their own myth."

"Like teach someone outside the family how to mesmerize," I murmured.

He nodded, and I could read in his eyes why he hadn't fallen into the same trap. He wasn't a Constantine like the others, and he could imagine doing things they would never dream of.

"Even so, it seems impossible they wouldn't at least suspect him."

Costas shrugged. "Perhaps they do, privately. But Uncle Ambrose and Barnabas are set on pretending everything is normal and we can continue our regular lives, and Ignatius is just as set on insisting King Marius is to blame for everything. Nobody wants to admit that we were attacked, but not by the Tartorans."

"How come Ignatius and Barnabas didn't run into Grey at his camp when they came to the mainland?" I asked. "They seemed genuinely surprised he was still alive."

"They were. But that's because they took a different route."

"There's more than one?"

"Of course. There are at least three. The one you would have taken is the simplest and leads to the most attractive harbor on the desert side. But the people who live in the crevasse parted from our ancestors with ill will a century ago, refusing to take ship to the island with the majority. We would never use that route, although we should have realized Aunt Chloe would flee straight to them. She shared many of their ideals, so I suspect they welcomed her with open arms."

"Did you know her?" I asked, finally able to indulge my curiosity about the topic.

"Only as a very young child. But I have snatches of memory of her still, and occasionally I've gotten Aunt Kendry to talk about her when no one else is around. She fell in love with a non-healer instead of the man assigned to be her husband. She defied the family and married her plants mage, and they wouldn't forgive her for it. She was merry and colorful and full of the sort of life that is missing from this island, and she wanted to change the way the family operated."

The story reminded me of Grey's original claims, although it was different in key respects. "So what happened?" I asked.

"Her husband died in an accident that was obviously not an accident."

"They had him killed!"

"My aunt snatched up her infant son and ran for her life. The only time she was truly happy on this island was during her brief marriage, so I don't think she was sorry to go."

"It's hard to sort out the truth from the fiction with Grey," I murmured. "But I think it's true that she arrived in the crevasse to find only a single elderly couple left. She would have been able to choose a house from the ones abandoned as their numbers dwindled, and the couple helped her get established and raise her son. She must have wanted a different life for him, but Grey doesn't seem to have taken after her. He heard her stories about life here and took a different message from the one she intended."

“Of course I did.”
The cold voice sent shivers down my spine.

CHAPTER

# THIRTY-ONE

I turned slowly, not wanting to confirm what I already knew. Grey had found us.

"She stole me away from the life I should have lived," Grey continued. "A life of luxury where I ruled like a prince. And for what? So we could scratch out a living in the desert, with only two doddering old fools for company, surviving on the occasional trading trip to Eldrida? We could have moved to Eldrida, at least. No one would have known our true origins, and with her ability, we could have made a comfortable life there. But she could never let go of the island. These people murdered my father, but it was like she both loved and hated them at the same time."

Costas and I were both frozen and silent in the face of Grey's simmering resentment. I wished there was some way to show him the burning look in his eyes, and to make him realize that his mother wasn't the only one to carry an unnatural, unhelpful obsession with her past.

"But that isn't what's important now," he said, his eyes fixed on me and his silky voice promising pain and suffering. "It seems someone has learned how to deceive me."

"Grey." Costas stepped forward, as if to confront Grey, but I pulled him back. He had no idea what he was dealing with and no experience with combat.

"Where did you leave Nik?" I hissed at him.

"Nik?" Costas glanced back at me, clearly confused and speaking far too loudly.

I winced at the flash of recognition and fury on Grey's face when he caught Nik's name.

"Didn't he find you and send you to me?" I whispered urgently to Costas.

Costas started to shake his head, and I quickly hurried on.

"In that case he must still be out there looking for you. Go quickly and find him!"

Costas hesitated, and I shoved him away, angling him as far from Grey's reach as possible. Finally picking up on my urgency, he sprinted away, plunging back into the party. The bright lights and chattering voices were only feet away but seemed like a separate world.

"Our rogue prince is here, is he?" Grey asked in the same dangerously smooth voice. "I suppose he was a stowaway."

I tried not to show my fear. I hadn't been sure Grey realized Nik's identity after the battle in Caltor. But clearly he had.

"Nicely played, young spy," Grey said. "But you do know the fate of spies, don't you?"

Moving lightning fast, he lunged forward and dug his fingers into my braids. I screamed as he dragged me along, but the sound was covered by the sound of merriment inside.

I tried to dig my feet in and shake him off, but his grip was iron firm, and the pain propelled me forward.

Dragging me into the garden, he flung me onto the ground on a stretch of lawn some distance from the lights of the party. I tumbled down, only just catching my fall. As I rolled onto my back, I sent my power racing to soothe the pain in my scalp.

Grey stepped toward me, his green eyes flashing. Bending over, he grabbed me around the neck and pulled me upward.

"This time you're not going to have a thought left in your mind that's still your own," he growled.

Forgetting about subterfuge or my own power to mesmerize, I reacted on instinct, throwing up my wall. Grey's power tried to snake into me, but it got nowhere. He tried again, grunting in effort as he struggled to break past my wall.

But just like in our experiments on the ship, he got nowhere.

"That wall!" he spat out, his tone turning the word into a curse.

I glared back at him, putting all my defiance into my expression.

"Don't look at me like that," he snapped. "You've misplayed this time. If I can't control you, then you're no use to me."

His fingers around my throat tightened, cutting off my air supply.

My hands reacted on instinct, flying up to try to prize his fingers loose. But my physical efforts weren't the focus of my attention. Wielding my power like a battering ram, I shoved it into him through the connection of his hands.

He felt it coming, though, and jumped back at the first whisper of my touch, shoving me away with such force that I fell again.

"You dare...!" he sputtered, but I could see he was shaken.

For the first time he was realizing that when it came to our power, I outmatched him. He had taught me his trick, but he hadn't been able to learn mine.

The knowledge only made him more dangerous, however. He pulled his sword from its scabbard with a ringing noise that echoed in my head. I drew my own knife in response, but its length was tiny compared to the reach of his blade. I would have no way to stop his sword reaching me.

Once again he moved too quickly for me to flee, leaping toward me and slashing his blade across my throat. My hand jumped up to the warm liquid already spilling out of me, but my ability was even faster, closing the veins and sealing the skin before too much blood could be lost.

Grey growled in frustration, preparing to attack again, but a new voice made him freeze.

"She's a healer?"

We both turned to face Ignatius. He was standing tall, fury on his face and two brawny men at his back. Both of them were armed with swords, although I'd seen no sign of guards previously.

"What else have you been deceiving us about, *cousin*?" Ignatius asked, his eyes focused on Grey. "How many of your other followers are not what they appear?"

I tried to use his distraction to my advantage, edging slowly sideways in a bid to escape. But one of his guards moved to block me, his stance experienced and his blade menacing. I paused again, trying to decide if it was worth attempting to flee anyway.

I looked across at Grey and saw resignation in his eyes. He knew it was over.

I relaxed as well, an instinctive reaction, but it was the wrong response.

Once again catching me off-guard, Grey closed the distance between us. Grabbing me roughly, he threw me with all his strength toward Ignatius.

I stumbled forward, totally out of control, and collided with the tall healer. He shouted as if I was white hot and my touch burned him, thrusting me away. Both of his guards responded, converging on me, and in the darkness I caught a glimpse of Grey fleeing back toward the party.

"I don't want to fight you," I cried, but none of the three were listening.

"Get rid of her," Ignatius hissed, and one of the guards grunted in response.

A blade bit into me, searing pain spreading through my leg as it severed a tendon. I threw my power at the injury, but it had no sooner healed than another burst of pain flared across my arm.

I stumbled backward, but the guards pursued me. Distracted by my healing, I didn't make it far before my foot caught on a root in the ground, and I went sprawling full length across the ground.

Both swords slashed at me at once, and I screamed, again throwing my power at the new wounds. I curled inward, throwing my arms up to protect my head and neck as I tried to keep the blades away from my most vulnerable regions.

My power was strong, and it could heal almost as quickly as they struck at me, but I could feel myself starting to weaken. My strength wouldn't last forever—I had experienced that firsthand.

But neither were my attackers going to stop. Not until I was dead.

My terrified, pain-dazed mind latched onto the thought. If I wanted it to stop, I had to die. Or appear dead, at least.

Another burst of pain, and another. I moved to block the pain and heal the worst of the injuries, but this time I left two surface wounds behind, leaking blood. Let them think I was already out of energy.

Another wound and then another. More wounds left on the surface.

But faking my death wasn't a simple task. My adversary was a healer, and a powerful one. He didn't want to risk touching me, but he didn't need physical contact to sense my heartbeat or the air scraping in and out of my lungs. Which meant I needed to stop them.

I let one more strike fall before sending what remained of my power to my lungs and heart, seizing them and holding them still. Almost immediately, my chest began to burn, but I found new depths of power and used them to soothe the sensation.

Another blow fell, but I remained limp, not responding to it at all. My eyes wanted to close, but I used my power to force the lids open, stilling their movement and dilating my pupils to their full size.

My vision went blurry, but I ignored it, holding absolutely still.

Only the use of my power allowed me to maintain the lack of movement. Already my body should have been spasming, forcing me to suck in air whether I wanted to or not. But I ruthlessly suppressed every sensation that would have forced that response.

"Stop," Ignatius called, finally bringing relief from the blows.

I waited another second and another. My thoughts were starting to grow fuzzy, my brain starved of air, and I felt strangely cold all over. But I had to hold on.

If I could maintain the ruse for long enough, then Ignatius would approach closer. The only way to be sure I was really dead was to touch me and see if he could reach me with his power. But the second he made contact, I would be ready.

A strange keening stabbed at my heart as a warm body threw itself at me. I had never heard Ember make that sound. A soft thud sounded as Phoenix landed beside her, his chattering call joining her distress.

I longed to sit up and reassure them, but I had to lie still.

I waited. And waited some more. Finally, I heard footsteps.

But instead of moving closer, they were moving away. The crunch of three sets of feet were returning to the party. He wasn't going to do a full check? Just how deeply ingrained was the Constantines' aversion to physical touch with another healer?

Another set of footsteps sounded, running toward me, and I froze just as I was about to release my fatal hold on my body. Someone was returning after all.

But I couldn't hold back my heart and lungs any longer. I might be a healer, but I still had limits. If my brain ceased to function, I wouldn't be able to rescue myself. I had to act now, or—

"No!!" The heartrending cry was part grief, part horror, and part raging anger.

My blurry vision showed someone falling to his knees beside me. Hands reached out to touch my cold face, but they were familiar hands. I didn't need to attack the body they belonged to.

Instead I turned inward, sending a spark of power to restart my heart. As soon as it was beating again, I let my fire spread out through me.

The effort took my whole attention as I restarted every function of my body. But dimly, somewhere in the back of my mind, I registered that Nik had let me go, that he had stood and left.

Usually, his departure left me feeling cold, but this time I felt a flood of warmth as my blood circulated through my body again, my lungs contracting in painful spasms as they sucked in air.

Slowly the fog in my mind lifted as my brain received the air it needed again. My thoughts cleared, and the remnants of my power easily restored the rest of my body to wholeness.

I was still coated in blood, my gown torn in many places, but underneath it, I was whole and well. Ember barked, jumping in her excitement, and nearly knocking me back down. Phoenix took off, however, apparently needing to spread his wings and feel the air beneath him in order to express his joy.

"But where's Nik?" I asked Ember, my trembling hands stroking her fur. "I'm sure he was here. I heard him and saw him."

Slowly my mind recreated the last image I had seen of him—the image I had been too far gone to process at the time.

In it, his face was dark and twisted, the grief raw and overlaid with seething rage. And he had been turning away from my body, stalking back toward the party.

Slowly I went cold again. I tried to get to my feet, but all of me was trembling now, and I couldn't seem to find my balance.

Unwittingly, I had recreated Grey's plan. He had intended to fake a death tonight, and I had done exactly that. But I had never meant Nik to see me.

I managed to find my feet at last, but all I could hear in my mind were Nik's words from inside the ship's hold, repeated again and again. *I really don't know what I'd do if someone killed you, Delphine...Someone might die at my hands...*

I'd told him then that he should never become a monster, no matter what happened to me. But he'd retorted that without me, he had nothing to live for.

I wanted to believe his thinking had changed since then—he'd come a long way in processing his past, and his behavior in the market had showed how much lighter he felt. I wanted to believe he wouldn't recklessly throw his life away or do something he could never come back from.

But I couldn't shake off the glimpse I had seen of his burning eyes, stark in his pale face. There had been rage there, beyond anything I had ever felt. I wasn't even sure he was in his right mind.

I stumbled forward, my steps slow and halting at first but then picking up speed. The sounds of the party had disappeared, but I didn't want to think about what that meant. Surely everyone had just gone home—fleeing perhaps from the distant sounds of our fight. Or perhaps Grey had collected his people when he ran from Ignatius. I was sure he would have been reestablishing his own mesmerizations, even as the Constantines tried to implant theirs.

The garden stretched impossibly far, my feet taking too long to carry me to one of the open windows. As soon as I reached it, however, I wished the journey had been even longer.

When I had left, the room was alive with movement and voices. Now it was still and deserted. But not everyone had left.

Scattered across the floor were bodies. Bodies broken and bloodied, their eyes glassy and hearts no longer beating. Everywhere I looked were fallen stones and rent floorboards, all of them splashed with red.

Only one beating heart remained. I wanted to look away, to cover my eyes, but instead they were drawn inexorably to the one warm body left.

Nik. My Nik.

He knelt on one knee, his sword dripping red, and his other hand coated in it where it rested on Augustine's neck.

"Nik." It was a strangled whisper, a sound I hadn't meant to make, but it was enough to catch his attention.

He looked up, his eyes meeting mine. Instantly his terrible expression changed, shock holding him immobile, only to be replaced with a radiant joy and relief that was out of place in this room of horrors.

I swallowed and forced myself to look around at the destruction before looking back at him. He followed my gaze, his eyes skimming over the bodies, and I saw the moment his emotions changed.

His expression twisted, filling with horror as if he was seeing his surroundings for the first time. He stood, starting toward me. His hand reached out for me as he called my name, his voice somehow twisted and tender at the same time.

I stepped back, stumbling away from him, and he instantly froze, his face twisting further.

"Delphine," he said again, and the sound of his voice broke my heart.

But I didn't go to him. I couldn't.

Instead I did what Ignatius hadn't bothered to do. I forced myself to pick a path through the stones, approaching each body and checking they were really dead, although the effort seemed futile.

Ignatius and his two brutish guards were there, but so was Kendry, the pale eyes which marked her as an outsider closed for the last time. And so was Grey's grandmother, her body looking frail and old now that the vitality of life was gone, the spark of calculation forever extinguished from her eyes.

Ambrose lay beside Augustine, as if the two brothers had been united only in their final moment of life, and Barnabas lay on the other side of the room. He appeared to have been fleeing for the door, but he'd never made it.

All the Constantines were here except one. Somewhere, dimly, I had enough feeling left to be grateful Nik hadn't killed Costas in his blind, unthinking rage.

As if summoned by my thoughts, Costas's voice sounded from the garden, calling for us.

I moved woodenly toward the window where I had entered, stepping outside.

"Nik! Delphine! You're still here!" Costas slid to a halt at the sight of me. Leaning over his knees, he sucked in gasping breaths. "I thought you might be gone."

"Gone?" I asked, too dazed to try to make sense of his words.

"With Grey."

That got my attention.

"I found Nik and sent him after you, but he raced off too fast for me to follow. Before I caught up, Grey appeared, running like hounds were chasing him. He went straight into the party and collected all his people. My father and uncle would have stopped him, but Grandmother said to let him be. Knowing Nik would rescue you, I thought I should follow and see where they were going. I couldn't believe it when he walked them straight down to the harbor, loaded them onto the boat, and just set sail."

He regained his breath enough to walk toward us. "I thought you might have somehow gotten onboard as—" A sharp intake of breath cut off his words as he finally came close enough to see through the window into the room beyond.

His face paled, his eyes jumping from the horror in the room to my blood-stained gown and finally to Nik's bloodied hands and sword. After a long, awful moment, his eyes turned back to his grandmother.

"What..." He stumbled back a step. "What happened?"

He couldn't take his eyes off Nik, his face displaying the same emotions that were tearing me apart. Is that how I looked, with those haunted, terrified eyes?

No wonder Nik kept looking at me with that heartbroken expression.

"Did you...I...My family..." Costas couldn't seem to finish a sentence, his thoughts fragmenting before my eyes. "It's over," he finally mumbled. "It's all over."

*What's all over?* I wanted to ask, but even before I formed the words, I knew the answer. Everything. Everything was over. It had all been obliterated past hope of fixing.

Costas must have come to the same conclusion because he sent one last wide-eyed look at me before turning and fleeing the way he'd come.

"Costas!" I took several steps after him, but he had already far outstripped me. The direction of his flight told me he was heading back to the harbor. Was there another boat there? A small one, perhaps, able to be crewed by one—as long as that one had both the necessary power to direct his course and knowledge of the route. A person such as the only Constantine with an elements affinity.

Somehow there was room for fresh horror. Costas had said Grey had already sailed, which meant Costas was the only one left on the island who knew the passage through the rocks. Was he abandoning us alone here?

The enormity of it crashed over me. For an overwhelming moment, I wanted to flee as well. Not toward the harbor or a boat or anything logical—just away. I wanted to leave this shattered mess behind and escape.

But even as I thought it, Ida stepped through the gate, staring at the abandoned garden with confusion. Her eyes found me, and our gazes locked, her confusion deepening when she saw my state.

Not all of Grey's people had left. Not someone like Ida who had only ever wanted a fresh start and a new life. Her he had left behind. I thought of Lumi and Fergus in the marketplace with their bright curiosity so at odds with the adults around them.

I was the only remaining strong healer on an island full of people who might fall sick or injure themselves at any moment. People who had always been led by healers and didn't know how to think for themselves.

I couldn't run away. Amara had taught me I had a responsibility to use my power to help people, and there was no clearer need than this. In Eldrida I had promised to respect my own limits, but I had also promised myself that in exchange, I would never refuse to give when I did have something left.

I wanted to find a way back to the safety of Amara and Hayes and our friends, but someone had to help these people rebuild from this destruction. And I was the only someone left.

"Delphine," Nik's tortured voice hit my already shredded heart, shattering it even further.

He stepped outside, coming closer, reaching for me. I stumbled backward, shaking my head.

"I'm sorry, Nik, I can't. Don't…" I shook my head, wishing I could turn off my emotions and feel nothing at all, if only for a moment.

But I couldn't afford to be weak in a moment that called for strength. I forced myself to plant my feet and stand strong, to meet his eyes without flinching.

The truth hurt—unbearably badly—but I could see everything clearly now. I had wondered if the spark between us would lift us up or burn us both to the ground, and now I had my answer.

I couldn't turn my face from it, though. I had too many witnesses filling my head, echoes of too many past Idas showing me the way.

Serena, telling me she would return to her old master, despite how she was now viewed in Tarin, so she could finish her apprenticeship and rejoin society.

The courage in the eyes of the couple who said they were selling their farm and leaving their whole life behind to give their injured daughter hope of a future.

The people of Eldrida, laboring through the violent storm to save their neighbors, and then coming out the next day to face the destruction and begin rebuilding.

"You're wrong about love, Nik," I whispered. My voice was quiet, but I knew he heard because I saw the words land, like blows across his face. "This isn't love. I know that you would burn everything and anything for my sake. But that isn't what I want. Love doesn't want to burn the world down. Love is willing to kneel in the ashes and build the world back up."

"Delphine," he tried again, but he couldn't seem to form a full thought.

I wanted to weaken, to run to him. But people were counting on me, and I couldn't give in to an impulse that was so clearly destructive.

"That's what I'm going to do here, for these people, as best I can," I said. "So if you can't help, stay out of my way, Nik. We're over."

I had to turn away from the look on his face, still afraid of myself and the love I couldn't help but feel despite everything. But my eyes landed on Ida who had stopped to pick up Ember and was now walking slowly toward me. And at the same time, a weight landed on my shoulder as Phoenix swooped in to land.

Slowly courage began to fill me. I might not have the strength for the task ahead, but I wasn't alone. Together we would find a way to do what felt impossible alone. Together we would free these people from the lies and find a way back to the mainland before Grey wreaked more destruction there.

I would see Amara again, and this time, when I did, I wouldn't have to be ashamed of my actions.

My heart thumped painfully, and I pressed a hand to it. Later there would be pain enough for all my past mistakes, but right now I couldn't give in to it. Right now, I had to think of the future.

I nodded at Ida and took Ember from her outstretched arms.

"Prepare yourself," I said. "It's going to be a long night."

# BONUS CHAPTER - NIK

READ THE END OF THE BOOK FROM NIK'S PERSPECTIVE IN THIS BONUS CHAPTER

"Grey!" Costas leaned over, bracing his hands on his knees as he sucked in breaths. "Grey is—" He panted again. "Delphine needs you!"

"What?" I grabbed his shoulders, pulling him upright as fear shot through me. "What are you talking about?"

Delphine was safely in the middle of the ballroom. She had to be. That's where I'd left her when I dashed off to look for the man now in front of me. Not that I'd found him myself, despite my exhaustive search. He'd been the one to find me in the end.

"Tell me," I said through clenched teeth. "What has Grey done? Where is Delphine?"

"In the garden," he said, still out of breath but at least recovered enough to talk properly. "We were talking, and Grey overheard us, and—" He gave me a worried look. "She shoved me away and told me to run and find you. It looked like Grey was dragging her into the garden."

"What?!" I let go of him and stepped back, my muscles trembling with tension. "The garden behind the party room?" I could barely hold myself in check long enough to see his nod of confirmation.

Sprinting through the mansion, I careened around corners as I headed for the closest door to the outside. As soon as I crashed through it, my pace increased even faster as I ran through the dark garden toward the section closest to the party.

There! I saw movement, the outline of three bodies showing against the dimmer light. I peered intently at them, slowing my pace slightly, but none of them were Delphine. Ignatius was at their lead, heading back to the party with two men that looked like guards—the first guards I'd seen on the island.

Was that a sword in one of their hands? My blood turned to ice, time slowing around me. I swerved, starting toward them, only to catch sight of a fourth figure collapsed on the ground behind them.

I turned again, moving even faster toward the horrible sight. It couldn't be Delphine. It just couldn't. She was a healer, a powerful one. She would never—

"NO!" The cry sounded distant to my ears although it had ripped from my own throat, deep and filled with fury. My legs collapsed, and I fell to my knees beside her.

She lay sprawled across the cold ground, her hair splayed out around her. Her clothes were torn in many places, and there was red everywhere. Too much red.

"Delphine," I tried to whisper her name, but my voice wasn't working anymore.

How could a girl who had always been so full of life be lying there so still? Pain pierced me, like a thousand blades cutting into me at once. Everything hurt, and my vision clouded as rage fired through my veins.

I reached out a trembling hand to touch her face, so cold and lifeless. I could see her bright smile clearly in my vision, and it was impossible to believe I would never see it again. She had been everything—all I had left—and now she was gone.

I had failed her.

For a second my strength deserted me, and I slumped forward, my shoulders curling inward. But a moment later, the anger burning through me straightened my spine as I remembered the three figures walking back toward the party. Ignatius. Ignatius had done this.

I surged to my feet. Turning away from her felt like tearing something inside me, and part of me wanted to drop back to my knees and never move again. But my feet carried me relentlessly forward, my rage fueling my speed.

There was one thing still left to me. Vengeance.

My pace picked up, and as I ran, I drew my sword. Dimly, in the back of my mind, I knew I would be bursting into a party, but I didn't care. Nothing mattered now that I had failed to protect the person I loved most in the world.

The darkness receded, the lights of the party spilling out onto the porch. I crossed it in two large strides and launched myself inside.

My eyes moved immediately, scanning the room for Ignatius, but the sight that greeted me shocked me momentarily senseless. I couldn't make sense of what I was seeing.

The scene inside the large room bore no resemblance to the party I had left earlier. Almost all the people were gone, and those that remained...

I shook my head, as if what I was seeing was a hallucination and I could shake it away. But the scene before me didn't change.

There were bodies on the floor already, and the same red from the garden had been spilled inside, marring the floorboards which had minutes earlier supported chattering, laughing people. My gaze locked onto the Constantine matriarch, standing on the other side of the room, her expression frozen in a look of shock. One of the two guards I had seen earlier stood in front of her, his arm pulled back, his blade ready to strike.

I reacted on instinct, knowing I wouldn't have time to reach them. Tearing a chunk of stone from the ceiling, I dropped it straight onto him. The man collapsed instantly, but I'd been a second too late. His sword had already been thrust forward, and his victim toppled to the ground with him.

"Kill him, too!" Ignatius shouted to his remaining guard.

I whisked my sword up just in time to meet his blade as he lunged toward me. Dancing back, I tore another chunk of stone from the ceiling, and then another. But forewarned by his comrade's fate, the guard dodged around them.

The man attacked with enthusiasm, but he had no depth of skill. In an ordinary sword fight, I wouldn't have needed to use my power. I could easily hold him off until an opportunity presented itself for me to disarm him without injury. But even as we thrust and parried, my eyes were darting around the room. Were any of them left alive, or was I too late to save anyone?

An abrupt movement caught my eye as Barnabas leaped up from where he had been huddled on the floor, dashing for the door into the rest of the house. Ignatius took off after him immediately, cold determination on his face.

I abandoned my attempts to focus on the blades and turned my attention to the floor. Sending my power sinking into the floorboards, I ripped them up in long rippling waves. There was no time for finesse.

The ground beneath my opponent's feet suddenly bucked, torn lengths of wood rising up to trip him over. He stumbled, attempting to stay upright, only to trip on another stretch of broken wood and fall backward, arms flailing.

His head hit the ground hard, and he lay still, but I didn't have time to check if he was alive or not. Throwing myself across the room, I tried to reach Ignatius before he got to his cousin, my power racing through the floorboards ahead of me.

But by the time the ground shifted beneath their feet, the two of them were already locked together, the bare skin of Ignatius's hands gripping the other healer's arm. Whatever battle they were engaged in was invisible to my eye, but just as I grabbed the back of Ignatius's clothes, tearing him off Barnabas, the other man swayed and crumpled.

One glance was enough to tell me it was too late for me to help him. Ignatius had used his guards' weapons to attack the others, exploiting a healer's vulnerability, as he had done with Delphine. But apparently he wasn't averse to getting his own hands dirty, now that his guards were no longer able to do the job for him.

Ignatius didn't stop to savor his triumph, however. Turning on me with a feral snarl, he lunged forward, fingers reaching for any inch of my skin.

I stumbled backward, bringing up my blade. But in my horror over his actions, I had forgotten the torn floorboards. I tripped and nearly went down, only just catching myself in time to keep my feet.

The misstep had given him an opening, however, and he latched his hands around my free wrist. I reacted instantly, doing the only thing I could to stop him sending his power into me. Swinging my other arm around, I buried my sword in his middle.

He cried out once in pain, letting me go. For a moment we stood frozen, eyes locked, and then he wrenched himself backward. I cried out a wordless, unthinking protest, but it was too late. The moment the blade was removed, his eyes widened in shock and horror. Ignatius might be a healer, but he had lived a sheltered life on the island. Apparently he hadn't known what happens when an object piercing you is suddenly removed. Unprepared, he succumbed to shock and moments later fell to the ground, unable to heal himself in time.

For two seconds, I stayed in place, panting as I stared down at him. So little time had passed since I arrived in the room that I still couldn't comprehend what had happened. And overlaying it all was an awful, deadening weight—the knowledge of what I had found in the garden waiting to pounce and incapacitate me.

But thoughts of Delphine bolstered me briefly instead of tearing me down, my heart still partially numb from shock. I knew what Delphine would do in this situation, and it wasn't stand around uselessly. I didn't have her power, I couldn't help people like she could, but I had to at least check if there was anyone still within reach of assistance.

I already knew it was too late for the cousins in front of me, so I turned back into the room. Driven by my new sense of urgency, I didn't even drop my sword before kneeling beside Augustine. I pressed my free hand to the wound just below his neck with a vague thought of trying to stem the bleeding. But even as I did so, I knew it was already too late.

"Nik," the strangled sound of my name reached my ears in the stillness of the room.

I looked up, my eyes beholding an impossible sight. Delphine. She stood in the doorway of the room, not only alive, but whole, only the mess of her clothes bearing witness to her earlier state.

Shock made me freeze, my thoughts sputtering to a halt at the impossibility of what I saw. She had been dead. I was sure she had been dead.

But clearly she hadn't been. Unlike Ignatius, Delphine had managed to use her power to claw herself back from death. She was alive. The reality of it hit me like a tidal wave. Delphine was alive.

Joy swept through me, more radiant than anything I had ever felt. I hadn't lost her after all. I might have failed her, but she had saved herself. She hadn't left me.

But while a smile was growing over my face, the relief wiping away all other thought, her face was still frozen in shock and what looked like horror. Swallowing visibly, she turned her eyes away from me. I followed her gaze, seeing the scene again through her eyes.

Looking down, I saw the red on one hand and the naked blade still gripped in the other. In dawning dismay, I realized how the scene must look to her. I had left her with rage in my heart, and now she was faced with this horror. I had even told her on the ship...

My stomach turned, and I leaped to my feet.

"Delphine." I reached for her as I crossed the room, still marveling at the sight of her alive, even as I went cold from the reality of our situation.

She stumbled backward away from me, nearly tripping on the uneven floor, and I froze. I couldn't blame her for her reaction, given how the situation appeared, but I couldn't help calling her name again.

She didn't come to me.

Instead, she did what I had known she would, visiting each victim to check for signs of life. She found none. Ignatius had been too impatient to wait for an uncertain future rule and had decided to take matters into his own hands, choosing the same night as Grey to make his move. But unlike his cousin, he had enacted his terrible plan too well. None of them had seen him coming.

A voice called for us from the garden, and distantly I registered it as belonging to Costas. He had finally come after me. A fresh surge of horror washed through me as I realized what this scene would mean to him. But there was nothing I could do to protect him from the truth.

I only half heard their words as he conversed briefly with Delphine, and from the corner of my eye I saw him flee from both us and his grief. But I couldn't look away from Delphine. The pain in her expression hit me deeply.

I had achieved nothing in this room. I hadn't managed to save anyone. Instead of coming here, I should have stayed by her side in the garden. As usual, my instincts had steered me wrong, and from the look she was giving me, I didn't know if our relationship would ever be all right again. But I had seen into the depths of my heart, and I didn't know if I deserved for it to be all right.

My emotions weren't listening, though. When I saw her standing tall despite everything, choosing strength instead of weakness, and rejecting the kind of darkness that masqueraded as love, I knew she was someone worth standing beside for a lifetime. If there was anything I could do to salvage our relationship, I would do it. And if there wasn't, I would still support her to the end. Because Delphine had proven herself someone worth everything.

# Acknowledgments

Somehow this middle book became the longest book I've written yet, despite being written during burnout recovery, and I'm so grateful to everyone who assisted in its creation and polishing—as well as all those who kept me sane in the process! No matter the length of the book or the timeframe required, my wonderful team never lets me down.

So, Rachel, Greg, Priya, Ber, Katie, Mary, Dad, James, Karri, Rebecca, Marina, Cheri, Shari, Brittany, Kitty, Aya, Lyra, and Marc—thank you from the bottom of my heart.

And thank you to God who helps us keep going when we think we have nothing left to give.

# TEMPESTS OF TRUTH

*For Marina
an excellent writing companion
and an encouraging friend*

CALINARA
LAKE ATERRA
ELDRIDA
CELADON RIVER
CELADON RIVER
VIRIDIAN RIVER
CALTOR
TARONA
KINGDOM
of
TARTORA
TOSTARIA
TARIN

CHAPTER

# ONE

I stood on the back porch of the mansion, taking a moment to admire the view of the mountain rising behind the town. The wisps of fog were already starting to burn off in the early morning light. Here on the island, it was hard to believe winter had already started. The season bore few similarities with the winters back home in Tarin.

It was hard not to enjoy the natural beauty and unfamiliar surroundings of the manor house, but I couldn't shake a sense of lingering guilt for taking the time to notice such things when I still hadn't resolved matters on the island—or even in the manor itself.

The servants should have been at the front of my mind, but I couldn't help my rogue thoughts drifting to Nik. He had moved into the manor house in the wake of the disaster, but I still barely saw him.

I wished I could take back everything about that day. If only I had found a way to show Nik I was still alive. If only I hadn't seen him in that room full of bodies and leaped to the worst possible conclusion without even asking a single question. If Nik had truly responded with uncontrolled violence, I could have been proud of myself for having the courage to push him away. But how could I have believed him capable of something so terrible, even for a moment? Why hadn't it occurred to me that his sword might be drawn because he had been desperately fighting for his own survival against the true attacker? Or that he might be crouched over Augustine desperately checking for signs of life?

Nik had been understanding of my mistake, of course—too understanding. His excuses for me only heightened my sense of guilt. And that guilt stabbed at me again every time the scene in the party room sprang back into my mind. I knew what had really happened now, so why was it so hard to shake that one horrible image of Nik?

My guilt was making me avoid Nik, but I was eaten up by the question of why he was avoiding me. I couldn't blame him after my lack of trust, but contradictorily, I also couldn't help being hurt. Our relationship had become a giant mess, and it was all my fault.

"Delphine!" The call came from inside the house, drawing me from both the beautiful scene and my dark thoughts. I sighed. My true responsibilities were waiting.

Ida stepped onto the porch, her expression lightening when she caught sight of me.

"I'm sorry," I said, forestalling her query. "I still haven't worked out what to do about the servants."

The Constantines had rotated new help in and out of the mansion on a regular basis since they couldn't risk anyone getting too close to them and seeing the truth behind their veil of mesmerizations. But the latest group had only started work recently and had all been contracted for at least two months. We no longer needed the services of so many, but they had been promised two months of work, and I couldn't take that away from them. And I certainly couldn't end their contracts early when I hadn't worked out how to pay their wage yet. I was relying on the extra time remaining in their service to find the necessary coin.

The Constantines might have manipulated and exploited the townsfolk— using their skill at mesmerization to lord over them—but they had always paid their bills in a prompt manner. Few things could cut through empty charm as quickly as unpaid gold. So I knew they must have had a stash of coin in the house somewhere, but I didn't have the least idea where. Exhaustive searching had failed to uncover it, and I found myself frequently wishing for Costas. I couldn't blame him for fleeing the murder of his entire family, but I could really have used one person who knew how the administration of the island functioned.

"It isn't the servants." Ida shook her head, and a sense of foreboding settled over me. "My hosts are ill."

"Oh!" I brightened. "They need a healer? Did you bring them with you?" I couldn't help feeling a sense of excitement at being presented with a straight-forward opportunity to use my healing power—a welcome alternative to managing the complicated vacuum left by the deaths of the entire Constan-tine family.

"They're not here." Ida's expression remained grave, and a rising tide of concern began to fill me.

I had suggested Ida relocate to the manor multiple times, but she had been steadfast in refusing, saying she felt more comfortable with the family who had billeted her on our arrival. If they were all too sick to travel, she must be greatly worried.

But perhaps they had remained at home for a different reason.

"Are they afraid of the manor?" I dropped my voice to a whisper. "After what happened here?" I barely managed to stop myself glancing toward the full-length windows that led to the scene of the massacre.

"No, it's not that. They're too sick to walk this far."

"It's that bad?" I winced, my hopes dashed. "You should have come to me sooner! Or did it come on very suddenly?" My mind whirled, running through various possible maladies that might fit with a sudden onset of illness.

"As to that." She cleared her throat, looking uncomfortable. "They didn't want me to come at first. And it seemed mild enough that I thought..." She frowned. "Clearly I should have insisted on coming sooner."

"How long have they been sick?" I asked, alarmed. "And how many are ill?"

"All of them." Ida grimaced. "Their youngest only started showing symptoms last night. I think they would have let me come sooner if he'd been sick from the beginning since they all dote on him so much."

"All of them?" I stared at her. It had to be something highly contagious. "Let's not waste any time!"

As we hurried through the house, I considered searching out Nik and suggesting he accompany us but decided against it. He wasn't a healer, so this was something I needed to handle.

I knew that wasn't my only reason for not searching him out, but I let my mental excuse stand. I didn't have time to consider the complicated dynamics of our relationship when people needed my help.

As we crossed the gardens that ringed the manor, a flash of movement pulled my eyes skyward. A small, feathered body was diving toward me. I stopped just long enough for Phoenix to land on my padded shoulder.

"Good hunting?" I murmured, and he preened, clearly satisfied with his morning's effort.

A quiet yip made me search the surrounding gardens, my eyes finding a small orange body. Ember was trotting toward me after her own hunting excursion. I stooped and ran a hand down her back. She also looked satisfied, her eyes already growing heavy. She shook it off, though, gazing up at me with what looked suspiciously like a questioning air.

"Go inside and sleep," I said softly. "Phoenix will keep me company."

She hesitated, her eyes moving to the merlin falcon on my shoulder. For a silent moment, the two animals stared at each other. Ember was the first to relax, pressing her body against my leg for a moment and then heading off toward the house. I smiled as I watched her go, despite my underlying worry about Ida's host family. Ember and Phoenix took better care of me than I would have believed possible for a fox and a bird of prey, and their companionship always lifted my spirits.

As we left the garden and entered the town, Phoenix in tow, I quizzed Ida on the illness.

"Is it something your host family recognize?" I asked. "Have they had it before?"

"They downplayed it at first, but now they're saying it's unfamiliar." Ida frowned. "It's not something I recognize either."

I nodded, but I wasn't entirely surprised. In order to maintain their mesmerizations, the Constantines had performed constant healings on the islanders. Not only had their doors always been open to them, but they had even instituted monthly checkups. Most illnesses encountered by the islanders would have been quickly nipped in the bud by the Constantines. There were probably many diseases whose later stages were unfamiliar to the townsfolk.

I had already canceled the schedule of monthly checkups, of course. There was no way I could keep up with them on my own, and just the thought of them was distasteful given they had been an instrument of control and repression. Through those checkups, the Constantines had regularly renewed the mesmerizations on the islanders, beginning their insidious manipulation almost from birth.

I had received no patients in the nearly two weeks since canceling the checkups, but I hadn't been especially surprised given they must all have been in good health at the point of the Constantines' death. But Ida's summons was making me question that assumption. How many others had hesitated to take their illness to the unknown new healer living in the empty house of their old rulers?

I glanced warily up and down the nearly empty streets. It had been over a week since I'd walked into town to the market, but something had changed. The atmosphere then had been somber, a haze of hesitancy and confusion hanging over the populace. The Constantines were gone, but their mesmerizations remained, and the same passivity we had first noticed in the islanders had only been exacerbated by the loss of their leaders. But while the people had all hung back from me then, this time was different. The people weren't dismayed or bemused—they were absent.

The few who did pass within view walked quickly, not appearing to even notice me as they busied themselves with their errands.

Unconsciously my pace increased.

"Go over the symptoms again," I commanded Ida, wanting to focus my thoughts before I started inventing catastrophes in my mind.

"They've been complaining of headaches, and most of them are coughing," she said. "I checked for fever from the start, of course, and they seemed warm but not excessively so. Their condition didn't seem too severe, or I would have come for you before now, like I said. But then this morning..." She grimaced.

I was about to ask for more details when she stopped outside a door. The house looked almost identical to the ones on either side, but Ida didn't hesitate as she let herself in, beckoning for me to follow.

I hesitated, jerking my shoulder upward. Phoenix recognized the signal and launched himself into the air. Bringing a falcon into someone's home was already questionable etiquette without considering that the family inside were ill. He would be better off waiting outside.

Phoenix flapped across the rooftops, looking entirely unbothered, so I stepped inside. As soon as I was all the way through the door, I flinched at the heat.

"First things first," I said, focusing on Ida. "Get all the windows open and some fresh air in here."

"Nonsense!" an old lady exclaimed, only to go off into a paroxysm of coughs. "It's winter!"

I barely refrained from retorting that there was nothing wintry about the temperature outside. Instead I dropped to one knee beside her chair.

"You need fresh air to aid your recovery. Please trust me, Grandmother. I'm a healer."

"A healer?" She squinted at me in suspicion. "You're that newcomer, then? From up at the manor?" She shuddered at mention of the Constantines' home. "Are you sure you're a healer?"

She regarded my face for a silent moment before her expression cleared. "I suppose you were going to marry young Ignatius. Or maybe young Barnabas." She nodded decisively as if she'd cleared up her own confusion.

I didn't bother to correct her. I already knew the tragic truth about healers on the island. Strong healers didn't make it past childhood unless they were earmarked as future spouses for the next generation of Constantines. If telling herself that story helped her to make sense of my presence, then I was willing to leave the misunderstanding in peace.

"May I examine you?" I held out a hand, my fingers hovering just above her wrist.

She nodded, her hesitation and suspicion apparently gone now that she had fitted me into her world.

I placed my hand gently against her skin and sent my power into her.

Within seconds, my mouth had turned down. My training at the hospital in Caltor had exposed me to a range of the most common illnesses, including some cases at later stages of disease. Those who lived more remotely, especially farmers like my own family, would often wait until an illness was severe before making the trek into a hospital for healing.

But whatever was ravaging this woman's body, it didn't feel familiar. I focused my attention, tracking down each area of her body that felt wrong.

For starters, there was nothing mild about her temperature. Even without my power, I could feel the heat radiating off her skin. And from inside her system, I could easily tell why her body was fighting so ferociously. There was inflammation in far too many places, and her lungs were struggling, her breath making an audible rattle.

We'd arrived only minutes ago, but she was already wilting visibly, clearly exhausted from the conversation. I sent a small burst of energy into her, but I didn't dare risk using too much power when I hadn't seen the state of the rest of the family yet.

"You need to be in bed," I said gently, fighting hard against the urge to pour my power into her and heal all her unfamiliar symptoms.

Ida cleared her throat significantly, and I finally examined the rest of the home. A large open room contained a dining table as well as cooking facilities. Two doors opened off the far wall, both propped wide to allow a view of the room beyond. One bedroom held a large bed that was already occupied by a man and woman. The other held two single beds. One seemed untouched, while the other was rumpled but currently empty.

I took a second look at the main room and noticed two pallets had been shoved against one of the walls, limiting the floor space. A young boy lay on one of the pallets, murmuring fitfully and staring at me.

"They insisted I take one of the bedrooms," Ida said. "So Grandmother and the boy have been sleeping out here."

I held out a hand, beckoning her to come closer. As soon as she was within reach, I latched onto her wrist. It only took a moment to ascertain she was healthy. I withdrew with a sigh of relief.

"It hasn't infected you yet. Until we know what's going on here, you're moving into the manor with me. And that way these two can move back into proper beds."

Ida nodded, making no protest this time given the circumstances. Launching into action, she helped the elderly lady into the untouched bed. While she did so, I knelt beside the child, chatting mindlessly in my softest voice as I sent my power into him.

By the time I withdrew, my frown had deepened. I helped him to his feet, leading him to the remaining bed. He wasn't in as bad shape as his great-grandmother, since his organs were mostly free of inflammation. But his temperature was raised and, even more concerningly, his heartbeat was slow.

"Does it hurt anywhere?" I asked him.

"My head." He moaned and then gave a cough. "And my tummy."

I frowned, my reply stalled by the sounds of someone thrashing and muttering incoherently in the next room. I handed the boy off to Ida with a quick look, hurrying into the other bedroom.

It was the man who was disturbed, so I went to him first, holding his arm firmly in both my hands. It didn't take long to recognize the same signs I had seen in the grandmother. In his case, the inflammation wasn't as bad—probably because of his younger age—but his fever was raging, as evidenced by the delirium. I sent enough power into him to cool him down and calm him, blocking his pain while I was in there.

He settled down at once, letting out a weary sigh. Cracking open his eyes, he frowned up at me.

"Who are you?" His voice was rough, but Ida appeared at my side with a cup of water which he accepted.

"I'm the healer," I said, and he accepted this statement without question.

"Do you think you could get up now?" I asked him, curious to hear his reaction.

He had propped himself up slightly to drink, and at this question, he attempted to pull himself all the way upright. He didn't make it before grunting and flopping back onto the pillow.

"Sorry," he muttered, a shadow crossing his face. "I don't know what's wrong with me. I haven't felt this tired since the fev—"

"Hush!" his wife snapped from beside him. Her voice was weak, but he still obeyed her command. Apparently she was less accepting of the new healer than he was and didn't like him giving me unnecessary information.

But he'd already said enough for me to guess what he was talking about. I exchanged a glance with Ida, my heart sinking all the way down to my feet, terror rising to take its place. I didn't know about her, but I'd already heard about the infamous fever from three winters before.

Usually the Constantines had intervened in health concerns early, but on that occasion, an entirely new illness had emerged from the jungle to sweep through the town before they realized what was happening. The islanders and their ancestors had carved a home here on this island, but much of it was still uninhabited and densely covered in a jungle-like forest. Environments like that could harbor new illnesses—ones previously unknown to healers— and those were always the most dangerous kind.

In the case of the fever, it had progressed quickly, and given its lack of familiarity, it had taken some time for the Constantines to work their way through the entire town, stamping it from existence. Some of the islanders must have been forced to wait for their healings, and clearly this family had been among their number.

A shiver trickled down my spine, traveling from my scalp all the way to my feet. Three winters ago there had been six powerful healers on the island, and it had still taken them time to handle a new, mystery illness. If the town had been hit by another new illness...

I drew a deep breath, reminding myself to focus on what was in front of me and not assume the worst. Circling the bed, I examined the mother, noting that while she appeared to be at a similar state of progression as her husband, she lacked his earlier delirium. In its place, she bore a nasty looking rash across her torso. I eased her pain as well, soothing the inflamed skin, but once again I didn't dare use enough power to heal her completely, regardless of the cause of infection.

When I let her go, I hesitated, wondering about the best way to proceed. A vision of empty streets intruded on my thoughts, but I pushed it away, trying to focus on practical steps.

The sound of the main door opening made me hurry out of the bedroom. Had others in the town heard I was here and come searching for me?

But as soon as I got a glimpse of the new arrival, I stopped.

The room had seemed large before, but suddenly it felt so constricted I could barely breathe. How could one man take up so much space?

Nik looked the same as he always had—his shoulders just as broad, and his dark hair still contrasting with the burning blue of his eyes—but his expression carried something less familiar. I still recognized it easily, however, and it did as much to shrink the room as his impressive height.

If his eyes had held even a hint of censure for leaving him behind, I could have met them with defiance. But I had no defenses against the sadness he was clearly trying to hide. I had left the mansion without even informing him of my departure, and he couldn't hide his reaction to my omission. Nik might be avoiding conversations with me, but given his choice, he would shadow me every time I left the mansion, taking the role of bodyguard. But he didn't just want to be by my side. He also wanted me to want him there.

And I did. Mostly.

The dynamic between us had become so complicated that sometimes I didn't know what I wanted. The unspoken weight of all that had happened hung in the air making it hard to breathe. I wanted to look at him and see nothing but Nik, but I couldn't stop myself from reliving that horrible moment in the party room—followed, as always, by the spear of guilt for my mistake.

The horror of that moment, and the resultant tangle of our relationship, filled my thoughts even now when something far more serious should have been at the forefront of my mind. Which was yet another reason why I'd been avoiding him while I tried to sort out the confusing administration of the island. It was already hard enough to keep my thoughts straight.

"One of the servants said Ida left a message for me—that I was needed down here?"

His deep voice sparked a visceral response that I immediately tried to tamp down.

He took a step toward me, concern flaring in his eyes. "Is something wrong?"

I let his words remind me of what was most important in the moment.

"I'm afraid there is." I pitched my voice low, trying not to disturb the patients in the two bedrooms. "This whole family is ill with an infectious condition I haven't seen before. And unfortunately it's already progressed significantly. I'm afraid..."

"The empty streets," he said quickly, obviously having noticed the same thing I had.

Hearing him reach the same horrifying conclusion should have made me even more afraid, but instead his words had the opposite effect. They steadied me, relief trickling in to counter the panic. I wasn't alone in this. Nik was here too.

"We need to find out what we're dealing with," I said. "I'll check the houses on either side, but can you and Ida spread further through the town? We don't have time to check every house, but I need to know the rough extent of this."

Given how sick this family already was, I suspected this area would be the epicenter of the spread, but I needed to know for sure.

"Of course." Nik looked at Ida who had entered the main room behind me. "You head toward the harbor, and I'll go back toward the manor?"

She agreed, the two of them murmuring several more clarifications about the routes they would each take. I had already tuned them out, though, hurrying toward the door to start my examination of the neighbors.

In the doorway, I paused to make a final comment.

"We'll meet back here as soon as possible." If things were less dire than I feared and this family was the worst hit, then I would be able to use my power to heal the three adults in this family at least.

Nik and Ida both nodded agreement, and I strode out into the street.

My optimism didn't last two houses. By the time I'd made it down one side of the street and back up the other, I felt as if I was carrying a pack filled with heavy rocks.

I had expected some of the families to show animosity toward an unfamiliar healer turning up unannounced on their doorstep, but no one had rejected me. And it was tragically easy to see why.

Every single household had someone in at least the first stage of the illness—like the young boy from Ida's host family—and some had members even worse off than the host grandmother.

From my questions, I had managed to track the rough course of the symptoms. In the first week, most patients had symptoms similar to the first boy I examined. After progressing to the second week, the symptoms increased in line with those I had seen in the boy's parents. Only a small handful of people had made it as far as the beginning of the third week, and most of them were even more sick than the first grandmother.

Those whose weakened bodies had succumbed to pneumonia or who had inflammation of the heart or brain were in a severe enough condition that I couldn't just walk away. I had tried to keep my healing to the minimal amount necessary to ensure the patient's survival, but there had been enough of them that even doing that much had drained me to a frightening degree. I didn't dare do anything to ease the suffering of those who were earlier in the illness, lest I end up collapsing like I had in Eldrida.

I tried to cling to some vestige of hope as I waited outside Ida's home. Those who reported being sick the longest had first come down with symptoms just before the Constantines' untimely demise. They must have only just missed having the Constantines heal them in the early stages.

I had thought this street might be the epicenter of the disease, but perhaps it was the opposite. If these families had been the last to get sick, the rest of the town might have already been healed before their illness could progress. If that was the case, and these were my only patients, then I could carefully stagger my healings, relying on power rather than knowledge or finesse to push through, and starting with those who were the most sick.

But the prospect still felt overwhelming, optimistic as it might be. Even Phoenix's appearance did nothing to lift my mood.

Nik returned before Ida, appearing at the end of the street and quickly covering the distance with his long stride. But even before he reached me, my desperate hope had died. One look at his face was enough to read the terrible truth.

When he stopped in front of me, he hesitated, apparently not wanting to put what he had seen into words.

"It's bad, isn't it?" I said softly.

He nodded slowly.

"Every house on this street has at least one person sick, and in some cases it's everyone," I continued.

Nik reached for me, as if he wanted to take my hands, or perhaps pull me close, but he stopped himself, letting his arms fall back to his sides.

"Every house I checked as well," he said reluctantly. "I did a fair sampling between here and the manor as well as a few streets on the western side of town."

I swallowed. It was even worse than I'd feared.

"So it's already made it through the whole town." My voice quavered with the unspoken words behind the spoken ones. This wasn't the sort of sickness you just recovered from on your own—not everyone, at least.

Nik's eyes never left my face, his own expression twisting as anguish filled his eyes. The sight of it leached all the strength from my legs, nearly making my knees buckle.

I knew him well enough to know that anguish wasn't for the islanders who were strangers to him. It was for me. And seeing his fear brought the stark reality of the coming future into horrifying clarity. The whole town was infected with a mystery illness, and there was only one healer of any strength on the entire island. Me.

People were going to die—possibly lots of people—and my only two options were to watch it happen, or else kill myself trying to stop it.

## CHAPTER

# TWO

I swayed in place, and this time Nik didn't stop himself from reaching for me, steadying my elbow and murmuring meaningless words of comfort. His voice was calm despite the raging fear in his eyes.

"This isn't your fault, Delphine," he said once I'd regained my balance.

He wasn't entirely right, though. I had taken responsibility for these people's health, but I had been too inexperienced for the task. I should never have canceled all the checkups so recklessly. I had assumed people would come to me if they needed a healer, but I had failed to consider the state of their feelings.

Their leaders—the ones they had been forced to revere since birth—had all died. And most of them hadn't seen me in person to judge if I was telling the truth when I claimed I wasn't responsible. None of them had attempted to attack me—not even verbally—and I had taken that as more significant than it actually was. Their passive response to me was only in line with their general passivity—a result of the subjugation forced on them. They could regard me with suspicion and hostility without actively launching an attack. And even to those who didn't regard me negatively I was still a stranger.

And into this worst possible moment, before we had the chance to get to know each other, disaster had struck. If the first to fall ill had come to me at once, I might have been able to head off the epidemic. But it was far too late for that now.

My assumption about them taking the initiative had been wrong, and now some of them would pay for my mistake with their lives. I should have checked on the town each day instead of allowing myself to be distracted at the manor. I had focused on the haphazard records left by the Constantines, as well as the management of the manor itself, instead of being focused where I should have been—the people of the town.

"If you push yourself too far, it won't help anyone," Nik said, the alarm in his voice easy to hear. "Without you, they'll be in an even worse position." His expression turned dark. "If anyone is at fault, it's me. If I had acted more quickly and saved some of the Constantines, you wouldn't be the only healer now."

"No." Strength returned to my voice. His useless self-recriminations highlighted the foolishness of my own negative thoughts. "The blame lies with the Constantines. And even that is beside the point. The important thing is how we're going to handle the situation in front of us."

But despite the confidence of my words, I had no idea how to follow them up. How could we possibly handle a disaster of this magnitude?

"Delphine! Delphine!" A high, childish voice made us both turn toward the end of the street.

Two short figures ran toward us, their eyes wide and expressions animated.

"Lumi? Fergus?" I frowned at the brother and sister. "What are you doing here?"

The two were the only non-mesmerized people I had met in the town. Their minds were unfettered because of their mother's avoidance of the Constantines, but that very caution should have placed them far from here. They had been the ones to tell me about the last fever. On that occasion their mother had fled with them into the jungle at the first sign of spreading illness, thus avoiding infection and the need for healing from the Constantines.

A fresh wave of guilt seized me. Had she failed to flee this time because the Constantines were gone?

"We were looking for you," Lumi said. "Mother is sick, and we remembered you're a healer too."

I winced, but Fergus jumped in.

"But never mind that!"

Lumi gave him a reproving look, but he just shrugged.

"She isn't *that* sick. Not like the Tergins down the street."

I winced again, but neither child noticed.

"We heard you were here, so we came to find you," Lumi continued, and once again, Fergus rushed to take over the story.

"We walked past the harbor on our way here, and you'll never guess what we saw!"

"The harbor?" I asked, sounding slightly dazed. My mind was too full of the epidemic to have room for any other topics.

"It was a ship!" Fergus proclaimed triumphantly. "But none of ours went out this morning."

I looked to Lumi, expecting her to refute Fergus's preposterous declaration.

"More like a boat than a ship," she said, "but he's right that it can't be one of ours. With so many people sick, none of the fishing vessels set out this morning."

She said it in a matter-of-fact way, as if she didn't understand the importance of any part of what she'd just said. But each of her words landed like lead in my stomach. The townsfolk were not only all ill, but they had also stopped gathering food due to their condition. We were in dire straits already, and now a fresh disaster was sailing into our shores.

My eyes met Nik's, wondering if he was thinking the same thing as me. From the angry flash in his eyes, he was. Grey had somehow gotten word of what had happened to the Constantines and had returned. And he couldn't have arrived at a worse time. With an epidemic underway, we had no time to deal with Grey as well.

"Show us," Nik said in the sort of commanding tones that were always obeyed.

The children nodded eagerly, happy to be caught up in the excitement. Clearly they hadn't yet grasped what was happening in their town.

Despite their exuberance, I managed to grab hold of both their hands, quickly examining their bodies. I heaved a sigh of relief when I found them both clear of the illness.

As we half ran through the streets, the brother and sister bickered over whether the arriving vessel was large enough to be considered a ship, and both Nik and I remained silent.

One glance at his grim expression was enough to tell me that he had no intention of allowing Grey to step foot back on the island unopposed. The Constantines were to blame for their own downfall, but Grey was one of them, and he certainly carried his share of the fault. He had done everything possible to upset the balance among his relatives, and he had succeeded beyond his wildest hopes.

I put on an extra spurt of speed as I spotted the end of the street and the glitter of the sea beyond. Everything would be easier if we could arrive before Grey and his people disembarked and disappeared into the town or forest.

From the sound of the siblings' argument, Grey hadn't returned in his full ship with all his followers in tow, so it was possible Nik might have the strength to hold them at bay and send them back the way they had come. Grey himself had no special strength without physical contact.

As soon as we burst onto the waterfront, my eyes scanned the water beyond the long pier. Sure enough, a wooden boat was closing the final small gap, ready to dock. I sprinted down the length of the pier, taking in the details before me.

The boat was a reasonably substantial, sturdy-looking fishing vessel, but it was a long way from a full-size ship. It didn't even have a proper cabin. But I forgot all about the boat itself once I saw the passengers. Coming to an abrupt stop, I burst into tears.

It wasn't Grey at all. Quite the opposite.

Floating in front of me were the people I wanted to see more than anyone else in the kingdom.

Nik halted beside me, his face reflecting the same shock.

"Is that really...?" he asked, not managing to voice the full question.

"I think so," I said, sobbing in relief.

He glanced at me, worry replacing the pleased surprise. I waved a hand reassuringly.

"I'm just happy," I managed to choke out, and he relaxed.

"Delphine!" Luna's delighted cry cut across the remaining distance.

The sound of her voice spurred me into action, and I hurried forward. By the time I reached the end of the dock, she had stepped ashore. As soon as I reached her, she pulled me into an enveloping hug.

"Am I glad to see you!" she said fervently. "Actually, I'm happy just to see land. I could kneel and kiss the dock."

I blinked, loosening my return hug and extricating myself from her grip. I couldn't imagine a passenger of Amara's having any cause to complain about the smoothness of the journey.

I looked past her shoulder, grinning like a fool at Hayes, Clay, and two men I didn't recognize who were wearing the uniform of royal guards and who looked almost as relieved as Luna. When my searching gaze fell on Costas, I gasped aloud, finally understanding how it was possible for the rest of them to be here.

I had assumed the new arrival had to be Grey since he was the only one who knew the route, but I had forgotten that one other Constantine was still alive. Gratitude welled up inside my chest. Costas might have fled after seeing the massacre of his family, but he hadn't abandoned us after all.

As he stepped onto the dock, my eyes jumped to the one person remaining on the boat. Amara. I had never been so pleased to see someone in my life.

She looked as poised as ever, but as she stepped toward me, I noticed the subtle signs of strain and exhaustion on her face. I frowned as I hurried the remaining distance toward her.

"Thank goodness you really are all right," she said in her calm way, as if she hadn't entirely believed Costas's report. "And you even have that bird with you still."

She eyed Phoenix with judgmental eyes, as if the falcon should have stopped me from haring off across the ocean without her.

"Of course I'm all right," I said. "But the town—"

My words cut off as a creaking sounded from the boat behind her. I leaned sideways to get a better view just as the entire vessel collapsed into planks of wood and flotsam that floated on the surface of the harbor.

My mouth fell open and my eyes widened as I turned to Amara, noting again the signs of exhaustion on her face.

"How long have you been holding that together with power alone?" I asked.

"Since we got caught in the storm two nights ago," Luna said in hushed tones.

"Two nights ago!?" I stared at Amara. "I know you did wonders in Eldrida, but even you couldn't expend that much power for days and nights without break."

She smiled back at me. "Which is why it's a very good thing I had help."

"Help?" I looked over my shoulder at the rest of the group, my eyes landing on Costas. "Oh! Of course!"

Costas smiled wanly. Now that I was properly focusing on him, I could see even more obvious exhaustion on his face than Amara's.

"It was actually nice to feel needed and appreciated for once." As soon as he said the words, he winced, looking reflexively uphill toward the manor, as if the reminder of his family and past was painful.

"You came back," I said quietly. "Thank you, Costas."

He met my eyes. "I'm sorry for running like that. I was in shock and not thinking clearly. I was most of the way to the mainland before I realized I had stranded you on the island."

"You never thought I was to blame?" I asked, surprised. It had been one of my biggest regrets that I hadn't been able to explain what happened that night to Costas. Out of everyone he most deserved to know about his family's end.

"I knew you weren't involved." He shot a dark look at Nik. "It was clear you were just as shocked and horrified as me. In fact, it looked like you'd been attacked as well. I've been berating myself for days for not taking you with me when I fled."

Nik stirred, as if he wanted to protest. He would certainly not have allowed Costas to haul me off and shove me on a boat. I sent him a warning look. Until the whole story was explained, the best thing he could do was stay silent. From the way his eyes slid from mine, his tense muscles slumping, he understood the shaky ground beneath his feet.

Amara put a hand on my arm, examining me from head to toe. "There weren't any injuries you couldn't heal? You're healthy now?"

"I'm fine. But it was a close thing. Ignatius ordered armed guards to attack me. Since their swords extended their reach so much, I couldn't get close enough to make contact and use my power. I had to let them wound me enough that they thought they'd succeeded in wearing me down."

Amara's face paled, but it was Costas who spoke.

"Ignatius attacked you?" He sounded shocked. "Not Grey? It took me so long to find Nik that I was afraid Grey might have killed you before we got back."

"To be fair, he did attack me first," I conceded. "But Ignatius did far more damage."

A slow light of understanding grew on Costas's face, and he turned to give Nik another look.

"So that's why Nik..." He didn't seem able to finish the sentence.

I shook my head quickly. "No! Of course he didn't! Nik isn't the one who massacred your family." Perversely, I felt incensed at the idea they had all been misjudging Nik, despite having made the same error myself.

"He wasn't?" He raised both eyebrows, sounding skeptical.

Amara lowered her hand from my arm, but her face didn't immediately relax. She looked across at Hayes. He nodded slowly to confirm he had sensed the truth of my words with his ability. Only then did relief fill her features.

"I was hoping there was a different explanation," she said. "I felt sure there must be."

"As did I." Hayes narrowed his eyes. "But I'd like to hear the truth from Nik himself."

I flushed at his oblique reference to the possibility that I had been taken in by Nik.

"I did not commit the massacre that happened that day," Nik said in a level voice.

Costas looked at Hayes, his brows lowered, waiting for his confirmation. When Hayes gave it, followed by a confirming nod from both Clay and Luna, he let out a long breath.

"They were all adamant that we return to find you both and seek out the true story." Costas made eye contact with Nik for the first time. "You have loyal friends."

"I think it's loyalty to my father more than me," Nik said caustically.

"Your father?" Costas frowned, clearly confused, and for the first time it occurred to me that he might not know Nik's full identity. That particular piece of information had been lost in the many revelations.

I glanced at Amara and read confirmation on her face. With a sick feeling, I realized she hadn't been quite as confident in Nik as she claimed. She had remained silent about his status, afraid of a powerful foreign mage finding out his family had been murdered by the son of Tartora's king.

But how could I blame her? I had been the first to accuse Nik, and I still couldn't shake the guilt of that or the echoes of the moment that still lingered in my mind. I should never have made such a terrible assumption, and I couldn't blame Amara for doing the same in the face of Costas's testimony.

"My hands aren't completely clean," Nik said in a low voice, bringing all eyes snapping to his face.

"But you were acting to defend yourself and others," I said quickly.

Surely he didn't feel guilty for defending himself against murderers who wanted to make him their final victim? Was that why he'd been acting so strangely ever since?

"You didn't attack anyone for revenge," I added.

"What does that mean?" Costas asked, taking a step toward me, his eyes intent on my face.

I hesitated, unsure how to tell him the full truth. I glanced beseechingly at Amara. "I'm not sure if this is the best place for this conversation. And I have some important things to tell you about what's happening on the island right now as well. Perhaps we should—"

"No!" Costas cut me off, not aggressive but firm. "I don't care how painful it is to hear, I want to know the truth without delay."

# THREE

I exchanged another look with Nik. Given what was happening in town —an ever-present pressure in the back of my mind—it would be best to get this whole conversation out of the way as quickly as possible. But that didn't make the words any easier to say.

Nik remained silent, indicating for me to continue with a nod. I sighed. I might not want to be the spokesperson, but I could understand why he thought it would be more sensitive for the story to come from me.

"Ignatius followed Grey and me out into the garden," I said.

"Ignatius?" Amara interrupted, looking to Costas.

"My younger brother," he said heavily. "And the heir apparent to the Constantines. Well..." He shifted uncomfortably. "He was heir apparent before Grey's appearance, at least. Although even then, not without opposition."

I sighed. "I can only assume that was the problem."

Costas looked at me, his forehead creasing. "What are you saying?"

"Sorry, let me start at the beginning. Ignatius overheard Grey and me talking and learned I'm a healer. Grey could tell his deceptions were all exposed, so he decided to sacrifice me to give himself time to escape." My face tightened at the memory, but I pushed myself to continue.

"As I already said, I had to pretend to be dead in order for them to leave, and I still appeared dead when Nik reached the garden and found me."

Amara's eyes widened, and I caught her uneasy expression as she looked toward Nik. I hurried on, all too aware of what she must be thinking.

"Nik hurried back to the party after Ignatius and his guards, but unfortunately he was just a little too late."

"Wait," Costas said, interrupting me again. "Who are these guards you keep talking about? My family never had any guards. They didn't need them," he added, his tone dark.

I paused, struck by his comment. It was true that I'd never seen any other guards before the party or since. In all the chaos, I hadn't given it much thought.

Nik spoke up, looking from me to Costas. "Grey chose the party as his time to make a move, but it appears he wasn't the only one of the Constantine cousins to think that way."

"What did my brother do?" Costas's face was pale, his look of exhaustion deepening.

Nik finally took up the tale, relating the part I hadn't witnessed.

"By the time I returned to the manor house, Grey had already fled, along with most of his followers. When I made it inside, only the Constantines were left. It seems your brother was sick of debating who would be the next heir, and he didn't want to wait to take his turn after his grandmother and father either."

"*Ignatius* killed them all?" Costas asked in barely more than a whisper.

Nik hesitated and then nodded his head. "His guards did, at his command. I tried to stop them, but I only arrived right at the end, and Ignatius ordered his men after me immediately. My power and training gave me the advantage—even over three of them—but the guards were able to keep me occupied long enough for Ignatius to finish the task himself before he also attacked me."

I thought of Barnabas, who had nearly made it to the door, and shivered. I still couldn't fathom how Ignatius could have done such a thing to his own family. The Constantines might have been the manipulators, but in the end, they had been just as twisted by their behavior as their victims.

"So, to be clear," Hayes said, his gaze trained on Nik. "One of the Constantines murdered the others due to some sort of internal family conflict. You were only responsible for killing the aggressor and his two guards after they attacked you as well?"

"That is correct." Nik held his gaze, his expression confident. But I could read something else lurking behind his apparent calm. Something about that night still tormented him, and whatever it was had been standing between us ever since.

"I'm sorry for your loss," Amara said formally to Costas. "But I am glad Tartora had no hand in it. I hope you won't hold what happened against our kingdom."

Costas nodded slowly. "I wish I could disbelieve Nikolas's account, but Ignatius was always so hungry for power. It always seemed foolish and unnecessary to me—what difference did it really make which of us ruled the family? But I could never convince him of that."

I nodded slowly. Even in my short time on the island, I had overheard an ugly argument between Ignatius and his father. There had clearly been no love lost between Ignatius and his relatives.

"As a healer I can assure you that Nikolas speaks the truth," Clay said, his voice gentle. "But I understand if you might prefer one of your own to confirm that. There may not be healers of strength left on the island, but even the weakest healing ability can truth tell."

Costas shook his head. "That won't be necessary. At first I was driven by shock, but I've had plenty of time to reflect since those first initial moments. As much as I regret every aspect of the situation, my family are guilty of terrible crimes. They lived a life of violence and deception, and I cannot be surprised they met the same sort of end."

"Yes, Ignatius made his choice," I said. "And he paid the ultimate price for it. He didn't know anything about Nik's presence on the island and had no idea what sort of opponent he might face. But I believe the ultimate blame lies with Grey. If he hadn't been deliberately stirring the situation up in preparation for his own coup, then Ignatius might never have made such a move. And Grey is still out there."

I looked to Amara. "What's been happening back in Tartora?"

She sighed. "We haven't seen any sign of Grey. When neither you nor Nik made any contact—" she paused to throw a disapproving look at both of us "—our whole party made our way to the crevasse to arrest Grey. You can imagine our surprise to find it completely abandoned. We were still debating what to do when Costas turned up."

"The route to the crevasse is the simplest," he said, "and since I was on my own, that was important. And I think a subconscious part of me was fleeing toward Aunt Chloe as well. Grey had said she was dead, but I still hoped…" He fell silent.

"Grey himself must have taken a different route," Amara said. "He never arrived at the crevasse. You can imagine our surprise when Costas showed up instead—and our even greater astonishment when he told us everything. I'm not sure if I was more shocked to hear about his family, the island, or your whereabouts."

I blinked, trying to imagine how that conversation had gone.

"You told them everything?" Nik asked Costas, and he nodded.

"There didn't seem any point in holding back. My family and our old life here are destroyed. The Constantine healers betrayed the townsfolk in the worst of ways, but they did look after them physically. Without them, the islanders are vulnerable. They need help, and I'm hoping Tartora will be willing to provide it, despite everything that's happened. Because none of it was my people's fault."

I nodded vigorously. "Yes, the people need help."

We had made it through the most important exchanges of information—the ones that couldn't be delayed—and I couldn't wait any longer to fill them in on the dire situation currently unfolding on the island.

But Amara spoke before I could continue. "You've been looking after them, haven't you." She didn't voice it as a question.

Tears sprang to my eyes. "Nik and I had no way to leave the island. But even if we did, we couldn't have just abandoned the islanders. These people have been affected by what was done to them—they can't think as proactively as you or I. And all their strong healers have been murdered. I'm only one person, but I thought I was at least better than nothing."

The words taunted me. I'd given myself a job and failed at it within two weeks.

"Delphine." Amara's voice was gentle as she wiped the single tear running down my cheek. "I know you would never abandon a whole town in need like that."

I gulped, trying to hold back any further tears. "I wanted you to have a reason to be proud of me this time. But—"

"Don't worry," she cut in. "I was the one to send you to Grey, and I even had the crown's permission to do it. And you couldn't have foreseen ending up trapped on this island. No one would consider you to have abandoned your apprenticeship—especially given we were separated for only a short time."

"My...apprenticeship?" I tried to follow what she was saying. Did she think I was crying out of fear of being branded a reneger? Was that why she had hurried after me at the first opportunity?

Becoming a complete outcast from society in all its forms would certainly be something to cry over, but the thought hadn't even occurred to me. My mind had been too full of everything happening on the island. And while the best of help had just arrived, even more was still needed.

I glanced dubiously into the harbor where the shredded remains of their boat still floated.

"I guess it will be a while before you've recovered enough strength to go back," I said.

"We will absolutely not be going back!" Luna shuddered dramatically. "You weren't out there in that storm, just one tiny boat among all those rocks. Even with the power of both Amara and Costas, I thought we weren't going to make it. No one is getting back to the mainland any time soon."

"What do you mean?" My eyes flew from her to Amara. "Why can't we get back?"

"That was the first of the winter storms," Costas said grimly. "We had two very strong elements mages for only one small boat, and we still barely made it through. It was a dangerous undertaking and not one worth attempting except under dire necessity. And besides, what about the islanders? You were the one who said you couldn't abandon them. I might have run once, but I don't intend to do so again." He crossed his arms over his chest, looking stubborn.

"Actually, we already discussed it on the way over and reached an agreement," Amara said to me. "Costas said none of the fishing boats are big enough to transport everyone, so the plants mages are going to need to work together and build us something bigger. With their power to aid the process, they should be able to have something serviceable by the time the season turns and the storms abate. We don't need something fancy like Grey's ship, since we don't care about creating an impression. Just something sturdy and seaworthy."

Nik looked warily at the flotsam floating nearby. I could easily read the concern behind his expression. Had that boat once been sturdy as well?

But my thoughts were focused elsewhere.

"You're saying we can't get back until the end of winter?" My dismay was evident, and everyone turned their eyes on me, their gazes reflecting varying degrees of worry. "So that means we're not getting any more help from the mainland before then, either. Not for the whole winter."

"Why?" Amara asked sharply. "Do we need more help?"

Tears sprang back into my eyes as the enormity of the situation hit me all over again.

"There's an epidemic on the island," I said. "I'm a terrible healer because I only just discovered it, and it's already spread through the whole town." My voice rose, assuming a hysterical edge. "And I can't even recognize what disease it is!" I swayed on my feet, the effect of all my power expenditure hitting me hard now that the initial shock and excitement had worn off.

Nik started toward me, but Amara was already at my side. She steadied me with an arm around my shoulders, her concerned gaze flicking to Hayes. "An epidemic?"

I tried to pull myself together to give them a proper report on the situation. "I've only examined the patients on one street so far, but I found multiple people in a dire situation. I had to heal them on the spot or they might not have lasted until I got the chance to return."

"It's that bad?" Hayes asked, clearly alarmed.

"I don't have much experience yet, so maybe you'll recognize it?" I quickly outlined the symptoms for him along with my limited understanding of the disease's progression.

Hayes and Clay exchanged a long look, both of their brows furrowed.

I leaned into Amara, guiltily relieved to no longer be the most senior healer present. I didn't have to be in charge anymore, and I'd never been happier to lack authority.

"It sounds like typhoid," Luna said hesitantly.

I tried to remember what I'd read about typhoid and failed. I'd certainly never encountered it in an actual person.

Hayes grimaced. "I'll have to examine a patient before I can say for sure. But it sounds like it has some similarities at least."

"Our mother is sick," Lumi piped up suddenly, making me start. I'd entirely forgotten the two children were still lurking nearby. "We could take you to her."

Hayes glanced at me, and I nodded. "Their mother kept them away from the Constantines. They're not like the rest of the town."

A shadow crossed Hayes's face, but he merely nodded and turned to the children with a smile.

"If you could do that, I would appreciate it." He glanced at Clay and Luna, and they both nodded, moving toward him.

I reluctantly pulled away from Amara, already missing her support. "I can take you to Ida's host family as well. They're the first ones I examined, and they have someone in every stage of the illness."

"No," Amara said firmly, making me frown. "Absolutely not."

"What do you mean?" I tried to work out what she was talking about. "No one else can—"

"I can take them there," Nik said. "I know this town as well as you, and I was at the house earlier. I'm also not exhausted from over-extending my power."

His eyes met Amara's, and for once they appeared to be in perfect agreement.

"I didn't overextend myself," I argued. "I'm still awake, aren't I?"

"Not for long from the look of you," Amara said. "You need to get some sleep before I'm allowing you to use another speck of your power. Otherwise we'll have you comatose for days again."

I grimaced, embarrassed at the reminder.

"I was careful this time," I said meekly, and her face softened.

"I'm sure you were. But you're also a single healer suddenly faced with an epidemic. I have no doubt you pushed yourself as far as you dared."

I bit my lip, unable to deny the truth of her words.

"Where have you been living?" she asked. "Is there room for us as well?"

"More than enough room." I glanced at Costas. "That is, if Costas doesn't mind."

"You're up at the manor?" He sounded a little surprised.

I shrugged. "It seemed the most practical place to stay while I was trying to sort everything out. But if it bothers you, I can—"

"No, no, it's a large house and the only place where we won't put anyone else out. It makes sense for us to stay there, especially if there's an epidemic underway."

I smiled, relieved I didn't have to come up with another living arrangement when I could hardly think straight.

"Delphine isn't the only one who's exhausted." Hayes gave Amara a stern look. "You and Costas need to get to bed as soon as possible as well. I'll find out what's happening in the town, and we can talk up at the manor once I get back. But only after you've had some rest! You've been holding on for days. You can safely hand over to me now."

She smiled, a softness in her eyes I'd never seen before.

"Thank you," she said softly. "This is your area of expertise anyway. But I'll try not to sleep too long."

"Take as long as you need." He hesitated, as if he wanted to say something further, but after a shake of his head he took off after Lumi, with Clay and Luna at his heels.

The two guards hesitated, looking from Amara to the retreating mages.

"Go with them," Amara said. "They may have need of assistance, whereas we'll all be sleeping. Nik, you too."

Nik also hesitated, although his eyes were on me. I gestured for him to go, sending him off with a reminder to try to find Ida while he was in town. We'd had to hurry off before her return, and she had to be worried.

Nik agreed and finally left to follow the others, sending one lingering look over his shoulder.

"There are several conversations still to be had," Amara said dryly, watching him go. "But they'll have to wait until we've all had some sleep."

"Yes, please," Costas said fervently.

More guilt picked at me as Costas led us through the streets toward the manor. The town was too quiet, and now that I knew the reason, the empty streets haunted me.

"I assume you came in the boat Costas took?" I asked, desperate for something to fill the unnatural silence.

Amara blinked, clearly distracted by other thoughts.

"Yes," she said at last. "We brought as many as could be crammed into it."

"And the rest of your group?" I asked. "You sent them back to the king?"

She nodded. "I wrote down everything Costas told us and instructed the guards to deliver it straight to the capital and directly into the king's hands. They had to return to Eldrida on foot, but they will have taken horses from there. They may even be in the capital by now."

"So Tartora has warning about Grey, at least," I murmured.

Amara nodded. "If King Marius and the Triumvirate believe it. I'll admit it's a hard tale to swallow."

I remembered my own astonishment on first learning that healers could mesmerize—and I had been offered firsthand demonstrations.

"I hope King Marius takes the warning seriously," I said fervently.

"He's a cautious king. He won't dismiss a message from Hayes lightly," she said. "But either way, there's nothing we can do about it until the weather changes. We only encountered one storm, and that was bad enough. I wouldn't want to try again any time soon."

CHAPTER
# FOUR

I woke up groggy. For a moment, my thoughts were muddled and confused, and then I shot out of bed as my memory fully returned. Scrambling into the first clothes I could find, I peered at the light coming in the windows. I had meant to sleep for just a few hours, but it didn't look like late afternoon. Apparently I'd slept through the rest of the day and the night as well. From Ember's warm presence curled in the sheets, I guessed morning must be well underway.

I hurried off in search of the others, but thanks to the size of the Constantine manor, it took me some time to track anyone down. Eventually I found Amara in the room we used for breakfast.

She smiled at me over a steaming cup of tea and gestured for me to take one of the empty seats around the table.

"Isn't it too hot for tea?" I asked, slipping into one of the places across from her and reaching for a slice of toasted bread. "I've barely drunk the stuff since I got to the island—and this is winter!"

"It's never too hot for tea." She assessed my face as she spoke, checking my condition.

I glanced uncomfortably out the window. "How long was I asleep?" I tensed as I waited for her answer.

"Just since yesterday," she replied, and I breathed a sigh of relief.

"You weren't in a comatose state from overusing your power," she added, "but you must have been pushing yourself a lot to need that much sleep. Now that I'm here, there'll be no more of that."

I shifted in my seat, considering her words. On one level, they were just what I'd been longing to hear. I couldn't wait to hand over responsibility for the island and its inhabitants. But I suspected it wasn't going to be that easy. Emergencies didn't care if you were an apprentice or a proficient.

"What's going on in the town?" I asked, sidestepping the issue of my exhaustion.

A cloud settled on Amara's face. "Hayes and Clay worked most of yesterday and then took shifts through the night. Luna, at least, was sent back here to sleep the night through, but she's already eaten and gone back into town this morning."

I straightened, stuffing the rest of the toast into my mouth. "I should be off too," I said around the mouthful.

"Absolutely not," Amara replied without any change in her steady tone.

"Amara!" I stared at her. "There are only three of them, and the whole town is sick. Four healers is better than one, but it's still not enough for an epidemic of this size and strength."

"I know you're powerful, Delphine, but you're still largely untrained," Amara said. "Even Luna is more experienced than you are, and Hayes and Clay are both masters. They can heal more people with less power than you can."

"Still," I said, clinging stubbornly to my point. "If they worked through the night, they must be getting tired. I'm sure they could use fresh assistance."

"*Fresh* is not a word I would use to describe you, even with all that sleep."

When I glared at her, she just raised an eyebrow, and I slumped back in my seat with a sigh. It had only been a matter of weeks, but apparently I'd already forgotten what it meant to be an apprentice with a master. It wasn't all positives.

Looking at my dejection, Amara relented, putting down her teacup and leaning forward.

"Costas and I were also tired enough to sleep most of the day and night, but I did manage a conversation with Hayes yesterday evening."

"What did he say? Did he recognize the illness?"

She shook her head, and my anxiety surged. So we really were dealing with something new.

"Apparently new illnesses sometimes appear out of the jungle," I said. "There was a fever a few years ago, but back then the Constantines..."

She nodded, allowing me to trail off uncomfortably. I still didn't know how to think or talk about the deceased Constantines who had lived terrible lives and met a terrible end.

"There is good news," Amara said. "It might be a new strain, but Luna was right that it bears many similarities to typhoid. So they aren't dealing with something entirely unfamiliar. By the end of yesterday, Hayes and Clay had finished their assessments and agreed on the best approach to treatment as well as a plan for general epidemic management."

"Already?" Tears welled behind my eyes.

Thank goodness two masters had arrived. I was used to relying on my strength to make up for my lack of knowledge and experience, but that could only get me so far. This had been a disaster far beyond anything my strength could compensate for.

"You'll be better off hearing the details from them. I admit I didn't absorb the finer points of it all. But the important thing is that the three of them have already recruited all those in the town with a healing affinity—however weak—and together they've made it to every household and completed a triage."

"That's incredible!" I hesitated. "How many are in immediate danger?"

She grimaced. "I don't know exact numbers, but since the situation is already so advanced, it's more than is ideal. And unfortunately a few have already died."

I paled. The townsfolk had started dying on my watch, and I hadn't even realized.

"The first deaths have only just happened," Amara said quickly, correctly reading my emotions. "It seems the real danger doesn't start until the third week of illness."

"That's something to be grateful for, at least," I muttered.

"At this point, we'll take any advantage, however small," she said. "Hayes and Clay spent the night doing limited healings on the most severely ill patients. Unfortunately, given how far the epidemic has already progressed, they can't do anything to get ahead of it—not yet at least. It will take everything they have just to help those in the most danger."

"Exactly!" I gave her a piercing look. "And that's why I should be out there helping!"

She ignored my words. "Thankfully, since the illness develops over weeks rather than just days, Hayes thinks that better management will eventually be possible. If the four of you can work through the worst cases quickly enough, you should eventually reach the point where you can start treating less advanced patients before they reach the danger period. That's going to take a while, and it will be much longer again until we can truly get on top of the epidemic, but time is the one thing we have."

My ears pricked up at her mention of the four of us. "You are going to let me go and help, then?"

"Tomorrow. As I said, this is a marathon, not a sprint."

"Not for those in immediate danger it isn't," I fired back. "How can you expect me to sit around at the manor doing nothing all day while people in the town might be dying?”

She surveyed me in silence for several moments.

“That does seem a bit much to ask,” said a friendly voice from the doorway.

I looked up to see Costas leaning against the doorframe, his eyes on Amara. How long had he been standing there?

“Shall we bring her with us?” he asked.

“That’s an excellent suggestion.” Amara stood, her manner turning brisk. “Some fresh air and exercise will no doubt be of value.” She looked at me. “How quickly can you be ready to go?”

“Immediately.” I jumped to my feet. “Where are we going?”

“Did you get as far as typhoid in those medical texts of yours?” Amara asked.

I shook my head. “I might have skimmed past it, but I don’t remember if I did. I’ve been focusing mainly on the anatomy books and those illnesses I encountered in the Caltoran hospital. But I haven’t even been able to do that for a while since my books are all back on the mainland.”

“While typhoid is infectious, it’s largely spread through contaminated food and water. Hayes and Clay are in agreement that this new illness is likely the same.”

“How can they tell?” I asked, fascinated.

“I can’t give you all the details,” she warned. “You’d have to ask one of them to get the technical reply. But I gather it’s a combination of factors. The nature of the illness and its close relation to typhoid is a clue. But also the way it has spread so evenly across the town. That suggests a communal source rather than a gradual spread from an initial infected patient. If it was spreading person to person, the most advanced cases would be grouped together in clumps of close associates.”

“That makes sense.” I frowned, considering her words. “So you’re going to search for the source of the infection?” I looked back and forth between them. “You must suspect it’s in a water source if the two of you are going?”

“We’re not making any assumptions,” Amara said. “I’ll be leading the investigation since I’ve helped in epidemic situations before, but we’re keeping open minds.”

“Which is why I’m coming along,” Nik said from behind Costas.

Costas came all the way into the room to make way for Nik who took his place in the doorway, his eyes on me.

“I’ll help in case the issue is coming from stored food, the soil, or a wild plant,” he said.

"And if you come along, Delphine, you can keep an eye out for an animal host as well." Costas sounded pleased.

I guessed he felt similarly to me. If we couldn't be in the town healing people, it was a relief to at least have something constructive to do. And he didn't even have the assurance I did that I would soon resume work among the infected. It had to be difficult not to have a healing affinity in situations like an epidemic.

Amara led the four of us out of the manor and to the edge of the garden. I was acutely aware of Nik's presence, but neither of us addressed the other directly. Just like in town the morning before, we needed to put aside the tension between us to focus on the epidemic.

"Ida!" I cried, distracted from thoughts of Nik by the arrival of the older woman.

She nodded at me, her face grave. But when she caught sight of Phoenix and Ember approaching, her expression lightened. Her fondness for the animals had only grown with each passing week.

She bent over to place a gentle hand on Ember's back. "Shouldn't you be sleeping, beautiful?"

Ember allowed the pat for a moment before slipping away to join me. It was unusual for her to be out of bed during the day, and I could only assume she'd sensed something unusual was going on.

"I'm sorry we rushed off without you yesterday," I said to Ida. "We got word of a boat arriving and feared it might be Grey."

She nodded. "Nik found me and explained everything. We are fortunate your friends arrived in such good timing."

I nodded fervently.

"I spent the day and some of the night helping Masters Hayes and Clay, and they are both highly skilled." Her expression of distaste didn't match her words, so I threw her a questioning look. She shook herself slightly.

"Sorry," she murmured. "Seeing them at work reminds me of Grey—the only other healing master I know. It's a relief to know they aren't all like him."

Her sour expression made it clear she had shaken off the last of Grey's hold and no longer held him in any reverence. It was a far cry from her attitude back in the crevasse when she had excused his lack of care for his people. I was sorry for all the terrible things that had happened to break the hold of her mesmerizations, but I couldn't be anything but happy that she was free of his lies.

"Are you coming with us?" I asked.

"Master Amara thinks I may be of help. Whenever I can, I've been exploring the mountain and the wilderness areas surrounding the town. This is a very beautiful place, and I enjoy the solitude and peace away from the bustle of the town. So I offered to act as guide since the locals are either sick or have sick family and friends to care for.”

“We’re heading into the jungle?” I looked from her to Amara.

“It’s not a true jungle,” Ida said. “Although it’s more like one than anything in Tartora.” She led the way into the dense trees that bordered the manor gardens to the north.

We all trailed behind her, coolness enveloping us as we stepped beneath the canopy. “But shouldn’t we be checking for contamination in the town first?” I stepped over a jagged branch that had obviously fallen a long time ago since it was half covered in moss.

“I did some initial investigations late yesterday, once we knew what we were dealing with,” Nik said, the familiar sound of his voice humming through my bones.

I could feel his presence at my back and didn’t dare turn to look at him. I longed to feel the comfort of his arms around me more than I was willing to admit.

“I couldn’t find anything amiss in any of the major food stores, or any obvious sources of poor sanitation that might be corrupting the environment.”

“For all my family’s faults,” Costas said, “—and they were many—they were still a family of healers. From the beginning, we’ve had a comprehensive sanitation system, and they always kept a close eye on the town’s food and water sources.”

“But Grey disrupted everything here,” I said slowly, considering his words. “Even from before our arrival, but especially after. They must have lost focus on the normal day-to-day issues.”

“The timing seems to line up,” Amara agreed. “I would guess the source of contamination first appeared shortly before their deaths.”

We were all silent for a moment as we considered the timing and everything that had happened on the island before and since that moment.

“Where are you leading us?” Amara asked Ida as we turned sharply west, following a trail that was so faint it barely counted as a track but which gave us a fairly straight passage through the trees.

“There’s an area just ahead that is well used by locals,” she said. “A number of families regularly forage among the trees there for the goods they sell at market.”

“What sort of goods?” I asked, frowning at the tall trunks and dense foliage around us. While the bright blooms were a pleasant sight, I couldn’t see anything that looked edible.

She glanced back over her shoulder. “All sorts of things. Mushrooms, for one. Plus various roots that grow at the base of the trees. And some of the leaves have health benefits as well.”

“Do they use it for medicine?” I frowned. “Didn’t the Constantines freely heal all ailments?”

“They eat them,” Costas explained. “Or make tea with them. My family encouraged the locals to take care of their health even outside their appointments.”

“Could something like that really be the source of such a virulent sickness?” I looked doubtfully toward Amara.

She shrugged. “If there’s a contamination source where they grow and they aren’t properly washed and cooked, perhaps? We don’t want to rule anything out.”

I didn’t need Ida’s announcement to know when we’d arrived. The dense tree trunks thinned, allowing much more sunlight through to the forest floor. In response, a profusion of bushes and other ground plants covered the area. In several spots I could even see freshly turned earth where some small plant had recently been pulled out by the roots.

“Let’s spread out,” Amara commanded. “Nik, you examine the plants and the earth. Delphine, please let me know if you sense anything wrong with any of the animals in the area.”

I stopped walking and reached out with my power, assessing the area around us. As expected, our immediate area was mostly devoid of creatures—our arrival having scared them away—but a few still lingered in burrows and nests, and further out the forest teemed with life.

There was only so much I could sense from a distance, but even so it was fascinating. My attention caught on a long snake hidden among the leaves of a tree a short distance from our location. I had never encountered anything like it—I had little experience with reptiles in general—and the unfamiliar feel of the cold-blooded creature fascinated me.

After a moment, I shook my head and forcefully pulled my focus away. I wasn’t here to learn about the local wildlife.

I spread my power out, skimming lightly over a myriad of creatures. While I couldn’t tell any details of their condition, I could feel the steady beating of the life inside them. I was confident that if any of them were in significant pain, I would sense it, as I had once done with Ember.

Nothing caught my attention, though. If any of the animals were ill, they were hiding it well.

I tried to push my power out, calling to the animals around me. If any of them could be coaxed close enough, I could make contact and get a more exact picture of their health.

The attempt brought back memories of trying to call to the trapped eagle.

Tears sprang to my eyes as I remembered how that incident had ended. And now there was more death around me.

I pushed harder, attempting to throw my power across the surrounding forest. It was a desperate, unfocused effort, but my ears caught a rustle in the surrounding ground coverage. I turned hopefully toward it, only to see familiar orange, white, and black fur as Ember appeared from between two bushes and rushed to my side.

I dropped to one knee and scooped her up. "Of course you came, old friend. You always do."

A small chip alerted me a moment before Phoenix flew in low beneath the branches, executing a tight maneuver to land on my shoulder.

"And you, too, fine sir." I ran a finger along his feathers. "You never let me down either." I sighed. "But it's your wild brethren I was hoping to meet. And I don't think the presence of the two of you is going to help in that attempt."

Phoenix cocked his head and regarded me with one beady eye. He didn't look in the least repentant, and I couldn't help smiling.

Amara strode toward me. "Have you noticed anything strange? Anything at all?"

"The animal populations look quiet as far as I can tell. I can try to get close enough to touch a few of them to confirm, but that might be hard to achieve with so much disruption to their normal environment." I glanced doubtfully around the disturbed section of forest.

"No, let's leave it there for now," she said, only half paying attention. "It was always an unlikely option that it might come from animals. They aren't carriers for traditional typhoid."

I nodded, relieved I didn't have to attempt to capture a selection of wild animals.

"Did you find anything?" I asked, hopeful despite her serious expression.

A startled cry made us both spin eastward, staring into the trees.

"Was that Costas?" I asked, and Amara nodded.

She took off without a word, heading in the direction of his voice, and I hurried behind. Had Costas been the one to find something?

CHAPTER
# FIVE

Phoenix took off from my shoulder, racing ahead of us, just beneath the canopy.

The forest had gone quiet again, but somehow that only made me more anxious. Was Costas in trouble and unable to call out?

We wound through the trees toward him, my straining ears picking up nothing except the sound of running water. Then came the glint of sunlight on water, followed by the sight of a small huddle of people standing on the bank of a small river.

Costas was there, looking unharmed, and Ida and Nik stood beside him. I slowed to a walk, huffing out a relieved breath as they turned to look at us.

"Sorry." Costas sounded embarrassed. "A wild boar took me by surprise. I didn't mean to bring everyone running."

"So you didn't find anything?" Amara sounded disappointed. "Did you check the river?"

He nodded. "Nothing to report, I'm afraid. The water felt the same as in the river beside town."

"That makes sense," Ida said, "since it's the same river."

"It's not actually," Costas corrected, making her frown.

"I suppose it's not exactly the same one," she acknowledged after a moment. "The main river bends westward, and it's only a branch that breaks off and goes south toward the town."

Costas shook his head. "I think you're getting confused, which is understandable. The town's river starts further south from here. It isn't a big one, and it starts from an underground source, so to all appearances it just springs out of nowhere not far above the town. It would be natural to think it comes from a larger river up north."

"I..." Ida paused, frowning, before giving a shrug. "Of course you would know the island better than me."

I looked between them, surprised Ida would be wrong on something of that nature. She was the sort of steady person who could be relied on to have accurate information and considered opinions. And while it was true that Costas had lived his whole life on the island, it was Ida who was serving as our guide because he had lived his life almost entirely separate from the regular islanders.

But then this was a matter of geography, not of where the islanders preferred to forage for herbs. As an elements mage, in particular, surely Costas would be familiar with the nearby rivers.

"Hmmm...I'm starting to regret not going with you to check the town's river," Amara said. "I won't be able to make a comparison with this one."

She knelt swiftly and plunged a hand into the flowing water. Her brow creased as she stared downriver. When she stood, it was slowly, the water flowing off her hand until it was completely dry.

She turned to Costas. "You really didn't feel anything at all unusual about this water?"

His brows shot up. "Did you?"

She hesitated. "Maybe?"

"Are you stronger than Costas?" Nik asked. "If you sense something he doesn't, could that be why?"

"I think we have a similar level of ability, actually," she said. "But there is one crucial difference." She turned to me. "Could you check the water, Delphine?"

"Me?" I stared at her. "I can, of course, but I don't know if I'll be able to sense anything."

"You think it's your cross-influence that's the difference, then?" Nik asked Amara in an intrigued tone.

"Cross-influence?" Costas asked. "What do you mean?"

"I have an elements seed," Amara said, "but I was activated by a healer."

"By a healer?" Costas stared at her in astonishment. "But that makes no sense. Don't you come from the Tartoran capital? Surely there was an elements mage available to do the activation for you?"

"There was, of course," she said, "but I preferred the healing master I chose—both for personality and affinity."

Costas's brow wrinkled, as if he couldn't understand what she was saying, and I remembered what Grey had told me about the island.

"They don't allow cross-influencing here," I said. "I suppose they had to do everything possible to preserve and strengthen their power, given their community is small and isolated."

"No cross-influencing at all?" Amara asked. "That's a loss."

"But what would be the benefit?" Costas asked. "We were taught it just weakens your ability."

"In the sense of brute force, it can," Amara agreed. "But there are many advantages to be received in exchange. I may not have proper healing power, but my power will always be tangled with traces of my influencer's power. It expands my ability in ways that are impossible for a straight elements mage. And in this case, it's given me an important capacity to sense life—however incomplete my sense might be compared to a true healer like Delphine."

"You think there's something alive in the river—something that shouldn't be there?" I asked.

"Possibly?" She sighed. "I can't be sure. I'm not familiar with what the disease feels like since I can't connect with a human body. I'm hoping you might be able to recognize it, though, since you're healing cross elements. I'm not sure a straight healer could sense life at such a minuscule level when it's suspended in water instead of inside a living creature. But I'm hoping my elements influence will give you that ability."

Kneeling, I leaned toward the water. As I neared it, I wobbled, nearly losing my balance and falling in. Someone caught me by the arm, steadying me, and I didn't have to look back to know it was Nik.

I could feel his warm presence beside me, but I forced myself to focus on the task at hand, merely murmuring a quick thank you.

As soon as my hand was immersed in the river's current, other thoughts fell away. I couldn't sense the water, exactly, but when I pushed out my power, searching for life, it slid eagerly and quickly through the water, latching on to the various river dwelling creatures with ease. I focused harder, looking for a different sort of life.

"Oh!" My exclamation made the rest of them crowd in close, peering over my shoulder as if my discovery might be visible.

"Did you sense something?" Amara asked.

"It's faint, but it's definitely there." I couldn't help sounding excited. "And it felt similar to the disease in the bodies of the townsfolk. I'd be surprised if such faint traces could make someone ill, but maybe it gets stronger downstream?"

"The two of you can put your hand in a river and sense traces of disease?" Ida looked at the two of us with hints of awe in her expression.

I was growing used to people looking at Amara like that, but I felt uncomfortable being viewed the same way.

"I'm sure any healing cross elements or elements cross healing mage could do it," I said.

"The important thing is that we find and eliminate the continuing source of infection," Amara said. "This river seems like it could be the answer, but we need to find out how the infection got from this river to the other one."

"Why don't we follow it south?" Ida suggested. "We can track its route as well as anything it comes into contact with."

Amara glanced at Costas before nodding. "That sounds sensible."

We quickly formed ourselves into a single file line with Amara at our head. She led us along the edge of the river for several minutes before holding up a hand to signal a stop. I put Ember down and peered around Costas and Ida, trying to see what Amara was doing.

Kneeling again, she once more put her hand into the flow of the river. This time she took even longer to rise, her eyes narrowing. When she said nothing, Costas copied her movements, also making contact with the water.

Almost as soon as he did so, his eyebrows shot up.

"You can feel the branch?" Amara asked.

"Of course. But where did it come from? That definitely didn't used to be there. I swum this river many times as a boy."

The melancholy tone of the final sentence brought to mind the image of an ostracized boy with an elements seed, seeking comfort in the water since he was unwanted within his healer family.

"Is it possible this new branch joins with the town's river?" Amara asked. "It seems to be heading in the right direction."

"Entirely possible." Costas looked up at Ida. "I apologize. It seems you were right. I shouldn't have dismissed what you were saying so readily. Something has changed since I was last in this part of the island."

"If this branch has connected the two rivers only recently, that seems like further evidence this is the source of infection," Ida said. "And it might explain why I'm still healthy as well. I didn't like to say anything to my hosts, but when we first arrived, I found the taste of the town's water unpleasant. I fell into the habit of boiling a pot for myself and letting it cool since I found it produced a more familiar taste."

"It must be the water source causing the problem," I said. "Everything fits. It even explains why no one at the manor is sick since we use a well on the grounds rather than traipsing across town to the river."

Amara stood, shaking water from her hand. "We'll follow the branch when it appears and confirm that it joins the town's river. But I now feel confident about what we'll find."

We resumed walking, but this time chatter passed up and down our line.

"How could a new branch suddenly form out of nowhere?" I asked.

"It happens more often than you might think," Amara said.

"Is it also normal for a new branch to carry a new disease with it?" Nik sounded skeptical.

"No. That bit isn't normal at all." Amara glanced back at us. "A new branch explains how the infected water is reaching the townsfolk en masse, but it doesn't tell us any more about the actual source of infection. How did it get into the water in the first place?"

"Between us all, I'm sure we'll find the source," Ida said with conviction.

I glanced back at Nik, but his face was carefully blank, giving no indication of what he thought of our chances. But when his eyes caught on mine, I glimpsed a fire raging beneath his calm exterior.

I whipped my eyes back to the front again. I was fairly certain that particular blaze had nothing to do with the epidemic or the town, and it was something I couldn't deal with right now.

But now that I'd glimpsed it, I could feel the warmth of his gaze on my back, making it hard to concentrate. When Ida stopped in front of me, I walked straight into her back, nearly sending us both tumbling into the river. We would have gone over if not for the cushion of air that pushed back against our momentum, righting us both. I threw a thankful look at Amara who was watching me with amused forbearance.

Ember was less impressed. Having only just managed to avoid my stumbling feet, she took off for the front of the line, apparently having decided Amara would be a safer walking companion.

I couldn't fault her since the near accident had clearly been caused by my distraction. I murmured a second apology to Ida, but she waved it off.

Once I was paying attention, I could clearly see why we'd stopped. The river bent sharply away to our right, while a small stream broke off and continued south, in the rough direction of the town.

After only the briefest of comments, we resumed our progress, but now following the stream instead of the main river. As we walked, I resolved to focus on the issue at hand, but the more I tried to force my mind away from Nik, the more aware I was of the heat from his body and the soft rise and fall of his breath. I stumbled slightly, and a strong hand steadied my elbow from behind. The touch was withdrawn again as soon as I regained my balance, but the tingle of contact remained, distracting me even further.

The flap of wings made me look up to see Phoenix zipping toward me. He was flying above the stream, as if it were a road for birds, its purpose being to clear a path free of trees. I shook my head at my own whimsy, but the thought of a path stuck in my head.

The ground beneath my feet was becoming easier to walk, as if someone had already started wearing out a track along the route. It would be natural for the townsfolk to do the same as Phoenix—following the course of the stream as they made their way to the best foraging ground. But this stream was new and the townsfolk had been falling progressively ill for the last couple of weeks. Was it possible they had already worn down the ground this much, even this far from the town?

A rustling in the undergrowth nearest the stream made me turn in time to see Ember come shooting out from between two bushes. She was moving fast enough that she might have slid into the stream if I hadn't scooped her up. I wasn't sure if she was afraid, but something had set her trembling. Whatever she had encountered in the forest had certainly caught her attention.

Making a fast decision, I changed direction, stepping away from the stream in the direction she had come. Nik immediately stopped as well.

"What is it?" He sounded concerned.

I didn't turn to look at him, just holding up a hand to ask him to wait. Closing my eyes, I sent my power out into the surrounding forest. Dimly in the background I heard Nik calling to the others ahead of us to stop, but I ignored his words as well as their replies, focusing on my search.

This time I ignored the feathered, furred, and reptilian populations I encountered, skimming over them as I looked for something else. Someone had made a path beside this stream, but what if it wasn't the townsfolk? What if someone else was here in the forest?

It was a large island, and the town only covered a small part of it.

I stiffened as my power brushed against the familiar feel of people. Nik's hand braced my elbow as he murmured a question I wasn't paying enough attention to catch. For once, his presence wasn't enough to distract me as I reached toward my new discovery.

"What have you found?" Amara's question—delivered in the voice of a master to an apprentice—broke me out of my focus.

I blinked, shaking my head as I turned to look at her. The others had abandoned their single line to cluster around me, all of their faces intent.

"There are people." I pointed straight into the trees. "Through there."

"We're still a way north of the town." Costas frowned in the direction I'd pointed. "But not everyone forages in the same place. They must be out gathering supplies. Perhaps they're hoping they can find something that will help with this disease."

"It's possible." I hesitated. "But would they bring sick people along on a foraging expedition?"

"Are they ill?" Amara asked, her voice turning sharp.

"It's hard to say for sure from this distance." I hesitated again. "I don't think they all are. But there's one—a child—who doesn't feel right even from this distance. I'm afraid she must be very sick for me to sense it from so far away."

"A child?" Amara's frown deepened. She exchanged a look first with Costas and then Ida. "Is it possible someone came out here in desperation and didn't want to leave their sick child behind? Regardless, it sounds unusual enough to warrant further examination." She turned to me. "Do you think you can take us to them? Are they moving?"

I checked again before answering. "They seem to be stationary, and I can certainly take us in their direction. But I can't tell what obstacles might be between us and them."

"I'll take care of any obstacles," Nik said in a matter-of-fact way, and I didn't doubt his ability to deal with anything the forest might throw at us.

I glanced up and down the river, considering the path that wasn't quite a path. My instinct told me these weren't townsfolk who'd come into the forest to forage. And if I was right about that, perhaps...

I stepped away from the river, pushing through the bushes in the same spot Ember had emerged from. At first I could see nothing but more trees and varied undergrowth. Nik strode through behind me, and I turned in time to see him stop abruptly.

Following the direction of his gaze, I sucked in a breath.

"I'm not imagining it, right?" I asked. "That's a path?"

"A path?" Amara reached us, following my pointing finger to see for herself. "Did you know this was here, Delphine?"

"Not for sure, but I wondered." I gave Ember a light squeeze. "Ember found something in this direction, and it occurred to me that whoever made that path," I gestured back toward the stream, "might have made more."

"Impressive." Amara smiled at me, and I couldn't help grinning back despite the seriousness of the situation. If I couldn't be in town healing people, at least I could be useful out here.

"If there's a path, we need to see where it leads." Costas took off, the rest of us hurrying to fall in behind him.

The narrow width of the path through the undergrowth kept us in single file again, but the conversation continued regardless.

"The path just ends abruptly back there instead of connecting with the path by the stream," he said, and for a moment I thought he was discounting my theory. But when I caught the look he threw Amara, I realized he had something else on his mind.

"You think they're hiding themselves, then?" Nik asked. "Would they have reason to do that?"

"I think you know the answer to that," Costas said in a tired voice, and Nik fell quiet.

"Are they hiding from us?" I asked, horrified.

The idea hadn't even occurred to me, but now it seemed to fit all too well, given the newness of the paths. Had our arrival driven some of the islanders from their homes?

I glanced back at Nik, and he frowned at the expression on my face. I expected him to say something comforting—however meaningless given our lack of information—but instead he turned a speculative look northward.

"Hold on a moment," he said, and we all stopped, everyone turning in his direction.

Plunging into the trees, he disappeared from view, only to call for us to follow him moments later. I had to wind my way around several dense bushes, but as soon as I was out of sight of the path, the undergrowth abruptly cut off, giving way to an unnatural clearing.

The trees had been cleared, as well as the undergrowth, replaced with neat rows of what looked like vegetables, and even a whole section of some sort of grain. I gaped at it, everyone else taking in the sight in equal silence.

"I thought I could sense something out of the ordinary through here," Nik said at last. Looking at me, he continued. "Whatever is going on here, I don't think it has anything to do with us."

I nodded, relieved, although my curiosity was now burning out of control.

"Look!" Ida pointed at a spot to our right. "That looks like a more established path."

"That makes sense," Amara said. "The stream is quite new, so the paths to and along it are also new. But this clearing has obviously been here a long time."

She led the way toward the second path, and we all followed. This track was much more obvious and had enough room for two people to walk side by side. From the look of the packed dirt beneath us, I suspected some sort of cart made regular use of it, as well as people on foot.

"How close are we?" Amara asked me.

"Very," I said quietly. "There are five adults and the sick child. I suspect two of the adults might be older, but they're not elderly enough for it to be obvious in their bodies from this distance."

"Sounds like a family," Nik murmured as he drifted closer to me. Despite his words, his hand strayed to his sword hilt.

Amara nodded. "Regardless of who they are, I feel confident we can handle the situation."

It was a reasonable assumption given the nature of our group. With two powerful elements mages, not to mention a strong plants mage, there were few people who would pose a risk to us.

"Relax," I whispered to Nik. "The last thing we need is more of that." I nodded toward his sword but regretted it immediately when his face paled.

He drew away from me, and I immediately felt the distance. I didn't need his protection, but I had appreciated his presence anyway. I bit my lip. How long would it be until the sight of Nik with a sword didn't bring back unwanted images of that awful night? I hated the lingering effects of what had been a misunderstanding on my part.

And as usual since then, I couldn't find the right words to bridge the gap that had sprung up between us. Nik had done nothing wrong—the horrible assumptions had all been mine, and it should be my responsibility to fix matters. If only I knew how.

"I'm sorry," I murmured, and he gave me a tight smile.

I wanted to say more, but it was hardly the time for a proper conversation.

"They're just ahead," I whispered, unsure if we were trying to hide our approach.

Amara nodded to show she'd heard but didn't stop walking. Ahead of her, the trees thinned and then disappeared completely, revealing another clearing. This second one was smaller, but it looked well established.

My mouth fell open as I took in a log cabin with another, smaller garden spreading in all directions around it. Whatever I had been expecting, it hadn't been this.

"How long have they been here?" I asked. "This isn't a camp but a long-term house."

"It certainly is. And the only polite thing to do at this point is knock." Amara walked up the neat path that led to the front door and rapped loudly on the wood.

A glad cry sounded from inside, and the door was wrenched open. A man appeared, but as soon as he took in Amara's appearance, his face fell, his expression changing from glad welcome to horror within seconds.

# CHAPTER
# SIX

"Please don't be alarmed," Amara said quickly. "We don't mean you any harm."

"Don't touch me!" the man said roughly, pulling out a knife and holding it up defiantly, although the hand that held it trembled.

I swayed forward, wanting to run to support Amara, but caution held me in place. I didn't want to cause the man to panic and attack.

"Don't worry," she said. "I'm not a healer." An unnatural wind swept past us and through the cabin door, clearly demonstrating her affinity.

The man relaxed slightly although he didn't lower his knife. Peering over her shoulder, he narrowed his eyes at where the rest of us were grouped together in frozen stillness.

"I did, however, bring a healer with me," Amara continued, making the man start violently. "And my healer tells me that someone inside this house is in need of medical assistance."

She met his gaze, her eyes steady, and I wasn't surprised to see him flinch. I had been the recipient of that gaze often enough myself to know its effect.

I finally let myself step forward to join her. Nik grabbed at my arm, his eyes on the knife blade, but I shook him off and he let me go.

"I'm Delphine," I said in as calming a tone as I could manage. "And I'm a healing apprentice." I nodded toward Amara. "She's my master."

His eyes widened. "You're cross-influenced? My grandma told me about that, but I've never met anyone who was."

I nodded. "Then you must know I don't come from the island. I'm not like the Constantines. All I want to do is assist the sick child."

He hesitated, glancing over his shoulder, and I could guess what was making him waver. From this proximity, I was certain the child inside was extremely ill. This family must have been avoiding healers for years, but now they had desperate need of one.

"Do you have any strength?" he asked roughly.

"My apprentice will be a master one day," Amara said with complete certainty.

The man's eyes widened as he gave me a second look. I shifted uncomfortably.

"I don't know about that," I said. "But I think I know what that girl in there has, and I'm certain I can help her."

I had encountered enough cases to know what the slow heartbeat and rattling breaths meant.

"You're sure?" he asked, and I could hear the indecision in his voice.

"Yes." I tried to look as trustworthy as possible. "But the sooner I help her, the better. I can't be sure without a proper examination, but she sounds like she's already well advanced in the illness."

"She's not the only one who's sick," Amara told him gently. "This disease has spread through the whole town. My apprentice may be young, but she knows what she's doing."

"Fine," the man said, "but she comes in alone. And she doesn't touch anyone except the patient."

I nodded eagerly, my concern for the girl growing as I heard her give a racking cough and sensed her heartbeat dip even further in response.

"Absolutely not," Nik said in a harsh voice.

He stepped forward to my side, and the man's eyes narrowed, his gaze taking in Nik's stance and the weapon on his hip.

"How about a compromise?" Amara said. "I will accompany my apprentice inside, and the rest of our group will remain out here."

The man's eyes flicked to the remaining two, but he was too distracted by Nik to give them more than a passing glance. If that distraction was the reason for him failing to recognize the one Constantine among us, then Nik's protective instincts had achieved some good at least.

"Very well," he said after a moment. "Just the two of you."

He stood back slightly, gesturing for us to pass him and enter the house. Amara went first, with me following close behind. The man shrunk back from me as I slipped past, clearly afraid of any contact, no matter how minor.

I winced but was soon distracted by the inside of the house. The first thing I saw was a second man stepping forward to provide backup to the one already in the doorway. He was a generation older than the first, and from the resemblance, I guessed them to be father and son.

This man also gave me a wide berth, clearing my view of the house beyond. A large, open room contained a wooden table with six chairs, a stove, a number of storage cabinets, and several more padded chairs. Unlike the smaller home of Ida's host family, the cabin had a number of doors opening off the central room. Judging from the different timbers used to make the various internal doors, I guessed the house had been expanded over time.

Two women—one older and one younger—sat at the wooden table, their postures stiff and their expressions torn between hope and fear. There was no sign of the child.

"Please take me to the patient." I'd barely finished the words when another round of weak coughs made me look toward one of the doors. "She's in there?"

The older woman stood and wrung her hands. "Please save our Nina." The look on her face almost brought tears to my eyes, and I nodded, determined.

Amara reached the door first, opening it for me and ushering me inside. The room beyond held two beds, one against each wall, a dresser, and a small table bearing a pitcher of water. Scattered across the floor and bed were a number of toys, each one clearly carved and polished with care.

But the small girl lying in one of the beds was too far gone to pay any attention to toys. Her eyes opened at the sound of the door, but from the glassy, unfocused look to them, she was barely conscious.

A woman lay beside her, her arms wrapped around the girl and a look of anguish on her face. The girl's mother.

"Please," she whispered, her eyes on my face. "Please."

Unlike the others, her face bore no hint of fear at our presence, and I guessed it was because a far worse fear already had her in its grip, leaving no room for anything else. She knew how close her daughter was to death, and she would clearly risk far more than our presence to save her.

I didn't waste any time on words, hurrying to the bed and kneeling beside it. Gripping Nina's thin arm with both of my hands, I pushed my power into her.

It only took seconds to confirm that our assumption had been right. This girl had the same thing that plagued the townsfolk, and her condition had already progressed beyond anyone else I'd encountered.

I didn't need my power to feel her burning up—my hands were enough to tell she was dangerously hot. I cooled her first, easing her pain while I did so. Just those two things were enough to get a response. She stirred, her eyes brightening as she regarded me with curiosity. But she didn't try to sit up, her condition still clearly extremely weak.

I sent my power to her brain next and her heart after that. With both essential organs in such a state of inflammation, she wouldn't have lasted long without intervention.

As I poured my power into her, letting my natural instincts guide the process, I wished I'd had a chance to talk to Hayes before we left. Not having learned the techniques he'd devised for treating the disease, I was going to have to expend a lot of power to save her. And as I poured it into her, I wondered how many other children in the town were approaching this level of illness.

Hayes and Clay had triaged the population, but sometimes conditions like this could progress unpredictably, and I preferred to keep as much of my power in reserve for other patients as possible. I didn't hold back from the healing, though. Considering the extent of her illness and the family's isolation, it seemed important to complete the healing while I had the chance.

By the time I had finished, the mother was shaking with sobs. When I let Nina's arm drop with a tired sigh, I reached for the mother's wrist, concerned. She waved me away, however, recovering herself enough to speak.

"I'm just so...grateful," the final word came out on another sob, but she pushed herself into a sitting position, helping her daughter to ease herself up as well.

"She'll still need recovery time." I stood. "Given the length of her illness, her energy reserves will be low, and her nutrient levels will be depleted."

The mother nodded, but she couldn't keep a beaming smile off her face.

"We'll take excellent care of her."

"Mama, I'm hungry!" Nina announced, her high voice strong, despite her recent ordeal.

Her mother swept her into her arms and squeezed her tightly. Meeting her eyes over Nina's head, I saw fresh tears spilling out.

"We tried so hard to coax her to eat and drink," she said. "But it was a struggle to get her to take anything. And we couldn't keep her temperature down. At first we were taking her to the water every few hours to immerse her, but even with the new stream so much closer than the river used to be, she got too weak for the journey."

Amara, who had been standing back near the door, straightened, her eyes focusing on the woman.

"You were bathing her in the stream?"

"Yes." The woman faltered before the intensity of Amara's expression, looking from her to me. "Was that wrong? We just wanted to cool her."

I rubbed the back of my neck and looked at Amara.

"Bathing a patient with a high temperature in cool water is often a good idea," I said carefully.

The mother remained tense, clearly understanding there was something more behind my broad statement.

"I'm hungry!" Nina repeated, escaping her mother's arms and sliding out of the bed.

Seeing her standing, I guessed her to be about five. Dropping to one knee, I offered her my hand and she shook it gravely.

As soon as she'd finished, she looked over her shoulder at her mother, her eyes bright.

"Did I do it right?"

"You did an excellent job," her mother assured her, then looked at me, vaguely embarrassed. "She hasn't met anyone outside the family, other than her ladyship, of course, but we've tried to teach her proper manners in case…"

She trailed off at the confused expressions on both Amara and my faces.

"Why don't we join the others," Amara said, "so we can talk properly, and you can get this young lady some food?"

Nina jumped in excitement and raced for the door. Her mother watched her go with the dazed expression of someone who'd just had a violent and unexpected shift in emotion.

Amara put a gentle hand on her arm. "Don't worry, she really is better. My apprentice might be young, but she's strong."

The woman flinched, pulling away, and Amara quickly removed her hand.

"Don't worry," she said. "I have an elements seed myself."

"You're cross-influenced?" the woman asked me, showing the same amazement as the man at the door.

"Yes, that's right," Amara said. "We're not from the island."

"Not from the island," the woman repeated slowly, as if she couldn't quite wrap her mind around the concept.

"I'm sorry to hurry you," I said. "But we need to talk to you about an urgent situation."

The woman still looked bemused, but she allowed us to lead the way out to the main room. Nina was already seated at the table, being plied with food by the two delighted-looking women there. Even the men at the door had relaxed since Nina's appearance. My healing had done far more than our words in convincing them of our intentions.

"Could the rest of our party come inside now?" Amara asked, looking from the matriarch of the group to the patriarch. "It sounds like there's a lot you don't know about the current situation on the island, and our time is limited."

Glances flew between all five of the adults, but after a moment the older woman nodded, and the two men slowly moved over to the table to join the rest of us. I hurried to the empty doorway and leaned outside.

Nik appeared in front of me before I could even wave them over. From the tension in his muscles, he had been poised and waiting to spring into action.

"You can relax," I told him. "I healed the girl, and everyone seems willing to listening to us now. She was close to death, so we arrived just in time."

"But who are they?" Costas asked, half to himself.

"I have no idea," I said. "But did you really not have any idea there were people living in the forest?"

He shook his head. "I've never heard of anyone living outside the town."

"It's a very sensible set up if you ask me," Ida said. "It must have been very peaceful out here without the Constantines breathing over them." She calmly entered the house and nodded a greeting to the group gathered inside.

There weren't enough chairs for everyone, but we gathered around the table anyway, some remaining standing. I would have liked to stand myself since my body was buzzing with nervous energy, but Nina's mother insisted I take her seat.

In the face of her earnest protestations, I couldn't refuse. But as soon as I was settled, their attention turned to the rest of my companions, and a reaction spread through them. Several of them leaned forward, the others exchanging whispers as they examined Costas.

He cleared his throat awkwardly. "Do you know me?"

"You look just like her!" The matriarch exclaimed. "Who are you?"

"Do you know where her ladyship is?" the mother asked in a rush, not giving him a chance to answer the grandmother's question. "Has anything happened to her?"

"That's your second mention of this ladyship," Amara said. "I didn't realize the island had any royalty or nobility. Is she the descendant of someone of rank in Calista from before the kingdom's fall?"

"Ah..." The mother looked at the older couple. "I'm not sure. That's just what we've always called her."

"She wasn't born into a noble family," the older woman said heavily. "But she married one of *them*."

A hush fell over the table. No one needed to ask who *they* were.

A strangled sound made me look at Costas. He had gone from slightly pale to an uncomfortable red, his hands tightly gripping the back of Ida's chair.

Ida turned to give him a confused look before surveying the others around the table. "Are you talking about Lady Isolde? My host family mentioned her once, but I thought she died?"

"Lady Isolde?" I looked from Ida to Costas, but his attention was on the matriarch.

"She did die," he said in a rough whisper. "When Ignatius was still a baby."

"No," the matriarch said simply. "She didn't."

Costas leaned forward, his eyes glued to her. "You're telling me my mother is still alive?"

This time the woman hesitated. "All I can tell you is that she was alive when we last saw her over a month ago. We expected her to be back before now, though, and we even went out looking when…" She trailed off, clearly uncomfortable at the level of emotion on Costas's face.

"I don't understand," he said, and this time he sounded dangerous. "Someone explain it to me right now."

Amara and Nik exchanged a look, Nik's posture shifting slightly in response. He had already positioned himself a step back from the table where he could see everyone and move easily, and he was clearly ready to take action if Costas was about to have a violent breakdown.

"My host family are convinced she's dead," Ida said, cutting through the tension in her matter-of-fact way.

I'd wondered about Costas's mother myself but hadn't dared ask since I was staying up at the manor instead of in the town. Part of me hadn't wanted to ask either, afraid the Constantines might have murdered their son's wife as they had their daughter's husband.

"Did the family not approve of her?" I asked tentatively.

"They were the ones to choose her since she's a powerful healer," the older man said, a note of either bitterness or disgust coloring his words. "But their lies can only take them so far. You can't make someone do what's not in them to do."

Nik shifted in place, and I shot him a look. He refused to meet my eyes, making me frown, but once again, we were in no position for a conversation about us.

"Hush, Pa," the second younger woman said, glancing at us fearfully. Her eyes lingered on Costas the longest.

"Did she live here with you?" Costas asked. "Until she disappeared a month ago, at least."

"Oh goodness, no," the matriarch said. "But she visited regularly. All the forest dwellers gladly house her when she comes past, and she could never bring herself to show favoritism by settling with anyone. Now there's a truly noble lady, whatever her blood."

"Ma!" the younger woman hissed, even more urgently.

"There are more of you?" Amara asked before holding up a hand. "Wait, no, don't answer that yet. I think I should start by letting you know what's been happening on the island. It sounds like this Lady Isolde was your link to news beyond this clearing, and much has happened in the last month."

"New arrivals to the island is news indeed," the younger man said, his gaze roaming over each of us.

"Perhaps more important, however, is that the Constantines turned on each other and are all dead," Amara said, keeping the news as concise as possible. "With the exception of Costas who has an elements rather than healing ability."

"Dead?! They're all dead?" The ringing voice from the doorway cut through the astonished exclamations of the rest of the group.

Everyone turned to see a middle-aged woman outlined in the doorframe. She had a wan, exhausted air, overlaid with an expression of deep shock. While we stared at her, the woman's eyes rolled up into her head and she collapsed.

Everyone at the table leaped to their feet, but Nik reached her first. He arrived just in time to cushion her head from the fall, and by the time I shouldered through the milling people, he had her lying flat on the ground.

I dropped down beside her and grasped one wrist. Someone behind me murmured a protest and someone else shushed them. I kept my eyes on the unconscious woman.

I could find no sign of injury or illness in her body, beyond a few minor scratches and a blister on both heels. I looked up at the others.

"Is she dead?" Nina asked, staring at us with wide eyes.

I shook my head. "Happily not. As far as I can tell, she collapsed from a combination of shock and exhaustion, nothing more."

I pushed some energy into her, and the woman stirred. As soon as her eyes fluttered open, she tried to push herself upright. I steadied her, holding her gently down.

"You've pushed yourself too hard," I told her sternly, adopting the healer tone I had learned in the Caltoran hospital. "I've given you some energy, but you need proper rest before you attempt anything strenuous."

The woman stared at me, her eyes even wider than they had been when I first saw her in the doorway.

"You're a healer?" she whispered.

Before I realized what was happening, her arm shot out, her fingers closing around my wrist like steel.

I tried to yank myself free as her power speared into me, but her hold was too strong. Throwing up my wall, I pushed her back out, but not before I felt the shape of her power inside me.

Nik, who had drawn back while I worked, appeared at my side. Grabbing the woman, he pulled her roughly away, using enough force to break her hold.

"Wait!" I cried, before he could do anything more drastic. "Wait! She wasn't trying to mesmerize me or hurt me."

"Of course she wasn't!" the matriarch exclaimed, clearly offended at the suggestion. "Lady Isolde would never do that."

"Lady...Isolde," Costas repeated in a numb voice. He alone hadn't left his original position by the table, although his eyes were glued on the woman. "You're my mother?"

# CHAPTER
# SEVEN

Isolde's eyes flew to Costas, and she gasped. The two were frozen for a moment, staring at each other while the rest of us watched them in an equally motionless state.

Slowly two tears slipped over her eyelids and tracked down her cheeks. "My son," she whispered. "My little Costie."

"How can you be my mother?" he said stiffly, clearly not recovered from the shock. "You can't be my mother. That's impossible!"

She struggled to her feet and started toward him, but he flinched back and she stopped.

"After a few months had passed, I couldn't remember what your face looked like anymore," he whispered. "I was too young. When I met you during my adventures in the forest, I thought you were someone from the town out foraging. I used...I used to imagine you were my mother. I would pretend I was a normal boy, and we were a family."

More silent tears ran down her face.

"I'm sorry," she said in a broken voice. "I wanted to tell you the truth every day, but I didn't dare. Too many lives were at stake. Possibly even yours after they murdered your uncle."

He shook his head violently. "No. No, it doesn't make any sense. It can't be."

"You know each other?" I looked back and forth between them, utterly confused.

"Sit down, your ladyship," the patriarch said, pulling out a chair and gently helping Isolde to sit. She allowed him to guide her, hardly seeming aware of her body's movements.

Once she was seated, however, she looked back at me. "You're a healer—a master level healer. And you brought my son to me. How is any of this possible?"

"That's exactly what we'd like to know," Amara said, resuming control of the conversation. "But first I must ask you not to touch or test my apprentice without her permission again." Her voice was ice, and the woman's eyes widened, a look of guilt coming over her face.

"I'm sorry! I didn't think. It's been so long since I've been around anyone who—" She cut herself off and shook her head. "I apologize. Please allow me to introduce myself. I'm Isolde—not Lady Isolde, just Isolde. I don't hold any rank—and officially I'm married to Augustine Constantine, although I haven't seen him in many, many years."

Amara's stiff stance softened. "I'm afraid I have to inform you that you are now a widow. Your husband was murdered."

"By your son," Costas said baldly. "Your son murdered his father, his grandmother, and everyone else he could get his hands on."

Isolde gasped again, her hand flying to her mouth. "Ignatius? Ignatius did that? But why...how...?"

I expected even more tears to flow, but strangely the news dried the last of them. Her brow furrowed, and I could almost see her turning the information over in her head, trying to make sense of it.

"He was such a chubby, beautiful baby," she said at last in a soft voice. "But he was a healer, so they shaped him into one of them. I knew from the beginning they would do that."

"So you just left?" Costas snapped. "You just abandoned him—and me?"

"No, of course not!" She sighed and ran a hand down her face. "Leaving you both was the last thing I wanted to do."

"Then why did you do it?" he asked in a quieter voice.

Amara cleared her throat. "This is clearly a very personal matter for the two of you, and I wish we had the luxury to respect that and offer you some privacy. But given the situation we all find ourselves in, I think it would be best if everyone was brought up to date on exactly what has been happening on this island."

Isolde nodded slowly. "I, too, would like answers about the current situation."

When she inclined her head toward the seats, the house's residents launched into movement, returning to the places they had occupied before. The rest of us followed, although Isolde was now in my seat. I lingered at the back, standing close to Nik, and this time no one took any notice of me.

"Let's progress in chronological order," Amara said, looking at Isolde. "You said you didn't want to leave your young children, so what happened to compel you to do so?"

"The Constantines have ruled this island from the beginning," she said. "But over the years they've become complacent and over-confident, too used to a docile population. I was one of those compliant townsfolk, once upon a time, and I was even flattered to be chosen as the future bride of Augustine. I knew that was my future from a young age, and I was delighted with it." She shook her head, as if unable to believe her youthful naïveté.

"But once I was actually married, everything began to unravel. Being in such constant contact with the Constantines gradually stripped away the mesmerizations that had been with me from childhood. At first I was confused and frightened—and even more so once Augustine explained mesmerization to me."

"So they taught you to do it too, after you were married?" Amara asked.

Isolde shook her head. "I'm not a true Constantine, so they didn't go that far. But they spoke openly in front of me, and when I asked questions, my husband answered them." Her face twisted in disgust. "I don't think it even occurred to him that I might be horrified by the information."

"So that turned you against Father and Grandmother and the others?" Costas asked. His eyes hadn't left her face the entire time she talked, as if he was weighing and measuring each word.

"Of course!" She shuddered. "Although in truth, I had already reached the point of being afraid and unhappy before that. I had worked out something was wrong, but I didn't understand what until the revelation about mesmerization. I thought I had just idealized them out of youthful ignorance or something."

"So you decided to leave?" The crease between Amara's eyes told me she was unconvinced by her own suggestion.

"No." Isolde's eyes were on Costas. "I would never have left my children just because I felt uncomfortable. And while I deplored the state of affairs on the island, there didn't seem anything I could do about it. But then they went too far."

"Of course they did," Costas muttered.

"There was a boy in the town who possessed a strong healing seed—one of those situations where a child is born with a much stronger seed than his parents."

I shifted on my feet, all too familiar with that situation. Nik glanced down at me, and I nodded slightly, managing to muster a strained smile.

"At first the Constantines did nothing," Isolde continued. "In retrospect, I think they were waiting to see if either Costas or Ignatius turned out to be a girl. If I had borne a daughter, the boy would have been marked as a future Constantine son-in-law. But my children were both boys, and Grandmother knew I didn't want any more."

"So they had to get rid of the child," Costas said bitterly. "They couldn't have any strong healers outside the family."

Everyone at the table stirred at his words, their faces twisting into various expressions of displeasure and grief. No one disputed his words, however.

"I see you've already worked out how the family ran things," Isolde said to her son. "I'm afraid I was slower to realize than I should have been. But the boy grew sick a number of years before reaching the age of activation, and I was the one sent to treat him."

My eyes widened, and Nik and I exchanged a look. The hubris of the Constantines really had grown beyond reason if they had sent an outsider to do a task like that.

"My instructions were to claim I had arrived too late and that he was beyond saving," Isolde confirmed. "But in reality, I was to use my power to end his life. Augustine mesmerized me himself just before I left, but he overestimated the effect of his lies. There is no truth under the sun that would convince me to use my power to kill a child. And any claim that the boy was a threat melted to nothing when I saw him weak and ill in his bed."

"Augustine forgot that he never had control of your mind," I murmured. "He could convince you of his lies—at least briefly—but he couldn't force you to do something so contrary to your nature. And especially not in the face of evidence to the contrary."

It made sense. There was a reason Grey had made so much use of his charm, despite his ability. He had tailored his mesmerizations around each person—to me he had spoken of a bloodless coup to save the kingdom, and to Ida he had promised a life of peace and safety.

Isolde turned to look at me, her brows drawing together. "I don't think I caught your name?"

"I'm Delphine," I said. "And I have more experience of mesmerizations than anyone should have."

Her brows rose almost to her hairline. "You know how to mesmerize? They taught you even though you're not a Constantine?"

I nodded and she sank back with a sigh. "I had hoped..."

"That the end of the line of Constantine healers meant an end to mesmerization?" I asked, and she nodded. "Unfortunately, not all the Constantines with a healing affinity are dead."

Her eyes widened. "But you said—"

"When I said all the healer Constantines are deceased," Amara interjected, "I meant all the Constantines who resided on this island."

Isolde gasped. "Chloe?" she asked, instantly understanding.

"My aunt died many years ago," Costas said, "but her son survives."

"Grey is alive and trained to mesmerize? But he was just a baby when his mother fled from her parents..." Isolde stared from Costas to Amara and finally to me. "Is he the one who trained you?"

I nodded. "And unfortunately, after instigating chaos on the island, he was able to escape to the mainland."

"The story has gotten out of order," Amara interrupted. "We now know why you fled, Isolde, but not how."

She shook her head, as if trying to put her thoughts back into order. "Yes, sorry. Obviously I couldn't kill the child. But I also knew he would never be safe in the town."

"So you smuggled him out to the forest," Costas breathed, looking around the house with fresh eyes.

"Lady Isolde was our rescuer then, and has been many times since," the matriarch said firmly. "My son would have been murdered without her intervention—and us none the wiser." Fury still blazed in her eyes at the memory of the long-ago crime.

"So you're a strong healer?" Amara looked at the younger of the two men in confusion.

I could understand her emotion. If he was a strong healer himself, why had they been in such desperate need of my services?

The man shook his head. "They're talking of my older brother. He died in an accident two years ago." Grief clouded his eyes.

"A strong healer died in an accident?" Ida asked, clearly confused at the idea.

"We were cutting wood and—" His voice choked slightly. "Death was immediate. There was no time for healing."

I swallowed. Healers had a better chance than most, but we weren't impervious to danger.

Nik tensed at my side, his eyes on my face, and I knew he was thinking the same thing, remembering all the times I'd been in danger. Careful not to look in his direction, I kept my focus on the people around the table.

"But he lived many extra years beyond childhood and even survived long enough to give us a beautiful granddaughter," the matriarch said in a muffled voice. Her eyes came up to meet mine. "We cannot thank you enough for saving Nina."

"Delphine had to heal Nina?" Isolde looked at me again. "She was sick with this new illness?"

"You know about it?" I asked.

"Of course." She ran a hand over her face, the exhaustion from earlier still showing on her features. "I discovered it several days ago and have been constantly on the go since. Because of where I started, yours happened to be the last house on my circuit."

"You pushed yourself too hard." Costas's voice softened for the first time since his mother's arrival. "You're fortunate Delphine was here to help you. Otherwise you might not have survived trying to heal Nina."

"These are my people," she said fiercely. "I couldn't leave any of them to die."

"So these people aren't the only ones you've smuggled out of the town?" Amara asked. "They were just the first?"

Isolde nodded. "I helped them pack up and flee as soon as it was dark. And then I returned to the manor and told them the matter was taken care of. So great was their confidence, they didn't even check on the family or notice they were gone. I thought I might have gotten away with it, but two weeks later, I tested a young boy and discovered he had a strong healing seed. I thought it would be easier to get him and his family out of town before they ever came to the Constantines' attention."

She sighed. "And that's when I discovered the difficulty of making solo trips into town and the forest without arousing suspicion. It took weeks before I got the chance to approach the child's family and get them out. I took them to a different location from my first evacuees—it's easier for individual families to escape notice than a whole second village—but on my way back, I checked in here."

"And she found me sick," the matriarch said. "We were unused to living in such a wild place, and I had been infected with something unfamiliar. By the time her ladyship arrived, I was stretched out on the bed too ill to move."

"I healed her, of course," Isolde said. "But I also realized that I couldn't bring these people out here and abandon them. They had no experience of living in a wilderness like this, and they had no strong healers of their own— at least not until their children grew old enough to be activated. And when that time did come, those children would need someone to activate and train them."

"And so you faked your own death," Costas said, his jaw tight.

"I made sure to go over the waterfall when half of them were there to see," Isolde said. "I needed to be sure they wouldn't come looking for me."

"Why didn't you take us with you?" Costas demanded.

Isolde shuddered slightly. "There was enough danger in what I did for an adult healer. I couldn't possibly have taken a small child or toddler over that waterfall with me. And besides, they didn't care about losing me—I'd fulfilled my purpose and delivered the next generation of Constantines—but their own blood would have been a different matter. For all I knew, they might have torn the forest apart just to find your bodies."

"Not me," Costas said bitterly. "They never wanted me."

Isolde sighed. "They were fools until the end if they couldn't see your value. But remember, back then you hadn't been tested yet, and they were still assuming you had a healing seed."

"And after?" he asked. "All those hours I spent in the forest alone. I'm not sure they would have even noticed if I never returned."

"I wanted to tell you so many times," she said. "But by then Chloe had married, lost her husband, and fled. I had seen just how far they were willing to go, and I was being more careful than ever to hide the existence of the forest families. I couldn't be sure they would ignore your disappearance, so I couldn't risk it. All I could do was watch over you when you were away from the manor," she said softly.

"I used to call you Forest Lady, and I thought you were so kind," Costas said quietly. "You were nothing like Grandmother or Aunt Kendry or Father. Whenever I came out, I would look for you, and I was always disappointed if you didn't appear with a kind word or special treat to share."

Fresh tears slipped down Isolde's cheeks. "It was all I could do for you, but it was far from enough. I'm painfully aware of that."

"So over the years you've been smuggling out families in danger and setting up a network of homes in the forest," Amara said slowly.

"Not a network," the patriarch said with a frown. "We've never met any of the others."

Amara looked doubtfully at the two younger women in the circle.

"Except for our daughters-in-law, of course," the matriarch said quickly.

"I kept everyone separate in case the Constantines ever stumbled on one of the families," Isolde explained. "Given their abilities, they would easily have extracted any secrets. This way none of them could betray the locations, identities, or even the total number of the others. And it also prevented the families from banding together. There are enough of them now that it would be dangerous for them to do anything as a whole group."

"So you travel between the houses, providing training for their young ones," Amara said.

"And also healing as necessary. Not all the families had to flee because they had a child in danger. Mesmerization can be broken, as I experienced myself, and it occasionally happens among the townsfolk—especially those who've served a term at the manor. I'll help anyone who wants to get away from the town and the Constantines."

"I understand that as a healer, you could easily test the town's young children before they even reach the age of official testing," Amara said. "Especially since it isn't something that needs physical contact. But how do you know about the discontented townsfolk?"

"Not all discontented people have actually fled the town," I said slowly, putting something together. Looking up, I met Isolde's eyes. "I'm guessing you know Lumi and Fergus's mother?"

She smiled. "I do. She is one of the few who chose to stay, and she acts as a go-between when she discovers anyone who wants to disappear."

"That's why she fled up the mountain during the fever," I muttered. "She wasn't just escaping infection but was fleeing to a healer who wouldn't mesmerize her or her children while healing them."

Isolde caught my words, her brows lifting. "You really do know her if you know about that."

"Actually I've never met her, only the children. They're so clearly different from everyone else in the town that they attract attention."

A shadow of fear crossed Isolde's face before she froze, her expression slowly changing. She had lived half a lifetime in fear, and it would take time to absorb that the source of that fear was gone forever.

"I'm one of those who realized something strange and terrible was going on after being a maid for several months at the manor," the second younger woman said in a timid voice. "Isolde found me and offered me the chance to escape."

She smiled first at Isolde and then at the younger man who was standing behind her chair. He squeezed her shoulders in response, smiling back at her, and I realized the two must be married.

"It was my parents who realized something was wrong," Nina's mother said. "They were concerned enough to keep me away from further healing checkups, but they were too scared to leave their comfortable life in the town for an unknown future in the forest. But once I finished my apprenticeship, I couldn't bear to stay in the town, surrounded by mesmerized people and watched over by the Constantines. Since I knew Isolde had offered my parents a different life, I set off by myself to try to find her."

She shook her head, as if recognizing her youthful foolishness.

"It was a blessed day for our family when our son found you wandering in the forest," the matriarch said with a warm look for both her daughter-in-law and her granddaughter.

Nina, who was seated in her mother's lap, still eating, looked up and beamed at her grandmother. Her mother wrapped her arms around her daughter and pressed a kiss against her hair.

"It was a fortunate day for me, too," she said softly. "I think I was already in love before I even reached the house."

The whole table went quiet, a communal shadow falling across their faces as they remembered their missing son, brother, husband, and father.

"How did the Constantines never notice?" Amara asked. "Didn't the other townsfolk ever say something about their missing neighbors?"

"Of course not," Costas said in a dark voice. "How could my family get rid of anyone they found inconvenient unless the islanders were mesmerized to accept disappearances or *accidents* among their neighbors without question? My family's behavior was so ingrained, that if any of them noticed a missing person for themselves, they probably assumed someone else in the family had dealt with them quietly and never bothered to even ask."

Nik made a quiet growling noise deep in his throat, his eyes on Costas and his expression thunderous. These were the people attacked during the party, and yet his instinct had still been to try to save them.

Was it any wonder he was upset that I had thought him a mass murderer —however briefly? Isolde had said not even mesmerization could turn her into such a person, and yet I had believed it of Nik without mesmerization even being involved.

"It's a relief to know that not all the missing children were murdered," Costas said. "But someone's going to need to visit the foresters to explain the current situation. From what you've described, I'm guessing there's still some quiet trade going on between the foresters and the town, so they need to know the entire town is about to disappear."

"They're what?" Isolde asked blankly.

The forester eyes were all firmly fixed on Costas, showing varying levels of shock.

"Actually, about that," Amara said slowly. "Perhaps it isn't necessary after all..." Her eyes were on Isolde's face as she spoke. "This discovery changes the situation significantly."

CHAPTER

# EIGHT

"What is the situation, exactly?" Isolde asked.

In succinct words, Amara summarized Grey's return to his mother's home and the dramatic events that had unfolded as a result.

"Grey has returned to the mainland, which means we need to get back to Tartora as soon as possible," she concluded. "But we couldn't abandon the population without any healers—especially not when they are now leaderless and ill equipped to take command themselves. So we thought we would need to take everyone back to Tartora with us. But now it turns out their forest is full of young, powerful healers—ones led by a strong, experienced healer. So tell me, Lady Isolde—are you willing to leave the forest and take your rightful place in the manor house again?"

Isolde's face slowly paled as she stared at Amara. "You want me to lead the entire island?"

"Why not?" Amara's level tone issued a clear challenge. "I can't think of anyone with a greater right. You might not have been born a Constantine, but you bear their name which will help the islanders to accept you. You have the power and experience, and you've amply demonstrated the necessary compassion. If you lead the way, will the other foresters follow?"

Isolde looked down into her lap, staring at her tightly clasped hands as she considered Amara's challenge. When she looked back up, her eyes went to Costas.

"The manor isn't empty," she said quietly. "One of the true Constantines remains. Whatever my reasons for doing so, I abandoned my young son, and I will not take his home or position unless he willingly opens the doors for me."

Costas gazed back at her, and I couldn't read his face. I held my breath until he spoke.

"I don't know if our relationship can be healed or not. I think only time will tell that. But I won't disadvantage the whole island for the sake of my pain. I'm not ready to lead on my own, and I can't keep the people safe without healers. I was planning to leave the manor as soon as the seas clear, so I can't bar its door now. If you will come, I will support your efforts to protect and lead the town as well as I'm able."

Tears welled in Isolde's eyes. "Thank you," she whispered. "You turned out far better than I could have hoped."

Costas's cheeks flushed despite his earlier words about their relationship.

Whatever hurt our parents inflicted on us, part of us still yearned for their approval. An image of my own father appeared in my mind. Would he be proud of the person I was becoming? For the first time since discovering his betrayal, I wanted to find out.

Amara gave a satisfied smile, but almost immediately, her brow creased again.

"That takes care of the longer-term future of the islanders, and I thank you for lifting the responsibility from our shoulders. However, we are still in the middle of an immediate crisis."

Isolde leaned forward. "The new illness? It's hit the town?"

"Unfortunately, yes," I said, still feeling guilty. "And it had spread through the entire town before we discovered it."

"The entire town?" she whispered, and from the horror on her face it was clear she knew what that meant. "What are you doing here, then, Delphine? They must have need of us..." She leaped to her feet, only to sway at the sudden movement.

"My apprentice is here under my orders," Amara said sternly. "And she's here for the same reason you need to be—healers have limits, and you'll help no one by pushing yourself past exhaustion."

Isolde collapsed back into the chair, reluctantly nodding her head.

"The town has not been abandoned," Amara continued. "Thankfully I was accompanied by three powerful healers who have already completed an initial triage and are working among the populace as we speak. Our role is to discover the source of the infection, and I believe we have done so."

Her eyes slipped momentarily sideways to rest on Nina.

The girl's mother pulled her closer, looking worried. "Are you suggesting my daughter infected the entire island? She's never even been into the town!"

"No, but she has bathed regularly in the stream," Amara said gently. "You may not be aware that this stream merges further down with the river that runs past the town and which is used by the townsfolk as their main source of water."

"They've been drinking downriver of this stream?" As a healer, Isolde didn't need any further explanations to be horrified.

"The people in the town have no idea anyone is living in the forest," Costas said. "It won't have occurred to them that someone might be contaminating the water upstream."

"And we didn't realize the stream ran past the town," the matriarch murmured. "We never thought we were doing any harm…"

"When I get back to that dolt," Isolde hissed through her teeth, her expression furious.

"Who do you mean?" Amara asked, instantly alert.

Isolde relaxed. "Oh, he didn't mean any harm." She sighed. "The most recent addition to the forester population is a young couple. They both have strong elements seeds, and the husband kept going on about how much easier it would be to source water for their crops if there was a closer stream. A few weeks ago, he decided to divert a small portion of the river. Between the two of them, they had the strength to do it, and he was convinced there was no harm done."

"And this is why elements mages are taught to be so careful about interfering." Amara gave her own sigh. "And this is why all three affinities are so important. Elements mages won't think of this sort of consequence unless they have healers to remind them."

"Is that where the stream came from?" the patriarch exclaimed. "We were pleased to discover it, but we couldn't imagine where it had sprung from."

"I'm amazed only Nina is sick," Isolde said. "Are you sure none of the rest of you have any symptoms?"

The rest of the family hurried to assure her of their health, but I agreed with Isolde. It was strange.

"I think you should all come back to the town with us," I said. "That way Master Hayes can examine you. He has far more experience and training than I do."

To my surprise, Isolde readily agreed. "I would like to meet this master for myself. While I was born with a powerful seed, the training I received was limited. I couldn't compare with a Tartoran master mage."

"How soon can you be ready to make the journey to the manor?" Amara asked, gazing around the table.

Several murmured conversations broke out, and it was soon decided that everyone would leave for the manor in an hour, with the exception of the childless couple. They would stay to prepare the house for a period of inoccupancy before taking Isolde's carefully written out directions and setting out to contact the other forester families.

"No one will force them to move into town," Costas said, "but they should at least come to see the situation for themselves. And if any of them are activated healers, we could really use the help right now. Naturally they won't want to leave their families behind unprotected in the case of a reinfection, so they are all welcome at the manor."

After that, the conversation gave way to a flurry of activity and movement as everyone prepared for departure. Nik took one look at the chaos and suggested we wait in the garden. We didn't have the chance for private conversation, though, since Amara and Ida accompanied us.

"Are we really free to go back to Tartora without taking the whole island with us?" I asked once the four of us were alone. It seemed too good to be true.

"I won't be entirely easy until I've seen how Isolde and Costas manage," Amara said. "But I feel optimistic. This really is excellent news for both the epidemic and the island as a whole."

"Of course we can't leave until the epidemic is over," I said. "But does this mean we don't have to wait the entire winter? We won't need a ship large enough for the entire population anymore."

Amara shook her head. "I wish we could go back earlier. I feel uneasy about what might be happening in Tartora in our absence. But I don't think it's possible. We don't need to take a lot of people now, but we've also lost Costas. I don't think we would have made it here without his assistance, and that was after encountering a single storm. One elements mage isn't enough to make that journey in winter—especially not when I'm unfamiliar with the route. It's just too far."

I slumped, disappointed. But I couldn't remain downcast for long. My situation had improved beyond all expectation. I was no longer separated from my master. I was able to hand over responsibility for management of the epidemic to more experienced healers. And now we had even found extra healers to assist. There was no reason for me to get discouraged about being temporarily stuck on the island. Tartora might not have experience with Grey, but they had warning and a whole host of powerful mages. It was foolish to think they were in desperate need of me, or even Amara. They would survive one winter without us, and we would clearly be busy enough here, even with Isolde and her healers.

It took more than an hour for everyone to be ready in the end, and I was more than eager to get moving again by then. I knew my impatience wasn't achieving anything—after completing a major healing on Nina during my rest day, Amara wouldn't let me anywhere near the town until the next morning—but I couldn't help my desire for action of some kind. Even if I couldn't help, I wanted to know what was happening with the epidemic.

Ida had departed ahead of the rest of us, heading for the town instead of the manor, so it wasn't a surprise when we arrived at the manor's door only steps ahead of Hayes.

"Ida told me," he said immediately. "You've found more healers?"

The combination of exhaustion and hope in his eyes made my heart sink.

"Deaths?" I asked, and he quickly shook his head.

"None since our arrival, but I'll be honest, we're hanging on by a thread."

I looked to Amara. "Couldn't I—?"

She shook her head, only to hesitate and glance at Hayes. "What do you think?" she asked him, inclining her head toward me. "I had intended to send her to you this afternoon, but we encountered a gravely ill child, and Delphine healed her completely."

I bit my lip. Now that the family was joining us at the manor, I was second-guessing that decision. I could have just done enough to keep her out of danger.

Hayes held out a hand, his eyes assessing me as I laid my wrist over his fingers. I felt his power press into me, skimming through me with a light touch before withdrawing again.

"Considering the circumstances, I think you could allow her to spend a few hours in town, at least," he said. "Luna will be here shortly because I've insisted she come back for food and some sleep. Delphine can take her place, just for a while."

"You haven't been eating or drinking in the town?" Amara clarified, and when he shook his head, she looked relieved. "That was wise."

We stepped inside the manor as Amara completed proper introductions between Hayes and Isolde.

"I understand you're to take charge of the island," he said. "I can explain what we've done so far, and you can—"

"No, no," she said rapidly. "I may have strength, but I lack your training and experience. Please continue managing the epidemic—I'll be watching closely and learning as much as I can."

He inclined his body in a slight bow, accepting the authority she was handing him.

"You should feel free to test me," she added. "That way you'll know how to put me to best use. And all my students as well, once they start arriving."

"You need to rest before being put to use," I said in my best impression of Hayes's own healer tone.

Hayes threw me a surprised look, and I smiled. "Said in my official capacity as her healer. She collapsed from a combination of shock and exhaustion not long ago and is only upright and functioning now because of my efforts.”

Isolde made a rueful face, not trying to deny it.

I glanced around, noting that the others had moved away to discuss accommodation with the manor's servants. I stepped a little closer to Hayes, lowering my voice anyway.

“You must be tired, but do you think you could examine the adults we brought out of the forest with us?”

Hayes frowned. “Do they have the illness too? None of them look severely ill, and if they're still in the early stages, I'm afraid they'll have to—”

“Actually, it's their apparent health that's confusing me.” I glanced at Isolde who nodded encouragingly. We had spoken about it during the walk to the manor, and she had been as confused as me. “The girl's condition was advanced—she must have been one of the first cases—and yet none of the others are sick. There's another couple who didn't come with us, so that's five adults total. I know that those who are more vulnerable usually succumb to the exposure first, but from what we've seen in the town, at least two or three of the others should be showing some symptoms by now.”

Hayes looked at the older couple who were standing nearby talking with Amara. “They have weaker healing abilities, don't they? Is it possible they healed themselves while the symptoms were still very minor?”

Isolde twisted her mouth to one side as she considered the possibility. “If it was so easily done by someone of their strength, one third of the town would be well right now. Is that the case? Do you have no healer patients?”

Hayes shook his head. “Unfortunately, we have many.”

“According to their account, they haven't had to heal themselves of anything lately,” I said. “So you can see why I'm confused. They both let me check them during the walk, but I can't see anything amiss. Even so, I was hoping you would check for yourself.”

Hayes nodded slowly. “It can't do any harm. If they're not sick, it won't cost me much in the way of energy.”

He strode toward the elderly couple, with Isolde and me following close behind. As he examined the woman in silence, a crease appeared between his eyes. When the expression slowly changed to one of surprise, I couldn't resist holding out a hand to the woman with a questioning look.

When she nodded permission, I made contact as well, sending my power to combine with Hayes's as I had so often done before. His power was in her abdomen, examining each of her organs, although they appeared healthy to my power.

I closed my eyes, concentrating harder. It was true her insides were healthy, but still—there was something there.

My eyes sprang open, and I stared at Hayes in shock.

"Is that...?"

He opened his eyes slowly, his expression thoughtful. "Yes, I believe it is."

"Am I sick?" the woman asked. "Can you heal me?"

"You're not sick," I said. "But also, you are. Sort of."

"What?" She looked to Isolde, who shrugged, clearly just as confused.

"I never would have noticed it," I said to Hayes, once again impressed by his skill.

"That's because you didn't know to look. It isn't something our power picks up instinctively like a wound or damaged organ. But I've seen it once before with a different illness."

"What is it?" Isolde asked.

"The disease is there inside her," I said. "It's just not making her sick."

"We call it being a carrier," Hayes said. "Some diseases are more prone to the issue than others. I hadn't even considered it for this epidemic, given how many in town are sick, so it's a good thing you discovered it early. If we heal only the sick and leave the carriers, then we'll just see constant reinfections. We'll need to heal everyone—symptomatic or not—before this will be over."

"There can't be many carriers in town, though," I said. "Almost everyone is sick."

"Hmmm...And you're saying five adults in this one family are all carriers?" Hayes let the woman go and stared at the far wall while he thought. "Is it something special about them, then? Something passed on by blood?"

"They're not all related, though," I said. "There were three married couples."

Hayes ran a hand along his jaw. "I'll have to examine the others to be sure they're carriers too, but if they are, then it must be environmental. Something they've consumed or been exposed to has protected them from symptoms."

"If we could find out what it is..." I said excitedly.

He nodded. "If it was something that could be replicated, it might be a big help in getting this epidemic under control. We'll still want to eradicate the disease from the population completely, but it would be helpful to be able to do it more slowly, without worrying about more and more people reaching a dangerous level of illness."

"I suppose you'd be looking for something Nina wasn't exposed to," the matriarch said consideringly. "I'll have a think and talk to my family and daughter-in-law. Between us, we should be able to come up with a list of possibilities."

"Thank you," Hayes said.

"I can lead the investigation," Nik said suddenly from behind me. "There's a good chance it's something they ate, so it makes sense to have a plants mage in charge. I'll probably need assistance from a healer at some point, though."

"I'll manage assigning you one," Amara said. "Costas and I are about to head out to cleanse the river, but once that's finished, my ability won't be of use to anyone, so I can take on a management role. You'll be the one making the overall decisions, of course, Hayes, but with the shortage of healers, you won't have the energy for purely administrative matters."

"Thank you, Amara," he said, with a speaking look.

She smiled back, a note of tenderness in her eyes that made me look rapidly between them.

"I know you healers well enough to know you'll need someone to remind you about taking regular rests," she said. "I'll oversee that and make sure no one is working themselves dangerously hard—and while you're each having a turn resting your ability, you can help out with searching the forest."

"We're very fortunate your boat turned up when it did," Isolde said. "The island would have been in trouble without you."

"We're not out of trouble yet," Hayes said grimly. "But I'm starting to think we have a chance."

CHAPTER

# NINE

The following days passed in a blur, day and night blending together as I slept when instructed and woke when told. Every waking moment was full of healing as I trailed either Hayes or Clay, learning how to better heal this particular strain and then immediately implementing everything I learned.

Two full weeks had passed before I once again had the chance to stand on the back porch of the manor and admire the dawn light over the mountain. And, just like the last time, Ida's voice calling my name interrupted me. I waited, letting her come to me as I enjoyed a final moment of peace.

As soon as she appeared, she handed me a piece of paper, and I scanned it quickly before giving another sigh. The list was still so long.

"I'll leave immediately," I told her, but she stopped me with a hand on my arm, her face concerned.

"Have you eaten?" she asked. "We don't want a repeat of last week."

I flushed at the reminder. The first few days had been chaotic as we scrambled to first identify and then harvest and distribute the plant which had protected Nina's family—the one she had hated and refused to eat. When I had collapsed halfway through my rounds, everyone had panicked, thinking I had driven myself past my limits. Most people had been relieved when they learned I had simply forgotten to eat for almost twenty-four hours—too caught up in my work to take the time for basic self-care. But Amara and Ida had both had stern words for me.

"I had a quick breakfast before I came outside," I assured Ida. "I'm not going to faint again."

She examined my face closely. "You're sure you're not pushing yourself too hard?"

I mustered a smile, wondering when I would be free of the bone-deep weariness that clung to me these days.

"I'm fine, I promise. I know we can't afford to have any of the healers out of action for multiple days. There are too few of us as it is."

Ida nodded fervently. "Thank goodness Master Hayes and Master Clay arrived when they did. As well as Isolde and her students. We wouldn't have made it this far without them."

I pondered her words as I hurried out of the mansion and into the town beyond. My resolution to stay and care for the people of the island seemed distant and foolish now. I could never have held back the current disaster on my own. As it was, we had passed the initial crisis but were still far from eradicating the disease completely, as evidenced by the list in my pocket of the next patients in line for healing.

"Delphine!" Hurrying footsteps from behind made me turn. When I caught sight of the man hurrying to catch up with me, I slowed to wait for him.

"What are you doing up?" I asked Costas. "Weren't you on night duty with Hayes?"

He shook his head. "Nik and I swapped, so he's just heading for bed, and I'll be accompanying you."

He spoke of the prince as casually as I did. Those of us residing at the manor had long since ceased to worry about formalities or honorifics. Island life was far from the realities of Tartoran position and rank, and all our efforts were focused on keeping the islanders alive and healthy.

"Sorry I didn't wait for you," I said. "I was already running late, and I thought Nik might be waiting in town already."

"No matter," Costas said with an easy smile. "Ida informed me you'd already left."

I was grateful he let the topic drop, making no comment about the awkwardness between Nik and me. The tension between us must have been obvious to everyone at the manor, but thankfully everyone was either too busy or too considerate to comment on it.

I cast a sideways glance at Costas, unable to put the matter out of my own head so easily. Why had he and Nik swapped shifts? Had it been Nik's request? Was he avoiding me again? I felt like I barely saw him these days, but my long hours in the town, paired with the never-ending exhaustion, provided an easy explanation for our lack of connection. I just wished I could believe that was all it was.

I couldn't stew on it for long, though. Once I arrived at the first house on my list, all my attention had to be on the patients inside. We had moved past the early days when we were pulling dangerously ill patients back from the brink of death. Those healings had required power and instinct, but not the finesse required for full eradication. Now that we were working on full healings, focused attention was needed.

At least I wasn't responsible for finding and healing the carriers. Those healings required even more skill and finesse, so I was happy to leave that work to the masters.

We progressed slowly, moving from house to house down our list. Costas charmed the inhabitants while I worked, too absorbed to be aware of my surroundings. Amara had decreed early on that we should work in pairs with a non-healer accompanying each healer. She said it was important that someone actually talked to the families while the healer was lost in their work, and after the first few visits, I appreciated her wisdom. Costas did all the explaining and socializing, and I was able to focus on the healing—something that became even more valuable as the session wore on, and I became more and more tired.

By mid-afternoon when I finally finished the final patient on the list, I was too weary to do more than muster a weak smile for the woman who had just been healed. She murmured a quiet thank you but wouldn't meet my eyes. I wasn't surprised at her manner—thanks to the mesmerizations, many in the town still viewed me with suspicion. Given my exhaustion, I was almost relieved, rising quickly to head back to the manor.

But when I looked around the house's spacious main room, there was no sign of Costas. The woman saw me peering around and muttered something about him leaving already.

He'd never left me alone mid-healing before, so I hurried from the house, concerned. Had something happened back at the manor?

I paused as soon as I got outside, looking up and down the street in case he had just stepped outside briefly for some fresh air. But the only person I saw was a boy skulking against the wall of the house with the sort of scowl some youths seemed to perpetually wear in those awkward years leading up to their activation and apprenticeship.

I turned in the direction of the manor and made it two strides before something solid hit the back of my head. Pain shot through me as I was flung forward. I hit the ground hard enough to rob me of breath, fresh pain spreading through my middle.

Rolling onto my side, I doubled over, wheezing as I tried to regain my breath. What had happened?

A shrill, chattering call made me look toward the sky. Before I could find Phoenix, however, I saw a solid wooden staff whipping toward my head.

Acting on instinct, I pushed my power through my body, letting it heal me without guidance as I rolled away from the descending weapon.

It never made contact. A hand appeared, catching the staff and ripping it from the grip of the youth. A second later a feathered arrow shot down from the sky, pulling up just before colliding with Nik and the boy.

Phoenix chattered again, somehow managing to sound approving this time as he swooped down to land on my stomach.

The boy fell back several steps before regaining his courage and standing his ground, rage twisting his face.

"You killed them!" he shouted, pointing at me. "Just admit it! It was you, wasn't it?"

I scrambled to my feet, sending Phoenix soaring skyward. A sick feeling rushed through me as I saw the look of naked fury on Nik's face as he advanced on the boy, his fist going white where he gripped the staff he had torn from the youth's hand.

"Wait, Nik!" I cried as he reached the boy, only to instantly regret my words.

I had reacted on instinct, the sight of him a reminder of that terrifying moment at the party, the one I couldn't shake from my mind. As always, the sudden memory had momentarily brought back the shock and fear I had felt then, but there had been no need for me to speak. Just as then, he wasn't going to attack indiscriminately.

Thankfully Nik didn't even seem to hear me. Reaching out with his free hand, he grabbed the boy's collar, lifting him slightly so that he was off balance. Throwing the staff down, he dragged the boy in my direction.

As Nik came, he turned his head and finally absorbed my reaction. The heightened color on his face immediately drained away, and I wished I could take back every moment of my reaction rather than see his anger replaced with pain.

Why did I keep hurting Nik? It was my own fault that I still saw echoes of that awful moment at the party when I saw him bending over Augustine's body. I now knew he had been checking Augustine for signs of life—something he had rushed to do without even dropping his sword—and I should have known it then, too. No wonder Nik was avoiding me when I kept letting my terrible mistake stand between us.

Recovering himself in an instant and hiding his emotion, Nik's face returned to a stony expression as he dragged the boy the rest of the way to face me.

"Look her in the face." He gave the boy a slight shake. "This is the woman who just healed your mother, and yet you struck her over the back of the head?"

"She claims she healed my mother," the boy said in a sullen voice. "But how do I know that's true? She's a murderer."

"Delphine is a healer," Nik said in an ice-cold tone. "She has never—and will never—murder someone. I was there. I saw it happen. Your precious Constantines turned on each other."

"You're lying!" the boy cried, his face twisting and showing a glimpse of something far more heartbreaking than his attack.

Beneath his aggression lay barely masked terror and confusion. It wasn't transient fear of Nik's larger frame and stronger muscles, but something far deeper. Already in the most confusing and tempestuous time of life, his emotions had been tangled further—first by the Constantines' mesmerizations and then by their abrupt and violent deaths.

All my anger disappeared, replaced with compassion and a bone-deep exhaustion. We could heal every person in the entire town and eliminate the epidemic, but how could they begin to heal from what the Constantines had done to them?

The boy exploded into sudden movement, trying to get to me, but Nik's grip only tightened further, holding him in place. He shouted further accusations, getting more and more worked up in the face of Nik's unyielding stance and blank face.

"You must know someone with a healing affinity," Nik said when the boy paused for breath.

The youth hesitated, giving Nik the space to keep talking.

"Of course you do. Have you asked them about this epidemic?"

The boy's eyes slid sideways, away from our faces, giving us our answer.

"Precisely," I said. "Believe me, we're not doing all this for fun. Any healer in this town, however weak, could tell you that the people who were sick have now been healed."

"Your own eyes could tell you that," Nik said with impatience. "And those same friends will be able to confirm I'm telling the truth about what happened to the Constantines. Shall we go find one right now?"

He took a step as if he meant to drag the boy off to find the closest person with a healing affinity.

The youth shivered, and for a moment I thought it was from fear or embarrassment. But when he shivered again, it racked his whole body in a way that made me hesitate.

"Wait," I said, putting a hand on Nik's arm. He stilled instantly. "Let me check something."

I put a hand to the boy's head, not even using my ability as I confirmed my sudden suspicion.

"He has a fever. No wonder he's acting so irrationally."

I sent my power into him, confirming that he had the illness, likely in the second week.

"How did you conceal this?" I muttered, mostly to myself. "Have you been hiding from the healers every time they came past?"

He shrank into himself at my words, looking guilty and scared.

"It's a good thing I discovered it now, or you could have ended up in a dangerous situation," I scolded him as I drove the illness out of his body. "Everyone who's ill needs to be monitored for disease progression—surely you know that by now."

As I healed him, my earlier discouragement and desperation rose up inside me. My power could easily drive the disease from his body, but what I really wanted was to drive out the lingering effect of the mesmerizations.

The Constantines might be gone, but the lingering echo of pain in my head told me people were still being hurt by them. How much longer did it have to go on? Would these people ever be free?

A protective instinct rose inside me, fueled by my anger. I stopped trying to hold it in, letting it fan into flame inside me as I did a final sweep of his body to check for any missed pockets of illness.

As my power tried to roll through him, something sprang up inside him, barring my way. A wordless exclamation fell from my lips as my power was abruptly expelled from his body.

I dropped back a step, as if I had been physically shoved, although the boy was still slumped limply in Nik's grip. Nik immediately let go of the youth, stepping to my side and examining my eyes.

"What's wrong?" he asked in a low voice. "What happened?"

"I...I'm not sure. I think...I think...Quick!" I shrieked as the boy attempted an escape. "Stop him."

Nik moved instantly, not losing any time to questions. He had the boy back in a firm grip before he'd made it more than half a dozen steps.

"Let me go!" the boy cried, some of the fire back in his voice.

"I'm sorry," I said breathlessly. "I just need to talk to you for a moment. I need to—" I held out my hand, hovering just over his skin. "May I?"

The boy opened his mouth, presumably to reject my request, only to pause, the words unspoken. A look of confusion came over his face, as if his own thoughts didn't make sense to him.

A heady, implausible possibility overtook me. Was it possible? Surely it couldn't be...

"Why did you attack me?" I asked, my tone coming out too eager. He gave me a wary look, and I tried to calm my manner. "What made you target me?" I asked.

Nik's hold loosened, but the boy didn't move, his earlier fury having completely disappeared. Reaching up, he scratched the back of his head.

"I'm not sure," he said at last. "Some people were saying you might have killed the Constantines yourself, and I was so..." He frowned as if the end of the sentence didn't even make sense to him.

"You were so angry?" I finished for him. "Because I might have killed them?"

"Yeah," he said weakly. "I suppose so."

"You were close to them, then?" I asked, ignoring the odd looks Nik was giving me.

"Well, not close to them exactly," the boy said hesitantly. "I didn't know them personally or anything."

"But you were enraged about their deaths because they were such good people," I suggested.

"Well." He rubbed the back of his head again. "I don't know about that. They did heal us, I guess."

"And now you're left without healers," I said.

He frowned, giving me a sideways look. "Not exactly. All of you people seem to be healers—aren't you?"

"We are!" I said with such excitement that he and Nik exchanged a confused look, united suddenly by bemusement over my odd behavior.

"But the important thing is that the Constantines were wonderful people and excellent leaders worthy of loyalty to the end," I said earnestly.

"I...suppose?" It was a question not a statement.

"Yes! Yes, yes yes!!" I jumped into the air, unable to contain my excitement.

My unexpected movement brought Phoenix winging back in my direction, one of his shiny eyes focused on me. I settled enough to allow him to land on my shoulder, stroking his soft feathers with one gentle finger.

"Thanks for warning me earlier, fine sir."

"Ah...Delphine?" Nik asked tentatively, placing a gentle hand on my arm. "Are you all right?"

"Absolutely wonderful!" I turned bright eyes on him. "We have to get back to the manor! No, wait! I have to check—"

Once again I held my hand out toward the boy, silently asking for permission to make contact. This time he willingly put his wrist into my fingers, although his expression was still bemused.

I cautiously pushed my power into him, but it encountered no barrier. I might have raised his wall, but it hadn't stayed in place once I lost contact with him. I activated it again, but this time when my power was shoved out of him, I maintained my contact with his wrist.

Trying a third time, I encountered a solid barrier, preventing my power from accessing him.

"Interesting!" I dropped his wrist and then repeated the entire experiment with the same results. "Very interesting!"

"What is interesting?" Nik asked, still in the same careful voice.

I burst into laughter. "Oh, Nik, you should see your face right now."

He smiled back, responding to my happiness, but looking adorably confused in the process. It felt good to laugh with him again, even if he didn't know the reason.

"Can I go now?" the youth asked, starting to edge away.

"Yes, yes, feel free." I wiped tears from my eyes as the boy took off at a run.

He didn't make it more than three steps, however, before he tripped over the discarded staff and went sprawling. Nik reached him in a single stride, reaching down to haul him back to his feet.

I stared at Nik, transfixed, as he thumped the boy's shoulder, shaking free some of the dust that clung to him. The boy had been flat on the ground, and for a moment Nik had been bent over him—the tableau a stark reminder of the memory that plagued me.

But this time when the emotions of that moment rushed back, they were overlaid with something different. This boy had attacked me, as the Constantines had done, and yet even so, Nik had helped him. When he reached down, it had been in the role of protector, and for the first time, I could feel that truth wound through my old memory. My mind had repeated the truth a hundred times, but now my emotions had finally caught up.

I remained in place, frozen, as the boy muttered something in an embarrassed undertone and rushed away. He disappeared into the house, closing the door firmly behind him.

I had no idea what emotions were showing on my face in the wake of my realization, but some of them must have been visible. When Nik turned to me, his brows drew down, his earlier look of confusion deepening.

"The boy must think all the healing has driven me over the edge," I said with a weak chuckle, worried it might be Nik who thought so, not the boy.

"It hasn't?" Nik asked, but his look of amused long-suffering told me he still had faith in me.

"Not in the least!" My earlier elation came rushing back as I remembered my discovery. "Did you hear that boy's responses?"

"He sounded about as confused as me." Nik gave a reluctant chuckle.

"Exactly! He didn't know what to think about the Constantines." I gripped both of Nik's arms and looked up into his face. "Do you know what that means?"

Slow understanding broke across Nik's face. "The mesmerizations broke?

650

How is that possible? Are they gradually fading away now that the ones who created them are dead? We haven't seen signs of that in anyone else who was under their thrall."

"No, we haven't, because mesmerizations will last forever without evidence to break them. Not having the Constantines around anymore actually made them harder to destroy since there was no way to show they weren't who they claimed to be."

"So what just happened, then?"

I ran back over the sequence of events in my mind. "I was just checking my healing when something changed inside him. I think…I think I somehow activated his wall, and when it pushed my power out of him, it pushed out the mesmerizations as well—just like my wall does for me."

"You made a wall in him?" Nik asked. "I thought you couldn't do that. Didn't you and Grey spend hours and hours trying?"

"Actually," I said, "I was never trying to activate someone else's wall for them. I was trying to teach them how to make their own. I don't think I've ever tried to do it for someone else before. It never occurred to me it was even possible."

"So what you're saying," Nik said slowly, finally realizing the full import of my discovery, "is that you can not only protect yourself from being mesmerized or attacked with healing power, you can also protect someone else?"

"As long as I have physical contact with them." A grin spread across my face. "And I can purge mesmerizations that already exist in others like I do in myself."

"Delphine," Nik whispered. "That changes everything."

CHAPTER

# TEN

I thought it might be hard to replicate, but to my joy it turned out to be much simpler than I expected. Like with my own wall, once I was familiar with the feeling, it was easy to reach for it again.

What wasn't so easy—what turned out, in fact, to be impossible—was teaching anyone else how to do it. I tried with Hayes, then Luna, then Clay, and even with Isolde. But just like with Grey and his followers, no one else could repeat my accomplishment.

When we finally gave up, the disappointment in the air was palpable. I knew Hayes and Clay, at least, were thinking about more than the islanders. My wall was useful against more than just mesmerizations since it could also protect against an attack from a healer. And calling up a wall for someone else was even more valuable than being able to create one for yourself, since it allowed those with other affinities to also be protected.

"I don't even understand how it's possible to do," I said to the other three healers in the wake of the failed lessons.

We were all gathered on the back porch, enjoying the mild weather as we worked. Even Ember had ventured out of my room for her sleep and was curled up at my feet, although Phoenix was nowhere in sight.

Due to our continued efforts to eradicate the epidemic, it was a rare event for all four of us to be together. But when my attempts to teach them individually had failed, Hayes had insisted on one final session all together, just in case that somehow brought a breakthrough.

"I always thought my wall was made from my healing power," I said. "How could someone from a different affinity create one?"

"We must have been wrong about its source," Clay said thoughtfully. "It must come from the body itself—it's just your power that controls bringing it up and down."

"If you think about it, it does make some sense." Hayes sounded fascinated despite our failure. "We know the body develops a resistance to healing power over time—both due to age and due to excessive healing. So we know everyone has the innate ability to resist our power. This must just be another aspect of that natural ability."

"Do you think non-healers could learn to activate their own wall?" Luna asked.

Hayes narrowed his eyes. "That's less clear. My instinct is no. Non-healers can't control their resistance to healing, unfortunately, so I don't see why they would be able to control this. Delphine uses her power to raise and lower the wall, but a non-healer can't connect with their body that way."

"Except a healer can't control their own natural resistance either, can they?" I asked.

Hayes and Clay exchanged a look, making my stomach sink, although I couldn't explain why.

"It's a bit more complicated than that," Hayes said. "Healers can't prevent the natural resistance of old age. If we could, we would never die except through the occasional accident. But when it comes to the resistance created by repeated healings, healers do have a heightened ability to push past it— particularly when healing themselves.

"That's good," I said, unsure why he and Clay looked so concerned.

"But there are still limits to that," Clay said gently.

I nodded. It made sense. No one had ever claimed healers were impervious to everything except old age.

"We're worried about you, Delphine," Hayes said when I clearly still wasn't getting it.

"Me?" I stared at him. "What do you mean?"

Hayes grimaced. "You've had an unusually dramatic apprenticeship."

"You certainly have!" Luna's expression caught up to the worry on the faces of the men. "I've nearly completed mine, and I've barely had to heal myself the whole time. I think at most I've intervened in the early stages of a few infections I picked up at the hospital. But you've had so many run-ins with Grey!" She shuddered.

"I'm particularly concerned about the attack from the Constantine son," Hayes said. "You did what you had to do to survive—and it was an ingenious solution, I must add—but it was far beyond a normal healing, even in the case of extreme injury. And it came after a number of other significant healings..."

"Have you noticed any difference since?" Clay asked. "Do you need more power when you heal yourself from small things?"

My hand moved of its own accord to rub at the back of my head where the youth from town had struck me.

"I don't think so?" I said hesitantly. "Not that I've noticed—although I haven't been paying attention."

"That's good." Clay sounded pleased. "Your natural strength should give you a high ability to push past the resistance. But you can't get complacent. You're young—very young—and you still have your whole life ahead of you. If things continue as they have been, you could soon find that even your strength isn't enough."

I gulped. "You mean it might get to the point where I can't even heal myself?"

"It's possible," Hayes said before rushing to add, "We don't mean to alarm you! But you need to be warned. I've already spoken to Amara about the matter, and she agreed that it made sense for us to talk to you about the issue."

"Oh." I swallowed. "Thank you for warning me. I'll try to be more careful."

I looked up, and my eyes caught on Nik, frozen in the doorway. From the horrified look on his face, he'd caught the latter part of our conversation.

I looked back at the others. "We're going to go back to the mainland and deal with Grey once and for all." I was speaking more for Nik's benefit than theirs. "And that will be an end to all the violence."

Luna agreed enthusiastically, but I wasn't sure if that was because she'd also seen Nik hovering in the doorway.

He cleared his throat, his expression closing off. "Amara asked me to fetch you all for the meal. She wants to take the chance to eat together to discuss where we're up to with the epidemic and the next steps for management."

Hayes nodded. "That's a good idea. We've come a long way, but we haven't reached the end of the business yet. And now that Delphine has discovered she can purge others, we'll need to make a plan for that as well."

"A plan?" I asked, still a little dazed from the unexpected turn of the conversation.

Clay nodded enthusiastically. "We'd hoped to be able to help with the task, but I'm afraid you'll have to do it on your own."

"I'm going to need to purge everyone before we leave," I said slowly, the answer obvious. If I had the ability to free people's minds, I couldn't walk away and leave anyone still trapped by lies.

"It will help that we've just surveyed everyone in the town," Hayes said. "It just means we'll have to start again and cover every single person all over again."

"And you'll be doing it alone." Luna linked her arm with mine, giving it a sympathetic squeeze.

"It's a good thing we have all winter," I said, trying to speak with a cheerful note.

It was an overwhelming task, but only days ago it was something we thought impossible. Despite the disappointment of my failed training attempts, it was still good news overall.

Luna glanced at Nik who hadn't made any move to return inside. Slipping her arm out of mine, she took hold of both Hayes and Clay's elbows and propelled them into the house with her.

"Come on!" she said cheerfully. "We can't keep Amara waiting."

Hayes had time to throw a single raised eyebrow in my direction, making me flush, before the three of them had disappeared into the manor.

Nik still stood motionless, his eyes on me.

"Every healing you have to do is putting you at greater long-term risk. And I let that youth hit you." I knew his anger and recrimination was directed inward, but it hurt me just the same.

"That wasn't your fault!" I said heatedly. "You weren't even supposed to be there at all."

It turned out the boy had planned the attack, getting one of his friends to lure Costas away at the crucial moment. I should have been totally alone, and yet Nik had been there to protect me as usual.

What I didn't know was why he'd been there. And why had he swapped shifts if he was worried enough about me to come into town to check on me during his rest time?

"No," Nik said softly. "I was supposed to be there. I should have been there from the beginning. And if I had been, that boy would never have touched you."

"You've been avoiding me." It wasn't a question, and he didn't deny it. "You're still affected by what happened...that day."

He swallowed visibly but didn't speak.

"Are you angry with me?" I asked hesitantly. "For creating the problem in the first place and then blaming you before I even gave you a chance to explain? I know it was terrible of me to assume the worst like that, and I don't expect you to just forgive me. I've been trying to give you space, but I've been sorry every day since."

"What?" He strode over and took my hands, moving as if he couldn't hold himself back. "Of course I'm not angry with you! How could you think I would blame you for that? You didn't ask to be attacked, and you must have been in a state of shock afterward. I know what that scene must have looked like."

A spark zipped through me from the place our skin touched, but I couldn't quite meet his eyes. "Then why? Why have you been avoiding me?"

He swallowed, letting my hands drop. But he didn't step away.

"I'd seen you injured before, but not like that." He looked away, the muscle in the side of his jaw jumping. "You can't imagine..." He shuddered, his voice dropping low. "I can't look at you without seeing you lying there, covered in blood. So still. Too still. Even now I can taste the panic and rage and fear of that moment."

"I'm sorry," I whispered, although the words were inadequate for the moment. I knew just what he meant because I had also struggled to escape the traumatic images of that night. A silent tear slipped down my cheek.

He reached up and brushed it away with his thumb, his hand cupping my face.

"But that wouldn't be enough to keep me away from you," he whispered in a rough voice. "Not on its own. If it was just that..."

"Then what?" I asked, my words hardly more than a breath. "What else have I done?"

"Nothing!" His response came quickly. "You've done nothing. It's what I've done."

He fell silent, and I knew we were both seeing the scene from that night.

"You didn't do that," I said in a stronger voice. "Ignatius and his guards did that. All you ever did was defend yourself and try to defend others. It isn't your fault you didn't succeed in saving them. It was over for the Constantines before you even arrived in the room."

"But it could have been me," he said in a low voice. "I walked into a scene of chaos and violence and reacted as anyone would. But what if I'd walked into something else? What if I'd walked into that room and everyone was talking and eating and laughing? I keep reliving that night and remembering the rage I felt as I walked across the garden. You were dead—lost forever, I thought—and I was pursuing Ignatius. I can't deny that."

"That doesn't mean you would have murdered him in cold blood!" I exclaimed. "Let alone murdered his entire family!"

"But how can I be sure of that?" he asked in a tortured voice. "I may not have murdered anyone that night, but that doesn't mean I'm not capable of doing it. The most powerful mages in Tartora are convinced I'm a terrible person. What if they're right?"

"Stop!" I took his face between both my hands, forcing him to look me in the eyes. "The Triumvirate didn't think you were suited for the throne— that's hardly the same as being a mass murderer. Do any of us truly know the depths of what's in our hearts? We can't judge ourselves by what we might have done if circumstances were different. We have to look at what we did do."

I tried to think how to make him understand and stop blaming himself. "Would you give yourself credit for something good you might have done if only you were in a different situation?" I asked. "If not, then you equally can't judge yourself for something bad you might have done if the surrounding circumstances were changed. It's our actions that matter. I've had plenty of time to think about it since then, and I trust you, Nik. No matter how angry you were, I don't believe you would have started killing people indiscriminately. And the very fact you feel this guilt now—despite doing nothing except defend yourself—proves you're not going to do it in the future. It was wrong of me to make such a terrible assumption, even for a moment."

He was shaking beneath my hands, but gradually the shivers ceased, his body going still.

"Do you really believe in me so much?" he whispered.

I held his gaze steady. "I do. I love you, Nikolas of Tartora. It doesn't matter what the Triumvirate think. You are a good man."

He gave a reluctant laugh. "They might be surprised to hear you say that."

"That's their loss, then. You may not be suited to be king, but you could be an excellent prince, if they'd let you."

His arms wound around my waist, pulling me close. "If that's true, it's because of you, Delphine. You showed me a different way to think about myself."

My hands slid up to his neck, my fingers curling in the hair at the back of his head. He closed his eyes and sighed with contentment.

"I wish we could always be like this," he murmured against my hair. "Just you and me alone here."

I pulled back slightly so I could see his face. "On this island? Do you like it so much here?"

His face clouded. "It's not the island specifically. I just like being away from everything—with you."

I bit my lip. "Don't you want to go home?" I hesitated. "You know we have to, right? We have to go and find out what's happened with Grey. I can block his mesmerizations, and even purge them, and for now I'm the only one who can do it. We can't just abandon Tartora."

He sighed again, but this time it sounded heavy and sad. "I know. And I would never seriously suggest we stay. I want this moment to last forever, but I know it can't."

He pulled further away from me, and the movement hurt with a pain that was in my heart, not my body. I could sense the movement was symbolic.

Despite clearing the air between us, despite reaffirming our feelings, Nik was still pulling away from me.

"Sorry," Luna said ruefully from the doorway, making us spring the rest of the way apart. "I gave you as long as I could, but Amara really does want everyone there for this meeting."

"No, no. Of course!" I flushed, hurrying forward to join her while carefully not looking at Nik.

He seemed less flustered, giving a low chuckle as I rushed past him. But he refrained from saying anything, picking up Ember for me and falling into place behind Luna and me as we hurried for the dining hall.

I thought I'd have to endure three more sets of knowing eyes when I reached the table, but Hayes, Clay, and Amara barely looked our way. They had fallen silent at our approach, but there was no denying the charged atmosphere in the room. I just couldn't tell if the tension lay between the three of them or was due to the interruption.

I faltered as I slid into my chair, glancing questioningly at Luna. She was looking between the three of them, an interested gleam in her eyes. I could almost see her leaping to her own conclusions.

I looked at the older three again, trying to see them from Luna's perspective. Amara did look less calm than usual—possibly even flushed—and Clay was determinedly looking out a nearby window. Only Hayes remained calm, although his gaze kept going to Amara's face, as if drawn there irresistibly.

"Do you think people can change?" Luna chirped into the awkward silence around the table.

Nik started noticeably, but Luna was too absorbed in the situation with the others to even look his way. Apparently, she wasn't talking about us or our conversation.

"That's a broad question." Amara took a bite of her meal, speaking with her usual calm, although I knew her well enough to recognize an underlying agitation.

"I guess I don't mean the people themselves," Luna clarified. "Do you think people can change what they want out of life?"

"That's a question I'd dearly love to know the answer to." Hayes was still looking at Amara, but she was staring fixedly into her plate.

"Why do you ask?" Clay raised an eyebrow. "Are you thinking of abandoning your plan to return to Calista once you graduate, Luna?" He seemed aware—and mildly disapproving—of whatever she truly meant, although I had no idea what it could be.

"No, of course not! I could never do that." She hesitated, as if realizing what she'd just said. "But that's not to say I might not change my mind one day—in the distant future, I mean. Maybe one day I'll return to Tartora. Life moves through seasons, however long or short they may be."

When no one immediately answered, Hayes gave her a repressive look. "I think that's enough life wisdom for a midday meal. I believe we need to make some plans for how we're going to get through every person on the island—twice—before the end of winter."

Luna subsided at the mild reprimand, but I could see from the twinkle in her eyes that she wasn't truly put off. Whatever was lurking in her mind was still bubbling just as strongly as before.

When the day finally ended, we headed for bed at the same time for once. We had been sharing a room ever since the manor filled with returning foresters, but we were usually on different schedules.

"What was that about?" I asked as I slipped into bed, turning on my side to face her.

"Huh?" She finished brushing her hair and dove into her bed in her usual exuberant fashion.

"At lunch. All that talk of life seasons and people changing. You weren't listening in on Nik and my conversation, were you?"

She giggled. "If you try to tell me he's fallen out of love with you because his devotion was just a phase, I'm not going to believe you."

I flushed. "No, of course not. I just wondered...What were you talking about?"

"Amara and Hayes, of course!"

I pulled my pillow into a more comfortable position. "What do you think they were all talking about before we came in?"

She sighed dramatically. "I wish I knew!" She sat up abruptly. "Do you think Hayes told Clay to back off? I know Clay's interested in Amara, but Hayes isn't doing anything about it!" She groaned and flopped back onto her pillow.

"What do you think he should do about it?" I asked.

"Declare his passionate love, of course," she said promptly. I laughed and she gave me a hurt look. "Don't try to say he doesn't love her because I know he does."

"Oh, he confided in you, did he?" I asked still chuckling.

"He doesn't need to," she said airily. "I can see it."

"Do you really find it so thrilling?" I regarded her curiously from across the room. She seemed so invested in the romance story she'd crafted in her mind.

"Can you blame me? Hayes has stayed loyal to her through all these years, and now circumstances have brought them together again." Her excitement fell away as she added, "I just really want it to work out this time."

I examined her face with a bemused smile. "You sound like you're worried about him."

"I am!" She gave me an earnest look. "Master Hayes has been nothing but kind and considerate since the moment he activated me. And not just me. He literally saved my people. I couldn't tell you how many of my friends and family would be dead right now if it wasn't for him. And when we arrived at the Guild, everything was so new and overwhelming, but he helped me to adjust—and my family as well. He looked after all of us."

"I understand," I said softly. "Amara has been the same for me, even if my family isn't involved."

The start of Luna's apprenticeship had been even more dramatic than mine, but I felt the same gratitude toward my activator as she clearly did to hers. I had only adjusted to the dramatic changes in my life because of Amara's care and understanding.

"It sounds like Hayes is on his way to becoming the Master of Healing, though," I said. "Why would you be worried about him?"

She gave an exaggerated sigh. "My two year apprenticeship finishes this winter, so I'll be officially graduating as soon as we get back to the Guild. And then I'll be returning to Calista. I'm excited to go back to my homeland and join in rebuilding it, but I don't feel like I can leave with an easy heart."

I tried to hide a smile at my nineteen-year-old friend's world-weary air as she considered the burden of caring for her more powerful and more experienced activator.

"Was he having such a hard time before he took you on as his apprentice, then?" I asked.

"Before he activated me, he was Master Colton's second, and seconds don't take apprentices," she explained. "So he'd been alone for a long time."

"You don't think he'll take on another apprentice after you graduate? Maybe even more than one?"

She pursed her lips. "He probably will. Affinity heads are expected to have a whole group of apprentices since they're so strong themselves. But that doesn't mean they're close relationships—especially since it's their seconds who do the heavy lifting of training and corralling the students. Besides, Hayes doesn't need more people who regard him with grateful admiration. He needs an equal who loves him. Someone who can help him take on the difficult role of guiding an affinity and helping to run the kingdom."

"And you think Amara is the right one for that role?"

She nodded, looking somehow both sad and hopeful. "After he gave his heart to her, no other woman has been able to measure up. It has to be her."

"They've known each other for so long, though," I said softly. "If either of them wanted to change the decisions they made back then, they've had plenty of opportunity. Maybe the barriers between them really are too large to ever be overcome.”

“No!” Luna sat up straight. “I refuse to believe that! There’s always hope for a better future.”

I lay on my pillow, staring at the ceiling for a long time after we finished talking. Nik didn’t want to go back to normal life, and I should have realized why immediately. He was both a royal prince and a reneger, forcefully outcast from society. What was there for him to go back to?

But at the same time, it was also true that we couldn’t stay here. So where did that leave us?

With nothing but hope that our situation might change.

CHAPTER

# ELEVEN

The weeks passed all too quickly. Knowing an uncertain future loomed in front of us, I tried to spend as much time with Nik as I could, but several things stood in our way.

Completely healing everyone in the town, even the carriers, was a massive undertaking since it sometimes involved circling back to the same people two or even more times due to our rationed resources and the chance of reinfection.

Isolde had also asked for our help with an education program designed to prevent such a widespread calamity from happening again. The healers in the town might not have significant strength, but they could be trained to look for and recognize sources of contamination.

And, on top of all that, I was solely responsible for visiting every person in the town and purging them of the Constantines' mesmerizations. Nik insisted I couldn't be alone even for a moment. If he wasn't free to accompany me, then Costas, Amara, or Ida were always at my side. And his fears were far from groundless.

The boy who had attacked me in the street wasn't the only one who blamed me for what had happened, and while everyone had been willing to accept healing, no matter who brought it, they were less willing to accept a checkup from the person they suspected and resented. I had thought the job would become routine, and the physical effort of activating their walls certainly became so. But the social problem of my task only grew as more and more of the town were freed from their mesmerizations. Removing the lies left an increasing number of people unsettled and dissatisfied, and their change in attitude provoked those who were still enthralled.

"The problem," Amara said one evening, "is how young they were when the mesmerizations started." It was a rare occasion where we were all eating the evening meal together, and the conversation had turned to the islanders' state of mind. "The effect of such early tampering went further than the specific lies implanted in their minds and impacted their whole patterns of thinking. The problem is a complex one, and it will take a long time for them to relearn and retrain their minds."

She looked across the table at Isolde. "I'm sorry we're leaving you to deal with the ramifications. But we have to head home as soon as winter ends, and Delphine can't stop freeing people just to make your job easier."

"And I would never ask her to," she said forcefully.

"Given the perpetrators are already dead," Amara said, "we'll leave it to you to decide when and how much to tell the general populace about mesmerizations. I know you won't be able to hide the truth forever—there are too many foresters who already know what was happening for that—but it might be strategic to wait until everyone is freed before explaining every-thing. There's no telling how those who are still under the mesmerization effect might react to what they would see as lies."

Isolde sighed. "That is a question that has been weighing heavily on my mind. But I appreciate your forbearance. The issue will need to be handled delicately."

"The people may end up turning against everything related to the Constantines," Hayes warned.

Isolde nodded. "If that is the case, I'll accept it. I didn't take on leadership because I thought it would be easy. And if the people end up deciding they want someone else to lead them, I'll gladly step aside. I would prefer to be a straight healer than deal with administration anyway." She glanced sideways at Costas. "But whatever happens, I have hope the people will recognize that the two remaining Constantines were never part of the plot against them."

I guessed from her expression that her hope went beyond that. I suspected she would happily hand over leadership to her son the moment he was ready to accept it.

"I'm relieved to hear you say that," Amara said. "But I still feel sorry. If we weren't so concerned about the state of affairs in Tartora, then I'd offer for us to stay and back you up for longer."

"You've already done so much," Isolde said. "We couldn't ask more of you."

"I hope you'll still feel the same way when it comes to negotiating an alliance and trade treaty with Tartora," Hayes said with a twinkle in his eyes.

"Or, if you prefer, I suspect King Marius would be willing to accept you all as subjects of the Tartoran crown—with the benefits and responsibilities that conveys."

Isolde raised her eyebrows. "That is definitely not a decision I could make on my own."

"Nor am I delegated to make any official offers," Hayes said. "But consider it food for thought."

"I certainly will." She glanced again at Costas who looked thoughtful.

Clay cleared his throat, gaining everyone's attention. "Actually," he said, "while we're on the topic, I've been considering the matter of our departure, and I'm unconvinced we all need to return."

Amara's brows lowered. "You want to stay?"

"I think I should—if the islanders would like me to, that is. I'm satisfied the epidemic will be eradicated by the end of the season, but the island's healers are mostly young, and none of them have undergone proper training. Isolde has done the best she can for them, but even she did not receive proper training in her youth. While the islanders are not currently bound by Tartora's strict laws around apprenticeships, I believe an apprenticeship of sorts would be of value to the stronger healers."

"You'd stay for two whole years?" Isolde asked, sounding shocked. "That's a very generous offer, and we'd be delighted to have you, of course. And not just for your healing strength and skill. We would appreciate your input on our unique administration challenges."

"I'm not an expert administrator by any means," Clay said, "but I'd be happy to help in any way I can. I just can't feel right about abandoning you all with the current state of the island."

He looked over at Amara. "I can't help you with the sea journey back, and given my lack of success in learning from Delphine, I can't help with Grey either. For now, at least, I think the island is where I am most needed and wanted."

Something unspoken passed between them before she bowed her head in acknowledgment.

Clay smiled in response, his face lighting up with his usual good cheer. "I'm sure my junior partner in the clinic back home will be happy to be rid of me for a while longer. He's been ready to take a more senior role for some time now."

Both Isolde and Costas gained a new animation after that, although the rest of us were subdued in exchange. If Clay was willing to stay, he could be of great assistance to the islanders, but it felt wrong to leave him behind.

"Do you think Clay will be all right here for so long?" I asked Amara and

Hayes later that evening. "Should we be trying to convince him to come back with us?"

Hayes grinned at me. "Is Luna's condition catching? Don't tell me you think you need to start looking after master mages as well now?"

I flushed. "No, of course not. It's silly of me, I suppose. I just feel bad. I was the one who led us all here in the first place…"

"Don't worry." Amara gave me a sympathetic smile. "Clay is more than capable of looking after himself, and he can make a big difference here."

"Do you think the island will want to become part of Tartora?" I asked. "I suppose Clay's presence might help sway them toward us."

"I couldn't say." Amara glanced laughingly at Hayes. "But I can tell Hayes would rather they became part of Tartora than Calista."

"We have done a lot for them," Hayes protested. "So there's no harm in planting the seed."

"None at all," she said, still with a chuckle in her voice, but I could see a sliver of hurt in his eyes.

If Luna was right, this was the problem that had stood between them from the beginning. Hayes wasn't a naturally ambitious person, but he had chosen to invest in the politics of his Guild and kingdom. Whereas Amara had been so scarred by her mother's power-hungry nature that she'd rejected politics completely.

Amara and Hayes might love each other, but their lives were incompatible. The discomfort of that thought weighed on me. They weren't the only couple whose love didn't match the practicality of their futures.

After finally purging the last islander of mesmerization, I walked home to the manor in pouring rain. Ida was my companion for the day, and she had enough elements power to keep the rain off the two of us, but the atmosphere was unavoidably gloomy.

My mood lifted, however, when I spotted Amara and Ember waiting for us just inside the door. Even Phoenix had come inside, unimpressed with the unrelenting wet outside, and Ember happily trotted over to join us.

As I bent to pick up the fox, Amara spoke. "I've been monitoring the situation for weeks, and I'm confident this is the last storm of the season."

I blinked, trying to work out her point. I had been focused on the rain, the completion of my task, and the difficulties facing Isolde in the town, so it took me a moment to realize the significance of her words.

"You're leaving?" Ida asked, catching on more quickly than me.

Amara nodded. "I've already talked to Hayes and Nik, and we'll be sailing the day after tomorrow. That should give us enough time to pack and say our goodbyes."

"So soon." I didn't know what to feel.

At the beginning, the winter had stretched before us, impossibly long. But the magnitude of our task had easily eaten the weeks. Now I couldn't believe it was already time to go home.

After a moment my thoughts caught up with me. "Wait, Ida. You said *you're* leaving. Aren't you coming?"

She shook her head. "Isolde has offered me a place here, and I already told her I would stay. I came here because I wanted to live in safety and peace. The island didn't turn out to be the haven I expected, but I still think I have as much chance of finding that peace here as anywhere. Whatever their reasons, the islanders welcomed me with open arms, and now they could use my help in return."

I swallowed, sadness clogging my throat. I had become used to Ida's solid, dependable presence, but I should have foreseen this possibility. I would miss her, but I was glad for Costas and Isolde's sake. Ida had stepped up to help me from the beginning, even before the others sailed in, and she had become as much an expert on the island's administration as Costas himself.

"I hope you can build the life you want here." I wrapped her in a tight hug. "But if you can't, you'll always be welcome with us in Tartora."

Ida smiled. "And I won't forget what you've done for me. If you ever want to come back, I'll make sure there's a place for you."

I smiled a wobbly smile. Ida had broken most of her mesmerizations herself, but she had still been ridiculously grateful to me for purging her mind completely.

"I'll miss these two." Ida stooped to run a hand down Ember's back. "I'd try to lure them into staying except I know it would do no good."

My smile steadied as I squeezed Ember tight. "Don't worry. I'll take good care of them."

Ember pressed into me, as if she understood what I was saying, and Phoenix made a small chip note that made us all smile. He didn't usually like coming into the manor, but he liked the rain even less.

The following hours passed too quickly. A final walk through the town and a farewell dinner with Isolde, Costas, and Ida had to suffice for my good-byes, and the rest of the time was consumed by sorting and packing my various belongings. I had come with very little, but somehow I had acquired more things during my stay than I could account for. It took time to decide what to take back with me, but at least I wasn't alone in having this problem, since Luna was even worse. Between the two of us, we filled five large bags.

"You must be especially excited to get back," I told her as we lugged our bags to the manor entrance on the designated morning. "You'll finally be graduating and returning home."

She had refused to tell me which winter day had marked her two years as an apprentice, saying we would celebrate together at her official graduation in the capital. She wouldn't even accept my apologies for getting her caught up in the entire mess with Grey. If she'd been back home, she wouldn't have had to wait to graduate.

"I'm excited and sad at the same time," she told me. "I can't wait to see my parents and all the progress in Calinara. All last year they were writing to me about the restoration work in the city, and I want to see it for myself. But then I think about leaving you and Hayes…" She stopped abruptly, dropped all her bags, and flung her arms around my neck, sobbing into my shoulder.

I froze in place, unable to put down my bags due to her tight hold and equally unable to keep moving forward.

"I'll miss you too," I told her, "although we're not saying goodbye yet."

She pulled away, mopping at her eyes. "It feels like a goodbye, don't you think?"

"It is a goodbye," I agreed, starting forward again. "But not between us two. And even once you do graduate, we'll see each other again. If you don't come back to Tartora, I'll go find you in Calista. I'll be free to travel once I'm a graduate too."

"Will you really?" Luna brightened instantly. "I'll show you everything! Promise!"

We reached the front door to find the others already waiting for us. Amara and Hayes were both watching us with amusement, but Nik turned away as soon as he saw me look in his direction. He didn't turn fast enough to hide his expression, though. One among us had no positive feelings about what was waiting for him back on the mainland.

He said nothing, however, and we quickly moved through the town toward the harbor. I threw a final glance over my shoulder as we left the manor and its beautiful gardens behind. Would I ever be back to the island? If they allied with Tartora, it was possible, although I couldn't imagine what the isolated community might look like in the future.

The islanders had gifted us a boat in gratitude for our extended service, and Costas had given Amara detailed instructions on the route back to the crevasse. She had traveled the path once before, but Costas had led the way on that occasion.

There were only five of us going back since both the Tartoran guards had elected to stay with Clay. They claimed to be staying to guard him, as if he was an official Tartoran delegate to the island community, but in reality we all knew they had more personal reasons for their decision. They had been chosen in the first place because they didn't have families waiting for them at home, and both of them had become attached to forester girls during the winter months.

For a while everyone was busy in the bustle of loading onto the boat and setting sail. But as the island dwindled to nothing behind us, I sat beside Amara on the small deck.

"Can you really do this on your own?" I asked.

She laughed. "Don't you think it's a little late to be asking that question?"

I grinned. "I suppose it is." I turned my face into the ocean breeze. "It's hard to believe we're really going home."

"Don't worry," she said after several minutes of comfortable silence. "With the winter storms behind us, I won't have any trouble navigating a boat this size." She gave a rueful smile. "I just might be very, very tired by the time we arrive."

True to her word, Amara barely slept for days as she negotiated us through the tricky passage. By the time land finally came into sight again, I was immensely relieved. My master was strict on my not pushing myself near exhaustion, but she was apparently willing to take herself right up to the line.

I wasn't the only one glad to see land. We were all sick of the confined space, with the tiny cabin providing the only relief from the elements. Even Luna had run out of topics of conversation, and Nik had barely spoken five words in at least a day.

As soon as we were positioned in a straight line for shore, Amara turned to Nik and gave a weary smile. "I trust you can bring us the rest of the way in?"

He nodded. "You can leave her in my hands."

I knew he was talking about the boat, but Amara still shot me an amused look before lying down right where she was on the deck and going to sleep. Nik frowned down at her, and even though he didn't say anything, I could see the concern in his eyes. As much as he might have fought it at first, Amara had worked her way into his inner circle.

Phoenix launched himself from my shoulder and winged straight for the distant land. Ember immediately padded to the boat's prow and stood watching him go.

"Don't tell me you miss him!" I took my place at her side, grinning down at her. "Don't worry. I won't tell him."

I laughed to myself, too delighted at finally finishing the interminable journey to care who might be listening to my nonsense.

The remaining distance flew past, the land growing closer and closer. At first we had been too far out for me to identify the crevasse, but soon I could clearly see the thin line of green standing out from the surrounding desert.

And by the time Nik brought us gliding gracefully into the dock—using his power on the wood of the boat and the wood of the dock itself to achieve it—I could see all the details of the slim crevasse that pierced the desert cliff.

It felt like years since I had sailed away, and yet at the same time only days. Everything looked just the same, all the tents still in place although they were no longer inhabited. The tall walls of the crevasse must have protected them from the winter storms.

Ember was the first to alight, with me close behind her. I took up a position on the dock, receiving the stream of bags that Luna tossed in my direction. Hayes unloaded the rest of the luggage in a more dignified manner while Nik secured the boat to the dock with firm knots.

No one woke Amara, although I saw Hayes throwing her concerned looks. When we were finally ready to leave the boat behind, he scooped her into his arms and carried her off the deck, still sleeping peacefully.

Luna, her eyes enormous, tugged on my arm, inclining her head toward Hayes's retreating back with an excited look. I watched them go myself, wondering what, if anything, Hayes's action meant.

If Amara did decide to change her mind about Hayes, I would be happy for her. But what would it mean for the rest of my apprenticeship?

"Are you all right?" Nik calmly took the many bags from my hands, swinging them over his shoulders like they weighed nothing.

"I'm fine." I smiled up at him. "And I'm also capable of carrying bags."

He just gave me a slow smile, but it didn't quite reach his eyes or dispel the tension in his frame.

Hayes's shout of surprise made us all freeze for a second before launching into action. Racing toward him, my thoughts moved even faster than my legs. Was there someone in the crevasse? We should have considered the possibility that Grey might return to reclaim his old camp.

I had almost reached Grey's house when I saw the source of Hayes's shock. As I had feared, we weren't alone.

Two strangers were waiting for us.

CHAPTER

# TWELVE

"Nik!" A short young woman, all motion and energy, threw herself into Nik's arms.

The bags went tumbling down as his hands closed around her. I froze, staring at them both as I tried to work out what was happening.

Nik didn't seem impressed, however, despite enduring the embrace without complaint. And as soon as she lightened her tight hold, he gripped her by both arms and pushed her away from him.

"What are you doing here, Gia?" he asked. "And where have you been for the last year? I didn't find a trace of you in Tartora."

Gia? I stared even closer at the woman. This was Princess Morgiana, Nik's twin sister? She looked different from how I'd expected—shorter and less regal, perhaps. And despite Nik's gruff greeting, she practically sparkled. They were clearly nothing alike in temperament.

"I've been in the nomad lands," she replied, undaunted by his cold expression. "And then Calista. And then the nomad lands again." She threw a glance at a tall young man who was standing slightly back, watching her with amusement. "When did we get back, Renley?"

"Didn't you know about the troubles we've been having here?" Nik asked, cutting off any reply the other man might have made. "We could have done with your help, Gia. Don't you care about your own kingdom at all? Or have you forgotten your people now that you married a Calistan? The people no longer matter to you since you're not taking the throne?"

I expected her to stiffen and take offense at receiving a bevy of accusations instead of a proper greeting, but instead her eyes widened and a smile grew across her face.

"Who is she?" Gia shook free of his hold only so she could grab his arms in what looked like an iron grip. "Is she here?"

Nik's eyes flicked toward me for the briefest second, but Gia caught the involuntary gesture. Twisting around, she peered in our direction, but since I was standing next to Luna, her eyes flicked back and forth between us. She looked back at her twin, her smile growing even larger.

"But this is amazing! You have to introduce me to her immediately!"

"I don't know what you're talking about," Nik said stiffly, all his earlier antagonism completely forgotten.

Gia shook him lightly. "Don't try that on me. I know you too well. All this talk about caring about our people—even without the throne. And you really seem to mean it too! Plus, I heard you've been working with Master Amara and Master Hayes of all people. Actually *collaborating* instead of sulking around the kingdom on your own."

Nik cleared his throat. "I don't know why that makes you think—"

"Ha! Didn't you hear me say I know you too well? The only person you ever listened to even a little was me—and I'm well aware that wasn't because I have any great wisdom. You listened to me because, despite yourself, you couldn't help loving your own twin. That little bit of softness was the only way I ever got through to you. So if you've suddenly started *listening to other people* and *learning things*, then obviously you've found a love that's softened you much more than I ever did. Something has made you open yourself to new ideas, and I want to know who she is. Immediately!"

Nik sighed loudly, but a smile was creeping across his face. I stared at him, fascinated by this new insight. I had always known he had a twin, but she had been a distant concept. A crown princess who had abdicated her throne. The one Nik could never live up to. I had never imagined someone who treated Nik like this.

"Well it isn't me," Luna said with a wicked grin. "Hello, Renley," she greeted the man standing behind the twins.

He smiled and waved back. "I'm glad to see you back in one piece, Luna. You've been keeping Hayes in line, I hope."

"I think that might be someone else's job now." She gave a significant look toward the cabin where Hayes had disappeared, still carrying Amara. Presumably he was finding her a bed so she could continue her much-needed sleep. I just hoped she wouldn't be disturbed by all the commotion outside.

Renley's eyebrows went up slowly, and he threw a considering look at the cabin. I elbowed Luna, glaring at her. She might speculate to me, but it was much too early to be making comments to strangers.

But as they continued to chat, exchanging news, it became apparent they were far from strangers. Luna finally noticed me staring.

"Renley and I grew up together in the Calistan settlement," she explained. "It was a small enough place that everyone knew everyone, but our parents were particular friends."

She turned to Renley. "And this is the dearest of my new friends, Delphine."

I couldn't help smiling at the label, but the expression froze when Gia whipped around to face me. She had been wheedling Nik in a quiet voice while Renley and Luna spoke, but she had clearly been listening for the introduction.

"I'm Gia!" She held out her hand, beaming at me with her whole face. "It's lovely to meet you, Delphine."

I stepped forward to take her hand, relieved to see my arm wasn't shaking. But when I began to bow over it, she snatched it away horrified.

"No, no, no! You can't do that!"

"I'm sorry, Your Highness," I said, startled.

"Please don't do that either," she begged me earnestly. "It's just an honorary title these days, you know. I left court precisely because I couldn't stand all of that. Just call me Gia."

I shot a glance at Nik, who was watching me intensely, something on his face I couldn't read.

"Very well, if you insist," I said, pulling myself together. Gia was probably the most important person in the kingdoms to Nik, and I wanted to salvage as good an impression as was still possible. "I'm Delphine," I added unnecessarily. "Master Amara's apprentice."

"The hero of Eldrida! I've heard of you," she said, making both my hands fly up and wave in protest.

"No, no, those stories are all exaggerated! I didn't—" My words broke off as I caught the mischievous twinkle in her eye.

"Please forgive my mannerless twin," Nik said stiffly. "She's well aware of how public opinion can distort matters."

"Oh, Nik." Gia sighed. "I'm glad you care about people now, but couldn't you also try being a bit more fun?"

He glared at her, and I moved to his side, offering him my silent support. He smiled down at me, his expression softening, and Gia gave a happy sigh.

His face immediately closed off again, but the damage was already done.

"I knew it!" Gia said, her eyes shining. "Delphine, I really am *very* glad to meet you."

"I'm glad to meet you, too," I said, warming to the intense girl in spite of myself. It was hard to resist her irrepressibility or her obvious affection for her brother.

"So you're elements affinity?" she asked, giving her brother a quick sideways look.

"Actually I'm a healer," I said awkwardly.

"Ooh, cross-influenced! Yes, of course, I should have remembered that from the stories in Eldrida. Interesting." She gave her brother another look.

A wave of irritation swept over me. "You don't have to keep looking at him like that. He isn't obsessed with elements anymore."

Gia's eyebrows sprang up to her hairline, and I flushed as I realized what I'd just said. I glanced apologetically up at Nik, but he was looking down at me in amusement.

"Healers can be fierce when roused," he said with a grin.

Gia's eyes widened at his reaction. "I really, really like you, Delphine," she said with a beaming smile. "I can barely recognize my brother."

I frowned, looking at him again. "Really? Maybe it's just that everyone always underestimated him."

Both twins laughed at that, making me squirm.

"Don't worry." Gia winked at me. "I'm sure he'll never entirely lose that dark and brooding thing he has going on. He just can't help himself."

"Gia," Nik said in a warning tone, but Hayes emerged from the cabin at that moment, interrupting the twins' reunion.

"Oh good, you're all still here," he said. "Amara will need to sleep for a while, so we have time to talk. I don't suppose you've been here long enough to prepare any interesting food?" he asked Gia and Renley hopefully.

Renley chuckled. "That we can help you with. Sick of ship fare, are you?"

The two led the way into the main room of the cabin, and everyone was directed to find seats around the table. I sat, running my hand along the wood and remembering the last time I had been here. This was the location of my first mesmerization, although I hadn't known it at the time, and I had expected the presence of Grey to linger. But somehow, with the room crammed full of familiar bodies and bits of conversation floating back and forth, it was hard to picture him at all.

We were a chair short, and Gia looked at her brother.

"Delphine can sit on your lap, can't she?" she asked innocently.

"Gia," Renley said in warning tones, pulling his wife onto his lap instead. "Your poor brother will be wishing you back in the nomad lands soon."

Gia just laughed, putting an arm around his neck and placing a fleeting kiss on his lips. "He's had a lifetime of putting up with me, so he's used to it."

Nik did have a look of long suffering on his face, but I also noticed he was carefully avoiding looking in my direction. I was glad because I could feel the flush on my cheeks. Gia and Renley were so comfortable and natural with each other, and it made my heart ache. Would Nik and I ever get to that point? Our relationship had been all heat and intensity with little room for the sort of relaxed familiarity I saw between his sister and her husband.

"If you've just come from the nomad lands, how did you end up here?" Nik asked Gia.

"We spent a year in Calista and the nomad lands," she said, "first recruiting for Calista, and then doing some negotiation for Father. So we were gone longer than I expected."

"Father trusted you to do negotiations for Tartora?" Nik asked skeptically.

She threw him an impatient look. "You're the one who has issues with Father, Nik. He knows I still want the best for Tartora—I just don't want to be tied down. It's not like it was a major trade treaty. Some things are best handled outside of the official channels."

I raised my eyebrows, but she didn't explain further, and I wasn't going to ask. Nik didn't ask either, his brows contracting as he looked at the table. Beneath its surface, where no one could see, I slipped my hand into his. He glanced at me and smiled slightly. His sister might not know his thinking about his father had changed, but I did.

"Calista isn't the most recent place we've been, though," Renley interjected. "We heard there was trouble in Tartora and hurried back to Tarona. That's when we heard you'd been found—and then lost again."

Gia rolled her eyes, as if she thought it very irresponsible of everyone involved. I had to stifle a smile since she gave the impression of being someone who would lose anything that wasn't attached to her.

Hayes leaned forward. "Do they truly believe we're lost? Didn't they get the information we sent about Grey?"

"Maybe you'd better let me tell the story," Renley said to Gia before turning to Hayes. "The guards you sent arrived promptly in the capital, and King Marius knows where you've been all winter. That's why we've been here waiting for you since the moment the last storm passed."

Hayes sat back slightly, but he didn't look that relieved. "So you worked out we were stuck there for the winter. But does that mean the king also assumed Grey and all the Constantines were stuck with us?"

I drew in a breath as I realized Grey might have been free to infiltrate the court all this time with no one on the watch for him.

"No, thankfully not." Despite Renley's words, his face remained grave. "His ship foundered close to shore just past the southernmost point of the desert. Some herders saw it and helped the passengers and crew reach land. Most of them scattered immediately, but a couple were injured and ended up being taken to local healers. The name of their leader and their place of origin made it back to some law keepers who knew Anka had been searching for Grey last year."

"You've caught Grey, then?" I asked hopefully.

"No." Renley's response made everyone in the room tense up again.

"I can understand his initial escape if there were only a few herders on hand," Hayes said. "But it's been months since then. How could they not have found him?"

"Finding him would require looking," Gia said flatly.

Luna propped her chin on her hand. "Let me guess, they're all holed up in the capital, afraid to come out in case they run into Grey?"

I frowned as something occurred to me. "Were you officially sent to meet us? Are you even supposed to be here?"

Gia and Renley exchanged a look, Gia chuckling. "Busted! You're quick, Delphine. I can see why Nik likes you."

Nik's hand tightened around mine beneath the table while Hayes sighed, rubbing his brows with his fingers as if he was developing a headache. "So you heard where we were and decided to run off on your own. As if we didn't have enough to deal with already with Grey on the loose."

"It's true that Gia was eager to see Nik," Renley said gravely, meeting Hayes's gaze. "But that wasn't our main reason for coming to find you. I know Gia has earned herself a certain reputation for recklessness, but I'm equally concerned about the situation in Tarona. We wanted to talk to you first—to prepare you for the situation and hear your perspective."

"It's that bad?" Hayes stared at him, clearly appalled. "Don't tell me Grey has wormed his way into court!"

Everyone around the table exchanged panicked glances as we imagined Grey mesmerizing the royal family and Triumvirate.

"No, no, it's not that bad," Renley said quickly.

A relieved sigh rippled around the table, and his face tightened in response.

Hayes frowned at his reaction. "What is going on, then?"

"The king and Triumvirate are extremely concerned about the possibility of exactly what you were just picturing," he said.

"Paranoid, you mean." Gia scowled.

"It's a real danger," Renley said, and I could tell from his tone that they'd had this conversation many times. "They're right to take the possibility seriously."

"They're right to be cautious, yes," Gia said. "But there's a difference between that and living in fear. While they're busy protecting themselves, where is Grey? The danger will never end unless we find him."

"The idea of having someone playing with the thoughts in your head is terrifying," Luna said quietly. "Surely we can understand their fear. Are you really saying they've done nothing?"

Gia snorted. "No, they've recalled Anka from Caltor so that the one senior official in the kingdom who knows what Grey looks like is sheltering at the capital with them, keeping *them* safe."

"Anka's at the capital?" Amara asked from the doorway of one of the bedrooms.

Hayes stood up, offering her his seat. "You should still be resting," he murmured as he helped her sit down, but he didn't try to convince her to return to bed.

She accepted the offered seat, her pale face betraying her underlying exhaustion.

"Master Amara," Gia said politely. "I don't think you've met my husband, Renley, yet."

Amara smiled and inclined her head toward both of them. "It's a pleasure to meet you, Renley, and to see you again, Princess Morgiana. I'm sorry I missed your wedding. I was traveling through the eastern hill country at the time, and I didn't receive the general invitation issued to all masters until it was too late to travel back."

"I'm glad you didn't inconvenience yourself," Gia said with an easy smile. "If it had been up to me, I would have gotten rid of all those formalities. There was no reason for you to uproot your plans to attend the wedding of someone you barely know."

Amara's lips twitched, and I could see Gia had a similar effect on her as she did on me. It was hard not to smile around Nik's vibrant twin.

"That is gracious, Your Highness," she said, and Gia immediately shook her head.

"Gia. Please."

Amara shot a glance at Hayes, and he nodded slightly. She looked back at the princess.

"Very well, Gia. I want to be sure I understand the situation correctly. The king and Triumvirate are aware of the danger from Grey and have taken measures to protect themselves. In particular, they have brought in Anka who can ensure he doesn't sneak into court under a false pretense. Is that the sum of it? Are you telling me they've done nothing to actively find Grey?"

"Of course it's not that bad," Renley said quickly. "Anka is working from court to head a kingdom-wide search for him. But he must be lying low because we've had no word of his location. He's certainly not stirring up public trouble like he was before."

Amara's shoulders relaxed slightly. "Some of Anka's people from Caltor know what he looks like, so even if she's not free to travel, she'll have sent them out, I'm sure."

"That depends," Gia said. "Were they mages? The Triumvirate have all but shut down the Guild. They're afraid of what will happen if Grey manages to enthrall enough mages of strength, so the mages are confined to the Guild and palace grounds or the capital at most."

"So Anka is leading a search, but she isn't allowed to make use of mages?" Hayes asked, sounding half bemused and half annoyed. "That's like searching with one hand behind her back."

"Exactly. I see you grasp the problem." Gia sighed. "I love my parents dearly, but they were raised to protect the throne and Triumvirate first and foremost. It's not that they don't care about the people—they just think the kingdom will crumble if the systems of government break."

"They're not entirely wrong," Amara said with a sigh. "There are many things I don't like about how we manage mages and the distribution of power in this kingdom, but I've also seen firsthand the ways they hold everything together. I don't think we even realize all the things that would collapse if the system itself broke down."

I nodded slowly, thinking of the literal collapse of the unsanctioned dam Amara and I had encountered early in our travels, and of the capital healers who kept Tartora's hospitals running. I had seen far less of the kingdom than Amara, but I knew what she meant.

"But the government isn't serving the kingdom if they're too focused on protecting themselves," Gia said. "They need to send out their best people and track this Grey down before he can twist more minds. It's the only right thing to do."

Renley grimaced. "It's awful to think that every day we delay may mean more minds forever tainted by Grey's lies."

"Actually...about that." Nik's hand tightened around mine again. "There's something Hayes and Amara didn't know when they sent that message. Delphine has worked out how to purge mesmerizations. So once we find them, we can free the minds Grey has touched."

Gia shot upright. "Really?" She stared at me. "But that's amazing news! Father can stop being so afraid and start actually doing something."

"It's certainly an unlooked-for boon," Hayes said. "But at this point, Delphine hasn't been able to teach anyone else to do it. So the skill is limited to Delphine herself."

Gia winced. "That's unfortunate." She shot a look at Renley. "Maybe we should hold off telling Father about this new development just yet."

"You want us to defy the king and go hunting for Grey on our own?" Luna asked in a neutral tone.

Hayes's frown deepened, and I caught the worried look he sent in her direction.

Gia waved her hand airily. "Oh, nothing as subversive as that. I'm merely suggesting that you aren't under any explicit orders to report directly to the capital, so it might be worth our while to take a more circuitous route there."

Nik nodded slowly, and Gia grinned.

"I like rebellious Nik," she said. "If I hadn't been so worried about you for the last two years, I would have been cackling and rubbing my hands in glee to see you go rogue."

This time it was my turn to squeeze Nik's hand. Hayes had clearly been right about Nik's family being worried about him.

"I'm not so sure about this." Hayes looked to Amara. "Anka is a trained law enforcement official, and she's very good at what she does." He turned back to Gia. "I don't know why you think we could do any better."

"Actually," I said slowly. "There's someone in Tartora who was tracking and studying Grey before Anka even knew he existed. The same person who found this camp when she couldn't." I looked at Nik. "And he's here with us."

Amara considered my words, looking thoughtful. "Nik certainly knows more about Grey than I do. So tell us, expert—if we were to entertain this plan, what would you be advising?"

Nik disentangled his fingers from mine so he could lean both his elbows on the table, his eyes narrowing.

"Did you talk to Anka?" he asked his sister. "What's her strategy?"

"They're assuming his goal is the capital—it's the only thing that makes sense given his ability," Gia said, glibly handing out what I could only assume had to be state secrets. "Grey doesn't need to spend time raising an army before attempting a coup. All he needs is direct access to those at the top."

"And so they've made a fortress around themselves," Nik murmured, his eyes narrowing. "But it's been an entire season, and Grey clearly hasn't managed to infiltrate the court. So what else have they been doing?"

"He's in hiding, clearly," Renley said. "So the theory is that he must be either laying low in some remote region, trying to avoid notice, or else he's lurking somewhere nearby, ready to make a move. So Anka has split her forces. She only has a few who have personal experience with him in Caltor, and she's sent some of them to circle through the more remote towns, while others have finished scouring Caltor and have now moved on to Ostaria, working their way out from the capital. Of course constant rumors about him crop up everywhere, but none of them have borne fruit yet."

"As far as they know," Gia said. "Because of course there's the constant fear that the people they sent to investigate may have encountered Grey and been forcibly turned."

Nik raised an eyebrow. "In that case, it's obvious. We should start in Eldrida."

"Eldrida?" Hayes asked.

"If I'd been in the capital, I would have recommended they start there, but instead it seems to be down the bottom of their list of places to focus."

"Why Eldrida?" Amara asked, her expression giving nothing away.

"It's not an obvious staging point for the capital," Hayes added, his eyes also fixed on Nik.

Nik shrugged. "Maybe not, but it's the place Grey knows best. He and his people must have contacts there. They were stationed at this camp for a long time, and Eldrida was their only trading point."

Gia jumped to her feet. "See! I knew there would be something we could do. And this is perfect. No one could criticize us for returning through Eldrida. It's basically on the way."

Hayes and Amara exchanged a look. Finally Hayes spoke.

"Very well, then. We can travel from here to Eldrida and from there to the capital. It would have been our likely route anyway."

Amara stood. "Given there has been no solid news of Grey, I can't see any rush for us to get to the capital. We can afford to spend a few days in Eldrida before moving on. But first, I need a proper sleep."

Everyone stood, moving away from the table, but Gia only moved around to latch onto Nik's arm.

"You will be coming with us all the way to the capital, won't you?" she asked quietly, her eyes fixed on his face.

"Don't worry, Gia. I intend to see this through."

"That's not what I mean, and you know it," she said fiercely. "It's been long enough, Nik. You need to come home."

He opened his mouth to speak, but she rushed on.

"I know what the Triumvirate did to you was awful. And Father treated you badly, too, in his own way. But he didn't know it was going to happen, and it wasn't as if he was offered a choice. He and Mother miss you. She's been so worried, not even knowing where you were."

"And so you wanted to make her feel better by leaving home the second your apprenticeship allowed and wandering the kingdoms yourself, then?" he asked, but it was amusement, not bitterness, lurking behind his words.

Gia had the grace to flush. "I understand why you had to get away. I had to as well, at least for a while. I'm just saying it's been long enough."

"Gia, stop." Nik cut her off gently. "I'm not avoiding Mother and Father, not anymore. I'm seeing what I started through to the end and making sure Grey can't hurt anyone ever again."

"So you'll be going to the capital with us?" she pressed.

He sighed. "I don't know what you're expecting. I've been gone a long time, and everything has changed. There's no place for me there, anymore. Or are you forgetting what I am now?"

She groaned. "Why couldn't you have waited to run off until after you finished your apprenticeship? Would that really have been so hard?" She gripped his arm with both hands. "But couldn't you ask them to take you back? If your master accepts you back, and you complete your apprenticeship, you won't be a reneger anymore."

He rubbed the back of his neck, giving a laugh that held a tinge of his old bitterness. "And you think Master Augusta will accept me back just for the asking? Unlike our parents, the Triumvirate always wanted me gone."

She bit her lip, her eyes worried. "But you could at least try."

He gently removed her hands from his arm. "I'll stay with you all the way to the capital, sister. But I can't promise you what will happen after that."

I stood frozen, hardly breathing since they seemed to have forgotten my presence. But as soon as Nik finished speaking, he flashed me a glance loaded with more emotion than I could name.

I stepped toward him, my mouth forming his name, but he was already gone, out the front door of the cabin and off into the greenery of the crevasse.

CHAPTER

# THIRTEEN

The trip due south to Eldrida was uneventful since it took us largely through desert. Gia took every opportunity to initiate conversation, quickly wheedling my entire life story out of me. She shared freely about herself as well, regaling me with stories from her childhood with Nik.

Nik, on the other hand, was clearly avoiding me. He never did anything pointed enough that I could protest, but neither did we have opportunities to talk unless there were several others present.

"Why does he have to sabotage his own happiness?" Gia asked sadly as we approached Eldrida on the final day. She was gazing at Nik, who was walking ahead of us in conversation with Renley.

I didn't pretend not to know what she was talking about or that the matter hadn't occupied many of my thoughts during our journey.

"I think he thinks he's doing it for me," I said with a sigh. "He knows I won't leave my apprenticeship and Amara—he wouldn't even ask me to—and he thinks that means it will never work between us. Like Amara and Hayes. So he's trying to create distance between us now, to minimize the pain."

Gia groaned. "That would explain why he's always looking at you."

"He is?" I frowned. I hadn't noticed him watching me. I was always the one looking at him.

But Gia nodded assuredly. "Whenever you're distracted and not looking at him, he stares at you like his life depends on memorizing every one of your features. Just seeing his expression makes my heart hurt—and that's despite thinking he's being a fool."

I looked down at my feet, my face burning. Did he really look at me like that?

Gia was right—he was a fool.

"Can't you straighten him out?" Gia asked. "I've tried, but he stonewalls me."

I sighed. "What am I supposed to say? What if he's right?"

"Don't you be like that, too!" Gia cried. "My brother has never cared about anyone the way he cares about you. We have to find a way for you to be together."

I sighed again. "If you have any suggestions, I'm listening."

When she fell silent, I gave her a look, and she winced.

"There's still time," she said quickly. "We'll find a way. Maybe Augusta will take him back."

"And what if she does?" I murmured. "Then he goes back to being a royal prince, and who am I?"

"Definitely none of that!" Gia exclaimed. "Look at Renley! He doesn't have a title or position. He's no different in rank from Luna."

I gave her a skeptical look. It had taken a few days, but I no longer felt awkward arguing back to a princess. "I think you're forgetting that Renley is Calistan, and from what I gather, he's a close ally of their new king and queen. Things are different in Calista—it's basically a new kingdom. Is there anyone of high rank? Since your marriage, you've become part Calistan, too. And that's given you freedom to distance yourself from being a Tartoran princess. But I'm only a very junior member of the Tartoran Mages' Guild. I don't have any alternative position or home to offer Nik. If he does finally reconcile with his family and take back his rightful place, how can I ask him to give it all up for a second time?"

Gia linked her arm with mine. "I'm sure it will work out. It has to."

I sighed and nodded, not wanting to dispute her words a second time. Especially when I was holding on to the same nebulous hope myself.

My eyes lingered on Nik's back, taking in the breadth of his shoulders and his easy stride, before slipping sideways to where Hayes and Amara walked, their heads bent close in conversation. Nik had been there for me from the start—from before I was even activated—and I desperately wanted him in my future too. But hadn't the same been true for Amara with Hayes? Their case proved that love wasn't always enough. You couldn't build a life together if circumstances forced you apart.

I tried to move forward to walk with Nik, but as usual he outmaneuvered me, and I ended up in the lead next to Amara. She took the opportunity to quiz me on what I had learned during the epidemic—an ongoing process that was being completed in snatches whenever we had the chance.

"It's not the teaching program I'd planned for you," she said. "But there's no denying that these constant crises are pushing you to develop your power far faster than an ordinary apprentice. You may be lagging behind on academic learning—Hayes tells me you still have plenty of memorization to do from both the anatomy and general medical texts—but you're far more capable than the average first year apprentice. Catching up on academic learning can happen easily enough later on."

"Even if I'd had my books with me on the island, I don't think I would have had the chance to open them," I said. "I feel like I barely drew breath the whole winter. But I promise I'll make more of an effort once we're reunited with our possessions. You left the bulk of them in storage in Eldrida along with Acorn, didn't you?"

Amara nodded. "I'm looking forward to that reunion myself."

"Have you missed the freedom of having your cart, Acorn, and an open road in front of you?" I asked. "I'm afraid taking me on as your apprentice has proven far more disruptive than you expected."

Amara gazed ahead at the walls of Eldrida, which were growing larger before us.

"A year ago I would have been itching to be off again after so long. But I actually haven't even thought about it. Although I will be glad to get to the capital."

"Really? I thought you didn't like Tarona?"

"It feels different now," she said thoughtfully. "So much is happening and changing in Tartora, and the capital is the hub of it all. In the past, I've always felt certain that the place I was most needed was in the smaller cities and towns. But now I feel needed in the capital. I suppose it's all this business with Grey."

She shook herself slightly and smiled at me. "Don't worry. Once everything has been resolved, we'll be back on the road again. I haven't forgotten that I promised you your apprenticeship wouldn't be spent at the Guild."

"About that..." I paused before continuing. "A year ago I thought differently, too. I'm not saying I want to be at the Guild, necessarily, but I now recognize how hollow my old prejudice against it was. If we need to stay there for some reason, I wouldn't consider it a betrayal."

Amara's eyebrows lifted slightly, her eyes distant. "I'll bear that in mind."

The sun was lowering toward the horizon as we approached the city, but the gates didn't close until sunset, so we joined the main western road without concern. But when we reached the gates, we found them closed and barred. Only a single door, cut within the left gate, was propped open. And standing in front of it were four armed guards wearing stern expressions.

Amara and I exchanged a surprised look. On our previous arrival at the city, the gates had been wide open and unmanned. On that occasion, the anomaly had been due to the storm, but this situation seemed almost as unusual.

"Are the gates closed for the day already?" Amara asked carefully, the others remaining silent as they clustered close behind us.

"That depends who's asking," the guard at the front said aggressively. "What's your business in Eldrida?"

"We're travelers seeking rest and shelter before we continue our journey," she said, making no mention of our identities.

I glanced over my shoulder and saw Nik and Gia had melted to the back of our small group, the other three attempting to block them from view. I quickly looked front again, hoping I hadn't attracted any attention.

"And what brings you traveling in these remote parts?" the same guard asked, clearly taking note of our lack of trading goods.

Amara shrugged, doing a good job of appearing unaffected by the strange situation. "It's not remote to our way of thinking. We've come south from eastern Calista."

"Calista?" The man glanced behind him, and one of the other guards nodded.

I realized, belatedly, that Amara had been picking her words carefully, wary of any guards with a healing affinity. And it looked like her caution had been called for.

The guard in front of us stood motionless for a moment, clearly torn about what to make of us. But two of the men behind him had started whispering, their heads bent together. The speaker was watching us with wide eyes, his words inaudible but rapid. The other started out frowning, but his eyes gradually widened as well, his gaze locking on us.

I shifted uncomfortably. If they intended to deny us entry, would they leave the matter there? Or would they attempt to arrest us? I couldn't imagine why they would do so, but nothing about the situation made sense. Travel around Tartora had never been restricted, and city inns relied on travelers to survive.

The speaker at the back had finished, and his listener responded by stepping forward to murmur something in the ear of the leader. This time he was close enough for me to catch the words *heroes* and *storm*.

Just like before, the leader's whole manner changed on hearing the whispered message. He peered first at Amara and then at me before dropping into an abrupt bow.

"We are honored!" he exclaimed. "Please forgive my earlier questioning. Of course the heroes of Eldrida are welcome in our city any time!"

My mouth fell open, but Amara took it easily in stride, inclining her head and smiling graciously.

"Thank you for your welcome."

"I apologize for not recognizing you at once," the leader said. "But I hope you can understand our caution. You must have heard the rumors and know there are dangerous people loose in Tartora. We can't be too careful in protecting our citizens and our city."

"An admirable goal," Amara said in a steady voice. If I hadn't known better, even I would have believed she found nothing about the situation odd.

The fourth guard had disappeared during the latter part of the conversation, and I realized his purpose when a loud creaking rang out. Slowly the full gate swung open, giving easy access to the city. All four guards jumped to attention, lining up on either side of the gate and bowing deeply as we passed through.

Amara led the way, the seven of us staying close together as we walked. I smiled at the guards as naturally as I could manage, but I wasn't sure how well I succeeded. We continued into the city in unnatural silence until well out of ear shot of the guards.

"It wasn't just me. That was weird, right?" I asked Amara. "I'm not even sure which aspect of it was more unsettling."

Amara nodded grimly, the calmly gracious expression she'd worn at the gate gone completely.

"So that was all about keeping Grey out?" Luna asked, but her voice made it clear she didn't find it a satisfactory explanation.

"So it would appear," Amara said.

"Or so someone wants it to appear," Hayes muttered, making me shoot him a horrified expression.

"Are you saying—?" I started, but Amara cut me off with a hand on my arm.

"Later," she murmured, and I nodded.

For several streets, I followed her with quick, jumpy strides, trying not to see a threat in every shadow. The people we passed appeared normal enough, going about the regular business of a coastal city. For the most part, they ignored us, although more than one took a second look at Amara and me before bursting into speech with their companions.

"I thought they would have forgotten about us by now," I said to Amara, acutely uncomfortable.

"A disaster like that storm isn't soon forgotten," she said. "And we can be grateful for it on this occasion. I honestly don't know if we would have gotten into the city if we hadn't been recognized."

"As long as it was only us who were recognized," I said.

I didn't know what was going on in Eldrida, but I was already uncomfortable about everyone soon knowing Amara and I were here. They didn't need to know both of King Marius's children were here too.

CHAPTER

# FOURTEEN

After another turn, I recognized a landmark.

"Aren't we going to the inn?" I asked Amara, sure that had been her intention. She had waxed poetic for several minutes during the morning about the warm bath waiting for us.

"Change of plans," she said shortly.

I didn't question her further, and neither did any of the others. After what had happened at the gate, I even felt relieved. Anyone who got word of our arrival would expect us to be at one of the city's inns. While I didn't know where else we could go instead, anywhere seemed better than there.

We had nearly reached the large central square—our route bringing back unpleasant flashbacks of the storm's destruction and violence—when Amara stopped abruptly in front of a large, closed wooden gate.

"What is this place?" Luna asked over my shoulder, looking at the worn wood with curiosity.

"It's a small, private stables," I said, recognizing it. "When we first arrived in Eldrida, the stable master was sheltering people from the storm. He kept Acorn, Ember, and Phoenix here while we went out to help. Oh!" I exclaimed, suddenly realizing what must have happened. "Has he been looking after Acorn while we've been gone?"

Amara nodded. "When we left for the desert, I organized for Acorn to board here until I came back. Since we were being labeled as heroes, he agreed easily enough, although I think his personal view was that I was pushy and self-righteous." She smiled slightly, obviously not offended.

"Why didn't you just leave her at one of the inns?" Luna asked. "Especially if you thought the stable master didn't like you."

Amara raised an eyebrow. "What difference does it make whether he likes me or not? Liking me isn't the measure of someone's worth. His first instinct during the storm was to open his doors and shelter as many as possible. And he even opened the doors a second time just because he heard hoof beats through the noises of the storm. And when I first came back to check on Acorn in the aftermath of the storm, she had been well groomed and looked fast on her way to becoming fat and happy."

Luna subsided, looking suitably chastened.

"I wish I could be so uncaring about whether or not people like me," she whispered to me, and I nodded agreement.

Amara had to rap on the wood several times, but eventually the large gate creaked open. The grumbles of the elderly man behind it ceased as soon as he got a good look at who was there.

"Oh, it's you," he said sourly, but his heart didn't seem to be in his ill temper. "I suppose you've come for that cantankerous mare of yours?"

Amara led the way inside, the rest of us trailing in behind her.

"Been causing trouble, has she?" she asked.

"See for yourself." He nodded toward a stall halfway down the short aisle. We peered over the closed half-door to see a contented Acorn feeding from a trough.

She hadn't looked up at the sounds of our arrival, but when Amara laughed, her ears pricked, and she turned her head. For a moment she surveyed her mistress before swishing her tail and returning to her feed.

"Who is that calm horse?" Hayes asked. "Do you think he swapped Acorn out with another mare with similar markings and a rounder belly?"

Amara chuckled again. "It's a good thing I have Delphine with me, or I'd never convince her to leave this stable."

I eyed the mare doubtfully. "I'm not sure my presence will be enough."

"I've never liked that animal," Hayes muttered, and Acorn pricked an ear, stopping eating. Turning her long neck, she gave him a look that could only be called a warning.

Luna and I burst into laughter while Hayes glared back at the horse.

"There you go!" I said. "It is Acorn after all."

"You were gone for long enough," the stable master said from behind us.

"Yes, we were held up for much longer than expected," Amara said. "Which is why I left her with you in the first place. I knew you wouldn't get rid of her when my original payment ran out. Of course I'll pay the balance now, with a bonus as well for your understanding."

The stable master's face lightened considerably, and he even nodded respectfully.

"If you'd like to earn a bit extra," Amara added, "I seem to remember you have several rooms on the second level above the stalls."

The elderly man eyed us uncertainty. "They're nothing fancy. You'd be more comfortable at an inn."

"Perhaps," Amara said lightly. "But we'd rather stay with Acorn if it's possible."

Out of the corner of my eye, I saw Hayes and Renley once again positioning themselves in front of Nik, attempting to block him from sight.

For a moment I wondered if they thought the man was a threat and why they weren't blocking Gia as well, if so. Then I remembered Nik's official status. He was a reneger—the kingdom's most famous reneger—and if the stable master realized his status, he would be legally required to refuse him service or lodging.

The man didn't even glance in their direction, however. Instead he started toward the stairs, gesturing for us to follow him. "Don't go saying I didn't warn you," he grumbled as he began the climb.

Next to the stairs, I noticed a bulky shape with a large length of canvas thrown over it. From the dimensions, I guessed it was Amara's cart. Apparently our remaining belongings had also been stored here in our absence.

Upstairs there were only two rooms available, so we split in half with men in one and women in the other. I wondered if Gia and Renley might protest, but they made no complaint about being temporarily separated.

"I didn't expect Nik to be proven correct so immediately," Gia said as we deposited our bags in the room assigned to us. "But I'm glad we came to Eldrida. Something is going on here that's worth further investigation."

"We have to keep an open mind," Amara warned. "It's still possible this is a reaction to the rumors about Grey and nothing more. It's easy to see things that aren't there when you're already suspicious. I suspect we'll find the capital equally tense."

She sent Gia a questioning look, and the younger woman shrugged.

"It isn't quite like this—or wasn't when we were there—but I can't deny it's been unsettled."

"What's the plan now?" I asked. "Are we going to head out into the city and see what we can discover?"

Luna bounded over and wound her arm through mine. "The two of us should go together," she announced.

"That's a good idea," I said before noticing Nik in the doorway, his expression disapproving. "And you're not invited," I told him. "Who's going to gossip with us if you're hanging around all silent and menacing?"

Luna nodded fervently. "Two female apprentices will get a very different reaction from any of the rest of you."

"I agree," Amara said calmly. "And beyond that, I am officially forbidding Nik and Gia from stepping foot outside these stables until we get a better idea of what's going on in the city."

They both began to protest, but she silenced them with a stern look. "I'm pulling rank on both of you, and don't try to argue you're royalty. Nik, you're a reneger, and Gia, you were the one to ask us not to consider your rank. As a master mage, I am the senior member of this expedition, and I expect both of you to obey this command."

She continued to stare them down until they both nodded reluctant agreement.

"I'm a master mage as well," Hayes said meekly from behind Nik. "Are you also pulling rank on me?"

She gave him a long-suffering look. "If you intend to cause trouble, I'll be forced to remind you that since you resigned your position as Colton's second, I'm back to being your senior due to having taken the mastery exams before you—at least until you're actually appointed the next Head of Healing."

"Yes, ma'am," he said meekly, and the corners of her lips tugged upward.

Nik cleared his throat pointedly, and the mood of the room shifted.

"Are you really going to let the two of them wander around alone?" he asked Amara, inclining his head toward Luna and me.

"Certainly. We have no immediate reason to think there's a physical threat lurking in the streets of the city, and you saw Delphine and my reception at the city gates. They're more in danger of being revered than attacked."

"And neither of them is helpless either," Gia added heatedly. "If two mage-level healers can't protect themselves, who can?"

Nik was reluctantly forced to concede, and I threw him a smile. I knew his concern stemmed from an excess of care rather than a lack of belief, and I couldn't bring myself to fault him for that. I also couldn't really blame him for thinking I would be safer with Amara than Luna. But Luna was right that we would create a different impression on our own—especially given Amara's hero status in the city. I had been dragged into the reverence due to my connection to her, but she was the much more recognized figure.

"The two of us will also go out." Amara indicated herself and Hayes. "We both have contacts in the city among different circles, and between us all, we can hopefully get a picture of what's going on."

She looked at Renley with a contrite expression. "I'll be leaving you to babysit these two. My apologies."

He laughed. "I think some quiet brother-sister bonding time is an excellent idea and long overdue." Both the twins rolled their eyes, but I also caught Gia shooting him an affectionate look. It was no wonder Renley was so calm and steady when he constantly had to balance out Gia.

Although the day was coming to a close, no one wanted to wait a whole night without doing anything, so we set out immediately. The two master mages disappeared quickly, heading for their individual contacts, while Luna and I strolled the short distance into the central square.

The day's market had almost wrapped up, with many of the stall holders busy packing away their remaining wares. We wandered around aimlessly, listening to snatches of conversation from both shoppers and sellers.

Unlike at the gates, nothing in the market gave the overt impression anything had changed. The salt tang in the air, slightly different from the one that had permeated the island, took me straight back to my previous stay in the city, and the people we saw were occupied with the usual business of life. But the longer we listened, the deeper the crease between my eyes grew.

"It's not just me, is it?" I asked Luna. "There's a different tone now from before."

Luna nodded slowly, her eyes scanning the closest row of stalls. "It does seem subtly different. More fearful and insular, maybe? And I haven't heard a single complaint about the guards at the gates, although some of these stall-holders must have traveled from out of the city for the market."

"Of course, it could just be because of the rumors about Grey, like Amara said." I frowned at a nearby clump of people who were talking animatedly.

"Yes, it's possible," Luna agreed, although she sounded doubtful.

"Do you think we should try approaching someone directly?" I asked as we neared the fountain at the center of the square. Whatever damage the feature had sustained during the storm had been expertly fixed, and several groups of people lingered around its enormous rim.

I eyed one of the groups whose members appeared around our age. One of the girls caught me looking and stared openly back. I was about to look away when her expression changed, her eyes going round.

She tugged at the arm of the boy beside her, saying something I couldn't catch.

"We might want to move on," I murmured nervously to Luna, but before we could do so, the girl called out loudly.

"Delphine? Luna?"

We both turned to stare at her as the entire group surged toward us. My eyes jumped from face to face until one of them triggered a memory, bringing the identities of all of them rushing to my mind.

"Oh!" I said. "From the hospital!"

The first girl laughed delightedly. "Don't worry if you can't remember our names. I don't know if we even got introduced. But of course we couldn't forget you—our own sleeping beauty."

I winced, flushing painfully while Luna laughed.

"Have you graduated yet?" Luna asked the girl. "Weren't you nearly finished with your apprenticeship last time we were here?"

The girl smiled. "Only ten more days!"

I frowned, confused by their familiarity, and Luna grinned in response. Prodding me lightly in the side with her elbow, she explained, "We worked together while you were slumbering, Hero."

I winced again while the others all jumped in, clamoring to know if Amara was with me and what we'd been doing since our departure from the city.

We answered as evasively as we could, Luna turning off many of their inquiries with questions of her own about the hospital and their work there. She couldn't shield me completely, however.

"Did you marry your prince?" one of the girls called from the back of the group, and most of them laughed.

I froze, remembering how they had exaggerated their own stories, making the tale more and more outlandish until they accidentally stumbled on the truth regarding Nik's identity.

Luna jumped into the gap on my behalf. "Not yet," she said breezily. "She's been too busy single-handedly holding off an epidemic."

I glared at her as the healing apprentices exclaimed among themselves. I didn't need her spreading more false rumors about my exaggerated heroism.

She just grinned back at me, clearly unrepentant. But her expression changed as the first girl began to press us with questions.

"There's been an epidemic? Where? We haven't heard anything about that."

Luna shot me a concerned look, recognizing her mistake.

"It wasn't near here," I said vaguely, and the girl looked relieved.

The boy next to her shook his head disgustedly, though. "An epidemic? If it's not one thing, it's another. The kingdom isn't what it once was."

My ears pricked up at his comments, and I tried to think how to keep him talking. But another boy jumped in immediately making any response from me unnecessary.

"Some days I think we really should just shut the gate completely," he said, and several voices murmured agreement.

When I frowned, the first girl jumped in quickly. "Not against you, of course! You're one of us now! The heroes of Eldrida will always be welcome in the city."

The rest of the group murmured their agreement, and one of the boys generously added, "You, too, Luna. Everyone who helped us in the storm is welcome here. Those are our true friends." The last was muttered with enough feeling to make me blurt out a question.

"What do you mean? Did some people not help?"

"Where was the capital when our city was being destroyed?" one of the girls said with feeling. "Not here, that's for sure."

"How could they have been here for the storm?" I asked, confused. "No one knew it was coming."

"Precisely," the girl said as if my point flowed perfectly from hers. "They claim everything would fall apart without the Mage's Guild, but where was the warning about the storm from the elements mages?"

"But the storm—" I cut myself off when I realized it wasn't my place to spill the truth about the storm to a group of random apprentices.

"As I said, *you* carry no blame," the first girl said earnestly. "We all saw how hard you worked. Our masters have all been holding you up as a cautionary tale ever since."

They chuckled among themselves, as I tried to hide my astonishment. We had been afraid of people wrongfully blaming the Calistans for the sudden killer storm, but I hadn't expected them to blame the Guild for failing to see the unnatural weather coming. The Eldridan mages must have known for themselves that there was nothing normal about that storm.

One of the girls hissed suddenly, pointing at where the sun had slipped below the buildings on the western side of the square.

"We have to get back to the hospital," one of the boys said, "or else we'll hear it from our masters." He sent us a questioning look. "Do you want to come with us?"

I shook my head quickly. "We have to get back to our own masters."

The other apprentices all accepted this without question, hurrying away in the direction of the hospital.

"I think we really should get back," I said to Luna. "I don't know how long the others will be out, but the market is about finished now."

She agreed without protest, and the two of us hurried back toward the stable that had become our temporary accommodation. I didn't know about Luna, but I had plenty of food for thought. And the more I thought, the less I liked the picture I was building.

CHAPTER

# FIFTEEN

Nik was waiting for our return in Acorn's stall. I caught his murmured voice before I saw him and peered in at him in surprise.

"She really has mellowed," I said with a grin when I saw how calmly the mare had accepted her visitor.

"You just don't know how much work I put in during our travels." Nik came out into the stable aisle, securing the door behind him. "Did you discover anything?"

"Maybe?" I glanced at Luna who shrugged. "It's hard to say."

He raised an eyebrow, but I just shrugged as well. "There was nothing definitive. Let's wait and find out what the others have discovered before I say anything."

He narrowed his eyes. "You have a theory."

I looked away. "Maybe."

It was unsettling how well he understood me. He was right that I had a theory, but I wasn't willing to say it out loud until I'd heard any other information on hand.

It took several more hours for Amara and Hayes to return. We had prepared a meal in the meantime, and as soon as everyone had finished eating, we gathered in one of the bedrooms.

Luna succinctly described what we had observed about the mood in the city, as well as the unsettling conversation with the other healing apprentices. She apologized for mentioning the epidemic, but none of the others seemed concerned.

"What did your contacts have to say?" I asked Amara.

"The elements mages I could find were withdrawn and cagey," she said.

"The ones you could find?" Gia asked with raised eyebrows.

Amara frowned. "Every time I asked for one of them, I was told he was at the law enforcement hall. It was always said as if I should understand the significance of that, although no one was willing to be drawn out on the topic."

Nik leaned forward. "He's been arrested, then?"

Amara shook her head slowly. "I don't think so. It didn't seem like it from their manner, anyway."

"Did they say anything about the storm?" I asked. "Why aren't they correcting the people's mistaken impressions?"

"All of them seemed weary of that topic," she said. "As if they've grown tired of explaining and being ignored."

"But why would the people ignore them?" Luna asked. "It doesn't make any sense."

"It does if there's someone they trust more telling a different story," Hayes said. "It sounds like I got straighter answers from the healers since they aren't directly involved in the matter. According to them, there's been a great deal of unrest since the storm, with many feeling the capital didn't send enough assistance in the aftermath. One or two loud voices started suggesting the city should have had warning from the capital ahead of time and claiming it showed how little Eldrida is valued and prioritized."

"That doesn't make any sense," Gia said hotly. "Even if it had been a normal storm and a warning had been possible, the warning wouldn't have come from the capital. Eldrida's own elements mages provide that sort of information."

"There's always someone who wants to be enraged about something." Hayes sighed. "And too many people died in that storm. The grieving populace would have been looking for someone to blame, and those in power are the easiest targets. Their own head law keeper was probably the first to be criticized—especially since he happens to be an elements mage instead of the more usual healing mage. So he was probably just trying to deflect blame away from himself, regardless of the consequences. That seems like Miro, from what I know of him."

"He never had the right temperament for the position," Amara said. "I told Anka that years ago."

Hayes shrugged. "There weren't exactly a lot of options. They wouldn't have assigned an elements mage—let alone him—if they had someone better suited who was willing to take the role."

"Which at least partially bears out the people's complaints." Amara sighed. "Eldrida is the furthest city of its size away from the capital, and we all know typical Tartorans have a tendency to look down on those who live east of the forest."

I stayed silent, unable to refute it. Even in distant Tarin I had encountered the occasional snide comment about easterners.

"How long has this issue been fomenting?" Nik looked across at Gia. "Why hasn't Father done anything?"

"Ordinarily he would have," Gia said. "But this is exactly the problem with the fortress mentality they've all adopted. With Miro stirring trouble in order to defend himself, they'd need to send out high level officials to address the issue. At any other time, he would probably have been recalled over this. But they're too afraid to let anyone of strength leave the capital."

"I actually overheard Anka having a conversation about it with some of her people," Renley interjected. "She seems to have reached a similar conclusion that Miro is transferring blame. While she took the situation seriously, it was prioritized below finding Grey, which is understandable. I think she would have come herself if she wasn't being kept chained to the court."

"That sounds like Anka," Amara said. "I wouldn't want to be the one telling her she has to stay sheltering in Tarona. I can imagine how that conversation went—even if it was with the king. There's a reason a mage as powerful as Anka had a position in Caltor, not the capital."

"They made her Royal Mage," Gia said simply. "Forcibly."

"They did what?" Amara stared at her.

Gia shrugged. "It's a position usually held by an elements mage, but there's no law that prevents a healer from taking the role, and Anka has the strength for it. If she'd cared to, she could have challenged Colton to become Master of Healing when the previous one retired. So there were no arguments she could make against the appointment. And as Royal Mage, she's part of the kingdom's government—the official liaison between the crown and the Triumvirate—so there was no question of her going rogue after that."

"Poor Aunt." Amara gave a pained chuckle. "Not only forced to the capital but chained to the heart of government. I wonder if they realize what they're in for by now?"

"But where does that leave us?" Luna asked. "Should we try to do something about the situation in Eldrida, or do we stay focused on trying to find Grey? Did anyone get word of him?"

Amara shook her head immediately, but Hayes hesitated before following suit. I focused in on him.

"Are you sure—*completely sure*—you didn't hear anything that could have been referencing Grey? Any hint at all?"

Everyone looked at me, surprised, except for Nik, who gave a small smile.

"Delphine has a theory," he said.

Amara raised both eyebrows. "Do you, now? Go on then."

"First I want to hear an answer to my question." I kept my attention on Hayes.

"I specifically asked after any new healers who'd come to the city since the start of winter," he said. "I figured other healers would be the most likely to know about a newcomer. But the only one mentioned was a younger female, a recent graduate of the Guild who I've met myself."

"But?" I said, given how he'd hesitated earlier.

"When they were complaining about the elements mages, a couple of them mentioned a newcomer who sided with Miro and promptly received a position in the law keepers' hall. He's elements affinity, though, not healing. And his vocal support of this nonsense was probably just his way of securing a desirable job despite being a newcomer. But since we're on the lookout for anything out of the ordinary and newcomers in particular..." He shrugged. "It did occur to me that the man in question might be one of Grey's followers acting as his agent."

A tight feeling in my chest robbed me of breath. "Anything else?" I asked, my voice barely above a whisper.

Out of the corner of my eye, I could see Nik watching me with concern, but I was too focused on Hayes to respond to him.

"My reception was markedly chillier than last time," he said, "which seemed suspicious in itself given how much assistance I provided during the storm. But then everyone knows my close connections with the Triumvirate."

"I'm sorry, Hayes," Amara said softly, no doubt comparing her own reception as a hero with his.

He smiled at her. "I'm hardly going to crumble due to a few unjust attitudes. But I grew curious enough to try going directly to the law keepers' hall myself."

Gia raised her eyebrows. "That was bold. What did Miro have to say for himself?"

"I don't know, since I wasn't permitted inside."

"What?" Amara straightened. "That can't be right. Law keepers' halls are required to be open and available for all to enter so that anyone can lodge a complaint."

"Officially, yes," Hayes said. "But who's going to reprimand them for not following the rules when Tarona has stopped sending senior visitors from the central law keepers' hall? From the state of things at the gate, Miro feels a similar fear to the king himself. He's created his own little fortress at the Eldridan law keepers' hall."

"That's one possibility," I murmured, hoping Hayes was right.

"Are you going to tell us the other possibility now?" Nik asked.

I took a deep breath. I had been hoping the others would dispel my fears, but instead their information had only strengthened my concern.

"I've been uncomfortable about something ever since we talked in the crevasse," I said. "I thought about it all the way here to Eldrida, and even so, I couldn't quite make sense of our theory about Grey's plans."

"What theory do you mean?" Hayes's tone was respectful, and he was obviously taking my concerns seriously which only put me more on edge.

"Everyone has been talking as if all Grey needs to do is get access to court, and he'll be able to take over the government and throne—like a puppet master in the background."

"Is that not the case?" Gia's eyes were fastened on my face with almost painful intensity. "That's the impression I had. Can't he use his mesmerizations to control someone's mind?"

"Yes and no. It's not that simple." I paused as I tried to work out the best way to describe it. "Mesmerizations aren't about controlling someone's mind. They're about lies and truth. Of course lies can be used as a vehicle to control someone, but there are significant limits—in particular that it won't last if the lie can be disproved. Just look at the island. It took an entire family of mesmerizers to keep one town subjugated, and even then they couldn't manage it completely. Isolde is a perfect example of the sort of limits I mean—and she was someone who'd been shaped by their lies since birth."

"Isolde?" Renley asked.

"Costas's mother," I explained. "Everyone thought she was dead, but it turns out she was in hiding, leading a sort of passive resistance." I briefly explained her story. "They told her a lie and ordered her to do something in line with that lie. But instead of compelling her to act according to their wishes, their order broke the mesmerization completely."

I tried to think of another example. "Take what the Triumvirate did to Nik. Imagine that Grey was there and had mesmerized both the Triumvirate and the king into believing Nik was a danger to Tartora. That lie would be enough to have them skip Nik in the line of succession in favor of Evermund —we know it's possible for them to act that way because they did it. But what if Grey said that since Nik's such a danger, King Marius should have him killed?"

"Father would never do that," Gia said with confidence. "Nik is his son, and he loves him."

I smiled at her, hoping Nik was hearing her words and believing them.

"Exactly," I said. "It doesn't matter what lies he tells the king, Grey couldn't compel him to kill his own son. And Nik's behavior would soon disprove the original lie, thus breaking the entire mesmerization. There are a hundred traps like that, situations where someone won't react to the lie as intended or where something unforeseen breaks the mesmerization."

"Grey could still cause a lot of damage and chaos," Renley said.

I nodded. "He could, of course, but what would be his motive? That's the part that had me confused all the way across the desert. As a single individual, he would have to work incredibly hard and incredibly carefully just to maintain a position that would always be insecure. And the attempt would be infinitely harder now that the court is on high alert. Everyone must be afraid of doing anything the least out of character in case others think Grey has gotten to them."

"He might just want to destroy Tartora," Gia said. "From what you've said, he destroyed his own family—and nearly their whole community along with them—and ended up with no personal benefit from it."

As little as I wanted to speak up for Grey in any matter, I couldn't accept the likelihood of her suggestion.

"Grey doesn't have any reason to destroy Tartora," I said. "On the island, he had a personal vendetta against the family who killed his father and caused his and his mother's exile. I dislike Grey as much as anyone—I'm the only one here who's experienced the stomach-churning reality of his mesmerizations—but he isn't some well of endless evil. He's motivated by his own advantage, and I just can't see how destroying the kingdom he wants to live in would be advantageous."

"He might plan to topple everything so he can take over and rebuild from the ashes," Nik said.

I shook my head. "Some people might want that," I said, "if their primary motivation is seeking power. But I don't think that's what Grey wants the most."

"You don't think he wants power?" Hayes sounded unconvinced.

"I think he wants adulation," I said, "which is similar, but not quite the same thing. If he seized power in the situation Nik described, he would hardly become a beloved leader—not when the majority of people would be beyond his ability to mesmerize."

"So you think we've all been focused on the wrong thing," Amara said. "You don't think he's planning to make a move on the throne at all. You think he has something else in mind."

I nodded. "Grey told me a lot of lies to start with, but on his final night on the island—when he realized I'd found a way to break his mesmerizations—his mask dropped, and he admitted a number of truths. In particular, he revealed his greatest grievance against his mother, which seemed to be the source of all his bitterness. Grey wanted back the life she had stolen him away from—not a life where he was head of a vast kingdom, but one he described as a life of luxury, living like a prince among the island's rulers."

"So you think Grey wants a life of wealth, respect, and comfort?" Nik said.

"Yes, and for all Grey's moral failings, he's never been a fool. I think he knows he won't easily find that life anywhere near the Mages' Guild or the court. In the time I was with him, I never heard him say anything about the capital. In fact, in his whole time in Tartora, he always carefully avoided it." I looked at Nik with a challenging expression. "Isn't that right? You tracked him the longest."

Nik brows lowered. "You're right. He never went near the capital."

"Isn't that a good thing?" Gia asked. "If Grey never actually wanted the throne, shouldn't we all be relieved? Why do you look so uncomfortable, Delphine?"

I grimaced. "He didn't talk about the capital, but he did mention somewhere else. Here. Grey spent his childhood and youth believing he and his mother should be living a life of comfort in Eldrida instead of scratching out a lonely existence in the crevasse. He believed his mother could have used her ability to mesmerize to make a place for them here."

"And Nik said from the beginning that Grey had contacts here—that it would be the most likely place for him to come," Amara said slowly.

"And now that we're here," I said, "we've found that the city is changing. They've closed the gates and all unrest is being directed toward the capital. People are complaining that Tarona doesn't care about the easterners and that they do nothing for Eldrida." I looked at Hayes. "You described Miro as turning the law keepers' hall into a fortress against Grey, but it seems to me it could be something else. Miro could be turning it into a palace."

Gia and Nik sprang to their feet simultaneously.

"You're saying Miro is trying to secede from the kingdom with the eastern part of Tartora?" Gia cried.

"I never liked him," Nik said in tones of contempt. "He was the sort to muss your hair and say something condescending just because you were a child."

"I'm not sure that makes him villainous," Luna said, earning herself a united glare from the twins.

"I agree with Luna," I said. "This Miro might be self-important and self-serving, but the timing is a bit too convenient, don't you think?"

"You suspect Grey has already mesmerized Miro and is working from the shadows?" Amara asked.

"That's what I'm afraid of," I said. "Who knows how many lies he's pumped him with? If Grey is happy with a high position and a luxurious life, he might be willing to lurk behind Miro's rule for the rest of his life, knowing his position of influence will always be secure. Grey has always been good at working out what motivates an individual and how that can be used to his advantage. If he's familiar with Eldrida, then he likely already knew Miro's nature. He would have known that Miro had the conceit and ambition to tear Tartora down the middle, if he only believed he could do it safely."

"The rest of the kingdom won't stand for it!" Gia said fiercely.

"Oh, they won't be happy about it," Hayes said. "But how far do you think they'll go to stop it? If Grey can use Miro and the other officials to convince the easterners they're better off on their own, it would mean all-out war to stop it."

Gia instantly deflated. "Father won't want to kill people in large numbers —not the soldiers he'd have to send, or the easterners either. Instead, he'll try to send a few powerful individuals to infiltrate Miro's circle and put an end to it at the top. But all he'll be doing is sending them into Grey's clutches."

"Calista are close allies, but they're also still in the beginning stages of rebuilding," Nik added. "They won't have the resources to aid us in a drawn-out conflict."

I glanced at Luna who was biting her lip and looking away. Nik was right.

"And the nomad tribes are used to doing things a different way," he continued. "They elect their monarchs, so if Miro can convince them he's acting according to the will of the people, they may side with him over us."

"But the people won't actually be better off," I said, remembering the islanders. "It's all lies about the capital not helping them. Grey himself is the one who first created that storm, and he's the one who provoked the Constantines into strengthening it. King Marius might not get everything right, but the very fact he won't attack proves he does care about the people. Grey, on the other hand, only cares about using them for his own gain. If Miro becomes king of the east with Grey behind him, no one in the new kingdom will ever be safe, even inside their own minds."

"We can't let that happen," Gia declared.

"But hold on," Hayes said. "The theory bears weight, but if Grey's here already, preparing a position for himself, shouldn't there be some sign of him? It can't serve his purposes to be too far in the background, not from what you're describing, Delphine."

"Actually," I said, "I think we already have had news of him."

Everyone frowned at me with varying levels of confusion.

"You were the one to hear, Hayes. You said there was a newcomer who immediately took up a position close to Miro."

"But he has an elements affinity," Hayes said. "Do you mean Grey is using one of his followers to stand in on his behalf?"

I shook my head. "Grey is wily, and even without using mesmerizations, he's well practiced at presenting lies in a way that will evade a healer's truth telling ability. In fact, this is one particular lie he's used before. When we first arrived on the island, he successfully convinced the rest of the Constantines that I had an elements affinity since he didn't want to confess I was a healer. What if he's done the same thing here for himself?"

"That's a sickening thought," Luna said in a horrified voice. "He's already here and right under our noses!"

"Coming to Eldrida seems reckless now," Amara murmured. "We didn't even consider that Grey might not only be here but in a position of power already." She looked at me, fear in her eyes. "We practically announced ourselves at the gate, and then we let you wander all over the city. If Grey hasn't already heard of it, he will soon."

"Me?" I stared back at her. "Why me in particular? We were all out and about."

"But you're the one person Grey must fear the most." Nik's eyes burned into me, hard and determined. "You're the one who not only knows all his secrets but is more powerful than him. He can mesmerize, but so can you— and you can block him and purge his lies as well."

"Thank goodness he doesn't know you worked out how to purge other people of mesmerizations," Amara said. "If he knew that, he'd tear the city apart to find you."

"Thank goodness for your foresight in coming to this stable instead of an inn," Nik said to her. "How many people know you left Acorn here?"

"No one, as far as I know. Unless the stable master told anyone."

"Someone will need to talk to him," Nik said, brisk and focused now that the threat had narrowed in on me. "He doesn't seem the loquacious type, though, so we might be fortunate."

"We need to get you out of the city, immediately." Luna's eyes were wide, her expression panicked. "But not through that gate. The guards might have orders to stop you. Does anyone know another way out?"

"Wait, stop!" I stared around. "Are you all serious? Do you really mean to smuggle me out of the city? What about stopping Grey and freeing Eldrida before he gets his claws the rest of the way into it? We can't just flee now!"

"We don't have to flee," Hayes said. "But you do. It's too dangerous for you here."

"I can't just leave! You all just said it. The only way to stop this turning into a proper war is to send someone to infiltrate Miro's so-called palace, and I'm the only one it's safe to send. I'm the only one who can protect myself against Grey, and the only one who can reverse his power."

"You want to walk straight into Miro and Grey's arms?" Nik asked, incredulous.

"Think about it," I said. "I can purge Grey's mesmerizations, which means all I have to do is get close enough to Miro to touch him and I can end this whole thing. Miro must be inclined to vainglory if he's ripe for Grey to use like this, but he never tried anything treasonous before. Grey must have convinced him of all kinds of things, including that he's not going to suffer repercussions from Tarona. Everything is playing into Grey's hands because with the capital locked down, there's no one coming to Eldrida to shake those lies. So we need to strip them away ourselves."

I looked directly at Nik. "You don't have to tell me you don't like the idea. I already know that. But it's the only plan we have that might actually work."

# SIXTEEN

The fight only ended when Nik stalked out of the room. I'd managed to convince everyone else—even Amara—but he was stubbornly resistant.

I watched him go with equal parts frustration and sadness. It might be easier if I thought he was being unreasonable, but who wanted the person they loved to throw themselves into danger?

"Is it wrong of me to be a little glad?" Gia asked in my ear as everyone got up and began to spread out, beginning the preparations for bed.

"Glad?" I turned to stare at her.

She gave me a cheeky grin. "I'm not saying the changes in Nik aren't great —they are. But it's nice to know he hasn't turned into an entirely different person."

"Gia." Renley gave her an exasperated look, but she just laughed.

"I like this new kind of selfishness, though," she said. "It suits him better than the old kind."

"Don't worry," I said. "He won't actually try to stop me from doing what needs to be done. He never has before."

Gia shook her head. "Just how much danger do you perpetually throw yourself into?"

"Far too much." Amara approached us with a look of long suffering. "I knew there was a reason I never took apprentices! I'll be gray by the time Delphine graduates."

I threw her a guilty look, and she smiled.

"I know, I know, you can't help yourself," she said. "And how can I stand firm against you when your motives are always so reasonable? I'm the one who chose an unusual apprentice and gave her the promise of an unusual apprenticeship. I can hardly quibble now when things have turned out to be so very unusual."

"Very sensible." Gia nodded approvingly. "My parents could have saved themselves a lot of heartache if they'd accepted it the first time I told them I was never going to fit their plans for me." She glanced toward the door. "Things might have turned out differently if they'd invested in Nik from the beginning and shaped him to be the future king."

Amara followed her gaze, letting her eyes linger on the empty doorway. "Actually, while the path may have been painful, I'm inclined to think things turned out just as they should have. I'm not saying Nik couldn't have been shaped into an adequate king, but I don't think he would have been either a great one or a happy one. Whereas now..." She paused for a moment. "Let's just say I have hopes for him."

Gia burst into laughter, causing both Amara and I to give her affronted looks.

"No, no, I perfectly agree." Gia wiped at her eyes, her mirth finally subsiding. "I just wish Nik could have seen your face and expression when you said that."

Amara gave a reluctant smile. "Your brother may be a powerful mage—officially or unofficially—but he is still a young man, and I know how young people view old fogies like me. Don't worry, I wouldn't say it to him directly."

"Old fogey?" Hayes leaned his head into our little circle. "Speak for yourself. There's never been a more youthful or in touch master mage than me. Just ask all of Colton's apprentices from back when I was his second and did most of their training."

Gia instantly went off into peals of laughter, regaling Luna with tales of how the apprentices had really viewed Hayes. Amara just smiled silently, her eyes meeting Hayes's with both humor and something warmer and more personal. I turned hurriedly away, feeling like an intruder in something private.

"Are you worried?" Renley asked me quietly. "The kingdom is in danger of being split in two, a whole people are blindly walking into the worst kind of subjugation, and you've just volunteered to take an enormous risk on your own, and here they all are—laughing."

I grinned back at him. "Isn't it excellent? How awful it would be if everyone was shuffling around in depression. When I think of everything that has been happening since the moment I got activated..." I shook my head. "Just think what a negative year I might have had if this group of people wasn't able to carry everything lightly!"

"That's the spirit." He smiled. "I know it can take some time to adjust to this crowd, though. I remember my own period of adjustment very clearly. But having a serious air isn't always the mark of those who actually take matters the most seriously when the moment of action comes."

His words reminded me of Clay, who would have been right at home in the center of this moment. Since the first time I'd met him, he had always been smiling and laughing, a cheerful presence in any situation. For the first time I wondered how much of that was his natural personality and how much was a purposeful approach to a life that was often unfair and difficult. When I was as experienced and skilled as him, would I still approach each new moment with the same relaxed good cheer? If not, I hoped I could at least match Renley, who lacked Gia's exuberance but was never a dampening presence. He was like the steady foundation that allowed her wildness to shine.

Gia's stories were still going, but I slipped away from the rest of the group. Descending the stairs, I entered the cold darkness of the stable. The quiet sounds of the horses surrounded me, the occasional swish of a tail, the munching of teeth, or the shifting of hooves. None of them stirred at my arrival, though, and I walked easily down the central aisle, peering into each stall as I passed.

The occasional lantern illuminated some more than others, and when I finally spotted Nik, he was inside Acorn's stall, sitting in near darkness. He looked up, meeting my eyes.

Jumping to his feet, he vaulted over the half door and landed in front of me in the light of the closest lantern.

"You've finished pacing up and down, then?" I asked with a small smile.

He ran a hand through his hair and gave me a rueful smile in return. "You know me too well. I thought I was going to lose my mind cooped up in that tiny room with so many people."

I refrained from pointing out that the rooms we had been given were hardly tiny. Instead I slid my fingers into the hair on either side of his head.

"I could see you were about to lose it in there."

He sighed, leaning his head slightly against my right hand.

"Do you know how many times I've wished you weren't the sort of person who considers the greater good before your own safety?" he asked. "And do you know what I always think next?"

"No, what?" I asked, playing along.

He slipped his hands around my waist. "I remember that I love you for the person you are. So how can I wish for you to turn into someone else?"

I ran my hands down the side of his head, cupping his face in my hands. "If you could take my place in this and go in my stead, would you?"

"In a heartbeat," he said instantly.

I smiled. "In that case, now that we've established we're *both* selfless people—in our own ways—shall we move on to more practical matters?"

"Practical matters?" His eyes had dropped to my lips, and he only seemed to be half listening.

"Yes. Namely, how are we going to infiltrate Miro's law keepers' hall?"

"We?" Nik's eyes sprang back to mine, his full attention restored. "When you say we…"

"You will come with me, won't you?" I asked. "I might be willing to risk myself in a situation as dire as this one, but I'd rather not go in there without any backup."

"Delphine!" He pulled me flush against him and pressed his lips to mine.

I leaned into the kiss, ready to let the rest of the world fade away for as many moments as he wanted. But all too soon he was drawing back, his eyes a little wild.

"Do you really mean it? You want me to come with you?"

I nodded, and he squeezed me close again, burying his face in my hair with a shudder.

"I've been down here trying to work out how to not lose my mind while you were off attempting to take on Grey and his minions on your own."

"I know." I smiled tenderly up at him. "I understand why you don't want me to go, and I also appreciate that you know you can't stop me. But most of all, I want us to do things together." I hesitated, afraid to keep going. "That's the future I want, Nik. Doing things together with you for the rest of my life."

I held his gaze, even as the color drained from his face, his arms going rigid around me. For a long moment we stayed locked there, motionless.

"I wish…" He shuddered again. "There's nothing I want more, Delphine. You know that, don't you?" He sounded desperate. "But I won't turn you into an outcast at my side. I can't do that."

I nodded slowly, fighting back tears. Did he really think it impossible he could return from being a reneger?

Swallowing, I forced a brisker tone. "As I said, we really do need to think about practical matters. It's all well and good for me to say I'm willing to go into the law keepers' hall to confront Miro, but how am I going to get inside? From Hayes's experience, we know they're not just letting people walk in."

"Especially not you," Nik said, relaxing slightly at the change in topic. "Of all of us, you're the one whose face Grey and his followers know best. Most of them still haven't actually seen me, and even Grey himself has only seen me briefly on a couple of occasions, both at night."

"So going in the front door isn't an option," I said. "And I'm guessing any back doors are sealed tight."

Nik let me go, pacing a few steps away and staring into the darkness of an empty stall, clearly thinking.

"If it was just me, I'm confident I could get in," he said. "All the law keepers' halls across Tartora are the same, and I've spent time at two of the ones in the capital. If you can climb up to the higher levels, the design of the windows..." He trailed off as he looked back at me.

"Given your height and all those arm muscles, I'm quite sure you could do it," I said. "Me on the other hand..." I held out my arms and did a spin on the spot. "We're going to need a different plan, I'm afraid."

A sudden throat clearing made us both startle. Nik strode forward to shield me with his body, but it was only the stable master who stepped out of the shadows.

"I wondered who was making a ruckus in my stables," he said gruffly, eyeing us disapprovingly.

I flushed, hoping he had only just come out to investigate and hadn't seen our earlier interactions.

"Apologies," Nik said curtly. "We'll return upstairs."

He took my hand, starting to lead me toward the stairs. But the stable master cleared his throat again, making us stop. A chill ran through me. Had he recognized Nik?

"I might be able to help with that problem of yours." He looked at us expectantly while we stared back at him blankly.

"Problem?" I asked tentatively when he stayed silent.

"Getting into Miro's lair," he said matter-of-factly. "Not you." He eyed Nik's height disapprovingly. "But I could get you in." He nodded at me.

Nik frowned, taking a step toward him. I wasn't sure if he intended the effect to be menacing, but I would have backed away if I'd been the other man. The stable master held his ground, however, looking unbothered.

"Couldn't help overhearing that last bit," he said. "The girl said she couldn't climb in, so seems to me, she'd be better off going through one of the doors."

"We understand they're not allowing people to just walk in anymore," I said cautiously.

"Aye, that's the case," he said. "But some people are allowed in."

I waited, eyebrows raised, and he sighed and continued. "My brother-in-law supplies fresh produce to the hall. He takes a hand cart all the way through to the kitchens and storerooms from what he's described.

"Why would you help us?" Nik asked. "Why would your brother-in-law?"

"I may be an old stable master in Eldrida," the man said, "but that doesn't mean I've never been anywhere else. I've visited the capital more than once. Seen the royal family, even, a number of years ago now."

Nik stiffened, and I gasped.

He gave a raspy chuckle. "I always had a way with faces. Your hair's changed, but your face is the same. And that sister of yours hasn't changed a jot. You can't fault a man for being curious about royalty, renegers, and master mages hiding out in his stable."

"You were listening upstairs?" I asked, mentally scrambling to remember everything we'd said.

He shrugged. "Didn't quite understand everything. This whole mesmerizing business is a mite confusing. But I got the gist, and it explains the strangeness that's been going on here lately."

Nik's stiff, threatening posture hadn't changed, but I placed a restraining hand on his arm, my eyes on the man as he continued.

"Not everyone likes what's been going on in the city," he said. "Ain't no good going to come from cutting ourselves off. And as for Miro and his cronies..." He shook his head. "They might not lie directly to the crowds, but I went to hear them speak myself, and there's no hiding the whiff of deception about them."

I raised an eyebrow. "Did you ever consider a career in law enforcement? Master Anka would be glad to have you." It wasn't surprising he had a healing affinity since he worked with animals, but he clearly had the sort of law keeping talent I'd heard Anka talking about.

The stable master chuckled. "That's a business for young heads like you two. Me, I've always preferred horses to people. They're more straightforward. No need to look for lies with them." He looked me straight in the eyes. "My brother-in-law has an elements affinity, and he's told me more than once that the storm came out of nowhere, and there's nothing the capital could have done about it. We both think this city would be better off without Miro. If you're going to put a stop to his nonsense, we'll do what we can to help you. Including turning a blind eye to this one." He nodded toward Nik.

I relaxed completely. "He's telling the truth."

I smiled at the stable master. It was nice working with another healer, even a weak one. He understood that I wanted to hear him state the situation clearly. After seeing Grey at work, I was becoming all too familiar with the ways people shaped words for deceptive purposes.

"If I get in via the produce cart, you're confident you can get yourself in?" I asked Nik.

He nodded, his expression determined.

"In that case," I said. "We should go talk to the others. I think we have a plan."

CHAPTER

# SEVENTEEN

The stable master's brother-in-law was next due to deliver supplies to the law keepers' hall the following morning, so we didn't have long to debate the details. But considering how much couldn't be known, I preferred it that way. Waiting around would only make me nervous and give more time for Grey to track us down.

When the stable master returned from an early morning visit with his relative and instructed me to come with him, Amara protested. She wanted to accompany us as far as the cart, at least, and Hayes only just managed to convince her to let me go alone.

I could understand her feelings. Hayes, Luna, and I could all sense the truth of the stable master's words, but she had to go on faith. If she wasn't so well-known in Eldrida, I would have been tempted to let her walk with us as far as the brother-in-law. But with her hero status, it wasn't worth the risk.

Nik would have volunteered in her place, of course, but he was already long gone. He had disappeared into the night the moment we agreed on the plan and was hopefully already inside the hall. I had been spending the hours since his departure trying not to picture him discovered and mesmerized by Grey. I could now understand firsthand why he hadn't wanted to be left behind with nothing to do but wait and wonder.

There was enough cool bite in the morning air to justify my wearing a cloak as we walked through the city, and it took all my self-control not to keep tugging the hood down further over my face. Instead I kept my head down as I wound through the streets in the wake of the stable master.

The morning was advanced enough that many other people were also out on various forms of business, and snatches of their conversation drifted past my ears. Some talked of their children or the day's prices for vegetables, but any time anyone mentioned the capital in a disparaging way, my insides clenched a little tighter. Did they really believe the throne and Guild were to blame for their recent woes, or had they already had the misfortune to run into Grey?

The stable master moved at a surprising pace given his age, and we were soon in an unfamiliar part of the city. When a tall, white marble building loomed before us, I jumped and came to a standstill. Staring up at it, I forgot to keep my face covered.

"What are you doing?" The stable master jerked my arm, pulling me back into movement.

I stumbled behind him, my thoughts churning. "Why are we at the law keepers' hall? Aren't you supposed to be taking me to your brother-in-law?"

Suspicious tension flooded my body, although I couldn't make sense of it. There had been no lie in his words when he had repeatedly stated his intentions and our destination. But I couldn't be mistaken in the building either. The law keepers' halls across Tartora had all been built in the same era to the same plans, and I had come to recognize one easily, even despite the similarity they bore to the public hospitals.

"My brother-in-law lives on the other side of the hall," the stable master said. "We'll be meeting him a few streets further on."

"Oh." The possibility was so obvious that I didn't know why I hadn't thought of it immediately. "Of course."

But now that my nervous tension had exploded, I couldn't easily get it to recede. I was practically trembling as we turned down a side street and passed down the side of the hall.

A plain, unembellished door swung open as we approached. I faltered, but the stable master kept moving steadily. I pushed myself back into movement as well, not wanting to draw attention to us, but my pace had slowed to a crawl.

My face was angled downward, keeping my features from view, but I couldn't resist a quick glance upward as two young men exited the building. They were moving slowly despite the air of excitement that clung to their frame and words.

"I thought you were just coming to keep me company," the first said. "I didn't expect you to sign up yourself!"

"How could I not once I heard the situation?" the second exclaimed. "If the capital won't assign us enough law keepers to ensure the city's safety, we have to step up. It's the only right thing to do."

"Won't your master be upset?" the first asked as I drew level with them.

"Mine has already signed on another apprentice. He couldn't afford to keep me on now that I've graduated since he would have to pay me wages and not just room and board. But yours was expecting you to stay and work with him, wasn't he?"

Neither spared me a glance as we passed each other, too absorbed in their conversation, but I caught the shadow of uncertainty cross the second's face. He quickly shrugged it off, however.

"I'm graduated now, just like you, which means I'm free to choose where I work. He has no hold over me. I'm sure when I explain the situation, he'll see that I'm doing this for the good of..." His voice faded as they turned onto the main street.

I looked forward again to find the stable master waiting for me, an impatient look on his face.

"Sorry," I murmured, hurrying to catch up with him.

A sick, churning feeling was growing in my gut. Miro was building a private army of youths, and something—or someone—was swaying them to sign up, despite their previous plans and intentions. I had to stop him before he started sending them off to die.

Nik's parting message echoed in my mind. He had leaned in to press a brief kiss to my lips, despite the presence of the others, and I had been so flustered I had nearly missed his quiet words.

"Protect yourself," he'd whispered, the words fierce. "Don't forget what Hayes told you. Every time you get injured, you're putting your future at risk."

I shivered at the memory, the words more frightening now than they had been then. Because now my mission had a face—two faces—and I couldn't afford to give up, no matter what risks were required.

I was still thinking of the two boys when my guide directed me into a small, fenced yard. A stoic-looking man, some years younger than the stable master, waited for us beside a sturdy hand cart that had been piled high with crates, barrels, and sacks of food.

"About time," he said, and the stable master grunted in reply. "All I have to do is get you in, correct?" he asked me.

I nodded. "Just get me inside the hall. I don't want you getting caught up in this any more than you need to."

The man nodded, looking satisfied with my answer.

I hesitated, clearing my throat. "Could you please—?"

The stable master elbowed the other man, whose frown turned into a look of begrudging understanding.

"I'm not looking for extra trouble, but I've seen the strangeness of things inside that hall for myself. They may all worship that Slate fellow, but I don't want him anywhere near me." He shook himself. "I won't betray you, if that's what you're worried about."

I nodded my thanks for his speaking his assurances out loud, but I couldn't resist questioning him.

"Slate?" I asked.

"That new elements mage Miro is so fond of. From the way everyone talks, you'd think he's keeping things running single-handedly, but I've never seen him lift a finger myself."

Slate. Grey. It had to be. My heart sank at the further confirmation of my theory.

"You'll just need to hop in here," the man said, driving out immediate thoughts of Grey.

"I'm sorry, where?" I asked, sure I must have misunderstood.

"You're a small enough thing, like me brother said. You should fit in," he said, as if climbing into a barrel was a perfectly ordinary thing to do.

"I thought you were just going to throw a blanket over me or something," I said.

"Not if you want to go undiscovered," he said. "I'll be met at the door and escorted to one of the storerooms where I'll receive assistance unloading the cart. You'll just need to sit right and tight until we've all departed. The lid won't be nailed down or anything, so if you give it a firm push, it will pop right off, and you can climb out easy enough. Look, there are even holes that will let the air in."

"An excellent plan." The stable master clapped him on the back, as if proud of his family member's good thinking.

I eyed the barrel dubiously. Although I could think of no solid objection, the idea of being restrained inside the barrel sent a bead of sweat running down my back.

But thought of the young soldier made me straighten. I could do this. I had to do this.

The barrel had already been loaded onto the cart, so I had to clamber up a fair way before I could lower myself into it. Both men offered me steadying hands, however, and the feat proved easier than I'd feared.

It was a harder task to make myself sit down, curling my body to fit the shape of the barrel, but that was due to mental resistance rather than physical difficulty. The brother-in-law had picked a good-sized barrel, and if anything, I would have to worry about flopping around when I was unloaded from the cart.

The lid went on, sending me into near darkness and muffling the sound of the two men exchanging final words. All too soon, however, we lurched into motion, sending me bouncing against one side of the barrel.

I was definitely going to have a problem when I was unloaded. If one of the helpers picked me up, they needed to believe there was grain or pieces of fruit in here, not one large, awkwardly shaped girl.

By the time I was dragged up a ramp and heard greetings being called out, I had finally arranged myself to my satisfaction, my arms and legs braced against the sides of the barrel. I waited, new pricks of sweat breaking out all over me as the cart was pulled through the back corridors of the hall.

When a thump finally sounded and we settled into stillness, my muscles were so tense I thought I was going to burst. I had to continue waiting, however, as the contents toward the back of the cart were unloaded first.

"What about this one, then?" an unfamiliar voice called out just above me.

I held my breath and squeezed my eyes shut, as if that would make a difference.

"That one's apples."

The man beside me grunted in response, the location of the sound suggesting he had squatted down. I strained my limbs against the sides of the barrel, holding myself in position as I was lifted suddenly into the air.

"Oof!" The man exclaimed as I was rocked violently from side to side, barely holding my position. "You really packed them in this time!"

"Only the best for the law keepers' hall," the delivery man responded, making the helper grunt again.

I dropped suddenly downward, barely suppressing a cry of pain as my rear end hit the ground. Tears welled in my eyes as I held another breath, waiting for the sound of footsteps moving away from the barrel.

Finally they came, and I allowed myself to relax, my arms and legs dropping limply. I couldn't relax for long, however. I needed to listen if I wanted to work out when everyone had left the room.

Now that my barrel had been unloaded, it seemed to take forever for them to unload the remaining supplies. But finally I heard the creaking of wheels as the cart was pulled out of the room, followed by a number of clomping feet and dwindling voices.

I remained motionless until I heard the door close, however, and even then, I made myself count to a hundred. When no further sounds reached my ears during that time, I placed both hands against the lid of the barrel.

Pushing upward, I displaced it, carefully keeping hold of the edges rather than letting it fall to the floor with a crash. I wanted to burst out of the barrel at all speed, but I forced myself to move slowly.

As soon as my head was free, I froze and examined the room. It was mostly dark, although some light leaked in from under the door and through the one dusty window in the far wall. But my eyes were already adjusted after the dim inside the barrel, and I quickly ascertained that I was alone.

The moment I reached this conclusion, I clambered the rest of the way out of the barrel, nearly knocking it over in my haste. I caught myself and it just in time, placing it carefully back upright and setting the lid in place.

Stepping back, I examined it and nodded. From the outside, it looked undisturbed.

I crept toward the door, wondering what I would do if I found it locked. Thoughts of a locked door made me think of Nik. He could easily take care of that problem, but where was he now?

He had to be inside the hall, but where had he chosen to hide? I looked over my shoulder, although I knew it was only wishful thinking that he might appear out of the depths of the room. It was better if I thought of myself as alone, anyway. It would make me that much more careful.

Pressing my ear against the door, I checked for silence before even attempting to turn the door handle. To my relief, it responded easily beneath my hand. Apparently the hall's residents trusted their own and didn't feel it necessary to lock away their supplies.

Easing the door open, I slipped out into the empty corridor beyond. I had spent some time in Caltor's law keepers' hall, so I was familiar with the location of the suite of rooms used by the head of the hall. But that did me little good when I didn't know my starting point. I had never had occasion to visit the kitchen or storerooms of Caltor's hall.

I had two options. I could keep my cloak and skulk around, keeping to back corridors and attempting to avoid running into anyone. Or I could leave my cloak behind and walk confidently through the hall, trying to look like I belonged. With the doors barred to outsiders, anyone already inside would be assumed to be a legitimate presence.

Taking a gamble, I folded my cloak and stashed it back inside the storeroom. Forcing my head high, I headed left, moving toward the main part of the hall. Once I reached the more public areas, I would be able to work out where I was and go from there.

The true test came when I heard footsteps. It was too late to change strategy, though, so I kept my pace steady, hiding my hands in my skirts to conceal their trembling.

The approaching people turned out to be servants. The older woman was too busy berating a timid-looking girl to pay me any heed. The girl glanced up as they passed me, a slight wrinkle appearing between her brows. But she quickly cast her eyes back down, making no comment. Even if she questioned my presence, she didn't look like she was going to say anything.

I breathed a little easier as I rounded a corner and left their sight. My spirits lifted even further when I recognized a staircase ahead of me. Hurrying up it, I finally found myself in a familiar corridor. Best of all, I didn't have far to go to reach Miro's office. They must have positioned his rooms so his food wouldn't get cold while it was being brought from the kitchens.

Hurrying down the corridor, I almost didn't hear the footsteps approaching from a side hallway. There was more than one pair of feet, by the sound of it, although they weren't moving in sync.

"Excuse me!" a strident male voice called. "Who are you?"

I froze, the blood draining from my face. But when I looked around, no one had come into sight. Both sets of footsteps had stopped, however, and I realized the man was addressing an unseen person in the side corridor.

Creeping forward, I peered around the corner to see an astonished-looking girl with a duster in her hand.

"I'm one of the maids," she said with a confused look.

The young man confronting her frowned deeply, clearly trying to look more important and officious than his years suggested.

"I don't recognize you."

The girl rolled her eyes. "I didn't realize new maids were brought to you for inspection before starting work."

The man bristled, clearly not appreciating her tone.

"Unapproved people are not permitted to wander the law keepers' hall," he said pompously. "If you are who you say you are, I'm sure you'll have no problem coming with me to—"

The girl put her hands on her hips and glared at him. "Of course I have a problem with it! We're behind work for the morning as it is. If you have an issue, you can go on your own."

The man swelled with wrath, his eyes bulging, but before he could say anything, another woman appeared from a side room.

"Where are—oh." She gave the man an unimpressed look. "It's you. I should have guessed. Stop harassing the new maid and let her get back to her work, or I'll have to report you again."

The young man drew himself up to his full height, but he couldn't entirely hide his chagrin.

"It is the duty of all law keepers to question the presence of anyone who might not belong in the hall," he said. "I was merely doing my duty."

"Well go do your duty on someone else's time," the woman said tartly. "I've had enough of your nonsense."

The girl with the duster laughed and hurried into the room behind the other woman, leaving the young guard sputtering alone in the corridor. I whisked my head back around the corner, my heart racing.

He was clearly the last person I wanted to run into, even before he'd been embarrassed and enraged by the two women. If he caught sight of me, there would be no one to shield me from his pompous meddling, and I might actually find myself dragged off to whatever authority figure he'd been intending to appeal to.

I glanced around wildly, my eyes landing on the smooth door used for storage closets. Prying up the ring that lay recessed in the wood, I pulled the door open and propelled myself inside, gently closing the door behind me.

It was nearly pitch-black inside, but I ignored the closet's contents, my attention on the door as the sound of the man's footsteps resumed. My breaths kept pace with his steps while my heart raced wildly ahead, pattering away as if I was already in his clutches.

Thank goodness he'd been held up in the other corridor, and I'd had the chance to see who I was dealing with. If I hadn't hidden myself away—

My thoughts cut off as the speed of his steps changed. Surely it was coincidence he was slowing down so near my hiding place. There was no way he could have seen me from around the corner.

"Why am I being asked to fetch supplies?" The indignant mutter reached my ears through the wood of the door. "It's a waste of a soldier and an insult to my dignity. If they knew what they were doing, they wouldn't—"

The door swung open, and the law keeper cut off mid-sentence. Taken by surprise, we both stood frozen, staring at each other.

CHAPTER

# EIGHTEEN

"What...?" the guard spluttered, his eyes roaming over the closet behind me. "Why are you in here in the dark?" A suspicious look descended over his face, and he lunged for me.

I moved at the same time, making a grab for his wrist. He was obviously inexperienced because he hadn't even considered the possibility I might be a healer. By the time he realized what I was doing, I had already latched onto the exposed skin.

For half a second, I considered the option of mesmerizing him. All I had to do was convince him he'd seen me cleaning the hall previously, and the problem would be solved without harm to anyone.

But before the temptation could properly set in, I rejected it. During the weeks I had spent purging the minds of the islanders one by one, I had made myself a promise. I was never mesmerizing anyone again, no matter what the reason. Reaching into someone's mind by force was a line that should never be crossed, no matter what.

If I decided it was all right to do it now in order to save lives, where did the argument end? Would I one day find myself enthralling my children to keep them away from any possible dangers?

But even without mesmerization, I was still a healer. As soon as I made contact, I pushed my power into his body. With only a small effort, I could easily end his life or even leave him permanently incapacitated. But this guard, no matter how officious, was not my enemy.

Instead of harming him, I used my power to put him to sleep. His eyes drifted closed mid protest, and he slumped forward onto me. I staggered back into a row of shelving, only just managing to catch him under his arms.

Struggling with his weight in the small space, I managed to get him down onto the floor and then onto his back. His legs sprawled out into the corridor, however, where they would draw the attention of anyone walking by. Leaping over him, I propped both of his knees up, but his legs immediately flopped back down.

I stepped back and considered the problem, my eyes landing on the door. Closing it part way, I wedged his feet against the wood so that as I pushed it closed, his feet moved back as well, pushing his knees up into a steeper angle.

I barely managed to get the door latched, stepping back with a sigh of relief. I had no time to waste, though. He might wake at any moment, and he would instantly raise the alarm when he did. I had to find Miro immediately.

Abandoning subtlety, I took off down the corridor at a sprint. When I tried to stop outside a door with an elaborate handle, I was moving so fast that I continued to slide forward. Spinning, I leaped back toward the door and pulled it roughly open.

Gasping for breath, I stumbled inside the room, pulling the door closed behind me. For a blank moment, I thought I'd come to the wrong place. The dark wood desk I had expected to see was nowhere in sight. Instead, an enormous, carved wooden chair with a high back and thick arms stood on the far side of the room. A row of simpler chairs ran down the room to the left and right, creating a space that felt far more like an audience chamber than an office. Even more shocking was the change from the familiar red carpet and curtains I had grown used to in Anka's office. In Eldrida, they had been replaced with a deep purple—a shade whose use was forbidden beyond the royal family and Royal Mage.

I gasped. If we hadn't already guessed Miro's intentions, the room clearly announced them. Its very brazenness took my breath away. How far had his plotting already progressed?

"And who might you be?" The oily voice, amused rather than shocked, made me spin toward the row of tall windows.

A middle-aged man stood in one of the windows, holding a document to the light. A second, younger man stood with him, but I recognized with sweeping relief that it wasn't Grey. The assistant stared at me with his mouth open, displaying all the surprise the older man lacked.

"Are you Miro, the head of this hall?" I asked boldly.

Both men raised their eyebrows at my impudence.

"I am," the older man said, still amused. "Do you have a grievance to bring to the law keepers?"

The younger man bristled. "If so, there are proper avenues! You can't come bursting in here."

I ignored him, my eyes on Miro. "I come with a warning."

"How fascinating." Miro looked me up and down as if I were some sort of unique specimen, briefly interesting but ultimately unimportant.

I edged slowly closer, eyeing the assistant. He looked like an administrator, not a soldier, but I didn't want to discover my mistake too late. It might be safer to put him to sleep before I attempted to make contact with Miro.

"I'll go and fetch someone," the man muttered to Miro who still hadn't looked away from me.

He started toward the door. I waited until he passed closest to me before lunging for him. He exclaimed, trying to evade me, but I was quicker. Thrusting my hand at his face, I made contact with his skin and put him straight to sleep.

He slumped to the ground so quickly that I barely managed to catch him before his head hit the ground. Laying him down, I immediately rushed back toward Miro, spurred on by the distant sounds of shouts and running feet. The guard in the closet must have woken up.

"You're more resourceful than I expected," Miro said.

"What—? No, never mind." I shook my head.

There was no point trying to have a conversation with him before I purged his mind. When I was finished, we could talk properly, without hurry, since he could call off the approaching guards.

I expected him to try to evade me when I reached for him, but he allowed me to take his wrist without protest. Brushing aside the strangeness of it, I pushed my power into him and called up his wall.

As it pushed my power out, I fell back physically as well, panting as I looked at him with wide eyes. He continued to look back at me with the same disquieting smile. I waited a breath and then another, ready for the look of confusion and horror to overtake him. Nothing happened.

"Slate said we didn't need to go looking for you, that you would come to us," he said conversationally. "But I didn't entirely believe him."

"What?" I asked, my thoughts stuttering at his unexpected reaction. "Don't you see? Slate is Grey, and he's been lying to you this whole time. We call it mesmerizing, and it's the reason you've been doing all this."

I gestured around at the transformed room, my breath coming heavily as I tried to make sense of what was happening.

"I'm not sure whether to be flattered at your belief in my loyalty or offended that you think I'm a mindless follower." His eyes narrowed. "I can certainly see how you might be useful, however. There's always value in an insurance policy. I wonder..." He tapped his chin thoughtfully, breaking off when the door to the room was wrenched open.

The man who walked in was clearly unwelcome, given Miro's startled, unhappy expression. His irritation was quickly swallowed by a welcoming smile, but his true feelings had been visible long enough for Grey to smile knowingly.

"Not quite ready to see me?" he asked mockingly. "However useful she may appear to be, Miro, she's not worth the risk. Take my word on that. Or has she already gotten to you?"

His mocking look made Miro straighten, his face turning cold.

"Of course not. I'm not such an easy target."

"Naturally not. My mistake." Grey bowed slightly, but in a negligent way that robbed the movement of any respect.

I stood motionless, staring across the room at Grey. I had thought my theories so clever, but I had made a terrible, fatal mistake. I had said we didn't know how many lies Grey had forced into Miro for him to choose this path, but it had never occurred to me that the number might be zero.

# CHAPTER
# NINETEEN

"You really are an appealing tool, Delphine," Grey said conversationally. "You have more value than all my other followers put together. Such a pity." He strolled closer but carefully stopped outside of touching distance.

I glared at him, my hands balling into fists at my side. "I am not a tool to be used at whim by others!"

"Yes, that is precisely the problem," he agreed, but even as he said it, there was a hungry look in his eyes.

"It rankles, doesn't it?" I poured every ounce of disdain and superiority I could into the words. "We both started out with a special skill, but I was able to learn yours and you could never learn mine. It must gall you to know you aren't the strongest person in this room."

Grey scoffed, but something unpleasant flashed in his eyes. Even so, he didn't step closer.

"Smart, strong, and beautiful," he said softly. "Are there any limits to what we could have achieved together? I think not. But you won't find me an easy target now. No matter how much you goad my pride, I'm too wily to offer you a contest." He flicked his arm, briefly exposing a flash of skin along his wrist while he watched me with a knowing smile.

My lips tightened, flattening into a thin line. I had walked straight into their trap, and now there was no easy way out. Everything had depended on Miro waking up from his enthrallment and turning on Grey in betrayed wrath.

Fear clawed at my throat, making it hard to breathe. But I couldn't give in to it now. If I was going to survive, I had to keep all my wits about me.

"An impasse, then?" I asked calmly, proud of my voice for not shaking.

"Oh, I hardly think that." Grey inclined his head toward the open door and two guards stepped into the room, determined looks on their faces.

Miro might not be mesmerized, but I would have been willing to bet these two were from the fanatical gleam in their eyes.

"You're really all right with this?" I asked Miro, desperation making my voice harsh. "You have no problem with Grey mesmerizing your people, as long as you get to sit on a pretty throne?" I glanced derisively at the elaborate seat.

"And why wouldn't I be?" he asked. "Marius's line is unworthy of the Tartoran throne—the Triumvirate themselves gave that ruling."

The slightest twitch of movement in one of the floor length curtains caught my attention. I kept my gaze on Miro, my heart somehow beating even harder as a terrible possibility occurred to me.

He was still talking, although I was barely listening.

"The Triumvirate's problem is that they're cowards!" he declared, working himself into a rant. "They recognized the problem, but they're too weak to look further afield than a cousin. I will never be given the recognition I deserve in Tartora, so why shouldn't I take something they don't even value and make it great? Who in the rest of the kingdom even values the east?"

The two guards nodded, as if they found this slightly unhinged spiel inspiring.

I flinched, the desire to look toward the curtain almost mastering me.

"I don't know how you escaped Ignatius," Grey murmured. "But I should warn you that I'm much more thorough than my cousin."

"Ignatius is dead," I said baldly. "Along with your entire family. The island is free of the lot of you now. Only the Constantines who actually cared are left."

Something flashed in his eyes, some glimmer of distant surprise and grief, but he shrugged it off quickly. "So poor, outcast Costas is on his own, is he?"

"Far from it," I said. "His mother is with him."

"Aunt Isolde?" Grey stared at me, his face blank for a moment before he shrugged and smiled again.

"The island is no longer my concern. I have a larger prize in mind now."

The guards behind him drew their swords, distracting me from Grey's face.

"Don't worry," he continued. "They've been trained how to deal with healers. It really hasn't been a pleasure, Delphine."

With one final mocking smile, he disappeared out the door, leaving a clear path for his guards to reach me. I backed up, putting myself closer to Miro, but he called out in a panicked voice and several more guards ran into the room, rushing to form a protective ring around him. His assistant had also woken and stood to join the guards, shaking his head as if to clear his groggy thoughts.

As Grey's guards advanced toward me, I pulled out the knife at my belt. It wouldn't do much good against their longer blades, but I wanted to go down fighting, at least. The feel of the hilt in my hand recalled the memory of when Nik gave the knife to me. I should have kissed him then. I wished I had. I wished I hadn't let any of our moments together slip away.

The curtains on the side of the room swung dramatically aside, and Nik lunged into the room as if pulled out by my thoughts. I dropped instinctively to the ground, curling into a ball as he leaped straight over me to meet the blades of my attackers with his own.

Miro gave a startled cry, and the guards surrounding him rushed forward to support the two now facing Nik. But Nik fought with a ferocity I'd never seen, his blade moving too fast to follow. Even so, his skill alone wouldn't have been enough against so many opponents. But Nik had more ways to fight than with a sword.

The chairs from the two rows shuddered into movement, their wood creaking as it responded to the pull of Nik's power. They rose into the air before flying across the room in every direction, exploding spectacularly into spears of wood as they collided with walls and people.

The guards shouted, some abandoning their weapons to shield their heads, while others went down, hit by one of the chairs. The two who had come in with Grey kept their focus, however. Ducking and weaving through the chaos, they closed in on Nik as he retreated toward the throne—the only chair not to have moved.

I looked around, wondering how I could help, and my eyes latched onto Miro. His earlier assurance had vanished completely, beads of sweat appearing along his brow. Inching along the wall, he was attempting to reach the door and escape the fighting.

Narrowing my eyes, I crawled across the floor, keeping below the smashed pieces of wood shooting across the room. Grey had already escaped, but I wasn't letting Miro get away as well.

He let out a sigh as he reached the door, pausing briefly to glance back over his shoulder at the chaos he was escaping. The brief pause gave me just long enough to reach him.

Stretching out my arm, my fingers latched around his ankle, burrowing until they found skin. He shrieked and tried to pull his leg free, but the effort only sent him toppling sideways.

I clung on as he fell hard, most of his body outside in the corridor. Dragged forward by my arm, my muscles strained to maintain contact as I sent my power spearing into him.

He stopped fighting instantly, his body relaxing into the ground as sleep took him. I took a deep breath and crawled forward to sit on his chest. The pounding of feet preceded the arrival of another column of running guards.

I grabbed Miro's floppy arm and held it aloft, my fingers curled obviously around his skin.

"I'm a healer!" I shouted in my loudest voice, and they all froze.

The men inside were Grey's people, and they wouldn't stop to protect Miro, but these were ordinary law keepers trained to respect their head of hall.

"Who are you?" called the captain at the front of the line.

"I'm an agent of the crown," I said, thinking on my feet. "And I'm arresting Miro on charges of treason against Tartora."

"And if we don't recognize your authority?" the captain asked in a hard voice.

"Are you a healer?" I asked, taking a gamble based on his rank.

He hesitated before nodding curtly.

"Then you can see the truth of my words. Any of the rest of you who are healers should listen closely too. You've been lied to, manipulated, and tricked by Miro and the man you call Slate."

The law keepers in the corridor shifted, looking at each other warily.

"You can't trust the thoughts in your head or even your own memories," I said.

"What are you saying?" the captain asked, but the tone of his voice had changed, a look of horror creeping into his eyes.

I focused on him. "From the look on your face, you've heard the official warnings from Tarona about the healer Grey."

The captain slowly nodded.

"Slate is Grey," I said. "And Miro knows it."

"Impossible." The man's voice sounded dry. "Slate is an elements mage."

"Tell me," I said. "Did you see evidence of that before you touched him for the first time? If your only memories are from after that time, they may be false ones, created by your mind to support his mesmerized lies."

"Captain," said one of the men tentatively. "What's she talking about? Everything she's saying has the ring of truth, but it doesn't make any sense. What's this about mesmerizing?"

As I had suspected, only those of sufficient rank had been included in the official warning from the capital. The king must be worried about creating mass panic if the story of Grey's powers spread freely across the kingdom.

"I can see you believe your own words," the captain said. "But that doesn't make them true."

A jagged spear of wood that had once been the leg of a chair flew through the open door behind me. Several of the law keepers dodged, only just avoiding it before it hit the wall of the corridor with enough force to damage the stone.

The men craned to see over each other's shoulders, all attempting to peer at the heated battle happening inside the room. I desperately wanted to look back myself, but I knew I couldn't afford the distraction. If Grey's guards were still locked in battle with Nik, they must have strong abilities of their own, and my best chance of helping him lay with the men in front of me.

A loud crash sounded behind me, and the knuckles on the hand holding Miro's arm went white as I fought to keep my focus.

"If you'll let me make contact with you, I'll prove it," I told the captain, desperate enough to take the risk of revealing my secret. "I have the ability to purge Grey's lies."

The captain hesitated, his eyes flashing from the unconscious Miro, to the battle behind me, to the men watching him with wide eyes.

"I swear I will do nothing but purge your mind of the lies," I said, knowing he would see the truth in my words. "I swear I will not harm you or use my power for any other purpose." Extending the risk even further, I added, "If you'll let me do this, I'll hand Miro over into your charge. If I'm proved right, I trust you'll arrest him yourself. If I'm wrong, he'll be free."

When he still hesitated, I put my whole heart into my eyes. "Have you ever been to the capital, captain?"

He blinked at the unexpected question and nodded. "Five years ago."

"Did you see the royal family?"

He nodded again.

"Then look into that room and tell me who's fighting Miro and Slate's men right now."

For a silent moment, the captain stared into the room, and I allowed myself a quick glance as well. Nik had leaped on top of the throne chair, using the higher ground it afforded as he held off multiple attackers, a haze of increasingly small wood shards whirling around him.

The captain swallowed, looking back at me with wide eyes.

"Very well," he said hoarsely.

A couple of the men behind him called out protests, but he ignored them, holding my eyes as he moved forward and held out his arm.

Using my free hand, I lightly brushed my fingers against his. Reaching into him, I called up his natural wall. His eyes widened as it sprang to life, driving my power out before it and Grey's lies along with it.

He fell back a step, breaking the remaining physical contact between us. One of his men stepped forward to steady him, glaring at me suspiciously.

"Captain! Are you all right?"

"Yes, I'm..." He cleared his throat. "I'm fine. It's...I don't..." He looked at me, and I looked back sympathetically.

"I've experienced it myself," I whispered. "I was once fooled by Grey as well."

He shook his head, a wild look in his eyes that felt all too familiar. He couldn't be putting more blame on himself for falling prey to Grey than I had when I first realized the truth.

"It's true," he said in a loud voice. "We've been deceived."

"Please." I stood, letting go of Miro. "Help the prince."

A murmur passed down the line of law keepers when I mentioned Nik's rank. The captain nodded grimly, gesturing for the men behind him to come forward and calling out orders as he did so.

"Wait!" I said. "Let me help them too."

I didn't stop for more debate. Reaching for the first bit of exposed skin I could see, I called up the wall of the person it belonged to. He gasped, jumping away from me, but I was already done. Reaching for the next person, I did it again and again. Several of them grabbed me back, but as soon as I'd purged their minds, they let me go, crying out in surprise.

Moving along the line, I reached for the next person only to realize there was no one left—at least for now. Turning back, I saw Miro awake and on his feet. He was spluttering and protesting, but both of his arms were gripped in firm holds, and from the careful placement of skin on skin, I guessed his captors were both healers. However strong his elements ability, Miro had little chance of breaking free from two determined healers who already had him in their grip.

"Nik," I murmured, running toward the door of the destroyed room.

When I stepped over the threshold, my feet crunched on wooden splinters. The debris littered the entire floor, heaviest around the throne which had somehow been split cleanly down the middle.

No more wood flew through the air, though, and the only upright figures I could see in the room were the captain and his men from the corridor.

"Nik!" I called more loudly, dashing into the room and spinning to try to see in all directions. "Nik!"

The captain looked up from where he knelt over a prone, blood-stained figure, and my heart nearly stopped. But as I raced toward them, I recognized the weak beat of a heart in the patient he was busy healing, and two steps later, I saw his face. It was one of the guards who had been attacking Nik.

I stopped, spinning again, as I peered through the people milling around. There! I caught a flash and then a second one as someone moved again.

Nik.

I raced to the broken throne, falling to my knees in front of Nik. He sat on a raised section of marble floor, his elbows on his knees and his head in his hands. His naked sword lay across his lap, and he was panting, his body streaked in dirt and blood.

"Nik," I said softly, and he looked up at the sound of my voice.

I took his face in my hands, sending my power searching through his body. A cut on his side was easily healed, although another on his arm was more serious. It still took me less than a minute to deal with it, and my heart lightened along with his expression as he responded to the healing.

"Well done." He nodded toward the guards who were busy arresting his opponents. "You got through to them, I see."

"I was so worried," I sobbed.

He carefully placed his sword on the ground before pulling me forward into an engulfing embrace.

"I'm not so easily defeated," he said, eliciting a watery chuckle.

"I see that now." I wiped at my face although I was likely only smearing it with dirt along with the tears.

"What about Grey?" Nik asked, and I stiffened.

"He was gone long before I got out of the room," I said, unable to believe I'd forgotten about him even for a moment.

Nik stood, pulling me up with him.

"We need to find him." He looked dangerous, the fire in his eyes only emphasized by the grime that streaked his face. "I'm not letting him escape this time."

# CHAPTER
# TWENTY

I tugged him over to the captain who had just completed his healing and risen.

"Do you have any idea where we can find Grey...I mean Slate?" I asked.

The captain frowned. "I know where his office is, but will he still be there?" He looked doubtfully around the wreckage.

"He left before this started," I said. "He might not know what's going on."

Shouts and running feet from outside the room's door made me wince. We'd created enough commotion to rouse the whole hall, so it seemed unlikely Grey wouldn't have realized something had gone awry.

We followed the captain down the hall, anyway. He stopped outside a much plainer door, gesturing silently at it before holding up one finger. One person inside. I could feel their presence too.

I exchanged a look with Nik. He shrugged and flung the door open, striding inside with his drawn sword in hand.

I followed so close on his heels, I nearly tripped over. The first thing I noticed was the size of the room, followed by the opulence of its decor, which seemed a mismatch with the plainness of the door.

But as soon as I caught sight of the man inside, all thoughts of the room itself fled. We had cornered him at last.

He had clearly been on his way from the large desk to the door. Apparently he had noticed the commotion outside, but not quickly enough to escape. Once again, his confidence had betrayed him.

His eyes widened as he took in not only my presence, but also Nik's. However, he recovered quickly and adopted a nonchalant pose.

"Perhaps I didn't give Ignatius enough credit," he said lightly, nodding in my direction.

I narrowed my eyes, and he chuckled, but he couldn't quite regain his earlier confidence. Grey had always known how to exude charm, but now there was an off-putting tension lurking behind his manner.

"I have followed you from one end of this kingdom to another, and even beyond its shores," Nik said. "It ends here."

"I had no idea I'd attracted such illustrious attention," Grey said in an attempt at his normal style, but he looked shaken.

At the beginning, Nik had kept to the shadows in his pursuit of Grey, and I was guessing Grey had been unaware of just how long Nik had been tracking him.

Grey's eyes swept past us to fasten on our companion, his expression growing stern. "I'm surprised to see you here, Captain. You should have put an end to this nonsense by now."

The captain met his gaze calmly, but I could feel the rage simmering underneath. "I'm in the process of putting an end to the nonsense going on in this hall. And it's to my shame I let it go on so long."

Grey's eyes widened, his heartbeat quickening. He was facing two healers, so no amount of acting could hide his underlying fear.

When his calculating gaze shifted to me, his eyes narrowed. I looked back, calm and sure, and he looked again at the captain.

Grey still didn't know about my new skill, so how did he account for the change in the captain? Did he think I had put my own mesmerizations over the top of his?

When he looked at me again, I was sure of it. And I saw something else in his face too. Grey had always surrounded himself with others, finding and exploiting their weaknesses while charming them in the process.

But now his followers had all been stripped away. He was facing us alone, and he no longer loomed larger than life. He looked small and pathetic, an empty shell of a man—all charm and no substance. Even with physical touch, I was now beyond his reach. Grey was weaponless, and he now seemed nothing but weak. Was he the villain we had feared for so long?

The fear I had felt of him drained away, replaced with nothing but contempt and beneath it a swelling sadness. Grey once had a mother who loved him, but he had rejected that love in favor of position and wealth, and now he was left alone with no one who knew his true self, let alone cared about him. It wasn't a life I would live for all the luxury in the world.

My emotions must have shown on my face because Grey's features twisted as he watched me, fury overcoming his polished mask.

In two long strides, he reached me, seizing me around the waist and pulling me tight against him. His other hand cupped one side of my neck, and I pulled up my wall. But he made no attempt to push his power into me, instead leaning over to whisper in my ear.

"You think you've won," he hissed, "but you haven't. You'll see. I've given you a gift you can't give back. You think you have the world right now, but you're the final successor in an illustrious line, and you should ask yourself what's happened to everyone else before you."

"Don't touch her!" Strong hands ripped Grey off me.

"No!" I cried, leaping after him, my hands reaching unthinkingly to pull Grey back. It was one thing for him to threaten me, but he couldn't be allowed to touch Nik.

Grey snarled, twisting nimbly out of the hold Nik had on the back of his jacket. I threw myself forward, convinced he was going for Nik's skin. Latching onto his closest wrist, I took a second to check my wall was in place before pushing my power into Grey. I should have put him to sleep while we had contact earlier, but I'd been distracted and thrown off balance by his words. I would rectify my mistake now.

But Grey pulled back so violently that he ripped his arm from my determined grip. His face had twisted into an expression I had never seen on him before—pure, unalleviated terror. He thought I was going to kill him, and he was ready to fight like a cornered rat.

I leaped after him, expecting him to retreat again, but instead he remained frozen in place. As my fingers circled his wrist again, I looked up at his face in confusion.

He was staring straight ahead, his expression frozen and eyes wide as if taken completely by surprise. I wanted to ask what had happened, but it wasn't a time for calm conversations. It was time to stop the fighting.

I pushed my power into him, but it smashed immediately into an immovable wall. I gasped, trying again and finding the same thing. Now I knew the reason for Grey's shock.

He had finally managed to make a wall of his own. All this time he had tried without success, and it had finally happened now, in the worst possible moment. I growled in frustration, and he grinned. The light that had been missing from his eyes earlier returned. He had thought himself cornered—even his backup plan in ashes around his feet—but now he had fresh motivation and hope.

I let go of his wrist and fell back a step, thrown off by the change. His unexpected discovery had galvanized him, whereas I felt paralyzed and confused at finding us back on equal footing.

As he looked at me, his eyes narrowed, and then he stooped. It took me too long to realize he was reaching for the knife in his boot. By the time I understood what he was doing, he was already lunging at me, his teeth bared and face locked into a grimace.

The blade flashed in my eyes, the steel sharp and the edge jagged. *I've been here before*, I thought numbly, bracing for the ripping pain.

But a body collided with me, pushing me onto the floor. Nik grunted as I heard the sickening sound of a blade plunging into a body.

I screamed, scrambling up. Running to his side, I grabbed one of his hands.

"What were you thinking?" I cried, tears running down my face as I saw his features twisted with pain.

"Had to...be...me," he panted. "You can't...have...more healings."

"And what about you?" I demanded as I sent my power into him. "How many have you had?"

He didn't answer, turning his face away. I tried to twist to see his expression, but my attention was caught by the flash of light on metal. Distracted by his wound, I'd forgotten all about our attacker.

Once again a blade was plunging through the air in my direction, but this time Grey's eyes were on Nik, his target the man next to me.

I lunged forward, my range limited since I was on my knees. I made it just far enough to grip his arm. Straining, I held it in place, hovering above Nik's torso.

He pushed downward, trying to put more force into the thrust, and I felt my resistance slipping. I was off balance, stretched as far as I could reach and unable to gain better traction.

Movement in my outer vision was the only warning before the captain yanked Grey back, pulling him away from Nik. I was still clamped onto his arm, however, so the sudden movement dragged me with him.

The two of us went down in a tangled heap. Grey had stopped pushing, but the momentum of my counter push remained. It thrust his arm back toward his own chest, my weight twisting it as we both collapsed.

When we landed with a thud, I was on top of him, the hilt of the knife digging into me. I scrambled off, grateful it had been the hilt, not the blade. But as soon as I was free, I realized I had been the only one to be so fortunate.

Grey stared back at me, his eyes wide as his hands clutched the hilt sticking out of his chest. He opened his mouth, but no sound came out. Instead a second groan from behind me made me spin back toward Nik. Grey was a healer. He could deal with the mess he had created.

Nik was in the process of pushing himself up to sitting, groaning all the way.

"Stop!" I cried. "I didn't finish the healing."

I pressed my hands against him again, sending my power toward his injuries. I took my time, making sure everything was fully healed before finally withdrawing.

When I had finished, I turned on Grey in fury. But the emotion faded instantly at the sight waiting for me.

Grey still lay where I had left him. He was utterly motionless, his hands still wrapped around the hilt of his dagger.

"But...what..." I tentatively touched the back of his hand, but it only confirmed what my power was already telling me. There was no heartbeat and no breathing rasped in and out. "He's...dead?" I stared blankly up at the captain. "But he's a healer! Why didn't he heal himself?"

"The blade pierced his heart," the captain said. "He was unconscious within seconds."

Nik slowly stood, coming forward to stand beside me. He gazed down at Grey, his face unreadable.

"You didn't help him," he said to the captain. "Aren't you a healer, too?"

A reddish tinge rose up the man's cheeks, but he held his ground, meeting Nik's eyes.

"I have a strong seed, but only non-mage level. Healing a wound like that is beyond me." He rubbed the back of his head. "To tell the truth, I thought he was healing himself at first. I didn't even realize he'd lost consciousness initially."

"So we just left him to die," I said softly, trying to process the thought.

"It wasn't as if we did it intentionally," Nik said firmly, pulling me to his side. "He brought this end on himself."

"On that we agree," the captain said. "And given his crimes, he would have been facing execution in the capital anyway."

"Still..." I rubbed my hand. "As healers, we are sworn to offer healing to all."

"And you did," the captain said. "A royal prince had been stabbed by a murderous traitor, and you were busy healing him. No one could fault you."

Nik squeezed me tighter.

"Is he really dead?" I whispered.

It was hard to fathom. He had been a specter hanging over my apprenticeship from before it even began. With Grey gone, I felt lighter than I could remember in a long time.

But a kernel of heaviness remained within. I had purged Grey's lies from my head, but his final words haunted me. He had left one part of himself in me—the knowledge of how to mesmerize. And there was nothing I could do to purge those memories.

I tried not to think about the other part of what he'd said. It didn't matter what had happened to the Constantines. I wasn't like them. I didn't seek to control anyone, and I would never use the skill again. I was done with mesmerizing forever, and with Grey gone, Tartora was also free of its insidious influence.

"Are you all right?" Nik asked, looking down at me with concern.

I shook myself and managed a wobbly smile.

"We're finally free of him. Right?"

"We are." Nik turned into me, wrapping his second arm around me as well.

I buried my face in his chest and wished I felt more comforted.

CHAPTER

# TWENTY-ONE

Even with the captain's help, it took time to sort out the chaos at the law keepers' hall. And, like on the island, I once again had to go through every single person connected to the hall to purge any mesmerizations Grey had left behind.

The captain agreed to take temporary charge of the hall until the capital could appoint a new head, and I suspected the king would be sending a whole team to straighten out the messy situation.

"Don't worry," Gia said when she caught me looking concerned. "It sounds like Grey stayed almost exclusively inside the hall. I guess he was worried about being identified if he ventured out into the city. So we only need to track those who came into the hall. And there's no need for you to stay here after you've freed the initial group. We can reassure the Eldridans that you're willing to travel back if they find more people in need of your assistance."

"Are we leaving soon?" I asked, and she nodded eagerly.

"We need to get to the capital as soon as possible to give them a comprehensive report. The unrest in Eldrida is advanced enough that they need to pay serious attention to the city."

"Attention?" I asked tentatively.

"Not like that!" She looked amused. "The last thing Father will want is to sow more unrest. He'll be looking to reassure the easterners that the rest of the kingdom values them. You can expect lots of resources to be sent east in the near future."

While I was relieved at her words, I didn't know how to tell her that my concern hadn't been over the possibility of needing to stay in Eldrida. It was going to the capital that worried me. My old prejudices against both the capital and the Guild were long gone, but the reality was far scarier.

"My parents must be very eager to meet you." Gia's eyes shone as she beamed at me.

Little did she know she had just made my fear worse.

"Do...do you think so?" I asked, trying not to sound as nervous as I felt.

"Of course! You're a valuable asset to the kingdom, you know! As the only person who can free people from Grey's mesmerizations, you've done Tartora a great service. Even though all the mesmerizers are now dead, there's still people left who've been mesmerized."

I stared at her, my mind skimming through our past conversations. It didn't take long to realize that no one had ever told Gia about Grey teaching me to mesmerize. She—and probably the rest of Tartora as well—thought the skill was gone. What would the king and queen think when they learned the truth?

"Plus, of course, they're parents too, not just king and queen." Gia gave me a sly look. "And you're the girl who brought their missing son back to them—the girl he loves. Of course, they'll want to meet you as soon as possible!"

A sick feeling started in my stomach. Gia seemed to have a very rosy view of a situation that was far from simple. Nik might have agreed to accompany us to the capital, but that didn't mean he was back to stay. He was still a reneger.

He clearly didn't feel Gia's optimism about his return given his avoidance of the topic. Even when we tried to discuss plans for the journey itself, he found a reason to excuse himself. I began to grow worried, finally catching him alone when I visited Acorn's stall and discovered him already there.

"You're not planning on backing out, are you?" I asked. "You did promise you'd come."

"And I'll keep my promise, of course," he said.

"Are you worried about seeing your parents again?" I asked softly.

He leaned one shoulder against the edge of the stall, looking down at his feet.

"So much has happened since the last time I saw them." He sighed. "When I left the capital, it was in a fit of anger. Part of me never wanted to see any of them again, and the other part thought I would prove them all wrong and return home in a blaze of glory. I dreamed of having my place reinstated and to hear everyone acknowledge they were wrong about me."

He shook his head. "I thought myself all grown up, but it was a childish fantasy. I can see that now."

I placed a hand on his arm. "You wanted them to change, but you were the one whose attitude changed instead. Of course there's some awkwardness. There's no shame in it, though. You were a child back then—legally speaking at least—and now you're grown up. Surely growth is natural."

He looked up and smiled at me. "You make it sound so normal and straightforward."

"Not quite that, perhaps." I tipped my head to the side, examining his face. "Acknowledging you were in the wrong doesn't mean saying they were entirely in the right, either. It just means maturing enough to recognize there were two sides to the situation. I think your parents will be proud of the man you've become. And even if it isn't the blaze of glory you dreamed of, you have done a great service to the kingdom."

He pulled me against him, resting his chin lightly on the top of my head. "Except you were the one who did it all, Delphine."

I laughed awkwardly, wondering if he'd picked up on my own nerves about going to the capital.

"I couldn't have done any of it without you," I said. "I wouldn't have survived long enough!"

He drew in a long breath. "I'm just glad that's all behind us. I never want to see anyone threatening your life ever again. It's happened far too often already."

"Don't worry." My arms wrapped around his waist and squeezed tightly. "I don't think I'm likely to meet another Grey."

"Thank goodness for that."

I tried to pull away, conscious of everything we still had to do before leaving Eldrida the next morning. He tightened his grip, though, holding me in place.

"Can we stay like this—just for another minute?" he asked.

I settled back against him with a happy sigh. "If it was up to me, we could stay like this forever."

***

Carriages and teams of horses were provided for our journey to the capital, and we were even given priority for the barge crossing. It was the most physically comfortable journey I'd ever made, but my nerves only strung tighter the closer we got.

Normally Nik would have been the first to notice, but I took extra care to hide it from him since I didn't want to feed into his concerns.

Amara took me aside to check in on me, but there was nothing she could do to ease this particular anxiety.

"There's no denying you've had a tempestuous romance," she said with a sigh. "And I can't promise there will only be smooth sailing ahead." She gazed at me, a thoughtful look on her face. "But I'll do the best I can to ease your way."

I gave her a surprised look, but she only smiled.

"I am your master after all. I should do at least that much for my apprentice."

Although she'd only spoken in generalities, her words comforted me somewhat. I was still only halfway through my apprenticeship, and no matter what else happened, I would still have Amara for a year yet. She had always managed to sort out every situation we'd encountered, so maybe she could somehow sort this one out too.

But when we entered the streets of Tarona, my tension started growing again. As the wheels rolled over the cobblestones, I peered out the window at a city far larger than any I'd visited so far. By the time we arrived at the stone wall surrounding the palace, my churning stomach was making me wish I hadn't eaten lunch.

Large gates opened for us, and we entered an enormous courtyard. I had expected to alight in front of the palace, but to my surprise the horseshoe building in front of us wasn't the largest of the structures within the walls. The towers and turrets of the palace loomed on our left, but the building in front of us was separate although built from the same gray stone.

"Welcome to the Tartoran Mages' Guild." Amara quirked one eyebrow, a slight smile on her face as she watched my reaction. "Does it meet your expectations?"

I gazed in some astonishment at the formal garden beds in the middle of the boxy horseshoe. The effect—which could have been grand—was broken by the occasional section of riotous growth and a sprinkling of odd-looking fountains.

Amara followed my gaze, nodding toward one of the areas where the garden was completely overgrown. "The work of the plants apprentices, of course."

It made sense, but something about it didn't fit the pretentious, image-focused concept I'd always had of the mages and the Guild.

"I don't know what to make of this place," I said at last. "But why are we here instead of the palace?"

The driver of the closest carriage peered down at us. "I thought you were all mages? Aren't you reporting to the Guild?"

I glanced at the other two carriages as everyone climbed out. Obviously he hadn't recognized the prince and princess.

"The Guild is fine," Amara said, and the man smiled in relief.

Whether because of the driver's mistake, or because our exact arrival time was unknown, there was no welcome party to greet us. I suspected it wouldn't be long before one arrived, however.

"What do you think of it?" Nik asked in a low voice from behind me, making me start.

I twisted to see his face, taking in the tight lines of his body and his set expression.

"It's very impressive," I said. "I can't imagine growing up in a home like this."

His eyes grew distant as he gazed across at the castle's towers. I wished I knew what childhood memories were running through his head.

"You can do this," I said in a low voice, gripping his closest arm. "You can do this, Nik."

His eyes dropped to mine, their expression softening as he slowly refocused.

"Of course he can!" Gia bounced over and grabbed him by the other arm. "It doesn't matter how you left. Mother and Father are going to be delighted to see you, Nik."

Looking at the gleam in her eyes, he relaxed further, snorting. "I can see through you, you know. You're planning to take all the credit for bringing me back."

"Of course!" she said with a mischievous grin. "I have to gain points wherever I can since I'm the daughter who turned her back on their legacy, married a foreigner, and spends her days flitting around other kingdoms."

"You know," Nik said thoughtfully, "when you put it like that, I don't seem like such a bad son after all."

"Which is just what I've been telling you!" Gia tugged on his arm, and I quickly dropped my hold on the other one.

As Nik let his sister drag him toward the palace, I watched them go with a slight smile. His sister knew how to ease this particular fear better than me, and she was the appropriate one to be by his side for this reunion. I would have my chance to meet the king and queen soon enough—too soon for my liking. I had no place in the first meeting between parents and son.

The rest of the group followed behind the royal siblings, moving toward the palace at a slower pace. I didn't move, however.

Amara glanced back and frowned when she saw me still motionless beside the carriage. When she gestured for me to catch up, I hurried to do so. But as soon as I reached her, I tugged on her sleeve, pulling her to a stop.

"I know Gia said her parents will want to meet me, but I want to give Nik space to reunite with them first without the complication of my presence."

She examined my face, as if looking to see whether my words were just an excuse to put off meeting the king and queen. After a moment, she nodded slowly.

"That's reasonable enough. Hayes and I need to consult with the Triumvirate immediately, and I'm sure they'll be eager to meet you once they've heard our report. But as an apprentice, we can't include you in the initial meeting."

She glanced uncertainly from the Guild building to the palace. "Luna has already run off to find her Guild friends, I see, but I'm sure there's somewhere you could wait in the palace. Or if you prefer, I could find out which suite will be assigned to us. The Guild keeps suites for the use of visiting masters, so you could—"

"Actually, I'd like to go out and visit the city." I glanced back toward the gates. "It's my first time in Tarona, and I don't know how much opportunity I'll have to explore the actual city."

Amara raised her eyebrows. "I suppose you can do that if you wish. But don't be gone for more than an hour or two."

"You're not worried about me?" I asked, surprised at her easy acquiescence.

She chuckled. "Tarona is a large city, but it's also home to most of the kingdom's mages. Even the criminals know better than to judge someone's strength by their outside appearance." She nodded at Phoenix, who sat on my shoulder as usual. "One glance at that fine fellow, and they'll know you're more than you appear."

I smiled, her words bolstering my confidence. Hayes had noticed her disappearance and stopped for her, so she left quickly. Given their serious expressions, I was glad not to be joining them in their upcoming meeting.

I still felt some trepidation stepping out of the Guild gates, but it wasn't about being alone in the city. Ember had even roused herself from her day's sleep, so I had two companions with me as I set off across the cobblestones.

My sense of anxious expectation came from my true purpose in exploring the city. I had family in Tarona—family I'd never met. It was time to remedy that situation.

I knew Amara, Luna, and Nik would all have gladly helped me if I asked. Even Hayes would have lent his assistance. But just as Nik needed to meet his parents on his own, this was something I needed to do by myself.

My uncle's trip to Tarona, and subsequent desertion of my father, had been one of the major shaping forces of my life. I might not know him personally, but his actions had affected me deeply. And even now, my father was back on our farm hurting because of what his brother had done. I needed to meet my uncle and ask why he never came back.

Since my uncle's strength had been just short of mage level, he wouldn't be found at the Guild or among the courtiers. But with a seed like that, he had to be in one of the nicer areas of the city. Unfortunately, I didn't know where those areas might be.

Since I had nowhere else to start, I asked the guards at the gates for directions to the central market. It turned out there wasn't only one market in such a large city, and they gave me directions to three of them. When I asked which one serviced the nicer areas of the city, they directed me to the closest of the three.

It didn't take long to reach it, and when I walked into the square, I almost forgot my purpose for being there. The rich scent of spices and cooking meat overlaid the bright buzz of the well-dressed crowd. Everywhere I looked, my eyes landed on fine fabrics and sumptuous wares.

I didn't dare touch anything, but wandering among the stalls admiring the goods for sale was entertaining enough. I couldn't let myself get distracted for long, though, not when Amara had given me a time limit.

"Excuse me," I said to a stall keeper whose display of leather goods was momentarily free of customers. "I'm newly arrived in Tarona and looking for my uncle. His name is Olan, and he has a plants affinity. I think he lives in this neighborhood. He might be a customer of yours?"

The woman listened politely before shaking her head with an apologetic expression. "I can't say I know an Olan."

I hesitated, disappointed, although in a city this large it was silly to expect the first person I questioned to know him.

"Have you had a stall at this market for long?" I asked.

She chuckled. "More years than you've been alive, I'm guessing." She eyed Phoenix on my shoulder with interest, her gaze dropping to the tell-tale color difference between his legs. "You're a healer, then? Did you train him yourself? I like what you've done with the shoulder of your dress. It's a convenient way to carry him in a crowd like this. But if you have need of leather gauntlets, you won't find any better quality than mine. All the palace and Guild falconers buy from me," she finished proudly.

"I can see their quality just by looking," I said, eyeing off the two pairs I could see displayed. "But unfortunately I don't have time for shopping today. Hopefully I can have a closer look next time I'm in the market."

The woman accepted my words with enough good humor that I resolved to do my best to come back at the earliest opportunity. Now that I was at the Guild, I was hoping to speak to some of the healing affinity's falconers and get some tips on caring for Phoenix. Quality gloves would no doubt prove helpful.

As I moved down the line of stalls, choosing ones free of customers to approach with my query, I was received with a range of attitudes. But whether gruff, surly, chatty, suspicious, or friendly, every one of them disavowed any knowledge of someone with my uncle's name and a plants affinity. And when I finally found someone who knew an Olan, further questioning established the man in question was barely older than me.

I was about to give up and head back to the palace when a hand pulled softly on my sleeve. I turned to find a small slip of a girl, at least five years younger than me, staring at me with shrewd eyes.

"I heard you asking around the market. You're looking for your uncle?"

"Yes, do you know him?" I couldn't help my voice quickening with eagerness. "His name is Olan."

"And he has a plants seed? Aye, I heard." The girl hoisted a large, wrapped bundle over her shoulder. "If you're wondering about trusting me, ask any of them." She jerked her thumb over her shoulder down the line of stalls and lifted her chin defiantly. "Any of them can tell you. I run errands for anyone who needs it round the market, and I'm known for being the most reliable."

A younger boy ran past in time to hear her remark, slowing enough to call a heckling challenge in her direction. He didn't stop completely, however, and was lost in the crowd as the girl pretended not to have heard him.

"So you actually know an Olan of the right age who has a plants affinity?" I asked, eager for a proper answer. "He would be coming up to five decades by now."

"Aye, I know one. But he don't live in this neighborhood. Likes to talk about his seed, though." She sniffed as if something about that behavior was unpleasant.

"Can you take me to him?" I asked, making a split-second decision. I was supposed to be heading back to the palace soon, but I couldn't let this opportunity slip away. If there was any chance this girl could take me to my uncle, I couldn't walk away now.

"That depends," she said.

"On what?" I asked warily.

"On if you can pay. I'm not trying to cheat you," she added defensively. "Anyone can tell you it's one coin to take goods or a message across town." She looked me up and down. "You're not exactly either, but I'll apply the same rates."

"Very well, then." I smiled at her. "I'll give payment when we reach this Olan."

The girl narrowed her eyes before making up her mind and giving a decisive nod. I was almost glad she'd asked for a coin. It made me less wary that she had some nefarious motive.

"Ember," I called, and the fox appeared out of the crowd.

The girl started, looking uneasily from Ember to Phoenix.

"How many of them creatures do you have following you around?"

I chuckled as I picked Ember up. "Only two. We're all here now and ready to go."

The girl turned without another word and led the way out of the square. I followed a few steps behind, keeping half my attention on her and half on the rest of my surroundings. But nothing suspicious appeared, and no one else appeared to be tailing us.

The girl didn't speak to me other than to give me a disparaging look when I offered to take a turn carrying her bundle. I didn't make the mistake of offering again, and we remained silent across half the city.

At least it felt like half the city. I had no actual way to measure our progress and would have been well past lost without my guide. If this Olan wasn't the right one, then I would have to pay the girl another coin to guide me back to the palace. If he was my uncle, I would have to trust in his good-will to show me the way back.

But as the houses around us grew more and more shabby, I finally spoke.

"Are you sure this is the right area?" I tried not to let the extent of my unease show in my voice.

"Nearly there," the girl puffed over her shoulder, switching her load to the other side. "And course I'm sure. His youngest attends classes with me in the morning."

I fell silent at this mention of cousins. I had always assumed they likely existed, but I had never expected to meet them.

"Here we are." She stopped in front of a tall, narrow building in a long row of buildings. This particular one appeared to be leaning against the one beside it, and I eyed its upper stories with concern.

"Don't worry," the girl said with a snort. "You're lucky. He's on the bottom."

She rapped loudly on the door, calling through the wood as she did so.

"Patti! Patti! There's someone here to see your Da."

When we heard shuffling from inside, she stepped back, looking satisfied.

The door swung open, revealing a middle-aged man. I gasped, my fingers digging tightly enough into Ember that she protested.

I relaxed my grip, my mind catching up with itself. This wasn't my father, no matter how much he resembled him.

Now that the initial shock had passed, I could see the small differences. There was no doubt about his identity, however. I looked from my uncle to the decrepit house on the rundown street and then back at my uncle.

This might be my Uncle Olan, but nothing else about the situation made sense.

# TWENTY-TWO

My uncle was still gaping at me, looking as astonished as I felt.

"She was asking all around the high market, trying to find someone as knew you," my guide said, nodding in my direction.

The man's face flinched at the mention of the market. Was he aware that he wasn't where he was supposed to be?

"Looking for me?" he said slowly, still regarding me with an expression of shock. "You're...you're Osan's daughter, aren't you?"

I nodded. Apparently my uncle wasn't the only one who resembled my father.

"That'll be one coin." My guide held out a hand.

I tore my eyes from my uncle to deliver the promised payment. "Thank you very much," I said with warmth. "I appreciate your help more than I can say."

The girl tucked the coin away. "Always happy to do business with them that can pay."

She nodded once at my uncle before disappearing up the street. I turned slowly back to the open door.

"What are you doing here?" my uncle asked after a painful silence. "Wait." He rubbed the back of his head. "I should ask your name first."

"I'm Delphine."

"Have you just graduated?" he asked, taking a guess at my age. "And come to the capital looking for work? If you thought I could help you, I'm afraid—"

"No," I said quickly. "I'm still an apprentice."

"An apprentice?" His brows drew together, and he took a step backward, retreating through the doorway. "You've not gone reneger!"

"No, no!" I shook my head emphatically, grimacing at how poorly the conversation was going. "Of course not. I apprenticed to a traveling master, and since our travels brought us here, I wanted to find…"

I trailed off at the expression on his face.

"Did you say a traveling *master*? You just mean that she's your master, I suppose?"

I shifted, realizing my mistake. "Ah, no, she's a master elements mage. Her name is Amara."

He gave a low whistle. "So Osan's daughter has a mage level seed—strong enough to attract the attention of a master, at that. So our family line did have it in us." I detected faint traces of an old resentment.

"I thought you had a strong seed yourself." My eyes narrowed. "At least that's how my father told it."

I ran my eyes up the unstable building, letting all my questions show on my face.

My uncle sighed, his face falling. "I suppose you'd better come in. My youngest is here, but my wife and sons are out at the moment."

I turned my head to murmur to Phoenix. "You wait out here. I'll be back out soon." I shrugged my shoulder slightly, indicating for him to take off.

He did so, his wing sweeping against me as he launched himself skyward. It looked like a small home, and I didn't want him cooped inside.

"How many sons do you have?" I asked as I followed my uncle into a narrow, dimly lit hallway.

"Three," he said. "My oldest two are twins and would be a little younger than you. They're about ready for activation. In fact, my wife is out talking to a potential master for one of them now."

"What's his affinity?" I asked, trying to wrap my mind around a whole collection of cousins I hadn't known existed.

"Plants, like me."

"You don't want to take him on yourself?" I asked as we reached a living space at the back of the house.

A girl of around twelve looked up curiously. Her eyes jumped from my face to Ember in my arms. She rose to her feet.

"Father doesn't want any of us stuck being builders like him. But who are you?"

"A builder?" I looked at my uncle in surprise. Construction was usually done by those with a plants ability due to their connection with both wood and stone, but I'd always imagined my uncle working with living plants.

He cleared his throat uncomfortably, ignoring my question to answer his daughter's instead.

"This is your cousin, Delphine. Delphine, this is my youngest, Patti."

"Cousin?" Patti's eyes grew even rounder. "Why didn't I know I had a cousin?"

"Because I didn't know myself," Uncle Olan said. "She's from Tarin. My brother's daughter."

"You have a brother still in Tarin?" From Patti's expression, it was clear my uncle hadn't told his children much about his history.

"Yes, my father still lives there on the family farm," I said.

"Family farm?" Patti stared at her father. "There's a family farm?"

"Uncle Olan and Father were supposed to run it together, after Uncle Olan finished his apprenticeship in Tarona. But he never came back." I tried to keep any accusation out of my voice, but it was impossible to do so completely.

"Father, what is she talking about?" Patti asked, a sharp edge to her words.

My uncle cleared his throat again. "I'm sure Osan was glad to see the back of me. He must have a bevy of children to assist him now." He looked at me for confirmation.

"Actually, it's just me." I held his gaze. "And now even I'm gone, as you can see. My father has suffered greatly from your absence."

"He's alone on the farm? Does that mean he needs extra help? Would he still want Father now?" Patti asked eagerly, taking a step closer to me.

"Hush, Patti!" Uncle Olan said sharply. "Don't talk nonsense."

I regarded them both with a creased brow. My uncle clearly felt ashamed of what he'd done, but he wasn't owning to his betrayal. I glanced around the room at the worn and sagging furniture. He certainly wasn't living the life of luxury imagined by my father.

"What happened to you?" I asked softly. "My father always thought… Well, he didn't picture your life like this."

"Reality rarely lives up to our expectations," my uncle said.

"But your seed—"

"Was strong, yes. At least by Tarin's standards. But potential doesn't always equate to success. Osan and I thought we'd saved up a vast sum, but it wasn't as much as we thought. I arrived in Tarona full of hope, but finding a master to take me on and activate me didn't prove as easy as I'd expected." His face assumed an expression so much like my father that I flinched.

"I had neither wealth, connections, charm, or experience to recommend me," he continued. "If I'd been strong enough to become a mage, it might have been a different story."

I shifted uncomfortably, remembering his earlier reaction, but he continued on without commenting on my status.

"In the end, I had no choice but to accept an apprenticeship with a builder, which was not what we'd planned. The experience I gained wouldn't be much use on the farm, but at least I would be activated and could return home once I graduated. Except after I was activated, I discovered my new master had misled me about his strength. The potential of my seed became meaningless once my power was capped at the strength of my influencer."

"Did you report him?" I asked, outraged.

He sighed. "He hadn't made any concrete promises or assurances I could point to—certainly nothing in writing. I was young, naïve, and desperate, without parents or community to guide me, so I was easily fooled. I had already used all my coin by that stage while searching for an apprenticeship, so I had to find a master quickly."

"How awful," I said softly, imagining what it must have been like for him alone in this big city. "But you were only bound to him for two years. Why didn't you go home as soon as you graduated?"

He grimaced. "That had been my plan. But unfortunately my master was a poor businessman as well as weak. He could barely afford to keep an apprentice, and there was certainly no coin left over to share with me. I needed to save enough to cover the journey home, but I couldn't start doing that until I graduated and found proper employment. It took me a while to accomplish that, and by then I'd met my wife."

"After that I suppose it was the twins," I said quietly. "You had more mouths to feed, which would have made it even harder to save. And the journey itself would have become more difficult and expensive as well. I suppose I can see how it happened. But why did you never write to my father, at least? He had no idea what had happened to you—he still doesn't!"

"Yes, I can see I should...ahem...I should have done that."

He wouldn't meet my eyes, and I could read the truth on his face. He had been the strong one—the one with the promise of a great future. But that future had failed to materialize, and he had been too embarrassed to own up to his true situation. Better for his brother to think him dead or absconded with their money than for him to know the truth.

I shook my head at the breathtaking selfishness of that attitude. I wanted to let go of my restraint and understanding and spew out a torrent of recrimination. His useless pride had nearly destroyed my life.

But I kept my mouth closed. This man might be related to me by blood, but we were currently strangers. I wasn't ready to tell him the most painful details of my past—perhaps I never would be. And there was nothing to be gained from recriminations. It might make me feel better in the moment, but the effect would be short. Nothing I could say now would change the past or the effect it had wreaked in my life.

I looked around the room again. My uncle hadn't traded his and my father's youthful dreams for a better life. He was already living the consequences of his choices every day. He didn't need punishment from me.

My uncle's eyes finally settled back on me. "Is your master good to you? You said she's a traveling master—where does that leave you when you graduate?" The concern in his eyes seemed genuine, burning away some of my earlier anger.

"My life is proof that a strong ability doesn't always lead to success," he continued. "You need to make decisions about your future carefully. I know it's too late to change masters, but you should make some connections while you're here in the capital, if you can."

A small smile tugged at my mouth as I thought of Hayes, Clay, Anka, and Luna—and then of Gia and finally Nik. Little did my uncle realize, but Amara's traveling lifestyle had allowed me to make many high-ranking connections already.

But imagining his reaction if I told him about my traveling companions kept my mouth shut. It would only complicate matters to tell him about my connection with the royals.

"Thank you," I said instead. "I'll keep that in mind."

He nodded, relaxing a little.

"And...is he well?" he asked tentatively. "Your father, I mean?"

"He was when I left. I haven't seen him in a year, though."

An unexpected surge of nostalgia caught me off guard. After everything that had happened, I actually wanted to see my father again.

From the wistful look on my uncle's face, I guessed he felt the same.

"I have a little coin of my own," I said slowly. "Not with me, but I could bring some to you later. You could send him a message—even go to see him yourself. I don't know if he would welcome you at first, but I think he would want to see you."

My uncle winced, clearly unsure about his potential reception.

"Go to Tarin? To our family's farm?" Patti gripped her father's arm with both hands. "Oh could we, Da? Could we? Please let us go!"

I watched her with bemusement. She was a number of years away from activation, but on a whim I reached out to test her. She had a plants seed of medium non-mage strength. Had she lived her whole life in this row of buildings? No wonder the idea of a farm was so appealing to her.

"Do all three of your sons have plants seeds like Patti?" I asked.

Both of them turned to me with expressions of mild surprise.

"Oh, I don't think I said, I'm a healer."

"A mage level healer?" My uncle's eyebrows shot up. "That must have been a surprise for my brother."

"It was a great shock for all of us," I said dryly.

"Will you really help us go to the farm, cousin?" Patti asked. "Could we stay there forever?"

"Patti," her father said warningly.

"I don't know," I told her. "That would depend on my parents. But—" I hesitated. "I'm never going back there to live. So they're going to need help from someone."

"Oh, Father, please may we go?" she begged.

The sound of the front door opening presaged a stream of new arrivals. A middle-aged woman was the first to appear, followed by three tall lads. All four of them stopped as soon as they reached the back room, regarding me with astonishment.

My uncle seemed to forget me for a moment, however, his eyes focused on his wife. "Did he agree to…?" His question trailed off at the sad shake of her head.

"Never mind that!" Patti exclaimed. "This is our cousin Delphine. She's a healing mage!"

"Actually I'm still an apprentice," I said uncomfortably as the new arrivals stared at me with even greater astonishment.

"And!" Patti added with increased enthusiasm. "She's been telling us about Da's family farm back in Tarin. She said we can go there!"

"I can help you pay for a visit at least," I said hurriedly. "Whether you can stay would be up to my parents."

The three boys remained silent, but their eyes lit up with the same light showing on Patti's face. Their mother turned to her husband.

"Your parents' farm? Could we really…?"

"Apparently my brother only ever had Delphine, and she's not sure she wants to live there," he said slowly.

"Actually, I'm quite sure I don't," I said firmly.

My uncle had bid me think about my future, and that was one thing I was sure on at least. But neither did I want to follow his advice and make connections in the capital with a view to settling at the Guild. It had only been a few hours, but I already felt the weight of the large city pressing on me. I missed the freedom of life on the road where I could focus on helping people instead of worrying about what impression I would make at court.

When my apprenticeship ended, would Amara be willing to let me continue on as her companion? We worked well as a team since we had different affinities and could cover different needs in the towns and cities we visited.

"Let me properly introduce you all," my uncle said. "This is—"

But before he could say the first name, the latch on the front door popped off, falling to the floor with a thud. The door was thrust forcibly open, bouncing off the opposite wall.

People poured into the cramped building, rushing down the hallway toward us. Patti screamed, two of the boys shouted, and the room became a chaotic muddle of movement and noise.

I remained frozen in place. The stream of arrivals were dressed in the blue and gold uniform of the royal guard, but I couldn't think what they were doing in my uncle's house.

Ember growled, going stiff in my arms. Her muscles tensed, as if she meant to leap down and attack the intruders, but I shushed her. In this chaos, she would only get stepped on. And if she did manage to bite someone, it might get my uncle into further trouble.

But the guards showed no interest in my uncle. They herded all of the house's residents against one wall with stern instructions to remain still. Only I was left in the center of the room, the remaining guards forming a wary circle around me.

Slowly it dawned on me that the guards weren't here for my uncle. They were here for me. Had Nik been worried about my safety and sent them out looking for me?

"You are Delphine, the healing apprentice of Master Amara?" the lieutenant asked formally.

I nodded, mystified.

He stepped forward, his stern expression not quite managing to mask what looked like nerves.

"In that case, you're under arrest. You need to come with us."

CHAPTER

# TWENTY-THREE

**M**y uncle and his family all gasped, but I was too shocked to pay them any attention.

"Under arrest? Me?"

"You will remain silent!" the lieutenant commanded, a line of sweat breaking out on his brow.

I stared at him, trying to make sense of what was happening. Scanning the rest of his men, I could see no familiar faces. What was going on?

The lieutenant indicated two of his men. They looked even more uncomfortable than him as they stepped forward to grip one of my upper arms each.

When I didn't resist, a third guard tried to remove Ember from my grasp. She snarled and snapped at him, and he whisked his hand away, looking to the lieutenant.

After a brief hesitation, the lieutenant indicated for him to leave Ember with me. I held the fox even tighter as the guards hustled me toward the hall.

Before they had me fully out of the room, however, I dug in my heels and stopped, twisting to look backward. The sudden resistance took them by surprise, and I managed to pull part way free of their hold.

"Go to Amara!" I said, my eyes on my uncle. "At the Guild. Tell her who you are and ask her to give you my coin. You have to go to Tarin and tell my parents—"

"Enough!" The lieutenant's shout cut across my words, silencing me.

The two guards recovered their hold, gripping me more tightly this time, and I was marched awkwardly up the hall. I managed one last look back over my shoulder at my astonished family who were still pressed against their living room wall.

Outside, a covered wooden cart awaited us. I was half thrust, half lifted into the back. The movement dislodged Ember who landed on her feet inside the cart, disappearing unnoticed into the shadows at the back.

Heavy gloves were placed over my hands before they were bound behind my back, and I noticed that the guards all wore gloves of their own. Other than their faces, they didn't have an inch of skin showing anywhere.

When I tried to ask what was going on, they all reacted violently, one of them shoving a heavy gag into my mouth. I made no attempt to resist since it seemed pointless. Even if I could get free from so many guards, where would I go? They were already taking me to the one place I wanted to go—the palace where Amara and Nik were currently located.

But when we arrived in the palace courtyard, there was no sign of either of them. The handful of servants and officials who were moving in and out of the palace and surrounding buildings all stopped to stare at me, but no one offered assistance.

The guards dragged me roughly off the back of the cart and hustled me through a side door and down a set of stairs hewn from stone. I could barely catch my breath with the gag blocking my mouth, and it was hard to see past the tears.

What sort of misunderstanding had sent the guards after me in such an intense manner? If they had just asked me to accompany them back to the palace, I would have come willingly.

Unbidden, Grey's final words came into my mind. I tried to push them away, but they took root, blossoming and growing along with the fear in my belly.

A clanking sounded as yet another guard opened the metal bars of a cell door. When they tried to thrust me inside, I struggled, wriggling from side to side and making garbled, muffled exclamations.

Once again they all reacted out of proportion to my actions, but when I twisted far enough to catch the eye of the lieutenant and thrust out my bound hands, he hesitated. Glancing at the others, he shrugged and removed my bonds.

As soon as the final knot came loose, I was shoved into the cell. Losing my footing, I sprawled across the straw-covered floor. I didn't bother to get back to my feet, merely rolling onto my back and ripping off the gloves. With them gone, I reached up and pulled off the strip of material holding my gag in place. The second I spat it out, I began coughing, sucking in deep lungfuls of air. The gag hadn't actually blocked my airways, but I had been fighting my panicked mind the entire time, trying to reassure it of that fact.

A distant shout made me sit up just in time to see a streak of orange slip through the bars of my cell. Despite everything, I smiled. I wasn't alone.

Climbing slowly to my feet, I picked up Ember and held her close, taking comfort from her warm presence. The cell door had been locked, and no one was in sight. Across from my cell was nothing but a stone wall. I pressed myself against the bars, trying to peer back down the corridor toward the stairs, wanting to see if I was truly alone.

I wasn't.

Sitting in a chair at the bottom of the stairs was a man. He wasn't dressed in the blue and gold livery of a servant or royal guard, and he didn't carry himself like one either. Even from this distance, I could see the quality of his clothes—far finer than a mere servant—and sense the indefinable air of power that hung around him. Even his age seemed too advanced for a guard. And yet he was clearly guarding the row of cells. Why?

He saw me watching and nodded, an unexpected courtesy in the setting. When I opened my mouth to call out to him, though, he shook his head sharply, his eyes conveying a warning. Remembering the gag, I snapped my mouth shut. There was no point talking if he didn't want to hear what I had to say, and I didn't want to end up gagged again. Neither did I want to bring more trouble on myself when I didn't even know what original crime I had committed.

Had the royal family been offended that I had gone into the city instead of coming straight to meet them? It was impossible to imagine they would react in such an exaggerated manner over an issue of etiquette.

Did they blame me for killing Grey, however unintentionally? Perhaps they had intended to question him after his capture and were angry to have missed the opportunity?

I stayed at the bars, waiting to see what would happen, but as the hours ticked by, I couldn't maintain a state of alert. At first I had thought my imprisonment a temporary measure and expected someone to arrive to speak to me at any moment. But no one came.

The old man remained in his seat as the hours wore on, and eventually I stretched out on the single, lumpy mattress that lay on the cell floor. Ember curled beside me, and thanks to her familiar presence, I even managed to doze, exhausted from the travel. But when the sound of an opening door echoed down the cells, I flew back to my feet, rushing to the bars.

But the person who came through the door wasn't an incensed Nik or outraged Amara. A man in the livery of a servant handed the old man on the chair a tray of food and immediately withdrew. The man carefully removed one bowl and plate from the tray before carrying the rest down the corridor in my direction.

"Stand back," he ordered in a deep voice that commanded instant obedience. "I'll only give you one warning."

I scrambled away from the cell door, snatching up a growling Ember as I went. I stared at him as he deposited the tray on the ground just inside the cell.

"What's going on?" I asked. "Why am I—?"

"You will remain silent!" he said in the same commanding tones, cutting across my question. But as he relocked the cell door, he relaxed a little, apparently caught in a moment of compassion.

"We have all been forbidden from speaking to you. But try to have patience. All will be explained in time."

I stayed frozen in place away from the door, hoping for more, but he simply sighed and strode off back down the corridor. I rushed to the bars in time to see him take his seat and pick up the bowl and plate he had left for himself.

Seeing him eat the same food I had been left gave me enough reassurance to consume the surprisingly appetizing meal on the tray. But I still monitored my body closely for hours afterward, watching for any sign I had ingested something unsavory.

Eventually, however, I found myself wishing there might be something secreted in my food. At least driving out the poison would have provided some alleviation from the boredom. Ember alone kept me sane, and I wished Phoenix could have been with us as well. For his sake, I was glad he wasn't, though. The falcon would have hated being restrained for so long without enough space to take flight.

My cell didn't afford any glimpse of outside light, but the regular meal deliveries kept track of the passing hours. Between the food and the two long stretches of slumber from the man in the chair—both punctuated by loud snores—I guessed I had been imprisoned for two days before something new happened.

I spent those days thinking longingly of Nik, Amara, and my other friends and brooding over Grey and his final words, which now felt like a curse over me. Had he known this would happen?

Gia had been convinced her parents would be pleased to meet me, but she hadn't known all the facts. We had never told her that with Grey gone, I was the only one left who could do mesmerizations.

Gia might not have known, but Amara and Hayes had obviously reported the full truth to the Triumvirate, and they would certainly have told the king. Once again, I had been recklessly sure of myself, only to find Grey had been one step ahead, even in death.

My thoughts ran in horrible circles, making it hard to sleep, so I jumped at any opportunity for variety, however small. The opening door had become familiar at mealtimes, but it had been only an hour since the last delivery when it opened again.

I immediately raced to the bars.

When I saw who was standing at the top of the stairs, I almost fainted with relief. Amara had finally arrived.

"I'm here to see my apprentice." She looked wrathful, commanding, and powerful, and my heart lifted just at the sight of her.

The man heaved himself to his feet, and I held my breath. Would he give way before her or attack—even if only with words? He did neither, however, instead sighing sadly.

"No one is permitted to speak to her."

"What sort of ridiculousness is that?" Amara snapped. "She needs physical touch to influence someone's mind. You might not be a healer, but don't pretend you don't know—"

"Their Majesties are not willing to take any chances." The man sighed again. "I know you're biased toward her. She's your apprentice, so of course you are. But you yourself reported that she has exceptional skill at using her power from a distance—more so than many master mages."

Amara snorted. "Yes, she's skilled in that area, but that doesn't mean her power can operate inside someone without physical touch. She's still a regular healer!"

"I'm sorry," he said simply.

Amara drew herself up, fury sparking in her eyes. "Delphine is my apprentice and therefore a member of this Guild! Does that really mean nothing, Master Drake?"

I stifled a gasp. Master Drake? The man on constant watch outside my cell was the Master of the Elements?

I shook my head. One of the affinity heads and a member of the Triumvirate had been on full-time guard duty outside my cell. For the first time, I realized just how dangerous they thought I was.

When Master Drake remained silent, Amara continued on. "She's done nothing wrong! We owe her our protection."

"Do you think I don't know it?" Drake spoke in a heavy voice. "It has been weighing on me the whole time I've been stationed here. But we cannot deny the very real danger—not just to the throne or the Guild but to the whole kingdom. You know what just two of those Constantines did to us."

Amara's shoulders slumped. Seeing her give in made me grip the bars until my knuckles turned white. I pressed myself against them, reaching out with one hand.

"Amara!" I shouted.

She jerked and turned, staring at me with wide eyes. It was obvious from their reactions that neither of them had realized I was hovering there, listening. Her weight shifted, as if she meant to rush toward me despite Master Drake's earlier prohibition.

But he moved to place himself in her way, his face growing stern. He no longer looked tired or old but instead full of the same inexorable strength as the tide.

"You cannot," he said.

For a moment Amara met his eyes defiantly, and then she deflated, her shoulders slumping for a second time. Tears pricked at my eyes.

I couldn't blame her, though. Master Drake might be old, but that only meant he had great skill and control. He was the master of her own affinity, and she couldn't possibly fight him.

Was this, then, why he had been placed here? Not to guard against me, but to block those who might try to reach me? My pulse quickened at the idea of who else might try to force entry, but Master Drake continued talking, distracting me.

"Delphine is safe in here for now," he said softly. "If you're concerned for her, expend your efforts where they'll be more useful."

Amara paused for a moment, her eyes measuring his, before she nodded once. She grew tall again, her usual straight bearing returning.

"You are right, of course."

She met my eyes over his shoulder and mouthed a silent apology. I nodded, waiting until she'd turned away to dash the tears from my eyes.

I had just slept, but I felt exhausted in the wake of her brief visit, tossed around on waves of conflicting emotion. Their final words had burrowed into my head, taking up residence there and replaying over and over. The Master of the Elements had issued no overt threat, but I couldn't shake the feeling that there had been danger hinted in his words. The implication that my future safety was in question. What battle had he sent Amara off to fight on my behalf?

And stronger even than my fear about myself was another thought, the one that had come to me earlier. Ever since my arrest, I had been thinking that no one knew where I was. But Amara had found me. And if Amara found me, then she couldn't be the only one who knew where I was. And if *he* knew...

The longing to see Nik was so intense it took my breath away. Every time I heard new footsteps, my heart leaped, sure it was him. Once he knew where I was, he would come.

But even stronger than the longing was my anxiety about what would happen when he did. Over and over, I silently told him not to come, wishing there was a way for him to receive the message. Wishing he would listen if he did.

Because when Nik came and Master Drake denied him entry, he wouldn't accept it and leave quietly like Amara. Nik would bring down the walls of this prison before he would allow me to remain imprisoned here without charge, trial, or crime.

It was true he had changed, but in some ways he remained the same. Never for a second did I doubt that Nik would throw his full strength into fighting to free me. And he had plenty of strength to fight with. Nik could literally rip out the stones keeping me here.

But he had never finished his training. Master Drake had decades more experience, as well as a host of guards to back him up. If it came to a fight, I feared for Nik. He wouldn't harm his own people, but he wouldn't hesitate to tear apart the prison itself, and they might well hurt him to stop that. And even if they managed to restrain him without causing him physical harm, he would be branded a traitor as well as an outcast. He would lose any chance of reconciling with his family and resuming his interrupted apprenticeship. He had finally agreed to come home, and the last thing I wanted was for him to ruin everything for my sake.

But neither did I want to be stuck in this cell for the foreseeable future. So it was impossible not to indulge daydreams of a dramatic rescue.

But the hours ticked on, and no familiar face or voice appeared. Eventually night fell, announced by Drake's snores, and then breakfast arrived again, and still no one came for me. I had willed Nik not to come, but sorrow crept over me at his continued absence. I was alone in this cell, with only my fear for company, and I couldn't deny how much I wanted to see his face and feel his arms around me again. He shouldn't come—I didn't want him to come— but my traitorous heart still called for him.

Finally, sometime during the afternoon, my straining ears heard footsteps that didn't belong to a guard. The approaching person was alone and moved briskly, their steps confident.

I rushed to the bars, gripping them eagerly with both hands.

But the figure that came into view was much shorter than I expected, a girl only a handful of years older than me. She threw a curious glance my way, smiling when she saw me watching. But she turned to Master Drake rather than trying to speak to me.

He surged upward, standing with an alert expression. I shook my head at the sight of the two of them facing off. Drake towered over the girl in height, bulk, and years, and yet she wasn't diminished by his presence. She might be young, but she carried herself with an authority that could only come from power in all its forms. Master Drake might be the rolling force of the tide, but she was the sweeping strength of lightning and thunder and gale force winds.

I sucked in a breath, transfixed by the sight of her.

"You've heard?" The girl didn't waste any time on greetings.

Drake sighed and nodded his head once, his stance slackening in the absence of an attack.

"It's utterly ridiculous," the girl continued. "They can't be serious."

"You know they are." The sorrow in Drake's voice made my stomach turn. What ridiculous decision had been made, exactly?

"Then we'll have to find a way to change their minds." The girl sounded resolute, but Master Drake remained silent.

She threw him a curious look. "I know you don't agree with them."

"Neither do any of them. Not really," he said, making both me and the girl frown.

"No one wants to be responsible for such an atrocity," he said. "No one wants to make the final decision. And yet no one is willing to set her free either. And so we remain stuck in stalemate, no one willing to move either forward or back." He gave her a knowing look. "I've been stuck down here for days, but I'm right, aren't I?"

She frowned. "It would explain why this is dragging on so long. What is everyone hoping for? That someone else will make the decision and absolve them of responsibility?" She sounded disgusted.

Looking my way again, she took in my desperate stance and wide eyes. She tried to muster a second smile but struggled.

"Is it really necessary for you to be down here the whole time?" she asked Drake. "If you could just talk some sense into the others!"

"I'm not sure how well they trust me after all my time down here," he said heavily. "I've carefully refrained from even speaking to her—any healer could see the truth of that if they bothered to ask me—but even so, I think they suspect me of being…influenced…"

This time they both glanced at me, and I rolled my eyes, unable to stop myself.

"That's nonsense!" The words flowed out before I could stop them. "Why hasn't Master Colton been consulted? I'm a healer! I can't influence anyone without touching them, and no one has been close enough for me to touch them since I got here."

For a moment both the Master and the new girl were still, clearly taken by surprise, as if they'd forgotten the barrier between us was erected by their rules rather than any physical impediment. Surely they had realized I could hear their conversation?

Master Drake cleared his throat and addressed himself to the girl again, although I saw his eyes flicking my way as he obliquely answered my query.

"Even if there's been no actual contamination, I believe there is some concern that I might be affected by her unprepossessing outside appearance." A rueful smile crossed his lips. "I've been here many hours after all."

That made me laugh, although I didn't feel much genuine amusement. Was I really such a sympathetic presence that even a captor might grow fond of me and be overcome by pity? I'd seen no sign of it since my arrival in the capital.

"They're afraid," the girl said roughly. "Well, except for Anka. I'm not sure that woman is afraid of anything. But she's playing her cards close—she's too wily to do anything else—so I'm not sure what she's thinking. But the rest of them are letting their fear overpower both their sense and their compassion. Especially Colton. I know he's afraid his entire affinity will be thrown into suspicion, but this is ridiculous."

She ran a hand down her face and groaned. "What a terrible time for Evermund to be away. I know he would do a better job of convincing them than me. But he'd already left for the northern farms before Nik arrived..."

Her voice trailed off, and although I held my breath, my heart beating in my ears, neither of them made any further mention of Nik.

"Airlie," Drake said gently, and I finally knew who the girl was.

Princess Airlie. Sister to the Calistan queen and princess of Tartora. And the greatest living elements mage. No wonder she could stand toe to toe with Master Drake without flinching.

"They know he'll disapprove." Her tone turned hard. "Why else would they be calling for a decision to be made before his return? There's no way Evermund would accept an execution."

*Execution?* The word rang through my head, everything else fading away as my surroundings grew fuzzy. Execution?

They meant to kill me. And I was stuck here, unable to do anything to defend myself, gagged even from speaking in my own defense.

"As you said, they're afraid." Drake's words pierced the muffled haze around me. "And can you blame them? They have reason to be. The chaos unleashed on this kingdom by the Constantines' insidious lies has already been great. You know how close we got to danger after they burned all those fields. Any further loss of crops, and we would have had people starving over the winter. As it was, it's caused great hardship to many. And all that pain and chaos was caused by only two people who were in the kingdom for mere weeks? Imagine how much worse the situation could get!"

"Of course I know all that. And I know Colton is afraid that lives will be lost if the populace lose trust in healers. But she didn't do any of that. It wasn't *her* who spread those lies!"

"No." He sighed. "And that is why I fear for our kingdom if we take this step. This leads down a road of darkness."

"And we've just got Nik back, too." She sounded close to tears. "You know he won't—" She cut herself off with a glance at me.

My awareness cleared, my thoughts going hard and solid again at the sound of his name. But, as before, they immediately let the topic drop.

Instead, the girl held my gaze. "I'm sorry." She spoke loudly enough that it was clear she meant to address me directly. "I apologize on their behalf, although I realize that must mean very little in the circumstances."

I wanted to reply, to plead my case, but Drake was already stretching the rules by letting her address me. If I pushed too hard—tried to engage in a proper conversation—he might call a halt to the whole thing. I remained silent.

"This really is unacceptable." Airlie's hands balled into fists. "There has to be something we can do. Hayes and Amara are both being treated as if they're already corrupted, but there has to be someone else—some ally we haven't thought of."

Drake sighed again and lowered himself back into his chair. "I wish I had your certainty that she isn't a danger," he murmured. "The certainty of youth."

She gave him an incredulous look. "I know you think this is wrong. You said as much in your message."

He looked my way, his expression weary and heavy, as if he carried the woes of the world on his shoulders.

"I have been helping guide this kingdom for much longer than you've been alive, Your Highness. The burden is starting to grow beyond what these old shoulders can bear."

Airlie snorted. "Don't try to fool me. You're a wily old man with the strength of ten storms followed by a hurricane."

He grinned, his deep chuckle sounding briefly. "I'll take that as a compliment."

"You should." She flashed him a smile, although her eyes were too tense to match the expression.

"I know this is wrong," he said after a moment, "but I couldn't tell you what would be the right decision in its place. And the others are all the same. They aren't bad people. They just feel the same weight I do, the same fear of getting it wrong and watching people suffer as a result. If any of us could figure out an alternative, I'm sure the rest would be easily convinced."

Airlie nodded. "I keep telling myself they won't actually go through with it. They're clearly reluctant to make the final decision. But every day that passes has me more worried."

She looked at me again, and I tried to pour my pleading desperation into my eyes. I must have succeeded to some extent because she flinched, her gaze falling away.

"It's all so pointless." The frustration poured out of her. "Delphine doesn't have a unique ability. She's just a healer, even if she's a strong one. For now, she's the only one in Tartora who knows how to use this skill, but how long will that remain the case? Now that we know something like this is possible, it's inevitable someone will come along with both the strength and the motivation to work it out for themselves. Getting rid of Delphine won't eliminate the threat—it will just ensure we don't know where the threat is coming from."

I slid down the bars to sit, suddenly too exhausted to remain upright any longer. Why had I never thought of that? I had been determined not to teach the skill to anyone—determined it would die with me. But Airlie was right. It had been done once, and that meant it would be done again. There would eventually be someone angry enough or greedy enough to seize at the possibility. I had thought I was the only one who could make a wall, but in the end, Grey had proved me wrong on that. Surely the same thing would happen again.

It didn't matter what the king did to me. He would never be able to eradicate this.

Dimly I heard Airlie leaving, but I didn't look up. My thoughts had turned inward, the futility of it all sparking a desperation that sent my mind flying, exploring avenues I hadn't considered before. Avenues I should have seen already.

This new skill existed now, and we couldn't change that. Others would work out how to do it, as Grey had worked out how to do my skill. But that didn't mean there was no hope. Quite the opposite—that certainty was my best source of hope.

Joy surged through me as I saw the way to save myself. Despair followed a minute later. Everyone of influence was afraid of getting close to me or even talking to me. The king and Triumvirate weren't going to allow me to stand before them and defend myself. They would decide my sentence behind closed doors, and there was no need for me to ever get close to them at all. In fact, they would almost certainly avoid me as carefully as if I was a known assassin.

Before I could sink too deeply into my fear, however, a face appeared in front of my mind's eye. I didn't know where Nik was right now, but I had no doubt that he would be either searching for me or fighting for me. And if he hadn't given up, I couldn't either.

I leaped to my feet, my hands on the bars as I fixed my eyes on the stationary figure in the chair.

"Master Drake!" I shouted the words.

He startled so hard he nearly fell out of his chair. Leaping to his feet, he whirled to face me, his brows knit. It was the first time I had ever called to him.

I didn't know how many words I would get, so I couldn't waste them.

"Amara. I need to speak to Amara."

The crease between his eyes deepened, and he didn't reply.

I rushed to continue, my words tumbling over each other as I tried to convey my sincerity.

"You said all you needed was a better option in order to convince the others to spare me. Bring Amara here—or if you can't bring her, bring Princess Airlie back—and I'll give you a better option, along with a way to keep Tartora safe."

CHAPTER

# TWENTY-FOUR

In the end, Drake summoned both of them. And the conversation that followed lasted for a long time. But at the end of it, Ember and I were swathed in a voluminous cloak and smuggled from the prison block.

Airlie went ahead to clear the path while Drake stayed behind to maintain the illusion I was safely in my cell. Only Amara walked beside me as I finally tasted fresh air and saw the sky again.

It was hard not to turn my face up to the sun, but I kept it down, hiding my identity as she hurried me across the short stretch of open ground and through a side door of the palace.

We were heading straight for the king, but Airlie reappeared before we could reach his reported location.

"You can't!" she hissed, making us both stop. "Not now. A delegation from the nomad tribes has arrived a day early and King Marius is in the middle of an audience with them. We'll have to wait until they've finished."

Amara groaned. "What terrible timing! What are we supposed to do now? Should we go back?" She glanced back the way we'd come.

"No," Airlie and I said at the same time, although I said it with considerably more force. I quickly fell silent, however, letting Airlie speak.

"We can't risk that. Drake said the others are suspicious of him already. What if they decide to put someone else on guard duty? She's free now, and there's no point moving backward. We just have to stash her out of sight until the delegation finish their initial business and retreat to their guest rooms."

"I'll take her to my suite," Amara said. "Only the steward knows which one I've been assigned—I don't think most people at the Guild even know I've returned yet—so I won't have any visitors."

Airlie looked uncertain but eventually nodded her agreement. "If someone does discover she's missing and raise an alarm, I'll try to get to you first."

Amara quickly described which suite she was in—a description that meant nothing to me—and then hurried me away. It took painfully long to cross the palace and Guild, but thankfully most of the corridors were empty due to the midday meal.

When we reached the suite, and Amara firmly closed the door behind us, I shrugged out of the cloak with relief. Ember jumped out of my arms and started exploring the room, apparently unbothered by the tension.

"Do you think we'll be waiting long?" I asked uneasily.

She sighed. "I hope not. I'm already nervous enough about this dangerous plan of yours. And I don't want to give Drake or Airlie a chance to overthink it."

"They're good people," I said, although I hadn't known them long. "They won't abandon us."

Amara sighed again but nodded. "If I didn't believe that, I wouldn't have agreed in the first place. I wish Evermund were here."

"Talking of people who aren't here," I said, trying to sound casual and failing.

"Nik's gone," Amara said, without my having to name him.

"Gone?" My heart rate picked up. "What does that mean?"

Had he tried to get to me in prison and been stopped? Had he already been cast out—maybe even from the entire kingdom this time?

"Relax," Amara said gently. "He's fine, or he was when he decided to leave."

"He just...left?" My brows drew together as I tried to make sense of her words. Nik had known I was in trouble, locked away without charge, and he had just left? There was no way that was true.

"He was very angry when he heard what had happened, and he grew even more furious when his father refused to relent," she said slowly, as if picking her words with care.

I relaxed slightly. Nik must have known he didn't have the strength to rescue me alone. Had he left in order to remove the temptation of trying anyway?

That thought didn't sit right, though. Amara and even Airlie had remained to fight for me, but Nik had walked away? I didn't believe it. And Amara clearly knew something more than she was saying.

But she was just as clearly remaining silent on purpose. I wanted to grab her by the shoulders and keep asking until she explained everything, but I couldn't. She was already risking a lot to support me, and I couldn't repay the debt by haranguing her, however desperately I wanted answers.

"What about Phoenix?" I asked. "Is he all right?"

She glanced toward Ember who was sniffing one of the curtains. "I thought he was with you this whole time, although I can see now that doesn't make much sense. A falcon doesn't belong in a cell."

"You haven't seen him?" I bit my lip, trying not to let my concern grow.

"Don't worry," she said, watching the expressions move across my face. "I believe you can make this plan work. And afterward—"

But before I could hear what was going to happen afterward, a knock sounded on the door. We both froze.

"Amara?" Hayes's familiar voice called through the wood. "Are you in there?"

Amara strode to the closest cupboard—a tall wardrobe—and silently pulled open one door. I remained motionless for a moment, taken too much by surprise to follow her lead. But when she gestured a second time for me to climb inside, I finally responded.

Scooping up both Ember and the discarded cloak, I bundled us into the wardrobe.

"Just a minute!" Amara called as she shut the door on me.

It was dark inside, except for the small bits of light that seeped in around the doors. I could hear perfectly, though, and was able to follow Amara's footsteps as she crossed the room to open the door.

"Hayes," she said in her usual calm way. "You were looking for me? I heard Their Majesties were greeting a new delegation. Are they finished?"

"Not yet, I believe." He stepped into the room, closing the door behind him. "But I couldn't put off talking to you any longer."

"What do you mean?" Amara sounded genuinely bewildered. "Is this about Delphine?"

"Delphine?" He sounded alarmed. "Don't tell me they've finally made a decision?"

She must have shaken her head because he continued in a calmer voice.

"Oh thank goodness. We still have time, then." He paused. "Actually, I came to talk to you about us."

"Us?" My confident master sounded unlike her usual self as she repeated his final word.

I wished I could close my eyes and will myself somewhere else. Clearly this wasn't a conversation I should be witness to. I could hardly start humming, however. Amara wanted me to stay hidden or she wouldn't have stashed me in the closet to start with.

"I know my timing is terrible, and that you're distracted with Delphine's situation, but the whole thing has made me think."

"How could it not?" she said softly. "You dedicated your entire life to serving this court. I remember how passionately you used to argue back in our apprentice days. You said the court was responsible for the good of the whole kingdom. And yet now they're so quick to discredit your judgment and experience."

"Oh, I don't mean that I'm offended," he said. "Not personally, anyway. If they believe I'm compromised, then their actions are reasonable enough. I'm not concerned that anyone is failing to value me as an individual."

He sighed. "I'm concerned at the failure of the entire system. I've believed for so long that I could do the most good by being here. But now I'm questioning that. I'm not sure how much good is possible here after all."

"Hayes." The soft sound of movement suggested Amara had drawn closer to him, perhaps even touched his arm. "You have always done good wherever you were."

He gave a half-laughing groan. "And you've always believed better of me than I deserve. In truth, I was already thinking about leaving court even before we got back to the capital."

"Leaving court?" Amara sounded alarmed. "What do you mean? Where would you go?"

"Wherever you are." The simple statement fell into stunned silence.

I was held frozen inside the wardrobe and could only imagine Amara was equally so out in the room. Was Hayes saying...

"I love you, Amara," he continued. "I've always loved you. You know that. And spending so much time with you again...I can't lose you a second time. I've lived alone all these years, and I don't want to do it anymore. I was young, and arrogant, and ambitious the last time, and it still hurt terribly. This time I'm afraid..." He drew a shaky breath. "I don't want to feel that pain again. I don't want to lose you. I've experienced firsthand the good we can do together. It doesn't matter if it's at court or elsewhere. I want to stay by your side and work beside you for the rest of my life. I want to marry you, Amara— if you'll have me. Even if that means giving up my life at court."

"You're next in line to be Head of Healing. Everyone says so. Would you really be willing to give that up?"

"I would sacrifice more than that," he said without hesitation.

I could hear the smile in Amara's voice and the tears clogging her throat. "You told me once that it was possible to have ambition without being like my mother. I guess you were right. I should have believed you then instead of running away. But I was so afraid of becoming like her.”

“You were never like her.” The sound of movement told me they’d come even closer together. “But I always understood why she had such an effect on you.”

“Of course you did.” Amara was clearly still smiling through tears. “You were always too good to me.”

“I dispute that,” Hayes said, the smile sounding in his voice too. “Never *too* good. Does this mean you’re going to marry me?”

“Yes,” Amara whispered, but I was so still inside the closet I caught the word. “I am.” Her next words came out stronger. “Because I already came to the same conclusion. Before we arrived in the capital I’d also decided on a major change.”

“What do you mean?”

“I mean that you weren’t the only one in pain after we went our separate ways all those years ago. And you aren’t the only one who has always remembered. I haven’t been unaffected by being with you again either. I decided weeks ago that I wasn’t saying goodbye a second time.”

“Really?” He sounded delighted. “Do you mean it? You’ve been feeling the same way? I should have said something earlier! I’ve been so nervous, afraid your feelings had faded into warm friendship after so many years.”

Amara laughed. “I thought they had. Until I saw you again.”

An unmistakable sound told me Hayes had finally taken firm action and given the appropriate response to her declaration.

But when they finally stopped kissing—much to my relief—their conversation merely resumed again.

“When you said you were planning a major change,” Hayes said. “Do you mean you’ve been thinking about remaining at the Guild? You know I wouldn’t ask that of you.”

“Actually, since arriving here, I’ve come to the opposite conclusion as you,” she said. “The king and Triumvirate responded badly to the threat from Grey. There’s no denying they should have caught what was happening in Eldrida, for one. And now this business with Delphine...” I could almost see her shaking her head. “The king and Triumvirate have been in their positions for too long. They’ve stagnated. And it’s clear that you were right about the impact that has on the rest of the kingdom. We need change, and I think it’s time I started working for that change here—at the heart of everything.”

“Do you really mean it?” Hayes sounded dazed. “You won’t come to feel resentful and constrained?”

“I can’t be sure of the future,” she said. “But I don’t believe so.”

"You're telling me I can stay in Tarona and have you too?" He laughed, an almost giddy sound. "That sounds too good to be true."

The sound of another kiss made me shove my hands over my ears, but it stopped much more quickly this time.

"You'd better come out, Delphine," Amara said loudly.

I startled so badly in response that Ember whined.

"Delphine?" Hayes sounded shocked, and I couldn't blame him.

Reluctantly I pushed open the wardrobe door and blinked in the bright light of the room. I could feel my cheeks growing hotter and hotter as I carefully stepped out of the closet. I couldn't bring myself to look at either of them until Amara chuckled.

"Don't look so mortified, Delphine. I'm sure you had some idea of Hayes and my history. Luna will have told you if no one else."

I gasped as I belatedly remembered my friend. "You have no idea how delighted she's going to be about this," I said, making both of them laugh.

"While I'm delighted to see you walking around freely," Hayes said, "I'm a little confused. What were you doing in Amara's wardrobe?"

I could see the concern slowly leeching away the joy from his face as he realized his new betrothed might be involved in something that bordered on treasonous.

"We're taking her to see the king," Amara said calmly. "But that delegation arrived at the worst possible moment so we ducked in here to wait."

"We?" Hayes asked.

"Airlie, Drake, and me. Gia and Renley by now as well, I'm sure. Airlie was going to speak to them."

He relaxed slightly at the other names, clearly relieved Amara had such powerful allies. "But why was she in the closet? You knew it was me at the door." Slowly understanding spread across his face, his expression falling. "You didn't know if you could trust me."

"Of course we trust you!" I cried quickly, but Amara was less quick to answer.

"I always knew you were on Delphine's side," she said. "You already risked your position and reputation arguing for her release. I never would have expected less. But defying the system is another thing altogether. While I knew you would agree with our intent, I was less sure you would agree with our methods. But then you said you were ready to walk away altogether. Then I knew you were safe to include in this."

Hayes sighed heavily. "I want to be offended that you didn't trust me from the beginning—that you didn't know I would always be on your side. But how can I be offended? I already chose the throne and Guild over you once, so I can't blame you for wondering if I would do it again."

"I'm not wondering anymore," she whispered, and he leaned toward her.

I cleared my throat loudly, and he moved away again, chuckling.

"So what exactly is this plan?" he asked. "Do you need my help?"

"If you're really certain you want to get involved," I said, "then I could definitely use your help."

CHAPTER

# TWENTY-FIVE

"They've finally left!" Airlie paused mid-step as she took in Hayes's presence. She threw a concerned look at Amara, but I answered for her.

"Don't worry. Hayes is safe. He's on our side."

Airlie looked relieved, but her mouth still turned downward. "I don't like this business of sides. Hopefully this plan will put an end to the matter."

"That's what we're all hoping for," Amara said.

"It's a risky attempt, though," Hayes murmured, making Airlie narrow her eyes.

"If you don't want to be involved..."

"No," he said quickly. "I'm with you. I'm just aware that some are more at risk with this plan than others." He threw me an obvious glance.

Airlie sighed. "It's not an ideal solution, no. But the one most at risk is also the one with the most to gain. If we had another solution, we would have already tried it."

"And that's why I'm with you," Hayes said. "I never would have believed King Marius or Colton could get to this point."

"It's this last winter." Airlie sounded sad. "You weren't here, so you didn't see the situation growing. One of the problems with fear is that it breeds more fear. I'm convinced that if they'd been presented with this situation out of the blue six months ago, they wouldn't have considered such a drastic path. Even now, none of them actually want to be the one to make the call. But we can't leave the situation hanging like this with Delphine at constant risk."

"We appreciate your care for Delphine," Amara said. "I feel terrible that I've been so helpless to rescue my own apprentice."

Airlie smiled at me, the gesture lighting up her face. "Of course we want the best for Delphine—and hope she has a long and prosperous life here in Tartora where her skills as a healer will always be needed. But I would do the same for anyone. We can't start punishing people for what they might one day do!"

"Should we be going?" Hayes asked. "How long do we have?"

Airlie started as if suddenly remembering her original reason for joining us. "Yes, we need to hurry! Drake is keeping Their Majesties and the rest of the Triumvirate in the throne room, but I don't know how long he can stall them."

Amara turned to me. "You're sure about this, Delphine?"

I drew a deep breath and nodded. However it turned out, I had to try something. I couldn't just sit back and let my life be taken away from me without fighting back.

"Where is that fascinating fox of yours?" Airlie looked around the room. "Do you think she would mind being left behind for this meeting?"

"She usually sleeps at this time of day anyway," I said, just before spotting her curled up and fast asleep on one of the padded chairs by the window. I smiled at the sight of her. "Looks like she won't miss us."

She didn't even stir as I wrapped myself in the cloak once again for the trip back into the palace. But with Princess Airlie at my side, no one would have questioned us anyway. From the looks of respect and admiration sent her way, she had obviously won her place in the palace, despite her humble origins.

My thoughts went to Nik again—as they all too often did. Even if the court was willing to accept a princess of humble birth, I had neither Airlie's extraordinary strength nor her temperament. I didn't think I could ever live permanently at court. The current situation might be unusual, but it was enough to put me off a political life forever. Airlie was the perfect wife for Evermund, but if Nik was going to reclaim his rightful position, I couldn't be the wife he needed.

All too soon we arrived at a set of double doors that clearly opened onto a room of importance. I would have preferred my confrontation with the king to happen somewhere less intimidating, but there was nothing I could do about it.

Airlie pushed both doors open without hesitation, making our entrance suitably dramatic. Hayes followed after her, and Amara gestured for me to go next, leaving her to bring up the rear. I appreciated the show of support they were giving me, but I still wished I could have slunk inside without making a fuss.

"Ah, Princess," a deep voice said from the far side of the room, "there you are." But whatever else he'd been about to say was lost when he caught sight of the rest of us.

Surging up from his throne, King Marius eyed me with alarm. His graying hair lent his features gravity, as did the formal circlet he wore, and I wanted to shrink back from his anger.

Beside him, on a smaller throne, sat an elegant woman with a circlet of her own. Standing at her side were Gia and Renley. The princess winked as soon as she saw me, her manner a shocking contrast with her parents. Clearly Airlie had managed to speak to her.

Standing in front of the dais were four more figures, two of whom I recognized. Given the presence of Drake, the Master of the Elements, and Anka, now the Royal Mage, this was clearly the Triumvirate, making the second man Colton, the head of my own affinity. And beside him, the diminutive second woman, whose hair was mostly gray but whose golden face was unlined and full of life, had to be the famous Master of Plants.

The king swung toward them. "What is the meaning of this? Drake?" He sounded furious. "You assured us all was well with your prisoner!"

"She looks quite well to me," Drake said blandly, ignoring the fire shooting from the king's eyes.

I gulped. Apparently Grey wasn't the only one adept at shaping his words around a healer's ability to truth tell.

"This has gone on long enough." Airlie had progressed calmly forward to take her place beside Gia. "You must make a judgment one way or another, and it is only fair that Delphine be allowed to speak in her own defense. You have both Master Colton and Master Anka to tell you if her words are true."

King Marius shot a look at Colton who was carefully avoiding catching my gaze. He might be worried for his affinity and the disaster I might bring on it, but he wasn't completely shameless. As my affinity head, he should have been the one defending me, not Airlie.

He cleared his throat. "I can certainly confirm any lies, Your Majesty." He finally looked in my direction. "You must answer questions directly and without prevarication."

Both Colton and the king glared in Drake's direction, but the Master of the Elements looked unmoved. He might not wear a circlet in his tight curls, but his height and the white of his hair against his dark skin conveyed a powerful combination of strength and age-won wisdom. I was fortunate in my allies.

"To begin with," Amara said, "let's clear up your most immediate concern. Delphine, is physical contact necessary to mesmerize someone?"

"Yes." The word came out shaky and quiet, so I repeated myself in a firmer voice. "Yes. Just like with regular healing, physical touch is necessary to mesmerize. From here I can tell your heart is beating, and your lungs are working, and I could recognize a lie or test a child's seed. But I cannot interfere with another person's body or mind from a distance. Mesmerization is bound by the same constraints as regular healing."

King Marius, Queen Celestine, Drake, and Augusta all turned to Colton. Colton was staring at me, but I couldn't read anything in his expression.

After a prolonged moment, he repeated the question.

"There is no possible way for you to mesmerize someone in any way without touching them?"

"That is correct," I said, holding his gaze steadily.

He looked at the king and nodded slowly. The king looked from him to Anka, who also nodded. Everyone in the room relaxed in response, even me a little.

"Well, then..." King Marius sat back in his throne and regarded me, his face weary and eyes sad. "The princess is right, and you should be allowed a voice in your defense. I apologize for not granting you an audience before now."

Part of me wanted to stammer out that it was fine, awed by my surroundings and company, but another part wanted to rage and scream abuse at his treatment of me thus far. I settled for a stiff nod.

"You were taught this skill by Grey, who is now deceased," the king said, waiting at the end of the sentence for my confirmation.

"That is correct," I said. "I saw him die myself and confirmed it with my ability."

Colton nodded again.

"To your knowledge, the only other ones who knew this skill were Grey's family, and all of them are now deceased as well?"

I hesitated, and the group around the dais tensed.

"As far as I'm aware, the Constantines never taught anyone outside their family the skill. However, not all the Constantines are dead. One of the grandsons had an elements affinity, and he remains alive. There is also a daughter-in-law who is a healer, but she was never fully accepted into the family and never taught to mesmerize."

Colton nodded a third time, and the king relaxed again. A hint of approval entered King Marius's eyes which I could only attribute to my detailed and specific responses. Apparently I was reassuring him with my openness and careful replies.

But his expression almost immediately grew heavier, his shoulders sinking. My heart sank with them. I had held onto the hope that my words could convince him, but it didn't look promising.

"Have you ever voluntarily planted a lie in another's mind?" he asked, and my heart dropped even further.

"Yes," I said reluctantly. "I mesmerized one of the Constantines at Grey's instruction. I didn't want to, but I felt I needed to allay his suspicions."

The king and queen exchanged a look, and I rushed to keep talking.

"But I regret having done so greatly. It seemed like a relatively harmless lie at the time, but it ended up having devastating consequences. I have sworn that I will never mesmerize again, no matter the circumstances."

"That is an admirable resolution," Augusta said. "But it is one thing to say so when everything is calm and another to hold firm to our intentions through the storm."

Amara shifted closer to me. "Delphine may still be an apprentice, but she has already weathered several storms and faced death more than once."

"Even to save myself, I will not mesmerize again," I said. "I have faced that situation already, and I believe I could face it again if necessary."

The king looked at Colton with a raised eyebrow and again received a nod. I breathed out, feeling hopeful for the first time, but the king's next words dashed the brief emotion.

"Even so…By your own admission, you have mesmerized before and accept some level of culpability in the deaths which followed."

Hayes stepped forward. "It is a credit to Delphine's sense of responsibility that she claims any guilt at all. The true responsibility for the Constantines' deaths rests at their own feet. They created Grey and set themselves on the path to destruction without any assistance from Delphine."

Colton gave Hayes a hard look, but Hayes continued talking.

"I must also remind you that what happened on the island happened beyond Tartora's borders and is out of our jurisdiction. We are not here today to assign guilt for those murders. If anyone is to seek justice on that account, it must be the islanders themselves. And on the island, Delphine was a protector, not a criminal. If we are discussing the island, we would do better to focus on the benefits of securing an alliance as quickly as possible before one of the other kingdoms beats us to it. And Delphine would be an asset in any such negotiations."

"We have already sent word to Master Clay to begin alliance negotiations," King Marius said. "But as much as we would value such a connection, the safety of our people must be our first priority."

I braced myself, waiting for what I knew would come next. As we had feared, no arguments could prevent the king viewing me as a danger. Seeing his kingdom nearly plunged into famine had clearly had a profound effect.

But before he could speak again, Queen Celestine leaned over and whispered something to him. I couldn't catch the words, but her eyes were on me, and I could have sworn I saw her lips form Nik's name.

The king winced visibly in response to whatever she'd said, and then slowly nodded. But from Gia's scowl, the queen's intervention hadn't provided any last-minute rescue.

"Delphine, many character witnesses have spoken on your behalf." The king's eyes traveled from Amara to Hayes and then back to his wife, making me wonder what private words had been exchanged between parents and son before Nik's departure. "Bearing this in mind, as well as your testimony today, I cannot in good conscience order your execution. While I would prefer the skill you possess be wiped from existence, that is too high a price to pay."

My whole body slumped with relief. It was good news after all. Except then he continued talking.

"However, regardless of your intentions, I cannot place my kingdom at risk. Therefore, you will be kept in a guarded location and forbidden from any future physical contact."

"Forever?" I asked, not quite grasping what he was suggesting.

He nodded ponderously.

"You will bar her from all physical contact with anyone? Ever?" Amara asked, her tone growing thunderous. "So she is not to be murdered but merely imprisoned for life and barred from using her ability?"

A shudder ran through me. I hadn't even considered that such an imprisonment would mean I could never work as a healer again. Could I spend my life locked in a cage, alone and unable to help no matter how great the need around me? What sort of life would that be?

I had hoped this audience wouldn't require any drastic action after all, but while my life might have been spared, I couldn't accept the future the king demanded. Which meant I couldn't hesitate.

Launching into movement, I leaped onto the dais and reached the king in a single bound. Before he realized what was happening, I had one hand wrapped around his throat. My touch was gentle, but everyone in the room knew what I could do with the lightest of touches.

"Don't move!" I cried. "You know I only need a second!"

King Marius had gone stone still beneath my hand, although his eyes jumped from Drake to Augusta. He had gone without formal guards for such a sensitive meeting, but he had done so knowing the strongest mages in the kingdom were at his side.

But when Drake moved, it wasn't to come to the king's aide. With two steps, he placed himself toe to toe with the Master of Plants. I had fought at Nik's side often enough to know what destruction could be wreaked by a plants master, but she had yet to make any move—no doubt taken by surprise and unsure of the danger I posed to the king.

"Drake," she said in a low, warning tone, but he didn't move.

Amara and Hayes stepped up beside him, the three of them forming a wall with their backs toward the dais. In front of them, blocked from approaching the throne were Augusta, Colton, and Anka. The king's eyes flicked to his daughter, but she shook her head sadly as she, Renley, and Airlie slowly retreated from the dais, leaving the king and queen alone with me.

"Sorry, Father," she said. "But what you're doing is wrong, and you know it. I can't stand with you on this."

"Gia!" the queen hissed. "Your father!"

But Gia just kept shaking her head with a mournful look.

I held my breath, willing my hand not to shake as I kept it in place.

The king met Airlie's eyes next. "We accepted you and made you a princess, and you repay us with treason?"

She remained silent, her face a careful mask.

The king turned his head toward me, speaking through gritted teeth. "I offered you your life."

"If you can call that a life," I replied, trying to sound scornful.

Augusta peered around Drake's crossed arms. "All you're doing is proving us right, girl."

"Perhaps," I said. "But I don't have much to lose at this point."

"And what do you hope to gain if you kill the king?" Colton asked. "If it's a swift death you're after—"

I laughed, the unexpected sound rendering him silent. "If I didn't want to live, I wouldn't be risking this now. But King Marius doesn't have to die. No one does."

"Of course not," Queen Celestine said, a strain in her lilting voice. "If you step away from the king we can talk further, and I'm sure we can—"

"Oh no," I said, shamelessly interrupting her. It had taken every bit of my determination to come this far, but it would all be for nothing if I couldn't brazen it out. "If we're all going to walk away from this alive, it's because Colton will save the king."

I met the eyes of the Master of Healing. "It's up to you to protect your king."

# TWENTY-SIX

Colton's brows contracted, his eyes meeting mine over Amara's shoulder.

"What do you mean?"

"Your Majesty," I said, "please extend your right hand away from the throne."

The king remained frozen for a long minute before reluctantly complying. When the arm opposite to me was fully stretched out, I looked toward Colton.

"That hand is for you," I said.

His eyes flashed as he understood my instruction to make contact with the king. But he clearly still didn't understand my intentions.

Amara stepped to one side, clearing the path to the dais, and Colton slowly approached. He took the king's outstretched wrist in a healer's practiced grip.

As I had expected, he immediately attempted to push his power into the king, no doubt wanting to be prepared to counter any damage I wrought.

I activated the king's wall in response, driving Colton's power out.

He gave a cry of surprise and jerked his hand back, the king's arm dropping limply from his grip.

"What is it?" Queen Celestine asked in alarm. "What has she done to him?"

"I...I don't know." Colton sounded lost. "My power couldn't connect with him."

"What does that mean?" King Marius asked, his voice tense despite the forced stillness of his body.

"That is your wall," I said. "Mesmerization was Grey's weapon, but I had one of my own. This is it."

From the corner of my eye, I saw Anka's face shift. Her narrowed eyes widened slightly. She had always been interested in my wall.

"You asked what I hope to achieve," I continued. "The answer is simple. King Marius intends to destroy my life although I've committed no crime. I need hope for the future. I could end both of us right now—taking my persecutor down with me—unless I have a reason not to do so. You're going to give me hope, Master Colton. And you're going to do it by learning how to activate someone's wall."

"A wall guards not just against a healer's regular power but also against mesmerization?" Anka's face had grown thoughtful as she watched me speak, her brows knitting together.

I nodded. "That's right. It blocks a healer's power from entering the body completely. If you raise someone else's wall, it will drop again when you lose physical contact with them, but, in the meantime, it will protect against another healer."

"That's a powerful tool," Anka said.

I looked from her to the king. "Even if I stay locked up forever, someone else will come along and work out how to mesmerize. Now that people know it's possible, someone will do it eventually. I understand you're worried about what a rogue healer could do, but there's a way to protect yourself against such a person—no matter their intentions. You see me as a threat, but removing all potential threats is an impossible task. The solution is to learn how to defend yourself."

"I thought you'd failed to teach anyone else how to make a wall," Anka said.

I shrugged. "That was true in the past. But I haven't tried to teach the Master of Healing himself." I met Colton's eyes over the king's head. "You're going to learn how to do it right now. And once you can, you'll have another option other than locking me up forever. I'll have a reason to choose hope. So like I said at the beginning: you're our only chance of all walking away from this alive, Master Colton."

One of Anka's eyebrows slowly rose, and I carefully didn't look her way as Colton swallowed. Thankfully his attention was fully focused on me and the king.

Slowly, he took the king's wrist again, and this time I let him connect, giving him time to ascertain that the king was unharmed. Then I activated the king's wall.

As before, Colton's power was immediately driven from Marius's body. But this time he was prepared, and maintained his hold on the king.

"It's remarkable," he said slowly, looking up at me. "But I don't know how you're doing it."

I shrugged. "It's not hard really. You just need to block your own healing power that's connecting with him."

"But how? I've never—"

The double doors creaked open, making him break off as the rest of us turned to look. A young man I didn't recognize strode through the narrow opening. His boots were coated in dust, and his clothes—while fine quality—were rumpled and dirty. On his heels strode a familiar figure in a similar state.

Nik had returned. And on his shoulder rode Phoenix.

The doors clanged shut behind them as the two men took in the scene before them.

"Don't come any closer," Anka called, although her almost lazy tone didn't match the seriousness of the moment. "As you can see, your father is being held at the point of a healer's sword, so to speak, and Colton is about to try his best to save him. Interference could prove...messy."

"What?" The unfamiliar man's eyes jumped to Airlie, full of questions, and I realized he must be her husband, the missing Prince Evermund. Only the heir to the throne would interrupt a meeting between the king and Triumvirate with such confidence.

Evermund had returned, and Nik had been the one to bring him. I met Nik's eyes, cold washing over me. The tables had been turned. Now he was the one walking in on me doing something apparently heinous. If he assumed I was truly threatening his father's life, I couldn't blame him.

But the confused look on his face faded as he held my gaze. The warmth filling his eyes ignited the same warmth in my chest. Regardless of the situation, he was as glad to see me as I was to see him. He didn't know what was happening, but he trusted me, and his trust filled me with fresh strength.

A sudden whoosh of movement made us all flinch as Phoenix launched himself from Nik's shoulder and flapped his way down the long throne room. The queen sucked in a breath as he swooped toward us, but he merely maneuvered himself onto his usual perch on my shoulder. Once there, he directed one bright eye toward the king. I tried to picture how we looked to others and decided a merlin falcon on my shoulder only helped with the impression I was trying to create.

"That's enough!" I snapped, letting my tension show. Hopefully Colton would think I was on edge at the arrival of fresh backup for the king. "It's time to end this one way or another." I put an edge of desperation in my voice as I added, "Colton, either you block my power right now, or it's all over."

"What?" Colton stared at me. "But I don't know how to make a wall."

I shrugged. "Then work it out. You have ten seconds."

"Wait!" Evermund cried, horrified, and his panic reverberated on Colton's face.

I thrust my power into the king, sending it toward his heart. I knew how Colton would react to my power being anywhere near that part of his body, and sure enough Colton's power was already there, waiting.

The second I reached his chest, my power collided with a solid force. Springing back like released rubber, I was driven instantly out of the king's body.

I pulled my hand away from his neck, joy spreading through me.

"He did it!" I could feel tears on my cheeks, but I didn't try to dash them away. "Master Colton made a wall!"

Cheers erupted from the direction of Gia and Renley, making Phoenix take off and wing around the room in a wide circle. I watched him go, my eyes falling on Amara. She looked deeply relieved. The situation had obviously strained her, but my eyes kept moving, drawn irresistibly to Nik. He still had no idea what was going on, but he ran across the throne room and leaped onto the dais, sweeping me into his arms.

I buried my face in his chest and cried in relief. I might be seconds away from being branded a traitor and dragged away, but at least I had a chance now. And perhaps more importantly, the healing affinity could now make walls. I had proven it could be done, and it was now only a matter of time before walls became commonplace.

Phoenix landed on a nearby urn, still unimpressed with the sudden disruption, but I was enjoying being in Nik's arms too much to care.

"Delphine." Nik murmured my name against my hair, pressing his lips against my head. "I'm sorry." His voice sounded thick.

I pulled back to look at him. "Whatever for?"

I wanted to tell him how much his faith in me meant—especially after I'd failed to show the same trust in him at the beginning of winter—but I was still too emotional for so many words.

"I'm sorry for not coming to you—for leaving you alone in there."

I shook my head. "No, I was glad you didn't come. I didn't want you to throw everything away for me."

He gave me an exasperated look. "Of course I would have come if it could have helped. Surely you don't doubt that?"

I flushed, but before I could respond, a snapped speech from Augusta made me pull away from him.

"Prince Nikolas is as foolish as ever, I see, but I expect better from you, Evermund! Everyone else may have lost their senses, but it is our responsibility to arrest the traitor who tried to kill the king."

Nik growled, his muscles tightening as he tried to pull me back into the circle of his arms. I resisted, and he settled for hovering protectively behind me.

"Of course Delphine wasn't going to kill the king," Anka said in a voice that was quiet but still commanding enough to cut through the tension of the room. "Can't you recognize a piece of theater when you see one?"

She looked with a raised eyebrow from Augusta to Colton, still standing beside the king and queen. "No? None of you?" She sounded disappointed, tsking quietly to herself. "This is why I'm needed as a *law keeper*, not playing dress up in purple robes."

"What are you talking about Anka? Were you in on this as well?" King Marius gripped both arms of the throne, his face white. But despite his obvious fury, he was reining himself in, waiting for answers.

His restraint demonstrated why he had been a successful ruler for decades. I didn't like the decisions he'd been making since learning about mesmerization, but he was capable of putting aside personal insult when it was politically necessary, and he was willing to consider the good and stability of the kingdom over personal revenge. He had proven that when he accepted the Triumvirate putting his son aside in favor of his nephew, and it was that trait I was placing all my hope in.

"Of course I wasn't involved," Anka said. "That should have been apparent. I suppose I wasn't deemed trustworthy enough." She gave Amara an unimpressed look.

"Nonsense, Aunt," Amara said briskly. "It wasn't a matter of trust. I couldn't ask you to get involved in something like this."

"If you didn't know about this ahead of time, then what do you mean?" Colton frowned in Anka's direction. "Are you saying you sensed she was lying when she threatened the king? Because I got no such impression."

Anka shook her head. "This is why I keep telling you that a regular healer is not the same as a law keeper—and why our affinity needs to put greater emphasis on proper truth telling training for all our apprentices."

I could tell from her tone that it was an old argument between them.

"Master Anka, please explain yourself," the king said in a warning tone.

"It's a classic strategy that wouldn't fool any law keeper worth their salt," she said. "The speaker says a series of true statements and allows the listener to assume that those statements are connected to each other."

King Marius frowned. "So in this instance..."

"Delphine said that you intended to destroy her life. True. She said that she needs hope for the future. True. She said that Colton activating a wall would give her hope. Also true. And then she said that without a reason for restraint, she might as well kill the person who was persecuting her. That's true, of course. Freed from all restraints, humanity has shown itself to be perfectly capable of murder. But most of us have restraints already—small matters like self-respect, value for life, and morality for starters. Plus in this case, you're both her king and the father of the man she loves. There was no chance a person like Delphine was going to kill you. She needed restraints to prevent her, yes, but she already had those. She just allowed you to assume that only hope for the future would be enough of a restraint to hold her back. In fact the two truths were never related." Anka looked to me. "Am I right?"

I nodded, impressed.

"But she said I was going to die if Colton didn't succeed in blocking her," King Marius said, looking from Anka to me with narrowed eyes.

"Actually," Anka said, "I think you'll find she said someone would die but never specified who. I believe it was herself she expected to die if she failed in her purpose here. Again, it was all the manipulation of assumptions. It was quite neatly done for a novice." She nodded respectfully in my direction.

"Yes, you're right on that point, too," I said, my whole body shaking with the aftereffects of my earlier bravado.

Nik pulled me against him, and this time I didn't try to stop him.

"I know none of us wanted to punish Delphine in the first place—not when her only crime was being forced to learn a skill she never wanted." Drake met everyone's eyes one by one. "I'm the one who told her that we were looking for another option—a way to mitigate the threat without punishing an innocent person."

"Please don't blame Master Drake or any of the others," I said to the king. "It was my idea. And I went into it knowing that threatening the king might be enough to see me executed, regardless of the outcome. I certainly knew that if I failed—meaning my skills remained an unmitigated threat—then my behavior here would certainly ensure my death. It was always my own death I was referring to, never yours. And while I know it's shameless of me, I beg you to forgive my actions now that you know you were never in any danger from me. Master Colton can make a wall—and hopefully soon other healers as well —so you have a way to protect yourself and others from what I can do. I'm hoping that will give you the reason you've all been looking for to choose a different path."

"Of course it will," Nik said in menacing tones, glaring at his parents. "No one *wants* to hurt you, Delphine."

"I'm not sure I'm following." Evermund had one arm wrapped around Airlie's waist, but his eyes were sharp as they jumped from person to person. "I don't suppose someone could explain what we walked in on?"

"It's quite simple, really," Airlie said. "The king and Triumvirate decided that Delphine should be locked up for the rest of her life without any physical contact for the crime of knowing how to mesmerize."

Evermund looked at Nik. "You were right."

I twisted so I could look up into Nik's face.

He looked grim as he replied. "It's better than I feared, to be honest. But you can understand why we needed to hurry."

"Is that why you disappeared?" Airlie asked. "You must have ridden day and night to fetch Evermund and get him back this quickly."

I frowned at Nik, taking in the lines of exhaustion I hadn't noticed earlier. Airlie had said all along that Evermund might succeed where she had failed. How hard had Nik driven himself in order to bring back the one person he thought could help?

"I talked to Amara," he said, focusing his reply on me. "And we agreed this was the most helpful thing I could do."

I felt a pinch at the memory of what I had once—however briefly—thought him capable of doing compared to the reality of his mature response on this occasion. But the feeling was gone almost as soon as it appeared. Nik had shown me in every way possible that he had forgiven me, and it was time to leave that tragic situation in the past where it belonged.

I looked across at Amara. "Why didn't you tell me?"

"I wasn't sure they would get back in time," she said, "and I knew how hard this was going to be to pull off. I didn't want you to think there was any other hope in case it made you buckle when the moment came."

"So you all hatched a plan to save Delphine?" Evermund asked. "By threatening the king?" He sounded skeptical, and I couldn't blame him.

"Just reckless enough to be believable," Airlie said. "That's what we decided anyway. Drake, Amara, Hayes, Gia, Renley, and I were all in on it, so there were enough of us to restrain the others so that the drama could play out."

"The drama being..." Evermund raised his eyebrows.

"I pretended to threaten the king," I explained. "I claimed I was either going to be saved by Colton learning to make a wall, or else I was going to die on the spot, taking the king with me for revenge. I would never have actually harmed him, though, no matter what happened."

Evermund glanced at Colton who slowly nodded, looking like it pained him to admit I was speaking the truth and he'd been fooled.

"But...why did you need to fake such a thing?" Evermund asked me, sounding bewildered.

"I've tried teaching others how to make their own walls before and always failed," I said. "But then Grey managed to make one during our final confrontation, and while I was sitting in my cell, I came up with a theory about why. Although a wall can be used to block the power of others, it's primarily about blocking a healer's own power. But our power is so central to who we are that it requires true desperation to cut it off. Curiosity, interest—even greed, as Grey previously discovered—aren't enough motivation.

"I was raised to hate and fear my power, and my first experience of it after activation was traumatic. So I started with the necessary desperation to separate myself from it. I had that desire before I had any knowledge of what should or shouldn't have been possible. Grey didn't start with that same desperation, but when he had his back against the wall and his life on the line, he was suddenly able to break through and create a wall as well.

"So I took a gamble that the same would be true for making a wall for others. I showed Master Colton a wall so that he understood the concept and truly believed it was possible, and then—"

"You provided him with sufficient desperation," King Marius said. "Am I supposed to be flattered that I was the chosen victim?"

I pulled free of Nik's arms to drop into my deepest curtsy. "It was the most believable and compelling scenario I could come up with. I apologize wholeheartedly for the distress it must have caused you and the lack of respect it showed."

"As to that…" The king paused and looked at his son who met his gaze challengingly. "I can see why it was necessary for me to be in the dark." He looked at Colton, and for the first time, an eager light showed in his eyes. "You can really do it now? As long as we're in physical contact, you could protect me from any attack from a healer?"

"I believe so." Colton also sounded enthusiastic. "Now that I've got the feel of it, I can bring my own wall up and down with ease."

"It's even better than that," I said. "If someone does manage to mesmerize you while you don't have a wall up, just bringing up the wall drives out the mesmerization. I've done it for myself many times, as well as for the people of the island and many in Eldrida."

"This changes everything," the king said before suddenly subsiding, as if he'd just remembered what had been required to reach this breakthrough.

"The healers among the royal guards will need to be taught it first," Anka said briskly. "And then my law keepers. But we're going to have to put some thought into how to manage the lesson. I don't fancy reenacting a similar scenario to this one a hundred times."

"I'll make it my first priority, of course," Colton said, and I felt a weight lift off my shoulders.

Someone better equipped than me was going to take over the burden I had been carrying. Colton knew how to make a wall, and he could be responsible for teaching others. Maybe—just maybe—I could go back to being no more than a healing apprentice.

"Father. Mother." Nik looked from one to the other. "I brought the woman

I love home to meet you, and you considered having her executed. Now that you know Delphine was never going to harm you—no matter what happened with Colton's wall—you can let this matter go. Can't you?" He paused, his eyes hard as steel. "Because if you can't, don't think I'll just stand by. Or that once we're gone, you'll ever see me again."

Marius exchanged a look with his wife before allowing his gaze to roam across the room. Anka and Colton had their heads together, discussing potential strategies, while Augusta was standing back, her eyes narrowed to slits as she took in the scene. But Drake, Amara, Hayes, Airlie, Evermund, Gia, and Renley were all watching the king, waiting to hear how he would respond.

If I had acted alone, I doubted I would have gotten away with threatening the king—whatever my intentions and whatever the outcome. But King Marius was a prudent man. Half his government, and most of his family were arrayed against him, and that would be enough to give more reckless men than him pause. It was certainly far too many people of importance—to both the kingdom and him personally—for him to consider punishing them all for treason. And if he wasn't going to punish them, then perhaps...

When even Anka broke off mid-sentence to look up and wait for his reply, he finally capitulated and nodded to Nik and me.

"Word of what happened here must not leave this group," he said. "This is not a situation that we can risk having repeated." He paused and looked at me. "But I am acutely aware that wrong has also been done to you, and I can understand why you felt driven to extreme measures. I accept the assurance of my healers that you were acting without malice in order to bring about an outcome that would benefit all. In light of that, I think I may issue a pardon for your actions. And Delphine, I hope you will accept my apology for locking you up and threatening permanent incarceration. And Nik—" He hesitated his voice softening more than I had yet heard it. "I'm sorry...for more than just this."

Nik nodded once, the movement rough, but I could feel his relief. It was nothing to how I felt, however. Fresh tears slipped down my cheeks, and Nik pulled me closer.

"Clearly banning all future physical contact wasn't going to work," the queen muttered, and I blinked, unable to process the humor in her voice as her eyes dwelt on her son's arm where it wrapped around me.

Her eyes jumped up to mine, full of concern and sadness. I tried to smile at her—reminding myself she was Nik's mother—but my mouth only twitched.

She stood and came closer, stopping with a hand on her husband's shoulder where he still sat on his throne.

"We have not had the best beginning, Delphine," she said in a quiet voice, "on either side. I'm sure our treatment of you will not be easily forgotten, just as your actions here today will not easily be forgotten by us." Her eyes moved to her son's face before returning to mine. "But we love Nik and have been sorely grieved by his absence. It is clear he has tied his future to yours, and I hope somehow we can find it in us to move past this and start afresh."

Her husband twitched beneath her hand, and she sighed. "Perhaps that is too much to hope for. Let's say instead that I hope we can start now to build a new foundation, and that it will one day prove stronger than this unfortunate beginning."

I thought of my own parents and the way my thinking about my father had changed over the past year.

"Thank you, Your Majesty," I said. "I would like that."

Nik's arm tightened around me, and the warmth of his smile as he looked down at me made the idea of forgiving his parents seem easy. I knew it wouldn't be a simple matter in reality—it had taken me a long time to overcome the image of Nik standing over the Constantines, and I had already been in love with him. But with time, I hoped Nik's parents and I could associate each other with something beyond the events of our first meeting.

## CHAPTER
# TWENTY-SEVEN

The king finally stood from his throne and stepped off the dais, joining the small gathering of men and women who formed both his government and his family. Anka and Colton broke off their conversation to look at him expectantly, and Augusta drifted closer.

"I won't deny a sense of betrayal to find so many of you involved in a scheme against me," he said.

"They wouldn't have been involved if the plan had involved any actual harm to you," Evermund said confidently. He hadn't even been in the city, but he clearly had total trust in his wife and her allies.

King Marius inclined his head in acceptance of Evermund's words. "Betrayal might be my first reaction, but it would be remiss of me if I looked no further than that. The very fact we were brought to this extremity means that collectively we have failed in our task of united government. The immediate crisis seems to be past, and Grey is no longer a threat, but it is clear that serious reflection on these events will be needed."

He looked at Anka. "Not all of those reflections are for right now, but I would like to start by apologizing to you, Anka. You have been a loyal and dedicated servant of Tartora for many decades, and it was wrong of me to force you into a position you didn't want. If you wish to resign as Royal Mage, I will accept your resignation with good will."

She regarded him in silence for a moment, her expression thoughtful.

"I accept your apology, Your Majesty. And at some point I will resign because I have always been a law keeper and always will be. However, I agree that changes are needed, and it seems to me that this isn't a time to be without a Royal Mage."

"Thank you, Anka," Evermund said, sounding relieved. "As always, your judgment is sound. An objective party—one with your wisdom and experience—will be a welcome asset as we repair what has been broken."

She smiled back, and the king nodded. I examined the crown prince. He was young compared to the others in positions of authority, but he was clearly comfortable in their midst.

If I remembered rightly, he had once been Royal Mage himself, and I could see why Airlie had wished for his presence from the beginning. Even with my extremely limited experience of this group, I could feel how the dynamic had changed with his presence. He would be a good king one day, and they all knew it. Already they afforded him some of the respect and authority of his future position.

I wrapped both my arms around Nik and squeezed. He had pushed himself to the edge to bring back the right person. He smiled down at me, but now that the immediate excitement was past, he looked even more exhausted.

"You need some sleep," I whispered, running my hand along the edge of his face.

"Seeing you is better than sleep."

"Today has taken some very unexpected turns," Augusta said acerbically, breaking into the various conversations.

I turned to look at her, my heart sinking as I saw her eyes were fixed on her former apprentice, now turned reneger—Nik. I had hoped she might be willing to take him back so that he could complete his apprenticeship, but her expression wasn't promising.

"While some rules have always been stretched for those of royal blood, some rules are immutable. I didn't speak previously because I am not totally lacking in compassion and wished to allow a family reunion. But word has been spreading that Prince Nikolas is back, and an example must be set. Renegers cannot be accepted into society, no matter what they might have done in the way of public service."

The queen flinched, her face paling as her eyes jumped to her son. Nik himself remained straight and unmoving, however, his face grave.

A moment of silence passed, and I held my breath, wondering if he would ask her to take him back. But he must have read the answer in her face because he made no such request.

"I do not deny your words, Master Augusta. And I did not come with the expectation that I could remain. Only the gravity of the situation brought me here in the first place. I will be gone by morning. I ask only that I be allowed to sleep before setting off again." He swayed slightly as he spoke, emphasizing the exhaustion behind his words.

"Nik!" For a moment I thought I'd spoken, but the voice had been his mother's. The distress on her face was obvious now, tears springing to her eyes. "You can't just leave again!"

The king put a gentle hand on her arm, looking at her with a set expression that was trying to hide his own distress. "My dear," he murmured, "Augusta is right. However much we want things to be different..."

"Surely there's something we can do." She glanced at Augusta, but the Master of Plants was still watching her old apprentice.

The king glanced at Augusta as well, his mouth tightening. "Perhaps in the future..." he murmured even more quietly than the queen.

The tempestuous events of the last few days hadn't placed the king in a good bargaining position. Of those around him, Augusta was one of the few who had been unwaveringly loyal, and he must be reluctant to pressure her into something she clearly didn't want to do.

I shook my head, a continuous movement that expressed everything I didn't have the words to say. Nik pressed me against him, whispering into my hair.

"I'm sorry." He sounded broken. "If there was any way I could stay..." His muscles jumped as he held me close. "But you know I will always do everything I can to protect you. Even if that means walking away and never seeing you again. With Grey gone, I've become the greatest threat to your future, and I won't drag you into my outcast status."

My heart broke at his words. The strength of his hold told me the words he would never say aloud. Nik would never abandon me. If he couldn't join society, he would remain in the shadows, watching for anything that might threaten me.

I couldn't bear the idea of that life for him. I wanted to tell him that I would give up everything and become an outcast with him. But I knew I didn't have that choice. Amara had risked everything to stand by me, and I had made a commitment to her. I still had a year of my apprenticeship, and I suspected we would spend at least some of that time with Anka, helping to train others how to make walls.

The king had just shown me great leniency, and I couldn't push the matter by declaring myself an outcast and attempting to leave society all together. They had accepted the risk I posed, but that didn't mean there wouldn't be eyes on me for the rest of my life. I couldn't blame them for that.

"I'm glad you brought up the subject," Amara said with a respectful nod to Augusta. "I had intended to organize a formal meeting to discuss the matter, but all the relevant people are present now so we might as well be done with it."

"I realize your apprentice has strong feelings on the subject," Augusta said, "but we cannot allow emotions to interfere on a matter as important as the status of renegers."

"I agree," Amara said calmly. "I had no intention of attempting to overthrow such rules. The matter I wish to discuss is Nikolas's formal graduation."

Her words sent a ripple through the group, and from Nik's reaction, he was just as surprised as me. Amara sent him a quick warning look, however, and he remained silent, his expression smoothing out.

"My apprentice has not returned to me to complete his apprenticeship," Augusta said coldly. "It doesn't matter what skills he has acquired on his own. He cannot become a proficient."

"No, of course skill alone is not enough." Amara remained unmoved by Augusta's opposition, her expression unruffled. "However, Nikolas has completed his apprenticeship under my guidance which is why I am now putting him forward for graduation."

"You are claiming to be his master?" Drake asked, clearly as surprised as I was. "You know that isn't how it works. Apprentices cannot change masters at will."

"In general they cannot, no," Amara said. "The law is clear that an apprentice must complete their apprenticeship under their influencer, except in the case of death or incapacity of the master. However there has always been a formal exception for royals—an exception that has already been put in place for Prince Nikolas."

"You mean the ruling that allows them to be activated by another royal but complete their apprenticeship under the Guild," Evermund said in an arrested tone. "It's true that ruling was used by Nik. He was adamant he be cross-influenced, so I was given permission to activate him, but the Master of Plants then took on his apprenticeship as had been initially intended."

"Precisely," Amara said. "In Nikolas's case, the law does not require his apprenticeship to be completed under his influencer but rather by the Guild. And I am a member of the Guild."

She slowly gazed across the assembled group, meeting each of their eyes with a challenging look. "Would anyone present like to argue that I lack the necessary strength to take on an apprentice of Nikolas's level?"

She let silence hang in the air as everyone shifted uncomfortably. Even Augusta wouldn't meet her gaze.

"I put forward that I am a member of the Guild and a registered master, and that I am therefore qualified to complete the apprenticeship of a royal student who has been activated by a family member."

"That exception is designed to allow the royal family to pass on their great strength to their children," Drake grumbled, "not to allow royal apprentices to jump from master to master. You know I acknowledge your strength, Amara, but you're one of my people. You don't even have a plants affinity."

"And my other apprentice is a healer," she said. "What of it? The prince is cross-influenced after all. His influencer was an elements mage, so it makes sense for his master to be one too."

"You have all been trapped on that island for the winter," Augusta said, "so you may well have supervised the prince during that time. But he was only halfway through his apprenticeship when he chose to abandon it. A single season is not sufficient to cover his remaining time."

"No, the winter would not be enough," Amara said. "However, I think you will find the prince has been with me far longer than that."

"What do you mean?" the queen asked, her voice eager.

"Prince Nikolas has been tracking Grey for a long time," Amara said. "Last spring, Grey abducted a friend of my other apprentice, and since that time, she and I worked together with Nik to find and free Miranda and then stop Grey. If anyone cares to track our movements, you will see our joint progress. After Tarin, we went to Ostaria, and from there to Caltor. Others can attest that Nik was seen with us in all three places. After Caltor, we traveled east across the northern half of the kingdom all the way to Eldrida. Nik traveled alongside us the whole way. And of course, we were all in Eldrida for the crippling storm before going north into the desert and eventually to the island. If anyone cares to count the months since we first connected in Tarin, I think you will find he has completed the necessary time."

Again, she gazed around the room, silently challenging anyone to deny her words. I was struggling to keep my mouth from dropping open. All her words were true—as a healer I knew no one would hear a lie on them. But she was stretching the truth as far as it could go, and everyone here had to know it. But one glance at the faces of the king and queen showed she was providing a solution they desperately wanted.

"If anyone doubts he has reached a sufficient skill level for a proficient, I invite you to test him," she said with a trace of humor. "I am confident you will not find him lacking in any way."

A dangerous smile spread across Nik's face. "I am more than willing to demonstrate my skill for any doubters."

"I don't think that will be necessary," Drake said dryly. He glanced at Augusta and Colton. "The Triumvirate will need to consult for a moment. If you will excuse us…" He gestured for the other two to step aside with him for a moment.

Hayes started a conversation with those of us who remained, but I wasn't paying enough attention to follow his words. And from the odd gaps in the replies, I wasn't the only one.

When the three affinity heads finally walked back from the other side of the cavernous room, Drake was smiling and Augusta looked resigned.

"We are happy to accept the graduation of Prince Nikolas to the official rank of proficient," Drake announced. "The Guild will publicly announce the successful completion of his apprenticeship and the lifting of his status as reneger as soon as possible."

Nik met his eyes. "Thank you." The simple words were full of depth.

Letting go of me, he crossed over to stand in front of Augusta. He towered over her small frame, but everything in his manner was respectful as he addressed her.

"Please accept my apology, Master Augusta. I disrespected you and your teaching by leaving in the manner I did."

"Well!" She raised both eyebrows, looking him up and down. "Never did I think to hear such a thing from you. Maybe there really is hope you'll turn into an asset to our kingdom."

Nik's lips twitched upward. "High praise, Master Augusta. I treasure it greatly."

She let out a bark of laughter. "Go back to your young lady, Prince, and don't go trying your charm on me."

Nik glanced at me, his eyes sparkling. Unable to resist, I ran forward and threw myself into his arms. It didn't matter about our audience or the drama of the last few hours. It might not be the right place, but I couldn't wait. After everything we had feared and endured, Nik was accepted back into society. He had a future again.

He swept his arms around me, lifting me completely off the ground and pressing his lips against mine. Lost in my joy and relief, I kissed him back, nothing in my mind but Nik.

Until a moment later when I remembered our audience. When I squeaked, Nik broke off the kiss with a chuckle and put me down.

"If you don't want all these important people to be scandalized," he said, "you'll have to let them know we're going to be married."

"Married?" I asked, the squeak reappearing.

For a second, a shadow marred the joy on his face. "You already know I want you in every part of my future," he said. "I thought you felt the same way?"

"Of course I do," I whispered. "But you just got reinstated as a prince. Aren't there... protocols?"

He grinned, the light blazing back into his eyes and filling me with an answering warmth.

"We can do a formal introduction now, if you like." He put an arm around my shoulders and turned me so we stood side to side, facing the group of bystanders. Phoenix chose that moment to swoop back in to land on my shoulder, as if lending his support to our union.

"This is Delphine," Nik said, "a future master healer and my betrothed. Does anyone object?"

"Would it make a difference if we did?" Augusta muttered.

Nik grinned at her. "Not in the least. I think I've already demonstrated I can walk away from royal life if needed."

"Wait a minute!" I gasped, his words bringing me back to earth. For a few minutes, I'd been thinking of nothing but Nik and the cloud that had been lifted off him, but I wasn't ready for the future he was implying.

"What is it?" The concern on his face was instant.

"I...I don't think I can be a princess and live at court and..." I glanced involuntarily toward the king and queen before quickly looking away.

Nik seemed to pick up on my meaning instantly. "Oh, is that all?" He looked relieved. "Don't worry. If I learned anything in my time away, it's that this isn't the life for me anymore either. I don't intend to settle at court."

"Nik!" Queen Celestine looked at him with disappointment. "Surely you don't intend to disappear again when we only just got you back? I know you were very unhappy with what happened after your arrival, but—"

"I'm not going to disappear, Mother." He gave her an affectionate look. "Gia doesn't live at court, but you still get to see her, don't you?"

"Yes, I suppose." She still didn't look pleased, but her momentary panic had subsided.

"It's not as if I have a role here," he said. "I can do greater good in the rest of the kingdom, especially if I have Delphine by my side. I've done enough travel with Amara to know what it means to the smaller towns and villages to have a master mage come through. And we've all seen how close Tartora came to disaster because the capital wasn't paying enough attention to the remoter parts of the kingdom. We need to increase the connection between the general populace outside the capital and the royal government. And what better way to do it than through a member of the king's own family? Besides," he added, "I am a plants mage after all. I belong in the farmlands, not in a city."

"You're suggesting you become an official royal emissary while fulfilling the same role as a traveling master?" the king clarified.

Nik looked down at me, still tucked against his side. "If Delphine agrees."

"That sounds incredible," I said, hardly able to believe he was suggesting something so perfect.

The king glanced toward the Triumvirate. Whatever he saw on their faces made him nod his head.

"Very well," he said. "Once Delphine graduates, the two of you can take on that role. You'll need to stay in the capital for a while, though. We need to show the court and Guild that you've been welcomed back and give them a chance to see you demonstrate your strength and control."

Nik glanced at Amara who gave him a small smile.

"Delphine and I will also be based here for the time being while we assist Anka," she told him.

Nik looked back at the king. "In that case, I'd be more than happy to stay. I'd like to take some time for study while I'm here. If I'm going to take on the role of a traveling master, I might as well officially pass the mastery exam before I leave."

Augusta's eyebrows shot up. "I see you haven't entirely lost your natural arrogance. You think you'll be able to pass the mastery exam within a year of becoming a proficient? Are you trying to set a new record?"

He gave her a provocative look. "I suppose that depends how well you teach me over the coming year."

She snorted, but I caught the answering gleam in her eyes. You didn't become an affinity head unless you relished a challenge.

"I'm sorry to abandon you the moment I graduate," I said to Amara, feeling a pang at the idea of leaving her.

"Don't be silly," she said. "Since I'll be here in the capital, I'll see you whenever you come back through. I'm actually relieved to know someone will be taking my place."

"You're finally going to settle down and stop all this roaming?" Anka's eyes immediately jumped to Hayes, her expression becoming amused when she saw the way he was beaming at Amara. "I'm glad to see the two of you finally managed to sort things out."

Her gaze shifted slightly to dwell for a moment on Colton. It flashed through my mind that perhaps one of the changes she wanted to see before she left the role of Royal Mage was a change in the Head of Healing. Master Colton had succeeded in activating the king's wall, and for that I would always be grateful, but he hadn't reacted well to the discovery of mesmerization. His desire had been to protect his affinity, but he had abandoned the ethos of a healer in his attempts to do it. Maybe it was time for someone with new vision to take on the role.

"Are you happy?" Nik's quiet murmur made me forget all about the politics of the Triumvirate.

"I've never been happier," I said honestly. "Would you really like to become a traveling master? You won't miss the life of a prince?"

"Once upon a time I thought gaining the throne was all that mattered," he said. "But now I would give up far more than a throne to have you by my side."

"I don't want you to have to sacrifice everything for me."

He shook his head. "Even without you, I wouldn't want to return to court. On Grey's ship, you challenged me to find the role I'm supposed to fill—since it was never that of ruler. I didn't know it then, but I think I'd already found that role while traveling the kingdom with you. Maybe it won't be forever—like it hasn't been for Amara—but it's what I truly want for now. And if the time does come for something different—that's a decision we'll make together."

"In that case," I said, "there's only one possible response."

Grasping the front of his jacket in both hands, I lifted onto my toes and pressed my lips against his, sealing our promises with a kiss.

# EPILOGUE

I gazed out the window at the changing leaves. Some trees were still entirely green, but others took my breath away with their fiery hues.

"I'm ready."

I turned to see another breath-taking sight. Amara's long, elegant gown trailed behind her by several feet, and her hair had been arranged on her head in an elaborate arrangement of braids and soft curls.

"You look beautiful," I breathed, making her smile.

"Thank you for helping me prepare," she said. "Both of you."

Luna beamed back at her, her eyes misty with unshed tears. "I would have come from further than Calinara to be at Hayes's wedding. Especially since he's marrying you! I couldn't have dreamed of a more perfect ending."

Amara laughed. "I hope it's not an ending! I like to think it's a beginning."

I chuckled as well. "You're forgetting. Luna is the center of her own story, and she's ready to leave us all behind."

"That's not true!" Luna cried, horrified, before she noticed we were both still grinning. Rolling her eyes, she pulled me into a hug. "I've missed you, Delphine!"

"Are you not enjoying it in Calinara as much as you'd hoped?" Amara asked.

"No, it's not that. I love being back with my family, and it's fascinating seeing the progress already made, as well as the new efforts underway. I just miss all of you at the same time."

"I think that might be the secret to adulthood that everyone was keeping from us," I said with a sigh. "You're always missing someone."

"I can see you've gained much wisdom since turning nineteen and becoming an adult." Luna gave me a cheeky grin. "But who are you missing? I know it isn't that prince of yours since I can't turn around without tripping over him."

"Her parents arrived yesterday," Amara said softly.

Luna's eyebrows rose. "You've reconciled with them, then?"

I nodded, remembering the long-awaited reunion.

In the aftermath of gaining my freedom, I had learned that my uncle had followed my instructions and gone to Amara. He and his family had received funds from her and left for Tarin before I emerged from my cell. I had sent an urgent communication after them to reassure my parents that I had been released and all was well, as well as to inform them of my betrothal. From their reply, I had learned that my uncle, aunt, and cousins had arrived safely on the farm.

My mother didn't go into detail on the meeting between the brothers, but I could read between the lines to know it hadn't gone smoothly. She seemed to be hopeful for the future, however, and with Amara and me stationed in the capital, my mother and I were able to exchange several more letters.

I learned from afar that my cousins had embraced farm life and that my uncle and father had slowly reconciled. By the time Amara sent my parents an invitation to her wedding, Uncle Olan and his family were sufficiently settled to run the farm in their absence. For the first time in my life, both my father and mother would be able to leave the farm at the same time for an extended trip.

I had thrown myself into the wedding preparations with fervor in an effort to distract myself from the wait for their arrival. Amara, in her usual perceptive manner, had understood my mindset and kept me run off my feet from morning to night until their arrival day finally came. Suddenly I had found myself without any tasks at all and no excuses to delay the meeting.

Nik had offered to be with me, but just like his own reunion with his parents, I knew it was something I needed to do on my own.

I had imagined how the interaction might go a hundred times, but I needn't have worried. The moment I saw them, all the pain and worry was overwhelmed by an entire childhood of memories.

I ran into my mother's arms without hesitation, tears streaming down both our cheeks. My father hung back, but when I finally finished hugging my mother, I turned to him with a smile.

"Thank you for coming, Father."

He cleared his throat. "Our daughter's influencer is getting married. How could we stay away? Even if she is a master mage."

I froze, but both he and my mother chuckled. Relaxing, I smiled back. If they felt calm enough to joke about it, that had to be a good sign.

"I'm sorry, lass," my father said softly, catching me off guard. "Your mother and I have had some long talks in your absence, and I know I was in the wrong with how I handled things."

"Obviously." My mother put her hands on her hips. "What am I going to do with the two of you? Of all the ridiculous things, keeping something like your squeamishness from me..." She shook her head.

"You've forgiven Father?" I asked, wanting to hear the reassurance, even though her manner made it clear she had.

She smiled. "He had to clean the henhouse on his own for a good month, but we got there in the end." She linked her arm through mine and squeezed. "You'll find out yourself soon enough, but you can't maintain a partnership through an entire lifetime unless you're willing to forgive each other along the way."

I nodded. Nik and I weren't even married yet, but we had already learned that lesson.

"Where is this man of yours?" Father asked. "He's not here to greet us?"

"He wanted to be," I said quickly. "But I wanted to meet you on my own first."

My mother nodded her approval, squeezing my arm again, but my father went quiet.

"I'm sorry, Delphine," he said. "I'm sorry for the way I treated you. I'm sorry for teaching you my anger and fear."

My mother nodded approvingly. "And he was sorry even before that brother of his showed up and made it even more clear how wrongheaded his ideas were."

"I forgive you, Father." I tried to surreptitiously wipe the moisture from my eyes. "I forgave you a long time ago."

My mother beamed at us both. "You were always a better daughter than I could have hoped for, Delphine. I've missed you, even if the house is full of people now."

"Are things going well with Uncle Olan?" I asked eagerly.

My mother smiled. "Better than I feared in the first week. Those cousins of yours have proved a mighty boon on the days my back aches."

"I'm so glad you finally have proper help," I said. "It makes me feel much better about not returning to the farm." I watched my mother's face, trying to gauge her reaction to my words, but she just chuckled.

"Don't look so worried. We already knew you weren't coming back. You outgrew the farm a long time ago."

"But not you!" I wrapped my arms around her, reveling in the familiar embrace. "I'll never outgrow my mother."

She chuckled. "I'm glad to hear you say it because I have every intention of spending a good portion of my old age bouncing my grandbabies on my knee."

"Mother!" I drew back and whacked her lightly, my cheeks heating.

She just laughed again. "So when do we get to meet Nik?"

"Right now, if you want," I said.

"And his parents?" my father asked gruffly, clearly uncertain about the prospect.

"They've invited us all to join them for the evening meal." I tried not to look as nervous as I felt at the idea.

"A meal with the king and queen?" My mother's eyes widened, and she glanced nervously at my father.

But despite all our fears, the meeting went better than expected. Nik's parents treated mine with more warmth than I anticipated, and my parents managed to overcome their awe at my future family's rank—at least enough to converse with sense.

"Delphine?" Luna bumped my hip with hers, startling my thoughts back to the present.

"Sorry." I shook myself and looked at Amara. "We shouldn't be talking about me. Today is your day."

"You're the envy of both the Guild and the capital, you know," Luna said cheerily. "Hayes was already the most eligible unmarried mage and that was before he became Head of Healing."

"Don't remind me about his new appointment." Amara sighed. "It's the reason we had to have a formal state wedding."

"Can you really begrudge us all the excitement?" Luna asked. "It's been a very long time since one of the Triumvirate got married."

"I heard Hayes is the youngest Triumvirate member in three generations," I said.

"Not that you're one to talk about youthful accomplishments." Luna snorted. "I overheard Augusta boasting about how that betrothed of yours is going to be ready to take the mastery exam by the start of winter."

I groaned. "Don't remind me. Nik's not only graduated, he's going to be a master before I'm even a proficient."

"He doesn't appear to mind," Luna said with a chuckle.

"It's not the difference in rank that's the issue." Amara was clearly trying not to smile. "Delphine has to graduate before they can be married."

Luna exploded into laughter. "Now that would definitely chafe Nik, if I know anything about him. I'm surprised he hasn't smuggled you off in the middle of the night."

"He would have both me and my betrothed to answer to if he tried anything of the sort," Amara said with a militant light in her eyes.

"Talking of your betrothed," I said, ignoring their teasing. "It's time for you to go and make him your husband."

Amara's face softened at the word, a glow radiating from inside her and making her even more beautiful. And the glow only grew brighter when the doors of the throne room opened, and she saw Hayes waiting for her at the end of a long stretch of red carpet.

I followed behind, but my eyes were on the man standing to one side of Hayes. Asking Nik and Evermund to be his two attendants had been a typical Hayes move —combining kindness with political acumen. His wedding had generated intense interest among both the Guild mages and the general populace, and Nik's inclusion had clearly demonstrated the former prince's return to favor and power.

Nik looked down the room and caught my eye. His smile grew as he watched me, and I sighed wistfully. It was right that Amara was getting married first, and I couldn't be happier for her. But spring seemed like a long time away.

The ceremony passed quickly, and all too soon, Hayes and Amara were swept up into a whirl of good wishes as everyone of wealth and power in the kingdom vied to congratulate them. I hung back, taking a moment to admire the white flowers that decorated the rows of chairs and the bright velvet of the carpet that had been used to form the aisle.

Arms came around me from behind. "That carpet will be purple the next time we're here for a wedding," Nik's deep voice said.

I smiled at the vision his words created. Hayes might be a member of the Triumvirate now, but only members of the royal family were permitted to walk down the aisle on a purple carpet.

A flash of the same purple caught my eye, drawing my attention to Anka. She was congratulating Amara, a delighted expression on her face.

She had been working hard for months but was finally starting to talk of retiring from the Royal Mage position. And I had an inkling who might be asked to fill it in her place.

"Do you think Amara will be happy in the capital in the long term?" I asked.

"Hmmm..." I felt the rumble of Nik's response in his chest. "I think she will be. But not as happy as we will be when we finally get back on the road."

A brush of movement near my feet made me flinch, but when I looked down, the sight of orange fur told me who had joined us.

I chuckled. "I'm not sure you're supposed to be in here, Ember."

"If the steward informed her of that fact, I don't think she was listening," Nik said. "No one ever manages to keep her away from you for long."

"I'm fortunate in my friends." I stealthily picked her up before leaning back into Nik's arms.

"She's not alone either." Nik pointed to an urn against the closest wall. Apparently Phoenix had taken a liking to the perch he'd found on his previous visit.

"Oh no," I groaned. Falcons were harder to keep hidden than foxes.

"Don't worry, today is about Hayes and Amara, and neither of them will kick him out. Isn't it fitting that he and Ember are here? They've spent almost as much time with Amara as you have."

"When you put it like that, I defy anyone to kick them out."

I leaned my head back against him and closed my eyes. For once, everyone I loved was together, and I intended to enjoy it while I could. Before long, I would be on the road, far from all but three of my loved ones.

When I thought about it like that, I knew the remaining months would fly by, especially given how much study Nik and I both had to get through. Before we knew it, our new life would be upon us. Tartora would wait for us, and we would be ready to explore every part of it when the time came.

# NOTE FROM THE AUTHOR

I hope you enjoyed Delphine, Nik, and Amara's story. If you missed the beginning of Nik's journey, you can read about how he ended up as a reneger in A Mage's Influence, starting with Seeds of Glory and Ruin.

Or for more adventure, intrigue, and romance in an academy setting, try the Spoken Mage series, starting with Voice of Power. Set in a world of written power, it tells the story of a girl who discovers she can wield power through spoken words.

To be informed of future releases, as well as A Mage's Apprentice bonus shorts, please sign up to my mailing list at www.melaniecellier.com.

And if you enjoyed A Mage's Apprentice, please spread the word and help other readers find it! You could start by leaving a review on Amazon. Your review would be very much appreciated and would make a big difference!

# Acknowledgments

I'm glad to finally reach a happy ending for Nik, and I want to thank all the readers who have stayed with me for the journey. I apologize for leaving you all hanging at the end of book two, but I hope you enjoyed how everything was wrapped up in this book.

And many thanks to my faithful team who have stayed with me through the series. Rachel, Greg, Priya, Ber, Katie, Mary, Dad, James, Karri, Rebecca, Marina, Cheri, Shari, Brittany, Kitty, Aya, Lyra, and Marc, I thank you every time, but it never seems like enough.

And, of course, a final thank you to God who is always ready to forgive our mistakes and help us find peace from our past.

# ABOUT THE AUTHOR

Melanie Cellier grew up on a staple diet of books, books and more books. And although she got older, she never stopped loving children's and young adult novels.

She always wanted to write one herself, but it took three careers and three different continents before she actually managed it.

She now feels incredibly fortunate to spend her time writing from her home in Adelaide, Australia where she keeps an eye out for koalas in her backyard. Her staple diet hasn't changed much, although she's added choc mint Rooibos tea and Chicken Crimpies to the list.

She writes young adult fantasy including books in her *Spoken Mage* world, her *Mage's Influence* world, and her various *Four Kingdoms* and *Kingdoms of Legacy* series that are made up of linked stand-alone stories that retell classic fairy tales.